Bobby's Bride

Bobby's Bride

A small town cop, damsel in distress, unlikely couple romance.

Heart's Destiny Book 3

Leah Mae Wright

Copyright

Copyright © 2022 Leah Mae Wright
All Rights Reserved.
Updated: March 2026.

No part of this book may be reproduced, scanned, or distributed in any printed or electronic format without the prior written consent of the author.

eBook ISBN: 978-1-968513-04-7
6x9 Paperback ISBN: 978-1-968513-05-4
Audiobook ISBN: 978-1-968513-32-0
Imprint: Leah Mae Wright

5x8 Paperback ISBN: 9798813199967
Imprint: Independently Published
Only on Amazon

This is a work of fiction. Names, places, characters, and incidents are the product of the author's imagination and are fictional. Any references to actual persons, living or deceased, events, organizations, or locations are used fictitiously.

Cover photo licensed through iStockPhoto.com.
Credit: sergeyryzhov
Stock photo ID: 148659629

Audiobook produced with Google Play Auto-Narration

www.leahmaewright.com

Contents

Dedication

To my wonderful husband, Mike. Thank you for supporting me in all my hopes and dreams. I love you.

Introduction

Bobby Burleson enjoyed the bachelor life and all the perks that came with being a member of one of the founding families of his small hometown. He had his own home on the Burleson Ranch, plenty of money in the bank from his dividends and salary as a board member of Burleson Incorporated, and his pick of the buckle bunnies that hung out at Tully's Roadhouse after the rodeo almost every weekend. Though his family money made him wealthy enough to never have to work a day in his life, he'd worked his way up from a small-town cop to the police chief position with the Heart's Destiny Police Department. Between his duty to the town and the extra work he did for his family business, Bobby didn't have time for his meddling mother and her friends' matchmaking mischief, much less the relationship they wanted him to find.

Brooklyn Brielle Barns was a mostly naïve heiress who lived a sheltered life, unaware of her inheritance from her mother. After her mother died when she was four, she was raised by the household staff, who provided her with a home-school education. Her father neglected her, except when he expected her to play the part of the dutiful daughter at social events. After earning her online degree in English with a special focus on creative writing, she was excited to start her career as an author of children's books. Before she could tell her father her plan for the future, he announced that he'd set up an arranged marriage for her. She was to wed one of his colleagues, a man more than twice her age, whether she liked it or not.

Brooklyn spent six months playing the part of the blushing, virgin bride, attending all the society events her father insisted she should with her unwanted fiancé, while secretly starting her writing career under the alias of Brie Brooks. She stashed her income in secret online accounts, only dipping into it so the household staff, who acted more like her foster parents, could help her buy a car to make her escape from the forced marriage. The unknown heiress became a runaway bride a little over a week before the wedding, hoping to stay hidden away from her oppressive father's evil plans.

When Bobby saw the kidnapped heiress headlines and heard the opinions of his family and friends on the young woman's fate, he felt compelled to investigate. Not because of his duty as a police officer, since a kidnapping in Georgia was way outside his jurisdiction, but because of the strange feeling in his chest when he saw Brooklyn Barns' photos. His inner alpha wanted to rescue the damsel in distress.

When Brooklyn's car broke down in a small Texas town, she felt a sense of safety and home that she'd never felt before. She accepted a job as a live-in cook and housekeeper on a ranch to supplement her author income. It was virgin instalove the moment she met her new boss, but she wasn't sure she could tell him who she really was without risking him sending her back to her unwanted old life.

When Bobby met the woman his mother hired to be his cook and housekeeper, he felt as drawn to her as he did to the images of the Georgia heiress that he no longer believed was kidnapped. As he got to know Brie, he started to see the similarities between her and Brooklyn.

Would he figure out that the two women he was drawn to were one and the same? Would the small-town hero be able to protect his lady in hiding? Could this unlikely couple find their happily ever after?

DISCLAIMER: This small-town cop, damsel in distress, unlikely couple romance book contains references to childhood neglect, profanity, and graphic sex scenes. It is intended for adult readers (18+) who are not easily offended.

Chapter One

Hazel Burleson woke up the day of Anthony and Kay's wedding shower from the greatest dream about finding a bride for her oldest son, Bobby. She'd been trying for years to find his perfect match, but every time she set up a situation where Bobby had to sit with one of her friends' daughters at town events, he showed no interest.

It was quite frustrating as a mother to have him so blatantly fighting every match she tried to make for him, but she thought that her dream had just shown her where she'd gone wrong. All this time she'd been trying to match him up with girls he'd known their whole lives, and thinking that one meal after church would be all that it would take for him to see them in a whole new light, as his future bride. In her dream, Hazel didn't make that mistake, though.

In the vision, Hazel met a pretty young blonde with the biggest blue eyes she'd ever seen. Understanding that the young woman was somehow in need of protection, Hazel hired her as Bobby's live-in housekeeper and cook. Her oldest son might be able to resist temptation for a few hours while at a church potluck or town hall meeting, but being cooped up in his house with a beautiful woman, who needed his help, for a few weeks would surely weaken his defenses and steer him toward a walk down the aisle.

She especially thought following the path laid out in her dream would work because she'd had prophetic dreams in the past. Early in her marriage, when she was starting to get discouraged about ever becoming a mother, she started dreaming about her six children and those dreams eventually came true. Not only that, but her youngest son had been having dreams about his soulmate and family for the last year, and Hazel believed they were just as prophetic as hers had been years ago. Anthony had not only found the love of his life, who he would be marrying in less than a week, but he'd also already adopted Kay's two daughters—the same two daughters he'd dreamt about when he was dreaming about Kay.

Now that she had two new granddaughters, Hazel was anxious to add more grandkids to the family, and she was hopeful that her dream the night before about Bobby's bride might just be the key to another son marrying and starting to help with finally filling her mostly empty house on the family ranch with grandbabies.

"Morning, Baby." Her husband, Bob, gave her a wake-up kiss like he'd done every morning for the almost thirty-three years they'd been married.

"Good morning," Hazel replied after their kiss ended. She wished they could spend some extra time cuddling in bed in the mornings, but running a ranch required them to get up early to start work. That was especially true on a special day like this, when they had to take care of the kids they'd kept in the bunkhouse overnight, so the out-of-town guests with children could go and enjoy the bachelor and bachelorette party the night before. Not to mention the fact that Hazel still had to make sure everything was ready for the wedding shower after church.

Hazel and Bob rushed through their morning routine, so Bob could go to the barn and make sure the animals were taken care of for the day and Hazel could go to the kitchen and start cooking for everyone on the ranch. *Thank goodness, I thought to have so many extra sets of grandparents staying to watch all the kids last night,* Hazel thought as she walked down the stairs, from the loft room where she'd slept, to the bunkhouse kitchen.

The Burleson Ranch was actually a lot more than just Bob's way of living out his childhood dreams of being a cowboy. It was actually ten-thousand acres of land that had been passed down through the family since the late eighteen-hundreds. It started as the homestead of Bob Rogers and his wife Lizzie.

In 1881, Jonah Burleson was on the train going to Laredo to find work as a cowboy. He saw Emma Rogers board the train in San Antonio and proclaimed her his heart's destiny. Instead of continuing his journey to Laredo, he got off the train at the no name station where Emma and her mother, Lizzie, disembarked. They were going to the homestead Emma's father, Bob, had set up a few years before.

Jonah ended up working for Emma's Pa and sleeping in the barn until they built a bunkhouse. A year later, after proving himself worthy to her father, Jonah married Emma and they built their own home nearby. Jonah and Bob worked together on both parcels of land and started raising cattle, eventually combining their properties, so when the elder Rogers passed, their property being willed to their only daughter, Emma, created the original acreage of the Burleson Ranch.

When Jonah and Emma's children and grandchildren grew up and married, they built several houses around the original homes on the ranch. More and more people moved to the area, starting a few more ranches, and eventually the town. In 1904, when the area had grown to a population of about five-hundred people, the town was incorporated with the name Jonah chose, Heart's Destiny, because it all started with him seeing Emma.

When the time came for Jonah and Emma to pass the ranch down to their kids, they didn't want it to end up divided into smaller parcels, or cause fights among their descendants over who got the bigger house, so they set up the ranch as a corporation, giving equal shares in the company to each of their children. As the generations passed it down, with some stock having to be passed back to siblings when an heir would die without any known descendants, the corporation changed its charter, so half the shares were divided equally between the oldest generation of the family, currently being Bob and his brother Jon, and half the shares were divided equally among the second oldest generation, currently being Bob and Hazel's six children and Jon and Susan's four children.

Hazel wanted to make sure that when the time came for the fifty percent of the company Bob and Jon shared to pass down to their grandchildren, that there were plenty of them to share the responsibilities of both the working cattle ranch, and the corporation that dealt with the oil wells on the back hundred acres, and all the other investments the company had become involved in over the years. All that responsibility just being carried by two brothers and their father for more than thirty years really had her worried about its toll on their health. Bob and Jon's father, Jerry Burleson died way too young in Hazel's opinion, when he passed two years before, and she thought it was because of the stress of so much responsibility.

Leah Mae Wright

With most of her children choosing careers outside the family business, and only really going to board meetings when they had to vote on something, she was worried that her husband, or brother-in-law, would have an early heart attack as well from too much stress. Hazel was hopeful that if she could get her children, nieces, and nephews all married off, they would all see how important it was to take bigger roles in running Burleson Incorporated. If so, then they would not only provide the next generation to leave the land and company to, but also help their fathers live longer by lessening their stress levels.

When Hazel got to the kitchen to start cooking breakfast for all the ranch hands, family, and out-of-town visitors, she put her plan together. She enlisted the help of Rosa Diaz, her friend who also worked as her assistant cook on the ranch, her sister-in-law Susan, and her other friends, Mandi Hunter, who lived across the main road on the east side of the ranch and ran the local bed and breakfast, Karen Walker, who ran the office for her husband Wyatt's construction company, and Lisa Walker, the middle school principle. Between the six of them, they had twenty-two children, and only Hazel's youngest, Anthony, had settled down.

Well, he was working on settling down anyway. He and his bride-to-be and new daughters had moved into the house closest to Hazel and Bob on the family ranch the month before, and were having their wedding on Saturday the twenty-fourth.

As soon as her friends heard her idea for Bobby, they jumped on board. They would each make lists of the traits they were looking for in the potential mates for their own children, and then they would get together after Anthony's wedding to brainstorm about who they knew in town that met those traits. They would also all be on the lookout for any young ladies who were new to town, who might be in need of a job, so Hazel could make her dream of the night before into reality.

While Hazel wanted to get started on her plan immediately, she knew she and her friends would all be too busy with wedding events and the Thanksgiving holiday to implement a plan immediately. With overseeing everything for the wedding for the next week, Hazel was having to trust Rosa to handle all the cooking and housekeeping jobs she normally performed herself. But maybe not having Hazel do the normal tasks that she did at Bobby's house would help him realize just how much he needed to hire a live-in cook and housekeeper, instead of relying on his mom to stock his fridge and keep his place clean.

Hazel hoped that one of her friends knew a woman who loved animals and wanted to live on a ranch, cooking, cleaning, and taking care of her husband and family, and would awaken Bobby's protective instincts. If they couldn't think of anyone they already knew who would be perfect for Bobby, Hazel was also making a list of places where she could advertise for the job as his live-in cook and housekeeper. *I'll interview all the applicants myself, so I can hand pick my future daughter-in-law,* Hazel thought. *The boy won't stand a chance of being disinterested when he's living with his perfect match!*

~~~

Thursday, November 22, 2018, Thanksgiving Day

It was two o'clock in the morning on Thanksgiving and Brooklyn Barns was supposed to be getting her beauty sleep in her lavish bedroom on the second floor of her father's mansion. *But is that what I'm doing? Nope!* Brooklyn thought as she silently slipped through the wooded area on the backside of the family estate.

Instead of sleeping in one of the silk nightgowns her father presented her with as part of her wardrobe for the role he'd cast her in as the virgin bride of his creepy old crony, she was dressed in head to toe black—yoga pants and tank top under a black hoodie with the hood up to cover her blonde hair, and black tennis shoes, all snuck in the house to her by her housekeeper because her father didn't think they were appropriate attire for a debutante—so she could sneak through the woods behind the house to the gardener's cottage at the back of the property without being seen. *Yeah, I'm running away from home, which seems silly to have to do at twenty-two years old, but I just can't stay here anymore. There's no way I can stand one more event where I have to pretend I'm happy to be marrying that old fart, Clayton Donaldson! Just the thought of him trying to kiss me again gives me the willies. Thank goodness he wasn't successful the first time.*

Brooklyn just couldn't make herself fake the role of the blushing bride to a man more than twice her age another time. She shuddered at
~~~

Leah Mae Wright

the thought of what she would've had to endure after the country club Thanksgiving dinner that afternoon, if she weren't running away right then. She wouldn't even let herself think about what would happen if she were still there the next weekend for the wedding. She was sure those thoughts would cause night terrors.

She made her way easily down the path that led through the wooded area between the main house and the cottage, and was happy to see Joe sitting on the porch in a rocking chair waiting for her.

Joe and Mary Turner were like her foster parents, even though she actually lived with her father. It wasn't that he was a bad father. He wasn't physically abusive as she was growing up. He was just very distant. Mostly, Brooklyn was to be seen but not heard, when he wanted to appear as the doting father, but he ignored her the rest of the time. Joe and Mary had always been there for her growing up. Technically, they were part of the household staff her father employed at his huge plantation-style estate in Macon, Georgia.

Her father was Bradley Stanton Barns, the third, and was the most pretentious person she'd ever known. Not that he deserved to be so uppity. It wasn't like he was part of an aristocratic family, or even one that had been well-to-do in Georgia for generations. His father worked for the railroad and only gave him the same name as his own because that was what his own father had done.

Brooklyn's dad worked his way up from a lower middle-class upbringing to a vice presidency at her mom's family company before he married her. Once they were married, he became CEO only because Brooklyn's mother passed away and left the position to her husband in her will. Before that, Madeline Ashbury-Barns was the CEO, stepping into the position when Brooklyn's grandfather retired as part of getting his affairs in order before he passed away from an aggressive form of cancer. Now her father acted like the company had been his all along, and that he built the empire that was Ashbury Enterprises.

As his only child, Brooklyn had been a disappointment to him because she was a girl. As bad as he wanted a son, she was surprised he hadn't remarried since her mother died to try and have his perfect heir.

Brooklyn was homeschooled because her dear old dad didn't want to waste the money on the prestigious private school all his friend's kids attended for an unworthy offspring. After high school, she convinced him to pay for an online college. He only did it because it would be an embarrassment to him if she didn't appear capable of completing a degree of some kind.

Her degree in English helped her to launch her career as a writer, even though her father didn't know about it. She'd written short stories for years, mostly her daydreams of a world where she could escape the prison of the plantation and explore the world. After graduating back in May, she published her first book. She set everything up under her pen name and stored everything in cloud accounts that her dad didn't know about.

She wasn't planning on being so secretive about it when she first started writing. But then her father had blindsided her by announcing that she was to accompany him to a gala to announce her engagement to his colleague that he'd arranged. That was when Brooklyn decided he didn't need to know about any money she could make and started saving up to be able to escape his plans. So, instead of publishing as Brooklyn Brielle Barns, she set up her online accounts as Brie Brooks, including online banking.

Over the last six months, she'd played her part acting as the blushing bride at all the parties and business functions her father forced her to attend, while secretly writing more books and saving every penny she made, so she could make this escape. Her royalties from the first book were enough to give to Joe to go buy her a used car, also in the name of Brie Brooks. As she packed her things to move to her *new home* in the weeks before she was supposed to get married on December first, Mary put the important stuff Brooklyn actually wanted to take with her in the car they'd hidden behind the cottage they lived in on the estate.

It was only a few boxes of her more comfortable clothes (well, as comfortable as the long skirts her father considered acceptable attire could be anyway), a few business-casual outfits in case she needed to interview for a job to supplement her income, several spiral notebooks of her writing over the years, and a photo album of pictures of her with her mother before she died. All the fancy clothes and jewelry that her dad bought to put on airs and present her to the world as a debutante leading up to the farce of a marriage he'd planned, she gladly left boxed up in her room to appear as if she were actually moving in with the dirty old man her father was trying to make her marry.

"Hey Joe," Brooklyn whispered as she walked up onto the porch.

"Hey Brook," he whispered back. "Do you have everything you might need for the trip?"

She patted the backpack that was slung over one shoulder. It held all the clothes she'd been holding back packing to wear that week, her laptop, and pretty much nothing else because she left her phone charging on the bedside table and her gaudy engagement ring sitting in the dish beside the bathroom sink. "Yeah, everything I need is here in my bag," Brooklyn answered. "I even managed to grab my birth certificate and Social Security card."

"Okay then." Joe stood from his seat. "Mary has some snacks for you she's packing up in the kitchen. Let me get them for you."

Brooklyn followed Joe as he walked into the cottage because she wanted to hug Mary one last time before she left. She was going to miss them both so much now that she had to leave the only home she'd ever known. She would always fondly remember all the days of learning to cook, especially the bakery treats they loved so much, from Mary, and Joe teaching her to drive, and so many other little things they'd taught her over the years, when she wasn't allowed to go out of the house without one of them with her.

"Oh, baby girl, I'm going to miss you so much," Mary cried as Brooklyn walked through the kitchen door.

"I'm going to miss you, too, Mary." Brooklyn hugged Mary. "I know it won't be safe to call, but I'll email you from my Brie Brooks account, so you'll know what's going on with me."

Mary squeezed Brooklyn so tight that she could barely breathe. They hugged for several long moments with tears coming to their eyes. It was such an emotional moment that it took all the strength Brooklyn had to find the courage to go before she chickened out.

She was scared about what life was going to be like, living on her own for the first time. The whole time she'd been growing up, she'd only had Joe and Mary. Her dad didn't want her leaving the house unless it was to go to one of his social functions, so she hadn't really had to interact with people often. At those company functions or country club galas, she was just supposed to sit there looking pretty, make sure she followed the rules of etiquette, and didn't eat with the wrong fork.

While she was looking forward to doing her own shopping, more than just the little bit she'd done when out with Mary, and the possibility of making new friends and exploring the world like her book characters, the thought of not having the safety of her bedroom to come back to and hide out in, when she was overwhelmed by not being able to talk to people or embarrassed by saying or doing the wrong thing around new people, was daunting. Finally, she choked back her tears and pulled away from Mary's embrace.

Of all the things she was going to miss about her old life, Brooklyn knew she was going to miss Mary's hugs the most. She didn't need her father's money or big house. She didn't need all the fancy clothes or jewelry. But she definitely needed the love and affection she felt whenever Mary gave her a hug. The most important lesson Mary had taught her over the years was that a hug may not be able to fix whatever your problem was, but it could make your troubles bearable when you had someone to help hold you together for a few minutes.

Brooklyn took the grocery bag Mary had packed for her as they all walked out the back door to the fifteen-year-old, faded blue, Honda Accord. They said their goodbyes and Brooklyn put the grocery bag of snacks, her backpack, and purse on the passenger seat and left home for the first time, and hopefully, the last.

She was bored out of her mind because the radio didn't work, but the car drove just fine down I-75 out of Georgia. When she hopped on I-10 to head west, Brooklyn was thrilled that she almost made it out of Florida before she had to stop for gas. She stopped at a Pensacola convenience store to fill up the tank and went inside to buy a cheap phone, since she left her old phone in Georgia in an attempt to keep from being traced through it by her father, or more likely the tech department at Ashbury Enterprises.

As she walked up to the counter to pay for the cheap phone, she realized that her father had been talking to the press. Her picture was on the television in the convenience store with the caption of "Kidnapped Heiress" under it. She was a little nervous when the clerk looked at her a little too closely, but apparently her hoodie and yoga pants, with her long blonde hair up in a ponytail, was enough of a disguise to keep him from recognizing her.

Leah Mae Wright

Just to be safe, though, Brooklyn rushed into Alabama as fast as she could. She was thanking her lucky stars that Walmart was open on Thanksgiving to start their Black Friday sales early. In addition to more yoga pants and tank tops that she planned to sleep in, she was able to find some black hair dye to cover her blonde hair, but she couldn't locate any colored contacts to cover her blue eyes. She checked in at a cheap motel on the outskirts of Mobile and got to work changing her appearance, so hopefully, nobody else would recognize her.

~~~

Bobby Burleson took his job as the police chief for the Heart's Destiny Police Department very seriously. So much so, that he wore his uniform to Thanksgiving dinner since he was technically the only officer on call for the holiday. Even the dispatcher and receptionist were off work, so any emergency calls the department received were being forwarded to his cell phone.

It was highly unlikely that he would be called away from the celebration in the ballroom of the Hunters' Bed and Breakfast, since all of the most prominent families of the town had been invited to join the Burleson family and all the out-of-town wedding guests for the holiday. The fire department was more likely to be called out when someone's deep fried turkey plans went awry, but there was always the possibility of a domestic issue arising when estranged and extended families got together. Since the town had grown to a population of a little over fifteen-hundred people, Bobby figured less than a third of them would actually show up for the festivities his family was hosting, so he wanted to make sure he was in uniform if he was needed by one of the other residents of the community.

Bobby mingled with a few prominent citizens, maintaining good relations with the mayor and fire chief before catching up with his best friend, Luke Walker, and his family before everyone started claiming tables and sitting down with their immediate family members for the midday meal. Bobby strategically sat between his brothers and cousins, narrowly avoiding being pushed toward his soon to be sister-in-law's single female friends by his mother.
~~~

Bobby loved his mother dearly, but he was long past being frustrated with her matchmaking shenanigans at every church potluck and community celebration. For a while, it seemed as if she never failed to seat him at a table full of husband-hunting women whenever he attended a meal other than their weekly family dinners on Sunday evenings. He'd somehow managed to avoid her matchmaking traps at all the wedding events so far, but only because she seemed more focused on fixing Kay's sister, Randi, up with James Hunter, and hadn't caught him sticking to sitting with the other guys.

"So, who's catching the cyber terrorists this week while you're on vacation?" Bobby's cousin, JJ, posed the question to Bobby's brother, Jake, who worked in naval intelligence with his super sleuthing computer skills.

"That would still be me, Cuz." Jake shook his head at their cousin. "I'm not actually on vacation. I've been working remotely all week."

"Really? I thought you had to be on base to work on the super computers." Their other cousin, Justin, gave Jake a dubious look.

"For some things," Jake replied with a shrug. "But I can still do quite a bit with my laptop and a secure internet connection."

"Oh, can you track people from your laptop?" Their sister, Charlotte, bounced in her seat, looking like she had someone in mind for Jake to track down.

"Yeah, why?" Jake replied to Charlotte. "You need me to track a boyfriend or something?"

"No, but maybe you could find that heiress that's missing in Georgia." Charlotte looked at their brother with hopefulness shining in her eyes.

"What heiress?" Bobby wondered what his sister was talking about, and why he hadn't been the first to hear about it as the top law enforcement officer in town.

"Brooklyn Brielle Barns," his cousin Jen piped in. "Her name almost sounds like European royalty."

"She's actually the heir to the Ashbury estate," his cousin Julie added, matter-of-factly. "We've had a few dealings with Ashbury Enterprises, the company she's supposed to inherit when she gets married next weekend."

"*If* she gets married next weekend," Charlotte interjected, putting special emphasis on the word *if* to indicate that the missing woman might not be found in time for the wedding. "Personally, I don't think she was kidnapped, like her dad and fiancé are spouting on the national news. I think she ran away, so she doesn't have to marry that guy who looks like he's her father's age."

A chorus of "oh yeah, she definitely ran away" and "for sure, she wasn't kidnapped" could be heard from around the table, specifically from the female members of the Burleson clan.

"Yeah, I'm not tracking a runaway bride." Jake shook his head at the women around them. "Besides, even if she was actually kidnapped, I couldn't legally look for her without being asked by the law enforcement agency heading up the case."

"It's too bad she's not from here," Bobby's sister, Becky, sighed, her shoulders slumping in disappointment. "Then Bobby could ask you to find her, and we'd get the real story of what happened to her."

"Yeah, well, since I probably won't be getting a call from the authorities in Georgia, you'll just have to follow the story on the national news to satisfy your curiosity," Bobby lightly chuckled at his baby sister. Even though he had no desire to feed into his sisters' and cousins' curiosity about the supposedly kidnapped heiress, Bobby made a mental note to look up what he could find on the case once he was back home or in the office. He knew he probably couldn't do anything to help the Georgia authorities locate the missing woman, but his devotion to law enforcement still drove him to want to investigate the case.

The subject was dropped when they were called up to fill their plates. Small talk resumed while they ate, but it was mostly about the wedding and the latest gossip around town. Once they were finished eating, Bobby once again mingled with friends while they all waited for the turkey and sides to settle, so they could gorge on the table full of desserts.

While he was sitting with the Walkers—and complementing them on the excellent job they'd done on restoring the old English style mansion in the middle of the Hunters' property in less than a month in order to have room for all of the out-of-town wedding guests and to host the various events in the ballroom—there was a commotion at the other end of the room. Bobby hadn't seen what had flown across the room to start the whole incident, but based on the way Kay's father was yelling at James Hunter about defiling his youngest daughter, it was obviously not something that should've been out in the open in a room full of families.

Bobby stood to walk over and diffuse the situation, figuring it was his job to be the peacekeeper as the chief of police. Before he even took the first step in the direction of the altercation, Randi Lee bolted from the room. He was halfway across the room when Charles and David Lee paused in their ranting at James long enough for James to say his piece. James finished what he had to say and followed Randi out of the ballroom just as Bobby approached the agitated group.

"Everything okay now?" Bobby looked back and forth between the Lees and Dean Hunter, who had been standing behind his brother. "Or do I need to go open up the jail to let a few tempers cool down?"

"I wouldn't say everything's okay." Charles was still red faced from his angry outburst. "But I don't think anyone needs to cool down in jail."

"Since the assault was only verbal and not physical, I'll agree to that for now." Bobby pointedly looked at the Tulsa County Sheriff, and hated that he was reprimanding a fellow law enforcement officer with enough experience to know better than to behave the way he'd just acted in a public place. "But let's all try to behave ourselves in a more professional manner from now on."

Charles gave Bobby a sheepish look as he nodded his head in agreement and turned back toward the table where his wife was sitting. David followed his father back to their family, so Bobby went back to chatting with his friends.

Speculation about whether or not Randi was pregnant replaced the earlier small talk about the missing woman from Georgia. Without another mention of the woman, Bobby put her out of his mind and enjoyed the rest of his holiday with his family and friends, grateful that he wasn't called out to work.

~~~

Saturday, November 24, 2018

"No, no, no!" Brooklyn shouted at her beat up junker of a car as it started sputtering while she was driving through San Antonio, Texas,
~~~

on Saturday morning. She was frustrated from spending the last couple of days on the road and staying in no-tell motels in her frantic flight from her father and his crazy idea of forcing her to marry one of his business partners. She shuddered at the thought of what she barely escaped. *I'm so grateful to Joe and Mary for helping me sneak away in the middle of the night,* she thought for the millionth time in the last two days.

She made it from Macon to Mobile on Thursday, and from Mobile to Houston on Friday with no trouble whatsoever. She'd even managed to make a couple of stops to dye her hair in Mobile and found some colored contacts to hide her blue eyes in Houston, thinking her easy disguise was a sign of her trip being blessed by a higher power. But she was only a few hours into her Saturday drive, and her car was making her wonder if she was going to make it any farther than San Antonio.

She got confused by the way the highways were laid out and somehow ended up turned around. She started to get worried when she couldn't see signs for I-10 anymore. She thought she was taking an exit from I-10 a while back, so she could find a service station to check out the knocking in her car's engine. Apparently, she ended up on I-35 and was no longer in San Antonio, since she saw a sign telling her how many miles to Laredo. *Laredo is on the border with Mexico, right? That sounds like a good place to hide from my dad. Nobody will be looking for an American trying to illegally cross the border into Mexico.*

"Please keep running long enough to get me to a garage," Brooklyn begged softly, trying to sweet talk her car. "You've been so good and running well for the thousand miles so far, but I really need another hundred miles out of you to make sure I'm safe, so please don't die on me now."

She reached out with her hand to pet the dashboard, and told her car what a good boy he was, like the car could actually understand her and appreciate the praise. Instead of being good and stopping the horrible knocking noise, however, the car sputtered and died instead. Luckily, she was in the right-hand lane and right at an exit ramp, so she was able to coast down it and get off the road before the car came to a complete stop. In frustration, she slammed her head into the steering wheel and screamed, "AAAAAHHHHH!"

Brooklyn took a few minutes with her head down to take some deep breaths and calm down. *Please, God, don't leave me stranded in the middle of nowhere,* she silently prayed. When she lifted her head, she realized that He was not only listening, but He was also still taking care of her because she could see a sign in front of her that read, "Welcome to Heart's Destiny, Texas, where we hope ya'll find your heart's destiny."

She got out of the car, grabbing her purse and the backpack she'd been using as an overnight bag while going into motels the past couple of days. She locked the car and started walking toward the gas station that she could see just about a hundred yards away from the end of the exit ramp. As Brooklyn walked up to the station, she worried that it might be closed because there wasn't another car in the parking lot.

It was a kind of rustic looking building, like a log cabin with wagon wheels around the gas pumps. It was really quaint and appealing for a gas station. The sign in the window proclaimed the store was "open," so she tried the door and was glad to find it was actually unlocked. A bell rang as she walked in and she heard a high-pitched voice call from the back, "I'll be right there!" She looked around at the quaint cowboy décor while she waited for the clerk to come out where she could be seen.

"Howdy, I'm Kenzie. How can I help you?" The clerk greeted her with a smile as she walked out from the doorway between the front counter and the soda fountain.

Kenzie looked to be about the same age as Brooklyn, early twenties, with light brown hair and green eyes. She was a little taller than Brooklyn's five-foot-three, but not by much. Kenzie's big, bright smile made Brooklyn feel like she was someone she'd like to be friends with, if she wasn't trying to hide who she was from the world.

"I, uh, I'm Brie," Brooklyn sputtered, hoping Kenzie didn't realize from her stuttering that she was lying, using her pen name instead of her real name. "My car broke down on the highway. You wouldn't happen to have a mechanic here, would you? I need to find someone to help me get it running again."

"No, we just have the convenience store and gas pumps here for people passing by between San Antonio and Laredo." Kenzie leaned against the front counter. "You'll have to go on into town to Luke's

Garage to find a mechanic, but I don't know if he'll be there, or if he's already closed for the day to get cleaned up for the wedding tonight."

Brooklyn felt her shoulders slump and the smile she'd managed to give Kenzie fell to a frown. *Just my luck that the only mechanic around is getting married, and I may not even be able to have him look at my car until he gets back from his honeymoon.*

"Is he the only mechanic around?" Brooklyn hoped he had some sort of backup plan for taking care of the townsfolk's automobiles while he was away. "Or does he have someone covering for him while he's away on his honeymoon? And is there a motel in town?" She decided that if she could get a motel room, she could wait until Luke came back from his honeymoon, if necessary.

"Oh, Luke isn't getting married, Anthony Burleson is getting married, but Luke is best friends with Anthony's oldest brother, so I'm sure he'll be going to the wedding," Kenzie babbled as she pulled her phone from her back jeans pocket and started scrolling through screens. "Let me call him and see if I can find out if he's still at the shop."

She thumbed a contact in her phone and put it up to her ear, while still looking down. Her lips were moving like she was saying a silent prayer that he would answer the phone. "Hey, Luke, you still at the garage? Yeah, I have a customer here whose car broke down on the highway and she needs to have it looked at." She looked up at Brooklyn with curiosity shining in her eyes. "Where on the road is your car?"

"It's right at the end of the exit ramp, directly in front of the welcome sign," Brooklyn answered.

"Yeah, it's not on the highway anymore," Kenzie relayed the information into the phone. "She got it to the end of the exit ramp by the welcome sign." She paused to listen to whatever Luke was saying. "Okay, yeah, and she'll need a ride to the B and B." She paused to listen again and then huffed, "Yeah, well, I have to finish my shift here and then rush home to change before the wedding, so I don't think I'll have time to get her there before they leave either."

When she stopped talking, Brooklyn heard Luke raising his voice but couldn't understand what he was saying. Whatever it was, it was obviously riling Kenzie up because she shouted, "Fine, you explain to the Burlesons why I'm closing the store early! Make sure JJ knows that it's because his cousin, the illustrious police chief, is too busy planning which out-of-town guest he's gonna hit on at the reception to come all the way over to the other side of Heart's Destiny to actually do his job and insure the safety of a stranded woman." Her finger poking on the end call button was probably not as satisfying as hanging up on him would've been on an old-fashioned landline, but she still made a growling noise in her throat that showed her irritation.

Brooklyn wasn't sure what to say to Kenzie as she stomped behind the counter. Having lived such a sheltered life with her only real interactions with other people being the staff at the house, she was what most people would call socially awkward. She had a few online friends, but they didn't really know her, and she'd never been in a situation with any of them when they were upset like Kenzie was right then. So, Brooklyn just shifted her weight back and forth from her right to left foot and back again, wondering if there was anything she could do to help Kenzie. She would've offered to help her by covering her shift, so she could go get ready for the wedding, but she knew she wouldn't know how to do the job, and there was no way she should trust a stranger to help that way anyway. Brooklyn hated being the cause of Kenzie being upset though, and wanted to do something to make her feel better.

If you'd have stayed home and done as you were told, Kenzie wouldn't be upset! You mess things up, even for people who don't know you! Brooklyn heard the inner voice that sounded like her father in her head.

She shook it off as best she could, trying to remember the lessons she'd learned in her online psychology class about maintaining a positive self-image. She tried to remember some of the positive mantras she'd learned in her online class and repeated them in her head. *I am only responsible for myself, not the thoughts, feelings, or actions of others. I am a good person. I know I'm not the person my father tells me I am. I am strong. I am smart. I can do anything I put my mind to doing. Now smile and show the world who you are!*

Kenzie came out from behind the counter carrying a purse on her shoulder, a piece of paper and tape in her left hand, and a key ring in her right hand. As she taped the paper to the door and locked up, Brooklyn realized that she was closing the store to take her to the bed and breakfast she'd mentioned on the phone. Brooklyn worried that she couldn't afford a bed and breakfast long term, so she stopped Kenzie before she could lead her out the back door.

"Um, you don't have to close early to take me anywhere." Brooklyn took a step back toward the front door that the other woman had just locked. "I don't want to put you out. If you just want to point me in the direction of the motel, I'm more than capable of walking. My car's locked and off the road, so if Luke can't get to it today, I can meet with him when the garage opens again."

"Oh, you're not putting me out," Kenzie insisted, grabbing Brooklyn's hand, and pulling her toward the back of the store.

Not used to people touching her that way, Brooklyn jerked her hand away, sure she looked like a big scaredy cat not wanting to walk into the back of the store with Kenzie. "Sorry," Brooklyn apologized when Kenzie looked at her like she was trying to figure out what she was thinking. "I, uh…" Brooklyn stammered, not sure what she should say.

Kenzie studied Brooklyn for a second before speaking. "Don't worry about it. I forget that some people don't like to be touched. I'm a very touchy-feely person. I hug everyone, and when I get an idea, I run with it, and often try to drag my friends along, literally. Sorry, I'll try to not do that again, for at least a few days until you can get used to me."

She smiled then and Brooklyn realized the other woman was just friendly in a way she wasn't accustomed to, and it made her feel guilty for being afraid a moment before. Brooklyn smiled back, though it wasn't as big as Kenzie's grin.

"Luke's my cousin, and he's driven me crazy for as long as I can remember. I forgot that you're new to town and don't know that, so you didn't realize that my irritability is directed at him and not you. I should've explained and told you what the plan is, instead of just trying to drag you out of here. No worries, I can do that now. I'm taking you to the B and B, it's the only hotel in town, and over five miles from here, so it's too far to walk. Luke is gonna pick up your car, but he won't do anything other than hook it up to the tow truck and take it to the garage today, so don't expect to hear from him about it until Monday. You able to stay in town until then? Or are you in a hurry to get to wherever you were going?"

Kenzie talked fast and said all that while walking quickly toward the back of the store. Brooklyn struggled to keep up with her as she followed, and she wasn't sure she actually caught everything the other woman had said. But she had to respond to her final questions, so she thought up a quick backstory to tell her.

"Yeah, I can definitely stay in town until Monday," Brooklyn acquiesced as they exited the back door. "But I'll need to go get a couple more bags from my car before they tow it, so I don't have to hunt down my clothes and stuff at the garage before then."

After they got in the truck Kenzie had parked behind the building and drove over to her car, so she could get all her clothes and other necessities, Brooklyn continued explaining her situation, or at least the cover story she was using. "I don't actually have a timeline or final destination where I have to be. I'm an author, so I can work anywhere. That's why I'm driving across the country, just to get a visual for different parts of the world to use as inspiration for my books."

"Oh, that's so cool!" Kenzie shouted. "Have you written anything I might have read?"

"I think you're a little older than my target audience," Brooklyn giggled. "They're more for preteens and young teenagers. *Mary Kate the Great* is my first book. It was published back in June. Then in August, *Mary Kate's Cotillion Catastrophe* was published. It's my second book. Last month, the third book, *Mary Kate's College Capers*, was released. I'm hoping to have the forth one written to publish before Christmas, but I need to see more of the world than my hometown in Georgia to have a good idea of how to describe the background of all the places she sees in *Mary Kate's Great Escape*, so it'll probably end up being published in January."

Brooklyn looked around as they drove through town, thinking that she should probably be taking some mental notes about the city, so she could describe the Old West vibe she got from most of the buildings. It was strange that the streets were paved, and the traffic lights were modern, but the buildings looked like they belonged in an Old West ghost town. The signs on the businesses were all carved wood, and Tully's Roadhouse, which was a block down from the Gas & Go where she'd met Kenzie, actually had swinging doors like on the saloons in old western movies. *How do they lock up at closing time?* Brooklyn wondered.

Kenzie was pointing out various places and telling Brooklyn who owned what and where to go to find whatever she might need while she was in town, but Brooklyn was unsure she was comprehending any of what she'd said because Kenzie was still talking so fast that Brooklyn couldn't catch but half of what she was saying. Kenzie was so friendly, Brooklyn hated that she wasn't able to return that friendship with as much openness and honesty.

After passing through the Old West themed downtown area, they went over a bridge that seemed way too big for the tiny stream down below it. The surrounding area was mostly flat grassland that looked like it would be ideal for a park and Brooklyn wondered why they hadn't put any playgrounds or sports fields there. That was what she would put there if she owned that land. Places for families to come to play and picnic.

But that was just the whimsical dreams of a woman who longed for a happy family, and she knew she'd probably never have one of those. As a little girl, she'd thought that's what she had—a happy family with Mommy and Daddy. But then her mommy died when she was four and her daddy left her at home with the staff and spent all his time at work. After a while, Brooklyn got used to only seeing him when he brought her a new dress and took her to a dinner party or charity event that he had to have her attend to keep up appearances.

Thankfully, Mary taught her at an early age how to behave at those fancy dinners, so she could use the right utensils and not embarrass her father. His expectation was that she was there to be seen and not heard, so Brooklyn followed the rules and watched everyone around her from whatever seat he directed her to for the evening. She was sure all his friends and their children just thought she was shy, since she never really interacted with anyone. But she honestly just felt so out of place and uncomfortable that she didn't feel like she had anything in common with any of them to have anything to say.

That was kind of how she was feeling right that moment in the truck with Kenzie. She was grateful that the other woman was so outgoing and friendly that she was talking enough for both of them. Brooklyn just hoped Kenzie didn't feel let down by her inability to adequately carry her end of the conversation.

Just past the park-like setting that Brooklyn had loved seeing, Kenzie turned into a parking area for the bed and breakfast. Beside the parking lot there was a huge, bright yellow house that was at least three stories with a wrap-around, covered porch and white porch rail and posts up to the additional porch on the second floor. *Is it still a porch on the second floor or is it a balcony?*

When they walked inside, Brooklyn was surprised to see the place appeared to be deserted.

"Oh, I bet everyone is over in the other building setting up for the reception tonight." Kenzie pulled out her phone and dialed a number. "I'll just call Mrs. Hunter and see where she wants me to take you until you can actually check in with her later."

"Um, okay," Brooklyn stammered, unsure what else she could do in such a strange situation.

"Hi, Mrs. Hunter, it's Kenzie Martin," Kenzie greeted the proprietress through her phone. "Yes, Mrs. Mandi, I'll try." Kenzie replied to whatever the other woman had said with a little giggle. "Yeah, I'm at your front desk with a woman whose car broke down on the highway right by the Gas & Go. She needs a room until Luke can get her car going again."

Kenzie paused to listen to the other woman for a long moment, while Brooklyn stood there worried that she wouldn't have anything available until after the wedding guests left.

"Yeah, I can bring her on around," Kenzie agreed with whatever she'd been told, smiling at Brooklyn, and giving her a thumbs up. "Thanks, Mrs. Mandi. See you in a few minutes."

Kenzie disconnected her call before telling Brooklyn what had been said on the phone. "Mrs. Mandi Hunter owns and runs the B and B. We're supposed to drive on around to the plantation house, so she can give you a room key. She's only over there for a few minutes though, just checking to make sure the ballroom is ready for the reception before going home to get ready to go to the wedding, so we have to hurry."

"Oh, okay, thanks." Brooklyn followed Kenzie back out to her truck, so they could drive around what appeared to be a huge property that included multiple houses. Brooklyn wasn't sure how many of the buildings were part of the bed and breakfast and how many were actually family homes, but she thought it had to be a mix of both.

When they pulled into the parking lot beside a ginormous mansion that reminded Brooklyn of the British country houses she'd seen on one of the travel shows she loved to watch on television, Brooklyn understood why the wedding reception was being held in the building. It made the mansion she'd grown up in on her father's estate look like a middle-class home in comparison.

Brooklyn giggled at the thought of how her father would react to his home being classified as middle-class. *Father would flip if he knew how I just thought of our house. Probably even more than he's flipping out about me being gone.*

Brooklyn knew she needed to do some research to figure out what all that heiress mess her father was telling the press was really about, but she couldn't mentally handle going there at the moment. She had to focus on what needed to be done, so she could have a bed for the night first and foremost.

As soon as they were parked by the mammoth mansion, Kenzie helped Brooklyn carry her bags into the foyer. Brooklyn stacked her things off to the side of the entrance and said a quick goodbye to Kenzie, who was rushing off to get ready for the wedding that appeared to be the biggest event the town had seen in years. At least, according to what Kenzie had said and Brooklyn overheard as she entered the building that the locals referred to as the plantation house.

"You must be the stranded motorist that Kenzie said she was dropping off." A brunette in her late forties or early fifties smiled as she approached Brooklyn. "Sorry, I didn't get your name from Kenzie, but everything's hectic here today."

"I'm Bro…" Brooklyn coughed into the crook of her elbow to hide the fact that she almost gave the woman her real name. "Sorry, I'm Brie. Brie Brooks."

"Mandi Hunter," the older woman introduced herself, extending her hand to shake. Brooklyn returned the strong handshake greeting, even though it wasn't how she was taught to greet new people at the society events her father took her to back home. "I'm gonna put you in room two-oh-one here in the plantation house. It's one of the rooms that has its own bathroom. Most of the others share a Jack-and-Jill bathroom with a second bedroom, but they're mostly occupied by the GWA crew here until Monday. I figure a single woman on your own won't wanna share a bathroom with a couple of wrestlers, right?"

"Um, yeah, right," Brooklyn stammered out, wondering what kind of strange alternate universe she'd stumbled into when her car died. *Wrestlers?*

"Sorry, there's no elevator, but we wanted to stick to as close to the original design as possible when we converted the old place into more of a hotel and event center, so it'll be a few months before we're able to extract enough of the same stone that was originally used to build this place in the eighteen-seventies to add an elevator to the north end of the building by the parking lot." Mandi motioned for Brooklyn to follow her as she quickly gave her a tour of the downstairs. "Luckily, the building inspector still allowed us to open for the wedding, since the ramps are done to make the first floor accessible and we have handicap accessible rooms in the other building for overnight guests who need them."

Once she'd shown Brooklyn the library, kitchen, a few rooms that looked like living rooms that were available as communal space for guests, and the ballroom that was being set up for the wedding reception, Mandi helped Brooklyn grab all her bags and finally directed her up the stairs to the rooms. Mandi pulled a key from her pocket when they approached the room Brooklyn would be staying in for a few days.

"I don't have time to do the normal check-in paperwork right now," Mandi explained as she put the key in the lock and opened the door to the room. "But we can do that tomorrow, either before or after church. You're welcome to join us at church and the reception tonight, since you don't have a way to go anywhere else to eat dinner and the kitchen here is gonna be in use by the caterers, so you won't be able to just grab something from there either."

"Oh, no, I wouldn't want to crash the wedding," Brooklyn protested, though she wasn't sure what she would do for food other than making an appearance at the wedding reception.

"Nonsense, the Burlesons made it known that any guests we had staying here that weren't already here for the wedding were more than welcome to attend." Mandi waved away Brooklyn's objections. "Hazel knows half the town is shutting down for her son's wedding, so she'll probably come looking for you to make sure you've eaten dinner as soon as she finds out you're here for the night. Besides, I imagine it'll be the first chance you'll get to actually speak to Luke about your car, since I know he didn't open the garage today."

"Well, um, okay," Brooklyn sputtered, feeling more than a little overwhelmed by the graciousness of the residents of this quaint small town.

"We'll all be heading over to the church for the ceremony in about an hour." Mandi turned to leave. "I'm sure anyone leaving from here will be glad to give you a ride if you wanna go, or you can just come down to the ballroom later if you prefer."

"Oh, um, thanks." Brooklyn awkwardly waved goodbye to Mandi's fleeting back. She took the key out of the door before closing it and setting her bags down on the bed. "I guess it's a good thing I packed a couple of nicer dresses to use if I need to interview for a job and not just my comfy clothes. I could probably wear one of the long skirt and blouse combos to the wedding reception tonight or church in the morning, but I definitely couldn't go in the leggings and hoodies I've gotten used to wearing the past couple of days."

Brooklyn spent the next hour unpacking and getting her stuff organized before grabbing a shower and getting dressed up to go to the wedding reception. *Surely, nobody will recognize me in this little town,* she thought as she fixed her now brown hair and put the brown contacts back in, where she'd taken them out to give her eyes a rest while she was alone in her room. *Even if they've seen the national news to know who I really am, I doubt they'll recognize me. I don't think my father could even identify me now.*

~ ~ ~

Bobby felt a little melancholy as he watched his youngest brother marry the love of his life. He was thrilled for his brother; glad Anthony had been able to overcome the trying times in his past to finally have the family he wanted so badly. But a small part of him wondered if he would ever be able to find the same happiness Anthony had found with Kay.

Bobby would never publicly admit to having a small sliver of his soul where he was jealous of his baby brother. Not that he had a thing for his new sister-in-law or anything like that. He was jealous that

Anthony had found someone to share his life with, someone who was just as in love with Anthony as Anthony was with her. Bobby had never felt love like Anthony and Kay shared, like his parents experienced, like his aunts and uncles felt, and like several other older couples in town knew.

Bobby knew true love and happily ever after existed because he saw the evidence of it every day in the love drunk town he grew up in, but he was beginning to think it wasn't in the cards for him. He was three months away from his thirtieth birthday and had never had more than a weekend fling with a woman. And women who lasted more than a one-night stand were few and far between.

He'd never lacked for female companionship when he wanted it, always able to pick up a buckle bunny at Tully's Roadhouse when they were in town for the rodeo, or a hottie for the night at one of the bars in San Antonio that he frequented when there wasn't a rodeo in Heart's Destiny. But having learned his senior year of high school that bringing a woman to his home for a bootie call was a bad idea, Bobby's hookups had almost always been in his truck, at the woman's place, or in a hotel in San Antonio. So, he never pictured any of them in his home, much less as his future bride.

The one time he'd made the mistake of taking Tammi Jo Willis to his house when he was eighteen and feeling grown up by living on his own, she'd tried to make it into more than it was, going so far as to try to move in with him. After he finally got her and all her shit off the ranch, Bobby hauled his bed, sheets, pillows, and all, out back and had a bonfire to exorcise all traces of her crazy ass from his home. He spent some time working for Luke's dad at the construction company after school and on Saturdays to earn the money to buy a new bed, so he didn't have to explain to his parents why he needed a new one.

Bobby was brought back from his musings of the past by the laughter around him as his youngest brother pulled their grandparents' wedding bands off the necklace around his neck, so he and Kay could complete the ring exchange portion of the ceremony. Since those were the only family heirloom rings that Bobby knew about in his family, he figured it was just as well that he'd probably never get married because he knew absolutely nothing about ring shopping to ever be able to propose.

The more he thought about it, the more he realized that he was pretty much married to his job and didn't really have time for a wife anyway. With having such a small police department, he was pretty much always on call. While there wasn't much crime in the small town he grew up in, Bobby kept himself busy with volunteering at the youth center in town and handling the security issues of Burleson Incorporated on his downtime.

The only reason he'd really had the opportunity to look up the details on the case of the missing woman in Georgia the day before was because it was Black Friday, and most of the people in town went into San Antonio to shop instead of causing a scene at the local businesses. Since he hadn't had a single call while in the office, and Burleson Incorporated was closed for the holiday until Monday, Bobby had spent his day researching everything he could find on Brooklyn Barns. Unfortunately, there wasn't a lot about her online. No social media, no personal website or blog. Just the news reports about her supposed abduction and the photos her father had released to try to find her.

Bobby had been blown away by the first picture he saw of the woman, feeling an instant attraction that he'd never experienced before, either in person or when looking at a photograph of a woman. It wasn't just that he got an instant erection when he saw her slender, lithe figure, long blonde hair, and vibrant blue eyes, though that did happen. He saw something in her eyes that called out to him, made him want to be the one to find her and rescue her from whatever made her look so distraught.

She was dressed to the nines in every photograph that her father had released to the media, like she never took a picture unless she was out at some high-society gala. While she was drop dead gorgeous in every single shot, her smile looked fake and never seemed to reach her eyes. Bobby wanted, just once, to see her real smile, but he knew that would never be in the cards for him.

It figures that the one time I actually think I'm having the "she's **The One***" feelings my family has described for as long as I can remember, it's for a girl I'll never actually have a chance to meet. Makes it pretty hard to believe I'll ever be able to really fall in love and have a wife and family of my own.*

As he followed the rest of the wedding guests out of the church and over to the plantation house at the Hunters' Bed and Breakfast for the reception, Bobby mentally catalogued the various reports he'd read online about Brooklyn's disappearance. With the case being out of his jurisdiction, he hadn't had access to the actual police reports, or any of the legal documents surrounding the estate she was supposed to inherit when she got married, so he'd been stuck with only reading the various news outlets' skewed accounts of her disappearance and snapshots of her life. And he knew better than to believe half of what was reported by the media.

No two reports that he'd read online actually agreed as to whether there was foul play involved in her disappearance. One claimed there were signs of a struggle in her room, but no signs of forced entry into the home. Another claimed there were signs of forced entry, but no signs of a struggle. Yet another article claimed that all her belongings were still in her bedroom, packed up and ready to be moved into her new home once she was married, and that was contradicted by yet another article that said her belongings were strewn around the room like someone had searched them.

Her father and fiancé both claimed that she'd been kidnapped by a business rival who wanted to stop her from taking over Ashbury Enterprises. *Fiancé*, Bobby gagged as he recalled the picture of the man old enough to be her father that he'd seen online the day before. *I don't believe him, or her father, with their conspiracy theories about this being a kidnapping to prevent her from taking over the company, unless the two of them are the kidnappers. Shit, maybe that's it! They don't want her to take over the company because they'll get caught with whatever dirty dealings they've had going on over the last couple of decades.*

Bobby's lightbulb moment about the possible motives for the case was quickly forgotten as he entered the ballroom for his youngest brother's wedding reception. Soon he was surrounded by friends and family making small talk as they awaited the arrival of the wedding party. Bobby found a seat at the back of the room with his best friend, Luke Walker, and several of their brothers and cousins, where they were all trying to avoid their matchmaking mothers.

Soon, the wedding party danced their way into the ballroom, with Anthony's boss announcing their entrances like he would announce the wrestlers who worked for him on their way into an arena. He laughed along with the rest of the crowd, but Bobby was secretly glad that Anthony had chosen his best friends to be his groomsmen and not his brothers. Bobby could two-step with the best of them, but he had no desire to be pushed toward one of the bridesmaids, like the Hunters were being pushed by his mom and her friends.

"What do you think of James hooking up with Kay's sister?" Luke lifted his chin in their direction.

"Better him than me," Bobby chuckled, shaking his head at his friend. Although he saw several similarities between Randi Lee and Brooklyn Barns, Bobby hadn't felt even a slight attraction to his brother's new sister-in-law in the week she'd been in town, much less the intense attraction he felt toward the missing woman he had no chance of ever actually meeting. "Actually, I'm surprised Ma's been pretty lax about pushing me toward the single ladies in town for the wedding, but I'm not gonna point it out to her as long as she keeps her matchmaking directed at anyone but me."

"Hey, I better not be included in that *'anyone,'* Chief." Luke used air quotes to emphasize the word "anyone" before continuing. "If your mom starts spreading her matchmaking and grandbaby fever to my mom, you're gonna hafta help me hide out, too."

"Speaking of matchmaking, what was up with your cousin thinking we'd be hooking up with women here?" Bobby referred to the conversation they'd had earlier when Kenzie had called Luke while they were getting a late lunch before going home to get ready for the wedding.

"She was just being typical Kenzie," Luke groaned, shaking his head. "She thinks we spend too much time at Tully's picking up buckle bunnies, and rags on me every time I talk to her. I'm surprised she didn't out-n-out call me a man-whore like she's done before. I guess she figures you're right there with me most of the time, so she assumed we'd be looking to hook up with the out-of-town wedding guests tonight. Like either one of us would hook up with someone who will probably come back to town to visit regularly now that Kay lives here."

Bobby didn't have a chance to respond to his friend as the speeches began and dinner was served. After they'd eaten, while the bride and groom were having their first dance, a beautiful brunette walked up to their table.

She was wearing a navy-blue dress that was a little on the casual side for a wedding, but Bobby didn't mind that it wasn't fancy with the way it hugged her curves. He also didn't recognize her as someone he'd met at one of the other wedding events, so he wondered if she was one of Kay's friends from out of town, or if she was another guest at the B and B that had been invited to the reception at the last minute.

Fuck, seriously, twice in two days? Bobby mentally questioned his body's response to the woman, who hadn't even had a chance to say a word yet. Just a glimpse of her and his dick was standing at attention, much like the way he'd responded to seeing Brooklyn Barns' picture the day before. *I thought these love-at-first-sight feelings were supposed to be limited to only one woman?*

"Um, which one of you is Luke?" The bombshell looked back and forth between him and Luke, making Bobby want to punch his friend for being the one she was asking about.

"That would be me, darlin'." Luke stood and extended his hand to the woman Bobby seriously wanted more than he'd ever wanted a woman before, even though he didn't even know her name.

"I'm Bro-Brie," she stuttered, taking Luke's hand, which he promptly pulled up to his lips.

Get your fucking lips off my girl, Bobby growled at his best friend in his head.

"I wanted to find out if you were able to pick up my car today." Brie pulled her hand back from where Luke had just kissed the back of it. "And give you the key if you need it to be able to figure out what's wrong with it."

"You're the one Kenzie called me about?" Luke questioned, looking like he was ready to kick himself for not going to help the woman immediately.

Bobby recognized the expression on Luke's face because he was mentally kicking himself for not leaving the Burger Barn to go pick up the stranded motorist as well. But since Luke told him it was a woman, he'd figured Kenzie driving her to the B and B would be less frightening than having him or one of his officers show up to drive her, especially since she hadn't been in an accident to need police attention about her car.

Brie nodded her head at Luke, but didn't verbally answer him, looking shy and nervous. Bobby wasn't sure why she was so nervous, but he liked the shy blush spreading across her cheeks. He only wished he'd been the one to cause it.

"Yeah, I picked it up." Luke scratched the back of his head. "But I haven't had a chance to look at it yet. It's still hooked up to the tow truck at the garage."

"Oh, okay." Brie shuffled from foot to foot like she was ready to bolt as soon as possible. "Well, here's the key. I'll be here at the bed and breakfast whenever you figure out what's wrong with it."

Brie handed Luke a single key on a keyring before turning and walking away from their table.

Bobby quickly jumped up from his seat and followed after her, needing to at least introduce himself and see if he could charm a smile out of the ravishing beauty. Being at least a foot taller than the petite dark-haired woman, Bobby caught up with her in three long strides.

As much as he longed to touch her, he would never do so without her permission. So, instead of reaching out to tap her on the shoulder, or clasp her hand to stop her forward momentum toward the door, Bobby stepped in front of her to block her path.

"Please don't leave without letting me introduce myself and welcome you to Heart's Destiny," Bobby pleaded as his hazel eyes met her caramel-colored orbs. *Damn, now I understand what Kay said about Anthony's eyes last weekend at the wedding shower. I don't think I've ever craved caramel as much as I do right now.*

"Um, okay." Brie nervously looked up at him.

Her words made Bobby realize that he'd stopped talking when he got lost in her eyes, so he cleared his throat of the lump lodged inside and lifted a hand to her as if he were going to shake hers as he continued introducing himself. "I'm Bobby, the police chief for Heart's Destiny."

"Oh," she gasped as she placed her small hand in his, her mouth forming a perfect O as she said the word. Just that small connection between them felt like so much more in a way Bobby wasn't sure he could explain.

Bobby lifted her hand to his mouth, lightly brushing his lips across the back of her hand, and feeling a tingle of electricity run from his hand and lips that were touching her straight to his overly engorged cock. He hated having to lower her hand and ultimately release it. "I'd love to show you around town. Help you keep from being bored and feeling cooped up in your room while you're waiting for your car to be fixed."

"Oh, no, that's not necessary," Brie declined his sly way of trying to get her to go out with him, looking down and no longer making eye contact with him. "Thank you for the offer, but I have to go now."

With that, she brushed by him and fled from the ballroom, leaving Bobby dumbfounded as to what had just happened.

"Dude," Luke drawled, dragging the word out to multiple syllables, as they both watched the doorway that Brie had just walked through as if hoping she would change her mind and return. "I never thought I'd see the day when a woman was able to resist both of us, much less that it would happen within five minutes of meeting us. I mean, I've been disappointed when a hottie like that gravitates more to you than to me, but I'm cool with that since the opposite happens just as often. But this," Luke waved a hand in the direction that Brie had just run away before finishing his sentence, "is an absolute first and not one I like."

"Yeah," was all Bobby uttered, not wanting to delve into the strange feelings he had being around Brie just yet, especially not with his best friend, who also seemed to be affected by the beautiful stranger.

Chapter Two

Sunday, November 25, 2018

Brooklyn was a little more comfortable eating breakfast the next morning than she'd been when she ate dinner at the wedding reception the night before. A couple of the women she'd met while eating dinner at the reception waved her over to their table as she exited the breakfast buffet line. Not wanting to be rude, she joined them to eat, but hoped they would dominate the discussion like they had previously, so she wouldn't accidentally out herself like she almost had several times since she'd arrived in Heart's Destiny, Texas.

It wasn't like she was intentionally trying to tell anyone who she really was. She just wasn't used to referring to herself as Brie Brooks anywhere but online. Several times the day before, she'd almost introduced herself as Brook or Brooklyn instead of Brie. That really could've been a disaster if she'd said her real name in front of the police chief, when she was talking to his mechanic friend.

And what was up with the flutters in my stomach when I looked into officer Bobby's eyes? Or feeling like I was struck by lightning when he kissed my hand? I didn't feel anything like that when Luke kissed my hand. Does that mean there's something special about Bobby that I should recognize? Is this what it feels like to have a crush on someone?

I really shouldn't develop a crush on the police chief, when I'm being hunted down by the Macon Police Department, and probably even the Federal Bureau of Investigation. And that's got to be what those crazy flutters and tingles are, right? Me crushing on the attractive cop, who I need to stay as far away from as possible.

She shook away those thoughts as she tuned into the conversation of the women around her. They were fascinating, and Brooklyn wished she could somehow record their conversations to be able to remember them better to incorporate some of them as characters in a book. Apparently, the couple who got married the day before were both employed by the Galactic Wrestling Association, so most of the people staying at the bed and breakfast were also employees of the sports entertainment company.

Brooklyn hadn't ever really watched wrestling on television before. But after meeting the women around her and their famous husbands, she wanted to check out their show, when it came on in a couple of days, to see if she could put some faces to the stories the women had told her over dinner, and now over breakfast.

When they asked her about herself, she'd actually found it pretty easy to talk about her books and her writing process, without delving too deep into the rest of her life back home in Georgia. That is, until their conversation took a turn that Brooklyn hadn't expected, and really wanted to completely avoid.

"So, Brie, where'd you say you're from?" Emily looked at her with a little too much scrutiny for Brooklyn's comfort.

"Georgia," Brooklyn replied before taking another bite of her scrambled eggs to, hopefully, hide her unease.

"Do you know that missing heiress?" Emily was still watching Brooklyn very closely.

Brooklyn shook her head, indicating a negative response as she chewed the massive bite of eggs that were suddenly tasteless in her mouth.

"Jeez, Em, Georgia might not be as big a state as Texas, but it's not like it's as small as Heart's Destiny, where everyone knows everyone else." Jana rolled her eyes at her friend. "Asking her if she knows that Brooklyn chick is like me asking you if you know the governor of Indiana's daughter. You might be able to find something about her online because of her being newsworthy, but you don't know her just because you're from Indiana."

Grateful for Jana's inadvertent defense of her when she couldn't respond with a mouth full of food, Brooklyn quickly swallowed and tried to cover for herself a little, praying she wasn't obvious in her blatant lie. "Yeah, there's over four million people in the Atlanta metro area and I only know about a hundred of them. And the only reason I even know most of their names is from interacting with them in my classes the past few years. The people I would say I really know and consider my lifelong friends, I can count on one hand."

"Yeah, don't mind Em and her true crime fascination," Jana waved off her friend's interest in Brooklyn's supposed kidnapping and changed the subject. "I wanna hear more about your books. Our daughters are eight and nine. Do you think they'd be something they'd be interested in reading?"

"Um, maybe," Brooklyn shrugged, not wanting to offend anyone by questioning the reading levels of their children. "They're really geared more toward twelve- to sixteen-year-olds, at least the last couple. They might like the first one, though. Mary Kate was eleven in it, so not too much of an age difference from them now."

"Oh, yes, which one is that?" Jana's eyes lit up with excitement as she pulled out her phone, as if she was going to search for the book and order it right then.

"*Mary Kate the Great*," Brooklyn replied. "It's about the imaginary world she makes up as she explores the family farm. The rest of the series follows her as she grows up. She's thirteen in *Mary Kate's Cotillion Catastrophe*, sixteen in *Mary Kate's College Capers*, and twenty in the final book that I'm currently writing, *Mary Kate's Great Escape*. Once she has her happily ever after, I'm planning to pick a new character to follow through their preteen and teenage years like I did with Mary Kate."

"Sixteen in college?" Emily looked confused. "That's a bit young don't you think?"

"Maybe?" Brooklyn shrugged. "But since I'm writing books for teenage girls, I wanted to give them a brilliant heroine to inspire them to study hard in school."

"It's not really that young." Jana gave her a bright smile. "Tia's not even thirteen and she's about to test out of high school, so she can start college classes next year. Maybe we should give her the whole series for Christmas or her birthday?"

"Wow!" Brooklyn couldn't hold back the exclamation, surprised by the age of the child they mentioned. "Thirteen and starting college, that's amazing. I hope she doesn't have as hard a time fitting in as Mary Kate did."

Jana and Emily went on to explain to Brooklyn about their friend Kay, who was the bride in the wedding the day before, and her daughter, Tia. Hearing that the young girl would be doing her college classes online with her new father figure was inspiring for Brooklyn. She wished she could spend some time with the young genius to get a feel for what it was like to be wise beyond her years.

Brooklyn certainly had no idea what that would feel like in real life. If anything, she was the opposite in her own life, feeling like her body was maturing at a much faster pace than her mind. That's why she wrote mostly stories about the preteen and teenage years. In her head, she still felt like she was younger than her years because she hadn't had the experiences of life to help her mentally mature.

But that's why I'm on this trip, Brooklyn mused. *To experience the world and grow into the woman I want to be. Escaping father's gilded cage is just a bonus.*

When they were finished eating, the other women rounded up their kids and husbands to go on an excursion into San Antonio while Brooklyn went in search of Mandi Hunter, so she could actually check-in to the hotel. It didn't take long to find the older woman, since she'd told Brooklyn to meet her at the front desk in the other building at nine-thirty to do the paperwork and get a ride to church that morning.

"Good morning, Mrs. Hunter." Brooklyn smiled brightly as she approached the desk. "Sorry, Mandi," Brooklyn corrected after receiving a pointed look from the proprietress of the bed and breakfast for her first greeting.

"Good morning, Brie," Mandi smiled back. "I was sorry to see you leave the party so early last night."

"Yeah…" Brooklyn let the word trail off, stalling for an excuse for why she ate and ran the night before, not wanting to admit to running away from the crazy attraction she felt for the local police chief. "Yesterday was long and tiring, so I took advantage of that glorious bed to rest up from my travels the past few days."

"I can understand that," Mandi lightly chuckled. "No worries, I'm glad you like the room. Now, if you'll fill out this guest card, I'll put you in our system."

Mandi handed Brooklyn a piece of cardstock slightly bigger than a standard index card. Brooklyn started filling out the information, using her alias, as Mandi quoted her the room rates. Brooklyn paused in her task as she did some mental math. She'd known that the posh hotel would be more expensive than the rundown motels she'd stayed in the first two nights on the road, but she wasn't quite prepared for more than double the cost of the motel rooms for an unknown length of time.

Maybe I can find a job that's close enough I can walk to work until my car is fixed? Brooklyn pondered. *I can cover that for a couple of weeks with what I currently have in the bank, but I won't have anything left to pay for my car repairs. So, either Luke has to be a miracle worker and fix my car tomorrow, or I'm going to need to supplement my income until my next royalty payment.*

"Everything okay?" Mandi arched an eyebrow when she noticed that Brooklyn had only filled in the first line on the form—her fake name.

"Yeah, sorry." Brooklyn shook her head before looking back down at the card on the counter and realizing that she didn't have much information that she could really fill in, since she no longer had a permanent residence or her old phone number. "Um, I'm not sure what to put on here. I, uh, left for this trip when my lease was up, so I don't have a permanent address."

"Oh, okay." Mandi looked at her quizzically.

Brooklyn quickly recited the same cover story that she'd given everyone else about being an author and needing to travel for research for story settings. When Mandi just smiled and said to leave those lines blank, Brooklyn filled in her Brie Brooks email address and looked at the cheap phone she'd bought three days before to get the number to list it on the card. Once she put the phone back in her purse, she pulled out the debit card, which she'd gotten for her Brie Brooks online bank account, and handed it to Mandi to make sure the other woman knew she had money to pay for her room.

"Oh, no, we don't collect for the room until checkout." Mandi smiled at her in a way that reminded Brooklyn of her mother's smile in the photos she had from her early childhood. "Especially since we don't know how long it will take Luke to get your car running. I hate having to run someone's card more than once, ya know. Too much to do in my day to spend half of it up here running cards for every guest on a daily basis."

"Oh, okay." Brooklyn felt her cheeks flush as she put her card back in her wallet. "Um, if you have that much work to do each day, maybe

I can spend some of my time here helping you with it? I wasn't planning for a big car repair expense so soon on my trip, so if I'm going to be in town for a while, I should probably supplement my book royalties with an actual job."

"Oh, yes, I can see how that might be necessary." Mandi suddenly had a broad smile spreading across her face. "I actually just filled all the positions I had open up with the expansion into the plantation house, but I have a friend I'd love to introduce you to at church. I believe Hazel is looking for someone to help her out with cooking and cleaning on the ranch. I'm not sure when she would want you to start, or if that would even be something you'd be interested in, but we can discuss it with her at the potluck dinner after church."

"Oh, yes, I'd definitely be interested." Brooklyn felt a little of the weight of the world being lifted off her shoulders at the prospect of finding a job locally. Especially since it sounded like a job she'd actually be qualified for, after her years of helping Mary at home.

Maybe if it pays well enough to cover the cost of rent, I can find an apartment in town. Heart's Destiny seems like as good a place as any to hide from my father and provide the backdrop for my next series of stories.

<div style="text-align:center">~~~</div>

Hazel Burleson pulled her phone out of her purse as it dinged indicating she had a text message, just as she was getting in the car to go to church with her husband, Bob, driving. She almost couldn't contain the squeal of delight when she read the message from her friend, Mandi Hunter.

> **Mandi: I'm bringing a prospect for your job opening to church this morning. {Male Police Officer Emoji} {Bride Emoji}**

> **Hazel: YES! Tell me all about her!**

> **Mandi: Her name is Brie Brooks. She's an author traveling for research for book settings and her car**

broke down on the highway yesterday. She's staying
at the B&B while Luke's fixing it. She asked me about a
job this morning because she wasn't expecting a big car
repair expense so early in her trip. She seemed really
interested when I told her about you needing help
cooking and cleaning on the ranch.

Hazel: You think she'll want to stay at the B&B, or will she
be open to a live-in housekeeper position?

Mandi: I got the impression that money is tight, like it
was either the B&B or her car repairs kinda tight. So, I
think she'll be relieved to find a job with room & board
as benefits.

Hazel: Awesome! I can't wait to meet her. But make
sure you don't introduce her to me when Bobby is
around. I still have to find a time to talk to him about
the need to hire someone.

Mandi: How about you come to the B&B tomorrow while
he's at work to meet her. That way we don't take any
chances of him getting suspicious at church.

Hazel: Perfect! I'll see you tomorrow around 2. I'll have
the girls with me, but they won't say anything to
Bobby. Actually, Tia will probably be too fascinated
with your library to stick by my side for our
introduction.

Mandi: Perfect. See you then. :)

"What are you grinnin' about?" Bob asked as Hazel turned the
sound off on her phone and put it back in her handbag.

"Just planning a late lunch with Mandi tomorrow." Hazel knew her husband wouldn't like the idea of her scheming to set Bobby up with his future bride.

"Uh-huh, sure you are." Bob shook his head but still smiled at Hazel. "I know that look, Baby, and I'm sure it means that one of our sons won't like what you and Mandi will be discussing at your late lunch."

"And why would our sons object to me hiring someone to help me with all the cooking and cleaning I do on the ranch?" Hazel playfully pouted at her husband. "I'm sure they've all noticed how I've had to push it all off on Rosa this last week and wouldn't begrudge me needing a little help."

"Of course not, Baby," Bob drawled, taking her hand in his and pressing his lips to the back of it. "But when you try to match one of them up with your new assistant, I'm sure they'll voice their complaints."

Hazel giggled, knowing she could never fool Bob into believing that she wouldn't do exactly what he'd just said. "Yes, well, Jake and Josh won't be home long enough to complain," Hazel replied. "And Anthony will be thrilled to know I'm hiring someone to help me keep his and Kay's place clean and stocked while they're at work, especially once Kay has to start cutting back on her activities as she gets close to giving birth."

"So, it's just Bobby that I need to avoid, so I don't get an earful about your matchmaking?" Bob chuckled.

Hazel just shrugged and smiled, glad that they'd arrived at the church, so she didn't have to disclose all her plans to Bob right then. *Once I find the right woman for Bobby, I'm sure Bob will get on board with the plan.*

~ ~ ~

Monday, November 26, 2018

Brooklyn was nervous as she got ready for her job interview. Mandi had explained that Hazel was preoccupied with her out-of-town guests not leaving until after church, and would need to leave the Sunday services early to take over watching her new granddaughters from her new daughter-in-law's parents while her son and new daughter-in-law were on their honeymoon, so she couldn't stay to meet her the day before. Therefore, they planned for Hazel to come to the bed and breakfast to meet with *Brie* about the job opening at two o'clock Monday afternoon instead.

After talking more with Mandi about the job, Brooklyn knew it would be an answer to her prayers. In addition to the salary, which Brooklyn thought sounded like it might be close to what Mary made each year working for her father, the benefits included room and board along with health insurance. She hadn't thought about needing to have healthcare coverage other than the policy she was on with her father through Ashbury Enterprises before she left Georgia, but now that she had, she was glad to find a job that would provide it.

And room and board being included means I can save most of my salary to cover my car expenses and not have to touch much of what I have in savings from my book royalties.

Having never really worked before, she wasn't sure what all she would need to fill out for employment paperwork, but hoped she could continue to do everything under her pen name, so there wouldn't be any kind of tax record with her real name on it to alert her father to her whereabouts. *Hopefully, I can use the tax identification number for Brie Brooks, LLC, and won't have to use my social security number.*

Once she finished fixing her hair, which was progressively getting lighter every time she washed it, Brooklyn sighed, not liking her reflection in the mirror. "I guess I should've picked the permanent hair color, instead of the semi-permanent," she vented to the empty room. "Who knew semi-permanent would fade in four days? I'll just have to find a way to get into town for another box soon. Or maybe go to an actual hairdresser, so I don't royally damage my hair by coloring it every week."

Resigned to not being able to do anything at the moment about her now medium brown hair, which had been just a shade shy of black when she'd arrived in Heart's Destiny on Saturday, Brooklyn finished putting on her makeup, got dressed in her favorite blue maxi skirt and shark bite hem top, put in her brown contacts to cover her blue eyes, and slipped on her favorite sandals. Once she was completely ready with no other excuse to stay in her room, she walked downstairs to the dining room, where she was meeting Mandi and Hazel.

She was thirty minutes early, so she wasn't surprised when there was nobody else in the room. Everyone from the GWA had left that morning, heading off to entertain the world, leaving her as the sole guest at the bed and breakfast as far as she knew. The place would've been eerily quiet if not for the sounds of the staff cleaning the rooms upstairs drifting down to the first floor.

Inspired by the grand mansion and needing something to occupy her mind, so she didn't stress out too much about the interview while she waited, Brooklyn sat at one of the tables and pulled a notebook out of her bag to write out the ideas for a princess story that popped into her head. Thinking back to the buildings she'd seen in town as Kenzie drove her through on Saturday, she laid out the plans for a new book series. She wasn't sure what her main character's name would be yet, but she imagined an English princess, who wished upon a star one night to wake up the next morning and find that her manor house had been transported across the pond and back in time to the rugged American west.

> *Unfamiliar with how to live without her cell phone and internet, the princess has to learn to survive amongst the cowboys and Indians.*

No, I can't use that term, it's not politically correct, Brooklyn realized, scratching out the term and continuing to write out her ideas.

> *Unfamiliar with how to live without her cell phone and internet, the princess has to learn to survive amongst the cowboys and ~~Indians~~. Indigenous people? Native Americans? **Research the current correct term.***

> *She has to learn to ride horses in a different manner than the side saddle version of her high-society days.*

She develops a crush on the cute cowboy with dark brown hair and soulful hazel eyes who teaches her to ride western style.

Brooklyn stopped writing when she realized she was describing the police officer, who introduced himself to her at the wedding reception Saturday evening, as her newest heroine's love interest.

No, Brook, don't think about him, she mentally chastised herself, rubbing her itchy eyes, and hating that she had to wear the contacts that irritated her eyeballs. *You can't develop a crush on a cop! He'll send you home to Georgia just as soon as he finds out who you really are. Besides, your characters are too young for crushes, so there's no need to describe the attractive officer as one of your book characters.*

She went back to her notebook, adding her next idea to the list she was compiling.

The Princess becomes best friends with a local cowgirl who teaches her to ride western style.

Before she could think of the next idea to write down, Mandi called out "Brie" from across the room. Thankfully, Brooklyn responded to the sudden noise and looked up due to the fact that the place was mostly empty. She wasn't sure she would've responded so quickly to her alias being shouted, if the room was still as crowded as it had been at breakfast before the wrestling company had left.

Brooklyn started to stand to greet the women who were approaching, but Mandi waved for her to stay seated. "Don't get up, you picked my favorite table in this room. I love the garden view out this window."

Mandi made quick introductions as she and Hazel took their seats on the opposite side of the table, so they could look past Brooklyn at the garden outside the window if they wanted.

"Did we interrupt your writing?" Mandi pointed at Brooklyn's notebook, which she should've put away as soon as she realized the other women had arrived for their meeting.

"Oh, no." Brooklyn smiled, shutting the notebook, and starting to put it back in her bag. "I was just doing some brainstorming since I was inspired by my surroundings. I tend to jot down ideas as they pop into my head, so I can remember them later when I'm actually sitting down to write."

"Mandi said you're an author." Hazel looked Brooklyn over. "What genre do you write?"

"I don't really fit into a specific genre," Brooklyn explained. "I suppose they could be classified as young adult novels, since that's the classification for readers between twelve and eighteen, but with some crossover to the middle-grades classification for the more advanced readers between eight and twelve. I only have one series out so far that follows the main character, Mary Kate, from her childhood adventures as an eleven-year-old to her early admittance to college at sixteen, at least until I finish the last book in the series that I'm currently writing. She'll find her happily ever after before she turns twenty-one and then I'll go on to a different series."

"Happily ever after at twenty-one?" Mandi arched an eyebrow questioningly.

"That sounds about right to me." Hazel smiled brightly. "I got my happily ever after at about that age. Besides, teenagers don't wanna read about people our age. So, is the next book a love story?"

"I'm not really sure yet," Brooklyn shrugged, enjoying talking to the two older women about her books. "I've only written the first half so far. The outline I have planned has her working in her dream job after escaping an unwanted arranged marriage, but my fingers have been known to hijack my manuscripts in the past. So, until I actually finish writing the whole thing, I can't say for sure if she'll just learn to love herself as I have planned, or if she'll find true love as well."

"Escaping an arranged marriage, huh?" Hazel gave Brooklyn a knowing look that made her feel slightly uncomfortable, like Hazel knew who she was from her plot mirroring her own life. "What an interesting concept. That's not really done much these days. Are you sure your readers will be able to relate to the character?"

"Unfortunately, it's more common than many people realize these days, especially overseas in more poverty-stricken countries," Brooklyn replied, glad she'd done her research for the book, instead of just basing it on her own situation. "In addition to wanting to write strong heroines to empower my young female readers, I want to bring attention to some of the issues in the world that, hopefully, the next generation will be able to eradicate."

Leah Mae Wright

"A very noble goal with your writing." Mandi smiled at Brooklyn, putting her a little more at ease.

"So, what did Mandi tell you about the job I'm looking to fill?" Hazel finally got them on track with the interview, which Brooklyn had almost forgotten about with their previous discussion.

"Just that you were looking for someone to help you with cooking and cleaning on the ranch," Brooklyn stated, matter-of-factly.

"And you feel comfortable with your cooking and cleaning skills to be able to do the job?" Hazel was still studying Brooklyn like she was looking for any little flaw in her to deny her the job.

"Yes, ma'am," Brooklyn replied. "My, um, foster mom, Mary, not only taught me to keep the house tidy, but she also spent hours upon hours in the kitchen teaching me to cook and bake. If I'm not writing, my second favorite activity is spending time in the kitchen trying new recipes."

"Excellent," Hazel exclaimed with a smile before asking, "Did Mandi explain that it would be a live-in position?"

"She said that the benefits included room and board." Brooklyn assumed that meant the same thing. "But she didn't say exactly where I'd be living, or anything specific about the salary and other benefits."

"Okay, well, nothing has been specifically decided as to any of that yet, which is probably why she was so vague." Hazel waved her hand as if to indicate the salary and such were no big deal. "I've been at least partially responsible for making sure the ranch hands are fed every day since I married Bob almost thirty-three years ago. At first it mostly fell on my mother-in-law's shoulders, with my sister-in-law and I helping her out. For the past twelve years, since my mother-in-law passed away, Susan, my sister-in-law, and I have not only had to handle all the food prep, but also the housekeeping duties for several of the houses on the ranch. We hired Rosa, our good friend, and the wife of our ranch manager to help us, but as we're getting older, and our families are growing, it's getting to be too much for the three of us. Our daughters are all good about doing their own housework, but quite frankly, our sons suck at taking care of their own homes."

Brooklyn couldn't stifle the giggle that escaped as Hazel described her sons' lack of housekeeping skills.

"In addition to preparing meals for all the ranch hands and keeping my own home clean, I've been cleaning the additional houses on the ranch for my sons and Susan has been cleaning her sons' houses. We keep their freezers stocked with food, dust, vacuum, that sort of thing. But with the wedding this last week, I haven't had a chance to take care of any of that extra stuff, and I'm not sure if Susan has either."

"How many sons do you have?" Brooklyn wondered just how many houses she might have to clean each week.

"I have four and Susan has two," Hazel replied. "But two of my sons don't live on the ranch full time anymore. They'd taken the house next door to me to share when they were eighteen, but it was mostly empty the last few years, since they went off to college and then joined the Navy. I still kept that house clean, along with my oldest son's house. I just didn't clean it as often when it was empty. My youngest son recently moved in there with his new bride and daughters. But while my new daughter-in-law does an excellent job of taking care of things while she's home, Kay and Anthony are only on the ranch three days out of ten with their work schedule, so I've been trying to make sure to go over there and clean up a little bit the day before they get home, so she doesn't have to spend her three days off work sweeping, mopping, vacuuming, dusting, etc."

"Not to mention the fact that she's not gonna be able to do all that in a few months when she can't see her feet past her baby bump," Mandi interjected.

"Yes," Hazel chuckled and smiled. "And now they're building a bigger house on the ranch, so it's gonna end up being more than I can handle on my own. So, I think it's time for us to hire someone to cook and clean for the boys and my very busy daughter-in-law. It would be four houses for now, until Anthony and Kay get their new house built, then it will be five. But the one next door to me will be empty then, so you could possibly move in there once they've moved out. In the meantime, I'm not sure what we'll do for the room accommodations, but I'm working out a plan."

"I'm sure I'll be fine in whatever spare bedroom you can find for me." Brooklyn hoped her ability to be flexible would help her get the job. "I don't need much space since everything I own fit in my little car. And when I'm not working, I'll probably spend all my free time in my room writing, so I won't be a bother if I have to stay in someone's spare room."

Leah Mae Wright

"That's probably gonna be the option we take, at least for a little while," Hazel smiled. "You can consider yourself hired, but you'll have to give me a few days to get all the details worked out with the family. Will you be ready to start working next Monday?"

"Yes," Brooklyn rapidly replied, without even thinking about the possible issues she could have come up in the next week.

"And I'll give her a ride to the ranch if her car isn't fixed by then," Mandi interjected, relieving Brooklyn of a worry she hadn't even considered.

They exchanged phone numbers, so Hazel could contact her once she had the salary and benefits finalized to make sure they were acceptable. Brooklyn knew it wouldn't matter to her how much they were actually paying her. With room and board included in the benefits, any money she made would just go toward her car repairs, and then into her savings. And with not having to drive to and from work, it wouldn't even really matter if her car was beyond repair.

Brooklyn felt nothing but positive about how her life was turning out since she landed in this quaint small town. She wasn't sure if she would find her heart's destiny there like the welcome sign had said, but her heart certainly felt more at peace since she'd met so many friendly faces there.

~~~

Thursday, November 29, 2018

Bobby was completely exhausted by the time he got home at three o'clock Thursday morning. The last three days had been really rough because he'd been having to coordinate with the federal Drug Enforcement Agency and Homeland Security on a bust of some cartel low life's, who thought his small-town police department would be easy to fool into believing they were a legitimate business. Little did they know that Bobby wasn't just a small-town police chief, but that he was also on the board of directors of one of the most profitable corporations in Texas.

Burleson Incorporated might have employed more cowboys than corporate executives for the majority of the years they'd been in
~~~

business, but the investments and diversification they'd done with the profits from the oil fields on the family land had not only made them rich cowboys, but had also shown Bobby behind the scenes of how big business really worked.

It was clear to him from the first day they opened the doors of their little store that it was a front for something shady. Only an idiot would believe a small-town bodega owner could afford to drive a Tesla. Bobby had reached out to some federal contacts his brother, Jake, had referred him to a month before when he first saw that car. It took longer to get through all the red tape to get the task force out to the small town of Heart's Destiny than the actual stakeout took to bring in the majority of major players in the Rodriguez Cartel. Unfortunately, they'd rounded up everyone but Roberto Rodriguez, the head of the cartel.

DEA agent, Trent Jones, seemed to think the man they'd given the code name of Rojo, might try to stick around town instead of going back to his compound in Mexico. He'd told Bobby to be on alert for the fugitive, but he didn't have any plans to leave agents in town to try to round him up. Bobby didn't think the leader of an international drug cartel would be able to hide very easily in his small town, where everyone knew everybody else.

Rojo might be able to stay hidden in San Antonio, but I doubt he'll stick around Heart's Destiny.

Regardless of where the ringleader of the cartel was hiding, Bobby was just glad his part of the current operation was done, so he could catch up on some sleep and get back into his normal routine of running the Heart's Destiny Police Department. He preferred his small town being mostly crime free, so the worst he normally had to worry about was teenagers joyriding or cowboys fighting down at Tully's Roadhouse.

Since the town was so small, there wasn't any place open in the middle of the night to get a bite to eat, so he made his way to the kitchen in the three-bedroom Victorian style house, where he lived on the family ranch. Bobby was the oldest of the youngest generation of Burlesons, so he got the first pick of the various ranch houses when he turned eighteen. He picked the one the farthest away from his parents' and aunt and uncle's houses. He lived there for a year while he finished high school.

Leah Mae Wright

When his great-great-great-grandparents' generation set up the school system in Heart's Destiny, they decided to try to keep their children home to help with farm chores as long as they could, so the kids there had to be six years old before they could even start kindergarten. That put most folks not graduating high school until nineteen or twenty years old, so they were living at home a year or two longer than people in other areas and could pitch in on the family farm. Bobby guessed he could understand why they did it, but being the oldest of six kids, he was sure ready to move out and have his own space at eighteen. Having several houses built on the family land in the last hundred-and-fifty years at least made that possible. Bobby still had to help with chores, though, until he graduated and went in the Navy.

He thought he was being smart in getting away from the hard work of farm labor, but he was wrong. He worked just as hard in the Navy, but he had to do it while fighting seasickness. As soon as his two years were over, he hightailed it right back to his comfortable house on the family ranch. Bobby signed up for the police academy over in San Antonio, which was only fifty or sixty miles from Heart's Destiny, depending on which way you drove. Since his Master-At-Arms training in the Navy carried over to the academy, it was only a couple of months later when his training was complete. That's when he joined the Heart's Destiny Police Department. That was eight years ago. Over those eight years, he'd worked his way up to the chief position, and enjoyed the benefit of having his mom keep his house clean and fridge stocked without having to do too many days of hard labor on the ranch.

Don't take that the wrong way. Bobby helped out on his days off from the Heart's Destiny Police Department, if his dad needed him. But if he had the option of helping his Uncle Jon with office work instead, he picked helping Uncle Jon a lot more now than he did when he was younger. Luckily for Bobby, the diversification of the investments at Burleson Incorporated meant there were a lot of background checks to do on employees, and security systems to set up for the various offices, refineries, and production plants that required someone with his background in police work, so he got to do them instead of his siblings or cousins being able to handle them.

The closer he got to turning thirty, the more he'd started backing off on some of the more intense cowboy stuff, like riding bulls in the rodeo and helping his dad train horses. He just couldn't recover from getting bucked as fast as he used to, and he didn't want to risk an injury that would keep him from riding a pretty cowgirl every chance he got. Though he did still enjoy teaching the kids at the youth center how to take care of the horses they kept in the stables on the other side of town.

Bobby was disappointed when he opened the fridge to see only a half-full tub of butter and a few condiment jars in it. "Where's the Tupperware full of leftovers?" He vocalized the question even though there was nobody to reply in the empty room. "I know Ma was busy last week with Anthony's wedding, and didn't have time to clean or drop off my normal supply of dinners. But he's been married for five days, and not home to keep her busy, so why hasn't she refilled my fridge yet?"

Bobby looked through the cabinets and couldn't find anything he could make into an actual meal. He decided to settle for a couple bags of microwave popcorn to fill his stomach, so he could get some sleep. "I'll make my own Tupperwares of leftovers at Sunday supper," he grumbled into his pillow as he crashed for the day. "Or maybe I'll go raid Mom and Dad's fridge when I wake up, so I don't starve before Sunday."

~~~

After sleeping most of Thursday away since he was so drained after being up for three days on that stakeout, Bobby took a quick shower and put on his favorite jeans, a green t-shirt, and cowboy boots. He brushed his teeth and combed his hair, and he was ready for a night out at Tully's after stopping at his parents' house for some food, and to find out what was going on with his mom.

Since he was planning to go to Tully's after eating, he drove his truck across the ranch to his parents' house instead of walking or taking an ATV. He went in the back door, through the mud room, and straight into the kitchen. It was almost nine o'clock at night so he didn't expect to see anyone there, since he knew his dad always went
~~~

to bed early, so he could get up and start working on the ranch at the crack of dawn. But Bobby was hopeful that his mother would have some leftovers in the fridge for him. Unfortunately, he was disappointed when he only found raw meat marinating and various ingredients stored in the fridge and no leftovers that he could heat up for dinner. Now he was really worried about his mom.

Bobby wandered through the house until he finally found his mother in the family room with his Aunt Susan and a couple of their friends. They were all seated around the coffee table with spiral notebooks in their laps, which they closed much too quickly when he walked in the room. *What are they up to?* Bobby wondered.

"Hey, Ma," Bobby greeted her as he leaned down and kissed his mom on the top of her head. "Whatcha' doin'?"

"Just starting the plans for the Christmas program at church," his mom, Hazel Burleson, replied as she patted him on the hand, which he'd laid on her shoulder as he half hugged her in greeting.

"Is that what's kept you so busy this week?" Bobby looked around and tried to make eye contact with her co-conspirators. None of them would meet his eye and he suspected he'd interrupted something other than planning the church Christmas program. Bobby groaned in his head at the thought that they were probably planning the seating arrangement for the potluck after the program and planned to have him at a table full of the most prim and proper, boring women in Heart's Destiny in their millionth attempt at matchmaking.

They really shouldn't get their hopes up that he would follow his little brother down the aisle. While Bobby was happy for Anthony, he wasn't ready to join the ranks of the happily hitched anytime soon. Bobby liked Anthony's new wife, Kay, and would gladly help him scare the boys away from his newly adopted daughters. Being a husband and raising a passel of kids was perfect for Anthony. But Bobby didn't have time for any of that, regardless of any of the jealous feelings he'd had when he watched his brother get married that he refused to even admit to himself.

Hell, I don't even have time to go grocery shopping or dust my furniture once in a while, so there's no way I have time for a relationship. I'm doing good to sneak in one night every few weeks to even go to Tully's and try to find a one-time hookup. And if I don't find some food fast, I won't even have the energy for that tonight.

"So, uh, Ma," Bobby stuttered, trying to figure out how to ask about his missing meals without sounding like an ungrateful ass. He knew his mother was doing him a huge favor in keeping his house clean and his fridge stocked, and he appreciated it a whole hell of a lot. If anything, Bobby felt guilty for being so busy that he didn't have time to take care of those things himself because he knew how much extra work it was for her, and he wished he didn't have to ask her to do it. "When do you think you'll have the time to restock my fridge with leftovers?"

"Oh, goodness!" Hazel dramatically smacked her forehead with her hand. "I haven't been to your house in a couple of weeks, have I? I just got so busy with Anthony's wedding and spending time with my granddaughters that I completely forgot. Rosa has been having to pick up my slack in cooking for the hands and just left all the food in the bunkhouse."

"Was that not what I was supposed to do?" Rosa looked back and forth between Hazel and Bobby. "Although, I'm not sure what I should've taken to Bobby's, since there haven't been any leftovers once the hands finish eating."

"No, I normally dish up a couple of meals for Bobby before I feed the hands because those boys will never leave leftovers," Hazel explained to Rosa before turning to look up at Bobby. "What have you been eating the last couple of weeks?"

"Well, the first week, I finished off the leftovers that had been moved to the freezer when I didn't eat them fast enough over the past few months. When I ran out of those, I've been grabbing something in town on my way home," Bobby answered her. "But I've spent the last three days on a stakeout, and then didn't get to leave the office until almost three this morning, so I'm currently starving from only having a few protein bars and bottled water while on the stakeout, and two bags of microwave popcorn when I finally got home this morning. Since there's no leftovers in your fridge either, I'm gonna head over to Tully's and eat them out of chicken fingers."

"Nonsense," Hazel protested as she got up from her seat. "I'll go make you something now. You sit down and relax after your stressful week. Ladies, make a list of all the things Bobby needs done around his house, all the cleaning that I've let lapse the last couple of weeks, how many meals he needs made each week. What am I saying? Ya'll know what to ask him."

Bobby knew better than to argue with his mom, especially when she was working on feeding him, so he sat down and answered the barrage of questions his Aunt Susan and his mom's friends asked about all the different things his mom had been doing for him for years. He felt slightly embarrassed, when he realized that the only reason his favorite jeans were clean for him to wear that night was because he'd only worn his police uniforms, and the suits he'd worn for Anthony's wedding and to go to church in the two weeks since his mother had last done his laundry. *Damn, I have to make sure she's able to do my laundry this weekend, or I won't have a clean uniform for Monday.*

Within a few minutes, Hazel was back with four large turkey sandwiches and a glass of sweet tea for Bobby.

"Thanks, Ma." He grinned at her when she handed them to him, and started eating while she sat back down and flipped her notebook open to a blank page.

"Alright, ladies," Hazel started, getting her pen in place to write in her notebook. "The four of us clearly don't have time to do all the cooking and cleaning Bobby needs done each week on top of what we already do, so I need you to help me write an ad to hire him a cook and housekeeper. I'm thinking it can all be done in one or two days a week. What do ya'll think?"

"Oh, yeah, one or two days a week should be doable," Aunt Susan agreed.

"Perfect, let's get something written out, and I'll put it on the church bulletin board Sunday, and hopefully, we'll find someone who can start on Monday."

Bobby started to worry a little about his mom hiring him a housekeeper from the pool of women she'd been trying to fix him up with for the last decade. But if they started on Monday and only worked one or two days a week while he wasn't home, then it wasn't likely that he'd actually have to interact with the woman, so he decided not to worry about his mom using this as a way to set him up.

It didn't take long for Hazel and her friends to write the ad, and Bobby tried to offer his help in setting the hours and pay. He really hoped that his mother was right in thinking she'd find someone Sunday at church.

"Now that we've got that handled, tell us about the stakeout." Hazel shut her notebook and laid it on the coffee table.

"Not much to tell you about," Bobby shrugged, not really wanting to tell her about the shoot-out, since he wasn't actually in the building to be at risk when it happened. "You know that new bodega that opened up last month over on Clydesdale, catty-corner from Tully's?" They all nodded, so he continued. "Yeah, it wasn't legit. It was a front for a drug cartel. I had to hang out in a building across the street for three days, cramped in the attic with a team from the DEA and FBI, watching people come and go. Then I coordinated with my guys to keep the street clear while the DEA and FBI guys went in to do the bust."

"That's all?" Aunt Susan shook her head. "That doesn't sound nearly as exciting as the stakeouts on television."

"Naw, police work in Heart's Destiny is never as exciting as on TV," Bobby chuckled, thinking that his Ma would've tried to forbid him from being a police officer if he wanted to work anywhere but Heart's Destiny because she thought it was too dangerous. He didn't even want to tell her there was a shoot-out that he wasn't even involved in, so she didn't worry unnecessarily.

"I hoped it would've been about that missing heiress from Georgia," Rosa sighed, changing the subject just when Bobby was contemplating telling them to be on the lookout for Roberto Rodriguez. "Her daddy is worried sick about who kidnapped her and has been all over the news since Thanksgiving."

"Yeah?" Bobby wondered what had happened with the missing woman since he hadn't had time to keep up with the story while working with the task force the past few days.

"Brooklyn Brielle Barns," his mother's friend Mandi chimed in with her name. "Don't you remember everyone talking about her at Thanksgiving?"

"Oh, yeah," Bobby nodded, covering for the fact that he'd sounded like he didn't know about the case. *Can't let these ladies know how interested I actually am in Brooklyn Barns and her whereabouts.*

"I don't think she was actually kidnapped. I think she ran away." Mandi shook her head and had a disgusted look on her face.

"I agree, Mandi," Bobby's Ma sighed. "I saw her *fiancé* on one of the reports today, talking about how horrible the kidnappers are for taking her right before their wedding." She said the word "fiancé" with a grimace that made Bobby think she was disgusted by the man. "He's at least twice her age, might even be older than her daddy."

They spent the next half hour talking about the fact that there hadn't been any new leads reported on the news and throwing out their theories about how she'd run away and was hiding out, so she didn't have to marry the dirty old man. Bobby hoped their theories were correct. He just wished that instead of hiding out in a big city like they all thought she needed to do to remain anonymous and not be found as easily, she'd have come to Heart's Destiny. No matter how ridiculous he felt for the strange urges her pictures stirred up in him, Bobby wished he could be the one to shelter and protect her from the world. Not that he would admit that to anyone, especially his matchmaking mother and her friends.

When they were done, Bobby decided not to go to Tully's. He was still tired from the lack of sleep and had to get up early enough to gather all his dirty uniforms to bring them to his mom in the morning before going in to work, so she could wash them all for him before Monday.

After a quick internet search for any new updates on the missing person's case, which he confirmed had no new leads just as his mother's circle of friends had stated, Bobby fell into bed to dream about the beautiful blonde. As he tossed and turned in his king-sized bed, Brooklyn's face morphed into that of the brunette babe he'd met at the wedding reception, Brie. He awoke just as he was about to kiss the gorgeous girl. He turned over in the dark and bunched up his pillow trying to get comfortable to go back to sleep, while making a mental note to check in with Luke the next day about Brie's car repairs.

I may never have the chance to meet Brooklyn Barns, but I can try to figure out some of these strange things I'm feeling with Brie Brooks.

~~~
~~~

Brooklyn felt like she'd had a productive week, even though the only time she'd left the bed and breakfast was to go to church with the Hunters the Sunday before, and when she went with Kenzie into town on Tuesday evening to grab supplies for their impromptu girls' night. In addition to the snacks and drinks they'd picked up for their movie watching party in *Brie's* room, Brooklyn had also picked up a few more boxes of the same semi-permanent hair color she'd used the previous week to disguise her blonde hair. She hadn't used the first one until the next day when Kenzie wasn't there, but Brooklyn felt much better about her cover by having extra on hand to reapply whenever the dark color started fading again.

In addition to staying in contact with her new friend Kenzie all week, Brooklyn had also gotten in touch with Luke Walker about her car repairs. On Monday, the first time she called the garage, he couldn't tell her anything because he'd just gotten it into the garage bay to start looking under the hood. He said he'd call her when he had an idea of what was wrong to tell her, so she didn't bother him again on Tuesday.

Brooklyn got lost in her writing on Wednesday and didn't think about calling again until well after when the garage would have closed for the night. So, Thursday morning she'd called Luke's Garage first thing. Luke had gone into detail, trying to explain what was wrong with her car, but Brooklyn didn't understand much of what he was saying. Eventually, he told her she had two options, replacing the engine, or having him rebuild the old one.

Since the rebuilding of the current engine was the cheaper plan, Brooklyn had picked that option, even though it would take much longer to complete the work than just replacing the engine with a new one. Actually, finding out that it would take several weeks for him to complete the work was a relief for Brooklyn. She needed those weeks to rebuild her savings with both her book royalties and the income from her new job.

If I ever get to start my new job, Brooklyn thought as she sat on her bed and opened her computer to work on her latest book. *At least Mary Kate is enjoying seeing the southeastern states as she runs away from her wedding to dastardly Donald.*

Brooklyn typed up a chapter about Mary Kate's adventures through Florida and Alabama, vividly describing the beaches she'd seen from her car window on her own drive the week before. Just as she was starting to veer off from her original plan into a side story about meeting a merman who looked like the handsome police officer she'd met at the wedding reception, her phone rang, stopping her from going off on a tangent that didn't fit with the age group she was supposed to be writing for at the time.

"Hello," Brooklyn answered the phone, trying to shake off her mental image of Bobby's captivating hazel eyes.

"Hi Brie, it's Hazel," the older woman's voice carried through the phone. "I finally have the details settled for you to start work on Monday. Does that still work for you?"

"Yes, ma'am." Brooklyn felt her shoulders relax, as if the weight of the world had just been lifted off of them.

"Please, none of that ma'am stuff. It makes me feel old," Hazel said through the phone, laughter evident in her voice. "Please call me Hazel."

"Sorry," Brooklyn apologized, feeling awkward. "Yes, Hazel. I can't wait to start work on Monday."

"Excellent!" Hazel exclaimed, sounding excited. "I know you'll have to check out of the bed and breakfast that morning, so I won't expect you to get here until about ten. Since your car is still in the shop, Mandi said she'd have someone bring you over. We'll meet at my house, and I'll show you around to all the houses you'll be responsible for cleaning, and get you settled into your room before we end up back at my house to finish up with lunch and dinner prep. I normally start breakfast at around five, so I can have it over at the bunkhouse by six and on the table at home by seven. Then I work on cleaning from eight to eleven, when I start lunch and dinner prep."

"Oh, um, okay, so Tuesday I'll need to be at your house at five to start with the breakfast prep?" Brooklyn tried to figure out how she would need to adjust her sleep for the next couple of days to be able to wake up that early.

"Oh, no, dear," Hazel giggled. "After talking with Susan and Rosa, we're rearranging our schedules and changing things up, so I was just explaining what my normal day looked like to clarify the changes to the routine for what you'll be taking off our hands. Since Rosa lives closest to the bunkhouse, she's gonna take over fixing breakfast for all the hands every morning in the bunkhouse kitchen. I'll still make breakfast at my house for anyone that wants to stop by on their way to work. That will include you starting next week."

Not sure if she was supposed to respond to the breakfast invitation or not, Brooklyn didn't say anything when Hazel paused to breathe before continuing.

"Rosa is gonna continue to keep the common areas of the bunkhouse cleaned, while Susan and I are just gonna clean our own houses. You'll be responsible for cleaning the boys' houses. Currently there are four, so you can just spend one day a week cleaning each place at your own pace. I'd recommend picking a schedule for which house you plan to clean each day of the week, but with Anthony and Kay's schedules, you might have to swap days around. I like to go through their place and dust and vacuum the day before they come home from work. Since they'll be home sometime Tuesday, I'll take care of that Monday morning after breakfast and before you get here."

"In addition to cleaning those four houses, and the fifth one when Anthony and Kay get their new house built, you'll be responsible for keeping the boys stocked with meals they can heat up at night when they get home or take for their lunches at work. That's why I want you to observe while Susan and I do the lunch and dinner prep for the ranch hands on Monday. It'll give you an idea of what you'll need to do to cook for yourself and three of our boys each day. Kay doesn't think she'll need you to cook for her family, but that may change when she goes on maternity leave."

"Kay is your new daughter-in-law, right?" Brooklyn clarified, trying to put a name to the face she remembered from the wedding reception. She'd met so many people in the last week that all of their names were scrambled in her head as to who was related to whom.

"Yes," Hazel replied. "She's six weeks pregnant, so the baby won't be here until July."

"Congratulations!" Brooklyn exclaimed, excited to hear of Hazel's impending grandmother status. "I'm sure you're looking forward to your grandbaby's arrival."

"Oh, yes, I'm thrilled," Hazel beamed through the phone. "I was already giddy at getting my two granddaughters when Anthony and

Kay met, but I love knowing their family is already growing even more."

Hazel went on to tell Brooklyn all about how her youngest son met his new wife only two months before, how they fell in love at first sight, and how Anthony adopted Kay's daughters from a previous marriage almost three weeks before he married their mother. She went on to tell Brooklyn about how the Hunters' son, James, had met Kay's sister the same night Anthony and Kay met. She talked about how the people of Heart's Destiny fall fast and hard when it comes to love, so she knew that James and Randi were having their own whirlwind romance while traveling the world working together with the GWA.

When Hazel asked if *Brie* had met anyone special since arriving in Heart's Destiny, Brooklyn replied with "only my new friend, Kenzie," completely pushing the mental image of Bobby from her thoughts. While she'd been instantly attracted to the tall, dark-haired man, who had the cutest dimples when he smiled, Brooklyn wouldn't let herself fall in love at first sight with a cop, who would probably send her packing back to Georgia if he found out who she really was.

"Oh, I didn't think to ask if you preferred women over men." Hazel sounded a little less enthusiastic than she had earlier in the call.

"Oh, no!" Brooklyn shouted, unsure why she was discussing her sexuality with her new employer, but not wanting Hazel to get the wrong idea about her either. "Kenzie is just a friend. I, I prefer men. Not that there's anything wrong with preferring whatever gender." *Shut up Brook! Quit putting your foot in your mouth, so you don't lose your job before you even start it.*

"I didn't mean to imply there was anything wrong…" Hazel trailed off, like she wasn't quite sure how to end her sentence. "I just wanted to make sure of your preferences, so I know who I should introduce you to, to help you find your heart's destiny. I don't wanna push you toward someone of the wrong gender for you to find true love."

"I'm, uh, not really, uh," Brooklyn stuttered out, trying to figure out how to avoid any potential matchmaking by her new boss, without losing her job by offending the woman. "I need to focus on my writing for now. I want to establish myself as a successful author before I look for true love. Besides, since I'm currently in the starving artist phase of my writing career, I don't have time to date while working during the day and writing at night."

"Yes, well, to keep you from being a starving artist, we should probably discuss your salary." Thankfully, Hazel changed the subject. Hazel quoted her a yearly salary that was more than double what *Brie* had earned so far that year in royalties, putting her mind at ease about how she would be able to pay for the repairs to her car after spending half of what she had left in the bank for her nine nights at the bed and breakfast.

Hazel also explained the pay schedule and how her check would be direct deposited every other Friday, one week after the end of the pay period. Her first payday would be Friday, December fourteenth, with the pay period ending on Friday, December seventh. It would only be for the one week since she was starting work in the middle of the two-week pay period, but it was still a much better turnaround than the sixty days of her royalty payments, so Brooklyn had no complaints.

Realizing that her royalty payment for the month of September should be hitting her online bank account any day, Brooklyn let out another sigh of relief after disconnecting her call with Hazel. With it taking two months to process her royalty payments for any book sales during the month, the current payment would still only be for sales during the month of September and for only the first two books she'd written. She was really looking forward to her royalty payment at the end of December, when she'd receive the first month of sales for her third book, as it had sold well to customers who came back to buy the next installment in the series.

In the first month of publication of each new book, her income seemed to almost double from the previous month of sales of her older books. If she could finish the fourth book to publish it in January as she planned, she could expect another bump in her royalty income at the end of March. If she could get started on the next series in time to publish the first book in April, she hoped she'd come close to depositing twenty-five thousand dollars in royalties between her initial June publication date for her very first book and the end of June for the following year.

She knew her father would laugh at her for being proud of such a low income, but unlike him, she didn't need much. He would probably still scoff at her total income, even with her new job bringing it up to double her royalty estimate for the year. But Brooklyn didn't need to make millions to be able to put on airs like her father. She didn't need fancy cars or high-society events. Though she did hope to one day be able to afford a home of her own, she wanted a modest home with maybe three or four bedrooms for her future family, not the thirty-thousand-square-foot mansion her father had kept her trapped in like a gilded cage.

Brooklyn pulled out her idea notebook and spent the rest of the day jotting down ideas for what she wanted in her home of the future. It may have seemed silly to others, but she knew that if she put her dreams on paper, one day she'd make them come true. For now, her dreams mostly consisted of writing goals and home plans, but in the back of her mind she couldn't stop thinking about adding a tall, dark-haired, hazel-eyed husband to the list.

<center>~~~</center>

Bobby's morning was hectic, even though it wasn't strenuous. After dropping off his clothes to be laundered and having breakfast with his mom, he went to his office at the police department and spent several hours getting caught up on all the paperwork scattered across his desk. In addition to the report he'd done in the wee hours of Thursday morning on his part of the drug cartel takedown, he had copies of the reports from the other agencies involved to review and make sure nobody had missed crossing a t or dotting an i.

Once that was done, he had to review all the reports from his officers for the week. Luckily, those were all minor issues, mostly speeding tickets issued, a disagreement at Tully's that didn't even come to blows between the two guys fighting over a woman who didn't want to go out with either of them, and a vandalism charge against a teenager for spray painting a declaration of love to his girlfriend on the town's water tower.

At least the kid was smart enough to profess his love in the wintertime, Bobby thought, chuckling to himself. *His community service of scrubbing down the water tower and all the signs in town, won't be near as much of a punishment this time of year, as it would've been if he'd pulled this stunt in the heat of summer.*

Once he finished tallying up the speeding fines that would be added to the community improvement budget, Bobby filed everything away,

60

finally able to see the wood of his desk again. He pulled up his work email to make sure there wasn't anything else he needed to follow up on for the feds, or any other law enforcement agency that he regularly worked with that might have emailed him about any new cases. He saw an email from Dean Hunter that had come in earlier in the week while he was working that stakeout. With a subject line that read, "Thought you might want to see this," Bobby didn't think it was a police matter, so he forwarded it to his personal email without opening it to see whatever photos Dean might have attached. It wouldn't be the first time one of his friends had sent him a picture that wasn't safe to open at work, so Bobby wouldn't take the chance of opening it in the office.

Once he finished going through the emails that had to do with actual police business and had replied to the ones that needed his immediate attention, Bobby felt his stomach grumble. As it was almost lunch time, he pulled out his cell phone to call Luke while on his way to the Burger Barn. *Maybe I can find out a little more about Brie and see about taking her to lunch?*

He waited for his phone to connect with the Bluetooth in his city-issued SUV before dialing his friend. Luke picked up the call before Bobby could even buckle up and get the vehicle started.

"Hey, Bro, where you been?" Luke answered. "Haven't heard from you all week. I was starting to feel neglected."

"Whatever, man," Bobby chuckled at the feigned neediness in Luke's voice. "I've been tied up with feds in town all week and couldn't get away to sleep, much less think about your needy ass."

"Feds?" Luke questioned. "Did they actually call you in to find that missing hottie from Georgia?"

"No," Bobby replied, wishing that had been the case he was stuck on all week. "But you know I can't talk about what I was actually working on."

"Yeah, yeah, I know," Luke chuckled through the phone. "If you tell me, then you'll have to kill me. I got it. So, why you callin' to bug me now?"

Fuck! This was a bad idea, Bobby thought, not sure how to go about asking his best friend about the new girl in town. "I, uh, just wanted to do my duty to protect and serve," Bobby blatantly lied through his teeth. "Make sure last weekend's stranded motorist was properly taken care of…"

Bobby trailed off as Luke roared with laughter. "You checkin' to see if I fixed her car and sent her on her way? Or you tryin' to find out if I was able to get anywhere with the beautiful Brie before you try to stake your claim?"

Asshole! Bobby mentally called his friend the derogatory name, shaking his head at how well his buddy knew him. "Seriously, man, I just wanted to check in with you about Brie's car." Bobby hated the next words to come out of his mouth. "You know I'm not gonna poach if you're interested in her." *No matter how fucking bad I want to.*

"Dude, I'm just yanking your chain," Luke cackled with laughter. "I knew the way you two were looking at each other at the reception that I was the odd man out there."

Thank fuck! Bobby thought. *Now I just have to endure a few more minutes of ribbing from him before I ask him for her number.*

"I've only talked to her a couple of times on the phone," Luke went on. "All one-hundred percent professional."

"Okay," Bobby drawled, dragging the word out to three syllables. "So, what's the deal with her car?"

"Her engine's fucked," Luke replied, bluntly. "And when I quoted her the cost to replace it, I thought she was gonna start crying over the phone."

"Shit!" Bobby exclaimed, hating that she was having money trouble and didn't seem like the type to let him step in and help her out.

"Yeah, I, uh, gave her the option to have me rebuild the current engine to cut the cost in half," Luke stammered, sounding like that was not his best idea. "But now that I've got the thing apart, I really don't think it's salvageable. I've got some calls in with my parts suppliers and a few junkyards to see if I can find a better used engine to rebuild for her instead, but I'm not having much luck."

"You give her a timeline of how long it will take?" The wheels in Bobby's head started turning on how he could help her without her finding out.

"At least a month." Luke's smirk was evident through his tone of voice, even though Bobby couldn't see it. "She mentioned getting a job and not needing it immediately, so I figured that would give her enough time to come up with at least part of the repair costs. Also told her we could work out a payment plan if we need to when it's finished."

"Yeah, well, if you can't find what you need to fix it up right for her within her budget, just put a new engine in it and I'll pay the difference." Bobby shook his head as he drove. Even though he wanted to just tell Luke that he'd cover the cost of the whole thing, Bobby knew that Brie would think he had an ulterior motive for the generous gift. Especially if he followed through on his plan to ask her out.

While he was very much interested in her and wouldn't turn down the opportunity to share her bed, his offer to pay for her car repairs had nothing to do with convincing her to have a fling with him while she was in town. Bobby would've made the same offer to cover the car repair costs of anyone down on their luck and stranded in town like Brie.

In fact, he'd worked several deals just like this with Luke over the last few years for families in town who couldn't quite afford to fix the family car in a timely manner, but who still needed the vehicles repaired as soon as possible to have a way to work and get their kids to school. Before he had the extra income he got from Burleson Incorporated, Bobby had recruited his dad and Pappaw Jerry to help him anonymously cover the costs of families in need.

The Burlesons had been blessed with so much that they were all happy to come to the aid of anyone who was down on their luck. They just preferred to keep their charitable work under wraps, not wanting to be in the spotlight for doing what any decent human should do for their fellow citizens.

Bobby continued to shoot the shit with Luke for a few more minutes, but he didn't bother asking for Brie's phone number. If he got her number from Luke and then covered the difference in her car repairs, she'd probably figure it out and never agree to go out with him. Naw, he'd bide his time with the beautiful brunette.

It's not like she can hide for long in a town this size, Bobby thought as he got out of his vehicle at the Burger Barn. *I know where she's staying and there aren't that many places she can get a job that she can walk to from the B and B. I'll let this play out organically. I know I'll be seeing her again soon. Hopefully, real soon.*

Chapter Three

Saturday, December 1, 2018

Brooklyn woke Saturday morning grateful for her surroundings in the Hunters' Bed and Breakfast. If she hadn't been brave enough to leave her childhood home in the middle of the night a little over a week before, she would've been waking up to her worst nightmare being a reality with her having to marry Clayton Donaldson that afternoon. She shuddered at the horrific thought of her former fiancé, cuddling down in the covers on the queen-sized bed for a little while longer, like she was cocooning herself in the warm blankets to block out the dreadful visions of what was expected of her on her wedding day.

She still couldn't figure out why her father had insisted on an arranged marriage for her, especially to a man thirty years her senior. *Was he just so sick of being responsible for me that he offered me up to anyone willing to take me off his hands?*

It wasn't like she had many prospects for actually dating. Her father had kept her isolated to the estate so much that even when she was required to go with him to one of the high-society events around town, she wasn't comfortable talking to her peers, much less flirting with boys her own age. Mary had given her the birds-and-bees talk when she got her first period, but she was useless when it came time to teach her how to interact with boys as a teenager.

Brooklyn had gone to a cotillion when she was thirteen, but she only danced with her father that night because it was expected of them. She hadn't danced with anyone else, even at the charity balls her father insisted she attend to be seen for their place in society. Being homeschooled, she hadn't had a prom or any other school dance experience. When she had to attend her engagement party, she'd been disappointed that her first real dance with a man would be with

Clayton, only to be relieved when she found out that he thought dancing was beneath him.

So, at twenty-two, almost twenty-three years old, Brooklyn had never even danced with a boy, much less had a real first kiss or any sexual experience. While she thought it was strange that, after one failed attempt at kissing her on the lips, when she'd turned her head just in time to prevent their lips from touching, her fiancé had only kissed her cheek at any of the events they'd had to attend together, Brooklyn was glad it had never happened. She might feel awkward at never having those experiences at her age, but she didn't want them to happen with a dirty old man either.

I'd much rather someone like Bobby be my first in all those ways. Brooklyn sighed at the thought of the handsome police officer she'd briefly met the weekend before. Though her sexual education was limited and her erotic experiences nonexistent, Brooklyn knew what she felt for the hot cop was a strong carnal attraction she hadn't even imagined she could feel before. Her fantasies about the man might be limited to kissing like at the end of a G-rated princess movie, but that was only because of her lack of knowledge and experience to be able to adequately set the scene in her head for the lovemaking she wanted to fantasize about. While she'd found pictures online to help her figure out where to touch herself to relieve her own need for pleasure of the bedroom variety, having only ever felt her own hand, she couldn't fathom how different it would feel to have his large, calloused hands touching her intimate areas.

I wish I could go to him for police protection, but I know he'd just have to report my whereabouts to the Macon PD. And since Father is friends with the upper echelon of power in the city of Macon, they'd just drag me home and make me get married.

In trying to figure out why her father was lying to the media and still pushing for her to be brought back to Macon to get married, Brooklyn had done a little research online the weekend before, wanting to figure out what was really going on back home. But while she'd felt safe searching her real name online when the boutique hotel was full of people the previous weekend, she hadn't wanted to be obvious with her searching when she was the only guest in residence at the beginning of the week. Now that the place was filling up again with more guests coming in for the rodeo that weekend, Brooklyn wondered if she could get away with doing another search to find out the latest news.

Maybe later, Brooklyn thought as she finally sat up in bed and turned on her television. *I'll just see if there's anything on the news for now. If I hear any of the other guests discussing my missing persons case when I go down for breakfast, then I'll do an internet search this afternoon, when I'll probably have the cover of others doing the same search.*

She settled in, leaning up against the headboard with a pile of pillows around her to watch the morning news. They weren't reporting any leads on her disappearance, which she thought was good for her being able to stay hidden away from them. But both her father and Clayton had given an interview that morning, professing their love for Brooklyn and pleading for her safe return.

"Why are they still pushing this?" Brooklyn beseeched her empty room, as if there was someone there to reply to her. "It doesn't make sense. If all Father wanted was to get me out of his house, he should be happy that I'm gone, not acting broken up about me not being there for the wedding. And Clayton professing his love is just asinine. I'm not sure he even likes women, and we have definitely not fallen in love. Ugh!"

Brooklyn scrunched up one of the pillows and hugged it to her chest as she watched the interview progress on television, completely confused by the out-of-character behavior of her father and former fiancé. When it concluded, the news anchor recapped the details of the case, again referring to her as a "kidnapped heiress," and listing out a few of the Ashbury estate assets she would supposedly inherit when she got married.

"But Father inherited all that when Mom died," Brooklyn stated to the image on the television like he could hear her. "I wasn't listed in her will, or Grandfather's, so none of that stuff comes to me, marriage or no marriage. And what's with this inheriting-when-I-get-married stipulation they're talking about? Even if I was listed in Mom's or Grandfather's wills, marriage clauses for inheritance aren't done in modern society."

The news changed from the national report to a local San Antonio station's program, which no longer mentioned her, so Brooklyn decided to get up and shower to get ready for her day. *Hopefully, the people here for the rodeo will be as interested in the case as the wrestlers were last weekend, so I can do an online search for more information without being traceable.*

~~~

Bobby woke up early Saturday morning so he could go have breakfast with his parents before diving into the background checks and security protocols he needed to review for Burleson Incorporated. If nothing else, he thought his being tied up with the federal agents earlier in the week would at least get him out of any manual labor on the ranch, since he hadn't been able to work on Burleson Incorporated business in his normal daily routine. But when he arrived at his parents' home to find that all the Burlesons who were in town were there for breakfast, he feared his plans for the day might have been changed without his permission.

"Mornin' everyone," Bobby greeted his family as he walked into the crowd in the kitchen, wondering why his Aunt Susan, Uncle Jon, both sisters, and all four cousins were there.

After a raucous round of "good mornings" went around the room, he got in line to make his plate and listened to the conversations around him to figure out what the special occasion was that he'd obviously missed hearing about. It was mostly useless gossip from the girls, so he tuned that out since he wasn't interested in who was dating whom in town. Justin and JJ were planning an afternoon on the Xbox, so Bobby bypassed their conversation too, having outgrown video games about the time his younger siblings took them over when he was a teenager.

His dad, Bob, and his Uncle Jon were discussing the field rotation for the herd to ensure their nutritional needs were met over the winter months. That wasn't the most interesting topic to Bobby normally, but it was better than getting involved in his mother, Hazel, and Aunt Susan's conversation, which he feared would turn into an opportunity for them to set him up with some unsuspecting local lady if he sat near them to eat. That was how he found himself sitting between his cousins and his dad once they all had their meals and were sitting down for breakfast.
~~~

Maybe I can at least get Dad and Uncle Jon to switch over to the part of the business I'm best equipped to help with? Or if Justin and JJ are through with their video game discussion, maybe we can talk about what's goin' on in their divisions that I need to know before the quarterly board meeting at the end of the month? Unfortunately, he didn't get the chance to change either subject of conversation because his mother did it for him.

"While we're mostly all here," Hazel shouted just loud enough to get the rest of the conversations in the room to come to a screeching halt. "Susan and I have been talking the past couple of days about the need to hire a full-time housekeeper and cook to help us with everything we've been doing on the ranch."

"Full-time?" Bobby was confused by how the conversation he'd had with them Thursday night went from needing someone for a one-or-two-day-a-week position to being a full-time job on the ranch. "I thought we decided Thursday that I only need someone a couple days a week."

"Yes, *you* need someone a couple days a week," his mother replied, putting special emphasis on the word "you" in a way that made Bobby's internal alarm bells ring to alert him of his mother's scheming against him somehow. "But I've also been going over to Anthony's house and making sure it's clean before he and Kay get home from work. And your Aunt Susan has been keeping Justin and JJ's houses clean in addition to her own. We're tired, and we'd like to cut all that extra cleaning off our plates."

"So, we thought we'd like to hire someone to rotate between houses," Aunt Susan added, pointedly looking at Bobby. "I haven't been putting together meals for my boys like your mom has for you, but I like the idea of having someone doing it, so they don't have to come to my house for dinner every night."

"Wait," Bobby's cousin, Jen interrupted, waving her hands around to get her mother, Susan's, attention. "So, because the boys are too lazy to cook and clean for themselves, you've been doing it for them all these years?"

"And now you wanna hire them a full-time cook and housekeeper?" Bobby's cousin, Julie, Jen's twin sister, continued, seeming to complete her sister's thought.

Hazel and Susan looked at each other before turning back toward the girls and saying, "yes," in unison.

"Why was this not an option when I moved out?" Bobby's sister, Charlotte, looked irritated. "Or can we get in on the housekeeping help now, too?"

"We might have to hire two people," Hazel shrugged, looking back at Susan with an expression that convinced Bobby that his mother and aunt were definitely up to something with the sudden need for housekeeping help on the ranch. "I mean, I'd already put together a schedule for one house a day for the first person I plan to hire. When Anthony and Kay finish building their new house, that will be a full five-day week for her."

"If we hire a second person, we can have them clean our houses as well as the girls' houses and maybe Rosa's if we need a fifth day for her," Susan suggested, clearly on the same page as her co-conspirator, Hazel, in their plotting. "But we have plenty of empty rooms on the ranch to be able to house more than one housekeeper."

And there's the scheme, Bobby realized. *They've both referred to the housekeepers as female and now they're talking about them living here on the ranch. No way on earth they'll "house" these women in their own homes or with the girls. They're trying to match them up with JJ, Justin, and I. Fuck! How am I gonna get outta this?*

"We do have an empty bunkhouse they can stay in," JJ pointed out, nodding his head.

Thanks for the suggestion, Cuz, but I don't think nodding like you agree with our moms will keep them from pushing one of these women at you.

"I'm assuming you want these new staff members to be employed by Burleson." Uncle Jon stated, referring to the family corporation by just their last name.

"Well, yes," Susan replied to her husband. "That seems only right since it will be a benefit to all the board members."

Bobby noticed that his dad was suspiciously quiet as Uncle Jon directed Jen to set up the new positions in the company in her capacity as the vice president of human resources. Bobby would have to pull his dad aside later to find out just how much he knew about the matchmaking portion of the hiring process before it was brought up to the rest of the family. Based on the expression on his father's face, he didn't think his mother's plans were much of a surprise to him.

While watching his father's reaction, Bobby missed part of the conversation, but when he tuned back in and realized they were discussing how many meals JJ and Justin wanted to be left at their houses each week, he didn't think he'd missed much. As the conversation went on, Bobby wasn't sure the way his dad and uncle had turned the planning of schedules and such over to the women so quickly was in his best interest. But when they turned to him to talk about the background checks they needed him to do, he really didn't have much of a choice in paying attention to them and not the details his mother, aunt, sisters, and cousins were hashing out for the new cooks and housekeepers.

As soon as they were through with breakfast, Bobby went with his father and uncle into the library that his dad used as a home office. He pulled out his laptop and started the background checks on the list of new hires they had for him, which was quite long since they'd just acquired a small tech company in Austin, including all of the people previously employed by the company that was now being rolled into the information technology division of Burleson Incorporated.

While doing background checks wasn't a complicated process, it did take a while when there were almost a hundred people being brought over from their old positions in the smaller company to new positions in the larger corporation. When Bob and Jon finished their portion of the corporate paperwork, they left Bobby there to finish the lengthy list of background checks while they went to play with their horses.

Bobby knew that technically his dad and uncle were training some new horses to replace a couple, who were getting too old to keep working long hours each day with the ranch hands who tended to the cattle. They just called it playing with their horses because they had too much fun connecting with their cowboy roots to consider it work.

While he didn't get as much enjoyment out of police work as his dad did playing cowboy, he liked to think of it as more of a calling than a job. He was just a natural protector, like wanting to keep others safe was ingrained in his DNA. He figured that was why his mind wandered to images of Brooklyn Barns as he tediously worked through the list of people he was doing background checks on, instead of trying to figure out what he needed to do to keep from falling victim to yet another of his mother's matchmaking attempts. That protector part of his DNA wanted to rescue her from whoever had her hiding away. And that deep seeded part of his psyche didn't care that her case was outside his jurisdiction.

Once he was done with the paperwork for Burleson Incorporated, Bobby texted his buddy, Luke, to meet him at Tully's that night. He had his detective on call all weekend, so he could cut loose and check out the buckle bunnies who were in town for the weekend, even if he did keep his alcohol intake on the lower side, so he could stay sober enough to drive home.

He made a quick stop at home to drop off his laptop and the four-wheeler he'd driven to his parents' house almost ten hours earlier. He changed out of his navy-blue t-shirt into an emerald-green button-down, knowing it would bring out the greener hues of his hazel eyes that the ladies seemed to rave about. Since he hadn't had to go work with the horses earlier, he decided to wear the jeans and cowboy boots he'd been wearing all day, but he opted to leave the hat at home. Too much cowboy paraphernalia would make it obvious that he was out bunny hunting.

Better to let them think they're the ones out lookin' for a hookup, Bobby thought as he got into the new Dodge Ram he'd bought earlier in the year and drove off the ranch for his night out. *I can't give the ladies the wrong idea that I want something serious by actively chasing after them. That just leads to a one-nighter turning into a clinger. Nope, not goin' through that again. I'll just play it cool and let the buckle bunnies chase after me for a night or two of mutual release, and then they can mosey along to the next rodeo town.*

Luke's brother, Leo, was behind the bar when Bobby walked into Tully's Roadhouse. It wasn't too busy yet, but the night was still young. Bobby went to the bar and ordered a beer, looking around the bar to scope out the crowd while he waited for Leo to finish fixing the drinks he was working on before getting Bobby's bottle.

"Luke's already in the back," Leo informed Bobby as he popped the top on a longneck before putting it on the bar in front of him. "And he's already got the first couple of bunnies back there with him to start the night off with a game of pool."

"Seriously?" Bobby chuckled, shaking his head at how fast his best friend worked when it came to picking up women. "He must've already been here when I texted him to meet me."

"Naw," Leo replied, chuckling along with Bobby. "He only got here like five minutes ago. Pointed to a pair of redheads while I was grabbing his beer and challenged them to a game. The way they were giggling as they followed him to the back makes me think ya'll are in for an early night."

"An early night?" Bobby raised an eyebrow quizzically at the bartender only a couple years younger than him.

"Yeah, either ya'll will leave early with them or you'll leave early to escape their annoying, giggly personalities," Leo smirked.

"Great," Bobby sighed, hanging his head as he made his way back to the pool tables. As he lifted his head back up, he found his friend standing by the wall of pool cues, helping two busty redheads pick their sticks for the night. "An early night indeed," he groaned as their incessant giggling pierced his eardrums from across the room.

As the night went on, Bobby couldn't make himself show any interest in any of the women around him. The redheads didn't stick around for more than one game when Bobby didn't say more than "hey" when they were introduced. He and Luke continued to monopolize the corner pool table they liked best, as the various women who were in town for the rodeo approached them off and on all night.

With each woman who tried to get his attention, Bobby found himself comparing them to the two women who'd captivated him the week before. *She's not as tall as Brooklyn, and her hair seems more brassy than Brooklyn's blonde,* he thought when approached by a strawberry blonde. *She's not as curvy as Brie, and her eyes are too dark, not like Brie's creamy caramel eyes,* he thought when a petite brunette approached him.

In the end, Bobby realized that he couldn't even think about having a meaningless hookup with a buckle bunny as long as his mind was occupied by Brooklyn and Brie. *Fuck, it's not even fair to have a fling with Brie when I'm still thinking about Brooklyn, too. Guess I'll be taking care of myself in the shower for the foreseeable future.*

~ ~ ~

Brooklyn was mostly excited to start her new job on Monday morning, but she also had to admit to a little part of her being afraid of how she could mess it up at the same time. She hadn't really discussed the dress code for the job with Hazel, but she didn't expect to have to wear a uniform like Mary did while working on the Ashbury-Barns estate. She also didn't think her sloppy cleaning clothes she wore at home when her father was at work were appropriate for a professional housekeeper, so she put on a purple skirt and lavender blouse to look semi-professional until she knew what Hazel expected her to wear at work. She had several of these long, stretchy skirt and loose blouse combos that were a compromise between her need for something comfortable to wear and her father's insistence that she "dress like a lady" at all times in case someone showed up for a meeting at the house in the evenings.

I wonder if he's looked through the boxes of my clothes to realize that I left all the stiff, stuffy outfits he's made me wear for the last six months and brought the comfortable clothes he let Mary help me pick out when I was a teenager? Does he realize that I only brought clothes I got to pick out for myself? Or does he even care that I need the freedom to be myself? Be myself? More like find myself—who I really am deep inside. I shouldn't be just recently learning things like how comfortable I am wearing leggings at twenty-two years old.

Pushing all thoughts of her father from her mind, she finished packing up all her belongings before calling down to the front desk to ask for assistance in carrying everything over to the other building, where she was meeting Mandi to check-out and get a ride over to the Burleson Ranch. She'd transferred her clothes from the boxes they'd been packed in when she left Macon into four duffle bags that first night, so she wouldn't look suspicious carrying boxes into and out of motel rooms as she traveled. She was really glad she had when she'd checked-in to the bed and breakfast because her things were a lot easier for her and Kenzie to carry in, and then her and Mandi to carry up to the room. Once again, with all her belongings in the four duffels and her backpack, it only took one trip to carry everything down from her room with the assistance of a member of the cleaning staff.

Without saying a word to Brooklyn, the maid placed the bags she was carrying into a vehicle that Brooklyn thought looked like a golf cart turned into a small truck. Brooklyn placed the two duffels she was carrying in the back of the strange looking vehicle as well, leaving her backpack on her back as she joined the maid on the seat of the vehicle to drive over to the other building. Brooklyn made sure to tip the maid for her assistance as they unloaded the bags to carry them to the front desk, glad she'd thought to get some cash when she went to the store with Kenzie a few days earlier.

It didn't take long for the check-out process, just a quick swipe of her *Brie Brooks* debit card to sign over half the money in her online account for the nine nights she'd stayed in the posh boutique hotel. Mandi insisted on personally delivering her to Hazel's house, which Brooklyn profusely thanked her for as they drove.

As they pulled up to the gate at the ranch, Brooklyn was excited to get her first glimpse of an honest-to-goodness cattle ranch. She knew they were still in existence to provide the beef she loved to eat, but she never dreamed she'd get to see one in real life, having grown up in the city. Even if she'd ventured into the rural areas of Georgia, she thought she'd only see large chunks of farmland used for peanuts or cotton, or maybe a peach orchard. Beef wasn't included in the listing of primary agricultural products she'd seen for her home state, so she hadn't thought she'd ever see cows up close while she was living there with her father.

"Hazel will give you your own gate code," Mandi informed her as she stopped the car at the wrought iron gate to key in a code on the keypad to allow them to enter the ranch. "They assign them to anyone who comes on the ranch regularly, so they know who is coming on the property. It's one of the security things they've implemented in the last few years. I don't think they've had problems with rustlers in at least twenty years, but I guess they think knowing who goes through what gate will help them figure out who's responsible if they ever do again."

"Yeah, that's the first thing here that reminds me of home," Brooklyn admitted, giggling at the realization. "Growing up in the city, I'm used to security codes on doors and gates like that."

"I imagine our little town has been a culture shock for you." Mandi lightly laughed along with Brooklyn.

"A little," Brooklyn agreed, smiling as they pulled up to a white three-story house that looked like it belonged in the movie *Gone With The Wind*, or maybe back in Georgia, since it looked more like the house she'd grown up in than any of the other buildings she'd seen in Heart's Destiny. "But that's a good thing. The whole reason I'm on this trip is to see different parts of the country to be able to use them as settings for my books. I've come up with so many story ideas this last week because of the unique atmosphere here that it'll be years before I can get them all written and published."

"Well, then I guess you'll just have to stick around for those years to stay inspired," Mandi suggested as they got out of the car.

Yeah, maybe, Brooklyn thought as she followed Mandi to what appeared to be the back door of the house. *If I can keep anyone from figuring out who I am, maybe I can stay here for a while.*

"Knock, knock," Mandi lightly shouted instead of actually knocking on the door as she opened it and walked right on in.

Brooklyn felt uncomfortable just walking in like she lived there, especially since it was her new employer's home. But she didn't see any other option, so she followed behind Mandi. They walked into a gorgeous, but empty kitchen, confusing Brooklyn even more.

"Oh, what time were you supposed to meet Hazel?" Mandi turned to Brooklyn but looked down at her phone that she'd pulled out of her pocket.

"Ten," Brooklyn answered, glancing at the clock on the wall to see it was just after nine o'clock.

"I bet she's still next door then." Mandi looped her arm through Brooklyn's and pulled her back out the door they'd just entered. "Since we're almost an hour early."

As they walked across the wide expanse of yard to a two-story white house with black trim, Brooklyn was glad she'd chosen to wear her ballet style flat dress shoes instead of heels with her skirt, so she didn't sink into the grassy terrain. Just as she had at the first house, Mandi walked in the back door without knocking. Brooklyn had no choice but to follow her. She just hoped her inward cringing at just barging into the home wasn't visible to anyone around her.

"Hazel!" Mandi exclaimed as they entered a quaint aqua-blue and light pink kitchen.

"Upstairs," Hazel called back to them. "Be right down."

True to her word, Hazel appeared a few moments later carrying a bucket of cleaning supplies.

"You're early," Hazel pointed out, smiling at Brooklyn as she sat the supplies down beside the kitchen island and greeted her with a hug.

"It didn't take as long as I expected to check out and drive over here." Brooklyn returned the older woman's embrace. *It's almost like being back home with Mary*, Brooklyn thought as she enjoyed the motherly squeeze of her new employer.

"Well, good." Hazel released Brooklyn from her hold. "We can go ahead and take your stuff down to the house where you'll be staying before getting started with everything."

They walked back over to where Mandi's car was parked, all three of them jumping in to make the drive down to the house Hazel described as the almost one-hundred-and-forty-year-old home that was originally built by the first Burleson on the ranch. Brooklyn wished it wouldn't be considered rude to pull out her notebook and take notes on the history of the ranch that Hazel was telling her as they drove. Though it wasn't her genre to write, the story of Jonah and Emma Burleson would make a great historical romance novel.

Wow, all the houses here are so big and beautiful, Brooklyn thought as Hazel continued with her Burleson family history lesson as they pulled up to a dark blue, Victorian-style, three-story home with white trim. The porch wrapped around from the front to the right side of the house, which was where Mandi pulled down the drive to park beside a detached garage that looked newer than the home, even though it was built to match.

"I figured I'd put you in the back bedroom," Hazel stated, as they got out of the car and grabbed all of Brooklyn's belongings to take into the house. "It's closest to the shared bathroom upstairs, not that you'll have to share the bathroom. My son uses the ensuite in the master bedroom at the front of the house. But, with the second bedroom between you, it will give you a little more privacy than putting you in the second bedroom."

"I'm good with wherever you want to put me," Brooklyn smiled, feeling a sense of awe as they walked into the house through a back door. After stepping through the mudroom, they entered the kitchen, which was gorgeous with light gray walls and white cabinetry.

"We updated this house about twenty years ago," Hazel informed her, continuing her mini-history lesson. "We replaced the old teak countertops with granite but kept as much of the original cabinetry as possible. We ripped out the butler's pantry to put in the laundry room, so we had to change the island to include the sink and dishwasher, but I think it still looks pretty close to correct for the time period when it was built, just with all the modern amenities we can't live without."

"It's beautiful." Brooklyn followed Hazel through the kitchen and up a set of stairs.

"This will be your room." Hazel walked across the hall from the top of the stairs to enter a bedroom. "I washed and changed the bedding right before everyone arrived for the wedding, but we didn't have to have anyone stay here then, so it should still be fresh."

They all put down the bags they were carrying on the bed before Hazel redirected them back out of the room. "The linen closet is right here, between your bedroom and bathroom, so you can find more fresh linens to change out the beds. My son's bed probably needs to be changed tomorrow when you'll be spending most of your day here cleaning, but since nobody is using the second bedroom, I wouldn't bother changing it anytime soon. And the fourth bedroom is pretty much empty, so there's no bedding to change in there. It was a sewing room way back when, but you might enjoy setting up your computer in there to write in the evenings."

Hazel showed them around the second floor, only pointing out the fourth bedroom that was once a sewing room beside the bathroom before turning them toward the front of the house to point out the second bedroom and the master bedroom. There was a second set of stairs outside the master bedroom that Brooklyn decided was the main staircase, as it appeared much grander than the back stairs they'd taken up from right outside the kitchen.

"The third floor is all attic space, so you don't have to worry about it most of the time. If you ever feel like you're completely caught up with all the other cleaning and wanna run a vacuum or dust rag over the space, that's fine, but probably not necessary more than once or twice a year."

They walked down the front stairs to the main entryway of the home. Hazel pointed out the half bath beside the front door, letting her know it was the only restroom on the first floor.

Leah Mae Wright

"Originally, this was a parlor," Hazel continued as they walked into the first room to the right of the front door. It was an unusually shaped room with a fireplace toward the center of the home and a rounded section that stuck out at the corner of the house that Brooklyn had thought looked like a castle turret on the front of the house. "Now I guess it would be classified as a formal living room, though I doubt it's used much."

I bet the master bedroom has that same strange corner, Brooklyn thought, realizing that the parlor was directly below the master bedroom that she'd only seen the doorway of before being directed downstairs. *I think those little alcoves would make great reading nooks.*

The parlor was sparsely furnished, with only an uncomfortable-looking sofa, two wingback chairs, and three small tables, but each piece looked antique, like it was original to the home.

"This next room was what they called a sitting room back in the day," Hazel explained as they continued walking toward the back of the house. "As you can see it's now more of a family room. Or a man cave for my bachelor son."

The family room looked a lot more comfortable to Brooklyn. It had a sectional sofa that covered almost all of two walls, with a big screen television on the third wall that wasn't broken up by the door into the room from the hallway. Instead of the artwork on the walls like in the parlor, there were pictures of an obviously large and loving family on the walls and side tables, making it feel much more lived in than the other room.

Diagonally across the hall from the family room was the dining room, which Brooklyn determined to be directly under the bedroom she would be using. It wasn't as formal as the parlor, but it wasn't as comfortable as the family room. There was a large table and chairs to seat at least eight to ten people. The dark wood of the dining set matched the china cabinet on one wall. It was all of a similar Victorian style as the furniture in the front room, but didn't seem as old with more modern upholstery than the pieces in the parlor. The chair seats were covered in a light gray silk fabric with a shimmery damask pattern that better matched the light gray walls throughout the house than the burgundy velvet that covered the chairs and sofa in the formal living room.

"So, you'll basically do all your cooking here," Hazel informed her as they reentered the kitchen. "Whatever you wanna fix for dinner is fine, the boys aren't picky. Just make sure you make enough each day for you and four others. Technically, two of those daily meals will stay here for my son, so if he's here to eat with you at dinnertime, then you just have to package up one for him a lunch later in the week, and one each for my nephews. I'll show you the containers I usually use this afternoon, so you can get an idea of how much to make."

"Okay, that sounds easy enough to keep track of." Brooklyn followed Hazel and Mandi back out of the house.

"Since Anthony and Kay have such a strange schedule, I figured it would be easiest to rotate the days their house gets cleaned between Mondays and Fridays, depending on when they're out of town. I was just finishing up when you got here for today, so you won't have to clean there until next Monday, the tenth. The following week, you'll clean their place on Friday the twenty-first. I'm not sure if Kay will want any help when they're home for Christmas and New Year's or not, but I'll let you know."

Wanting to make sure she didn't forget any of the dates Hazel was mentioning, Brooklyn pulled a small notebook out of her purse, which she'd thankfully remembered to get out of her backpack before leaving everything else in her new bedroom. She was taking notes of what she needed to do, and when she needed to do it, as Hazel listed out the specific areas she should clean in each home.

"Your schedule will be more stable on Tuesdays, Wednesdays, and Thursdays," Hazel continued as they got back into Mandi's car to drive back to the other houses on the north part of the ranch. "Tuesdays you'll stay here cleaning." Hazel pointed with her thumb back at the house they'd just left, where Brooklyn would be living. "And when I say cleaning, I mean just the same things I said for Anthony and Kay's house, dusting, vacuuming, sweeping, mopping, cleaning the bathrooms and kitchen, but in addition to washing the bedding, you'll also need to do laundry for the boys. Kay does the laundry for her family, but the rest of the boys have still been relying on Susan and I to do it all."

"I'm assuming there's a central location in each of their homes where I can find their laundry to be able to wash everything."

Brooklyn didn't remember seeing a hamper in the laundry room when she'd peeked in there at her new abode.

"Yes, hopefully," Hazel smiled warily. "I have mine trained to put his dirty clothes in the hamper in the master bathroom, but I can't say for sure that's where you'll find my nephews' clothing."

"I'm sure it won't be too hard to find." Brooklyn smiled back.

"The smaller white house with black trim on our left is the house you'll clean on Wednesdays." Hazel pointed to the first house on the left as they came back into the cluster of homes where most of the family lived. "And the two-story brick house beside it, you'll clean on Thursdays. Whatever you fix for dinner tonight, you can drop off in Tupperware for each of them tomorrow morning. If you wanna cook in bulk, so you don't have to drop off a meal a day to each of them, just make sure they get seven meals a week each. And fourteen meals a week for my oldest, who you're rooming with."

"Do I need to plan desserts with any of these meals?" Brooklyn hoped she would get to spend some of her time baking since she loved it so much.

"Entirely up to you," Hazel smiled. "The boys will eat whatever you put in front of them."

They pulled back into Hazel's driveway, but Mandi didn't pull all the way around to the back of the house this time. "I have to get back to the B and B, but I'll see you both later." Mandi waved them off as both Brooklyn and Hazel exited the car.

"Thank you." Brooklyn stopped at Mandi's car window to lean down and give her a goodbye hug. "For everything you've done to help me this last week. I really appreciate it. Thank you."

"Oh, anytime, sweet girl." Mandi returned Brooklyn's one-armed embrace.

As Mandi pulled back out of the driveway, Brooklyn followed Hazel through her elaborate home and back toward the kitchen she'd briefly seen when she first arrived. Hazel's home reminded her a lot of her childhood home. In addition to sharing the plantation style that was so popular throughout Georgia and the rest of the southern states, the interior was elegantly decorated much like her family home back in Macon.

When they made their way through the house to the kitchen, Brooklyn met Susan and Rosa, who were both there to make lunch for the dozen ranch hands that lived in the north bunkhouse. Once that was all prepared and packed up, Rosa took it with her to meet her husband, who was also the ranch manager, and feed the men out where they were working.

Brooklyn enjoyed chatting with both Hazel and Susan as they ate their own lunch, but she was starting to wonder what was up with Hazel not referring to her oldest son by name as the two older ladies told her story after story about their children. Brooklyn had determined that Hazel had six kids, and Susan had four, from the stories they'd told.

She knew the names of all four of Susan's kids. Jon Jr., who went by JJ, lived in the two-story brick house that Brooklyn would be cleaning on Thursdays. Justin lived in the single-story white house with black trim that Brooklyn would be cleaning on Wednesdays. Both of her daughters, Jennifer and Julia, who went by Jen and Julie, lived in the large two-story home diagonally across from Hazel's that looked a lot like the house Brooklyn would be staying in on the south side of the ranch.

She'd also learned that Hazel's youngest daughter, Rebecca, who went by Becky, lived in the same house as Jen and Julie. Hazel's oldest daughter, Charlotte, lived in the single-story brick home next door to her sister and cousins. And, of course, she couldn't forget that Hazel's youngest son, Anthony, lived next door to Hazel with his new wife, Kay, and their daughters, Tia and Maria.

She also heard stories about Hazel's middle sons, Josh and Jake, who were twins. They were currently relegated to their childhood bedrooms at Hazel's house when they came home to visit while serving in the Navy, but they would probably be moving back to the house Anthony and Kay lived in currently, once their new home was built south of the home where Brooklyn was staying.

I wonder if that's why I'm staying down there instead of in one of the houses in the main cluster of homes on the ranch? I guess it makes sense for me to stay so far from the three houses I'll be cleaning here, since I'll be cleaning two houses down there eventually and the majority of the meals I have to make each week are for Hazel's oldest son. I just wish she'd mention his name, so I'd know who to expect to meet tonight when I go back to cook dinner.

Leah Mae Wright

As much as Brooklyn wondered about her new roommate, she couldn't bring herself to ask Hazel what his name was, thinking it would make her seem like she hadn't been paying attention when Hazel mentioned him. So, she just kept quiet for the most part, enjoying the comfortable feeling of comradery with the two women she was getting to know while helping them with making dinner for all the ranch hands.

Once everything was prepped and in the oven for Susan to watch, Brooklyn rode with Hazel into town to stock her new kitchen with groceries.

Thank goodness, I have all Mary's recipes stored in the cloud, so I have plenty of things to choose from to make, Brooklyn thought as she picked out the staples she knew she needed and ingredients she could remember for the first couple of meals she was planning to cook, Brunswick stew and chicken-n-dumplins, and, of course, a peach cobbler.

She'd found almost everything, her grocery cart almost as full as Hazel's, but she couldn't find the pulled pork she needed for the Brunswick stew. "Do you know where I can find pulled pork?" Brooklyn looked at Hazel for guidance while standing in the middle of the meat department.

"We don't really eat much pork on the ranch," Hazel confessed, looking around the area like she wasn't sure where to even find pork, much less pulled pork. "What are you making? Can you replace it with beef? We can get any cut of beef you want back on the ranch."

"Oh, um, maybe," Brooklyn stuttered, not quite sure how to explain that she'd only prepared her stew with already barbecued meat in the past. *How do I explain that my family never had a cookout, or that the only reason I know about Brunswick stew is because Mary taught me when my father wouldn't be home for dinner?* "I'm making Brunswick stew. Some people make it with chicken, but since the other meal I planned was chicken-n-dumplins, I thought it best to go with the more traditional barbecued pork. I don't have any experience actually barbecuing anything, so I might need you to teach me how to prepare whatever cut of beef would be easiest to shred to go into the stew."

"Oh, that sounds like fun," Hazel gushed, her eyes lighting up as she pulled Brooklyn in for an unexpected hug. "My girls never wanted to learn how to cook from me, insisting their home economics classes and Memmaw Judy taught them all they needed in the kitchen. It's nice to have someone who actually wants to learn from me."

Brooklyn returned Hazel's embrace, only feeling slightly awkward at how the other woman was treating her like a member of the family instead of an employee. Hazel reminded Brooklyn so much of Mary that her motherly hugs brought tears to her eyes from missing the woman who'd raised her. *I really wish I could do more than send Mary and Joe cryptic emails about Mary Kate's adventures to stay in touch with them.*

"If you have everything else you need, let's hurry home, so we can have the guys bring over a brisket for you and I'll show you how to make it in the oven just as tender and barbecuey as if it was done in the smoker. I'll even give you my homemade barbecue sauce recipe, so you don't have to use that jar sauce." Hazel released the tight grip she had on Brooklyn and turned to push her shopping cart toward the front of the H.E.B.

"I would love to learn your homemade barbecue sauce recipe," Brooklyn choked out as she blinked back her tears and followed Hazel to the registers.

"My niece is bringing me all the employment paperwork tonight," Hazel mentioned as she started unloading her shopping cart, placing the items on the conveyor belt to be rung up. "You can fill them out at breakfast tomorrow and then we'll get you a card for our household account for any grocery runs you need to make."

"Oh, okay," was all Brooklyn could say, unsure how she was going to make grocery runs without her car.

"Don't look so downhearted, dear," Hazel commanded, smiling at Brooklyn over the cart between them. "I know your car is in the shop. We have plenty of vehicles on the ranch to make sure you're able to get to town whenever you need to. Between my son and nephews, I'm sure you'll have plenty of offers to drive you, but don't let those boys get their way. I'll show you where the keys are to my son's extra vehicles when I drop you back home with him, so you can do some of your own exploring around town for your book research, and don't feel trapped on the ranch."

"Thank you," Brooklyn choked out, unsure how Hazel knew she was feeling slightly uneasy with not having a way off the ranch whenever she wanted.

It wasn't that she really wanted to go off the ranch all that often. Or even that she thought she needed to be able to go get groceries without having to get a ride with Hazel or one of the other women on the ranch. It was all psychological. After years of feeling confined to the estate where she grew up, not being able to leave the grounds without her father's permission or an escort, Brooklyn needed to know that she could leave wherever she was if she wanted to, so she didn't feel imprisoned again.

"Good afternoon, Mrs. Burleson," the cashier said as she started ringing up Hazel's items, bringing Brooklyn back to the moment from her wayward thoughts. She noticed that there was space at the end of the conveyor belt for her to add the items from her own shopping cart, so she started moving the groceries from the basket to the belt to be rung up with Hazel's.

"Tammi," Hazel snapped, her voice sounding curt with a hint of annoyance, which was very unlike what Brooklyn had seen from her all day.

They all stood there awkwardly without saying another word until the cashier had finished ringing up Hazel's things and stopped, giving Hazel a total without ringing up the items Brooklyn had put on the conveyor belt.

"Actually, Brie is with me," Hazel pointed out, motioning toward the rest of the items to be purchased. "While we do need her things bagged separately to go home with her to my son's house, it can all go on the same ticket to be charged to our ranch household account."

"Oh, I thought your new daughter-in-law's name was Kay." Tammi gave Brooklyn a once over as she started scanning the rest of the items.

"Yes, and I'm sure Anthony and Kay will be in to do their grocery shopping tomorrow or Wednesday when they get back into town," Hazel retorted, giving Brooklyn a beaming smile before turning back to Tammi. "I do have more than one son with a home on the ranch, ya know."

Tammi's mouth opened as if she was going to say something, but instead she snapped it shut and glared at Brooklyn without saying another word as she finished scanning the grocery items. Brooklyn wasn't sure what the history was between the Burlesons and Tammi that might have caused her to have an attitude with Hazel and anyone associated with the family, but it was obvious that she'd finally met the one person in town who wasn't friendly and welcoming.

Yeah, I'll just make sure I look at who's working the register before I check out here again, Brooklyn thought as she and Hazel pushed their carts of groceries out to the waiting SUV to head back to the ranch. *I don't want to get in the middle of whatever that obvious hostility is about.*

~~~

After his mother's Sunday supper announcement that she already had the first person lined up to start work as the housekeeper and cook who would rotate between the ranch houses, Bobby was looking forward to coming home Monday evening to find his house cleaned and his dinner in the refrigerator waiting to be heated up.

Hopefully, whoever Ma hired is done and already settled for the night in the bunkhouse, so I don't have to worry about feeling awkward watching her work, Bobby thought as he drove down the driveway to park his cruiser between the house and the detached garage.

His garage only held two vehicles, his pick-up truck that he drove for any ranch work and whenever he wasn't on duty around town, and his classic Dodge Charger that he and Luke had fixed up back in high school, which he only drove when he was going out in San Antonio for an evening. So, that meant the city-issued police cruiser had to be parked in the elements, but luckily for him, the only risk of weather damage to the city vehicle was the occasional hail storm or possibly a tornado. Since he hadn't had any damage to his city-issued vehicles in the eight years he'd worked with the Heart's Destiny Police Department, Bobby wasn't too worried about the possibility of damage now that his vehicle was labeled as the chief's, instead of just a patrol car like he drove when he first started with the department.

He was exhausted and took a moment to just sit there when he turned off the vehicle, resting his head on the steering wheel. It wasn't
~~~

that his workday had been strenuous by any means. The most strenuous thing he'd done all day was his morning run, a five-mile loop around the pastures closest to his house. After that, he'd gone into the station and made sure everyone had their paperwork done that morning. Then he spent the afternoon patrolling the town to maintain a peacekeeping presence.

After work, he'd gone to volunteer at the youth center in town, where he filled in wherever he was needed a few evenings a week, be it supervising the kids in the agricultural program as they worked with their animals, or tossing the ball in a pickup game of basketball with whoever might be through with their other activities and still needed to expend some excess energy.

He was going to start teaching a class there on Monday evenings in the new year, which might be a little more mentally draining when he finally figured out a topic. But even though he'd spent an hour on the basketball court with the high schoolers after work, his exhaustion wasn't from the kids wearing him out that night. He wasn't tired from the work he'd done with his dad and uncle over the weekend either, since that had all been reviewing reports and running background checks, even though there had been almost a hundred of them.

The reason Bobby felt so worn out was because he hadn't been sleeping well recently. Other than the previous Thursday, when he'd slept like the dead all day after only catnapping the three days before, Bobby hadn't gotten three solid hours of sleep in a row, even though he'd been in his bed by ten o'clock every night. He spent those nights tossing and turning, dreaming about two women he felt immensely attracted to, and he had no idea how to deal with the unusual feelings they were stirring up in him.

Knowing that he would probably never get a chance to even meet Brooklyn Barns, he wished he could block the missing woman from his mind. He thought he could do that by not searching for updates on her case daily. But even though he hadn't looked her up since the previous Friday, her image would pop into his head at random times throughout the day, and especially in his dreams at night. He'd dreamt of screwing her six ways to Sunday and wasn't sure he'd be able to go the rest of his life without knowing how accurate his dreams were of how combustible they'd be in bed together.

Get it together! It's completely warped to be lusting over a missing person like this, Bobby mentally chastised himself. *Especially when I'm having similar dreams about Brie, who I might actually have a chance with, if I can get Brooklyn outta my head long enough to track her down and ask her out.*

Fuck! I may not have any experience with being in a relationship, but I'm not a douchebag who thinks about another woman when I'm with one of my one-nighters either. It's not right to pursue Brie, and try to start even a short-term fling, when I'm not able to focus solely on her.

Maybe it's a good thing I haven't seen Brie out and about around town yet. Until I get Brooklyn outta my head, I can't ask her out, so seeing her now probably wouldn't end well for me.

Fuck! Fuck! Fuck!

After beating his head against the steering wheel with each of those mental expletives, Bobby finally unbuckled his seatbelt and got out of the cruiser to go into his house. He shed his hat, jacket, and boots in the mud room before stepping into the kitchen.

His phone beeped, alerting him to a text message, so he pulled it from his pocket and was looking down at the screen when he stepped through the door between the mud room and kitchen and didn't notice the woman bent over, looking into the oven.

Luke: This engine is kicking my ass. I need a beer. You in?

Bobby: Just got home. Too beat tonight but call me if you need a ride later.

"Fuck, I hope his brother gives him a ride if he gets drunk tonight," Bobby grumbled as he hit send on his response to his friend.

Before Bobby could put his phone back in his pocket and look up, he heard a high-pitched squeal and the clang of metal hitting metal from the other side of the room. He jerked his head up just in time to see a blur of purple spinning around over by the stove.

"What the fuck?" Bobby shouted without thinking, fumbling his phone in surprise at having an unexpected woman in his kitchen.

"You?" The woman looked scared, stopping in her tracks to look up at him, her brown eyes wide in shock at seeing him. "You're Hazel's oldest son?"

Bobby could only nod, not sure how to respond to finding Brie in his kitchen. *Of course, Ma would have to hire her when I'm not ready to ask her out yet. Fucking Hell!*

After a moment of just staring into each other's eyes, Bobby finally let his gaze wander down from her brown hair that was up in a messy bun on the top of her head, down the column of her neck to take in the swell of her breasts as they pressed against the light purple shirt she was wearing. With the kitchen island between them, he couldn't see her lower half, but when he looked down toward her waist, he noticed how she was cradling one arm with the other in front of her abdomen and realized that she'd burned herself when he startled her by speaking when he first entered the room.

Knowing he'd caused her to injure herself quickly deflated the instant erection he'd gotten from seeing her once more. *Fuck!* Bobby mentally swore, hating that he'd caused her harm rather than protecting her from it.

"Shit! Brie, are you okay?" Bobby rushed toward her to examine the burn on her arm. He dropped his phone on the island as he rounded it, not taking the time to try to put it back in his pocket. He noticed the stockpot on the stove and the open oven door with a large metal serving spoon resting on it before he got to Brie's side, but he didn't bother picking up the spoon or closing the door before he took Brie's uninjured hand and guided her over to the sink in the island.

Bobby felt a bolt of lightning shoot through his body at the contact, traveling from where their hands were clasped together straight to his cock. *No, stay down. Now is not the time for a boner*, he mentally chastised his rapidly growing erection, hoping that would be enough to redirect the blood flow, which was currently speeding to his dick, back to his brain, so he could focus on how to treat her wound.

"I'm fine," Brie protested, pulling back against him as he turned on the cold faucet and reached for her injured arm to hold it under the flowing water. "It's not that bad a burn."

"Maybe not, but we still need to treat it." Bobby held her arm under the running water as she continued to try to pull away from him.

"The water has cooled it off completely," Brie argued. "That's all the treatment it should need."

"No, we're gonna dry it off, put on some burn cream, and bandage it," Bobby commanded, turning off the water with the hand not holding on to Brie. He reached for the hand towel that was hanging off the drawer beside the sink and started drying the wound before continuing. "Now stop fighting me and let me take care of you."

"I don't need you to take care of me," Brie protested, stomping her foot like an indignant child. "I'm more than capable of applying burn cream and a bandage myself."

"I'm sure you are," Bobby agreed, stifling his laugh at her adorably insolent behavior, and not wanting to imply she was incapable of taking care of herself. "But I caused the injury, so I'm gonna take care of treating it."

He let go of her arm long enough to get the first aid kit out of the cabinet on the other side of the room. When he turned around to walk back over to her to finish treating the burn, he shook his head at her using the hand towel he'd just dried her arm with to pick up the spoon off the door of the oven.

"That can all wait," Bobby demanded as Brie closed the oven door and dropped the spoon in the sink.

She opened her mouth as if she was going to argue with him again, but quickly snapped it shut when he set the first aid kit down on the island. He focused on finding the supplies he needed instead of on her beautiful, argumentative face.

Neither of them spoke as he deftly treated the small burn on her forearm, where she'd apparently hit it on the oven rack when he startled her, causing the spoon to fall from the edge of the stockpot. Bobby felt guilty as fuck for causing her injury, but he was also irritated at her being there when he'd expected the new cook to already be gone for the day by the time he got home from work. Since he was unable to settle between the two feelings, he skipped over his apology because he knew it would come out as insincere at the moment.

"How much longer before you're done here tonight?" His words came out in a sharper tone than he intended as he put away the first aid kit.

"Oh, um," Brie stammered, her eyes bouncing around the kitchen and not seeming to settle on any one place in the room. "The chicken-n-dumplins are done, so we can go ahead and eat them for dinner. Then I'll package up the leftovers for your lunch tomorrow and to take to Justin and JJ's houses. All I really have to do after that is finish the dishes before I can get out of your way in here. I'll still need to come down to check on the brisket a couple times overnight, but I'll be as quiet as possible, so I don't disturb you when I do that."

"You're plannin' to walk over from the bunkhouse a couple of times in the middle of the night to check on the brisket?" Bobby wondered why the hell she didn't just cook it in the oven at the bunkhouse, so she wouldn't have to traipse around the ranch in the dark.

"No, I'll just come down the stairs from my room." Brie looked at him with confusion written all over her face. "I don't know anything about a bunkhouse."

"The bunkhouse is where you're supposed to be stayin' at night," Bobby told her, his words coming out a little more forcefully than he probably should've been speaking to her.

"No, the bunkhouse is where the ranch hands stay," Brie argued, putting her hands on her hips, and drawing Bobby's attention to her curves that weren't well hidden by her dark purple skirt. "I was given a room upstairs by Hazel when I first arrived for work this morning."

"Un-fucking-believable!" Bobby shouted, throwing up his hands in exasperation. "I knew this was just another one of Ma's misguided attempts at matchmaking. I should've made it damn-fucking-clear that I don't want anyone else living here, but did I? No! I was too fucking tired and distracted and actually thought she'd agreed with the suggestion to use the second bunkhouse for the housekeeping staff she's hiring. Fuck!"

When he stopped ranting and stomping around the kitchen, Bobby noticed that Brie had taken a step back from him and was looking down at the floor instead of up at him. She'd also wrapped her arms around her midsection, like she was trying to comfort herself to be able to handle listening to his tirade.

Fuck! Bobby mentally screamed, hating that he'd verbally lashed out at Brie when she didn't deserve it.

"Sorry," he muttered, fighting the urge to take her in his arms to comfort her. He knew that would do more harm than good. "I didn't mean to yell at you. I'm just frustrated at my mom and her scheming to push all the wrong women at me. It's nothing against you. She's just crossed a major line by moving someone into my house without my knowledge or consent."

"Oh, okay," Brie stuttered, still not looking up at him. "I, uh, I'm sorry for whatever inadvertent part I played in making you feel that way today. I'll ask Hazel tomorrow if there's another room in either JJ or Justin's houses that I can stay in, since I'll be cleaning their places, too. And I'll get out of your way as soon as I can get this cleaned up tonight."

Fuck no! She's not moving to JJ or Justin's! Bobby fumed as Brie turned her back to him and started pulling plastic containers out of the cabinet to package up the chicken-n-dumplins. *Just because I'm not ready to explore the attraction I feel for her, doesn't mean I wanna give her the opportunity to move on to someone else.*

He stood there watching her dividing the chicken-n-dumplins into a dozen containers, stoically taking a moment to breathe and think before speaking. He took in everything he could see of the beautiful woman with her back to him, from the messy bun of her hair that seemed lighter than it was the first time he met her, down the elegant line of her neck to her shoulders that seemed tense as she scooped the food out of the stockpot with a clean spoon. As he watched her work, his eyes ventured lower, noticing the nip in at her waist before her hips flared out slightly.

I wonder if her bra and panties match the purples of her skirt and top? Bobby stopped himself from continuing that train of thought, trying to keep his cock in check, so he didn't give her another reason to run from him by sporting an obvious boner. As he continued his perusal of her backside, he noticed how petite she was, at least a foot shorter than his six-foot-five, and probably no more than half his body weight. *Fuck, it's a wonder she didn't run away in fear when I was yelling because of our size difference alone. How am I gonna make this right?*

When his gaze finally landed on her bare feet sticking out from under the long skirt she was wearing, Bobby couldn't help but notice how she was standing on her left foot and rubbing the top of it with her right foot, like she was self-soothing to be able to get through the next few minutes in his presence. *First, she was hugging herself, now she's rubbing her feet together. She needs a comforting touch from a friend, not a hot-headed asshole like me, scaring the shit out of her by yelling at her for someone else's shenanigans.*

When she finished emptying the stockpot into the plastic containers for him and his cousins to be able to reheat the meals later, she turned toward him to place the pan and serving spoon in the sink. Before she could turn back to the counter where she'd stacked the packed-up meals, Bobby stepped forward, instinctively reaching out to tilt her chin up, so she had to look up at him.

"I'm sorry," he adamantly apologized, hating that she froze at his gentle touch. "You don't have to go stay somewhere else. I'm just…" His voice trailed off as he tried to come up with a reasonable excuse for his earlier behavior. "I'm an asshole. There's no excuse for the way I just lost my shit, other than the fact that I'm an asshole. I'm sorry. I'll try my best not to be that guy around you."

"Oh, okay," Brie stuttered, her eyes watery where she was obviously holding back tears. She quickly turned away from him to pick up the first stack of containers to carry them over to the refrigerator, absolutely gutting Bobby when she tore her gaze away from his.

Not knowing what else to do, he moved to carry the rest of the food to the icebox for her. "Um, aren't we supposed to eat some of this for dinner?" He lifted the stack slightly to show her he was referencing the food in his hands when he got to about a foot behind her where she was stacking containers in the freezer.

"Ya-yes," Brie stuttered, her posture stiffening when she realized he was right behind her. "I'm only freezing the extra portions. The ones for your dinner tonight and lunch tomorrow and the ones I'm supposed to take to JJ and Justin's tomorrow, I was planning to put in the fridge. But if you're ready to eat now, please go ahead and take one of the containers before I put it away."

"And when are you gonna eat?" Bobby inquired as she slowly turned around and started taking containers from the stack he was carrying to put them in the freezer.

"I, uh, nibbled as I was preparing everything," Brie obviously lied, not making eye contact with him, even as she was taking a container off the stack he was holding. "Totally ruined my appetite with the veggies I was cutting up for the salad that's in the fridge to go with your dinner."

Once there were only four meals left in his hands, she took three of them and placed them in the refrigerator. Leaving him standing there holding his dinner, she stepped around him to go back to the sink to wash up the dishes.

"This is more than I'll eat in a sitting," Bobby lied, holding up the container that held at least three bowls worth of chicken-n-dumplins, hoping he could entice her to at least have a little of the dinner with him. "Surely, you can at least eat a small bowl with me?"

She didn't answer, just went about her business washing the dishes as if he wasn't even in the room. He hated seeing her starting to shut down on him. He felt like a total ass for being the reason she was going to skip dinner.

There's no way she got full on rabbit food, Bobby thought, resolving to figure out a way to get her to eat a little something for dinner.

He placed the container down on the island before going to the cabinet and getting out two bowls and two plates. He went back to the refrigerator and got out the salad and both bottles of salad dressing. Using the serving spoons, which she'd just washed, he served them up a portion of each, making sure to keep her serving small, so she couldn't argue that it was too much for her to eat. He put away the leftover food, leaving the salad dressing bottles with her food on the island so she could pick which she preferred.

"You're welcome to join me at the dining table," Bobby implored her in the softest voice he could manage as he picked up his own plate and bowl to carry them to the dining room. "But I understand if you'd rather eat in here. Just make sure you eat, please."

Damn, these are good, he thought as he dug in, enjoying the meal she'd made. A few minutes later, he realized he'd forgotten to get anything to drink, so he went back to the kitchen to make himself a glass of water. He was shocked to find an empty kitchen; Brie obviously having vacated the room as soon as she finished the dishes. At least her plate and bowl were gone too, and the salad dressing bottles had been returned to the fridge.

How the hell did I miss her going up the squeaky-as-fuck stairs right outside the dining room? Bobby wondered as he made his drink and went back to take his seat at the dining table. *Ma must not have mentioned the no-food-in-the-bedrooms rule to Brie. And if the only way I can get her to eat is to let her sneak food up to her room, then I'm damn sure not gonna mention it to her now.*

He ventured into the kitchen a second time to refill his bowl of chicken-n-dumplins, finishing off the rest of the first container. He thought back over the events of the evening as he finished his meal and rinsed off his dishes before going upstairs to bed.

Fuck! I can't believe how bad I screwed things up with her tonight, he fumed as he stopped at the top of the stairs and noticed the light under the closed bedroom door at the opposite end of the hallway from his master bedroom. He briefly placed his hand on the door, wanting to reach out to her and knowing he couldn't yet, before walking down the hall to his own room.

And fuck if I know how I'm gonna fix it. Maybe knowing she's sleeping in my house, just down the hall from me in my big empty bed, will be enough to keep me from dreaming about anyone but her tonight. Maybe this is just what I need to be able to block out my gut feeling that I'm supposed to save Brooklyn, so I can focus on exploring the attraction I feel for Brie.

Chapter Four

Tuesday, December 4, 2018

Bobby didn't usually go eat breakfast with his parents on workdays, opting to grab a dozen donuts at Kara's Kakes to take into the office to share with his staff instead. But after the way he'd screwed things up with Brie the night before, he knew he needed to catch his mother before Brie did, so she wouldn't have a chance to move out of his home. It felt completely wrong to go along with his mother's matchmaking scheme, but he couldn't take a chance on Brie being redirected toward JJ or Justin, so he didn't have another choice.

As he was getting ready for the day in the ensuite bathroom attached to the master bedroom, he noticed that Brie hadn't cleaned it the day before and decided that finding out her cleaning schedule would be the opening he would use to talk to his mother about her. He paid more attention as he walked through the house as he was leaving for the day, and realized the only room she'd obviously cleaned the day before was the kitchen.

He hadn't ventured into her room or past her room to the little office space or second bathroom at the back of the house on the second floor to know if she'd cleaned any of those rooms, so he wasn't a hundred percent certain she'd spent her whole day in his kitchen the day before. But after he'd had to coax her into eating dinner the previous night, he didn't think she would've focused on cleaning her own space first.

Fuck, I still can't believe she was gonna go without dinner, so she could get out of my way sooner. She's obviously had a rough upbringing to be so programmed to putting other people's needs before her own, Bobby thought as he got in his cruiser to drive over to his parents' house before going to work. *Maybe if I can get my shit figured out soon, I can be the man to take care of her, since it doesn't appear as if anyone else ever has.*

His short drive was filled with ideas of how he wanted to take care of Brie. In addition to the little things like doctoring her burn and getting her to eat like he'd done the night before, he envisioned talking to her for hours on end to get to know everything about her, so he could help her achieve all her hopes and dreams. He kind of shocked himself when he realized that he was mostly thinking of ways he could be a good friend to her, instead of the sexually explicit things he dreamt about doing to her every night since he'd met her.

He pulled into his parents' driveway before he could go back and analyze the content of his dreams the night before to determine if having Brie sleeping just down the hall had helped him dream less about Brooklyn and more about Brie. *I'll have to figure that out later*, he decided as he got out of his vehicle and walked in the back door to his childhood home.

"Oh, Bobby, what a nice surprise," his mother, Hazel, exclaimed, pulling him in for a hug just as soon as he got within arm's reach of her. "Is Brie with you?"

"Mornin' Ma," Bobby replied, returning her hug, and realizing she was using it as cover to look around him for Brie. "No, uh, I don't think she was up yet when I left."

"Oh." Hazel released Bobby and looked up at him quizzically.

"I mean, I don't know if she was up or not," Bobby backtracked, feeling scrutinized by his mother's appraisal. "Her bedroom door was closed, and I didn't hear her moving around when I walked by to head down the back stairs, so I didn't wanna disturb her if she's used to sleeping in a little later than we do."

"Well, that's very considerate of you." Hazel turned back to her breakfast prep. "Did you happen to show her where you keep your spare car keys last night? Or the ATVs? I forgot to when I was there showing her how to start the brisket after we went grocery shopping. And I hate to think of her walking the whole way because of not knowing what vehicles are available for her to use."

"Uh, no," Bobby stammered, unsure how he felt about his mother offering the use of his personal vehicles to anyone without his knowledge. While he didn't think it was a big deal for Brie to have access to his vehicles, he wasn't sure who the second housekeeping person to be hired would be, and didn't like the idea of a stranger driving his classic car. Pushing the bizarre idea of feeling okay with Brie driving his Charger out of his head, he forged on with his original plan to talk to his mother about Brie's sleeping arrangements. "I was kind of shocked to find out she was staying with me last night. I was looking forward to coming home to a clean house with dinner in the fridge, not her still working in my kitchen without having done anything in the other rooms."

"Oh, no, you're not on her cleaning schedule until today," Hazel waved him off, not acknowledging his shock at Brie staying in his home. "Mondays and Fridays she's helping me with cooking lunch and dinner for the hands when she's not needed cleaning at Anthony and Kay's house. Tuesdays she's cleaning your house, Wednesdays at Justin's, and Thursdays at JJ's. She has Saturday and Sunday off, unless she didn't make enough meals to last ya'll through the weekend earlier in the week."

Bobby understood why Brie had stored the eight extra containers of chicken-n-dumplins in his freezer the night before after his mother's last statement. Distracted by that thought, he didn't get the chance to go back to the sleeping arrangements portion of the conversation before his father and sisters appeared in the kitchen to join them for breakfast. Luckily for him, the girls were doing a quick fly-by to grab a bite before work and didn't stay long enough to sit down with their parents for a full meal.

Once the girls left, with their bacon and eggs smashed between the layers of a biscuit so they could eat and drive, Bobby redirected the conversation with his parents to Brie's sleeping arrangements.

"So, um, I thought the housekeepers were gonna stay in the south bunkhouse," Bobby hinted, leaving his question implied.

"Well, that was the plan." Hazel diverted her eyes sheepishly. "But when I went to get it cleaned up and ready for them, I found the whole thing flooded, so I obviously couldn't put them out there."

"Uh-huh," Bobby's dad, Bob, grumbled, shaking his head.

"Wait a minute, I'm confused." Bobby tried to figure out how the bunkhouse flooded when they hadn't had rain recently, and none of the other buildings on the ranch were having similar problems. "How'd the bunkhouse end up flooded?"

"I think one of the kids left the water running in the upstairs bathroom when we had the sleepover there," Hazel shrugged. "With nobody going in there for two weeks, that little trickle of water ended up causing a whole lot of damage. I called Karen Walker and she sent Dalton out to make sure the water was turned off into the building, but it'll be six months before they can get it gutted and rebuilt since they're having to work it in when they have openings between other construction jobs."

"Wow, that bad, huh?" Bobby was completely dumbfounded by the way his parents were nonchalantly reacting to such massive destruction. "Well, that explains why you had to have Brie stay with one of us, instead of in the bunkhouse."

Bobby rubbed the back of his neck, not quite believing that what he was about to say to his parents was actually coming from his mouth. "So, um, I might not have taken the surprise houseguest as a good surprise at first last night."

"Oh, Bobby, what did you do?" Hazel covered her mouth with her hand, having a much stronger reaction to his mealy-mouthed statement than she had to the damage at the bunkhouse.

"I might have made her a little uncomfortable when I complained about it being a set-up for one of your matchmaking schemes," Bobby hesitantly admitted.

"You're not wrong there," his father, Bob, chuckled between bites of his breakfast.

"But it was just my knee-jerk reaction to being surprised at first," Bobby professed, practically choking on his next words. "After thinking about it, I kinda like being set-up with Brie. I know I'm gonna hafta do some massive damage control after the way I first reacted last night to get her to even speak to me, much less agree to go out with me, but I'm willing to do it. I just need your help to make sure I have the chance to convince her."

"Oh, Bobby!" Hazel shouted, jumping out of her seat to nearly strangle Bobby with a hug around the neck. "I knew she was perfect for you. Of course, I'll help you win her over. What do you need me to do?"

"Thanks, Ma," Bobby choked out, patting her back to return her affection. Once she released him and went back to her seat, he beseeched her, "Just don't let her move out of my house, if she asks for a different place to stay."

"Oh, you must have really put your foot in your mouth if you think she's gonna ask to move," Hazel chided, shaking her head as she smiled at her son.

All Bobby could do was nod his head as he shoveled his eggs into his mouth. Luckily for him, they went down a lot easier than his pride had at admitting his interest in the same woman his mother wanted him to date. *Date? Hell, Ma's probably already planning the wedding. And if I tell her I'm not ready for that because I still feel drawn toward another woman, she's liable to push Brie toward one of my cousins or brothers instead of me. Yeah, I definitely hafta get my shit together as soon as fucking possible.*

~ ~ ~

Brooklyn waited until she heard Bobby leave for work before she opened her bedroom door to come out and get started on her day of work. She'd felt uneasy every time she'd sneaked out of her room overnight to check on the brisket and return her dinner dishes to the kitchen, not wanting to run into him when she knew he didn't want her in his home.

She'd originally planned to have everything packaged up and put away before he got home, so she could spend the evening in her room without intruding on his nightly routine. But after not catching the name of Hazel's oldest son while spending the entire day with the older woman, Brooklyn was just too curious about who he was to wait until the next day to ask his name. She thought it would be okay to be finishing up when he got home from work, so she could at least meet him to find out his name.

I should've known better than to stay downstairs, so I could meet him. Trying not to be embarrassed by asking Hazel her oldest son's name really came back to bite me. Interacting with Bobby was much more humiliating than asking Hazel to name off her kids again would've been.

Brooklyn still couldn't believe she was staying in Bobby's house. Bobby, the police officer who would probably have to send her home to her father's horrible plans for her future. Bobby, the man she'd secretly crushed on since she first saw him across the room at the wedding reception over a week before. Bobby, the only man who had ever given her goosebumps and butterflies. Bobby, the man who clearly wasn't attracted to her and made it abundantly apparent in his rant the night before.

Brooklyn thought back to his comments and cringed.

"I knew this was just another one of Ma's misguided attempts at matchmaking. I should've made it damn-fucking-clear that I don't want anyone else living here."

"So much for the attraction I thought I saw in his eyes at the reception," she complained to the empty house as she got started with her day. She ate one of the peaches she'd bought to make a peach cobbler for breakfast as she removed the brisket from the oven, and sat it on top of the stove to cool down enough that she could shred it for the Brunswick stew she planned to make them for dinner that night.

Her mind drifted back to the night before as she cleaned the rest of the peaches and got started making the cobblers.

"Sorry. I didn't mean to yell at you. I'm just frustrated at my mom and her scheming to push all the wrong women at me. It's nothing against you. She's just crossed a major line by moving someone into my house without my knowledge or consent."

"Yeah, really nothing against me," Brooklyn huffed as she took out her frustration on the innocent fruit she was cutting up. "I'm just one of those *wrong women* his mom is trying to push on him by moving me into his house without his consent."

She continued to fume as she finished getting the food started for the day, not understanding why she was so angry. "I mean, it's not like I'm really in a place in my life where I can fall in love or have a relationship with him, so why am I so mad at him for not being interested in even having me around? I should be happy he doesn't want me here, so I won't have a chance to get close to him only to have my heart broken when I have to move on from here."

The phone on the wall behind her rang, startling her out of her thoughts. She wasn't sure if she should answer it or not, seeing as it wasn't really her home. *If anyone needs to reach me, they'll call my cell,* Brooklyn thought, knowing that the only people who had her cell phone number were Kenzie, Mandi, Luke, and Hazel. *But my cell is upstairs in my room. Would Hazel call me on the house phone if she couldn't reach me on my cell phone?*

The phone stopped ringing before Brooklyn could decide to answer it, so she finished putting the cobblers in the oven, thinking she'd go check her cell phone once she got to a stopping point in her current task. Just as she was shutting the oven, the phone on the wall started ringing again. Worried it might be Hazel, Brooklyn quickly crossed the room and picked up the phone.

"Hello," she tentatively uttered.

"Brie, we missed you for breakfast," Hazel gushed, making Brooklyn glad she'd listened to her gut instinct and picked up the phone.

"Oh, sorry, I ate a little something here while getting started on my tasks for the day," Brooklyn replied, wondering if she'd screwed up by not attending the Burlesons' daily breakfast in her attempt to avoid being around Bobby.

"Good, when Bobby said he let you sleep in, and I realized I'd forgotten to show you where the car keys and the ATVs are down there, I was afraid you might try to walk the five miles up here." Hazel's worry for her was evident in her tone, even through the phone. "The keys are on the hook beside the phone in the kitchen."

Brooklyn looked around at the wall beside the phone she was currently using and saw a strip of metal hooks between the phone and the doorway into the mud room, which had a keyring on each of the five hooks. "Yes, I see them," Brooklyn told Hazel.

"Good, the top one is for the truck, the one right below that is the keys to the car," Hazel informed her. "They're both in the garage to the right of the house when you go out the back door. The next two are to the four-wheelers, and the bottom one is to the mule."

"The mule?" Brooklyn questioned, confused by why they needed a key for an animal.

"Yes, that's what I'd suggest you use to deliver the food to JJ and Justin's houses."

"Um, I don't even know how to put a saddle on a mule to be able to ride it, much less how to strap down the stack of food containers I'll be carrying up there this afternoon," Brooklyn confessed, thinking she was definitely in over her head if she was expected to use a mule for transportation.

"Oh, goodness," Hazel laughed. "Not a four-legged mule, a four-wheeled mule. It's like a jacked-up golf cart that has a truck bed instead of a back seat."

"Oh, okay," Brooklyn laughed along with her boss. "I actually rode on one of those for the first time yesterday when I checked out of the bed and breakfast, but I didn't know that it was called a mule. Not something we see a lot of in the city."

"You fit in so well here, I forgot you're a city girl," Hazel confessed, still lightly chuckling. "Anyway, the four-wheelers and mule are all in the shed behind the garage. I know you wanted to finish up a couple days' worth of food before delivering it today, but when you do head this way, don't forget to stop by and get your HR paperwork to fill out for me."

"I won't forget that," Brooklyn replied. "I'm just going to work on cleaning here while the cobblers and stew are cooking and then I'll take a break to deliver the food before coming back to finish up the cleaning here."

"Sounds like an excellent plan." Hazel's smile was clear in her tone of voice. "Call me if you have any problems with getting the mule started and carry your cell with you in case you get lost trying to navigate the ranch."

"Will do," Brooklyn assured her boss, glad for the reminder to get her phone since she wasn't familiar with the ranch roads yet. "Thank you."

"No, thank you for taking such good care of our boys," Hazel replied. "See you later, sweet girl."

Hazel hung up before Brooklyn could muster the courage to ask about moving to a different house on the ranch. *Crum bunnies! I should've said something about needing to stay with someone other than Bobby*, Brooklyn thought as she went to the closet where the cleaning supplies were stored to get started on the biggest task of her day.

It'll be fine. I'll just make sure I'm done with everything for the day and in my room for the night before he gets home from work. And if I can't figure out how to ask Hazel to move out of his house by the weekend, when I have the day off, I'll go see if I can find a coffee shop in town to be able to work on my book where I won't be at risk of seeing him.

Besides, I kind of need to go find a place with lots of people using the Wi-Fi to keep anyone from tracking me down through my internet searches for information about what's going on at home. I certainly can't do those searches from the home of the top cop in town.

~~~

Saturday, December 8, 2018

After a week of almost zero communication with Brie, Bobby was not a happy camper when he went to his parents' house for breakfast. All week he'd hoped to catch her in his kitchen again, so he could start trying to get to know her. But after his asinine behavior on Monday, she'd stayed holed up in her room the rest of the week whenever he was home.

Tuesday evening he'd gotten home to find his house spotless and a barbecue flavored stew in his fridge for dinner that he thought could be his new favorite meal. Not to mention the excellent peach cobbler for dessert. But if it wasn't for the sliver of light escaping under the door and the light clicking of keys he heard when he walked past her room, Bobby wouldn't have known Brie was even still staying there at night.

When he left for work on Wednesday morning, her door was still closed, and there were no sounds coming from the room, when he put his ear to the door to check on her. That night when he got home, he found containers of beef roast, potatoes, carrots, gravy, and homemade yeast rolls waiting for him. It was a delicious and filling meal that went well with the leftover peach cobbler from the night before. He really wished he could've shared the meal with Brie, but she was already in her room for the night.

Thursday and Friday it was more of the same. The nightly meals changed to a chicken and broccoli casserole with a chocolate cream pie for dessert on Thursday, and a smothered steak and potatoes dish with pound cake for dessert on Friday, but Bobby was still stuck eating them alone. Brie seemed to only come out of her room when he left
~~~

for the day, and always made sure to hide away again before he returned.

With the extra meals in the freezer to feed him for the weekend, some of which having disappeared, presumably to go to JJ and Justin for their weekend meals, Bobby knew she was technically off work until Monday. He hoped she wouldn't spend the whole weekend in her room, but thought it was pretty likely if he didn't leave the house for her to feel safe coming out.

Fuck! I hate knowing she's hiding in there just to avoid me, Bobby thought as he got into his truck to drive to his parents' home. *Hopefully, I'll get done with everything Dad needs me to do this morning fast enough to catch her out of her room this afternoon. Even if I'm not ready to act on the attraction I feel for her, since I'm still dreaming about Brooklyn too, I at least want to start making some progress with her as a friend.*

The whole family was there for breakfast that morning, with the exception of his two middle brothers, Jake and Josh, who were both still in the Navy. Bobby had been surprised that they'd both gotten almost two weeks off at Thanksgiving and were able to be at Anthony and Kay's wedding. It had been nice to have the whole family there for the normal Sunday supper that his mother insisted everyone attend.

Since Anthony, Kay, and their daughters were leaving for the airport right after breakfast, they weren't going to be there for Sunday supper the next day, so Bobby figured that was why his mother had insisted on everyone's breakfast attendance this morning. Bobby smiled, thinking about how much he loved having at least one meal a week with his whole family. With as much as he'd complained about needing his space away from them when he turned eighteen to be able to move out on his own, though, he would never admit to them how much he enjoyed hanging out with everyone regularly. His sisters wouldn't let him live it down if he did.

After the usual greetings and filling their plates to go be seated around the larger table in the dining room, the conversation turned to everyone's plans for the next week. Bobby didn't feel like he had much to contribute to the conversation since he was just doing the same ol' same old at the police department with nothing specifically scheduled after work or for the weekend.

Instead of zoning out to think about Brie, Bobby's ears perked up when he heard his niece, Tia, was going to be staying with his sister all week. *That's weird. Why would Tia wanna go to Heart's Destiny Middle School for a week, instead of traveling with her parents and working with her usual tutors?* He didn't get a chance to verbalize his questions before his mother cleared them up by asking her own.

"Have you been studying hard for the acceleration tests you're taking in Char's classroom this week?" Hazel questioned Tia.

Ah, acceleration tests. That makes sense. Tia's certainly smart enough to skip a grade or two.

"I don't need to study, Memmaw," Tia replied with her usual serious tone that sounded years older than her actual age. "I have an eidetic memory. Even if the questions are about books I haven't read for years, I can just close my eyes and read them again in my head to know the answers."

"Wow, that's cool." Bobby's sister, Charlotte, turned to ask Tia a follow-up question. "Can you remember other stuff like that or just books you've read?"

"I remember almost everything that way." Tia slightly lifted one shoulder in a half-shrug. "I just have to close my eyes and think about what day something happened, or where I was when something happened, and it kind of plays out like a movie in my head." Tia turned her attention back to her food, quickly taking a bite like her exceptional memory was no big deal.

"Almost everything?" Bobby's sister, Becky, looked at Tia in awe. "Like, how far back does your memory go?"

Tia finished chewing before answering. "I don't remember being a baby or learning to walk, or talk, or anything like that," she confided, waving her fork around like it was an extension of her hand as she spoke. "But I remember sitting on the ugly brown shag carpet playing with building blocks on the day Mom and I moved out of Grandma and Grandpa Lee's house into the house around the corner with the green shutters when I was two."

"I can't believe you remember that carpet!" Kay blurted, barking out a laugh. "That was the first thing we replaced when we moved in there. I forgot about it within a few months of living there."

"I don't think you forgot it, Mom," Tia smiled at her mother. "I think you intentionally blocked it out of your mind because of not knowing if the previous owner's dog had left poop stains on it like you told Grandma Lee that day."

"Poop stains?" Anthony arched an eyebrow at his new bride as he and several others around the table chuckled.

"Hey, don't laugh," Kay scoffed, playfully swatting away Anthony's hand, where he was leaning in like he was going to tickle her. "That carpet was a weird pattern of all different browns, with the darkest spots looking remarkably similar to doggie doo."

Bobby couldn't contain his own laughter at the humorous conversation. Though he was shocked to see his parents laughing and not changing the subject away from animal excrement at the breakfast table.

After the laughter died down and the rest of the family had talked about the various things going on in the coming week, the discussion turned to the family business, and scheduling the quarterly board meeting for the end of the month, when everyone would be in town for the holidays. Unless Josh or Jake had something come up to prevent them from coming home on leave, like had happened the previous two years, it would be the first time since their grandfather passed away that the entire board would be physically present for a board meeting.

Two years before, when Pappaw Jerry passed away, Anthony had also been in the Navy and deployed on an aircraft carrier in the Mediterranean Sea. He'd had to Skype in for the funeral as well as the first few meetings that their generation had as new board members. With three of the Burleson brothers being in the Navy, at least one of them had needed to Skype in for the board meetings in the first six months of them inheriting their interest in the company, unable to get leave on short notice.

After Anthony's accident, he'd only been present for one meeting before starting work with the Galactic Wrestling Association as a pilot. In the year and a half since he started that job, he'd still only physically attended half the meetings, Skyping in from his hotel room, or whatever arena where the GWA was performing, for the ones that were held while he was working.

Josh and Jake had gotten better at trying to put in for leave the last week of the quarter to be able to be at the meetings, but with Josh being a Navy SEAL and Jake working in naval intelligence, it wasn't always feasible for them to schedule time off. They'd both missed out on several holidays at home in the eight-and-a-half years since they'd graduated high school and entered the Naval Academy.

While Bobby had done his two-year stint in the Navy, he'd realized he missed his family too much to want to stay in for a full career like his brothers. In the summer of 2010, he'd come home to the family he missed only to realize that they were all starting to leave home. His sister Charlotte had gone to college the year after he left for the Navy, so she wasn't on the ranch often in the first three years he was back home. About the same time he got home from his time in the Navy, Jake and Josh left for the Naval Academy, where they spent four years as active-duty midshipmen while getting their college degrees before following their career paths into the current positions they were serving in as naval officers.

In the summer of 2011, a little less than a year after Jake and Josh left home, Anthony dropped out of high school, got his GED, and joined the Navy. He got his college degree online, the same way Bobby had, taking CLEP tests for several subjects, so he could finish his degree faster than the normal four years. He completed his degree and flight school in the first three years he was enlisted, and then spent three years flying fighter jets before an explosion on board the aircraft carrier where he was stationed ended his Navy career in the spring of 2017. Even with Anthony being out of the Navy for the last year and a half, his career as a pilot still kept him away from home too much for Bobby's liking.

When Becky went off to college in 2012, two years after Bobby returned home from the Navy, Bobby spent the next year feeling extremely lonely, being the only Burleson of their generation living full-time on the ranch because even his cousins were all off at college. Thankfully, his sister, Charlotte, and cousin, JJ, both came back from college to live on the ranch again when they graduated college in 2013. His cousin Justin came back to the ranch after graduating in 2014, with his sisters, Julie and Jen, following in 2015. Bobby's sister, Becky, was the last family member to complete a college degree and return to the ranch in 2016, right before their Pappaw Jerry passed away.

Having his sisters and cousins come home from college to live on the ranch and work locally, lessened some of Bobby's feelings of separation from his family. But with all three of his brothers choosing to work in jobs that kept them away from home most of the time, he still missed them. So, he savored the extra time he had with Anthony that morning as they laughed and joked around as a family, even if he wouldn't admit it to anyone around him for fear they'd try to revoke his man card for being so sappy and sentimental.

Once breakfast was over and his siblings started to disperse, Bobby followed his dad to the stable, opting to do any background checks they needed at Burleson Incorporated once he was back at home. He wanted to take the time they were alone while working with the horses to talk to his dad about the unusual feelings he'd had the last couple of weeks. Being a lot like his quiet and reserved father, however, they spent most of the next hour silently caring for the two new horses that still needed to be convinced to take a saddle before they'd ever work with a rider to be able to work on the ranch.

After they'd each finished grooming the two horses Bob Burleson had purchased a little over a week before, Bobby went over to the stall where his father was working, knowing he'd only want to take them out on a lead rope one at a time to help keep them calmer.

"So, you gonna tell me what's got you suddenly wanting to help me train horses again?" Bob only glanced at his son as they walked the brown and white American Paint horse out to the paddocks where they could work with him.

"I've never totally stopped helping you with the horses," Bobby replied, feeling guilty for all the times he'd ducked out of the manual labor of the ranch to work on his computer for Burleson Incorporated instead. "I just normally have other things that seem more important to get done when you're out here with the horses."

"Uh-huh, sure ya do." Bob turned to face the horse instead of Bobby. He rubbed the horse and spoke softly to the animal for a few minutes before starting to walk him on a lead rope around the paddock they were in.

Bobby felt kind of foolish standing there doing nothing while his dad walked the horse around, but he still hadn't figured out how to explain the way he was feeling to be able to talk it out with his father like he wanted.

"I'm assuming whatever you wanna talk about that has you standing around here, instead of walking the other horse, is about

Brie," Bob prodded as he completed his first lap around the paddock with the Paint.

"How could you tell?" Bobby chuckled, shaking his head at how well his father knew him.

"I've seen the look you have on your face a few times over the years," Bob smiled at his son as he walked past him with the horse. "On my own face, on my brother's face, on your youngest brother's face, and even on a few of my friends' faces. It usually has to do with a woman and being overwhelmed at what you're feelin' for her."

"Yeah, overwhelmed sounds about right," Bobby admitted.

"So, are you still tryin' to figure out what you feel for her? Or do you know she's *The One*, but she won't give you the time of day to start winning her over?"

"Maybe a bit of both," Bobby shrugged, feeling like a cad for what he was about to admit to his dad. "I mean, I already know the attraction I feel for her is more than what I normally feel for a girl, but, um, she's not the only woman I'm feelin' drawn to right now. So, while it's drivin' me nuts that she won't even come out of her room when I'm home, so I can talk to her, I'm not really sure I'm ready to pursue her either. At least not until I can get this other girl outta my head."

"Okay…" Bob drew out the word like he was trying to wrap his head around what Bobby had just said before formulating his comments on the situation. "I saw Brie catch your eye at the wedding reception. When did you meet this other girl? And who is she?"

"I haven't met her," Bobby confessed, running a hand through his hair in frustration at how Brooklyn had captivated him from only a picture. "You remember hearing about that Georgia woman who disappeared on Thanksgiving?"

"Yeah." Bob nodded his head and stifled a chuckle when the horse seemed to nod along with him. "No need to agree with me, Patches. You weren't even here on Thanksgiving."

Bobby chuckled at his dad's interaction with the horse. *He's got such a way with horses. I hope my kids will get to see this fun side of my dad one day.*

"Well, the day after Thanksgiving, I didn't have a whole lot to do at work, so I did a little research on the case," Bobby finally confided. "I had that first *She's-The-One* feeling the first time I saw Brooklyn's picture on my computer. Then the next day, I met Brie at the reception and had the same feeling. I've been dreaming about them both ever since. But instead of feeling drawn to Brooklyn like a cop who's supposed to help her, I'm feeling the same attraction to her that I am to Brie."

"Huh?" Bob huffed, sounding as confused by the way Bobby was equally attracted to the two women as Bobby felt himself. "Maybe neither one of them is *The One* for you."

"Then why do I feel like they both are?" Bobby wanted his father to clarify his last statement.

"Well, I've known guys who are equally attracted to more than one woman, but that's usually when they're still playin' the field, not ready to settle down. Once you meet *The One*, it's almost like nobody else exists. She's the only woman you wanna be with, or can even think about most of the time."

"Yeah, well, I've tried puttin' Brooklyn outta my head. I mean, I know I'll probably never even meet her, so I wanna pick Brie and focus on her, but I can't stop the dreams at night when they morph back and forth from one to the other."

"Like one minute you're with Brie and the next you're with Brooklyn?" Bob looked quizzically at his son over the top of the horse's back where he'd started trying to get Patches ready for a blanket and then a saddle on his back.

"Yeah." Bobby nodded his head as he moved to the other side of the horse, so they could both pet the animal to acclimate him to being touched and having weight on his back. "I mean, other than hair and eye color, they kinda have similar facial features. Heart-shaped faces, button noses, and pouty lips."

Bob didn't say anything, but the tilt of his head on the other side of the horse prompted Bobby to continue his description of the two women.

"Brie has brown hair and brown eyes with fair skin, where Brooklyn is a platinum blonde with blue eyes and more of a tan skin tone," Bobby elaborated, picturing the two women side by side in his head. "Brie seems to be the same height as Ma and curvy. The news reports on Brooklyn aren't consistent, listing her as anywhere from five-foot-three to five-foot-six, but the pictures I've seen make me think she's taller. I'm guessing she's probably closer to five-five but wearing heels to look even taller next to the men she was photographed with. And she doesn't appear to have as much of an hourglass figure as Brie."

"I guess all that police training has made you extra observant when it comes to describing people," Bob chuckled at the way Bobby had just described the two women so completely that he could picture them in his head.

"Yeah, I guess," Bobby laughed with his dad at using his observational skills in a way not really intended in the training he'd received in his Navy Master-At-Arms training or in the police academy. "At least as much as I can tell from pictures on a computer screen. I'm sure the hair, eye, and skin colors can vary dramatically in the same picture when viewed on different monitors, so there's a little margin of error there."

After a few minutes of silently working with the horse, Bobby finally asked, "So, what do you think I should do, Dad?"

"Give it time, son," Bob advised, a knowing look in his eye that Bobby couldn't quite interpret. "I agree that you shouldn't pursue something romantic with Brie if you're still having dreams about another woman. But that doesn't mean you can't be her friend while you're trying to figure out which one of them is really the woman for you. Remember, friendship is the best foundation for building a relationship. And who knows, maybe if you start spending time with her as a friend, getting to know her better might just make your choice clear."

"That's exactly what I've been thinking the past few days," Bobby admitted to his dad, glad for the reassurance that he was on the right track by following his instincts. "Now I just have to figure out how to get her to talk to me again, so we can actually become friends."

"How 'bout you start by knockin' on her bedroom door and inviting her to church in the morning and Sunday supper tomorrow evening," Bob suggested. "Maybe she won't be as uncomfortable around the whole family as she seems to be when ya'll are alone at home."

"Thanks, Dad." Bobby was glad for his dad's excellent advice. "I will definitely do that."

After spending the rest of the afternoon working with his dad and the two new horses on the ranch, Bobby went home to find his house quiet and empty. Brie's bedroom door was open, so he could see that her bed was neatly made, but she wasn't in the room. He checked the other rooms at the back of the house before going to his ensuite bathroom to wash away the sweat and grime from working with horses all day.

As had become his daily habit since meeting Brie at his brother's wedding reception, Bobby palmed his cock as soon as he stepped into his shower. Prior to then, he only jacked off in the shower on the weekends, when he couldn't go pick up a one-nighter to relieve his need for release because of being on call at the police department. Back then, he'd picture a random woman, or one he'd made up in his head, to provide the mental component he needed to get off. Since his brother's wedding, he'd been alternating between images of Brie and images of Brooklyn during his shower jerk sessions.

Maybe if I can focus on only picturing Brie while I'm stroking my cock, Bobby thought as he lubed up with a couple drops of his bodywash. *I'll be able to push Brooklyn outta my head enough that she won't show up in my dreams anymore either.*

With his new plan in place, he leaned back against the wall and conjured up her perfect, petite little body in the shower with him. Normally, his fantasies leaned toward doggie style or fucking against the shower wall, something hot but impersonal, just like his hookups. But Bobby wanted more with Brie. He wanted the intimacy that he usually didn't allow when he was with a woman. So, he started his fantasy off with kissing every inch of Brie's compact curves. He may have stopped kissing the girls he hooked up with when he started having sex in high school, and had never once gone down on anyone he fucked, but he imagined how he'd eat her pussy if Brie were really in his shower with him.

He'd have her sit on the bench at the back of the shower and spread her legs. Then he'd go down on his knees to kiss her pretty, pink lips before trailing his tongue down to her tits. He imagined spending several long minutes lapping the shower water off her peaked nipples before moving lower. *Fuck, I wonder if she's waxed? Or shaves? Or maybe leaves a little patch of brown curls I'll have to try not to choke on while I'm eating her creamy cunt?*

Bobby couldn't keep his tongue in his mouth, acting out the movements as he pictured himself licking through her folds to fuck her with his fleshy, muscular, oral organ. *Thank fuck, nobody can see how ridiculous I must look imitating what I wanna do to her with my tongue while jacking off.*

Brushing away the fleeting thought to focus back on his mental cunnilingus, Bobby could almost imagine the taste and feel of her coming undone on his tongue. *I bet she tastes sweet, not fishy like some women smell.* He envisioned finger-fucking her to stroke her G-spot to make her come while he sucked lightly on her clit. The thought of Brie's O-face almost took him over the edge, and he was still only lightly stroking his dick.

He squeezed his length tighter as he imagined himself standing, so she could suck his cock. He'd never really had a good blow job, since the one girl who attempted it in high school had barely licked his shaft before injuring her jaw because he was too long and thick to fit in her mouth. Bobby knew Brie probably wouldn't be able to suck him off either, but reality had no place in his fantasies. He imagined her pouty, pink lips wrapped around his dick with no problem. He tried to mimic the pressure of her lips around his thickness as he pictured his hands in her hair to control the bobbing of her head up and down his length.

Fuck! Brie! Bobby mentally shouted as his orgasm rocketed through his body. He'd wanted to move the fantasy on to actually fucking her tight pussy, but the vision of her sucking his dick like a porn star was more than enough to make him spray his shower with at least a half-dozen jets of his white, sticky cum. With each spurt of cum, he repeated his outburst of the expletive and her name, unable to control how he cried out for her in pleasure.

He stood there, still clutching his spent cock, for several long moments while he caught his breath. Once the spots in his vision faded from the image of Brie to just his empty shower, Bobby grabbed his bodywash and a washcloth to clean himself up. When he was done bathing, he used the washcloth to wipe up the remnants of his semen that hadn't already been washed down the drain by the spray of the shower. As soon as the evidence of his masturbation was eradicated, Bobby quickly finished up with his normal routine in the bathroom, hoping Brie would be home when he exited his room.

Where the hell is she? Bobby wondered as he wandered through the house after getting dressed. He grabbed his laptop to do her background check while he ate another container of the stew from earlier in the week. *And how the hell did she leave when I know she doesn't have her car back yet and all my vehicles are here?*

Entering her information from the email his cousin had sent him as the only new hire this week into the computer to run her background check, Bobby was taken aback as he realized she was seven years younger than him. *Damn, that's more of an age difference than I expected. Though I guess I haven't really seen her without makeup to get a more accurate idea of how old she really looks. I just thought she was closer to Becky's age.*

Is seven years too much of an age difference? Naw, Anthony's almost eight years younger than Kay, so surely it's okay for me to go out with Brie, even though I'm seven years older than her. Right?

He was so distracted by thinking about how he would be perceived for dating a woman so much younger than him that he didn't realize the report generated by entering her tax identification number was for the Brie Brooks limited liability company and not for Brie Brooks the person. He noted no criminal record and attached it to the email back to his cousin. Since he didn't really get any new information from the criminal background check, he went over to his internet browser and searched for her online presence. He found her website and author pages on several social media platforms, but not any personal pages.

All the pictures on her pages were of her book covers, none of her like he'd hoped. Dejected at not finding much about the beautiful woman who was currently living in his house, Bobby put his things away and went to bed early. He figured with the way Brie was avoiding him all week, she wouldn't come home until she saw that he'd turned off the lights for the night, so she could sneak back in without running into him.

<center>~~~</center>

Brooklyn felt like she'd done a really good job all week with settling into her new routine and avoiding any interaction with Bobby Burleson. It was surprisingly easy to hear where he was in the house to be able to sneak back and forth between her bedroom and bathroom without him knowing she'd even opened her bedroom door. So, she made sure to get all her work done and have all her meals between when he left for work early in the morning and when he returned home from work late in the evening, leaving her only having to take a break from her writing to go through her nightly bathroom routine after he'd retired for the night.

She had a plan already for how to avoid him on Saturday when he would be on the ranch all day. As soon as he left to go to breakfast at his parents' house, Brooklyn called Kenzie to get directions to the coffee shop in town, planning to go hang out there and catch up on her online book promotion and internet stalking of her missing person's case in Georgia. Instead of having to take one of the Burlesons' vehicles as she'd dreaded she'd have to do, Kenzie insisted on picking her up and hanging out with her all day. Brooklyn didn't get to do any of the things she'd planned to do online, but she enjoyed a day off with her new friend.

They started off going to the coffee shop, but Brooklyn didn't pull her laptop out of her bag. She was too busy soaking up the scenery of the town and especially the interior of the Caffeinated Cowpoke. Like the rest of the businesses around the town square, the wooden façade of the building was straight out of the Old West. While the interior was more modern with the fancy espresso machines and all the amenities of a twenty-first-century coffee shop, the décor still gave off a country vibe with rustic wood tables and rodeo pictures on the walls.

She was enjoying getting to know more about Kenzie when two women approached their table. "Hey, girl, who's your new friend?" asked the woman with long straight black hair who took the seat beside Brooklyn.

"This is Brie. She's the author whose car broke down that I was telling you about a couple weeks ago." Kenzie introduced Brooklyn to her friends. "Brie, these are my two best friends, Ashley Myers," she pointed to the woman who'd sat down beside her as she said Ashley's name before pointing to the woman seated beside Brooklyn and finishing her statement, "and Heather Deere."

"Nice to meet you." Brooklyn felt a little uncomfortable, even though both women were smiling and appeared to be as nice as Kenzie.

"Nice to meet you, too." Ashley pushed her brown hair behind her ears.

"I hope your welcome to Heart's Destiny has gotten a little better since you first arrived," Heather commented before sipping her coffee.

"Oh, yes, everyone in town has been so welcoming and friendly." Brooklyn hoped to hide her ingrained shyness to be able to make two more new friends.

"So, are you just passing through and stuck here until your car gets fixed, or are you actually moving to town?" Ashley leaned back in her seat as she assessed Brooklyn.

"Well, I was just passing through, but since it's going to be a while before my car is fixed, and I've felt so welcomed here, I'm now planning to be here a while longer," Brooklyn admitted, not sure yet if her move to Heart's Destiny could possibly be permanent, or if she would have to move along to keep from being discovered by the investigators her father had after her.

"She actually got a job on the Burleson Ranch," Kenzie informed her friends. "So, I'm hoping she'll stick around, if for no other reason than to give me several opportunities to hang out at the ranch with her, so we can enjoy the eye candy of the Burleson boys."

"Are you actually living on the ranch?" Ashley's hazel eyes lit with excitement.

"Yes." Brooklyn didn't really want to elaborate on her current housing situation in case one of the other women was interested in Bobby Burleson. She didn't want her inappropriate crush on him to cause a rift between her and her potential new friends during their first conversation.

"We've definitely got to plan some girls' nights with you on the ranch," Heather smiled widely. "Especially when Jake and Josh are home for the holidays."

"It's such a shame that the two hottest Burleson boys are always off serving our country, instead of home where we can ogle them," Ashley added, sighing wistfully.

"JJ and Justin are home though, and they are just as hot as their cousins," Kenzie interjected with a dreamy expression on her face.

"So, what are you doing on the ranch to get to hang out with all those hotties?" Heather asked Brooklyn.

"I'm cooking and cleaning houses," Brooklyn replied, unsure if she should mention that she hadn't actually met any of the Burlesons that the ladies seemed to be crushing on or not. "But I've only hung out with Hazel, Susan, and Rosa, not any of the younger generation of the family."

"I'm sure that'll change soon," Kenzie giggled. "It's no secret around town that Hazel and Susan are on the hunt for their kids' future spouses. I'm sure she's got a plan to fix you up with one of the boys. In fact, that's probably why she has you staying at Bobby's house."

"You're staying with broody Bobby?" Heather turned to look at Brooklyn with an expression of utter shock.

"Ya-yes," Brooklyn stuttered. "Since I started work on Monday."

"And our illustrious police chief hasn't kicked you out yet?" Ashley's shocked expression matched Heather's.

"Well, he wasn't exactly thrilled with the situation on Monday when I met him," Brooklyn admitted with a slight shrug of her shoulders. "But it's a big house and I've easily avoided any further conversations with him by being in my room for the night by the time he gets home from work."

"Oh, that's hilarious," Heather giggled. "I bet that's driving him nuts, knowing you're there as part of his mom's matchmaking schemes, and not being able to scare you off because you've figured out how to avoid his grumpy ass already."

"Has Hazel tried to match him up like this before?" Brooklyn wondered if any of the ladies around her had been pushed toward her hunky housemate in the past.

"Not exactly like this," Kenzie replied, shaking her head. "But she's put him at a table full of eligible women at every town event with a sit-down dinner for as long as I can remember."

"Ugh, don't remind me," Ashley groaned. "I got stuck sitting next to him at the Independence Day picnic this year."

"That's your own fault for not being brave enough to tell Hazel you really wanted to sit by Josh," Heather teased Ashley.

"Yeah, but I did let Bobby know I was interested in his brother and not him," Ashley confided, turning to look at Heather. "But instead of telling me more about Josh or helping me get moved to his table, broody Bobby just sat there and ate in total silence. I finally gave up trying to have a conversation with him and rushed through eating, so I could get up from the table and go hang out with anyone else."

Brooklyn wasn't sure she could picture Bobby Burleson just sitting and eating without protesting the seating arrangements if he really wasn't interested in the girl he was being forced to sit with. But as the girls went on to describe more of Bobby's antisocial behavior at various town festivals and church potluck dinners, she was starting to question how much she really knew about him from the two very brief interactions she'd had with him.

"So, does he just not date?" Brooklyn was curious about the man she knew she shouldn't be interested in. "Or does he just not date the women his mother tries to fix him up with?"

"He avoids the women his mother tries to fix him up with," Kenzie chuckled. "And like my cousin Luke, his dates are usually buckle bunnies, who are only here for the weekend when there's a rodeo in town."

"Yeah, I wouldn't classify those as *dates*," Heather laughed. "More like random hookups while parking on a back road in his truck."

"Actually, since he had the Walkers put gates on the trails off of Clydesdale across from Lover's Lanes, he's been seen goin' to the girls' rooms at Aunt Mandi's B and B on rodeo weekends," Ashley informed them.

"Okay, I'm confused, who are the Walkers?" Brooklyn queried, trying to dissect everything she'd just learned from Ashley's last statement. "Why do these trails need gates? What's Lover's Lanes? And is Mandi Hunter your aunt?"

"The Walkers are my cousins," Kenzie started answering Brooklyn's questions. "Well, half of them are my cousins. My dad's sister, Karen, married Wyatt Walker, so their three sons, Luke, Landon, and Leo are my cousins. But I'm not blood-related to Aiden, Dalton, Hayden, or Hudson, who are Wyatt's brother Tully's kids."

"Years ago, when the town was first founded, the Walker family had a parcel of land as big as the Burleson Ranch, but they sold off half of it and built houses for all the oil workers who moved here when the Burlesons struck oil," Heather continued answering. "The northern part of the land still owned by the family is a wooded area of trails that's bordered by Clydesdale Street to the north, Rogers Road to the east, and Hereford Road to the west. That's where all the teenagers used to go parking, until a few years back when Bobby caught one of his sisters parking there with a boyfriend she'd brought home from college, and he made the Walkers put up gates. So now only the Walker boys can go parking there."

"And Bobby since he's Luke's best friend and has the gate codes," Kenzie added, finishing her friend's statement. "And Lover's Lanes is the bowling alley on Clydesdale across the street from the now gated-off parking area."

"They named the bowling alley Lover's Lanes because it was across the street from where everyone went parking?" Brooklyn assumed, thinking it was an oddly appropriate name.

"Yep," Ashley replied. "And Mandi Hunter is my dad's sister, making her my aunt, which is how I know not all of Bobby's hookups have been on the Walkers' trails in the last few years."

She didn't need any reminders of her current housemate and his long history of one-night stands to spoil her good mood from feeling like she was fitting in with her new friends. It had been awkward enough explaining to the girls that she was working as the live-in cook and housekeeper for the Burlesons. So, when the girls started talking about Bobby's double standard for who should be allowed to go parking on a dirt road, Brooklyn changed the subject to ask them about their boyfriends and the other men in town.

"No boyfriends," Kenzie replied. "Though not because we're not looking. We just normally avoid talking about my brother and the Walkers because I'm related to half of them and feel like I'm related to the other half."

"And we don't normally talk about the Hunter hotties because they're my cousins," Ashley added.

"So, we mostly drool over the Burleson boys since none of us are related to any of them," Heather giggled. "But catch me when these two aren't around and I'll gladly tell you all about the man candy they won't mention."

"And we'll tell you about the dashing Deere men," Kenzie continued, motioning between herself and Ashley. "When Heather's not around to be grossed out by us lusting after her brother and cousins."

"What we're saying is that if Hazel doesn't successfully get you hooked up with one of the Burleson boys, we'll help you find your Heart's Destiny hottie." Ashley wagged her eyebrows suggestively. "Especially if you're willing to help us make time with the Burleson boys."

"Well, Hazel said they're still looking for a second housekeeper to clean the houses on the ranch that I don't have time to get to," Brooklyn offered, happy to help her new friends try to spend some time with the Burleson boys she hadn't even met yet. "I'm not sure where they'd have you stay on the ranch since the bunkhouse flooded, but I know both Justin and JJ have spare bedrooms because I cleaned them earlier this week. Maybe that could be your in?"

"Yeah, Mom and Dad would be furious if I quit working with them at Heart of the Home." Heather shook her head. "So, I'll just wait until you've worked at the ranch long enough to be able to invite us over to go horseback riding, or when they have another big barbecue like they did the week of Anthony's wedding, to ogle JJ and Justin."

"And I already work for the Burlesons at the Gas & Go," Kenzie shrugged.

"I have to admit the job sounds tempting," Ashley confessed, tilting her head, her expression showing deep contemplation. "And if it were Josh's full-time house with a spare bedroom I'd be asked to stay in, I'd probably jump on the chance. But I have a feeling my Aunt Mandi would whup me for taking a job as a housekeeper after paying for my culinary school."

"You work at the bed and breakfast?" Brooklyn wondered why she hadn't met Ashley during her stay there.

"Yeah, I helped her and Meemaw cook on weekends and summers when I was in high school," Ashley explained. "Then after culinary school, I took over as the head cook, so Aunt Mandi could focus on other things. I ended up having to have her hire some kitchen help when I found out Meemaw didn't actually work there. And now that she's got the plantation house all renovated, we're talking about using that dining room as a full restaurant open to the public, instead of just the breakfast service for guests we've been doing."

"Yeah, I bet she would definitely be upset if you quit to be the Burlesons' housekeeper when you're her head chef now," Brooklyn chuckled along with her new friends.

The ladies continued chatting late into the afternoon, discussing hobbies and favorite things, and really making Brooklyn feel welcomed into their close-knit group of friends. When the coffee shop was empty except for their little group and the employees, they decided to take Brooklyn to Lover's Lanes, since she'd never been bowling.

While she got more gutter balls than all three of her new friends combined, she had a wonderful time learning a new activity. Even though she'd only known Kenzie for two weeks, and had just met Ashley and Heather that day, Brooklyn felt like she'd known them forever. They became fast friends, exchanging phone numbers at the end of the night, so they could text all week and plan for another girls' day the following weekend.

She couldn't explain why she felt so at home in this small Texas town, or the instant connections she made with the people there, but she knew in her heart that she belonged there in a way she'd never felt back home. That feeling of belonging didn't go away when Kenzie dropped her off late that night. Brooklyn quietly crept up the back staircase, trying not to make a sound, so she didn't disturb Bobby in case he was already asleep. But even that was her attempt at being a courteous houseguest, and not because she felt like she didn't belong in his home. After a week of cooking and cleaning in the spacious Victorian, Brooklyn felt right at home.

Before going to sleep that night, Brooklyn pulled up her laptop and sent another email to Mary and Joe.

To: MaryTurner@GAemail.com

From: BrieBrooks@BrieBrooks.com

Subject: Mary Kate's Great Escape

Mary & Joe,

Thank you for your previous feedback on Mary Kate's adventures along the Gulf Coast. As opposed to emailing the next chapter for you to proofread and critique, I'm writing to ask your opinion on how I should proceed with writing it.

As you know, Mary Kate's car broke down at the end of the last chapter, stranding her in a quaint town that's a wonderful blend of the Old West with all the modern amenities. In order to fund her car repairs, I've started the next chapter with her getting a job as a live-in cook and housekeeper on a local ranch. The owner of the ranch where she's staying is also the local sheriff, whose name I've yet to decide on for the book as I'm not sure yet if he'll be a prominent character.

She's also met several of the local women, who she's starting to bond with in ways she hadn't expected. There are three motherly women, who are married to the other men living on the ranch, who've taken her under their wings. When she's not busy cooking and cleaning for the sheriff, she spends her time with them cooking for the ranch hands and sharing recipes. They've made her feel as much a part of their family as she feels with the motherly figure her father had hired to raise her.

In addition to the three older women she's bonded with, she's also met three women her own age in town. They've welcomed her into their tight-knit friend group and started introducing her to new things to do, like girls' nights and bowling. Mary Kate isn't very good at bowling, but she had a great time trying to learn the game with her new friends, and can't wait to go back and practice, so she'll eventually get better.

I'm planning to fill the next chapter with her experiences in making friends in the small town where she's currently staying. But I'm torn as to whether or not I should let her get too close to them. On the one hand, I can see her feeling so at home that she decides to live the rest of her life there with her new friends. But on the other hand, I worry that if she gets too close to the local sheriff, she'll be at risk of him having to send her back to her unwanted wedding with dastardly Donald.

Does the risk of being found and sent back outweigh the potential benefits of having close friends who feel like family? Is being too close to the sheriff really a risk? Or do you think he'd go against the out-of-state law enforcement agencies, who are looking for her, to keep her safe there with him?

I look forward to reading your opinions and incorporating them into Mary Kate's future plans.

Love & Hugs,

Brie

Chapter Five

Brooklyn laid in bed Sunday morning, contemplating her life and future plans after making two more new friends the day before. When she accepted the job to cook and clean on the Burleson Ranch, she hadn't planned on it being a permanent position. She'd thought she'd just work there long enough to earn enough money to fix her car, and save up some to be able to continue her journey across the country in a few months. But the more time she spent with the people she met in town, the more she wondered if she could stay hidden there, living as Brie Brooks for the rest of her life.

It wasn't just that Kenzie, Ashley, and Heather made her feel like a long-lost sister with the way they'd treated her the day before that was compelling her to stay. Though she loved feeling like she finally had a close group of friends, she wasn't sure she'd instantly bonded with them so strongly that she'd miss them if she had to move on to find new friends in a different town. But having never had close friends before, she couldn't be certain of that.

She did know that she missed Mary and Joe, even though she'd cryptically emailed them under the guise of asking their advice on the plotline of her new book. If anyone ever read their email from the children's book author, asking the older couple their thoughts on the adventures Mary Kate was having as a runaway bride, they'd probably realize pretty quickly that the Turners weren't really beta readers for the books that were way below their age group.

Brooklyn just hoped her father never read their emails because she knew he'd probably figure out her alias immediately and narrow down her whereabouts to Texas, even though "Brie" didn't mention any specific cities in her adventure updates. She probably shouldn't have mentioned "Mary Kate's" car breaking down in an Old West town and her going to work on a ranch to pay for the repairs, but it was too late to change the message. She only hoped Mary was savvy enough to delete the messages as soon as she replied.

Regardless of the risk, emailing Mary and Joe helped Brooklyn not miss them nearly as much as she would without any communication between them. And after spending several days with Hazel in the last week, Brooklyn knew that she would miss her, too, if she left the little town of Heart's Destiny after spending a few more months working with her. *Who am I kidding? I'd miss her if I left today.*

In addition to spending all day with Hazel on Monday, Brooklyn had visited with her, Susan, and Rosa for a couple of hours on Tuesday, when she was done cleaning Bobby's house and went to deliver the meals to JJ and Justin's houses. She'd thought she would just pick up her human resources paperwork and bring it back after filling it out, but the ladies had convinced her to stay and help with dinner for the rest of the ranch.

Brooklyn had ended up having to go back to Hazel's house after cleaning Justin's house on Wednesday to pick up the paperwork she'd accidentally left there on Tuesday. That meant another hour hanging out with the ladies that all reminded her so much of Mary. She actually remembered to take the paperwork with her that night, but then she had to return it on Thursday after cleaning JJ's house, and ended up visiting with them for another couple of hours while cooking with them.

Then Friday, since she didn't have a house scheduled to clean, she spent the whole day with Hazel, going grocery shopping a second time and stocking the freezer and pantry with enough food to feed an army for a month. In addition to enjoying her time with Hazel, Brooklyn had been relieved to not have to drive one of Bobby's vehicles for that grocery run.

She'd only gotten her driver's license because it was expected of her growing up. She hadn't really had much experience driving after getting it, since she usually rode with Mary or Joe when she went with them on errands, and her father had insisted on them riding in a chauffeur-driven limousine when they went to the various society events he needed her to attend to keep up appearances. With her lack of experience behind the wheel, she'd been exceptionally nervous driving when she had to in order to escape her unwanted wedding, and that had been in her own used car. The thought of operating one of the pristine new or like new automobiles on the Burleson Ranch was extremely daunting. Brooklyn didn't want to take a chance on damaging one of them due to her inexperience driving, so she was trying to avoid it for as long as possible.

Luckily for her, Hazel hadn't been able to get her a card for the ranch accounts to be able to go grocery shopping on her own yet, so Brooklyn was able to plan her shopping trips with the Burleson matriarch. In addition to shopping together, they'd swapped recipes and made memories baking together like Brooklyn had with Mary growing up, bonding to the point that Brooklyn knew she'd always think of Hazel as yet another surrogate mother, and she couldn't stand the thought of moving away from her.

But as much as she wanted to stay in the quaint, little town with her new friends that felt like family, living with Bobby wasn't the most ideal situation for her to be in either. It was difficult living with a man who didn't want her in his home, especially when she couldn't stop herself from having a massive crush on the guy, but it was all she could do at that moment in time. When she'd asked Hazel about the second bunkhouse that Bobby had mentioned that first night, she was told about how it had recently flooded, and wouldn't be repaired to livable condition for at least six months.

Brooklyn hoped it wouldn't take six months for her to earn enough money to repair her car and save up enough to find an inexpensive apartment in town. But even if it did take her longer than that to be able to completely stand on her own two feet, she at least knew she'd only have to live in Bobby's spare room until the bunkhouse repairs were completed.

Her plans to avoid him completely until the time came for her to move out of his home were dashed when he knocked on her bedroom door, instead of leaving for the day as she'd expected. She was still lying in bed in a pair of sleep shorts and a tank top, and really wished she'd bought a long fluffy robe when she bought the new sleepwear in Houston, so she had something to cover her body more before talking to him.

Maybe if I'm really quiet, he'll think I'm still asleep and will go ahead and leave for the day, Brooklyn thought, covering her head with the quilt on her bed, just in case he opened the door.

"Brie," Bobby called out as he knocked again.

Just pretend to sleep. Don't acknowledge him.

"Rise and shine, Brie." Bobby had a cheerful quality to his voice that Brooklyn hadn't heard before. "I've been given strict orders to bring you to church this morning, so I need you to get up and get ready."

I guess I can't keep feigning sleep, Brooklyn realized as she pushed down the quilt and started to sit up in bed. Before she could call out to tell him she was up, she saw the door start to open and his large body fill the doorway as he stepped into her room.

"I'm up!" Brooklyn squealed, pulling the quilt back up to her neck, so he couldn't see how her braless breasts responded to his presence in her room. She quickly closed her eyes, knowing it would be disastrous for her if he saw her without her colored contacts in to disguise her bright blue eyes. But not before she got a good view of his bare chest where he was walking around in only a pair of pajama pants.

His broad, bare chest with a light dusting of chest hair, Brooklyn thought, trying not to sigh at how hot the man was, so she didn't give away her attraction to him.

"Uh, sorry," Bobby apologized, slowly backing out of her room. At least Brooklyn thought he was backing away from her based on the way his voice was receding from the room, since she couldn't tell for sure with her eyes closed. "We're leaving in an hour. I hope that's enough time for you to get ready."

Unable to verbalize a reply, Brooklyn nodded her head, hoping he would understand her affirmative response to being ready to go in an hour.

When she heard the door click shut, Brooklyn finally opened her eyes and let out a breath she hadn't realized she'd been holding. That was a little too close of a call for her. She waited until she heard the master bedroom door shut before she jumped out of bed, grabbed her clothes for the day from where she'd hung them in the closet, and took off for the bathroom to get ready for the unexpected outing with her hunky housemate.

I should've realized after spending so much time working with Hazel this week that I would be expected to attend the Sunday services while living on the ranch. If I had, I could've been up and ready without risking him seeing my real eye color.

But then I probably wouldn't have gotten a glimpse of his broad shoulders, perfect pecs, and sexy six-pack abs. Brooklyn didn't contain her sigh as she started her shower and got undressed, imagining what it would feel like to run her hands over the muscular planes of his body. *And I can't complain about the fantasy material I just saw. I just wish I could've gotten a better look at what he's hiding under those pajama pants before I snapped my eyes shut.*

Even though Brooklyn had been too sheltered to have any real-life experience with the opposite sex, she'd done enough online exploration to learn a little more than the basics Mary had told her about intercourse. While she still believed she should wait for the love of her life before having sex, like Mary had taught her, she also knew that she could alleviate some of her body's need for pleasure through self-stimulation in the meantime.

Seeing Bobby's naked torso for a much too brief time that morning was certainly more stimulating than all the pictures and videos she'd looked at online in the past. It didn't take but a few minutes of remembering what he looked like shirtless and imagining how his skin would feel under her hands, while standing under the hot spray of the shower with one hand kneading her breasts and the other softly rubbing on her clit, for her to release the pressure building up in her body from being near him and unable to touch him.

Just before the waves of pleasure broke over her body, Brooklyn released the grip on her breast to reach over for the soft gray washcloth she'd hung on the bar on the shower door. She sped up the strokes of her fingers against her clit, biting down on the washcloth just in time to keep from screaming out her orgasm for her sexy housemate to hear.

This ride to church is going to be awkward enough already. I don't want to make it worse by having him hear me screaming his name as I come when I'm supposed to be getting ready.

<div align="center">~~~</div>

Holy fuck! Brie has the most perfect, pebbled nipples on her luscious, round tits, and I can't believe I could almost see every detail of them through her tight, white tank top, Bobby thought as he speed-walked

128

back to his room after waking Brie up. *If only she hadn't covered them up with the quilt and closed her eyes, so she didn't have to look at me.*

Fuck! If only, what?

It's not like I can follow through with my fantasies about her right now. And she obviously doesn't want me to, either, based on the way she tried to hide under the covers and block me out of her sight by closing her eyes.

Hell, she couldn't even talk to me after I scared her awake by barging into her room. I hope that nod of her head means she'll be ready on time to go to church.

Even though he knew his attraction to her was not reciprocated, Bobby couldn't stop himself from palming his cock in the shower to a fantasy of fucking her bountiful breasts. At almost thirty years old, he thought he had a fairly good handle on keeping his cock under control to not have inappropriate erections anymore, like back when he was a teenager and popped a boner every time he saw or thought about a pretty girl regardless of his surroundings. Having already willed his morning wood to recede, he thought it was safe to peek in on Brie when he couldn't get her to wake up through the bedroom door without risking a reappearance.

But not only was he wrong about being able to control his reaction to seeing her, he was also wrong when he thought he could make his cock shrink back to a non-aroused state by just walking away from the sexy-as-sin woman sleeping in his spare bedroom. Even as he tried to think of other things to deflate his erection while standing in the coldest shower possible, the vision of her sitting in her bed with her perfect peaks practically poking through her shirt kept playing on repeat in his head. He really had no other choice but to stroke himself in the shower to alleviate his incessant need to fuck her.

"Fuck, yes, just like that, Brie," Bobby imagined himself saying as he ran his fingers through her long brown hair, using it to guide her mouth up and down his length. He could almost feel her tongue working over the underside of his dick as her lips clamped down around him while she sucked him to the back of her mouth.

As he felt that familiar tingle spread from his spine down to his balls, he pulled her off his cock and bent his knees to go down low enough to go back to fucking her tits. He cupped her breasts, squeezing them together over his dick while pinching her nipples between his forefingers and thumbs.

"Play with your pussy, Brie," he commanded as he looked down to see her fingering her smooth folds. "Be a good girl and come with me, Brie."

"Yes, Bobby, yes," she replied as they both went over the edge to ecstasy.

They continued chanting each other's names as rope after rope of his cum spilled over her chest and her whole body spasmed in release.

When Bobby caught his breath after one of the most intense self-induced orgasms he could ever remember, he cleaned his cum off his hand and the shower wall before actually completing his normal shower tasks. After washing his hair, he did a little manscaping on the off chance that he was wrong about Brie's lack of interest in him, wanting to be neatly trimmed for her if he ever got the chance to live out the fantasy he'd just had in the shower. Or at least the part where he fucked her tits until they both came, since he knew he'd never really get a blow job from her, or anyone else, after the trauma of his one and only oral experience. He finished up by scrubbing his body with the ocean-scented bodywash he'd used since he was a teenager.

He pulled one of the gray bath sheets from the cabinet right outside the shower to dry off, running it over his short hair a second time after drying off the rest of his body. Since he kept his hair in a traditional men's business cut, he didn't have to do anything other than to comb it into place after a shower. He'd tried to do the long hair thing like his brothers and friends back in high school, but he hated having to primp like a girl with a blow dryer and hair products, so he stuck to a style similar to his father and uncle, other than when he'd had to wear it high and tight the two years he was in the Navy.

After shaving his face, combing his hair, and brushing his teeth, he hung his towel over the bar on the shower door before going back into his room to get dressed. As he went to pick out a suit to wear to church, he noticed the one he'd worn to Anthony's wedding was still hanging in the closet where he'd placed it to be taken for dry-cleaning, alongside the two he'd worn to church since then, and the one he'd worn to church the week before the wedding. While plucking his last suit from the back of his closet, he made a mental note to mention the dry-cleaning to Brie later, hoping that he could adequately describe the location in his closet without having to actually show it to her. He wasn't sure he could handle seeing her in his bedroom to show her where he hung things to go to the dry cleaners without being too tempted to spread her out on his bed.

Fuck! Go down, damn it! Bobby mentally chastised his cock for standing at attention at the brief thought of Brie in his bed. *You've had all you're gonna get today, Thor, so hide the hammer before you scare the girl away.*

Once he was dressed and ready to go, Bobby went downstairs to have a cup of coffee while waiting for Brie to finish getting ready. He focused on thinking about everything but Brie, trying to keep his cock at no more than half-mast. Unfortunately for him, his mind wandered to Brooklyn, causing a similar response in his pants to his earlier thoughts about Brie. It took everything he had to block them both from his mind while he sipped his coffee and waited to drive to his parents' house for breakfast before church.

Surprisingly, it only took Brie thirty minutes longer than him to get ready, even with doing her hair and makeup. So, she actually walked into the kitchen ready to go exactly an hour after he'd woken her up. He stopped himself from blurting out how gorgeous she looked in a blue skirt and top similar to the purple ones she'd worn on Monday, knowing she wouldn't appreciate the compliment coming from him. Controlling his mouth did nothing for stopping his eyes from perusing her from her sandal covered feet, up over her luscious curves, to the curly caramel-colored tresses flowing down past her shoulders.

Fuck, it's gonna be hard, not to stay hard, all through church with her looking so fucking hot, Bobby thought, standing to rinse his coffee cup and discretely adjust himself without her noticing, thanks to the island between them.

"Ready to go?" Bobby turned back to look at her as soon as he felt back in control.

"Yes, Sir." Brie clutched her purse to her side and walked toward the back door without looking up at him.

Yep, I'm just gonna be hard as a fucking rock all day, especially if she keeps calling me Sir in that breathy tone of voice.

Instead of grabbing the keys to his Dodge Ram that he would normally drive around town on a Sunday morning, he pulled the keys to his 1969 Dodge Charger off the hook in the kitchen before following her to the back door. He quickly caught up with her, unable to stop himself from guiding her to the garage with a hand on the small of her back.

"Is black your favorite color?" Brie looked around the garage as he opened the passenger door for her to get in the car.

"No, why?" Bobby was confused by her question.

"All your vehicles are black," Brie pointed out, waving her hand toward the front of the car, then in the direction of his truck, and finally outside the garage toward the police cruiser that was also black with white city decals, "so I figured it must be your favorite color."

"I can see why you'd think that," Bobby chuckled as she sat down in the car. He shut her door and walked around to get in the driver's side before explaining. "Black vehicles are more stealthy on the road, which is why our cruisers are black. They're also less likely to be pulled over than brighter colors, which is why I painted this one black when I was a teenager, instead of red like I really wanted."

"Oh," was all she said, not continuing the discussion by asking his favorite color as Bobby had hoped she would.

She turned to look out the window as Bobby drove to his parents' house. As much as he wanted to ask her all her favorite things, and use the short drive to start getting to know her better, her body language made it obvious she didn't harbor any of the same sentiments toward him. So, he filled the silence with the sound of his favorite country radio station playing on low as he drove.

Brie looked confused when he pulled up to his parents' house, but she didn't ask why they were there, so Bobby didn't say a word. He just did his gentlemanly duty of opening first the car door for her, and then the back door to the house, guiding her forward with his hand on the small of her back because he couldn't resist the temptation to touch her. He hoped she felt the electricity between them when they touched, no matter how platonic it seemed to anyone observing them.

"Oh good, you brought Brie in time for breakfast," Bobby's mother, Hazel, exclaimed as soon as they stepped into the kitchen.

"Well, that was what you asked me to do," Bobby replied to his mother, pausing in his walk toward the food to bend down to kiss her on the cheek before standing back up straight and guiding Brie over to the island, where everything was laid out for them to make their plates.

"Thank you for inviting me," Brie softly whispered, looking directly at his mother. "I've really enjoyed the services when I attended with the Hunters the last two weeks. I thought I was going to have to miss them until I get my car back from the shop, so I really appreciate you thinking of me and making sure I have a ride."

"Of course," Hazel smiled at Brie. "I'm glad you've enjoyed the services so far. Being a non-denominational church, not every newcomer does. What church did you attend back home?"

"I, uh, didn't really," Brie slightly stumbled over her words, turning her focus toward making her plate like she was embarrassed at the admission. "I vaguely remember my mom taking me to a big church when I was little, but she passed away when I was four, so I was too young to remember much about it. My, uh, fa-foster parents didn't really go to church, though they did quote the Bible on occasion."

Foster parents? Damn, I hate that she had to grow up in the system. Hopefully, she didn't get stuck in an abusive home. Though, that would explain why she cowers and hides away in her room. I wonder why I didn't see anything about the foster system when I did her background check last night? Maybe I can do some more research on her later to see if I can figure out how to help her recover and come out of her shell a little bit.

"Did you have a lot of foster parents? Or just the couple you were telling me about earlier this week?" Hazel undoubtedly realized she was getting Brie to open up more than Bobby could on his own. He silently thanked his mother as he finished making his own plate and directed Brie toward the dining room to sit down with the rest of the family.

"No, just Mary and Joe," Brie replied as they walked out of the kitchen and down the hall to the dining room.

"Hmm?" Hazel arched an eyebrow inquisitively as she followed them from the kitchen. "I don't know much about the foster system, but it seems unusual to stay with the same family so long without being adopted."

"I guess I just got lucky to be able to stay with them," Brie shrugged as they took their seats. "Even though my biological father wouldn't ever sign away his rights, so they could adopt me."

With his sisters and niece at the table, the conversation quickly switched from Brie's childhood to her book series, leaving Bobby with more questions than answers about any possible abuse in her past. Brie seemed really excited to hear Tia's opinion about her books, offering to gift her digital copies, so she could read them on her tablet while traveling with her parents while they were at work. Bobby was so tuned in on the conversation between Brie and Tia that the rest of the conversations around the table faded to the background as if they weren't even there.

"Thank you for the offer, but I've actually already read them," Tia smiled at Brie, after wiping her mouth with a napkin. "When we moved in next door back in October, Memmaw Hazel stocked our bedrooms with a bunch of books, including all three of the books in the *Mary Kate* series."

"Really?" Brie's voice came out at a higher pitch than normal, like she was excited to hear a live review of her books from someone in her target demographic. "What did you think of them? And please be brutally honest. I need to know both the good and the bad about my books, so I can make the next one better."

"They're really good for a quick, fun read," Tia smiled at Brie like she was hoping to soften the blow of her next words. "But I think they're more geared to kids younger than me, like my sister, Maria's age. In fact, Mary Kate really reminds me a lot of Maria, especially in the first two books. When I saw Mary Kate was going to college in the last one, I thought it might be something I could relate to more, since I'm testing this week to be able to start my college classes in January. But the pranks were all things we did at slumber parties when I was in elementary school, and there weren't any references to real issues on college campuses, like underage drinking or date rape, that young women really need to be made aware of to be able to take precautions and protect themselves when they go to college."

"Oh." Brie's shoulders slumped in disappointment.

Bobby desperately wanted to wrap his arm around her and console her from the criticism, but he didn't think she'd accept it from him. Before he could think of something to say to try to ease the blow Tia had inadvertently delivered, his niece offered some advice that brought Brie's smile back.

"But I'm not your average twelve-year-old." Tia reached over and patted Brie's hand to give her the comfort Bobby wished he could deliver. "I've been reading at a collegiate level since I was seven, so I have a hard time finding new books that are age appropriate and still on my reading level. My friend Britany, who's a little over eight months younger than me, loved all three of them. So, my only suggestion to be able to sell more books would be to market them as middle-grade books, which is the category for ages eight to twelve, instead of as young adult books, which is the category for ages twelve and up."

"Oh, yeah, I will definitely be changing my marketing strategy for the first three books," Brie agreed, turning her hand over under Tia's, so she could clasp them together. "I thought I was bringing the third one up to relate to the older teenagers by using the university setting, but I guess getting my degree online didn't really give me the on-campus college exposure to make my character's experiences in college seem realistic."

"You did your degree online?" Tia's eyes lit with excitement as she looked at Brie.

"Ninety-nine percent of it." Brie nodded her head at Tia. "I only had to go to campus to buy my books and take final exams, and even those were online for most of the classes."

"Well, that makes me feel better about starting college online next month," Tia smiled at Brie. "None of the college classes I've done online before actually counted toward a degree, so I was worried that I wouldn't be able to take all the classes I'll need for my degree online. I just got my Daddy and I want to be able to stay living with him and Mom for a few more years before I have to move off to a dorm, which I'll probably have to do once I finish my undergrad and go to law school."

"Ya'll ready to go?" Hazel interrupted all the other conversations going on around the table to get the family motivated to finish eating and head over to the church.

They all quickly finished eating and cleared their dishes from the dining table, dropping everything in the sink to take care of after church.

As the family walked out of the house as a group to go to the various cars they'd take to church, Bobby lightly tugged on Tia's ponytail to get her attention. "Hey Tia," he grinned when she turned around and poked him in the belly for pulling her hair. "Why don't you ride with us, so you and Brie can finish your conversation about her books."

"Thanks, Uncle Bobby." Tia gave him a one-armed side hug as they walked toward his car. "Letting me ride in your hot rod has earned you favorite uncle status for the day."

"Only for the day?" Bobby feigned being hurt by the limit, miming pulling a knife out of his heart, before opening the passenger doors for both Tia and Brie. "Since I'm the uncle you see most often, and the only uncle home with you all week, I should at least get favorite uncle status for the week."

"You're not the only uncle home with me this week," Tia disagreed as she got in the car. "Uncle JJ and Uncle Justin are here on the ranch, too."

"They're your cousins, not your uncles," Bobby corrected her, chuckling as he closed her door, then closed Brie's door, before walking around to get in the driver's seat.

"They're too old for me to think of them as cousins, so I call them uncles instead," Tia shrugged. "And I actually see Uncle James and Uncle Dean more than you, since I train with them seven days out of ten and I only see you five days out of ten with Mom and Dad's work schedule."

"James and Dean aren't your uncles either," Bobby playfully pouted, winking at Brie when he caught her giggling at his antics. *Yes, letting her see me as the fun-loving uncle might just give me an in to being more friendly with her.* "I'll concede that James might be your uncle one day when he marries your aunt, but that title's not legal yet."

"It doesn't have to be legal," Tia argued, shrugging. "It's an honorary title given after the heart adoptions Memmaw taught me about."

"Yeah, well, I don't think favorite uncle status can be given to people with only honorary uncle titles," Bobby grumbled playfully, finally starting the car to pull out now that the other cars around him had already started pulling away. "What do you think, Brie? Since I'm the only legal uncle she's mentioned all morning, I should be her favorite uncle all the time, right?"

"Don't ask me." Brie held her hands up like she was pushing the issue away from her. "I don't have any uncles, so I don't know the rules for earning favorite uncle status."

They all chuckled at her response, lightening the mood, and making Bobby feel like he'd broken down a little of Brie's walls between them, giving him a little better chance of getting closer to her. Once their laughter died down, Brie changed the subject back to writing, leaving Bobby to silently listen as he drove them to church.

"Tia, would you be interested in helping me with the next book?" Brie turned in her seat to look at Tia in the backseat. "Maybe read over what I have of my first draft to help me make it more appealing to teenage readers?"

"Yeah, I can do that," Tia replied, sounding excited at the thought of assisting with writing a book. "But you might get better feedback from my mom than from me. She actually studied writing in college before she had me and had to drop out. But she's going back to writing now, working on a book of her own when she has some free time."

Damn, I guess Kay is actually using the birthday present Anthony got her after all. I wonder if Brie writes her books like that? Maybe I can get her a couple of those blank books to write in for Christmas to start showing my interest in her?

"The more the merrier." Brie flashed a beaming smile back at Tia. "I'd love to have both of you look over my stories and give me feedback."

"Cool," Tia grinned, just as Bobby pulled into the church parking lot. "I'm free after three all week to read what you have for the next book already, and Mom will be home next weekend for you to ask her, too."

The girls made plans to meet up at Tia's house on Monday afternoon when Brie would be there to clean, so Tia could read what Brie already had written for the next book, while Bobby got out of the car and walked around to open their doors. He got a few strange looks from friends as he escorted Brie and Tia into the church, but he didn't care. Bobby just puffed out his chest as he guided Brie to their seats with a hand on the small of her back to make sure all the other men in town knew she was spoken for, even though he technically didn't have a claim on her yet.

A few more days like today when she can see me for the gentleman I really am instead of as the jackass I was last Monday, and I'll be set to stake that claim just as soon as I can get Brooklyn outta my head.

137

~~~

Brooklyn couldn't believe how much fun she was having hanging out with the whole Burleson family after church on Sunday. They'd stayed at the church for the potluck dinner after the services, where Hazel made sure she was properly introduced to the family members she hadn't met yet. Even though Hazel was obviously trying to push her and Bobby together by seating them side by side, Brooklyn had focused on speaking mostly to Tia, loving learning how the young girl's mind worked.

When the festivities at church finally broke up late in the afternoon, they all went back to the ranch and piled into the family room at Hazel and Bob's house for family time. Brooklyn followed Hazel and Susan to the kitchen when they went to fix Sunday supper, feeling more comfortable helping them cook than infringing on the family time of the rest of the family. But she wasn't allowed to hide out in the kitchen the whole night. As soon as the food was prepared, everyone gathered in the dining room to eat dinner together, including Brooklyn as if she was one of the family.

When she thought she could help with the dishes and dinner clean-up, Tia grabbed Brooklyn's hand and dragged her into the family room, insisting she was needed to make three equal teams of three for Pictionary. Having never played the game before, Brooklyn protested, saying, "I don't know how to play, so I'm not sure you really want me on your team."

"Nonsense, it's an easy game." Tia practically pushed her down onto a couch beside Bobby. "We take turns drawing whatever's written on the cards and the rest of our team just has to guess what we're drawing. Easy-peasy."

"Oh, um, okay." Brooklyn suddenly felt tongue-tied from sitting so close to Bobby.

"It's really not that bad," Charlotte assured her, sitting down on the other sofa across the room with her cousins, JJ and Julie. "We're making the twins split up to separate teams, so it'll be a fair game even though you're teaming up with the least artistic of my brothers."

"Hey, I resemble that remark," Bobby quipped, pointing at Charlotte while playfully pouting.
~~~

How am I supposed to stop crushing on him when he's so cute in the way he interacts with his family? Brooklyn silently questioned her ability to back away from the handsome man seated beside her.

"We can use my phone to pick our words, instead of having to go upstairs and rummage through the old games to find the Pictionary deck," Jen directed them from her spot on a bean bag chair between her brother Justin and cousin Becky, who were seated in the recliners positioned at one end of the two sofas, creating a U formation of bodies around a central coffee table. "What categories do we wanna pick?"

"All of them," Becky declared, pointing to the list on the app Jen was setting up to play the game.

"I'll put all of them but celebrities," Jen acquiesced. "This thing comes up with ones I don't even know, so I'm sure it will spit out a celebrity that Tia doesn't know and mess up the game."

"Agreed." JJ nodded his head at his sister. "Becky only wants celebrities because she's the only one who knows who they are."

"What difficulty level?" Jen inquired.

"Medium," all the Burlesons said in unison, making Brooklyn giggle at the obvious love between them all.

"All right, we're all set up." Jen stood up to walk over to where Brooklyn was seated between Bobby and Tia and handed her the phone. "Since you've never played before, Brie, you get to start us off. Just push this button to get your word or words once you're over at the whiteboard. You can't write words or say anything, just draw whatever pops up. And don't let anyone see the screen to guess."

"Okay," Brooklyn smiled as she took the phone and saw the button to push for a new word. She walked up to where a dry-erase board was set up on an easel in the opening of the U they were seated in. She pushed the button where the words "Police Officer" popped up under the category of "Persons." She placed the phone on the ledge at the bottom of the board with the screen facing the board, so none of the other players could see what she was supposed to draw.

"You are supposed to tell us the category and how many words are in the phrase," Tia informed her, smiling at her from her place on the couch next to her uncle. "Otherwise, Uncle Bobby and I won't have a clue where to start guessing."

"Oh, the category is persons and it's a two-word phrase." Brooklyn picked up the dry-erase marker to start drawing.

"I'll start the timer when you start drawing." Charlotte held up her phone with a stopwatch app showing. "They have two minutes to figure it out before we can steal the points by guessing."

Brooklyn uncapped the marker and started drawing her best version of a stick figure as Charlotte started the timer. Once the stick figure was done, she started drawing the gun belt she'd seen Bobby wear into the house on Monday night. It looked kind of weird on a stick figure, but it was the best Brooklyn could do.

"Construction worker," Tia guessed.

Brooklyn shook her head and realized her gun, handcuffs, and baton looked a lot like tools in a tool belt. She moved away from the gun she hadn't figured out how to draw clearly in the holster and moved up to the chest where she drew a star to represent the police badge.

"Sheriff's deputy," Tia shouted, making Brooklyn hate having to shake her head, since she was definitely on the right track.

"Police officer," Bobby smirked. Brooklyn nodded and said, "yes."

"Of course, Bobby would get that one," Becky playfully chided her brother.

"Hell, I'd have to fire myself from my job if I missed that one," Bobby laughed with his siblings and cousins.

"Swear jar, Uncle Bobby." Tia pointed at Bobby as Brooklyn took her seat for the next person to go up to the board to play the game. She sat on the opposite side of Tia from her uncle, hoping she could keep her attraction to him in check by putting the preteen between them.

"What swear jar?" Bobby looked around the room as if he was trying to find the swear jar Tia mentioned. "I don't see a swear jar anywhere."

"You know it's at my house." Tia poked her uncle in the side. "You also know I'm keeping track of how much you owe the jar when we're done here."

Bobby reached into his back pocket and got out his wallet, pulling a twenty-dollar bill from the inside and handing it to Tia. "Here, Squirt, consider me paid in advance for my next seventy-nine slipups."

Before Brooklyn could figure out how much each swear word cost to the swear jar, Julie stepped up to the board and picked up her sister's phone to get the next word for the game. She erased Brooklyn's police officer drawing while Charlotte reset the timer.

"The category is animals and it's only one word," Julie stated, looking at JJ and Charlotte, who were on her team, before starting to draw what looked like a fluffy ball to Brooklyn.

"Dog," JJ guessed, causing Julie to shake her head and continue trying to draw.

"Cat," Charlotte postulated, to which Julie shook her head again.

"Kitten, mouse, rat," JJ rattled off, not giving Julie a chance to really stop shaking her head before saying the next guess.

"Ferret, guinea pig," Charlotte added.

"Guinea pig is two words, Aunt Charlotte," Tia corrected.

"Racoon, rabbit, coyote," JJ started in with more wild animals.

Julie started drawing squiggly lines up from the fur ball she'd drawn just as the timer went off.

"Skunk," Jen shouted as soon as it was allowed for the other teams to steal the point, getting a nod of her sister's head to confirm their team's stolen point.

Becky was up next with a one-word phrase in the persons category. Her ability to draw people was lightyears better than what Brooklyn had drawn as the two people she drew were obviously a couple in a tuxedo and wedding dress.

"Couple," Justin exclaimed.

"Newlyweds," Jen shouted.

When neither of those were the correct answer, Becky drew arrows to just the male figure.

"Groom," Justin guessed as Jen shouted over him with "bridegroom."

When the buzzer went off, Tia hollered, "husband," to steal their point.

Tia took the next turn to draw, furrowing her brow when she looked down at her word. "Um, can I give my team the specific category for this word instead of the broad category the app is listing?" Tia looked around the room at the group as a whole.

"What's the category that's used in the app?" Charlotte obviously slipped into teacher mode with her niece.

"Animals, but most people only think of mammals when they think about animals," Tia sighed, looking deep in thought. "And while this is technically part of the animal kingdom, the phylum, class, order, family, subfamily, and genus are all pretty far away from mammals."

"Do you know the phylum, class, order, family, subfamily, and genus for the word you're supposed to draw?" Charlotte smiled at her niece.

"Yes, am I allowed to list those out for my team?" Tia answered her aunt's question with a question of her own.

"Um, I don't think that info will be much help, at least for me," Bobby shrugged.

"Then by all means, please list the specific classification for the word, so maybe we can steal Bobby's points," JJ smirked at his cousin.

"The phylum is arthropoda," Tia started listing matter-of-factly. "The class is insecta. The order is hymenoptera. The family is vespidae. The subfamily is vespinae. And the genus is vespa."

So, it's a bug? Brooklyn gathered from the class of insecta which sounded like an insect to her ears. *Tia's mind is amazing to know all that, but wouldn't it have been easier to just say that there should be a separate category for insects?*

Tia started drawing as Brooklyn started guessing every kind of bug she could think of. Once Tia added wings, she started listing off only the flying insects she could think of. Bobby apparently caught on to the insect theme and started doing the same, eventually saying "hornet" to get the point just before the buzzer went off.

"You only got that because your teammate is smart enough to understand all that phylum and class stuff to get you started guessing insects," Becky huffed, tossing a pillow at Bobby.

"Hey, not my fault you put me on the team with the two smartest people in the room." Bobby tossed the pillow back at his sister. "I'm more than happy to increase my own intelligence, and our score, by following their lead."

The game went on for a couple of hours with words as abstract and hard to draw as "shave" and "study" mixed in with more people, like "surgeon" and "paleontologist." There were some easy animals, specifically "elephant," but Brooklyn's favorite word of the game was when Bobby got flustered trying to draw the action "suck," and turned beet red when his sisters and cousins told him the straw he was drawing looked way too phallic for a game with Tia playing.

He drew a glass of liquid around it to make it more obvious, but with his cousins picking on him about his ice cubes making it look like a dick and balls in a glass, they were all laughing too hard to actually guess the action.

After both the original two-minute timer for his team to guess and the second one-minute timer for the other teams to steal the point went off, Bobby threw up his hands in exasperation. "I should've started drawing each of your pictures," he grumbled, pointing specifically to JJ and Justin. "Because ya'll suck. That's the word, suck."

"So, the phallic references were a good way to go," Tia shocked them all. When she noticed all their jaws dropping as they stared at the youngest person in the room, Tia just shrugged. "What? Ya'll think I don't know about that stuff? I'm almost thirteen and I've already audited college level biology and anatomy. Mom wouldn't let me audit the human sexuality class, but I did have sex ed in sixth grade, in addition to what she'd already told me about the birds and the bees. Plus, I've just spent the last two months traveling the country with a group of professional wrestlers, who don't always realize there are kids present when they're having adult conversations. Not to mention having to have the TV on all night to drown out Mom and Dad."

Brooklyn couldn't stifle her giggles at the reactions of the Burlesons to Tia's revelations. Some were still showing signs of shock while others were chuckling like Brooklyn.

"I don't wanna hear about what my baby brother does at night," Bobby groaned, pointing at Tia. "And since you shouldn't have to hear it either, I'm buying you and Maria some earplugs for Christmas."

"Earplugs? You're going to lose that favorite uncle status with earplugs for our Christmas presents," Tia chortled, picking on her uncle who was sitting back down beside her.

"Noise cancelling, Bluetooth headphones, so you can go to sleep while watching Disney movies on your tablet?" Bobby suggested.

"Much better, Uncle Bobby," Tia replied, nodding her head, and hugging her uncle.

Leah Mae Wright

As the game continued, Brooklyn not only enjoyed getting to know more of the Burlesons, but she also felt her attraction to Bobby growing based on how he treated his niece, sisters, and cousins. It had been easy to avoid him all week when she pictured him as the grumpy, growly guy who didn't want her living in his home, like he'd been on her first night of work. Seeing the softer, funny, happy-go-lucky side of him, who obviously loved his family, was making her resolve to avoid him seem like an impossible task.

She could easily see herself falling in love with him if she spent very much time around the man he was showing her today. And even if he reciprocated her feelings, falling for Bobby Burleson could only end in disaster for Brooklyn Barns. They couldn't have a happily ever after, when she couldn't even tell him her real name.

~~~

Monday, December 10, 2018

Brooklyn reflected back on the enjoyable day she'd had the day before, when she hung out with the Burleson family all day, as she was preparing lasagna for that night's meals. She'd been extremely nervous about going with Bobby to church and bungled her feeble attempt at small talk on the ride over to his parents' house for breakfast. He hadn't seemed as awkward as she felt. He went into detail to answer her questions, even though she mentally stumbled and couldn't think of a follow-up question to continue the conversation. She'd half expected him to chastise her for her silence and inept social skills, like her father would have, but he hadn't. Instead, Bobby acted like the perfect gentleman, treating her with the same respect he showed for his family and friends.

Every time he'd opened a door for her, or placed his hand on the small of her back to guide her to where she was supposed to be going at his parents' house and the church, she'd almost felt like they were on a date, acting as a couple instead of boss and employee. She felt like she'd seen a different side of Bobby than the serious police officer and angry bachelor she'd previously met. The way he playfully interacted with his niece had made him infinitely more attractive,
~~~

which wasn't necessarily a good thing for Brooklyn's ability to keep her distance between them.

I have to go back to staying in my room to avoid him when he's home, Brooklyn thought as she finished covering the fourth baking dish of lasagna with mozzarella and started putting them in the oven to cook. *If I have any one-on-one game nights with him like we had with his sisters, niece, and cousins yesterday, I'm liable to give in to my crazy, intense urge to kiss him. And I definitely can't do that when I have to hide my real identity from him. If only he weren't a police officer, who has to report my whereabouts to the Macon authorities, who are looking for me, if he figures out who I really am.*

Brooklyn let out a huge sigh as she started cleaning up the dishes she'd already dirtied that morning, wishing she was attracted to one of the other Burleson men she'd met the day before, instead of the one with a legal obligation to turn her in to her father's cronies.

As wonderful as the whole family was when I met them yesterday, I could probably tell any of them who I really am, and they'd help me stay hidden, if it weren't for the fact that Bobby works in law enforcement. I could probably confide in Kenzie, Ashley, or Heather, too, but I don't want to get any of my new friends in trouble for keeping my secrets. I just hope they'll all understand my reasons for not telling them who I am if it ever does come out.

While she was sifting and measuring flour to start mixing up the dough for the garlic knots she would let rise all day and bake just before dinner time for all the guys, Brooklyn realized that she was still just as alone in the world as she'd been back in Georgia. Even though she'd met so many new friends, and felt more at home in this new community than she'd ever felt in her old life, she wouldn't truly feel the connection she longed for with the people around her as long as she couldn't tell them her real identity.

She'd felt guilty every time she talked about her life back in Georgia, and had to lie about being from Atlanta instead of Macon, or claiming Mary and Joe as her foster parents when they were actually her father's employees. While she was slightly relieved that there wasn't a confessional in the Heart's Destiny Community Church, so she didn't feel compelled to confess her lies to the priest, she'd definitely spent some time the night before praying for forgiveness from above before she went to bed.

Brooklyn was only making herself depressed by dwelling on the lies she had to tell to escape from the hell of being forced to marry a man she could never fall in love with, so she thought about Tia's suggestions for her books while she finished what she could of the meal prep for the day. Once she had the garlic knots all rising, the pans of lasagna cooked and divided into the plastic containers to go to the various houses for dinner that night, and all the dishes done, she put her laptop and idea notebook in her backpack to take with her to Anthony and Kay's house. She threw in a sandwich, a couple pieces of fruit, and several bottles of water to have for lunch and to stay hydrated while she cleaned.

She grabbed the keys for the mule as she practically skipped out of the house, excited to get Tia's input on her current book to help her grow as an author.

Even if I can't tell any of them my real name, I can still share the real me, who I am inside, with all the new friends I'm making here. Well, everyone but Bobby. If I share too much of who I am inside with him, he'll see through my alias and figure out my real name. So, no matter how much I'm crushing on him, and really, really want to kiss him, I have to keep my distance.

I hope Tia will be able to come back to his house with me at four, so I can bake the garlic knots while we're going over the book stuff. If I take her and the food back to the houses on the north side of the ranch at five, I should have just enough time to fix a plate for myself to take to my room in case Bobby gets home at six like he did a few times last week.

~~~

After the way Brie had come out of her shell while hanging out with his family all day Sunday, Bobby was looking forward to having dinner with her now that the ice was broken between them. He'd been in a great mood all day and was even whistling as he walked in the back door of his house. He was instantly hit with the smell of fresh garlic bread as he stepped into the kitchen, but was disappointed to not see it or Brie when he looked around the room.
~~~

He checked the key hooks to see that they were all there, so Brie wasn't still up at one of the other houses on the ranch. He went upstairs to lock up his badge and gun before stripping off his uniform to wash off the day, noticing as he walked by that her bedroom door was shut again, like it'd been most of the week before when he got home from work.

Yeah, I'm not gonna let her keep hiding from me after how great we got along yesterday, Bobby thought as he went through the motions of his nightly routine. *Like it or not, she'll be coming back downstairs to eat dinner with me tonight, and every night from now on. Spending time with her yesterday helped me keep my dreams focused on her, and only her, last night, so I need to spend more time with her every day to keep that up. I'll probably still feel a little bit of guilt for not doing anything to help Brooklyn, but I'm choosing Brie as the woman I wanna pursue a relationship with. So, she's just gonna hafta quit hiding from me, so I can actually pursue her.*

Once he was through in the shower, he threw on a t-shirt and workout shorts, not bothering to comb his hair or brush his teeth before going to knock on her door.

Damn, should I have brushed my hair and teeth before talking to her? Naw, no point in brushing my teeth right before eating garlicky food. I'll just have to brush them again right after dinner. And maybe the messy hair will make it seem like I'm keeping things casual and friendly, and not trying to impress her by primping like it's a date.

Yeah, that's it. Play it cool. Just be a friend for now. Pushing too fast for the romantic stuff will just scare her off.

"Hey, Brie," Bobby called out as he wrapped his knuckles on her bedroom door. He wanted to walk in like he'd done the morning before, but he didn't want to push his luck and piss her off by invading her space.

"Just, a, just a minute," Brie stuttered.

He heard some indistinct noises as she moved around the room and wondered what she was doing. *Fuck, is she naked and having to get dressed before she opens the door?*

Bobby ran a hand through his already messy hair, trying to keep from tenting his shorts at the thought of Brie in the buff with only a thin door separating that vision from his sight. *You already got your hand job for the night, Thor. Go back down, so you don't scare the girl off. 'Cause you're definitely not gettin' any of her anytime soon.*

"How can I help you?" Brie opened the door just wide enough to reveal her face, hiding the rest of her body behind the door.

"I, um, have some stuff I wanna talk to you about." Bobby tried desperately to keep his eyes locked on hers, instead of letting them wander downward to try and get a glimpse of her body to see what she was wearing. "I figured we could talk while we eat dinner."

"Oh, I, um," Brie stuttered.

Damn, she's cute when she's nervous.

"I'm already almost done eating." Brie blushed so prettily that Bobby had to fight to keep from reaching out and running a hand over her pink cheek. "I brought my dinner up here, so I could work on my next book while I'm eating."

"Yeah, that's one of the things I wanna talk to you about." Bobby decided at that moment that he'd use his mother's rule about no food in the bedrooms to get Brie to eat with him every night. "We have some ranch rules that Ma obviously didn't tell you about this last week. One of which is that food stays in the kitchen, or dining room, or outside when we have a cookout."

"Oh." Brie's mouth formed a cute little O shape as she softly whispered the word. "I'll bring my plate right down then."

She closed the door in his face, and he heard some more rustling around in her room, so he figured she had to be changing clothes before joining him downstairs.

It's probably bad form to tell her that she doesn't have to wear clothes to the dining table, huh? Bobby chuckled to himself at the mental image of how Brie would react if he actually said that to her as he walked down the stairs to the kitchen to put together his own plate.

By the time he had his first plate of lasagna and garlic knots dished up and heated up in the microwave, Brie was seated in the dining room with her plate that was mostly salad and a bottle of water. Grabbing his own bottle of water from the fridge, Bobby went and sat across from her, so they could talk without him invading her space too much by sitting next to her. *And so Thor is less likely to make an appearance and frighten her back up to her room.*

Once he was seated and starting to eat, Brie finally looked him in the eyes. "What other rules do you need to tell me about, so I quit breaking them?"

"Well, I think you figured out last night that Sunday supper at my folks house is mandatory," Bobby stated when he finished chewing his first bite. "As is breakfast on the weekend. I honestly think the only reason I get out of breakfast with everyone during the week is because Ma knows I'm picking up donuts for the whole station on my way to work."

"Oh, yeah, I guess Hazel did invite me to breakfast that first day, but I didn't understand it was a requirement to attend," Brie acknowledged before taking another bite of her own.

"The other things aren't really rules," Bobby explained between bites of the most delicious lasagna he'd ever tasted. "More like things I need done that I don't think you were told about."

Brie just sat there nodding her head as she ate, not saying anything in response to his statement, so Bobby continued. "I actually prefer sweet tea with dinner, so I need you to keep a gallon made up in the fridge for me. And I have a section in my closet where I put clothes that need to go to the dry cleaners, instead of putting them in the hamper with the stuff that can be washed here. I have five suits hanging there now since Ma hasn't had the time to take them recently. I'm guessing she didn't mention them when she gave you the laundry instructions for each of us."

"No, she didn't mention anything about dry-cleaning," Brie admitted, blushing. The way her cheeks turned bright pink made Bobby wonder what she was thinking about that was so embarrassing for her. Before he could ask, she continued speaking. "She didn't really give me any instructions for doing your laundry, just told me to do it for you, JJ, and Justin, but not at Anthony and Kay's house. I honestly worried I'd put your things away in the wrong places last week."

Fuck, is that blush from thinking she'd put my clothes away incorrectly, or from remembering putting away my underwear? And why the fuck am I getting a boner from thinking about her touching my underwear when she does the laundry?

"Yeah, I, uh, didn't notice anything out of place, other than all my suits piling up on the bar to the right of the closet door because they haven't been dry-cleaned." Bobby shook his head, trying to clear his thoughts. He was also trying to keep his erection under control, so he could get up from the table for seconds without Brie seeing how he was responding to sitting and talking to her. "I wasn't sure if Ma had told you it's okay for you to use one of my vehicles to go to town for stuff like dry-cleaning and grocery shopping. Or if she'd given you a card on my account to be able to pay for any of that stuff."

"She did tell me it was okay to use your cars, but I don't really feel comfortable driving someone else's vehicle," Brie confided after finishing her last bite of food. "She also mentioned getting me a card for household expenses on my first day, but since it wasn't ready last week, I just rode to the store with her, and she paid for enough groceries to last at least a couple of weeks."

"Okay, well, I don't know what account she was gonna get you a card on, but we'll go to the bank in the morning, and have you added to my checking account, so you can pay for my dry-cleaning and anything else you need to do for me," Bobby informed her, feeling oddly at ease about adding Brie to his bank accounts. "Since I have to be there to authorize it and you have to be there to sign the signature card to get your own debit card, I'll go into work late, so I can take you first thing. We'll stop and drop off my suits too, so I can show you where the dry cleaners is, but I'll need you to pick up my suits when they're ready later in the week. Otherwise, I won't have a clean suit for church on Sunday."

"Um, we might have a problem with me being able to drive to town." Brie shyly looked down at her plate before looking back up at him sheepishly.

"Seriously, don't worry about driving one of my vehicles," Bobby assured her, reaching across the table to pat her hand, hoping she would take it as reassuring the way he intended and not as an inappropriate form of touching her. "I really don't mind you using them."

"It's not just that I prefer driving my own car," Brie confessed, tentatively smiling up at him, but not pulling her hand away from his. "Though the size of your truck compared to my car is why I don't really want to drive it, I noticed yesterday that your car is a manual, and I don't know how to drive a manual."

"And my truck is a manual too," Bobby chuckled at the realization that she wouldn't be able to drive either of his vehicles until he taught her how. "Okay, I'll pick up my suits later this week, and I'll teach you how to drive a manual on Saturday, so you aren't stuck on the ranch until your car is fixed."

"You really don't have to do that," Brie protested. "I'm sure your mom will let me drive her vehicle, if she's not free to give me a ride to town. While her Jeep is bigger than I'm used to driving, it's not huge like your truck, and I'm sure it won't be too hard for me to drive, since I know it's an automatic."

Yeah, I know Ma won't mind Brie using her Jeep, Bobby thought, trying to figure out how to convince Brie to let him teach her to drive his car instead. *Hell, she could probably take Kay's Jeep if Ma's busy with hers, since Kay's gone for work most of the time. Why do we have to have so damn many automatic vehicles available to her on the ranch?*

"Yeah, I'm sure Ma won't mind you using her Jeep." Bobby hoped she wouldn't point out the faulty logic behind his next statement. "But with the way she's changing her schedule, you never know when she'll be off shopping, or having lunch with a friend, and neither she, nor her Jeep, will be available. So, I'd still feel better teaching you to drive a manual, so you can take my car whenever you wanna go to town without worrying about anyone else's schedule."

"Okay," Brie conceded, drawing out the word like she wasn't quite convinced. "But I can't do it this Saturday. I already have plans for the day."

"Really? What kind of plans?" Bobby tried to keep from looking as upset as he felt while thinking of her having plans with another man. *Fuck! She better not have a date for Saturday. I'll strangle Luke if he's used fixing her car to score a date with her.*

"Kenzie is going to come get me to hang out with her, Ashley, and Heather again," Brie smiled as she mentioned the friends she'd made in town. "Like we did this past Saturday."

"Ah, I wondered where you were when you weren't here when I got home from working with the new horses Saturday." Bobby felt the tension release in his shoulders, feeling relieved that she was hanging out with female friends and not dating. "What all did you do

Saturday? And are you planning to do the same things this week? Or something different?"

"We just got to know each other while hanging out at the Caffeinated Cowpoke most of the day." Brie appeared more relaxed as she talked about meeting her new friends. "Then when the coffee shop started to close, they tried to teach me to bowl the rest of the night. I totally suck at bowling, so I could really use the practice if that's what they want to do again this week, but I'm not really sure what they have planned. They said something about showing me some of the other things to do around town, but I don't know what. And I have to find a place in town to add minutes to my phone before I can check in with them to find out what the plan is for Saturday."

Other things to do around town? Bobby mentally questioned, knowing that the only places open late on Saturday nights were Lover's Lanes and Tully's Roadhouse. *Fuck! They'd better not take her to Tully's on the weekend, when I'm on call and can't go have a beer to keep an eye on her. The guys will give me hell if I go up there in uniform to hang out drinking bottled water all night in case I get a call.*

"There's not that much to do in town," Bobby smiled at her, wanting to continue their conversation as long as he could without her realizing he was still holding her hand. "The rodeo was last weekend, so it'll be a couple more weeks before another one comes through."

"Yeah, the girls mentioned it last week," Brie smiled back at him. "That's why they wanted to go bowling, instead of to the bar. They said it would be full of cocky cowboys and buckle bunnies trying to hook up while they were in town for the rodeo, and they'd rather go when it was only locals who wouldn't be put out by them trying to teach me to line dance. While I don't think I can use any of the things I'll see for the first time as research for my young adult books when we go to the bar, it's still exciting to have all these new experiences in life."

Goin' to a bar and learning to line dance are new experiences for her? Fuck! Maybe there really is too big of an age difference between us. And what was that about adding minutes to her phone?

"Yeah, um, what exactly did you mean about needing to add minutes to your phone?" Bobby realized he needed to get her phone number, so he could check in with her during the day when he was at work.

"I, um, didn't really use a phone much before," Brie shrugged. "So, I just bought a cheap prepaid one to have on hand in case of an emergency. But with giving the girls my number, I've used up all my minutes, and need to find a store that sells the prepaid minute cards to add more to it."

She has a fucking burner phone? Nope, not happening on my watch.

"I don't know of any place in town to get a prepaid phone card," Bobby lied, shaking his head. "But since I need to get your number to be able to call you if I need something done here at the house while I'm at work, we'll stop and get you a new phone on my plan tomorrow morning, too."

"You don't have to do that," Brie protested. "I'm sure I can look it up online and order a prepaid card for the one I have."

"No, Brie," Bobby barked, his voice taking on a commanding tone like he sometimes had to use while working. "My house, my rules. As long as you're living here and taking care of my home, I'll provide you with everything you need to do it, including a cell phone that won't be out of minutes or lose reception when you're going back and forth between the houses you're cleaning on the ranch."

"Oh, okay," Brie mumbled, demurely dipping her head in agreement.

Fuck, I hate seeing her cower like that, Bobby thought, trying to come up with a way to change the subject to bring her lighter, happier personality forward again.

"So, did you get to meet up with Tia today to work on your next book?" Bobby hoped talking about her book would bring her back into the conversation.

"Yes," Brie nodded, lifting her gaze to his, excitement lighting her eyes. "Did you know that in addition to being brilliant, she's also a speed-reader?"

"No, but I'm not surprised," Bobby chuckled.

"She read through my whole first draft and had notes on every chapter within an hour," Brie beamed, smiling, and shaking her head.

They talked for a while longer, mostly about the ideas she had for her next book after her afternoon with Tia giving her suggestions for how to make it more appealing for older teenagers and more advanced readers. Then about the ideas she had for her next book series and how she came up with them from looking at the architecture around town since she arrived in Heart's Destiny.

Bobby hated having to break their connection by releasing her hand to go to the kitchen for seconds of lasagna, but it wasn't too bad since Brie stayed downstairs talking to him the rest of the evening. When they were both finished eating, he followed her to the kitchen to continue their conversation while she washed their dishes, and he dried them. The evening was way more domestic than Bobby had ever experienced with another woman, but he liked the way it felt to spend time with her.

Even though we're only starting to become friends for now, this has been the best night of my life. But Dad always says that friendship is the best foundation for forever, so maybe we'll build to more between us in the coming months.

Chapter Six

Brooklyn had failed miserably at avoiding Bobby in the last couple of weeks. Ever since seeing his softer side on Sunday the ninth, when she spent the day with him and his whole family, he'd found a way over the walls she tried to put between them. They sat down to dinner together almost every night since, talking about everything and nothing at the same time. They talked about their favorite things and shared childhood stories. Well, what Brooklyn could share while pretending to be Brie anyway. Though she didn't think she'd given away her true identity with anything she'd shared, she thought he might be suspicious after figuring out that she colored her hair every Wednesday.

Lord, I hope he really believes that the light brown shade it fades to by the Tuesday after I've colored it is my natural hair color, Brooklyn prayed as she laid in bed, remembering him commenting that her natural hair color was so pretty that she didn't need to cover it up every week.

After the first five nights of alone time with Bobby, when they got to know each other over dinner, Brooklyn had really needed to find some excuses to put some distance between them. He was so sweet and charming all the time that she was having a hard time not acting on her attraction to him. She wanted to kiss him so badly that she was not only dreaming about him at night, but she was also daydreaming about him while she worked every day, especially the days she cleaned his bedroom.

She'd had to stop herself from spending an hour just sniffing his sheets when she'd changed them the week before. They smelled like him—a mix of his ocean-fresh bodywash and his natural musk—and the scent was obviously filled with pheromones that entranced her. When they'd ended their evenings watching movies on the large sectional sofa in his family room, she'd found herself unconsciously sitting closer and closer to him each night just to get a whiff of his intoxicating aroma.

Her formerly once-a-month self-release sessions in the shower had quickly morphed into a twice-a-day habit because of how being around him increased her libido. She fantasized about Bobby teaching her all the carnal ways they could pleasure each other as she touched herself every morning in the shower and every night as she laid in bed.

Since she'd opened up more to her new girlfriends the previous weekend, what was previously only schoolgirl-style innocent kissing fantasies had transformed into much more graphic sexual visions. Now that her eyes had been opened to some other possibilities, Brooklyn wasn't sure how much longer she could resist the urge to kiss the cowboy cop, who'd somehow stolen a part of her heart.

Though I doubt he'd be very receptive to my inexperienced advances, Brooklyn wallowed in self-doubt, remembering what her girlfriends had told her about Bobby's sexual escapades. *I'm sure he wants a woman who already knows how to please him, not a little girl in a woman's body that she has no idea how to use. I doubt even all the advice and pointers the girls have given me so far would be enough to entice him with the way I'd probably fumble through trying to seduce him.*

When she was hanging out with Kenzie, Ashley, and Heather on Saturday the fifteenth, they'd gone to get their hair, nails, and makeup done before going out dancing that night. Brooklyn had yet another new experience with how girlfriends gossiped at each of the three places they went for their mini makeovers.

She'd only gotten a trim at the Cut & Curl, but the girls had gotten her to talk about what life was like on the ranch. After telling them about the previous Sunday, when she'd played Pictionary with three of the six Burleson boys, and how she'd had dinner with Bobby every night since, they were all convinced that she was definitely starting to fall for him.

While they were sitting in the massage chairs and getting pedicures at Nailed It, they started asking her when she thought she'd start sleeping with him. Brooklyn had tried to claim that she would never sleep with him, but the girls didn't believe her. When she tentatively admitted to still being a virgin and too shy to ever let him know she was interested in him being her first, the girls had given her a whole new experience in sex education.

I still can't believe how graphic they were describing things in a public place, Brooklyn thought, shaking her head at how she'd turned beet red when the nail techs had joined in on the conversation, and they all started comparing techniques for giving blow jobs and ranking their favorite sexual positions. It was all way more advanced than Brooklyn ever thought she'd be sexually.

After their manicures were done, when Brooklyn thought the sexual conversation was over, they started talking about taking her lingerie shopping in San Antonio and giving her ideas for how to seduce Bobby. When she told her new friends that she didn't think she could ever be made over into a seductress like they all seemed to be, they started talking about taking her shopping for sex toys, so she could at least have more satisfying orgasms, even if they were only when she was alone in bed. At least when Brooklyn turned beet red then, nobody could tell because of all the makeup they'd put on her in Beautiful Destiny.

Once they were all done with the beauty regimen for the day, they all went back to Kenzie's apartment to change into jeans and cowboy boots, insisting Brooklyn's leggings and sneakers weren't appropriate for the country bar. Luckily, all four girls wore the same size shoes and jeans even though Kenzie and Heather were an inch taller than Brooklyn and Ashley. They tried to convince her to change into a tied-up western shirt, but when she took off her sweatshirt to reveal the tank top underneath it, Kenzie pulled out a loose weave, off-the-shoulder sweater that would allow the tank top to show through without appearing too slutty by showing off her flat stomach.

Based on the outward appearance of Tully's Roadhouse, Brooklyn had expected to walk into an Old West Saloon. But the country bar was more modern inside than she'd envisioned. The bar on the right side of the front room was wooden, but well-lit with hanging lights shining down on it about every three feet. The barstools were all padded with actual backs on them, instead of the plain wooden stools she'd imagined. The tables and chairs positioned around the room were of a similar style. They were mostly hugged up to the bar and walls on the back and left side of the space, leaving the center of the room open for the dance floor. There was a stage set up on the front wall with a band setting up for the night. There was also a jukebox on the left side of the room, probably for nights when they didn't have a live band playing.

As her friends led her over to the table on the left side of the room closest to the jukebox and stage, Brooklyn noticed an archway in the back wall that looked like it went to a back room with a few pool tables visible from where she ended up sitting. She wondered if she'd get to learn another new game, but the girls were set on dancing and drinking all night, and never ventured into the back room to teach her how to play pool.

Kenzie was acting as the designated driver for the night, so Ashley and Heather were pushing Brooklyn to drink the harder stuff with them. Not wanting to risk getting drunk and revealing her secrets, Brooklyn ordered one glass of wine and switched to bottled water after that, much to her new friends' disappointment.

She was really glad she'd stayed sober when she spun on the dance floor where the girls were teaching her a line dance and saw Bobby in his uniform watching her from the bar. The girls teased her mercilessly about her hot cop chaperone keeping the other guys from asking any of them to dance, but Brooklyn wasn't convinced that was the case. Bobby didn't approach her at all as she danced to the live band, but when they were through playing, he did insist on giving her a ride home, so Kenzie only had to get Ashley and Heather home at the end of the night.

Brooklyn still couldn't believe Bobby had shown up that night. She didn't have any idea why either, even a week later. Once they got home, she quickly changed and went down to launder the clothes she'd borrowed, so she could return them at church the next day. But she didn't stay downstairs to have a conversation with her hunky housemate, just in case her one glass of wine loosened her tongue a little too much.

That Sunday had been similar to the previous one, only instead of playing games as a family, the Burlesons coaxed her onto the back of a horse for her very first trail ride. Brooklyn was disappointed that Tia had flown out with her parents and sister to see her aunt start her wrestling career at a pay-per-view show that weekend and wasn't there, but she still had an enjoyable time getting to know the other women on the ranch a little better as they chatted on the trail. *Thank goodness the girls took pity on me, and insisted on it being a family trail ride and not just Bobby teaching me to ride, like Hazel suggested.*

They'd set it up with Bobby leading the ride, his sisters lining up behind him, then Brooklyn, followed by all their cousins. She wasn't sure if there was a reason the men were either leading the ride or bringing up the rear, keeping all the women in the middle of the pack, as if they needed to be protected from whatever they might come upon as they rode or what might come up from behind them, but she certainly felt safe in her central position.

It had been an enlightening experience learning how to take care of the horses after the ride was over, making her want to spend more time with the animals to find that peace inside her that she hadn't known she could tap into by brushing a horse. She also wanted to learn more about riding and use it all as research for a future book.

Though she hadn't completely avoided being around Bobby on that Sunday, at least their interactions weren't nearly as intimate as the nights they ate dinner alone together. When Tia and her family arrived back on the ranch on Monday while Brooklyn was up working with Hazel, Susan, and Rosa, she did finally find a way to avoid one night of those intimate dinners with Bobby. She ended up spending the evening talking with Kay about books and writing.

While Tia had been insightful with ways to improve her books for young adult readers, Kay was more interested in hearing about her historical romance ideas. Apparently, the book Kay had started writing was more contemporary romance, but her taste in reading material encompassed all romantic genres, so she wanted to read any historical romance novels that "Brie" penned in the future. When Brooklyn explained that she didn't feel experienced enough to write more adult content, Kay had pulled out her tablet and started making a list of books for her to read to expand her knowledge, and prepare her for gaining that experience.

Brooklyn had added a couple of them to the Kindle app on her computer and started reading that night when she got home. They were a lot racier than the books Brooklyn normally read, but with the way her new friends were so open when talking about sex, she thought they might be exactly what she needed to be able to hold her own in any future conversations. *Even if I never put any of this new knowledge to practical use with Bobby.*

Unfortunately, in addition to helping her feel more confident in her ability to talk about sex, they were also filling her with fantasies like she'd never imagined before. And Brooklyn could only picture Bobby in the role of her pleasure partner when she let herself indulge in those fantasies while touching herself daily.

Having dinner with him every night the rest of the week certainly didn't lessen her attraction to him either. Lingering over dinner, sitting on the sofa watching movies, and talking with him for hours after they were over wasn't just making her feel closer to him than she thought it was safe for her to be. All that time with Bobby was also seriously cutting into her writing time.

I wonder if I can get out of these driving lessons today by telling him I need to spend my day writing? Maybe if I go ahead and get up to go to breakfast with him at his parents' house, then I'll be able to convince him that I need to come back here right after to have a quiet day of writing because I'm behind schedule for my deadline to publish the next book?

Or maybe I can enjoy spending the day with him and recap it tonight by writing a new chapter for Mary Kate as she falls in love. If only Kay was coming home today, instead of going to Oklahoma for the first half of their Christmas break. I bet she could help me figure out how to navigate these feelings I have whenever he's around, and translate them to add a light romantic angle to my book.

Maybe when she gets home on Thursday, I can ask her how to let Mary Kate fall in love without getting my heart broken in the process.

~~~

Bobby had really enjoyed the last couple of weeks getting to know Brie, even though he'd kept it strictly platonic. He liked how easily they'd transitioned to being friends with their nightly talks and knew they were building the foundation they needed to have a good relationship in the future. Physically, he was beyond ready to take the next step in their relationship, having to jack off in the shower a couple times a day to quell his primal desire for her. Mentally, however, he
~~~

knew he needed to hold off until he was able to banish all thoughts of Brooklyn from his head.

With all the time he'd been spending with Brie, he thought it would be easy to put her first in his mind and not think about Brooklyn anymore. Unfortunately, it wasn't as easy as he'd hoped. Brooklyn still crept into his dreams at night and flashed into his head at random times during the day. The dreams didn't bother him nearly as bad as the thoughts about her when he was wide awake because he knew it was impossible to actually control what a person dreams about when they're asleep. He just hated feeling like he wasn't strong enough to control his thoughts when he wasn't sleeping.

The worst was when he was actively focused on Brie and something about her would remind him of Brooklyn. That had been a real issue the previous Saturday when he'd gone to Tully's to make sure nobody caused any trouble while she was there with her new friends in town. He'd seen Brie out on the dance floor with her face covered in more makeup than she normally wore, and the stage lights cast a yellow glow over her brown hair making it look lighter. For a moment, Bobby thought it was Brooklyn on the dance floor instead of Brie.

He'd always thought they had similar facial features, but with their coloring being so different, he hadn't thought they looked that much alike before. Since they were both from Georgia, he wondered if they had an ancestor in common that would account for the similarities between them. Kind of like how he and his brothers and cousins all looked similar, even though their heights, body types, hair colors, and eye colors differed.

Regardless of why they resembled each other, it'd made him feel weird to imagine Brooklyn when he was looking at Brie. Like the worst kind of creep, who wanted them both and was combining them in his head, so he could have them both at the same time. It was totally messing with his mind in a way he wasn't sure he could handle.

Thank fuck she uses that dark wash stuff on her hair every week, Bobby thought as he observed Brie over the breakfast table. *If it stayed her normal light brown all the time, I'd probably see her as Brooklyn more often than just those few times last Saturday.*

Bobby shook off his wandering thoughts and tuned back into the conversation going on around him. The rest of the family had been discussing the Christmas pageant that was being performed the next day at church.

"I hate that Tia and Maria weren't able to participate," Hazel sighed as the meal was winding down. "Maybe next year we can get their travel schedule early enough to coordinate with everyone, so they can be in the play."

"Hopefully, next year they'll actually have a weekend off in December to be able to rehearse with us." Becky crossed her fingers like she was hoping to be able to work with their nieces in the play she was producing for the church starting this year.

"They were technically off last weekend and this weekend," Hazel informed them, shaking her head at her youngest daughter. "But Kay had already committed to being at her parents' cabin for Christmas between now and the twenty-sixth, so they wouldn't have been able to participate tomorrow, even if they had every other weekend off in December."

"With them being in Oklahoma on Christmas, when are we going to celebrate with them?" Charlotte looked to their mother to answer her question. "Most of the stuff under my Christmas tree is for the girls."

Charlotte set up a Christmas tree at her house? Bobby wondered. *I mean, I understand why Anthony set one up for the girls at his place, but I thought all the rest of us just put our presents under Mom and Dad's tree like always. Should I have put up a tree at home for Brie? Shit, should I have planned to give her presents to her at home when we're alone, instead of at Mom and Dad's on Christmas?*

"With Anthony not scheduling them to fly home until the twenty-seventh, and then ya'll planning the board meeting for the twenty-eighth, I figured we'd do a second Christmas with the girls on the twenty-ninth," Hazel explained.

"Do we want to wait and just do all our gifts then?" Becky looked around the table at the rest of the family. "I'd rather have everyone here for one celebration instead of splitting it to multiple days."

Bobby looked over at Brie to see that she seemed to be shying away from the discussion about their Christmas celebrations. *Fuck, I hope she knows she's invited to whatever we decide to do for Christmas as a family.*

When she stood and started clearing her dishes from the table while the family discussed the holiday plans, Bobby picked up his own empty plate and followed her into the kitchen.

"You know it's your day off, right?" Bobby teased her when he noticed Brie was starting to wash the dishes.

"Yes, but I can still get things started, so your mom doesn't have as much to do later." Brie continued with the task at hand, not looking in his direction.

"Well, at least let me help." Bobby rolled up his sleeves to rinse what she'd hand washed before putting it in the dishwasher for a sanitizer cycle.

"Thanks." Brie continued shyly looking down at what she was washing, instead of up at Bobby like he longed for her to do.

"You know we probably should've stayed in there to get a vote on what we wanna do for Christmas." He bobbed his head in the direction of the dining room. "Now we're gonna be stuck with whatever the rest of them decide for when we open presents."

Brie looked up at him then, but instead of the affection he hoped to see in her face, she looked panicked. "I haven't bought any Christmas presents," she whispered. "Instead of teaching me to drive your car, can you take me shopping today? And maybe give me some ideas about what to get everyone, since I don't know any of your family well enough to have even the slightest clue what to buy them?"

"Sure, I can do that," Bobby happily agreed, smiling down at her. "But we might wanna head out soon, so we can go into San Antonio and have enough time to hit every store in the mall before it closes."

They quickly finished up the dishes that were in the kitchen and walked back to the dining room to find out the family Christmas plans before leaving.

"So, what's the plan?" Bobby inquired as soon as he and Brie stepped back into the room. "One Christmas or two?"

"One and a half," Becky replied, obviously trying to annoy her older brother by not answering in a clear manner.

"How can you have half a Christmas?" Brie queried from beside him, looking confused.

"We're having a family dinner to be together on Christmas day," Hazel explained, smiling at Bobby and Brie where they were standing so close together. "But no presents until the twenty-ninth, when we'll have a second Christmas dinner when Anthony, Kay, and the girls are home to celebrate with us."

"Cool, we'll be there for both," Bobby nodded, referring to himself and Brie as if they were a couple without even realizing it. "But we've gotta go now."

"Go?" Hazel looked surprised that Bobby and Brie had plans for the afternoon.

"Where ya'll goin'?" Justin gave Bobby a skeptical look.

"Brie needs to head into San Antonio for some things, and I figured it's as good a time as any to teach her how to drive a stick, so she's not stuck at the house until her car's fixed," Bobby elaborated.

"At some point this week, I need to go over some discrepancies with the background checks you did a couple weeks back." Jen pointed at Bobby.

"Discrepancies?" Bobby didn't remember anything unusual with any of the background checks he'd done recently.

"Yeah, I'm not sure we were given the correct information on several of the Dalton Tech employees," Jen clarified. "I think they were actually independent contractors instead of employees and gave their business tax ID numbers instead of their social security numbers, so there's no personal information in the background checks you ran."

"Huh? I'm surprised you got anything on them with business ID's." Bobby scratched his head as he tried to remember seeing any weird reports. "I should've gotten an error message with using anything other than social security numbers."

"Maybe you need to have Jake check out your system when he gets here tonight," his Uncle Jon suggested, obviously concerned with the reliability of the information Bobby was able to obtain with the system not seeming to function properly.

"Yeah, I'll definitely do that." Bobby turned to direct his next comments to Jen. "I'll have him go through my laptop and the desktop at the station and then we'll re-run all of them for this month. I'll let you know once he's done with the computers, so you can show us the specific files that you found discrepancies with, but it might be after Christmas before we can re-do them all."

"That's fine," Jen replied. "I didn't bring the files home this weekend anyway, so it was already gonna be Wednesday at the earliest that I'd have them for you to look at."

Bobby noticed that Brie was exceptionally quiet as he finished the Burleson Incorporated business discussion with his uncle and cousin, but he brushed it off as her lack of interest in the company and nothing more. They quickly said their goodbyes and made their way out to his car, where he opened the passenger door for her before getting in to drive.

"Alright, I know you're not ready to get behind the wheel and drive into San Antonio," he started as they were putting on their seatbelts. "But I'm gonna spend our drive teaching you to listen to the engine to be able to shift at the right time, so if we get back before dark you can take a few laps around the ranch to try getting used to it."

"Okay," Brie sighed, looking nervous at the prospect of driving later.

Once he started the car, he explained using the clutch and the gear configuration before shifting into reverse and backing out of his parents' driveway. Once they started toward the gate, he had her listen to the sound the engine made when it didn't like staying in too low a gear before shifting into second.

"So, basically, I'm supposed to shift to the next gear whenever the car makes that noise?" Brie looked a little more comfortable with being able to shift gears.

"Yes, that sound means you're trying to go faster than the gear you're in can handle." Bobby went on to explain slowing down by downshifting, engaging the clutch when stopping to keep from killing the car, and making sure the car is all the way back in first gear before trying to take off from a stopped position.

She asked questions as they went along and only looked scared to shift the first time he asked her to reach over and shift gears while he engaged the clutch. He knew shifting left-handed didn't quite feel the same as shifting right-handed while driving, but he wanted her to get a feel for shifting and the pattern of the gears memorized before she was actually behind the wheel. If she messed up while he was driving, he could easily cover her hand with his to make sure they were in the correct gear to protect the engine and transmission from any potential damage of improper shifting. *If I can quit imagining her hand on my cock instead of the gearshift, I might be able to deflate my dick before we get out of the car, too.*

By the time they got to the mall in San Antonio, Brie seemed extremely confident in her ability to shift, but she still didn't want to practice behind the wheel until they were back on the ranch, where she wouldn't impede traffic as she tried it all the first time. Remembering back to his first time driving a stick shift, he couldn't agree more with practicing on the ranch first before attempting to drive on the road with other vehicles.

"So, what kind of gifts do you normally exchange with your family?" Brie questioned him as they walked into the mall.

"It depends," Bobby replied, not quite sure what to suggest she buy for anyone. "Like for Kay's birthday, back in October, we all got her music boxes."

"Music boxes?" Brie looked at him like she wasn't familiar with them.

"Yeah, she collects them, and her collection had recently been destroyed when her house in Tulsa was vandalized," Bobby explained, smiling at the memory of Kay's surprise birthday party. "So Anthony told us all to buy music boxes for her when he was planning her surprise birthday party. I didn't have time to get into San Antonio to find any of the musical jewelry and trinket boxes like the rest of the family, so I had to improvise with a Big Mouth Billy Bass from the Tackle Box."

"That's the singing fish on the wall in their music room, right?" Brie giggled.

"Yep," Bobby replied, grinning at her. "But I was actually able to order her a real music box for Christmas. None of the rest of us really collect anything like that to be easy to shop for like Kay."

"So, what did you get for everyone else?" Brie looked up at him quizzically.

"I got earrings for all the girls and watches for all the guys," Bobby shrugged, knowing he sucked at buying gifts. "I'm probably not the best person in the family to ask for help buying presents."

"Is that how everyone else usually buys gifts?" Brie asked as they stepped into the first department store. Bobby didn't clearly understand what she was asking, so when he didn't answer, she elaborated. "Picking an item and buying one for everyone."

"Yeah, pretty much," Bobby finally replied, remembering back to previous holidays with his family to realize that he wasn't the only one who wasn't good at personalizing gifts. "The girls tend to buy clothes for everyone a lot. They seem to have a thing for matching pajamas for the whole family, which is why if you end up doing anyone else's laundry besides mine, you'll probably see we all have matching sets."

"That explains some things," Brie giggled and blushed.

"Last year, my brothers, male cousins, and I were all put on notice not to do gift cards anymore, because we all suck at picking out presents," Bobby chuckled with a self-deprecating smile. "That's why I decided to up my game by getting jewelry for everyone. Figured the girls couldn't be disappointed with diamonds."

"You did at least make sure they all have pierced ears before you bought earrings, I hope." Brie's eyes widened as she smiled up at him.

"Yes, I know they all have pierced ears," Bobby chuckled at her recognizing his one potential error in shopping. Bobby had also noticed that Brie's ears were pierced, but he'd already bought all the earrings for his female relatives before he met Brie, so that wasn't what he had under the tree for her.

He'd seen her flipping through a couple of notebooks when she was typing on her manuscript for her next book, and realized that she would appreciate the blank, journal-type books, like Anthony had given Kay for her birthday, to be able to write out some of her future ideas. So, he'd gone to the Book Nook and bought one of every style for her, along with several different colors of pens, since she'd had a rainbow of colors in the notebooks she'd already mostly filled with her ideas.

He also saw her using her computer to read the eBooks Kay had recommended from her Kindle app, so Bobby had hopped online and ordered her a tablet, thinking that would make the eBooks easier for her to read without having to carry around her heavy laptop, if she wanted to relax and read somewhere other than where she had a table to put her computer on. He might not be good at personalizing gifts for everyone, but with writing and reading being her primary hobbies, he thought he was successful in picking out personalized Christmas presents for Brie.

Hopefully, she won't think they're lame gifts, Bobby thought as they looked over various items, trying to find some gift ideas for Brie to buy.

Bobby noticed as they shopped that Brie was being frugal with her selections, and wished they were far enough along in their relationship that he could offer to pay for her purchases without offending her. *How soon into dating someone is it okay to combine our accounts, so she doesn't have to spend any of her own income? I guess I've kinda already done that even though we aren't really dating, so she can use my account to buy my groceries and stuff. I wonder if I can convince her that everything she's picking out for my family for Christmas is a ranch expense? I mean, she wouldn't be buying any of this stuff if she wasn't working on the ranch, so it should all count as ranch expenses, right?*

No matter how much he argued the point, Brie was not convinced. She insisted on using her own money for everything. She ended up settling on funny graphic t-shirts for everyone, trying to personalize them by picking sayings that she thought matched the individual. Bobby had to text his mom to get everyone's sizes, and tell her a little about his two brothers that she hadn't met yet to help her pick them out, but she'd eventually found one for everyone but him.

"I promise I won't look, so you can go ahead and pick out mine." Bobby covered his eyes with his hand, but left an obvious gap between his fingers to pretend to be peeking at her choice of funny t-shirt for him.

"Oh, no, mister," Brie impishly scolded, shaking her head and laughing at him. "I'm not buying you a Christmas present while you're shopping with me. I'll have to get comfortable driving this afternoon, so I can go to town for the other idea I have for you on Monday."

"You're not getting me a t-shirt?" Bobby playfully pouted. "But there are so many of them I like, and really want you to get me for Christmas."

"Yeah, well, be a good boy, and quit pouting, and maybe you'll get lucky enough to get them for your birthday," Brie smiled at him as she paid for the rest of the shirts she was buying.

"Fine," Bobby huffed as if he were really disappointed. "I guess I can wait two months for you to buy me some funny shirts. Can you remember my size that long?"

"Yes, I think seeing the two XL in all the shirts I've washed for you in the last three weeks has ingrained your size in my brain," Brie deadpanned. "If I haven't already memorized it, I'm sure the next two months of doing your laundry will solidify it in my head forever."

"Just makin' sure." Bobby threw an arm over Brie's shoulders to walk out of the mall. *Damn, I love how she's coming out of her shell and letting me see the smartass she really is deep inside.*

~ ~ ~

Sunday, December 23, 2018

After only dreaming about Brie the night before, Bobby felt like he was finally getting closer to being able to step things up between them. He wanted to say it was because of how close they'd gotten in the last couple of weeks with all the time they'd spent together, especially the fun day they'd had the day before while shopping and teaching her to drive a stick shift. But he knew that was only part of the reason why he desperately wanted to ask her out on a date. He knew a much bigger part of his desperation for Brie was the fact that he focused exclusively on her as he fantasized while jacking off in the shower on a daily basis.

Thankfully, we aren't Catholic, so I don't have to confess to thinking about getting her naked while sitting here in church, Bobby thought as Pastor Harrison asked everyone to bow their heads for the prayer, dismissing the services.

He said his own silent prayer, asking for clarity to know when to proceed with pursuing a relationship with Brie, and for forgiveness if his lustful thoughts were sinful. Bobby wasn't quite convinced that lusting after a woman was a sin if she was *The One*.

When the service was over, Bobby followed along with the rest of his family out of the chapel and into the fellowship hall, where the whole congregation met for a potluck lunch. Bobby had always considered the food his mother and aunt contributed to the potluck as enough to cover for the whole Burleson family. But for the past two weeks, Brie had insisted on making something to contribute to the meal as well, making him realize that he probably should've been contributing something else all along. She'd made a huge pot of her Brunswick stew the night before, and Bobby couldn't wait to dig into it for lunch, having loved it the first time she'd made it for him almost three weeks prior.

Bobby wasn't sure if he should point it out to his family and friends, so they could all praise her for her culinary abilities, or if he should keep quiet about how good it was, so he could bring home leftovers after the potluck was over. As they sat around talking while eating, Bobby ended up pointing out that Brie had made the barbecue stew everyone was raving about, and took the ribbing from his friends for going back for seconds and thirds, resigned to the fact that it was too good for there to be any leftovers. *I'll just have to ask her to make it again soon.*

"Hey, Bobby." Dean Hunter walked up to him as he was disposing of his trash after he finished eating. "I wanted to ask you what you thought of the email I sent you last month."

"What email?" Bobby only vaguely remembered forwarding something from his departmental email to his personal email without actually opening it.

"I sent you an email the day we left after Thanksgiving," Dean reminded him. "While we were on the plane from here to Tampa, a couple of the guys' wives were talking to Randi about that missing heiress and the girl who showed up at the wedding reception possibly being the same person, so I emailed you the pictures they had, so you could investigate her before she left town."

HOLY FUCK! Bobby screamed in his head. *No fucking way!*

"Yeah, I vaguely remember getting the email, but I was covered up with a federal drug bust that week, so I didn't ever go back and actually read it." Bobby tried to maintain his composure while standing in church with a huge audience who didn't need to see the wheels turning in his head. "Can you recap their theory for me?"

"There wasn't much to their theory." Dean scratched his head like he was trying to remember everything to go over it with Bobby. "Just that they looked alike, and their names were similar. When they were looking at the pictures on the plane, they said something about how she could've come up with an alias from her name. And Randi wondered if she'd dyed her hair and worn colored contacts to change her appearance enough to not be recognized. The email was just the pictures a couple of the guys' wives sent me of both Brooklyn and

Brie, and asking if you thought they could be right about them being one in the same."

Hell yeah, they could be one in the same! Bobby fumed, questioning his own investigative abilities at not seeing it sooner. *That would certainly explain why I feel drawn to both of them.*

"Yeah, I'm not sure," Bobby drawled, hopefully covering his own inner turmoil with his bland expression. "I'll definitely look into it now, though."

"Cool. Let me know what you find. We have a whole bunch of people dying to figure out the real story," Dean informed him before turning to walk back over to where his family was gathered on the other side of the room.

"Yeah, I will," Bobby mumbled to Dean's retreating back. *After I decipher what the fuck is going on.*

Bobby was quiet the rest of the time they were at church, too busy reviewing everything he knew about the Brooklyn Brielle Barns case in Georgia and comparing it to all the conversations he'd had with Brie Brooks. *Fuck, I should've seen through her alias the first day I met her!*

No wonder she has to redo her dark hair color every week. That stuff's supposed to last like at least a month, but probably only on hair that's naturally closer to the color she's using.

And I bet all those time's she's made me wait when I've knocked on her door, the rustling around I'm hearing is her putting in the colored contacts. Shit! How did I not put this together on my own before now?

Especially with all their similarities. Not just in looks, but the strange coincidences of both of them having their mother's die when they were four. And her stories about only seeing her biological father when he faked being a doting father to try to get ahead with his colleagues. I bet those were actually references to her dad needing her to make public appearances at the society events where every picture I've seen of Brooklyn were taken.

Fuck! We've been getting so close. Why wouldn't she tell me who she really is? Did I really screw up so bad that first night that she doesn't think she can trust me?

And how the fuck am I gonna ask her about it without losing my temper and scaring her away from me even more?

Leah Mae Wright

When everyone started talking about their plans for spending time together as a family the rest of the afternoon, Bobby finally spoke up and made excuses for he and Brie to go home, change clothes, and do another driving lesson first before coming back to his parents' house later for supper. Brie had proven to be very competent driving his car the day before, so she didn't really need another lesson, but she didn't argue or contradict him in any way.

While I hate to see her revert to acting so subservient, like she was when she first moved to the ranch, I'm glad she's not pushing back, so I can ask her about this privately and not in front of the whole damn family.

Neither of them said a word as they drove home, the uneasiness between them so thick he thought he could cut it with a knife. *I guess at least it's not sexual tension for once.* Bobby slightly shook his head at his own desire for them to revert to being awkward because of attraction.

Once he'd opened the passenger door for her to exit the vehicle, Bobby grabbed the large stock pot out of the back seat, insisting on being the one to carry it in, just as he'd carried it out for her on their way to church. He followed her in the back door, unable to stop watching the sway of her hips regardless of how upset he was at her deception.

He dropped the stock pot in the sink to wash later before stopping her from going upstairs to change clothes by saying, "Wait, we need to sit down and talk for a few minutes before we figure out what we're really doing this afternoon."

"Um, okay," Brie sputtered, stopping just before walking out of the kitchen, without turning around or making eye contact. "What do you want to talk about?"

Fuck, I can see how tense she is just from the set of her shoulders. I can't just spring this on her. I need to get her a little more relaxed before I ask her what's really going on.

"Lots of things." Bobby tried to put some playfulness in his tone of voice to help put her at ease. He cautiously walked up beside her, reached out to take her hand, and interlaced their fingers before guiding her to the comfortable sectional sofa in the room he'd previously considered his man cave. Since Brie had been living there,

Bobby had thought it would end up more of a family room eventually. He hoped that would still be a possibility after their conversation.

Once they were seated side by side on the sofa, Bobby turned to face her, so he could see her facial expressions as they talked. Knowing he couldn't just jump into figuring out her real identity without freaking her out, and possibly causing her to bolt, Bobby decided to let her know how he felt about her first. He hoped she might share some of his feelings and would figure out that she could trust him with her secrets without being scared that he would be mad at her for keeping them.

"I know I was an ass the first night you moved in here," Bobby started, earning a small smile from Brie. "But I hope the last couple of weeks have shown you that I wasn't really acting like myself that night."

"Yeah, I know," Brie nodded, squeezing his hand where he hadn't been able to release his grip on her.

"But I'm not sure you really understand the reason why I was such an ass that first night." Bobby ran his free hand through his hair as he tried to figure out how to word what he wanted to say to her. "I was fighting my own feelings because I was so confused by them back then."

"Okay." Brie drew the word out to three syllables, like she wasn't really clear on what he meant by his last statement.

"Since you've been in town, have you heard how Heart's Destiny got its name?" Bobby thought maybe he'd have to explain his family's penchant for falling in love at first sight before she would understand how he felt torn in two by seeing her in pictures as Brooklyn and then in person as Brie.

"Yes, your mom told me about Jonah and Emma my first day on the job." Brie tentatively smiled at Bobby. "Kay and I were talking the other day about how their story would make a wonderful historical romance novel."

"Yeah, if ya'll go to pen that one, make sure you get Ma and my sisters to bring out the family albums and tell you more than just how they met," Bobby chuckled at the thought of the two writers turning his family history into one of the books his Pappaw Jerry had referred to as bodice rippers back when Bobby was too young to understand what the adults around him were talking about.

"Kay's probably more likely to write that one than me," Brie smiled and looked more relaxed with the change of subject. "That's not really my genre."

"I'm sure you'd write it beautifully, regardless of it not being your normal genre." Bobby hoped the compliment would be well received and relax her a little more before he went back to his original point.

Brie blushed but didn't say a word, so Bobby decided he'd better get their talk back on track.

"Anyway, back to what I was trying to say earlier," Bobby smiled. "So, you know Jonah and Emma were my third-great-grandparents and their love-at-first-sight story is how the town got its name."

Brie nodded her head in agreement before Bobby continued. "They're not the only couple in my family who fell in love at first sight. That's how it happens for pretty much everyone in the Burleson family. Their son, Joshua fell for my second-great-grandmother, Sarah, the first time he saw her. Joshua and Sarah's son, Robert, who my dad and I are named after, fell in love with my great-grandma, Sylvia, the first time he saw her. Robert and Sylvia's son, my Pappaw Jerry, fell in love with my Memmaw Judy the first time he saw her. My dad fell for my mom the first time he saw her, and if you listen to any of his stories, he went through hell waiting five years for her to be old enough he could ask her out. Uncle Jon and Aunt Susan, same thing, though she was at least of age the first time they met."

"Wow, that's like your whole family tree," Brie exclaimed, looking at him with awe written across her beautiful face.

"Yeah, pretty much," Bobby affirmed, turning serious to make sure she understood his next words. "And this generation of Burlesons is no different."

"Kay told me how she and Anthony fell in love at first sight," Brie confirmed before he could declare his feelings for her.

"Yes." Bobby cleared the lump in his throat before continuing. "And the night I met you, I knew what I was feeling because of spending my whole life hearing all the stories of how my family felt when they first fell in love."

"You, uh, you felt, uh, oh wow," Brie stuttered, pulling her hand from his grasp, and covering her face with both of her hands.

"Please look at me, Brie, and let me finish explaining." Bobby reached out to pull her hands down, clasping them both in his and resting them all on the sofa between them.

"I, uh, oh wow," Brie sputtered, looking up at him with wide eyes.

"Don't say anything yet." Bobby tried to keep his voice soft and soothing. "Let me finish explaining."

Brie nodded that she was ready for him to continue.

"Like I said, I knew the way I was drawn to you, when you came to give Luke your car keys at the wedding reception, was more than just a passing attraction. It was exactly what everyone in my family described feeling when they met *The One*. But I was confused because it wasn't the first time I felt that way."

"Oh." Brie looked surprised, slightly pulling back from him when Bobby paused his speech to breathe.

Once he calmed his racing heart, Bobby continued. "I felt the same intense draw the day before when I saw a picture of another woman. With nobody in my family ever having mentioned feeling drawn to two different women at the same time, I've been really confused about why I've been feeling torn between you. That's why I was such an ass that first night. I wasn't ready to pick between you. I've been trying to put her outta my head ever since, so I can focus on only you. I didn't wanna come to you with my feelings until I could be sure I was giving you one-hundred percent of my heart."

"And you've finally gotten over her, so that's why you're telling me all this now?" Brie questioned.

"Not exactly," Bobby admitted. "I just figured out that the woman I saw in that picture the day before we met is actually you. I haven't really been drawn to two different women. I just fell in love with one woman, who has two different identities."

Her jaw dropped and her eyes widened to the point they were practically saucer sized. Bobby waited patiently for her to gather her thoughts and say something, but she floundered for a while before finally breaking down.

"Please don't send me back to Georgia," she begged as tears streamed down her face.

"Oh, no, Darlin'." Bobby pulled her across the sofa and into his lap before releasing her hands to wrap his arms around her. "It's okay. You don't have to go anywhere you don't wanna go. I promise."

She wrapped her arms around his waist and cried into his chest for quite a while. Bobby tried his best to comfort and soothe her, rocking gently as he rubbed one hand up and down her back, while he weaved the fingers of his other hand through her hair to cradle her head to his chest, right over his heart.

"You don't have to worry, Sweetheart," Bobby softly whispered, grazing his lips over the top of her head as he spoke. "I've got you. I meant what I said about falling for you the first time I saw you, both in a picture and in person. Now that I've found you, I'm not about to let you go. Even if you tell me you don't feel the same for me, I'm still gonna do everything I can to help you live the life you want, not what anyone else is trying to push you into. Who knows, maybe along the way, you might even start to fall for me, too."

When her sobs subsided, she pulled away slightly to look him in the eyes. "You're really not going to arrest me and send me back to Georgia?"

"No." Bobby adamantly shook his head, hoping to reassure her. "I mean, I don't know the whole story to know for sure, but I don't think you've done anything illegal, so I have no reason to arrest you."

"But don't you have to turn me in?" Brie still looked a little nervous. "My father has local, state, and federal law enforcement all looking for me."

"You're an adult," Bobby explained, smiling at her. "It's not illegal for you to move out of his house without his knowledge of your whereabouts. If anyone's at risk of being arrested, it's him for giving a false report of a crime because I don't think you were really kidnapped."

"No, I wasn't kidnapped," Brie admitted, looking unsure of what else she could tell him.

"Why don't you start from the beginning and tell me the real story," Bobby suggested, still rubbing her back to try to help her feel safe to open up to him. "Not the lies that have been put out to the media by your father, or the cover story you've given all of us for the last month."

"I really tried not to lie to ya'll." Brie stiffened in his arms. "I really am an author and use the pen name of Brie Brooks. I even made sure to use my tax ID number from my LLC to report my income from working here on my taxes."

"Yeah, I bet that's one of the reasons Jen wants to go over those background checks with me next week," Bobby chuckled.

"Sorry, I thought that was how to keep things legal without exposing my real identity and risking having to go back to Georgia," Brie shrugged and gave him a small smile. "And all the stories I told you about my childhood are mostly true. Joe and Mary did raise me like they were my foster parents. Technically, they're my father's gardener and head housekeeper. The only real lies I told were when I said I was from Atlanta instead of Macon."

"And I completely understand keeping details vague to cover who you really are," Bobby reassured her, looking deep into her eyes to make sure she saw that the truth in his matched his words. "What I don't understand is why you're so afraid of having to go back to Georgia. Can you please tell me what's really going on that has you so scared?"

"My father is trying to make me get married when I don't want to," Brie disclosed, looking irritated. "I'm not entirely sure why. I mean, I know he's never really wanted me around, but I can't help that I was born a girl and not the boy he wanted. Growing up, I learned to stay quiet whenever he was home. I learned what I needed to do when he had to have me accompany him to a society event, and only got my degree online because it would look bad to the people he did business with if I was too stupid to go to college. I thought when I graduated that I'd be allowed to move out and get a job, so he didn't have to support me anymore. But instead, he arranged a marriage to Clayton Donaldson, who's thirty years older than me. I was grossed out at the thought, but I didn't have any money of my own to be able to move out immediately."

A single tear slipped out of Brie's eye, and Bobby reached up to wipe it away, so she could continue with her story.

"So, I didn't tell him when I started writing," Brie continued. "I set up everything online under my pen name, so he couldn't track it. As soon as I had enough in royalties, I had Joe go buy my car and hide it where my father wouldn't see it. I kept pretending to be the perfect daughter and bride-to-be, while secretly writing more books to earn more royalties to be able to have some money saved up to cover my expenses when I left. When I was having to pack up my stuff to move to Clayton's house after the wedding, I had Mary take the boxes of stuff I wanted to keep and stash them in my car. I really wanted to wait to get my royalty payment the last day of November to leave, but when my father told me what he expected me to do on Thanksgiving, I couldn't wait any longer. So, at two in the morning, when he was sound asleep, I crept downstairs and over to Joe and Mary's cottage, where they had everything ready for me to be able to escape."

"What did he expect you to do on Thanksgiving?" Bobby knew he probably didn't want to hear all the details.

"He expected me to go home with Clayton, so he…" her voice trailed off as she started sobbing again. "So, so, he, he could…" She stuttered, unable to actually get the words out.

"It's okay, Brie," Bobby consoled her, hugging her to his chest for his comfort as much as for hers. "You don't have to say the rest."

Fucking Hell! Her own father was sending her over to that pervert's house, so he could start raping her before the wedding. Bobby hadn't ever been prone to violence at any previous point in his life, but in that moment he could gladly kill both her father and former fiancé with his bare hands.

"I won't let either one of them near you again, Brie," Bobby promised, whispering the words in her ear as he held her while she cried.

When the tears finally subsided and she started to regain her composure, Brie pushed off of his chest to look up into his eyes again. "I just don't understand why. Why spend all this money on clothes to send over to Clayton's house? Why spend so much on the elaborate wedding they were planning? If he just didn't want to be responsible for me anymore, why couldn't I just move out and save him the exorbitant expense of this farce of a wedding? Not to mention all the lies about me being kidnapped by a business rival, so I don't inherit the business. My father was the only one listed in my mother's will, not me. I have no claim on her family business, so none of that makes sense to me."

"Did you actually see your mother's will?" Bobby realized she'd probably been told some serious untruths about her rightful inheritance.

"No, but I was four when she died, so there's no way she would've left me the company." Brie shook her head.

"What about her parents?" Bobby wasn't sure how the business was structured as to who was the owner at the time of her mother's death to say for sure if that was when ownership would've passed to anyone, much less Brie or her father.

"I don't remember them," Brie shrugged, shaking her head. "I just assumed they died before her from what little Mary said to me about them. And if they passed before Mom, then they would've left everything to her as their only child."

"Okay," Bobby sighed, the investigative wheels in his head turning as to how to best approach the situation to learn the truth for Brie, while still keeping her safe from whatever other plans her father had for her. "I think the first thing we need to do is talk to my brother, Jake. He can use his computer skills to access all the public records to verify who is supposed to inherit what and when. And then if needed, he can hack into the company computers to find any correspondence between your father and Clayton to see exactly what their plans are, giving us an idea of how to clear up the mess with the media and law enforcement, so you don't have to be scared of them anymore."

"Okay," Brie agreed, looking up at him quizzically. "Um, do we need to finish our earlier discussion about, um, the feel-feelings you were talking about?"

Based on the way she was slightly stuttering, Bobby didn't think Brie was really ready to explore the relationship he wanted to have with her just yet. "Don't worry, Brie-Baby, we'll get back to that," he smiled at her. "But I think you might need a little time to process everything else that's going on right now before we do."

"Yeah, you're probably right about that," Brie agreed, giving him a shy smile.

"Let's go change clothes and I'll let you drive the Charger up to Mom and Dad's, so we can get the rest of the family caught up with what's going on, and looking into the situation from different angles," Bobby suggested, brushing his lips across her forehead before helping her up from his lap.

~~~
~~~

Leah Mae Wright

Brooklyn was nervous as she and Bobby made their way into the dining room at Hazel and Bob's home, where the whole family (minus Anthony, Kay, Tia, and Maria) were gathered for Sunday supper. It wasn't that she didn't think she could trust them with her secrets. She'd thought for weeks now that they could all be trusted and would help her stay hidden from her father if she told them her real identity. She was just afraid they'd be mad at her for lying to them in the first place.

She was still shocked that Bobby didn't appear to be mad at her for not telling him sooner, but she figured that probably had to do with his earlier confession about feeling drawn to both versions of her. *Is that why I felt so weird around him at first too? The butterflies and goosebumps and instant attraction. Were they the signs of love at first sight that I didn't comprehend? And if he's right that there's more between us, then why isn't he mad at me for making him feel torn in two for the last month?*

Not that she could focus on figuring out her feelings for Bobby at the moment, even though he was making her tingle where he had his hand on her low back to guide her into the dining room of his family home. She had to suck up her pride and confess her true identity to this family that had made her feel like one of their own for the last three weeks. *Yeah, I don't think the t-shirts I bought them for Christmas will be enough to make up for my deception.*

All eyes turned to them as they stopped to stand in the opening of the U made up by the three tables that were arranged around the dining room, so the whole extended family could sit together. Brooklyn really wished she could crawl under a rock and not have to tell them what she'd done. Obviously noticing her trepidation, Bobby reached over and took her hand in his, offering his silent support. Unfortunately, even the comfort of having him holding her hand wasn't enough to help her feel brave enough to open her mouth.

"Oh, goodness," Hazel exclaimed, clutching her hands together over her heart. "Please tell us that the way ya'll are holding hands means I get to plan another wedding soon."

"Geez, Ma," Bobby groaned, shaking his head and chuckling. "Can you please let me actually take her on a date or two before you start pushing for a wedding?"

Several people in the room started laughing and teasing Hazel for her matchmaking, lightening the mood in the room. Brooklyn let out a breath she hadn't realized she'd been holding, and felt a little less tense than she had when they first walked into the room. Unfortunately, her slight relaxation was short lived, as Bobby cleared his throat and got everyone's attention again.

"Actually, Brie and I do have something to tell ya'll," Bobby announced, turning to look down at Brooklyn. She could see in his eyes that he was silently asking her if she wanted to tell them or if she wanted him to. Unable to form words at that moment, Brooklyn just nodded to him, hoping he understood her meaning for him to tell them. "Her real name is Brooklyn Barns, and she needs our help to figure out why her father is trying to force her into an arranged marriage."

There were several gasps of surprise from around the room. Among the looks of shock and astonishment from most of the people present, Brooklyn noticed that Hazel didn't look like they were telling her anything she didn't already know. *It's almost like she's known who I really am all along,* Brooklyn thought as she watched the older woman smile meaningfully at them.

As Hazel walked over to where they were standing, the room seemed to shrink down to just the three of them—Brooklyn, Bobby, and Hazel. Brooklyn no longer heard the questions flying at her from all around the tables. "You knew," Brooklyn muttered, pointing at Hazel. "How? How did you know?"

"Oh, sweet girl, don't you worry about that." Hazel pulled Brooklyn in for a hug.

"You knew who she was before you hired her?" Bobby glared at his mother.

"Of course, I wouldn't have hired her if I hadn't known who she was before she ever left Georgia," Hazel disclosed, releasing one arm from around Brooklyn to wrap it around Bobby and pull them both over to the table to sit down.

"I thought it was weird that you hired a brunette when you said you'd dreamt about a blonde for Bobby." Susan shook her head at Hazel.

"Yes, well, I was a little uncertain that it was really her when I first met her because of the dyed hair and colored contacts." Hazel turned to explain to Susan. "But then her contact slipped to the side when we were doing the interview and I recognized her blue eyes from my dream."

"Seriously, Ma?" Charlotte questioned her mother. "More prophetic dreams?"

"Why can't I have some of these dreams?" Becky huffed, but nobody answered.

"How did your dream and her slipped contact lead to you knowing her identity?" Bobby looked confused by his mother's revelation. "And why didn't you tell me who she was, so we could've helped her outta this mess sooner?"

"Well, when I first dreamed about her, I didn't know her name," Hazel started her explanation of how she'd dreamed about the perfect woman for Bobby the night of Anthony and Kay's bachelor and bachelorette party. "In the dream she came to the ranch needing help, but she didn't explain what kind of help. Then she and Bobby fell in love when we gave her a job and moved her into his house. I didn't actually know who she was until Thanksgiving day, when I recognized her from my dream when I saw her picture on the news."

Hazel turned to look directly at Brooklyn before continuing. "I really hope we can get this all fixed soon, so you can quit coloring your hair and wearing the brown contacts. Your natural coloring suits you so much better."

"She's beautiful either way," Bobby bellowed pointedly to his mother. "So, how 'bout you just let her do whatever she wants with her hair and eyes."

"Actually, the contacts are kind of irritating," Brooklyn giggled with a smile at Hazel. "So, if I can ditch those soon, I'd really appreciate it."

"Before we can make any decisions about when she can lose the disguise," Bobby's brother, Jake, who Brooklyn had only met that morning at church, interjected, garnering all their attention. "Shouldn't we evaluate the likelihood of someone looking for her here?"

"Yep, and you're just the brother I was gonna ask to do just that," Bobby confirmed, smiling at his younger brother. "Along with digging up the public records of her mother's and grandparents' wills and snooping into any electronic communication between her father and Clayton Donaldson that might shed some light on what they're really up to."

"You think they're up to something shady with Ashbury Enterprises?" Bobby's Uncle Jon inquired. Brooklyn had only been formally introduced to Susan's husband once, but she got the impression that he was a shrewd businessman.

I wonder if he's dealt with Ashbury Enterprises as part of his job at Burleson Incorporated?

"Maybe," Bobby answered his uncle. "At the very least, I think there's something in one of those wills that will lead to Brie being able to take over the company and they're trying to keep it under their control by controlling her."

"Is that why the news is reporting about me inheriting it when I get married?" Brooklyn wondered, remembering the reports she hadn't comprehended when she saw them. Bobby nodded his head to her. "But they don't really have marriage stipulations in wills anymore, do they?"

"Oh, yeah, that's actually pretty common," Bobby answered her, taking her hand in his again, which she found very comforting. "In fact, Pappaw Jerry's will has a marriage stipulation for getting our trust funds."

"Really?" Brooklyn was shocked that it was so common that the Burlesons of her generation were all nodding their heads in agreement.

"Anthony's the only one of us who's gotten it so far," Charlotte confirmed. "Because he got married. Otherwise, we all have to wait until we turn thirty to get them."

"Wow, okay," Brooklyn murmured, starting to understand what might be her father's reasoning for arranging a marriage she didn't want. "So, if either my mom's or grandparents' wills have a stipulation that I inherit their estate when I get married, that's probably the motive for pushing me into this arranged marriage. And if I'd have gotten married back on the first of December, like my father wanted, I'd have probably been forced to sign over my inheritance before the ink even dried on the marriage license."

"That's my theory," Bobby declared, squeezing her hand, and giving her a sad smile. "But I'm not gonna let that happen. I won't let either one of them near you, Brie-Baby."

Bobby lifted their joined hands to his lips, brushing a kiss across the back of her hand. Though it was an innocent touch of his lips to her skin, Brooklyn felt tingles throughout her body as if it were a much more intimate kiss. She couldn't focus on that tingly feeling or think about what it meant for her and Bobby in the future, as she was inundated with questions from around the room.

She ended up regaling them with her life story as they ate dinner, hoping that knowing every detail she could share would help the Burlesons in their investigation into what was really going on with her father. It was a long, exhausting evening, but with Bobby by her side and constantly reassuring her with innocent, comforting touches, it was easier to get through than Brooklyn had previously imagined.

Chapter Seven

Monday, December 24, 2018

Brooklyn practically had an extra day off for the Christmas holiday because Hazel and Susan insisted their daughters help them with the meal prep, instead of Brook and Rosa. Since she didn't have a house to clean that day, only having to make dinner that evening as part of her job, Brooklyn had some free time that she needed to fill on Monday. With doing a little picking up around the house she shared with Bobby every night, she didn't even have much she could do there, so she took advantage of the extra free time that morning to call her new friends to set up a lunch time present swap with them. Ashley and Heather both had to work that morning, but they planned to meet her for lunch at Millie's Diner. Kenzie had the day off and couldn't wait to hang out with her new friend, showing up at Bobby's house less than fifteen minutes from when the women hung up from their call.

Since Bobby had left for work early that morning, Brooklyn invited her friend in for coffee, not even thinking about the fact that she hadn't put her contacts in to disguise her eye color, after the discussion the night before when the Burlesons agreed that she was probably safe in not wearing them while she was on the ranch.

"There's something different about you this morning." Kenzie studied Brooklyn in a way that made her feel slightly uncomfortable. "Are you wearing colored contacts?"

No. No, no, no! Brooklyn screamed inside her head. *Guess I'm not keeping my identity as much of a secret as Bobby suggested until he can find out how likely it is that my father knows where to look for me. But I can trust Kenzie, right? Just like I can trust the Burlesons. I just hope she's not mad at me for not telling her sooner.*

"Um, no," Brooklyn reluctantly admitted. "You actually caught me before I put them in for the day."

"Seriously, girl, why would you cover those gorgeous baby blues with brown contacts?" Kenzie looked shocked that the brown were the colored contacts instead of her natural eye color.

"Um, well," Brooklyn stalled, nervous she might lose her new friend with her revelation. "I, uh, kind of needed to wear them as a disguise."

"A disguise?" Kenzie arched an eyebrow, looking confused for a moment before blurting out, "Are you in the witness protection program or something?"

The wide-eyed way Kenzie asked the ridiculous question caused Brooklyn to burst out laughing. "No," she sputtered, shaking her head as her laughter died down. "Technically, I'm a runaway bride who doesn't want to be found by my father, and forced to marry his business colleague who's thirty years older than me."

"Shut up!" Kenzie shouted, slapping her hand down on Brooklyn's where it was resting on the dining table, where they were having their coffee. "That sounds like the story line for a movie, or one of your books!"

"Yeah, well, I'm kind of making it into my next book," Brooklyn shrugged. "But it's true. My name's not really Brie, either."

She spent the next few minutes explaining her situation to Kenzie, who freaked out when she realized that her new friend was the missing woman who'd been plastered all over the national news for the last month. Instead of being mad at her as Brooklyn had expected, Kenzie understood why she'd hidden her real identity until they got to know each other better, saying, "of course you couldn't tell me until you knew you could trust me," as if it was the most natural thing to have happened.

Once the surprise portion of the morning was over, their conversation turned to who all she could trust with her secret identity, leading Brooklyn to reveal that she'd told all the Burlesons the night before. After she told Kenzie about her conversation with Bobby, when he'd revealed that he figured it out, their girl talk turned much more personal.

"So, that's why he was such a jerk the first night," Kenzie's expression turned to shock once more. "Because he was confused by having instant feelings for both Brooklyn and Brie and not knowing how to handle them?"

"Yeah, that's what he said," Brooklyn confirmed. "But we haven't talked about what those *'feelings'* actually are or what they mean for us going forward." She used air quotes around the word "feelings" to make it clear to Kenzie that she wasn't sure exactly what he meant he felt.

"Oh, it was definitely love at first sight," Kenzie blurted, her voice high pitched with excitement. "It's no secret that the Burlesons all fall fast and hard. That's why us local girls know we don't stand a chance with any of them, since we've known them forever without any of them showing an interest in us."

"Yeah, he told me a little bit of the family history of love at first sight," Brooklyn admitted. "But I think I was too overwhelmed with realizing he'd figured out who I am to comprehend what he meant when he was talking about all that. And he seems to want to fix everything back home for me, so I don't have to live my life on the run from my father, before we talk about any feelings between us again."

"So, are you finally willing to admit that you have feelings for him?" Kenzie alluded to the way the girls had been teasing her about having a crush on Bobby the last couple of weeks.

"I'm willing to admit that I think he's hot," Brooklyn confided, feeling herself blush at the admission. "But I'm not sure what I really feel for him."

"Pul-ease!" Kenzie dramatically drew out the word. "I've heard the way you get all breathy when you talk about the conversations you have with him over dinner every night. And I can clearly see the dreamy expression on your face when you're thinking about him now. You may not believe you're in love with him just yet, but you're definitely in lust with him."

"Yeah, well, I've never been in lust with anyone before, so how am I supposed to know that's what I'm feeling?" Brooklyn mirrored Kenzie's dramatic body language. Both girls burst out laughing, giggling like the teenagers they were just a few short years ago.

"Okay, okay," Kenzie croaked, waving her arms about as if that would stop their giggles. "Now that we've figured out that you're definitely in lust and well on your way to in love, it's time to figure out what you're gonna do about it."

The thought of acting on her lustful urges with Bobby quickly sobered Brooklyn up, stopping her schoolgirl giggles in her throat. "Nothing," Brooklyn choked out. "Like I told you the other day, I'm never going to be comfortable being a seductress like you, Ashley, and Heather."

"Girl, we are not seductresses," Kenzie laughed. "We're just not afraid to wear sexy lingerie and flirt a little now and then. And we'll eventually wear you down and get you more comfortable doing the same. Now, let's start by heading into town and letting me show you the back room at Destiny Dresses, where Louella keeps all the lingerie."

"Actually, I need to go into town and find a Christmas present for Bobby," Brooklyn admitted.

"Yes, you in lingerie sounds like the perfect Christmas present for Bobby," Kenzie squealed, jumping out of her chair to push Brooklyn into getting ready to go to town.

What have I gotten myself into? Brooklyn questioned her own sanity, as well as that of her friends, as she left the ranch with Kenzie to go shopping and meet up with their other friends for lunch.

<div style="text-align:center">~~~</div>

As Bobby went for his early morning run around the ranch, he thought back through all the conversations he'd had with Brie over the last few weeks, and especially what he'd learned as she told his whole family all about her life the night before. Even knowing that she was really Brooklyn, he still referred to her as Brie in his head. His family may have started calling her Brook, like she'd asked them to call her, since that's what Joe and Mary had called her all her life. But Bobby didn't like the reference to her former life in Georgia and didn't want to bring up any bad memories of that time by referring to her as Brooklyn, or even Brook, so he continued to call her Brie.

Brooklyn was the heiress trapped in the gilded cage of her father's estate, who was almost forced to marry a dirty old man. Brie was the fun-loving, writer with the wild imagination that had stolen his heart. Thinking back to how she'd smiled at him when he called her "Brie-

Baby" the day before, made him hopeful that he'd be able to use the pet name for her for many years to come.

While he was glad to finally feel like he knew everything about her, it had been hard hearing about her life in Georgia. He hated how she'd felt trapped in her father's house her whole life, unable to go out and make friends, much less have the normal experiences of life growing up in a loving family like he had. He wanted to give her all the love and affection she'd wanted but didn't get earlier in life, while showing her all the wonderous things she'd missed in the world.

I wanna take her to amusement parks and aquariums and on all the fun dates she's never been on before, Bobby thought as his feet pounded the dirt of the pasture he was running through. *Fuck, being homeschooled and isolated like she was, I bet she's still a virgin. No wonder she looked so nervous when I was talking about falling for her so fast. She seemed to relax on my lap when I was holding her while she cried, but she probably wouldn't have if she'd have been sitting closer than on my knees and felt how fucking hard I was for her right then.*

I'm definitely gonna hafta take it slow with her, Bobby pondered his plan for moving their relationship along. *I think I did alright yesterday, with holding her hand and rubbing her back to comfort her while she was telling her story. I'll just keep up the innocent affection to ease her into more. As much as I prefer to take control, especially in the bedroom, I'm gonna hafta hold back on my dominant desires with her. She hasn't had control of anything in her life so far, and I'm not about to scare her off by being too aggressive now. I'll bide my time and wait for her to make the first move. I'll let her feel in control of our relationship, until she seems ready to let me take over, even if that means taking way too many showers every day to relieve my need for her.*

Hell, even after she makes that first move, I'm still gonna hafta go super slow with her. I'll have to spend extra time getting her ready for our first time. I just hope I can be gentle enough not to hurt her too bad.

Bobby was seriously worried about his ability to make her first time enjoyable. He'd never been with a virgin before, not even when he lost his virginity almost fifteen years ago. His first time had been after the homecoming dance his freshman year of high school. Heart's

Leah Mae Wright

Destiny High School had a tradition of electing a prince and princess from the freshman, sophomore, and junior classes, with the king and queen coming from the senior class to make up the homecoming court. Bobby had been the freshman prince, but he was already taller than the upperclassmen, though he was only fifteen at the time. His impressive height, combined with all the hard work he did on the ranch to define his muscles, made him attractive to all the girls in school, regardless of their grade level.

Instead of leaving the dance with the freshman princess—and having to get a ride home from one of his parents since he was still too young to legally drive—Bobby rode home with the homecoming queen, Melissa Martinez, after spending a couple hours in the back seat of her car while on the trails on the north side of the Walker Ranch. He spent the next three years of high school hooking up with several older women, not going out with a girl his own age until his senior year.

Thinking back on his sexual history as he finished his run and got ready for work, Bobby realized that he hadn't hooked up with a younger woman until the last couple of years, and the few of those that there were had only been a year or two younger than him. He wasn't quite sure how he felt about the seven-year age difference between him and Brie. Only knowing one other guy who was in a relationship with a large age gap, Bobby opted to text his youngest brother to ask if there were any issues he'd need to watch out for in pursuing Brie.

Bobby: Hey, Bro, you free to chat w/o anyone reading your texts?

Anthony: Yeah, why?

Bobby: Need some brotherly advice & you're the only one I know in a similar situation.

Anthony: Needing to know how to pop the question w/ Brie?

Bobby: Not yet. But wondered if I need to watch out for any issues from our age difference when I'm ready to actually ask her out on a date. Figured since you & Kay have about the same age difference as Brie & I, you might have some insight for me.

Anthony: Well, our situation is different with her being older than me, but it doesn't seem to be an issue for us.

Bobby: Thanks, that helps a lot. {GIF of a guy holding a piece of paper with the word "sarcasm" written on it}

Anthony: Sorry, Bro, I'm an old soul who's met my match. Since you're still a kid at heart, you should be good with a younger woman.

Bobby: Seriously, ya'll haven't had things pop up that you don't see eye to eye on because of the age difference? Or had issues with anyone saying something about ya'll's age difference?

Anthony: Only Kay the night we met. But once I convinced her that I looked older than her, nobody else has said anything. Not that I'd care what anyone else thinks. And you shouldn't either. Ask Josh & Jake if you don't believe me.

Bobby: Thanks, Bro.

Josh: Ask us what?

Jake: Dude, you freaking out about Brook being so young?

> **Bobby: Did Anthony not explain when he added you to our chat?**

Josh: Nope, only got his last message.

Figures our baby brother would just toss them in the middle of the conversation without explaining, Bobby thought, unable to keep texting since he had to drive to work. By the time he got to the station, his brothers had blown up his phone with messages and even added in his male cousins and a few of their best friends in the group chat. He waited until he was ensconced in his office behind closed doors to read through the rest of the messages.

Anthony: Bobby was asking me about issues with age differences in relationships. I think he's worried about being too old to ask Brie out.

Jake: Dude, you didn't tell Anthony that Brie is really Brooklyn?

Josh: Baby bro should have been at Sunday supper last night to hear the news.

Anthony: Brooklyn? As in the kidnapped heiress from Georgia the women have all been yapping about since Thanksgiving?

Jake: The 1 & the same. But don't tell anyone but family for now. We're trying to figure out everything that's going on in Georgia to make it safe for her to be herself again before we reveal where she's been for the last month.

Anthony: My lips are sealed. But we should probably just refer to her as Brie until it's safe for her to be herself

again. Especially since I think we need a few more opinions on the age difference between her & Bobby.

Josh: Agreed. Should we add our cousins to this chat, or maybe the Walkers & Hunters?

Jake: Just added them all. Hey, guys, what do ya'll think of Bobby asking Brie out? Or is he too old for the young hottie?

JJ: Go for it, Cuz.

Justin: Seemed like ya'll were already dating at dinner last night.

Luke: I'm surprised he hasn't asked her out yet. I've expected it to happen every day since the wedding reception when he met her.

Dean: Exactly how young is the hottie?

Jake: 22.

Josh: And Bobby's almost 30.

James: I don't see a problem with it. That's about the same age difference as Anthony & Kay.

Aiden: Are ya'll suggesting our Police Chief should be corrupting a beautiful young woman?

Hudson: Maybe I should ask her out since I'm so much closer to her age.

Hayden: Yeah, how did we miss meeting her at the reception?

Leo: If ya'll had seen the way Bobby was guarding her at Tully's the other night, you wouldn't be thinking about hitting on her.

Dalton: This the new chick hanging out with Kenzie, Ashley, & Heather on the dance floor the other night?

Leo: Yep.

Landon: It was kinda funny how Bobby growled at anyone who even looked at them.

Anthony: So, now that ya'll know who we're talking about, what do you think of Bobby asking her out?

Dean: Since Bobby's thinking about dating her, I guess he's figured out the girls' theory about her is wrong?

Jake: Shit, who all already knows?

Anthony: Dean, we'll discuss that later, privately.

Luke: Knows what?

Josh: State secrets that we'd have to kill you if we found out you knew & could expose things that need to be kept private for now.

Dean: I don't have a problem with their age difference, as long as there's no conflict of interest between them with his job & her secrets.

Aiden: Dude, I don't want to know about any secrets, especially ones you might want to kill me over.

Landon: Age is just a number, so don't worry about that. Ask her out if you want, Bobby.

Hudson: Better hurry it up, Old Man. Or else I'll ask her out first.

Fucking numbskulls! Bobby thought as he read through the conversational thread, suddenly worried that he would be the next person in town to get the "Old Man" moniker, like Old Man Thompson, for being so much older than his wife. *None of these guys actually understand what I originally asked Anthony. And if they're not careful, they'll expose Brie's real identity before we know it's safe for her.*

Bobby: I asked Anthony if there were issues I needed to watch out for when dating someone with such a large age difference between us, not whether or not I should ask her out because of the age difference. I want to make sure I don't do or say something to make her uncomfortable. I couldn't care less what anyone else thinks about me dating a younger woman. Now quit blowing up my phone, so I can actually get some work done.

Bobby closed out of the group chat before turning on his computer and going over the business of the day. His phone pinged a few more times, but he ignored it as he went through his email and looked at the reports from the weekend. Once that was done, he checked his phone just to make sure the message alerts were just the idiots in the group chat and nothing important. Luckily, the notifications were all just the guys offering him encouragement about dating Brie.

Just as he was about to go check with his staff to see if there was anything else he needed to work on before going on patrol, there was a knock on his door.

"Come in," Bobby called out, sitting back down in his chair where he'd just stood.

Bobby was surprised to see his brothers, Jake and Josh, walk through the door into his office. They shut the door behind them and offered their "good mornings" as they sat down in the chairs across from his desk.

"I take it you have some information for me," Bobby eyed Jake, once the greetings were concluded.

"Yeah, not something I felt comfortable discussing over the phone," Jake confirmed, pulling his laptop out of the messenger bag he'd carried in with him. "I got copies of the Ashbury wills this morning."

"Yeah?" Bobby questioned, impatient to hear what his brother had found in the wills. "And?"

"And it appears to me that your theory, about why her dad is trying to make her get married, is correct." Jake clicked through some screens on his computer before turning it toward Bobby for him to read the wills for himself. "But in addition to inheriting the company and the bulk of the Ashbury estate when she gets married, she should've been receiving a rather large monthly stipend to cover her living expenses until then. For the last eighteen years since her mother died. According to what I read, her father was to manage that money for her until she turned eighteen, but she should've had full access to it on her eighteenth birthday."

"But he didn't give her access to it, did he?" Bobby skimmed through the first will on the screen.

"No," Jake admitted. "And from what I've seen so far of their financials, Bradley Barns has been draining the account set up for Brooklyn every month for the last eighteen years. I haven't tracked where he's transferring the money to yet, but it's not goin' to his primary household account that he pays the utilities and household staff out of."

"You think he's been stealing it from her?" Bobby finally got to the point in her mother's will that spoke about her monthly stipend of fifty-thousand dollars. "Like transferring it offshore somewhere to hide it from both her and the IRS?"

"That's what it looks like." Jake nodded his head.

"How much money are we talking about?" Josh looked back and forth between his brothers.

"Total? About eleven million," Jake confirmed Bobby's mental math. "And that's just from Brooklyn's monthly stipend. If he's willing to take that from his own daughter, I bet he's taken more from the company coffers."

"Damn," Bobby swore at the same time Josh cursed out, "Shit." Obviously, both brothers were on the same page with their astonishment at the potential loss for Ashbury Enterprises with Bradley Barns at the helm.

"I think we need to talk to the feds about our suspicions, instead of just hacking into the company to find out all of Barns' and Donaldson's misdeeds," Jake suggested, looking conflicted about using his ability with computers to uncover everything.

"Yeah, you're probably right," Bobby admitted. "Anything you find without a warrant would be considered fruit of the poisoned tree and inadmissible in court to prosecute them for their crimes."

"You wanna reach out to your FBI contacts, or you want me to reach out to mine?" Jake asked Bobby.

"Maybe you should," Bobby sighed, hating that he couldn't be the one to fix the situation for Brie. "With you being based right outside DC, it'll be less likely for her dad to get wind of her being here if he has anyone in the bureau in his pocket."

"Will do." Jake nodded his agreement. "I'll wait until I go back to base in January, so there's no chance anyone will figure out it's information I gathered from home."

"And what are we supposed to do to help her now?" Josh inquired. "Or while the feds are dragging their feet with investigating the embezzlement?"

"I've got some feelers out to see where the Macon PD is with their investigation into the '*kidnapping*' and should know soon if anyone in Georgia has a clue where she's at," Jake informed them, using air quotes when he said the word "kidnapping" as he grinned at the inaccurate case description. "As long as she stays in disguise when she's not on the ranch, I'm pretty sure she'll be able to stay safely hidden until her father is arrested and we're ready to alert the media and authorities as to her whereabouts."

"You really think we need to wait until her father is arrested to tell the world where she is?" Josh smirked at Bobby like he had another plan.

"That's the safest thing for her for now," Bobby replied to his younger brother, only slightly curious as to what Josh's idea was for changing the timeline.

"Or you could just marry her and take her back to Georgia to claim her inheritance," Josh suggested, still smirking. "That would not only thwart her father's plan, but it would also give you the authority to investigate everything else, so we don't have to wait for the feds to drag their feet."

"No, we're not there yet in our relationship," Bobby disagreed, shaking his head at his younger brother. Even if he could picture himself marrying Brie in the future, he didn't think she was ready to tie the knot just yet. He had to be patient and take things slow with her because of her sexual inexperience. At the very least, he had to take her on a few dates and work up to doing more than giving her chaste kisses before he could talk to her about being an exclusive couple. Then it would probably take a few weeks, or maybe even months, before she'd be ready to talk long term like marriage.

"It would help speed things along to clear everything up," Jake grinned at his older brother.

"Even so, I doubt she'd agree to marry me when we haven't even gone on a date," Bobby argued, shaking his head at his brothers. "She's too sweet and innocent for me to push things along that fast. I'm gonna hafta take my time and woo her for a while before she'll be ready to talk marriage. Besides, asking her to marry me to gain control of her family business is too close to what her dad and Donaldson tried pulling on her. I don't wanna give her any reason to think I'm anything like them."

"True," Josh admitted, bobbing his head as if he was trying to think of another plan. "So, how are you gonna woo her?"

"For now, I'm just gonna keep being a friend." Bobby's shoulders slumped at the thought of having to stick to the friend zone for a while longer. "I'll gain her trust by being there for her and slowly increase the affection until she starts to return it. Then I'll ask her on a real date."

"You mean like the way you were holding her hand last night?" Josh looked at Bobby quizzically.

"Yeah," Bobby agreed. "Ya know, friendly hugs, and maybe putting my arm around her on the couch when we're watching TV at night, that kind of thing. But nothing too aggressive or overtly sexual. I'll wait for her to make the first move to take it to the next level as more than friends. She's got a lot on her plate right now, and I don't wanna overwhelm her by pushing for more than she's ready for, ya know."

"Yeah, I get it," Jake acknowledged as Josh nodded along in agreement. "She hasn't had control of much in her life, so you're gonna let her be in charge of your relationship."

"Wow!" Josh exclaimed, smirking again. "Never thought I'd see the day when one of my brothers would let a woman take the reins. But now I'm seeing it from both you and Anthony."

"Whatever, jackass," Bobby scoffed, grabbing a piece of paper off his desk, wadding it up, and tossing it at his brother's head. "Just wait 'til you meet *The One* and then you'll understand that a real man will do whatever his woman needs him to do to make her happy."

Josh batted the paper away as he chuckled, "Yeah, don't expect that to happen anytime soon."

They continued chatting for the hour it took Jake to update the computers at the police station, so Bobby wouldn't have any more trouble with the background checks he was doing for Burleson Incorporated. Bobby had him stick around to make sure there weren't any more issues as he redid the background checks that were problematic when he'd done them earlier in the month. When that was all done, Jake closed his laptop and slipped it back in his messenger bag as the brothers said their goodbyes for the afternoon.

Damn, I'm gonna miss those two jokers when they go back to base after the holidays.

<div align="center">~~~</div>

After an uncomfortable shopping trip to Destiny Dresses on Appaloosa Avenue right across the street from City Hall, Brooklyn was glad when Kenzie went around the corner on Angus Avenue and took them to the Caffeinated Cowpoke for a coffee break, before showing her around the rest of the town while looking for ideas for things for Bobby for Christmas.

She'd broken down and bought a pretty light pink bra and panty set as they'd looked through the lingerie section at the back of the dress shop. It was the only set of underwear she owned that wasn't virginal white and plain cotton. While she liked how the satin and lace looked, she wasn't sure she'd ever actually wear it. She just bought it to get Kenzie to quit hounding her about it, so they could leave the store and still have enough time to shop for Bobby before they were meeting their friends for lunch.

Once they had their mid-morning caffeine fix, they walked next door and browsed through the Book Nook. Brooklyn had loved seeing her books on display in the young adult section of the store, but she didn't find anything there that would be an appropriate gift for Bobby for Christmas.

From the Book Nook, they walked around the corner to the Knick Knack Shack on Mustang Lane. Most of the things in that store were collectables and decorative items that really didn't fit with Bobby's masculine vibe. She did find a cute mug, though, that read, "Behind every good Police Officer there is a supply of coffee and donuts," that she bought him, thinking she'd have to find a donut recipe to make him for breakfast soon.

When Brooklyn wasn't sure that the mug was enough, Kenzie drove her across town to Charolais Street to look around the Farm & Feed store, the Tackle Box, and Hunt'n Stuff, insisting that Bobby would love getting the supplies for more manly activities as a present. Not familiar with any of those activities or Bobby's need for any of the supplies for them, Brooklyn declined picking anything from any of the three stores.

They ended up going back toward the center of town on Appaloosa Avenue, stopping just after they crossed over Brangus Street to go into a store named Boots & Britches. While Brooklyn wasn't sure she'd find anything in the store when they first walked in, she was surprised to find several button-down shirts that she thought would look nice on Bobby. She ended up picking a green one that would bring out the vibrancy in his hazel eyes, along with a pair of jeans for herself, so he wouldn't tease her about wearing leggings the next time they went to ride the horses.

Finally satisfied that she had an appropriate gift for Bobby for Christmas, the girls made their way back toward the center of town to

Millie's Diner on Longhorn Lane. Ashley and Heather were already in the large circular booth in the corner waiting for them when they arrived. Knowing they were planning to exchange Christmas gifts while they were there, they insisted that they needed the biggest booth in the restaurant to make room for them and all their gifts.

Overwhelmed by food options she'd never even heard of before, Brooklyn decided to get her friends' opinions. "What's the best thing on the menu that I just have to try?"

"The patty melt," Kenzie replied, just as Heather called out, "the Texas caviar."

Not knowing what either of those were, Brooklyn looked to Ashley to see if she had another suggestion.

"Don't look at me." Ashley held her hands up in surrender. "I like everything on the menu, so it depends on what you're in the mood for to know what to recommend. If you want a full dinner, go with the chicken fried steak or the meatloaf. If you want something vegetarian and lighter, go with the Texas caviar, which is just a bean salad. And if you're in the mood for a burger, go with the patty melt."

Not wanting a super heavy meal with having to go home and cook dinner and not thinking a bean salad sounded super tasty, Brooklyn opted for the patty melt. Having not had many opportunities to eat burgers growing up, she was looking forward to the meal, and wasn't disappointed when her burger was served on thick toast with cheese adhering the meat to the bread.

"So, tell us how things are going with Bobby," Heather prodded. "Since you ditched us Saturday to go shopping with him, I expect to hear all the juicy details."

"Um, well, Saturday was just two friends shopping," Brooklyn shrugged, not really sure it was safe to tell her friends about all the revelations on Sunday while out in public. She looked around the room to make sure the rest of the people in the restaurant were far enough away from their booth that they wouldn't hear her whispering about her real identity to her friends. She lowered her voice, leaning in and motioning for them to all lean in too, so she could confide in the rest of her new girlfriends. "Ya'll have to promise to not say a word to anyone about what I'm about to tell you."

"Of course." Heather made an X across her heart. "Cross my heart, it'll go to the grave."

"Your secrets are safe with us," Ashley murmured, also crossing her heart as a sign of her promise.

"And you know I'm not gonna say anything, since I think you've already told me what you're about to tell the girls," Kenzie whispered, grinning like the cat that ate the canary from already knowing the secret.

When the other two looked hurt by not being in the loop before now, Brooklyn tried to console them by saying, "Yeah, but only because you showed up this morning before I had my contacts in and started to figure it out."

"Contacts?" Heather reached over to turn Brooklyn's head in her direction, so she could see into her eyes. "Are those colored contacts?"

"Yes," Brooklyn replied. "I have to maintain my disguise by coloring my hair and wearing colored contacts until Bobby and his family can figure out how to make it safe for me to be myself again. I'm really Brooklyn Barns. Brie Brooks is my pen name for writing my books."

"Whoa!" Ashley whisper-shouted. "No wonder I thought you looked familiar but couldn't place it. You've been all over the news for like a month now."

"Shush!" Brooklyn hushed her friend, trying to covertly make sure nobody else heard her. "If it gets out who I am and where I'm staying, my father will send in an army to take me back to Georgia and force me to get married. Please, you can't blow my cover."

"Sorry," Ashley whispered, looking contrite.

"Since you said Bobby and his family are working on making it safe for you to come out of hiding, I take it you told them all who you are," Heather inquired, still leaning in conspiratorially.

"Actually, Bobby figured it out yesterday," Brooklyn admitted.

"And professed his feelings for her when he told her he knew," Kenzie whisper-shouted, like she couldn't hold it in any longer. "He was conflicted because he fell in love at first sight with both Brooklyn and Brie and didn't know how to handle falling for two different women. Now that he knows they're one in the same, I expect he'll step up his game when it comes to pursuing Brie."

"Wait." Ashley held up her hand to stop the conversation while she got something cleared up in her head. "Are we supposed to still call you Brie? Or would you prefer we call you Brooklyn?"

"Stick with Brie in public," Brooklyn smiled at her friend who obviously wanted to make her feel most comfortable. "Once I'm safe to be me again without the hair dye and colored contacts, you can call me Brook."

"Cool." Ashley sat back in the booth and raised her voice a little as the waitress brought their food. "So, Brie, now that Bobby has professed his love for you, it's time for you to tell us how good of a kisser he is and when you expect to do the deed."

Brooklyn felt her cheeks heat and knew she was flushing from the waitress hearing that question. She couldn't have made herself respond if she had to with how embarrassed she was from such a blatant sexual question in front of others. She covered her face with her hands and took a moment to breathe and regain her composure before looking back at her friends after the waitress had left their meals in front of them.

"I haven't kissed him yet," she finally admitted in a tone just above a whisper, after swallowing her first bite of the heavenly goodness known as a patty melt. "Though having him hold me and rub my back while I cried yesterday was very nice."

"Oh, you lucky bitch," Heather blurted, slightly louder than a normal conversational tone. "What I wouldn't give for a cuddle from one of the Burleson boys."

"You and me both," Ashley grinned. "Though Bobby wouldn't be my first choice, I bet his big strong arms felt amazing around you."

"Amazing would be a pretty good description," Brooklyn admitted with a sigh, almost feeling his arms around her again as she remembered sitting on his lap while he comforted her the day before. "And last night at dinner with his family, he kept holding my hand, or putting his arm over my shoulders. It was all innocent touching, nothing even remotely sexual, but I loved feeling like he was showing me that he was there for me to lean on if I needed him while I told them everything."

"There's that dreamy look again," Kenzie teased, pointing at Brooklyn with the hand not holding her patty melt. "It's so obvious how far gone she is for him every time she talks about him and gets that look on her face."

"So, after dinner with his family, did he at least ask you out on a date?" Heather looked hopeful on Brooklyn's behalf.

"No," Brooklyn replied with a shrug. "But we pretty much have dinner together every night, so I don't really expect him to ask me to go out somewhere else to eat."

"Oh, no, don't you dare let him get away with that." Ashley pointed at Brooklyn with her fork. "You make him ask you out on a date before you let him go past holding your hand. Fixing dinner is part of your job, not a prelude to him getting in your panties."

Brooklyn choked on the bite she'd just taken at Ashley's outrageous statement. Heather slapped her on the back, helping her dislodge the lump in her throat before she washed it the rest of the way down with a drink of her tea.

"I don't think I'll ever get used to the way ya'll talk about stuff like that so easily," Brooklyn confessed when she could finally speak again.

"Yeah, you will," Ashley smiled. "And if Bobby's half as good as I've heard, you'll be walking bowlegged by New Year's and be more confident in speaking sexual innuendo than all three of us by Valentine's Day."

"That is so, not, going to happen," Brooklyn denied, shaking her head at her friends.

They continued their conversation as they ate, with the girls specifically asking for an invite to the ranch later that week while Jake and Josh were home for the holidays. Brooklyn told them that they were all welcome to come have dinner with her and Bobby anytime they wanted, but she didn't feel comfortable inviting them to the dinners happening at Hazel and Bob's house with the whole family, as she wasn't a member of the family to have the right to invite anyone there.

Once they were finished eating, they exchanged gifts. Brooklyn felt a little lame when they all opened t-shirts from her, and they all gave her lingerie. The girls explained that without boyfriends, they didn't have the prospect of getting lingerie as gifts from anyone but each other, so that was what they normally exchanged as gifts. After apologizing for not telling her in advance of the tradition, they told her she could redeem herself on Valentine's Day when they would do another girlfriend gift exchange.

Thank goodness, it's just sexy nighties and not actual sex toys they expect me to shop for next time, Brooklyn thought as she was putting her new things away when she got home. *Although, I suppose I could order those online and not be embarrassed by having to go into a store to buy them. If Bobby doesn't at least kiss me soon, I may have to order one for myself to alleviate the ache I have for him to kiss and touch me everywhere.*

~~~

Tuesday, December 25, 2018, Christmas Day

After another enjoyable night talking with Brie over dinner and then watching a movie that led to her falling asleep and leaning over into his side half the night, Bobby was exceptionally aroused when he awoke on Christmas morning. She'd cuddled so nicely into his side as she slept that Bobby hadn't been able to disturb her by moving when the movie was over. Instead, he turned slightly, so he could prop his legs up on the extension of the sectional, and spent the night mostly sitting up cradling her to his chest. He hadn't gotten much sleep, but waking up with her wrapped in his arms was worth the lost z's.

Apparently, they'd moved somehow overnight, so they were both laying on their sides with his back pressed against the back of the sofa and her back pressed into his front. She was using his bottom arm as a pillow, while his top arm was draped across her midsection. He had to resist the urge to pull her back into him to get closer. Still, it was all he could do not to grind his rock-hard cock into her perky ass when they were laying so close.

Damn, now I understand why people talk about liking to spoon their partners, Bobby thought, realizing it was the first time he'd ever spooned anyone. *This is really nice. And I bet it'll be even better when we can do it naked.*

Not wanting to alarm her with his obvious arousal first thing, he took the throw pillow out from under his head and slowly slid it under her head as he pulled his arm out from under her, trying to be as gentle
~~~

as possible. It wasn't easy for him to manipulate his six-foot-five, two-hundred-and-thirty-pound frame out from behind her on the couch without waking her, but he somehow managed.

He went upstairs and changed into running clothes, all the while telling his over-eager cock to wait until he got back and in the shower for his morning release. Instead of running his normal loop around the south pastures, he ran to his parents' house, so he could pick up one of the presents he'd gotten for Brie and left under their tree with all the gifts for his family. Since he'd wrapped them as two separate gifts, he decided to give her the journals at home on Christmas morning, knowing he would still have the tablet under the tree for her when they opened presents with the family on Saturday.

When he got back from his run, he found fresh coffee in the coffee pot in the kitchen and Brie no longer asleep on the sofa. He heard her shower running as he made his way upstairs and groaned as he walked toward the front of the house to his own bedroom and bathroom. He couldn't hold it in when the thought of Brie naked and wet in the shower instantly brought back his morning wood.

Maybe I should've taken care of this before the run? Bobby wondered before quickly ruling it out as a useless endeavor. *I'd still be hard and need to jack off again now, even if I'd already choked the chicken this morning. Damn, that's a terrible analogy. Let's rephrase that to even if I'd already shook hands with Thor this morning. Yep, much better.* Bobby chuckled to himself as he dropped Brie's present on his bed before stripping off his running shorts and t-shirt to get in the shower.

While imagining Brie on her knees in front of him in the shower and her pretty, pink lips wrapped around his cock, it only took a few minutes for him to temporarily relieve his need for her. Though he knew it probably wouldn't ever happen due to his size, Brie sucking his cock had quickly become his go-to fantasy because it was guaranteed to get him off almost instantly.

"Fuck, Brie," he growled out as he released his load all over the shower wall, hoping he wasn't so loud that she could hear him. He grabbed the handheld shower nozzle and rinsed his swimmers down the drain before actually washing up.

Once he'd finished his normal routine in the bathroom, he threw on jeans and a green Henley in honor of the holiday. He paired his casual clothing with cowboy boots in case they decided to spend any time with the horses before or after their family dinner that afternoon. Normally he would've put on a uniform for the holiday, since he was technically on call. But since Dusty Deere, Bobby's only detective and second-in-command in the Heart's Destiny Police Department, was first on call for Christmas Day, he decided it would be okay for him to keep it casual. If he got a call, he could always grab his badge and gun before taking his cruiser to the scene without really having to wear the whole uniform.

When he went downstairs, Bobby found Brie carrying down wrapped packages that he knew were the gifts she'd purchased with him the previous Saturday and wanted to take up to his parents' house early for the gift exchange the following Saturday.

"Is that everything?" Bobby motioned to the stack of presents on the dining table.

"No, there are a few more upstairs still," Brie smiled at him as she put the stack she was carrying down alongside the others and turned to walk back upstairs to get the rest.

He followed quickly behind her to help her carry the rest of the presents down, enjoying the view of her heart-shaped ass, hugged nicely in a pair of jeans. *Damn, I should've gotten her a pair of cowboy boots, so she wouldn't have to wear those sneakers the next time I get her on the back of a horse. Though I suppose I should be glad she listened to me when I told her she needs jeans for on the ranch, and bought a pair that clings to her curves so nicely.*

Bobby felt an unusual pang in his chest at not being the one to buy the jeans for her. He wasn't sure what was up with his sudden desire to shop for her, but he thought it might have something to do with his inner caveman that his dad had told him about that needed to provide for his mate. Shaking off the strange predilections, he held out his arms and told Brie to "load me up" with the packages that still needed to be carried downstairs and out to the car.

She laughed at his insistence in carrying a stack of presents three times the size of the stack she'd previously carried down, and Bobby reveled in the joyous sound coming from the beautiful woman in front of him. Once he had everything carried down, he stopped Brie before they went to take the packages to the car.

"Before we go to Mom and Dad's," Bobby implored her, picking up the box he'd brought back from their place earlier that morning and handing it to her. "I want you to go ahead and open this one today. There's still a second one for you under the tree for Saturday, but I wanted you to have something on the actual holiday, too."

"Oh, wait," Brie exclaimed, not taking the box from him but rummaging through the boxes she'd carried down first before handing him a small box as well. "I bought you two presents, too. So, this is perfect for us to swap today and Saturday."

They each took the gift from the other one, but Bobby didn't open his until after he watched Brie open hers. He shook his head and chuckled as he watched her carefully open the present without tearing the paper. *She and Kay are both in for an eye-opening experience when our family rips into the presents on Saturday,* Bobby thought, deciding his sisters and female cousins had to be different than most women when opening presents, since both Brie and Kay were so delicate when they opened them.

"Oh, Bobby, this is perfect," Brie gushed, reverently running her hands over the books and multi-colored pens in the box. "How did you know I'm almost out of space in my idea books?"

"I've just seen you flipping through them," he shrugged. "Figured even if you didn't need new ones immediately, you'd use them eventually."

"Well, thank you," she smiled, putting the box down on the table and going up on her tiptoes to press a kiss to his cheek.

No, that was perfect, he thought, still feeling his face tingle where her lips had brushed as he moved to open the gift she'd given him. He wasn't near as careful with opening the package as Brie had been. Once the paper was ripped off and fluttering to the floor, he opened the box to find a coffee cup with what looked to be a homemade book of some sort inside it. He pulled the booklet of papers out first, flipping through them to see a couple dozen coupons that read, "Donuts for breakfast tomorrow."

"Read the mug and those will make more sense," Brie insisted, smiling shyly up at him.

Bobby pulled the mug out of the box and read it, chuckling at her cop and donut reference. "So, are you gonna make me these donuts or go get them from Kara's?" Bobby referenced the coupon book still in his hand by lifting it a couple of inches higher than he'd been holding it.

"Make them, of course." Brie gave him a beaming smile. "I found several recipes for them online yesterday, so I'll have a variety of types for you to try until we figure out which ones you like best."

"Thank you, Brie." Bobby put his mug and coupon book back in the box and sat them on the table beside her gift. *If she can kiss me as a thank you, I can kiss her as a thank you, too, right?*

Bobby mentally reminded himself to keep it chaste as he tilted her chin up and bent down to brush his lips across hers. It took every ounce of willpower he possessed to keep from pushing her further than she was ready to go, wanting nothing more than to pick her up and press her against the wall while he plundered her mouth with his tongue.

Fucking put the hammer away, Thor. There will be no pounding into her today. Bobby silently told his engorged cock as he pulled back from the all too brief kiss. She stood there for a long moment, appearing to be as dazed as he felt from their short smooch, before turning her attention back to the things she needed him to help her load into the car to go to dinner with his family. *Thank fuck! Maybe it won't be as long as I feared before we're doing more than innocent kisses.*

~ ~ ~

Brooklyn was floating on cloud nine after her all too fleeting lip lock with Bobby before they left to go to his parents' house for Christmas dinner. She couldn't believe she'd finally had her first real kiss, and it was with the most attractive man she'd ever seen. *Though was it a real kiss since it didn't include our tongues? It wasn't a peck either, like the cheek kiss I gave him to thank him for his thoughtful gift. There was definitely lip movement, and not just my lip movement, so I'm counting it as my first real kiss. I can't wait until he kisses me again. And next time I might even be brave enough to open my mouth, so we can use our tongues.*

She'd been so dazzled by the experience that she almost forgot to take the cake she'd made the day before with them when they'd finished carrying out all the presents. They were actually a couple hours early for dinner, having left their house at ten a.m., but everyone was already milling about talking about taking a trail ride as a family before eating at noon. *Is it really dinner when it's being served at lunch time?* Brooklyn wondered, thinking the word "dinner" signified the evening meal.

Brooklyn helped Bobby carry the presents in and put them under the tree in the formal living room before they carried the cake to the dining room.

"Brook, Bobby, I have some news for ya'll," Jake greeted them as soon as he saw them enter the family room, where the rest of the younger generation of Burlesons was gathered.

"Damn, that was fast, Bro." Bobby slapped a hand on his brother's shoulder as soon as they were within arm's reach.

"You know I don't waste time," Jake grinned at his older brother.

Brooklyn took a moment to compare the brothers while they were standing side by side, finding it strange that she was only attracted to Bobby when they looked so much alike. Bobby was a couple inches taller than Jake and a little more muscular, even though they were both pretty lean for their over six-foot-tall heights. They both had dark brown hair and similar facial features, right down to the dimples when they smiled, which wasn't nearly often enough as it should be in Brooklyn's opinion. Other than their eye color difference—Bobby's being hazel and Jake's being brown—they looked more alike than Jake and his twin, Josh. When Brooklyn really thought about it, Jake and Anthony looked the most alike—other than their approximately three-inch height difference and Anthony's lack of dimples—since they both had the same color hair and eyes. Josh actually looked more like his cousin Justin with their lighter brown hair and lighter eyes.

"Did you catch any of that, Brie?" Bobby got her attention, bringing Brooklyn back to the moment and out of her mental comparisons between the Burleson boys.

"No, sorry." Brooklyn shook her head, hoping she didn't blush at being caught ogling the men around her.

"I found the offshore account where your money's been hidden," Jake informed her, referring to the money Bobby had told her about the night before that was supposed to be a monthly stipend for her living expenses from her mother's will that her father had been keeping from her for the last eighteen years since her mother had passed away. "I've got all the info you should need to give to your attorney to be able to get it back when this mess is all cleared up. Technically, law enforcement can't use what I found to prosecute him without getting a warrant and finding it on their own, but you can use it in a civil suit against him as the aggrieved party, who hired a private investigator to track down the money he stole from you."

"Oh," was all Brooklyn could say, still reeling from the way her father had deceived her all her life and stolen the money her mother had intended to go to her. Thankfully, Bobby must have recognized her lost, lonely, little girl expression and wrapped his arm around her shoulders, instantly making her feel stronger with his support beside her. She didn't know why she felt better when he innocently comforted her, but she was grateful he was there for her when she felt like she had nobody else to help ease the burden of her old life.

"I'd recommend waiting to do that for now, though," Jake advised. "Let us get the feds on the case to make sure he's prosecuted for what I suspect he's been embezzling from Ashbury Enterprises as well, so you can get him removed as the trustee of your inheritance first."

"Yeah, okay," Brooklyn agreed, taking a deep breath, and leaning into Bobby for support. "You'll keep track of all that in case he tries to move the money when he realizes the feds are looking at his finances?"

"Definitely," Jake smiled at her reassuringly. "I set up a backdoor hack, so I'll be notified if any money is moved into or out of that account. I don't think anyone will notice it if they go snooping in it behind me, but just in case, I didn't do the same when I looked at the Ashbury Enterprises accounts. I wanna make sure the FBI can prosecute him for what it looks like he's stolen from there, so I didn't wanna leave my virtual fingerprints where they might jeopardize the case."

"You think he's embezzled a lot from Ashbury?" Brooklyn felt disgusted at the thought of her father being capable of stealing from the company built by her maternal grandfather that was passed down to be her mother's legacy.

"Yeah," Jake affirmed, scratching his head like he was uncomfortable with what he was about to say. "And I don't think it was just him. I didn't dig too deep to follow the money trail out of

Ashbury, but there were definitely unusual transfers going out to more than one offshore account. I'm thinking the marriage wasn't the only arrangement between your father and Clayton Donaldson."

Brooklyn closed her eyes and sucked in a deep breath, counting to ten as she blew it out trying to calm the wild emotions running through her at the moment.

"It's okay, Brie-Baby," Bobby consoled her, squeezing her into his side. "I've got you. You don't have to worry about them anymore. We'll figure it all out and fix it for you."

"Thank you," Brooklyn choked out, desperately trying not to break down and cry on his shoulder again. Regardless of what might or might not happen between them in the future, Brooklyn was grateful to have Bobby at her side to help her get through the ordeal that had become her life.

~~~

Wednesday, December 26, 2018

Brooklyn was busy on Wednesday, trying to make sure everything she'd not gotten done the day before at Bobby's house was finished, as well as the cleaning she needed to do at Justin's house. She should've realized that she needed to do some laundry at home on Monday, but she was too preoccupied with needing to have time off the ranch for shopping and visiting with her friends that it had slipped her mind. That meant she didn't have time to take breaks to write down the story ideas that popped into her head, even though she spent the whole day imagining different tales taking place in the make-believe world in her mind, instead of dwelling on her problems.

Since she'd started hanging out with her new friends, who talked about sex a lot more than she'd ever been around before, and started reading the romance novels Kay had recommended, Brooklyn's characters were living out more risqué storylines in her head. *It's probably a good thing I haven't had time to write down any of those ideas,* she thought as she was pulling the rolls from the oven that she'd made to go with the baked ziti she'd made for dinner that night. *If I*
~~~

ever write a book like that, I'll have to do it under a new pen name, so none of the kids who've read my other books accidentally read it.

She packaged up the portions of dinner that would go to Justin and JJ the next day, along with the one set aside as Bobby's lunch for later in the week. She'd just put those in the refrigerator when Bobby walked in the back door. The butterflies in her belly fluttered around like crazy the instant she saw him in his way too sexy police uniform.

Seriously, when did I become the girl who thought of a uniform as sexy? I've never thought anything like that before. It must just be because it's him wearing it. He's sexy, so therefore, whatever he wears is sexy. Now I just have to figure out how to keep myself from drooling all over the man, so we can have dinner without me making a fool of myself.

"How was work?" Brooklyn moved over to the cupboard to take down a couple of plates to start dishing up their dinners.

"Not too bad," Bobby replied, his smile making her stomach feel like it was doing somersaults in her belly. "We had a couple calls about some unruly teenagers breaking into the high school gym because they didn't have anything better to do with their time off for the holidays. So, we carted them over to the 4-H building and put them to work mucking stalls in lieu of arresting them for breaking and entering."

"What's the 4-H building?" Brooklyn wasn't quite sure what Bobby was talking about. "And is putting them to work like that actually legal? Don't they have to be convicted of a crime and imprisoned before you put them on a work detail?"

"4-H is the youth center over by the rodeo arena on Charolais," Bobby answered while pulling down two glasses to pour them each a glass of sweet tea to drink with dinner. "And it wasn't like a prison work detail. They're bored kids, who just wanted to go in and play basketball for something to do. Since there was no malicious intent, I gave them the option of what they wanted to do. I could arrest them for breaking and entering, or they could go to the youth center and do something productive with their day. They were smart enough to choose the option that wouldn't go on their permanent record and risk their futures. Plus, they got snacks and supervision at the youth center to go along with the information about the different programs they can participate in there to not be bored, including access to the basketball courts at the center, so they won't be tempted to break into the gym again."

"You're a total softy, Bobby Burleson," Brooklyn teased, grinning at him. "Nothing like the grumpy, hard-nosed cop everyone warned me about when I first arrived in town."

"Hush now," Bobby playfully admonished, shaking his finger at her and making a stern face that just made her giggle. "Don't be spreadin' stories around town about me being soft on crime. I need to maintain my grumpy, hard-nosed, crime fighter image to keep the townsfolk in line."

"Sure," Brooklyn squeaked out between giggles. "Your secret, softy side is safe with me."

Bobby broke character, where he was trying to act dour and tough, chuckling with Brooklyn as they carried their plates and drinks to the dining room to eat dinner.

"So, how was your day?" Bobby inquired once they were seated and starting to eat. "Get any breaks to get some writing done?"

"Busy with catching up on what I missed doing yesterday on top of my normal routine for Wednesdays," Brooklyn stated between bites. "But I got it all done, even if I didn't have time to jot down my story ideas in between tasks."

"Oh, you, uh, need to write them down now?" Bobby gave her a look of concern that she wasn't quite sure how to interpret. "So you don't forget them?"

"Oh, no," Brooklyn waved off his suggestion. "None of the ideas I had today would work for my current book, or even the characters I'm developing in my head for the next series, so it's no big deal if I forget them."

"You sure?" Bobby arched an eyebrow at her, holding his fork in midair, so he could speak before taking his next bite. "It may not seem like a big deal to forget these ideas now, but who's to say they won't be best sellers for you in a few years?"

"No, they're not really right for my demographic," Brooklyn explained, feeling herself blush at the memory of what she'd pictured in her head earlier in the day. "I'm sure I'll remember them well enough to tell Kay about them next time I see her. I think they might work better in the books she was telling me about wanting to write."

"Ah," Bobby drawled, giving her a knowing look. He shoveled a big forkful of pasta into his mouth and grinned with his mouth closed as he chewed.

Please don't ask me about the books Kay wants to write, Brooklyn thought, taking her own huge bite, so she couldn't speak if he did ask. *I can't talk about romance novels and the steamy sex scenes in them with the man I'm crushing on. It's hard enough talking about them with Kay and my other female friends.*

Think, Brooklyn, think! What can I change the subject to before he finishes chewing to get us away from potentially embarrassing discussions?

Brooklyn was apparently too slow in coming up with a new topic and was still chewing her pasta when Bobby swallowed his. "She's writing romance novels, right?"

Grateful for her full mouth, Brooklyn nodded her head. She was hopeful that the acknowledgment would be enough to drop the subject, but her hopes were soon dashed.

"Brie-Baby," Bobby drawled out in a low, sexy tone of voice that made Brooklyn's nipples harden and her thighs clench together to cover the desire building in her core. "Were you thinking about dirty book scenes today?"

Brooklyn was mortified at even the thought of answering Bobby's question truthfully. She sat there in shock for several long moments, unable to move, much less respond to his inquiry. She was so frozen in place that she forgot to chew, swallow, or even breathe.

"Hey, you okay?" Bobby looked at her with concern, but she barely registered it as the room started to fade out. "Breathe, Brie-Baby, breathe. Shit, you're pale as a ghost."

Bobby got up from his seat across the table from Brooklyn, coming around the end to kneel at her side and start rubbing her back. He continued speaking in a low, soothing tone, but Brooklyn couldn't comprehend the words. After a few minutes, all the color that had drained from her face started to return.

"There you are," Bobby crooned, bringing Brooklyn's attention back to him, where he was kneeling beside her chair and gently rubbing her back with one hand while holding her hand in the other. "Sorry, I didn't mean to freak you out by teasing you a little."

Brooklyn quickly finished chewing the bite of pasta that was still sitting on her tongue, wanting to safely swallow it before she tried to speak. She rinsed it down with a drink of her tea before turning to look Bobby in the eyes. His hazel orbs still showed his concern for her, but they also held a twinkle of something Brooklyn couldn't identify.

"Sorry, I, uh, don't know what happened just now," Brooklyn muttered tentatively, not quite sure how to classify that episode. *Was that a panic attack? Or just an extreme case of embarrassment that froze me in place?*

"I'm not sure either," Bobby admitted, making her wonder if she'd spoken her thoughts aloud. "One minute I was trying to flirt by teasing you a little and the next minute I thought you were gonna pass out. I was a little worried you'd choke on your delicious dinner, so I got into position to be able to catch you if you went out and Heimlich you if needed. Do you have a history of absence seizures?"

"Nah-no," Brooklyn stuttered. "Is that what just happened?"

"That's what it looked like to me," Bobby shrugged, still looking concerned. "But I'd rather call Doc Hayes and have him evaluate you to make sure."

"No!" Brooklyn exclaimed, horrified at the thought of Bobby calling a doctor out to the ranch when she wasn't sure she could reveal her true identity to him. "I, uh, I mean, I've never had a seizure before, so I don't think that's what that was."

"No?" Bobby tilted his head as he observed her. "What do you think it was?"

"I think I just froze up," Brooklyn confessed, feeling her cheeks heat, and knowing she was blushing at her admission. "Extreme embarrassment can trigger the fight, flight, or freeze response, so I'm sure that's all it was, not a medical emergency by any means."

"Damn, Brie-Baby, now I'm really sorry," Bobby apologized, squeezing her hand in his much larger one. "I obviously suck at flirting and should've known better than to think we're at the point in our relationship where we can share our sexual fantasies without freaking you out because I'm moving too fast."

"Oh," was all Brooklyn could say to his inadvertent revelation about having sexual fantasies that included her. As she processed his words, her curiosity got the better of her and before she could stop herself, she blurted, "How soon in a relationship do you normally share your sexual fantasies with a woman?"

Apparently, it was Bobby's turn to blush since his cheeks pinkened under his slight five o'clock shadow. "Um, I, uh, don't really," he stuttered, much like she had earlier. "I don't really have relationships."

"So, you haven't, uh, you know…" Brooklyn started to ask, her voice trailing off when she couldn't figure out how to ask if he'd talked dirty to his hookups without turning as red as the tomato sauce she'd used in their dinner.

~~~

Fuck! I don't wanna tell her about all the random one-night stands I've had over the years, Bobby thought, hating how he was going to have to answer her question. *I can't exactly let her keep thinking I'm a virgin either, though. Fuck!*

"No, I have," he exclaimed, his voice going up an octave higher than normal like a pubescent teenager. "Way more than I'm proud to admit."

Fuck. Fuck. Fuck! Spit it out, jackass!

Bobby sat back on his heels, removing his hand from Brie's back to run it through his hair. He looked down at the floor before finally speaking. "I've just never wanted to lead a girl on, so I've kept my hookups to one or two nights for mutual release and nothing more."

"So, you're, uh, used to talking about s-e-x?" Brie blushed as she spelled out the last word. "Like the first day you meet them?"

"Yeah, pretty much," Bobby reluctantly admitted. "But that's because I knew that's all it would be with them. You're different. Special."

Fuck! I'm screwing this up. Why do I feel so tongue-tied and unable to explain clearly what I want for us in the future?

"Special?" Brie questioned. "How? How do you know whatever this is you think you feel for me will be more than one of your hookups?"

"I, fuck!" Bobby shouted, jumping up and walking back over to his seat at the dining table before trying again to get the words out. "I
~~~

don't know how to explain it. I just know we're meant to be. You and I, we, we're gonna go the distance. Have a long life together like my mom and dad, and my grandparents, and several generations of my great-grandparents before them."

Bobby reached across the table and took Brie's hand that was resting beside her half-eaten plate. "You are the most beautiful woman I've ever seen," he told her imploringly. "And I definitely wanna get to the sexual stage of our relationship. But I know it's more important to build a strong foundation that will last us through the years than to jump straight into bed together. So, I'm really trying to take things slow with you. But sometimes, hell a lot of the time, it's really hard to hold back everything I imagine doing with you."

"Oh," Brie breathed out the word, her mouth forming a perfect O and holding there, like she was stuck there trying to comprehend everything he was saying.

Just as Bobby was about to suggest they plan their first date to start easing their toes into the relationship waters, Brie blurted, "I'm a virgin." She quickly slapped her hand over her mouth, almost as if she was shocked she'd said the words. Her beautiful blue eyes were wide as she looked at him across the table.

Bobby's lips turned up in the corners in a slow, seductive smile. "I kinda figured that out from everything you've told me about your life before coming here," he confided, winking at her, and squeezing the hand he still held to try to reassure her that he was okay with her virginal status. His inner caveman actually loved her being a virgin, wanting to be the only man to ever be inside her. "Yet another reason why I wanna slow things down and court you properly before we move to the next stage in our relationship. I wanna make sure you're one-hundred percent comfortable with everything we ever do together. So, I will gladly wait until you're ready for us to do more than hold hands or chastely kiss."

"What if I want to do more than hold hands or chastely kiss, but I don't know what steps come between that and going all the way, which I know I'm not ready for?" Brie shyly looked down at her plate instead of at him.

"Then we'll start with dating." Bobby leaned across the table and pulled her hand up, so he could kiss the back of it. As he gently laid their joined hands back down on the table in between them, he continued. "And I'll teach you one thing at a time, sticking with whatever you're comfortable with for as long as we need to, until you're ready for more."

"Okay," Brie agreed, giving him one of those genuine smiles he'd longed to see on her face since the first time he saw her picture. "What do you want to teach me first? And when do you want to start teaching me?"

"I thought we might go on our first date on Friday." Bobby was already formulating a plan to take her to a restaurant on the RiverWalk in San Antonio, so she wouldn't have to cook dinner for him Friday night. "But we can practice cuddling on the couch while watching movies tonight if you're ready to get started on maybe some more advanced kissing techniques."

"You're the teacher," Brie smiled coyly at him. "I'm good with following whatever lesson plan you set."

Fuck! Don't even think about progressing to teacher and naughty schoolgirl role play, Bobby chastised himself in his head. *I'm definitely gonna hafta take care of this hard-on in the shower before we get comfortable on the couch.*

"Then let's hurry up and finish dinner," Bobby advised, picking his fork back up to eat the baked ziti that Brie had made them for dinner. "I'll need a few minutes to wash off the day and change out of my uniform before we can start a movie, too."

"Sorry, I guess I should've kept this warm for you to go get comfortable before dinner," Brie apologized, slightly blushing as she started eating again.

"Naw," Bobby disagreed, grinning at her. "I kinda like coming home to find you barefoot in the kitchen with dinner hot and ready."

Damn, I hope that didn't sound too much like a sexist pig, who wants his little woman to have dinner on the table as soon as he gets home from work.

"Not that I mind having to reheat it after changing out of my work clothes when you cook earlier in the day either," he added, hoping to sound less like an ass than he thought his first statement came out. "Whatever works best for your schedule with everything else is fine with me, Brie-Baby."

"Why do you call me that?" Brie thankfully changed the subject, so Bobby could quit putting his foot in his mouth.

"Brie? It's who you introduced yourself to me as, so that's who I think of you as," Bobby shrugged. "And since it's the alias you're currently using, I figured I should keep using it, so I don't accidentally call you Brooklyn when we're out in public and tip off anyone who doesn't need to know where you are yet."

"No, I understood the needing to keep using the alias thing." Brie shook her head, still looking at him quizzically as they continued to talk while they ate. "But you've called me Brie-Baby several times over the past few days. Why?"

"I guess it's just my twist on a pet name for you," Bobby confessed with a self-deprecating lift of one shoulder. "My dad calls my mom Baby, and Anthony calls Kay Baby. I guess I'm not creative enough to use a different term of endearment than the rest of my family, but I still wanted to make it special for you. Why? Do you not like it? I'll change it if you don't like it."

"No, I like it," Brie blurted, her smile beaming through her eyes. "I just wondered where you came up with it. It's different than the darlin' I've heard most Texans use for everyone they meet."

"Like I said earlier, you're special," Bobby smiled after finishing the last of his dinner. "I wanna call you something nobody else does."

And hopefully none of the guys will ever ask me about it, Bobby thought as she smiled at the sentiment. *Because they'd revoke my man card for being so sappy.*

Chapter Eight

Brooklyn wasn't getting much done on the book she was supposed to be finishing soon. Instead of writing, while she waited for the turkey tetrazzini she was cooking to take to JJ and Justin's houses to finish in the oven, she was daydreaming about the last two nights of cuddling and kissing with Bobby. She didn't have to cook dinner for Bobby, since he was taking her out to eat that night, so she'd decided to prepare the other Burlesons' meals first thing that morning. Then she'd check in with Kay to see if she needed anything done at her house that afternoon, when she delivered them to the houses on the north side of the ranch.

Normally when she was caught up with the cleaning and only sitting around waiting on meals to finish cooking, she would set up her laptop and work on her book. But since she'd had her first kiss with Bobby on Christmas day, all of her creative output had too much kissing included to be appropriate for her young adult readers. Especially after the last two nights, when they'd missed most of the movies they'd tried to watch while practicing French kissing.

She'd been a little worried on Wednesday night when Bobby suggested starting with more advanced kissing techniques, thinking she'd put too much garlic in the ziti for swapping spit to be tasty. But she'd taken advantage of the time Bobby needed to go get changed out of his uniform and into a t-shirt and workout shorts to go upstairs and brush her teeth, so she wouldn't ruin their first tongue kiss with bad breath. Thankfully, Bobby had done the same, so her first open-mouthed kisses were all minty fresh.

Maybe Kay can help me figure out how far to let Mary Kate go with the cowboy cop who rescued her from dastardly Donald? Maybe it'll be okay to have them kiss a few times in the book, and end it with them getting married and living happily ever after without being too graphic for young readers?

She thought the kisses she'd shared with Bobby recently were probably okay to describe, especially since they never actually touched each other's private parts. They hugged, but it was always with her arms around his waist or neck and his arms around her torso. Their hands were limited to touching the other's back or hair, not anything really inappropriate. And even when they hugged, they didn't press their bodies together enough to even have more than the barest incidental contact between her breasts and his chest.

The only reason she knew he was aroused by their kissing sessions was because she could see his bulge in his athletic shorts. He never let her get close enough to his manhood to feel it pressed against her in any way, no matter how much she wished he had.

I hope he doesn't wait too long before he starts teaching me about more intimate types of touching each other. Surely, we can touch each other over our clothes without it being too much. Right? I mean, I know I want to learn more than just kissing from him. I'm not sure I completely believe everything he's said about it being love at first sight, and a forgone conclusion that we're meant to spend the rest of our lives together, but I do know I like him enough to want to explore what we could be, eventually.

With everything up in the air back in Georgia, it's impossible to know if we'll be able to stay together once everything is cleared up. If my father and Clayton are both arrested for embezzlement, I may have to go back to Georgia to take over running things at Ashbury Enterprises. Not that I know how to run a company like that, or have any desire to be the one in charge, but I'll do what I have to in order to save my maternal family legacy.

It's not like Bobby can quit his job as the police chief to go to Georgia to help me figure it all out, either. His job is too important for him to walk away from like that. So, if I have to go back when it's safe for me to be there without my father forcing me to step in line with his plans, then it will all be over for us.

I wish I could call Mary and talk to her about what to do. She was awkward when talking to me about sex, and would probably still insist I wait until I know I'm truly in love first, but she'd also be able to help me figure out if all these butterflies in my belly and the goosebumps I feel whenever Bobby touches me are signs it's true love. Maybe I can covertly ask her in an email? Her previous reply for "Mary Kate" to trust the sheriff and her new friends with her real identity to enlist their help in fixing her situation was spot on, so surely she can help me with this, too.

After closing out of the manuscript for her next book on her laptop, Brooklyn pulled up her Brie Brooks email account and quickly typed up the message.

To: MaryTurner@GAemail.com

From: BrieBrooks@BrieBrooks.com

Subject: Mary Kate's Great Escape

Mary,

Thank you for your valuable feedback on the latest plot twists in my work in progress. I'm at a point in the story where Mary Kate has started to develop feelings for the cowboy sheriff who is protecting her from dastardly Donald and would like your opinion on how she can determine if her feelings are true love, or just appreciation for his protection.

Some background on the cowboy sheriff, Adam Appleton: He's tall with dark brown hair and piercing hazel eyes. In addition to his time working as the top law enforcement officer in the little town that Mary Kate has settled in, he volunteers his free time with the local youth center, trying to keep the local teenagers occupied, so they stay out of trouble. His athletic build doesn't come from working out in a gym, either. That's a result of the hard work he does every weekend on his family ranch.

He and Mary Kate got off on the wrong foot when his mother hired Mary Kate to be his live-in cook and housekeeper without his knowledge. But after that first uncomfortable evening, he apologized, and has spent the past few weeks befriending her. He's been torn because of his family history of everyone falling in love at first sight with their spouses, and while he thinks that's what he's feeling for "Katie" (Mary Kate's alter ego to stay hidden from dastardly Donald), he's also had the same feelings when looking at pictures of Mary Kate on the news reports of her disappearance.

Since he figured out that "Katie" is really Mary Kate, he's been insisting that he knew she was the one for him regardless of her alias or disguise, and wants to pursue a relationship with her. He's using his professional resources to investigate dastardly Donald and Barnaby Stanton (Mary Kate's father, who arranged the marriage with Donald and has been stealing her inheritance since she was a child) while keeping Mary Kate safe in his home on the ranch. He's also asked Mary Kate on a date, which she agreed to go on, but she's nervous about being more than his friend.

Mary Kate gets butterflies in her stomach anytime Adam is in the room and feels goosebumps and tingles throughout her body whenever he holds her hand, but she's not sure what those mean. She's felt the butterflies ever since the first time they met, so she wonders if they're a sign of love at first sight like he claims. And when he gave Mary Kate her first real kiss, she felt like her toes curled from the electricity shooting through her whole body. It was better than she'd ever imagined a kiss could be. Is that true love? Or

just a little hero worship for everything he's doing
for her?

I'm still trying to figure out how to end the book
and would love your thoughts. Should she be the
strong independent woman and go out on another
adventure after Barnaby and Donald are dealt with
by the authorities? Or should she stay in the small
town where she's feeling more at home than she's
ever felt anywhere else in her life to live happily
ever after with her cowboy sheriff?

Love and Hugs,

Brie

Just as Brooklyn finished her email to Mary and clicked send, the oven timer went off, alerting her that it was time to get everything ready to go to the north side of the ranch. It didn't take her long to have the food packed up and her laptop in her backpack to take to Kay's house, in case she was free to look over the new chapters of the book. She grabbed the keys to the mule and loaded everything up for the drive that was now second nature to Brooklyn.

She parked the mule between JJ and Justin's homes, delivering their dinners first thing. Once that was done, she drove over to Kay's house and pulled around back to go in through the mudroom and kitchen at the back of the house. While she'd been instructed to just walk in when she was there to clean, she still knocked as she opened the door and announced herself before just walking in, since the family was home. She didn't want to accidentally walk in on the newlyweds in an intimate moment, so she thought the warning of calling out to them as she walked through the mudroom and washroom into the kitchen was her best option for alerting them without offending them by not walking on in as she'd been instructed.

"Hey, Brie," Kay called out from her position at the kitchen counter where she was pouring what looked like flour into her mixer bowl. "What's up?"

"Just coming by to see if you need help with anything around the house today," Brooklyn replied.

"Not really, but you're welcome to stay and play with us," Kay smiled as she started the mixer. "My sister and I are making Christmas cookies while the girls are with Anthony this afternoon."

"Alright, I found Mom's recipe," a blonde woman announced, walking into the kitchen from the hallway toward the front of the house. When she looked up and noticed Brooklyn, she dropped her phone on the kitchen island and extended her hand to introduce herself. "Oh, hi, I'm Randi, Kay's sister."

"Oh, hi, uh, Brie," Brooklyn stuttered, shaking the other woman's hand. *Oh no! I didn't put my contacts in since I was staying on the ranch. I figured it would be okay to tell Kay who I am since the rest of the Burlesons know, but I'm not sure about her sister. I should've asked Bobby who all it's safe to tell.*

"Brie?" Randi arched an eyebrow at Brooklyn, her tone sounding like she was questioning where she recognized "Brie" from and making Brooklyn uncomfortable. "You're the girl whose car broke down the day of Kay's wedding, right?"

"Yes, that's me," Brooklyn replied, not quite able to make eye contact, and hopeful that the other woman wouldn't notice her eye color because of it.

"You can relax," Kay informed Brooklyn as she turned off the mixer and swapped out the bowl, so it was ready to start another type of cookies. "Randi already knows who you really are, Brooklyn."

"Yeah, it was my boyfriend's brother who sent Bobby the email about the theory we came up with about your identity on the GWA plane when we left after the wedding last month," Randi smiled reassuringly, gathering the ingredients to start a new batch of cookies from the recipe on her phone. "Don't worry, none of us will spill your secret. Once everything's settled, Rick might wanna buy the rights to your story to use for a wrestling gimmick, but we won't say a word before then."

Brooklyn could see the other woman was joking with her and relaxed. "Yeah, your boss will have to be disappointed since I'm already writing my story for my next book," Brooklyn laughed along with the other two women as she washed her hands to be able to assist them in the day's baking. "Unless he's got a movie division and wants to license all four of the books for movies, then I might be interested in talking to him."

"Oh, oh, oh! Rick doesn't have a movie division, but Burleson Incorporated has an entertainment division that might expand to making movies," Kay blurted out, grinning as she hand-stirred a bag of chocolate chips into the first batch of cookie dough. "We'll have to pitch turning all our books into movies at the next quarterly board meeting. Too bad we didn't think of that before today's meeting."

"Today's meeting?" Brooklyn was confused by what Kay was talking about. So much had happened in the last week with her identity coming to light and the change in her relationship with Bobby, from just friendly interactions to kissing and planning to date, that Brooklyn had forgotten hearing about the Burlesons' board meeting the previous Saturday over breakfast.

"Yeah, the board meeting all the Burlesons are in right now," Kay confirmed while rolling the chocolate chip cookie dough into balls and putting the balls on a cookie sheet. When Brooklyn still looked confused, Kay went on to explain the structure of Burleson Incorporated and how ownership of the company was divided among the two oldest generations of the family. She explained that her daughters had gone with Anthony to the board meeting, so they could prepare for what would be expected of them in the future. She made a joke about Tia possibly telling Anthony how to vote now, but Brooklyn thought it was entirely possible for the prodigy she'd gotten to know a couple of weeks before to already be smart enough to run the whole company.

"Well, that explains why Bobby was so insistent on bringing them in to look at what all is going on at Ashbury Enterprises," Brooklyn realized, finally putting all the puzzle pieces together in her head as she assisted Kay in filling the cookie sheets with chocolate chip cookies. "I thought it was just Jake's cyber skills that he needed to look into things, but I bet he's planning to bring in anyone else, who has the business knowledge to review the details that Jake finds, once he's able to get all the info after the federal investigation."

"Oh, yeah, you have the whole family ready and waiting to help you figure out whatever you need to fix at Ashbury," Kay assured her, putting a couple of cookie sheets in the oven to bake. "Especially with Bobby staking his claim on you."

"Wait," Randi interjected, holding up her hands in a stop motion after turning out her cookie dough onto the flour-covered counter.

"You're dating broody Bobby? Why didn't anyone give me this update?"

"Sorry, I just found that out last night," Kay grinned, moving over to the sink to wash her hands. "I told you as soon as I found out her real identity on Christmas Eve, but nobody mentioned the sparks flying between them, until we got home last night and asked why they weren't at dinner with the rest of the immediate family."

"What dinner?" Brooklyn looked back and forth between the sisters, confused as to why she and Bobby, or at least Bobby, weren't invited to the dinner Kay was talking about. "Nobody told us about a dinner last night."

"Yeah, it wasn't planned." Kay waved off her confusion, getting a set of cookie cutters out of the cabinet before walking back over to the island where her sister was rolling out the second batch of dough. "We got in right at dinner time and went next door instead of having to cook after traveling all day. Jake and Josh were already there, since they're staying with their folks while they're home for the holidays. We waved at Charlotte and Becky when we saw them as we were walking over, and all ended up having dinner together."

"Your mother-in-law doesn't get irritated with you just dropping in to eat unexpectedly?" Randi questioned Kay, as the three of them worked together to cut out Christmas-themed shapes from the rolled out dough.

"Oh, no, we weren't unexpected," Kay chuckled, shaking her head. "Hazel always cooks enough for an army, and insists we eat with them the first night we're home, and every morning we're here. Didn't you have to go eat with James's family last night?"

"No, we got pizza when we got in last night," Randi shrugged. "We're doing Christmas dinner with them tonight, since you insisted we have to come to the Burlesons' Christmas tomorrow to exchange gifts."

"Did you make sure Amy knows she's supposed to be coming tomorrow, too?" Kay inquired, pointedly looking at her sister. "Hazel said to make sure she knows she's expected at every family dinner and event now that she's living here in town, whether we're here or not."

Brooklyn was confused as to who all the extra people were, who would apparently be at the Christmas gift exchange the next day, but the other women quickly filled her in on the friend of theirs that had recently moved to town and didn't have family in the area. Kay elaborated more on how Hazel was insisting that not only Amy, but also all the wrestlers and the new English teacher that were staying at the bed and breakfast for the holidays, had to attend the festivities to try to work some of her matchmaker magic on them with her kids, nieces, and nephews.

Kay also verified what Brooklyn already knew about Hazel moving her into Bobby's house as her way of trying to push them together. *I wonder if Mary would be joining in on the matchmaking schemes with Hazel and her friends if she lived here?*

She never seemed to think anyone was good enough for me to consider dating, but there weren't really any men in father's circle of friends' children who were as good natured and down to earth as the Burlesons either. I bet if I could ever get her out here to meet this family, she'd feel as at home as I do and wouldn't want to leave.

Yeah, she'd probably settle down here and be right in the thick of all the matchmaking shenanigans with Hazel, Susan, Rosa, and Mandi.

When there was a lull in the conversation as they finished discussing the various people coming to dinner the next day, Brooklyn finally got brave enough to ask her new friends for some advice. With Kay being married to Bobby's brother, and Randi actually dating Mandi's son, she figured they were much more likely to have good advice for dating than the single friends she'd made in town.

"So, um, Bobby and I are going on our first date tonight," Brooklyn blurted somewhat awkwardly. "It's actually the first time I've ever been on a real date, and I'm a little nervous about what I should wear and what I should expect to happen."

"Oh, how exciting," Kay beamed. "Do you know where he's taking you?"

"Not really." Brooklyn shook her head. "Just to a restaurant in San Antonio is all I know."

"Let me guess, he did like James did on our first real date and didn't even give you an idea of the dress code for the restaurant?" Randi smiled as she obviously remembered back to her first date with James.

"Not even a tiny hint," Brooklyn admitted with a smile of her own. "I figured I'd wear a dress, just in case. I mean, if it's a nice place, then a dress will be required, but if it's more casual I figured a dress wouldn't be too out of place. But then I got to thinking that if it's any place like Tully's, maybe I should wear jeans since a dress would be way out of place in there."

"We wore skirts there for the bachelorette party." Randi motioned between herself and Kay. "And I don't think we were too overdressed."

"Really?" Brooklyn was surprised at hearing that, considering that wasn't what she'd seen everyone wearing at Tully's. "Everyone was in jeans the night I went with my friends from town. I was really glad they'd insisted on dressing me for the night because I wouldn't have fit in at all if they hadn't."

"Yeah, but we were in kind of casual skirts and tops, not a fancy dress by any means," Kay clarified.

"What did you end up wearing on your first date with James when you didn't have any idea what to wear?" Brooklyn hoped maybe Randi could give her a better idea of how to dress, thinking maybe Bobby would take her someplace similar to where James took Randi.

"Boots, jeans, and a sweater." Randi's smile widened at her memories. "But we went for a picnic in the woods for lunch first and then walking around the RiverWalk in San Antonio before having dinner at a fairly casual restaurant. I dressed for hanging out during the day and planned on changing before going to dinner, but James insisted it wasn't necessary."

"Oh, that sounds like a fun date," Brooklyn sighed at the mental image of her and Bobby doing something similar.

"It was an excellent date," Randi smirked. "Until he got all quiet when he saw the pregnancy test I bought for this one." Randi pointed at Kay with her thumb. "We went from hot and wild in the back of his truck in the middle of the woods at lunch to barely a kiss goodnight because he thought I needed the pregnancy test. I was so confused thinking we'd end up back at his place that night, but I didn't realize he'd seen the test, and was freaked out about possibly being a daddy before we're ready."

"Oh, so you were ready to go all the way on your first date?" Brooklyn practically whispered, wondering if that was normal and what she should expect from Bobby that night.

"Actually, James and I went all the way the night we met," Randi gloated. "But James is the only person I ever felt that comfortable with so fast. Before him, I had to date a guy for at least six weeks before I'd do more than give them a goodnight kiss. And most of my dates didn't even get that."

"Oh." Brooklyn was relieved that it didn't sound like most people jumped into a sexual relationship on the first date. Kenzie, Heather, and Ashley seemed to think Brooklyn should be trying to sleep with Bobby already, so she was starting to worry that her hesitation was abnormal. "What about you Kay? What was your first date with Anthony like?"

"We didn't really do the traditional dating thing," Kay confided sheepishly, her slight blush surprising Brooklyn. "We went to breakfast at a diner after meeting at a bar, which is what Anthony says is our first date. I still say it was just extending our time together that night, so I could decide whether or not I would go on a date with him the next week when he came back into town."

"I agree with you, Sis." Randi nodded her head. "I don't count the night James and I met as a date either, and still say the Monday before your wedding was our first official date, since it was planned as a date where he came and picked me up, and the whole nine yards. But James claims all our Skype sessions while he was traveling and I was in Tulsa were virtual dates."

"Yeah, well, ya'll were having Skype sex, so I can see why he classifies them as dates," Kay giggled at her sister. "Anyway, back to Anthony and I's lack of dating. The next week when he came to Tulsa to pick me up for our first official date, we ended up taking the girls to play mini-golf, instead of going to dinner as planned. Then we flew out the next day to start traveling together all the time with me working with the GWA a few days later. He claims all our outings with the girls were dates, but they weren't what I'd call a date because we weren't alone to do anything romantic. We didn't actually go on what I'd call a real date until after court the day Anthony adopted the girls, while they were with our parents."

"Oh, wow, okay." Brooklyn was kind of surprised by the way Kay and Anthony fell in love without dating. Brooklyn already had a lot of respect for Kay and wanted to ask her how long she should wait to do more than kissing with Bobby, but she was too embarrassed to admit her inexperience again. "So, um, I know you said it was love at first sight, but how long after ya'll met before you had sex? Was it faster than normal because of being in love so soon?"

"Two weeks," Kay admitted, grinning like it was a wonderful memory for her.

Only two weeks? I've known Bobby over a month, Brooklyn thought, wondering just how long he actually wanted to wait. She felt herself blush as she hoped he was more like his youngest brother and would want to move a little faster than they were currently. Hopefully, sometime soon.

"Oh, sweetie, Bobby's freaked you out with the way the Burlesons fall in love at first sight, hasn't he?" Kay wiped her hands on a hand towel and pulled Brooklyn into a hug.

"Maybe a little," Brooklyn admitted, not wanting to explain why she was blushing, while hugging the shorter woman back as best she could with cookie dough on her hands.

"It's not just the Burlesons in this town," Randi giggled, embracing both of the other women in a group hug. "I didn't wanna admit it to James, but it was instant for us, too."

"So, you think Bobby's right about it?" Brooklyn wondered aloud as the girls pulled back from each other and went back to rolling out cookies. "That the butterflies I felt the night we met are because it was love at first sight?"

"Sounds like what I felt the first time I looked into Anthony's eyes," Kay smiled knowingly.

"Same here," Randi nodded.

"But Bobby's the first boy I've even kissed," Brooklyn admitted shyly. "How am I supposed to know it's really love?"

"I think the butterflies are a pretty good indicator." Kay shook her head and chuckled under her breath before continuing. "I mean, I kissed a whole lot of frogs and never felt the butterflies until I found my prince."

"Yeah, I think some of my previous boyfriends were toads, not even good enough to rank frog status," Randi quipped, laughing. "And I never felt butterflies for anyone but James."

"So, maybe you're one of the lucky few, who found your prince on the first try without having to risk getting warts," Kay giggled at her own joke, but obviously meant what she said about Brooklyn being lucky to find love with the first boy she kissed.

"Maybe," Brooklyn pondered aloud. "But I still can't help but worry I don't have enough experience to keep him interested over time. What if we do more than kiss and find out I'm actually bad at the sex stuff?"

"Then he's not the right man for you," Kay stated, matter-of-factly. "I used to think I was bad at the sex stuff, too, but it turns out the problem was that I wasn't with the right man. My ex had me convinced that I was asexual, totally lacking any interest or ability in the bedroom. But that all changed when I met Anthony. He showed me that when you're with your soulmate, it's impossible for sex to be bad."

"You can still have a mishap like falling off the bed, though," Randi smirked. "If you try a new position that you don't fully comprehend."

"That's only because you and James keep trying to turn wrestling maneuvers into sexual positions," Kay teased, pointing at her sister with a ball of cookie dough, where she'd gone back to the chocolate chip cookies while Randi rolled out another lump of sugar cookie dough for them to cut into shapes. "While Bobby might be like his brother and want to explore some kinks, I doubt he'll try to make her tap out while he's tapping her."

"Oh, I hope not," Brooklyn squealed as they all cracked up at Kay's analogy. "I haven't even made it to second base playing sexual baseball. I'm nowhere near ready to try erotic wrestling."

Once their laughter died down, Brooklyn finally got brave enough to ask what she really wanted to ask them. "So, um, what do I need to wear and do tonight to move us past kissing?"

"Well, with not knowing exactly where he's taking you, I'd recommend going with a casual skirt and top, so it's acceptable if you go someplace fancy, and not too dressy if you go someplace casual," Randi advised while swapping out cookie sheets in the oven. She started transferring the cookies to the cooling rack before adding, "And your sexiest undies if you want him to see them at the end of the night."

I guess it's a good thing the girls got me some for Christmas then.

"As for what you should do, just relax and have fun," Kay suggested before transferring her cookie dough cutouts to the now-empty cookie sheet. "As much as Anthony tried to fight it when we first got together, I think all of the Burleson men have a strong dominant streak in them. Bobby will want control in the bedroom…"

"And maybe outside the bedroom," Randi interrupted her sister to add.

"Probably more than maybe," Kay giggled. "Let him take control and he'll lead you to where you need to be when the time is right. I'm sure he sees your need to take things slow for now, so he won't push you past your limits."

"Oh, yeah, I know he won't ever push me to do more than I'm ready for," Brooklyn defended him, making sure Kay knew Bobby wasn't that type of man, as if she hadn't already known that about all the Burleson men. "I'm actually more worried about him going too slow. All we've done for the past two nights is kiss, and I'm ready to move on to a little more touching, too."

"Well, then, if all he's doing is kissing you, either tell him you want to do more, or let your hands wander a little when you're kissing," Kay recommended, her lips turning up in a half smile that looked rather conniving. "He'll get the hint."

They spent the next few hours baking and talking, until Brooklyn had to leave to go get ready for her date with Bobby. Kay and Randi were a wealth of advice on how and where to touch and tease to excite a sexual partner. Brooklyn didn't think she'd use a tenth of the information they'd given her during their talk while on her date that night with Bobby, but she was looking forward to touching him a little more than she had previously.

I can't wait to feel how hard the muscles of his chest and arms are tonight, she thought as she showered. She tried to practice casually touching her own arms and chest, but as soon as her fingers stroked over her sensitive nipples, she instantly imagined what his calloused hands would feel like in place of hers. Picturing him in the shower with her in only those pajama pants he'd worn the day he'd awakened her when he wasn't wearing a shirt, Brooklyn was soon fantasizing about kissing him while he used his fingers to bring her to climax.

As she touched herself, in her mind it was Bobby touching her, stroking through her folds, lightly pinching her nipples, and finally applying just the right amount of pressure to her clitoris to make her cry out his name as her body convulsed in orgasm. Once she caught her breath, she made quick work of shaving, washing and conditioning her hair, and scrubbing her whole body.

Thank goodness, he's not home yet to have heard me. That would've been sending a signal I'm not quite ready to send him yet.

~~~

Bobby heard Brie using the blow dryer in her bathroom as he walked up the back stairs when he got home Friday evening. The thought of her being naked in the bathroom as she got ready for their date instantly aroused him. He hadn't planned on taking a second shower when he got home, since he'd spent the day sitting in an office at Burleson Incorporated instead of on his normal patrol for the police department, but he absolutely had to go deflate his dick before their date or he was likely to embarrass himself with an uncontrollable erection all night.

Maybe I should actually wear a suit instead of just slacks and a dress shirt? Bobby mentally questioned as he stripped out of the business casual attire he'd worn all day while in the office. *At the very least, the jacket will keep Thor covered if this isn't enough to appease him until we get home.*

As he'd already done once that morning and every morning and evening for the past few weeks, Bobby palmed his cock as soon as he stepped into the shower. Instead of the typical fantasies of her in the shower with him, he imagined her spread out on his bed, waiting for him to explore every inch of her delectable body. He pictured her hair as the dark dye faded, her honey-colored tresses draped over his pillows. But instead of picturing her wearing the caramel-colored contacts that he'd previously associated with Brie, he envisioned looking down into her sky-blue eyes.

He still couldn't believe he'd been blinded by his desire for both Brooklyn and Brie, and hadn't realized they were actually the same woman. *I guess Thor knew,* Bobby lightly chuckled to himself. *Maybe he should be running the police department, since the head in my pants is so much more observant than the head on my shoulders.*

Blocking out his wayward thoughts, Bobby went back to his fantasy of exploring Brie's body, teasing her with light touches and
~~~

open-mouthed kisses to every erogenous zone he could find before settling in with his head between her thighs. *Fuck, I wonder if she shaves her pussy? Or if she just trims enough to keep her bush from showing when she wears a bathing suit? It's fucking torture waiting to find out.*

Thinking about her lack of sexual experience made him groan as he imagined pushing his tongue and fingers inside her for the first time. *Fuck, she's gonna be so tight. I'm gonna hafta spend hours getting her off and opening her up before I'll actually be able to fuck her. But if I can get her opened up enough to take three fingers with ease, then the only pain she'll feel when I replace them with my cock will be when I break her hymen. It'll be worth the torture of waiting to fully be with her if it keeps her first time from being too painful.*

Mentally walking through his plan for making love to Brie the first time, Bobby squeezed down tight on his cock, imagining how snug she would feel around him the first time. He held his hand still, increasing the pressure on his dick, trying to estimate how long he'd have to keep still inside her for the brief moment of pain to pass before he could start to thrust in and out of her little, wet cunt.

The vision in his mind quickly became too much, causing him to explode the instant he loosened his hold to start stroking himself as if he was plunging into Brie. "Fuck!" he screamed as his orgasm caught him off guard and overtook his whole body. *Brie-Baby, fuck, yes, Brie,* he mentally shouted as he bit down on his bottom lip to keep from actually shouting out her name as he continued to shoot rope after rope of cum over the wall of the shower.

"Fucking hell," Bobby practically whispered as he held himself up with one arm against the wall because he felt weak in the knees after that intense climax. "If the orgasms are better than I've ever had before when I'm just fantasizing about her, I don't know if I'll be able to handle how extreme they'll actually be when I'm really with her."

Once he finally caught his breath and no longer felt like his legs were wobbly, Bobby cleaned up and got dressed in his favorite navy-blue suit with a white button-down shirt and solid red tie, taking special care to make sure he looked his best for their date. He grabbed the flowers he'd picked up at Flora's on his way home and had dropped on his dresser when he first got upstairs, glad he hadn't left them in the kitchen as he'd originally thought, so Brie wouldn't see them until he handed them to her.

He wanted to give her the whole first date experience, but he wasn't sure it really felt like he was picking her up for a date when they lived in the same house. *Would it be too cheesy to sneak back out of the house and ring the doorbell like I was picking her up from a house where I don't live?*

"Yes, total cheese dick move, Bro," Bobby imagined his best friend, Luke, saying in his head.

Yeah, I'm not gonna risk the ridicule by actually texting anyone to ask. I'll just go hang out downstairs and wait for her to come down when she's ready to go.

He sat on the sofa in the room he'd previously considered his man cave, but had started to think of as more of a living room when Brie had started watching television with him in there after dinner most nights. He flipped on the TV, but he didn't register what was playing as he remembered their make-out sessions the two previous nights.

It had been all he could do to limit where he touched her while their lips and tongues tangled. Somehow, he'd managed to keep from pulling her in close and grinding his erection into her center when she was sitting on his lap Wednesday night. Her innocence was evident in her timidness the first time he parted her lips with his tongue, reminding him to rein in his inner caveman to keep from frightening her away.

The second night, they'd progressed to laying on the couch, which made it harder for him to keep his hands on her back with her laying on it. But being on his stomach with only his chest, shoulders, and head hovering over her allowed him to press his cock into the couch instead of rubbing it against her like he really wanted. She was a little bolder the second night, actually sticking her tongue in his mouth to return his passionate kiss more than she had previously.

Fuck, I can't wait to kiss her again tonight when we get home, Bobby thought just as Brie stepped into the room. Her hair was down, cascading over her shoulders in waves, instead of up in a ponytail or messy bun like she normally wore it. He ached to run his fingers through the soft tawny tresses. She wore a little more makeup than she normally applied on a daily basis, but it wasn't as overdone as it had been in the pictures he'd seen of Brooklyn, or when Brie went to Tully's with her friends from town.

He hated that she had to put the caramel-colored contacts in because they were leaving the ranch. Especially when he realized that the blue in her blouse would have really accented her natural eye color. As his eyes wandered down the rest of her body, taking in the way her breasts filled out her top and her hips flared out under her skirt, he realized that her navy-blue skirt was a very close match to his suit.

"Wow, you look amazing!" Bobby was in awe of her beauty. He stood from his seated position and extended his hand, which was holding the bright yellow daisies, to her. "These are for you."

"Oh, thank you," Brie smiled shyly as she took the flowers from his hand. "I, uh, should put them in water before we go."

Bobby followed her to the kitchen, watching her as she pulled out a vase and filled it with water before unwrapping the flowers and arranging them in the vase, and feeling like an awkward teenager going on his very first date.

Get it together, man! He mentally told himself, wanting to end the awkwardness of the night immediately, starting with his own anxiety.

"Ready?" Bobby smiled at her when she'd finished with the flowers, extending his hand to hold hers as they walked out to the car.

"Yes," she barely breathed out the word, lacing their fingers together and walking by his side.

Thankfully, once they got on the road, the clumsy conversation seemed to morph into their normal relaxed repartee. They talked about books that had been made into movies and how Brie was torn between wanting her books to be made into movies for the additional enjoyment of people around the world, and at the same time not wanting to have the stories drastically changed like movies made about books tended to be altered versions of the original stories.

Bobby wasn't surprised that the money she could make from licensing her books to be made into movies didn't factor into her thought process about whether or not she'd ever sell the movie rights to her books. She may have been raised as Brooklyn Brielle Barns in an expensive-as-fuck mansion, and hobnobbed with high society when required to by her father growing up, but that had all been fake, more like window dressing covering up her true self. Deep inside, she was Brie, a down to earth woman without a greedy bone in her body.

As long as she made enough money to cover her expenses, she was happy. She wasn't a writer because she wanted fame and fortune. She was a writer because she wanted to share her stories with the world, making other people happy by giving them entertaining anecdotes.

It was refreshing to be around a woman who didn't look at him for his bank account or birthright, like he felt all the women his mother had tried to set him up with had in the past. *Hell, not even just the women Ma's tried to set me up with,* Bobby thought as he listened to Brie sing off key with the radio while driving into San Antonio. *Even a few of the buckle bunnies and random hookups have had ulterior motives when trying to get my attention.*

Brie is definitely a rare gem in a mine full of fool's gold. That's why I have to be mindful of everything going on between us and not push too fast, so I don't risk losing her.

~~~

Brooklyn felt like she was living a dream as she and Bobby walked hand in hand around the RiverWalk after a romantic dinner where their table sat overlooking the water. She'd been nervous as she'd gotten ready, and reading Mary's reply email telling her that it sounded like "Mary Kate" was feeling the first flutterings of love hadn't quashed her excitement for the night. If anything, Mary's words of encouragement to *"enjoy the feeling of falling and embrace love's potential"* had amplified her anxiety over what might happen between her and Bobby as the date progressed.

Their conversation had been stilted at the beginning of the evening, with Brooklyn hiding her giddy schoolgirl reaction to being given flowers for the first time under the elegant persona she'd had to portray every time she went with her father to an event. But as soon as Bobby had taken her hand to walk her out to the car, the high-society mask she'd donned fell away and they were back to their normal friendly banter.

The conversation flowed easily between them. They'd talked about Bobby's day at work, the pros and cons of having a book made into a
~~~

movie, and even enjoyed their own impromptu carpool karaoke while listening to the country station Bobby preferred and Brooklyn was growing to love.

Bobby was very attentive all night. The only time he didn't look her in the eyes when she was speaking was when he had to keep his eyes on the road while they were driving. Even then, she still knew he was actively listening to what she was saying because he offered his opinions and asked her thought-provoking questions to dig deeper into the topics they were discussing.

His attentiveness wasn't just limited to his listening skills either. He'd also been very affectionate, constantly having some form of contact with her. He'd held her hand while they drove and as they were walking to and from the car. When they got to the restaurant and the space between tables was too narrow for them to walk side by side, he'd guided her in front of him with his hand on the small of her back. Once they were seated—with them side by side so they could both look out over the water—Bobby had either held her hand or draped his arm across the back of her chair and stroked her shoulder with his thumb.

All those tingly feelings throughout my body whenever he's touching me have to mean something special, right? Surely, having him hold my hand wouldn't make my nipples hard and my core quiver, if we weren't meant to be more than just friends. He wouldn't be so openly affectionate in public, if he didn't want to get me worked up for more later tonight, would he?

Between his normal gentlemanly behavior of opening doors and pulling out chairs for her, his additional attention and affection, and the way he seemed to be protecting her by placing his body physically between her and any potential danger, Bobby was making Brooklyn feel special in a way that she'd never felt before. It was like he really loved her, cherished her, and wanted to be there with her. It was more than a little overwhelming to be the recipient of all his tender loving care.

"You've gotten awfully quiet over there." Bobby's words pulled her attention back to the present from her mental ramblings about the meaning behind all his actions earlier in the night.

"Sorry," Brooklyn apologized, looking up into his eyes as they strolled hand in hand along the RiverWalk. "Just trying to take everything in, so I don't forget a moment of tonight."

"I thought you might be getting tired." Bobby's lips lifted in a slight smile, not quite enough to bring out his dimples. Before Brooklyn could protest that she wasn't tired, Bobby continued. "We're almost back to where we parked, if you're ready to head home for the night."

"I'm not really tired," Brooklyn admitted, smiling shyly up at him. "But I wouldn't mind going home and finding something else to occupy us there for the rest of the night."

Like kissing and touching each other more than we can do in public, Brooklyn thought, hoping Bobby understood her implications because she didn't think she'd ever be brave enough to blatantly tell him she wanted more to happen that night.

"Yeah, I have some definite ideas for things to do at home that we can't do here," Bobby hinted he was on the same page, his grin widening and his dimples popping out.

Oh, I hope that grin means we're going to do more than kissing, Brooklyn internally squealed as they made their way back to his car to drive home. Realizing that she was thinking of Bobby's house as her home kept her pondering how possible that could be for her future as they drove. Luckily, they had another round of carpool karaoke on the way home, so Bobby didn't notice how deep in thought she was as she pictured potentially getting married and raising babies with him on the ranch.

Maybe once everything is settled in Georgia, I can find someone trustworthy to manage everything in Mom's estate, so I won't have to live there full time, just go visit for quarterly meetings, like the Burlesons meet for their board meetings? If that happens, then maybe Bobby's right about us being meant to be together, and we can actually plan a future together.

His house is perfect for raising a couple of kids. Though if we have more than two, we might need to convert some of the attic space into bedrooms for them. I wonder how many kids Bobby wants?

Growing up as an only child and being lonely most of her life, Brooklyn had always dreamed of having a large family. She'd written in her book of future plans that she wanted at least four kids, but she was open to more than four as long as she could have them in even numbers. She wanted her children to always be able to pair up with a built-in best friend, and not feel like the odd one out as she had by being an only child. Learning during their nightly talks that Bobby had moved out of his childhood home as soon as he turned eighteen to get some peace and quiet after growing up with five brothers and sisters, made her wonder if he would really want a big family like she did, though.

Yeah, I'm not going to ask him how many kids he wants on our first date. I'll wait to broach the subject of kids when we actually start doing things that might create them.

"So, um, you wanna change clothes when we get home?" Bobby momentarily glanced over at her as they were exiting the highway in Heart's Destiny. "Or just go straight to the couch to make out?"

"I'm pretty comfortable in what I'm wearing," Brooklyn replied, trying not to blush while thinking about what she was wearing underneath her clothes.

She'd barely been brave enough to wear the skimpy bra and panties. There was no way she'd be so daring as to leave them on if she went up and changed into a t-shirt and leggings like she normally wore around the house. Not that she thought there was really any chance of Bobby seeing them that night, but she thought maybe wearing them while they kissed would help her feel sexy enough to try touching him more than she had previously.

Her anxiety ramped up the closer they got to the ranch. She was sure Bobby could feel her leg shaking under their joined hands as they went through the gate and made their way to the house. She was afraid he was going to have to carry her in because she wasn't sure she could walk on such shaky legs, but she somehow managed to maintain her composure as they walked hand in hand back inside in much the same way they'd walked out to the car earlier in the night.

As soon as they stepped inside the house, Bobby surprised her by scooping her up in his arms and carrying her straight to the family room. He was obviously as ready for their make-out session to get started as she was and wasted no time in pressing their lips together before he even got them settled on the sofa with her on his lap.

The kiss started much like their first kiss, with just soft, gentle movement of their lips on one another. But as soon as they were seated, so he could release his hold under her knees, Bobby's hand plunged into her hair, tilting her head back, so he could deepen the kiss. Brooklyn didn't hesitate for a second before opening her mouth to his plundering tongue. She met him lick for lick as they explored each other's mouths.

Brooklyn had wrapped her arms around Bobby's neck when he'd first picked her up, but as their kiss progressed, she let her hands start to wander. First weaving her fingers through the short strands of hair on the back of his head. Then pressing her palms down his neck and across his shoulders. Even through the layers of his shirt and suit coat, she could feel the solid muscle of his upper back and shoulders.

As they pulled back momentarily to take a breath, Brooklyn trailed her hands down his arms, marveling at the strength she felt in his biceps, even through his clothing. She twisted on his lap, trying to move to be able to face him straight on, but she was stopped in her movement by his next toe-curling kiss. She moved her hands to his chest, pushing under his jacket, so she could feel the thickness of his pecs with only the barrier of his shirt between them. She felt his nipples pebble under her palms, just like hers did when she touched herself while thinking of him in the shower. Instinctively, she moved her hands to lightly pinch his nipples the way she liked when she touched herself, and really wished she could see what she was touching without the impediment of his shirt.

Brooklyn couldn't believe how Bobby was keeping one hand on her back and the other in her hair while they were kissing, just like he'd done the previous two nights. She was starting to worry that her hands wandering over his body wasn't enough of a hint for him to move things along like she wanted when he started to pull away.

"Fuck, Brie-Baby," he groaned as his hands moved to her hips. He shifted her on his lap, so she was straddling him, her skirt bunching up at her thighs. "If you keep touching me like that, we're gonna go a lot farther than I think you're ready for tonight."

"But I want to touch you," Brooklyn whined, her voice sounding different, huskier than normal, making her wonder if it was because she was aroused. "And I want you to touch me. Please."

"Fuck," Bobby growled, closing his eyes, and tightening his grip on her hips. "You're absolutely killing me, Brie-Baby."

Brooklyn continued massaging his chest as he sat there seeming to fight his own desires.

"Fine," he barked when he opened his eyes. "But you have to tell me if it starts to feel like too much. I don't wanna pressure you into doing more than you're ready for, ever."

"Bobby," Brooklyn sighed, moving her hands up to his jaw and holding his head still, so their eyes could meet. "I promise I'll tell you if it feels like too much, but I don't think you'd ever pressure me into doing more than I want."

She pressed her lips to his again, not giving him a chance to say anything more. He responded by taking over the kiss, tangling their tongues like he couldn't get enough of kissing her. He slid his hands up her sides, settling them right over her ribs. Though their kiss felt passionate and intense, he was tentative as he lightly caressed her breasts with his thumbs.

Her nipples felt as hard as diamonds, like they were ready to cut through the thin lace of her bra to get closer to Bobby's touch. She was afraid the matching little lace panties wouldn't be able to contain the flood of moisture she felt between her legs. He'd barely touched her, and she was more aroused than she'd ever been in her life. But it still didn't feel like enough. She needed more than just his thumbs lightly grazing the underside of her breasts.

"More," Brooklyn begged into his mouth, not wanting to break their kiss, but needing to encourage him to go further. "Please."

Apparently, please really was the magic word. Brooklyn barely got the word out before Bobby moved his hands up to cup her breasts. He miraculously found her nipples, pinching them between his thumbs and forefingers as he trailed his mouth across her cheek, so he could whisper in her ear.

"I'm only gonna touch you where you touch me," Bobby whispered, his breath tickling her ear. "Keep showing me what you like, Brie-Baby."

"Yes, Bobby," Brooklyn replied, sliding her hands back down to his chest to continue touching his powerful pecs and kissing her way down his neck as she felt her orgasm building from their nipple play alone. She involuntarily started rocking her hips, bringing her core in contact with his very impressive erection.

Brooklyn felt overwhelmed by all the sensations flooding her body. Between the way they were licking and sucking on each other's necks, alternating between pinching and palming each other's nipples, and the way his hard length was grinding against her clit, it didn't take long for the pressure to build up in her core, causing her to explode in the most intense orgasm she'd ever experienced.

"Oh, Bobby," she shouted as her body convulsed in climax.

Bobby pushed her just far enough away from him that their eyes could meet, before dropping one hand to her butt to hold their pelvises tightly together. "Fuck, Brie-Baby," he yelled along with her as she felt his erection pulse against her center.

They didn't break eye contact as they floated on the waves of their mutual release, until Brooklyn collapsed into Bobby, too drained by the experience to hold herself up any longer. He wrapped his arms around her, cradling her to his chest, where her head rested right over his rapidly beating heart.

"That was…" Brooklyn breathed out, her voice trailing off. She couldn't think of the right word to describe how she was feeling in that moment.

"Wow," Bobby finished her sentence for her.

They laid there for a while, cuddling, and catching their breath, before Bobby finally broke the silence by asking, "Was that your first orgasm?"

"Um, maybe," Brooklyn sheepishly admitted, hoping he couldn't see her blush with her face still resting on his chest. "I mean, I thought I'd come before while touching myself, but those were nothing compared to what we just did. That was definitely my first man-made orgasm."

Brooklyn inwardly cringed at using the expression she'd learned from her new friends in town while talking to Bobby. He chuckled at her revelation, easing her anxiety over the admission.

"Is it always that good?" Brooklyn relaxed in Bobby's embrace. "Like actual sex produces more intense orgasms than the do-it-yourself ones I've had before?"

"I think it has more to do with who you're with," Bobby chuckled, squeezing her tight against him. "My recent do-it-myself ones have been more intense than I've ever had before, but I think that's because I've been thinking about you at the time. And this was definitely the most intense orgasm I've ever had, and the only time I've ever come from dry-humping. I'm pretty sure that's just because of being made for each other."

Yeah, we're made for each other, Brooklyn thought, barely processing Bobby's words as she drifted off to sleep.

~ ~ ~

Saturday, December 29, 2018

Bobby couldn't believe he'd fallen asleep holding Brie on the couch again. He'd only intended to sit there holding her for a little while to give them time to catch their breath after their intense orgasms. But when Brie started softly snoring in his arms, he couldn't bring himself to disturb her sleep, no matter how bad he needed to clean up the mess in his pants.

Speaking of unbelievable, Bobby thought as he felt her starting to stir in his arms. *The fact that I came like an untried teenager from dry-humping is pretty un-fucking-believable. Hell, I didn't even come from dry-humping when I was a teenager.*

"Oh, um," Brie sputtered, seeming unsure what to say as she lifted her head off his chest. In the middle of the night, they'd somehow rotated to lay on the couch, with him on his back and her laying on top of him, making it impossible for Bobby to hide his morning wood from her.

"Good morning, Brie-Baby," Bobby smiled up at the disheveled woman pulling up out of his arms.

"Good-good morning," Brie stuttered, looking like she wasn't sure how to politely maneuver off of him.

Not wanting her to feel uncomfortable in their semi-scandalous position, Bobby gripped her waist and lifted her as he sat up, smoothly placing her on her feet beside the couch at about the same time his feet hit the floor on either side of hers.

"I don't know about you, but I really need to go clean up before I even attempt to make coffee this morning." Bobby stood as soon as she took a step back, so he could do so without running into her.

246

"Yes," Brie nodded in agreement, turning toward the door. "Definitely need a shower before anything else."

She'd barely left the room before he heard her running up the stairs, making him chuckle.

Guess we're not gonna have a repeat of last night to take care of my morning wood, he thought as he made his own way upstairs to his shower. He hoped her shyness that morning wasn't an indication of them needing to go back to just kissing.

He stripped out of his suit, hanging the pants, jacket, and tie up to go to the dry cleaners later before tossing his shirt and socks in the hamper in the bathroom to be washed. He stepped into the shower still wearing his boxer briefs. Knowing he'd need to rinse them out before putting them in the hamper anyway, Bobby opted to use the sprayer nozzle in the shower to cut through the glue-like stickiness adhering his underwear to his erection.

Once he'd safely removed his boxer briefs without taking a layer of skin off his cock from being stuck together by his cum from the night before, Bobby cleaned them out as best he could and hung them to dry over the shower door, so he could finish his shower. Though it wasn't nearly as satisfying as making out with Brie the night before, Bobby palmed his cock for his morning release. He wished Brie would've joined him in the shower. Even if she wasn't ready for more than what they'd already done, he thought watching each other masturbate in the shower could've been a pleasurable morning without pushing her completely out of her comfort zone. *Maybe?*

Since he wasn't sure he'd be welcomed if he walked naked down the hall to ask if she wanted to share a shower, Bobby just pictured her there fingering herself while he jacked off. It didn't take long before he was able to move on with the rest of his normal shower routine, including manscaping, just in case he and Brie moved faster than he expected.

As he got ready for the day, he thought about how he wanted to progress with her. He didn't want to push too much, but he also didn't want to fall back too far either. So, he planned to continue with the way he'd been affectionately touching her, only adding in a little more kissing even when the rest of the family was around. He wouldn't push to touch her more like they had the night before, opting to wait for her to not seem as embarrassed as she was that morning before going there again. But he also wasn't going to keep things completely chaste either.

He wanted to start taking her out to places around town, and making it known to all the single guys in town that she was his. He wasn't sure she'd appreciate his possessive caveman tendencies, especially if he started insisting she only go out in public with him to protect her. That meant he had to get her comfortable with him kissing her in public, and not just a little peck of a kiss, so he could show the other men in town that she was his to keep them from hitting on her when he wasn't around.

Once he'd showered, shaved, brushed his teeth and hair, and dressed in his favorite jeans and a red Henley, Bobby shoved his size thirteens in his cowboy boots and made his way downstairs. Brie was already downstairs, surprising him by being ready before he was that day. She had her hair twisted up in a knot on the top of her head and very little makeup on, which was probably why she didn't take as long to get ready as he did. That and the fact that he'd had to spend some extra time dealing with the mess in his pants from the night before.

She was also wearing jeans and a red sweater, making them mostly match except for her tennis shoes instead of boots. "You know if we keep dressing to match, my family is gonna pick on us for doing it on purpose," Bobby quipped, chuckling as he motioned between the two of them to indicate the jeans and red shirts matching.

"Oh, goodness, this is like the second day in a row, huh?" Brie giggled and smiled brightly. "Guess we should start actually telling each other what we're planning to wear, so we don't do it again. Though I don't think I've seen a purple shirt in your laundry, and I know I'm wearing purple to church tomorrow, so I think the streak will end today."

"Or maybe I just need to run to town and buy myself a purple shirt this afternoon," Bobby teased, winking at her as they both laughed. "I mean, if I already know I'm gonna be ragged on for matching my girlfriend, I may as well embrace it and make sure we always match."

"Girl-girlfriend?" Brie stuttered questioningly.

Not giving her a chance to argue the point, Bobby reiterated the label, "Yeah, my girlfriend." He wrapped his left arm around her, pulling her into his body before tilting her chin up with his right hand. He bent down and gently kissed her. It was just a light brushing of his lips over hers, but it was enough to arouse him in an instant. Not wanting to go to his parents' house for their second Christmas celebration sporting an obvious boner, he quickly pulled away. "I know you're not ready for more than that yet, and I'm willing to wait for as long as you need before we take the next step. But I need to make sure you know I'm serious about us, that we're exclusive, boyfriend and girlfriend, for as long as it takes until you're ready for more."

"Oh!" Brie's mouth formed that cute little O he loved to see because it made him think about how her lips would look wrapped around his cock, even though he knew he'd never actually ask her to do that. "Okay."

She still looked a little dazed by his declaration, but she didn't protest when he led her out the back door to go to the car. It was a quick drive to his parents' house, where he found not only his immediate family, but also all his extended family, honorary family, and a few surprise guests who were new in town or visiting for the holidays.

Bobby wasn't entirely surprised to see the Hunters, figuring they came with Kay's sister, Randi, since she was dating James Hunter. But everyone else they brought with them were surprise guests for Bobby.

He remembered meeting Amy Lawton the month before, when she was in town for Anthony and Kay's wedding. She was Randi's college roommate and best friend, who would be starting work at Burleson Incorporated the next week. He also remembered meeting several of the wrestlers from the GWA that were there, but he didn't know any of the other people with them.

Unsure of who they were or if they could be trusted with finding out Brie's true identity, Bobby pulled Brie along with him as he cornered his mother in the kitchen to ask, planning to take her home to put her brown contacts in if he needed to in order to keep her safe.

"Uh, Ma," Bobby started interrogating his mom as soon as they were sequestered in a corner away from prying eyes and ears. "Who are the couple with the little boy who came with the Hunters?"

"That's the new English teacher at the middle school," Hazel informed him, smiling brightly as if it was great to have strangers at their family gathering.

Leah Mae Wright

Bobby vaguely remembered Charlotte mentioning that the other
English teacher at the middle school, Fiona Harrison, who was also the
daughter of the Heart's Destiny Community Church pastor, had taken
the job as the English tutor for the GWA back at Thanksgiving. She
was scheduled to work the rest of the semester, but she would be
flying out with Anthony's family to start her new job on New Year's
Day. Bobby hadn't realized the middle school had already hired a
replacement, but he supposed they had to in order to have a teacher for
the next semester starting a little over a week away.

"Ian Campbell, and his sister, Cait, who's helping him raise his son,
Brody," Hazel continued. "They're staying at the bed and breakfast
until he can find them a house here. I'm thinking about asking Cait to
fill our other housekeeping position, so she can earn a little extra
money and I can act as Brody's honorary grandma."

"Do they know who Brie is?" Bobby gave his mother a pointed
look and hoped she understood his concern, while ignoring her
potential matchmaking for his siblings and cousins to get herself
another grandbaby.

"Oh, no, of course not," Hazel replied, waving off his worry as if it
were nothing.

"Do I need to go put my contacts in?" Brie looked nervously
between Bobby and Hazel. "I wasn't thinking about needing to be in
disguise today."

"No, I don't think so." Hazel shook her head, giving Brie a one-
armed hug to soothe her nerves. "They'll be meeting so many new
people here today, they won't remember who all they met, so I doubt
they'll figure out who you are. We'll just make sure you sit on the
opposite side of the room from them when we eat, and you should be
fine."

Bobby wasn't quite as sure about the newcomers as his mother
appeared to be, and really wished he had his laptop with him to do a
quick background check on them, but he kept his mouth shut. He kept
his arm around Brie as they made the rounds talking to his family and
friends, vowing to protect her if anyone said something they shouldn't
during the celebration.

True to her word, Hazel sat he and Brie on one side of the room
with Anthony, Kay, their daughters, Kay's sister, and James Hunter
surrounding them, and his Aunt Susan sat the newcomers on the other

side of the room with his other siblings, cousins, and the GWA wrestlers, with all their parents, aunts, and uncles in between them. Bobby wasn't sure how much of that had to do with protecting Brie's identity, and how much was pure Hazel Burleson matchmaking.

It certainly seemed his mother had a plan up her sleeve for each and every person in attendance. Right down to having a stack of presents for everyone to open, even the people he hadn't known were going to be there.

Thank fuck, I found Brie when I did, Bobby thought as he observed the room. *Otherwise, I'd have been stuck in that convoluted mess with the rest of my siblings and cousins, being pushed toward whoever our mothers think we should date.*

Unable to hold back his appreciation for the woman beside him, Bobby leaned over where he had his arm around Brie's shoulders and kissed the top of her head, not caring if he interrupted the conversation going on at the time. When Brie turned to look up at him and returned his affection with a kiss to his cheek, Bobby couldn't contain his smile.

He was thrilled that she was openly claiming him in front of his family, instead of wanting to hide their relationship as he'd feared. He'd still take things slow, waiting for her to push for more than kissing again since she'd been so embarrassed that morning, but he didn't think it would be too long before they were going to the next level.

Chapter Nine

Brooklyn was getting frustrated with the way Bobby seemed to be putting the brakes on her sexual awakening. Friday night was the best night of her life so far and she really wanted to repeat the experience. Unfortunately, Bobby seemed to think they needed to go back to just kissing the next day.

She'd thought he would be ready for more when they got home from the Christmas party on Saturday evening, especially since he'd kissed her more than once in front of his whole family that day. But when they got home, he pushed her to get on her laptop and work on her book while he did some work on his computer for Burleson Incorporated. He'd given her a fabulous kiss goodnight, but they'd still gone to bed in their separate rooms without touching anything more than their lips and tongues.

Sunday had been another family day with church that morning, the potluck after church, horseback riding in the afternoon, and Sunday supper that night. While Brooklyn loved Bobby's family and enjoyed the time she got to spend with them, especially getting to ride horses with Tia and Maria to see the delight of childhood on the girls' faces, she missed her alone time with Bobby. Ending the second night in a row with only a kiss goodnight seemed like a step backwards for them.

When she got downstairs Monday morning, she was disappointed that Bobby had already left for the day, so she didn't even get to kiss him goodbye before he left for work. As she went to pour herself a cup of coffee, she found a note from Bobby beside the pot.

Brie-Baby,

Sorry, I forgot to mention it earlier, but there's a town wide New Year's party I want to take you to tonight. Please go to Destiny Dresses this afternoon and pick out a dress and shoes to wear. I'll have everything set up with Louella, so she'll have a selection of things for you to try on, so we can match tonight.

I should be home at about 6 p.m., but we don't need to leave until 7, so you'll have plenty of time to get ready.

See you soon,

Bobby

P.S. Don't argue with Louella when she tells you I've already paid for your outfit for tonight. Just pick what you like best.

Brooklyn wasn't sure whether to be giddy and excited about her second date with Bobby, or nervous about how fancy the event was and worried about fitting in, since she'd never felt like she fit in at the society events she'd attended back in Georgia. Blocking out the harsh voice of her father that threatened to make an appearance in her head, she pulled out her new cell phone and sent a text to her friends to enlist their help in getting ready for the event.

"I'm going to choose to be giddy and excited about tonight," Brooklyn declared as she typed on the fancy phone Bobby had insisted on getting her, so she never risked being out on the ranch without a signal.

> **Brie: Bobby wants me to go get a dress for the New Year's party tonight. Are any of you going? Are you available to help me pick something out to wear this afternoon?**

Kenzie: I'm working all day so I can go tonight. But text me pics & I'll give you my opinion on the dresses you try on.

Ashley: I'm swamped with prep for the party. Catering it tonight but hope to get free to celebrate before midnight.

Heather: I'm at work, but if you go to Destiny Dresses, I can take my break & go next door to help you. ;) Maybe I'll find something new for me to wear tonight too.

Brie: Thx! See you soon!

Brooklyn finished up her meal prep that morning, not wanting to risk running late for her date by cooking that afternoon. Since Kay had told her to wait until the seventh to clean at her house, basically skipping that week, Brooklyn went ahead and cleaned the bathrooms there at Bobby's house, so she wouldn't have to do them the next day, in case he insisted she take the day off for the holiday, like he had on Christmas. She could sweep, dust, and do laundry later in the week while cooking if she needed to in order to make up the day of work.

She took her shower after cleaning the bathrooms, knowing that chore always made her feel dirtier than the rest of the cleaning duties. Once she'd done her hair and makeup and put her colored contacts in, she got dressed and went to town. She still felt a little uncomfortable driving Bobby's car, but he'd insisted she was fine driving it, so she quit arguing the point. She did make a mental note to call Luke when she got home to see how much longer it would be before her car would be fixed. Between the two paychecks she'd gotten from Burleson Incorporated and the royalty payment she'd received for her book sales in October, she thought she had enough to pay for the engine rebuild without any problems.

As soon as she pulled up in front of Destiny Dresses on Appaloosa Avenue, Brooklyn got out of the car and walked to Heart of the Home to see if Heather was able to take her break or not before going into the dress store. Heather introduced "Brie" to her parents, Brent and Honey, who owned the home goods store, before they walked next door.

Brooklyn tried to hide her embarrassment at buying lingerie the last time she'd been in Destiny Dresses when she was reintroduced to Louella, but she wasn't sure she was successful.

"Um, Bobby told me he was going to have you pull some dresses for me to try on to match what he's wearing tonight," Brooklyn informed Louella, knowing her cheeks were probably redder than Rudolph's nose based on how hot they felt.

"Oh, yes," Louella smiled at her before walking over to a rack of dresses and pulling out half a dozen in a rainbow of colors. "He's actually wearing a black tux, so I'm supposed to get him a tie to match whichever dress you pick out and send it home with you for him. We'll take these to the dressing room and let you try them on first."

Brooklyn followed the older woman to the dressing room where she was left with several dresses to try on. She looked over the selection, thinking they all reminded her too much of the gowns she'd had to wear to various events with her father back in Georgia.

Darn it! I was hoping a side benefit of getting away from my father would be avoiding having to wear a girdle again, Brooklyn thought as she tried on the first dress, a sapphire sheath that didn't quite skim along her curves like it would on taller, thinner models.

"Um, do you happen to carry girdles?" Brooklyn took off the first dress and moved to the red one beside it on the rack in the dressing room.

"We do." Louella drew out the word like she was skeptical of the need for the restrictive garment. "But none of those dresses should require one, unless Bobby guessed the wrong size for you."

"I think he guessed the wrong size," Brooklyn announced when the second dress also clung a little too tightly to her body.

"Step out here and let me see," Heather insisted, sounding like she was right outside the dressing room door.

Brooklyn opened the door, but she didn't want to step out of the dressing room in the too tight garment.

"Wow, he got close," Heather smiled.

"Oh, girls, you should've seen him in here trying to decide on the right size," Louella laughed as she walked up with another selection of the same dresses, but apparently a size larger than Bobby had guessed. "He was holding his arms up like he was hugging you to show me the right size. When I had him look at the dresses to pick the closest size, he couldn't tell the difference between a six or an eight. He actually suggested I get mannequins in all the different sizes, so guys like him could come in and hug them to determine the right size to buy for their girlfriends."

"Wow, you've really done a number on our police chief," Heather laughed along with Louella. "I can't imagine broody Bobby hugging mannequins to figure out a dress size."

"Oh, yes, it was definitely a fun-loving side of Bobby Burleson I haven't seen since he was a kid," Louella agreed, swapping out the dresses in the dressing room for the ones she was carrying over, except for the one Brooklyn was still wearing.

"Oh goodness," Brooklyn giggled with the other ladies. "Please don't tell anyone else about it. He's made it clear that I'm not allowed to let anyone else know he's really a big softy, so he can keep crime down in town with his surly attitude."

Louella and Heather both laughed even harder, as Brooklyn shut the dressing room door and went to try on the bigger size dresses. Once she tried on the dress in the correct size, she decided to go with the red, since it was Bobby's favorite color.

Heather picked out a purple dress in a similar style, so Brooklyn was less self-conscious about being too overdressed and not fitting in at the party. They picked out shoes and then went into the back room to find undergarments to match. It felt strange to Brooklyn to pick out a red strapless bra and matching thong to wear to a fancy affair, instead of the nude-colored shapewear she'd had to put on under every dress she'd worn to an event in Georgia since she was sixteen.

But it'll be a lot more appealing to Bobby if I can get him to help me out of the dress tonight, Brooklyn mused as Louella was bagging up her purchases. *And maybe my whole body won't blush as red as the lingerie if I get brave enough to let him see it.*

~~~
~~~

Bobby couldn't believe how many people had come out for the New Year's Eve party in the ballroom of the Hunters' Bed and Breakfast. With it being such a popular party night, he had the whole department working. The phones were all forwarded to the dispatcher's cell phone first and rolling to their receptionist's phone second, so they could relay the calls to whoever was needed all night. They were all in plain clothes, with he and his officers carrying their guns in shoulder holsters with their badges clipped to their belts, so they could all fit in wherever they were celebrating that night. They were also all driving their official police vehicles to have their presence seen on the roads around town to deter drunk driving as much as possible.

Wearing his badge and gun under his tuxedo made Bobby feel a little like James Bond, but he wasn't about to admit to anyone that he was living out one of his childhood fantasies by pretending to be an international spy as he spun Brie around the dance floor.

Forget childhood fantasies, Bobby pondered as he looked down at Brie in the sexy red dress she was wearing. *Brie role-playing as my Bond Girl definitely makes what I'm thinkin' about tonight into adult fantasies. Thank fuck for long tuxedo jackets covering erections.*

He'd probably gone a little overboard with the tux and elegant dress, since the majority of the people at the party were dressed more like they were going to church or for casual Friday at an office. He didn't care though. He wanted to dress up for Brie, and he wanted to be the one to buy her a fancy dress to make her feel as gorgeous as he thought she was in the yoga pants and tank tops she wore most days.

He might not have ever been in a relationship before, but he had sisters and knew that women always felt better about themselves when they got to dress up for a special occasion. Brie had been coming out of her shell and not acting as timid as she'd been when she first got to town. But still, Bobby wanted to do everything he could to reinforce her positive self-image, so she was less likely to revert to the frightened, subservient woman she'd learned to be growing up.

Hearing her confession earlier in the night that she'd never danced with anyone but her father at her cotillion when she was thirteen had made him glad he'd thought to make it a special night for them. He loved being able to be her first in so many ways, but he hated how much she'd missed out on earlier in life. *I'll make sure she never misses out on anything she wants to do in the future,* Bobby mentally reiterated his vow to her just as the song was coming to an end.

"It's almost time, folks," the lead singer of the band announced into the microphone. "Grab your glasses and midnight kissing partners as we count down the last two minutes of two-thousand-eighteen."

"If I forget to tell you later, thank you for bringing me tonight, Bobby," Brie smiled up at him as they made their way off the dance floor and over to the table they'd been sharing with a few family members most of the night. "This is way more fun than the ball drops I've watched on TV the past few years."

"No need to thank me, Brie-Baby." Bobby pulled her chair out for her. "Thank you for giving me the honor of escorting you tonight."

A waiter stopped at their table, offering them all glasses of either champagne or sparkling grape juice. Since he was technically on duty, he'd opted for the grape juice, but was surprised when Brie chose the same.

"You know you can have a glass of champagne." Bobby motioned toward the other tray of drinks. "Just because I have to stay sober while on duty, doesn't mean you have to do the same."

"I know." Brie blushed slightly as she smiled up at him in his seat beside her. "But I want to stay sober, so I don't forget a moment of tonight."

Bobby heard the countdown spreading loudly around the room, but he didn't join in with his fellow revelers. He focused on looking into Brie's eyes, leaning in for his very first midnight kiss.

He may have had a lot of experience in hooking up with women over the years, but he hadn't really kissed anyone since middle school, until recently with Brie. Kissing was just too intimate for a hookup. He felt the same about oral. He'd been happy to get a woman off with his fingers or his condom-covered cock, but never cared about anyone he was with before to want to share bodily fluids of any kind.

Brie was different though, and he couldn't wait to do everything with her that he'd never wanted to do with a woman before. Not just kissing or oral either. He wanted to be inside her bare, planting his seed and making a family with her.

Their lips touched at the stroke of midnight, but Bobby didn't stop with a chaste kiss, like most of the people around them. He pulled her practically into his lap as he plunged his tongue into her mouth. He weaved the fingers of his right hand through her hair to cradle the back of her head, while his left hand rested on the small of her back, pulling her as close as possible while still seated in his chair.

She wrapped her arms around his neck, her hands making a mess of his hair as she returned his impassioned kiss. They were so lost in each other for the first few minutes of the new year, they didn't even hear the noisemakers going off around the room or the band playing **Auld Lang Syne**. It took Luke slapping him on the back and screaming, "Happy New Year," in their ears for them to come up for air.

"Happy New Year, Brie-Baby," Bobby crooned as soon as their eyes met when their lips parted.

"Happy New Year, Bobby," Brie whisper-shouted back, smiling up at him.

They toasted the new year a few minutes later than the rest of the people in the room, but Bobby didn't care.

They didn't have time to share well wishes for the new year with their friends because Bobby's mother appeared and pulled them away to where she had Tia's birthday party set up in the library on the other side of the plantation house. Since Tia would be flying out with her parents that afternoon to go back to work, the family had decided to surprise her with a birthday party as soon as the clock rolled over to her birthday.

"Is this normal for celebrating a family birthday?" Brie leaned into him as they walked down the hall toward the library.

"Naw, Ma would've never let me celebrate just after midnight when I was a kid," Bobby chuckled, pulling her into his side with the arm around her shoulders. "I think she's going senile in her old age."

"Nope, not going senile," Hazel protested from in front of them where she was leading the way to the birthday party. "Grandkids are just special and can get away with a lot more stuff than just plain ol' kids."

"I think she just called you plain," Brie giggled as they walked into the room where the rest of his family was already gathered.

"So much for the first born being special," Bobby sighed, shaking his head.

"There you are," Anthony admonished as soon as the door shut behind them. "What took ya'll so long?"

"I thought we were gonna hafta dump the champagne on them to get them to break their lip lock," Hazel joked with her sons.

"Bobby, you realize that a New Year's kiss is supposed to be at midnight, and when in public it shouldn't last until twelve-oh-five, right?" Anthony quipped, slapping Bobby on the shoulder.

"Sorry. It was my first New Year's kiss, so I didn't know the rules," Brie apologized, shocking Bobby, and causing a roar of laughter from the family around them.

"Alright, enough, quit pickin' on me and let's get to singin' to the birthday girl," Bobby redirected their focus, trying to get his family back on track for the rest of the celebration.

"It's okay, Uncle Bobby." Tia gave him her ornery smile. "I can wait to celebrate my birthday while Memmaw puts you in time out for canoodling when you're not old enough to yet."

"What?" Bobby chuckled at the precocious new teenager.

When they stopped rolling with laughter, his brother and sister-in-law told Bobby and Brie about the lesson on canoodling that Tia had gotten back in October when Hazel, Susan, and Rosa had been talking about Anthony and Kay. Apparently, when Anthony walked in on the conversation, he'd made it clear to the girls that they had to be at least thirty years old to canoodle, which they classified as anything more than chaste kissing.

"Yeah, well, I'll be thirty in six weeks, so I think I'm close enough," Bobby joked, putting his arm around Brie's shoulders.

"Too bad I'm seven years and four weeks away from thirty," Brie shrugged, smirking up at him. "Don't know who you're going to be canoodling with, since I know an upstanding police officer such as yourself would never corrupt me into canoodling before I'm of legal age."

"Seems you've met your match, Bro," Jake chortled before Bobby could reply.

"Yeah, I have," Bobby admitted happily, looking down into Brie's eyes, which were full of mischief and maybe a little inkling of love.

Once the thirteen candles were lit on Tia's birthday cake, the family sang ***Happy Birthday*** to her. They enjoyed a slice of chocolate cake with chocolate frosting while Tia opened her presents. Tia and Maria were pretty tired from not being used to staying up so late, so the party broke up a little after one in the morning, which was perfectly fine with Bobby. That meant he could take Brie home sooner, and hopefully, spend a little more time canoodling without being called into work.

Canoodling, Bobby chuckled under his breath as he pulled up beside the garage when they got home. *Gotta love my family and their goofiness.*

He helped Brie out of his city-issued SUV, wishing he'd been able to drive her to the party in something nicer than the rolling deterrent to drunk driving he'd had to use, just like all the other officers who worked for him.

Brie had been filling the silence of the drive by going over everything that had happened that night that she wanted to commit to memory, allowing Bobby to ponder his plan for spending more time with her when they got home. But as soon as he helped her out of the vehicle and started walking her toward the house, she got very quiet and seemed to be slightly blushing in the faint moonlight.

Is that because she knows I wanna do more tonight than we've done previously, and she's not ready yet? Or is it because she's thinking about what she wants to do when we get inside? Fuck! Should I back off and just kiss her goodnight like I've done the past couple of nights? Or should I push for a repeat of Friday night, so I can get her more comfortable with me touching her to be able to move us to doing more carnal activities sooner?

Unable to decide what course of action to follow, Bobby chose to bide his time by saying, "I need to go lock up my gun for the night," and making a beeline up the back stairs as soon as they got inside.

Fuck! I'm such an idiot, he mentally chastised himself as he removed his tuxedo jacket and started taking off his shoulder holster. *I'm acting like I'm the fucking virgin, unsure what to do next with her.*

Just as he was putting his gun in the lockbox in his closet, he heard a soft knock on his bedroom door. He quickly closed the box and engaged the lock before walking to his bedroom door to open it for Brie.

"Um, can I get you to, um, help me," Brie stuttered out shyly.

"Of course, Brie-Baby," Bobby replied, smiling at her in the hopes of putting her at ease, so she wouldn't be so nervous. "I'm more than happy to help you with whatever you need."

"I, um, got my hair caught in my zipper," Brie informed him, turning around, so he could see a few strands of her long hair stuck in the top of the zipper on the back of her silky red dress. "Can you, maybe, get it unzipped for me?"

"Sure," Bobby choked out, his voice breaking like a pubescent teenager at the thought of seeing Brie's exposed back when he got the zipper undone. Any success he'd had at controlling his cock that night vanished in an instant as soon as his fingers brushed across the skin of her upper back and neck to push the majority of her hair over her shoulder and out of his way.

It took him a little longer than he would have liked to get her hair detangled from the dress, and his cock seemed to grow an extra inch for every extra second he was touching her skin to skin. Once he got most of the hair out of the zipper, with only a couple strands breaking to stay lodged in the teeth, he attempted to unzip the dress. Unfortunately, those couple strands of hair made it difficult to get the zipper moving, prolonging the contact between them.

"Fuck, Brie-Baby," Bobby groaned, bending down to trail open-mouthed kisses down the back of her neck, rapidly losing control of his need to touch and taste her.

"Oh," Brie moaned, leaning back into him.

Bobby took her slight movement as a green light to keep going, so when her zipper finally parted, he dropped to one knee to be able to trail his mouth down her exposed spine. He slipped his big hands under the slinky fabric, pushing the straps of the dress off her shoulders, and fully exposing the back of her red lace bra.

"Tell me to stop, Brie-Baby," Bobby whispered against her skin, continuing to kiss her back as his hands moved around her torso to cup her lace covered tits. "I don't wanna do more than you're ready for, but I don't know that I can control myself much longer if I keep touching you, kissing you like this."

"No," Brie protested breathlessly, placing her hands over his and pressing them harder into her bountiful breasts. "Don't stop. This feels too good to stop."

He continued to knead her breasts, enjoying the perfect handfuls while kissing every inch of her back. Needing her dress out of the way, so he could see the rest of her hot little body, Bobby released his hold on her breasts and moved her hands down so the straps could slip off her arms. As soon as the upper half of the dress was freed from her body, the whole thing slid down, forming a ruby pool at her feet, and exposing her rounded ass, the split between her cheeks barely covered by her red lace thong.

"Fuck, you're so hot," Bobby groaned, resuming running his hands over her curves and kissing his way down across the small of her back to the gorgeous globes. "And you taste so sweet. I have to know if you taste this sweet everywhere. Please, Brie-Baby, will you let me taste your sweet pussy?"

"I, oh, yes, Bobby," Brie panted as Bobby kissed his way over her ass cheeks.

"Bend over, Brie-Baby," Bobby commanded, needing better access. "Grab the stair rail and spread your legs for me."

She followed his instructions to the letter, giving Bobby the best view he'd ever seen in his life—her heart-shaped ass in the air, with her pretty, pink pussy barely covered by the red lace thong that was already wet with her arousal.

Bobby put both knees on the floor and sat back a little toward his heels, so he could bend low enough to get his face between her thighs, inhaling her natural musk mixed with her fruity floral scent. *Fuck, I can't wait to find out if she tastes as good as she smells.*

He gripped her hips, holding her in place as he licked her ass cheeks and thighs, teasing her a little before running a finger under the lace covering her pussy. She was soaking wet and smooth as he ran his finger through her folds for the first time.

"So, fucking, wet," Bobby moaned as he ran the tip of his tongue along the side of her thong, barely grazing her outer lip. "Is that all for me, Brie-Baby?"

"Yes, yes, Bobby," Brie answered as she pushed her creamy cunt back against his face.

"Such a good girl," Bobby praised her as he pushed her thong to the side, exposing her shaved mound for him to lick the slit. "You taste amazing, like sweet honey over tangy fruit. I can't wait to hear you screaming my name when you come on my tongue."

Unable to hold back a moment longer, he devoured her, licking and sucking on her clit before pressing his tongue inside her. She was so tight, he couldn't get in very far, so he went back to focusing on her clit with his mouth as he started to open her up with a single finger.

He took his time, gently pushing inside her while using the mix of his saliva and her cream as lube to work his way in, stopping momentarily as he passed the first knuckle. He could feel the extra tissue of her hymen and had to feel around for the small opening in it that had previously only allowed her menstrual flow through.

Fucking hell, she's tight, he thought as he worked his digit into the opening. He sucked on her clit, hoping that would increase her desire enough to relax her some while he massaged her internal tissues to start opening her up enough to take more than his single finger.

He knew he wasn't going to fuck her that night. But he wanted to start preparing her for when he was finally able to stick his dick in her, so his size wouldn't be too much for her to handle. Wanting to make sure he was arousing her as much as possible, he reached up with his free hand and fondled her breasts, pulling the cups of her bra down to be able to lightly pinch her bare nipples.

If only I could see her tits too, he thought, second-guessing his choice of position for the first time.

"Yes, Bobby, yes," Brie chanted as her hips rocked against his mouth and hand.

He wanted to talk her through the orgasm he knew was building inside her, get her used to the way he liked to talk dirty during sex, but that was impossible with his mouth full of her perfect pussy. So, he backed off a little with his mouth while he pumped his finger in and out of her. "You like that, Brie-Baby? Having your pussy eaten? Being finger-fucked?"

"Yes, Bobby, yes," Brie panted out, matching the movement of her hips with the strokes of his finger in her tight, little channel. "Feels so good, so full."

"Oh, you're not full yet, Brie-Baby," Bobby chuckled, his breath blowing across her clit. "My finger's nothing compared to how full you'll be, when I finally get my cock in your tight, wet cunt."

"Oh, oh gawd, Bobby," Brie shouted as her pussy started convulsing around his finger.

Bobby circled her clit with his tongue before sucking it into his mouth, not wanting to miss a drop of her sweet cream as she came. As her vise-grip on his finger relaxed, Bobby started working a second finger inside her, continuing to alternate between licking and sucking her clit to work her up to a second orgasm.

Thor was hard as steel, trying to hammer his way out of Bobby's pants to take his turn in her warm, slick sheath. But Bobby refused to acknowledge his own carnal needs. He couldn't believe she'd allowed him to go as far as he had and knew she wasn't ready for the way he ached to fuck her. At least not yet. A few more times of him pleasuring her with his mouth and fingers should get her to the point they could start sharing his bed nightly, though.

Thinking of how good it was going to feel when he was finally able to be inside her almost made him come in his pants again as he took her over the edge for a second and third time before backing away. He pulled her down into his lap, spinning her around, so he could suckle her tits while she came down from her euphoric, orgasm high.

When she caught her breath, she started trying to unbutton his shirt, but Bobby stopped her hands. "No, Brie-Baby, not tonight." He gripped her hips and helped her stand back up.

"But I want to touch and kiss you like you did me," Brie pleaded, looking at him imploringly as he got to his own feet.

"And I would love for you to do that," Bobby admitted, grasping her hands again when she moved them back to the buttons on his shirt. "But if you touch me right now, I'm not gonna be able to stop until I'm balls-deep inside you, and I know you're not ready for that yet."

Her eyes widened at his confession and her mouth formed a little O, even though she didn't make a sound. Bobby bent down and picked up her wrinkled dress that he'd been kneeling on, holding it up in front of her to hide the temptation of her body from his eyes.

"Go get ready for bed, Brie-Baby," Bobby directed her, tilting her chin up, so he could give her a quick kiss before stepping back.

"But, uh, don't you…?" Brie pointed at his crotch with the hand not holding her dress up in front of her as her voice trailed off as if she couldn't figure out how to finish her question.

"I'm good, Brie-Baby," Bobby assured her, just as he heard his phone ringing. His over-eager erection quickly deflated when he realized he was being called in to work. "I'm just glad we got to take care of you before I had to leave for work."

He quickly turned and walked into his room, retrieving his phone from his jacket pocket. Seeing his dispatcher's name displayed on the screen, he moved to get his gun back out of the lockbox as he answered the call.

Leah Mae Wright

"Bobby Burleson," he barked into the phone as he started strapping on his shoulder holster.

"Bobby, we have a drunk and disorderly at Tully's with possible firearm discharge," Paisley informed him, sounding flustered by a rough night of calls.

"Thanks, Paisley. On my way," Bobby replied, knowing he needed to quickly clear her line, so she could receive any other calls they got that night.

He didn't take time to change out of the tuxedo pants, shirt, and tie, but he did put on his uniform jacket, instead of the tux jacket before leaving. Brie was still standing in the hall, though she'd slipped her dress back on without zipping it up.

"Everything okay?" She looked up at him with concern written on her face as Bobby stepped out of his room.

"Yeah, just a typical start to the new year," Bobby reassured her, dropping a kiss on her forehead as he passed her in the hallway and headed toward the back stairs. "Get some rest, Brie-Baby. I'll be home as soon as I can."

"Be safe," she implored him, as he bounded down the stairs.

"Always," he shouted back up to her before heading out for a long night of dealing with drunks.

~~~

Tuesday, January 1, 2019

Brooklyn was worried when she ventured through the rest of the house after showering and getting dressed to find that Bobby's bedroom door was still standing wide open, and his bed didn't look slept in. She quickly pulled out her cell phone and sent him a text, needing to know he was safe even though he wasn't home. Not wanting to let on just how worried she was for him, she took a deep breath before carefully wording the message.

**Brie: Good Morning, Bobby. Just wanted to check in and
see if you need me to bring you some food or anything**
~~~

> **since it looks like you're stuck working straight through**
> **from last night.**

Bobby: Morning, Brie-Baby. No need to bring me anything. I'm almost done here. Should be home in an hour or so.

> **Brie: Want me to have breakfast ready when you get**
> **here?**

Bobby: 2nds of what I had to eat before leaving early this morning?

Brooklyn blushed at the insinuation that Bobby would be repeating the oral activities of the early morning hours when they first got home from the New Year's party. She still couldn't believe how wonderful it had felt to have him bring her to orgasm—multiple times—with his mouth on her sex.

Thinking back to the feel of his hands on her body and his finger inside her as he licked her intimately was almost enough to bring her right back to the edge. She'd thought she'd alleviated the need for release with her fumbling in the shower while reliving the experience. But apparently, just thinking of Bobby and his talented tongue was enough to excite her all over again.

She tried to think of how to reply to Bobby's text without wetting her panties while remembering the way he made her feel earlier. But she was unable to come up with a response before the phone beeped with another message from him.

Bobby: The only thing I'm hungry for right now is you, Brie-Baby. But I might need a couple hours sleep before I can taste you again without losing control.

> **Brie: Then I'll go get your bed ready for you. We can go**
> **for 2nds once you wake up. ;)**

Bobby: You're too good to me. ;) See you soon!

Brooklyn rerouted herself, heading straight for the linen closet, so she could change Bobby's bedding first thing. She set the clean sheets on the dresser before stripping the bed. Once she had the fresh sheets in place, she went back to the linen closet to grab a clean quilt to cover the sheets.

After making the bed, she second-guessed her decision to turn down the bedding for him to have easy access to sleep before finally grabbing all the dirty linens to carry down to the laundry room. She started the first load of bedding washing before grabbing the vacuum cleaner, wanting to do as much of the loud cleaning as she could before Bobby would need her to be quiet while he slept.

She'd just finished vacuuming the carpeted bedrooms when she heard Bobby's police cruiser pulling down the drive. *Perfect timing,* Brooklyn realized as she put the vacuum cleaner away. *I should be able to sweep and mop downstairs without being too loud and waking him up when he needs to catch up on his sleep after working all night.*

She met her tired man in the downstairs hallway, where he was apparently looking for her in every room on the first floor before going up to bed. "Oh, Bobby, are you okay?" She was concerned by how exhausted he looked.

"I'm better now that I'm home with you," Bobby smiled, pulling her into his arms and brushing his lips across hers.

"You need to go up to bed," Brooklyn advised, pulling back from their brief kiss.

"Shower first, then sleep." Bobby pulled her along as he walked toward the stairs. "But I might need your help in the shower, so I don't fall asleep and drown."

Brooklyn blushed at the thought of getting in the shower with Bobby. Even if it was only to keep him awake while he got cleaned up, she couldn't think of seeing him naked for the first time without her cheeks turning pink.

"Don't worry, Brie-Baby," Bobby chuckled, kissing the top of her head before releasing his hold on her at the top of the stairs. "I'm not too tired to shower alone. I know you're not ready for what I'd do if we were both naked in there. So, I'm gonna let you go back to writing while I clean up and take a nap."

"You sure you don't need anything to eat?" Brooklyn was worried that he'd missed breakfast.

"Positive," Bobby insisted, his lips barely turning up as his eyelids started to droop. "I'll eat when I wake up."

"Okay," Brooklyn sighed, wishing there was something she could do for him as he turned to walk into his room. He'd given up sleeping the previous night to take care of his town; now she wanted to take care of him.

When he closed the door between them, Brooklyn resigned herself to the fact that the best thing she could do for him was leaving him alone so he could rest. She went back downstairs and finished up the rest of the chores that she could do without making too much noise. When she had to carry the clean linens back upstairs, she used the back staircase, so Bobby wouldn't be disturbed by her using the stairs right by his bedroom.

She set up her laptop on the kitchen island, so she could write while cooking dinner, spending the rest of her afternoon working on the final chapter of her next book. It still needed to be proofread and edited, but she was pretty happy with how her characters found their happily ever after.

Just as she was bending over to check the casserole in the oven, Bobby walked into the kitchen. "Damn, Brie-Baby." Bobby's voice was husky from sleep. "As much as I love the view of your sexy ass in those tight yoga pants, it's too bad you're not wearing one of your skirts."

"You prefer me wearing skirts?" Brooklyn stood back up and turned to look at Bobby. She was instantly defensive, half expecting a tirade about how women were supposed to dress, like her father would have lectured her if he could see her choice of clothing at that moment.

"Brie-Baby, you look sexy as fuck, no matter what you wear," Bobby proclaimed, calming her defensiveness with his lusty look and dirty words. "But if you were wearing one of those skirts you like to wear on Sundays, I could push it up outta the way and eat you for an appetizer while you're finishing up dinner."

"Bobby!" Brooklyn gasped, knowing she was turning beet red at the thought of him with his head under her skirt while she was trying to cook. "That sounds like a good way to end up with a burnt dinner."

"And I would relish every bite," Bobby promised, grinning, and pulling her into his arms. "I mean, it seems only appropriate that my worshiping you for the goddess you are, would lead to you serving me burnt offerings as if I were a god."

Brooklyn couldn't help but giggle at the ridiculousness of the man, who could easily pass as a Greek god, making such a statement. She wrapped her arms around his waist, returning his embrace as they enjoyed the moment of levity.

"Seriously, though," Bobby stated, brushing his lips over the top of her head. "How long do we have before dinner's ready? Think I have enough time for a Brie-Baby appetizer?"

"No," Brooklyn admonished, pulling back even though Bobby didn't seem to want to let her go. "It's almost done. Like, on the table in less than five minutes, almost done."

"Fine," Bobby huffed, finally releasing her. "I'll just have to have you for dessert, then."

Brooklyn hid her blush by turning away from him to remove the casserole from the oven. *Hopefully, he'll think I'm pink from the heat of the oven, and not think I'm too inexperienced to want to keep doing the things he's suggesting.*

Bobby walked over to the cabinet and got out plates and utensils to set the table, while Brooklyn carried the casserole dish to the dining room. Soon, they were sitting there dishing up their plates and chatting as if it was any other night, without any further sexual innuendo or flirty banter to bring out Brooklyn's blush.

Part of her was glad, hating that she couldn't control the physiological flushing that signaled her slight embarrassment when talking about sex. But another part of her was worried that Bobby was backing off on the flirtatious, sexual repartee because he was also going to be backing off from actually doing anything sexual with her. Too shy to ask Bobby for more of what she really wanted, Brooklyn settled in and listened as he told her about all the drunk and disorderly calls he went on after leaving her standing in her orgasm-induced stupor in the upstairs hallway.

"Thankfully, the firearm discharge was just Old Man Thompson," Bobby sighed, shaking his head.

"Firearm discharge?" Brooklyn gasped. She'd realized that Bobby's job was dangerous, but she hadn't really thought it was too risky in the small, friendly town. Hearing that he went on a call where someone was shooting a gun, even if it wasn't at him, frightened her in a way she hadn't ever experienced before.

"Not a big deal, Brie-Baby," Bobby assured her, reaching over to squeeze her hand in a comforting gesture. "Kenneth Thompson has had a thing for pulling out his BB gun to scare the boys away from his daughter, Kara, since she started high school more than a decade ago. Worst he's ever done was when he clipped Leo Walker in the ass, when he kissed Kara goodnight on Prom night."

"Wait, Kara? From Kara's Kakes?" Brooklyn questioned, making sure she knew who Bobby was talking about.

"Yeah," Bobby chuckled.

"But she's an adult, a few years older than me," Brooklyn clarified. "And he's still trying to scare the guys away from his daughter with a gun?"

"Only when he's drunk," Bobby grinned. "And only Leo Walker. Which is why it's a good thing he only goes for his BB gun, since Leo's the bartender at the only bar in town."

"But he's still going after someone with a gun," Brooklyn protested Bobby's lackadaisical attitude toward the crime. "That's still a dangerous situation that he should be arrested for, right?"

"He was arrested," Bobby informed her, shaking his head. "Along with several other drunks last night. And if it were anyone other than Old Man Thompson, a BB gun could still be dangerous. But his arthritis is so bad nowadays that he can barely get one pump into his old Daisy rifle, and it requires at least three or four pumps to produce enough air pressure to do more than drop a BB out of the end of the gun."

Not understanding how guns worked or the differences between the various types to know what Bobby meant by his explanation, Brooklyn just looked at him in confusion. Bobby ended up spending the rest of the meal teaching her about air guns in comparison to what she considered regular guns. He even offered to pull his old BB gun out of the gun safe in the attic to teach her how to shoot it to try to make it more understandable for her. But Brooklyn declined the offer, not having any desire to fire a weapon.

"So, how much writing did you get done while I was sleeping?" Bobby changed the subject as they stood to take their dishes to the kitchen.

"I finished my book," Brooklyn beamed, excited about completing the series.

"Yeah?" Bobby arched an eyebrow, grinning at her as he sat the casserole dish on the island while she put their plates in the sink. "Does that mean I can read it now? Or are you gonna make me wait until it's edited and published first?"

"You want to read my book?" Brooklyn was surprised that he'd want to read a young adult story. "It's not too juvenile for you? It's nowhere near the crime thrillers you usually like to read."

"I wanna read everything you write, Brie-Baby," Bobby grinned, turning to grab the Tupperware containers out of the cabinet for Brooklyn to put the leftovers in to take to Justin and JJ the next day. "It doesn't matter what genre it is; it's your words I wanna read."

"Oh, okay." Brooklyn wasn't sure why she was blushing at the thought of him reading her books. She pointed to her laptop that was still open on the island. "The manuscript is still open on my computer if you want to read it now. But I haven't even proofread it yet, so don't be surprised if you catch a lot of typos."

Bobby sat down on the stool at the island that she'd been using to sit and type earlier. He read while she finished cleaning up. She nervously watched as he read, observing how he only used the arrow key to scroll through the document, and didn't appear to be correcting any errors he found.

She wasn't sure if she should ask him to fix her mistakes or not. She was too worried that he wouldn't like the story to care if he caught any typographical errors in her first draft.

He didn't say a word as she put away the leftovers and washed all the dishes. When she was done with all she could do to kill time while he read, she walked around the island to see how far he was able to read. *Wow! He must be a speed reader,* Brooklyn thought when she noticed he'd gotten almost halfway through the book in the time it took her to clean up after dinner.

"Done?" Bobby looked up from the screen to look into her eyes.

"Yeah, but I can come up with something else to do while you finish reading."

"I have a better idea." Bobby stood up and scooped Brooklyn up into his arms. "I'll read the rest after I have dessert."

"I didn't make dessert tonight," Brooklyn admitted as she looped her arms around Bobby's neck. She wasn't sure what Bobby's plans were for the rest of the night, but she was enjoying the way he was carrying her, and not acting like he was backing off on their physical relationship as much as he had during dinner.

"No, Brie-Baby," Bobby chuckled, wagging his eyebrows suggestively as he carried her back into the dining room. "You're dessert tonight."

"Wha-what?" Brooklyn stuttered, shocked at Bobby setting her down beside the table and deftly sliding her yoga pants and panties down her legs before gripping her waist and placing her on the table where his plate had just been an hour before.

"You're my dessert, Brie-Baby," Bobby declared, locking their gazes as he took his seat. He finished removing her clothing before gripping her by the nape of her neck to pull her in for a passionate kiss.

"I know you're not ready for me to take you to my bed just yet." Bobby's voice deepened with desire as he trailed his mouth down her body. "But I intend to get you ready for me by eating your pussy every chance I get."

"Oh," was all Brooklyn could choke out as Bobby latched onto her breast. He had her completely naked in front of him for the first time and seemed determined to taste every inch of her exposed skin. She felt off balance seated precariously on the edge of the table, but instead of leaning back onto her hands for stability, she ran them up Bobby's arms and over his strong shoulders.

She wanted to remove his t-shirt and athletic shorts, so she could touch and taste him the same way he was her. But the exquisite way he was teasing her with his tongue kept her request lodged in her throat. All she could do was moan in pleasure and enjoy the way he reverently caressed and kissed her in places she hadn't realized were erogenous zones while working his way down her body to the areas she longed to feel him.

As his hands swept down her thighs, Brooklyn would have sworn she felt an electric current scorching her in their wake. When his large palms reached her knees, he gently pushed them apart, spreading her legs open to fully expose her sex.

"Oh, Bobby," Brooklyn moaned as he grazed her nipple with his teeth. The erotic sensation felt like lightning striking from her breast to her core, blowing up any last vestige of a dam holding back her arousal from flooding out of her.

She couldn't think rationally enough to worry about whether or not her bodily fluids would damage the wood beneath her. The pleasure coursing through her was drowning out all thoughts and worries from her mind. She couldn't ponder the possibilities of their relationship or where it would go from there. She couldn't worry about the outcome of everything with her father back in Georgia, or how it might impact her future. All she could do was feel.

The light suction of his mouth as he trailed open-mouthed kisses down her body. The gentle pinch of his fingers on her nipples as they replaced his mouth that was now moving farther south. The light tickle of his breath on her belly as he licked his way down toward her mound. Even the slight scratchiness of his stubble on her skin felt amazing in her sexually charged state.

As Bobby bent lower to trail butterfly kisses over her pubic bone, Brooklyn weaved her fingers through the soft, short strands of his dark hair. She loved the way he kept his hair cut short that allowed her to mess up the tresses while it still looked like it was styled. She also loved having his hands in her hair as much as she loved her hands in his.

Love. Maybe that really is what I'm feeling. And not just for his hair or the way he touches and tastes me.

Brooklyn's train of thought was lost as Bobby's lips closed over her clit. He suckled softly, causing her eyes to fly open in surprise. Their gazes locked as he started to tease her with his tongue.

"That's it, Brie-Baby," Bobby reverently whispered, his warm breath titillating her bundle of nerves as he spoke. "I want you to watch me eat your pussy. See how much I love licking all this sweet cream from your cunt."

"Oh, oh, yes," Brooklyn panted, watching as he licked through her folds before tightening the muscle of his tongue to push it partially in her slit. He mimicked what she imagined he would eventually do with his penis, bobbing his head and stroking in and out.

"Tell me what you like best, Brie-Baby," Bobby commanded, pulling his tongue out of her to lick back up to her clit.

"I li-like it all, Bobby," Brooklyn moaned, feeling her climax building deep in her core.

"Do you prefer it when I fuck you with my tongue?" Bobby poked her opening with his hardened tongue. "Or do you prefer it when I lick every crevice of your cunt?"

Brooklyn could barely breathe, unable to speak as he once again demonstrated what he was asking her about.

"I think your favorite is when I suck on your little clit," Bobby growled before demonstrating once more.

"Yes, Bobby, yes," Brooklyn cried out, the suction on her bud taking her over the edge to oblivion. The waves of pleasure crashed over her like a stormy sea against a rocky shoreline. Hard, fast, and seeming to be never ending.

When she thought Bobby was backing off to let her come down, he pushed a finger inside her, and found a spot that took her right back up to the heights of ecstasy. He pushed the digit in farther than he had his tongue, and kept rubbing the mysterious button inside her that had her screaming his name as she came harder than she'd ever come before.

It was all she could do to keep her eyes open and on his, as her whole body seemed to spasm in orgasmic bliss.

"Fuck, yes, keep coming, Brie-Baby," Bobby ordered in that deep, gravelly voice that only seemed to come out when they were intimate. Her body obeyed his command, even as he pushed a second finger inside her, stretching her inner walls as they clamped down on his digits.

"Keep those beautiful blue eyes on me, Brie-Baby. I want you to know exactly who's making you come so fucking hard. Only me. No one else will ever make you come like this."

"Yes, Bobby, yes," Brooklyn exclaimed as he took her over the edge once more.

"You're all fucking mine," Bobby growled, gentling his strokes as he brought her down from her climax.

"Yes, Bobby, I'm all yours," Brooklyn barely breathed out, feeling like she was about to collapse from the intense multi-orgasmic experience.

Observing her jello-limbed state, Bobby sat up and pulled her down into his lap. He cradled her there as she caught her breath, stroking one hand over her head and the other over her back. As she came back into her body from the other realm where he'd taken her, Brooklyn noticed the large ridge in his shorts pressing against her behind.

She sat up and kissed him as she twisted in his lap to straddle him. When he deepened the kiss, she tasted her arousal on his tongue. It wasn't a flavor she expected. Not as sweet as Bobby had claimed during their first oral exploration in the wee hours of the morning. But it also wasn't as unappealing as she'd read about online either.

Brooklyn ran her hands along the planes of muscle on Bobby's torso, working her way down to the hem of his shirt and wanting to remove it as she rocked her still wet center on the bulge in his shorts.

"No, Brie-Baby," Bobby barked, pulling back from their kiss to stop her from lifting his shirt.

"But I need you naked," Brooklyn protested, "so I can touch and taste you, too."

"Fuck," Bobby groaned, drawing out the word to multiple syllables. "As much as I want that, Brie-Baby, it's not happening tonight."

"Why?" Brooklyn felt hurt by his denial of her reciprocation.

"Because I can't guarantee I'll be able to maintain control if you touch me," Bobby insisted, his eyes pleading for her understanding. "I hafta keep my clothes on until you're ready for me to be inside you."

"But it's not fair that I got to come like a half-dozen times and you haven't," Brooklyn whispered, still wishing she could do something to make him feel as good as he'd just made her feel.

"Trust me, Brie-Baby," Bobby smirked. "I enjoyed watching you come more than I've ever enjoyed coming myself. I'm good. And Thor will be fine waiting 'til you're ready to meet him."

"Thor?" Brooklyn giggled. "You named your penis, Thor?"

"What can I say?" Bobby shook his head and smiled. "I was really into Marvel movies and when I got my first erection I thought it was as hard as Thor's hammer. Since I'm not sure of the proper pronunciation of the name of the hammer, I figured Thor was the better name to use."

"I can't believe you named your penis," Brooklyn squealed, laughing outright at the silliness of the situation.

"I can't believe you keep saying penis, instead of dick or cock," Bobby laughed with her, tickling her to keep her laughing when it started to die down.

"Stop, stop, stop," Brooklyn shrieked, squirming in his lap until they both almost fell out of the chair.

"I'll stop when you say cock." Bobby rolled them out of the chair to land on the floor with her on top of him.

"Cock, cock, cock," Brooklyn screamed to get him to stop tickling her.

Bobby stopped tickling her to pull her down for another amazing kiss. When they broke the lip lock, Bobby shocked her by saying, "Now let me up, woman. And quit distracting me with your nudity. I need to go finish reading your manuscript before bedtime."

<div align="center">~~~</div>

Saturday, January 5, 2019

Bobby was glad to have a day off after spending the first few days of the new year making court appearances for all the drunk and disorderly arrests he and his officers had made in the early hours of the new year. While he'd still made sure to spend some time each evening with Brie to touch and taste every inch of his woman, a few hours a day with her were just not enough.

As impractical as he knew it was, he wanted to have her with him every minute of every day. Even having to share her with his family at breakfast on the weekend was better than how he missed her presence while they were working during the week.

Maybe once everything is cleared up in Georgia, she won't feel like she has to work on the ranch to pay her own way, Bobby thought as they left his parents' house to go pick up her car. *If she can go back to just writing for her job, then maybe I can convince her to do that in my office, so we can be close while we work.*

Looking over at his independent woman in the passenger seat of his truck, Bobby realized that keeping her by his side twenty-four-seven was extremely improbable. With the way Brie had insisted on going to pick up her car, which he thought should've gone to the junkyard instead of to the repair shop, he knew she would be too stubborn to stay within his sight at all times. She needed the freedom to go off and do her own thing, after years of feeling imprisoned by her father, so Bobby was fighting his inner caveman to keep from making her feel similarly imprisoned by his need to be with her.

Leah Mae Wright

"Where am I going to need to park when we get my car home?"
Brie smiled at him as he turned into the parking lot for Luke's Garage.

At least she's thinking of my house as home, Bobby realized,
smiling as he parked. *I suppose I can't really ask for more than her
wanting to live there with me, at least for now. Fuck! I gotta quit
trying to jump ahead to marriage and babies, when I haven't even
convinced her that she loves me yet.*

"I'll move the cruiser over beside the garage, so you can park where
I normally park it," Bobby replied, turning off the truck and getting out
to go around and help her down from the passenger seat.

Bobby took the opportunity to steal a quick kiss before setting her
on the ground. He shut the passenger door and hit the lock button on
his key fob before pocketing it with one hand and grabbing Brie's
hand with the other.

"Are you sure?" Brie gave him a curious look as they walked hand
in hand into the garage. "I can park beside the garage instead."

"No, Brie-Baby," Bobby demanded, shaking his head as he held the
door open for her to precede him into the office of Luke's Garage.
"One good rain and your little car would be stuck in the mud on the
side of the garage. The four-wheel drive on the cruiser is better
equipped to park in the grass, while you need to stay on the
pavement."

"Yeah, I'd suggest new tires before she even takes the gravel roads
on the ranch," Luke interjected, stepping into the office from the
maintenance bays of the garage.

*Fuck! How bad are her damn tires that Luke doesn't think they can
handle the gravel road between our houses?*

"What's wrong with the tires?" Brie looked confused. "I thought it
was just the engine you had to fix?"

"It was just the engine to get it running again," Luke corrected, his
mouth a grim line. "But running and in decent enough shape to
actually go anywhere are two different things."

"Fuck," Bobby swore loudly. "Let me see this car to see if we're
gonna finish fixing it, or trade it in for something else."

Luke pointed to the back door, directing Bobby and Brie to the
fenced-in lot behind the garage, where he stored the vehicles he was
working on until their owners came to pick them up. Brie didn't
protest when he pulled her by the hand to go look at her car, but she

was obviously irritated by him taking over the decisions about her vehicle. As bad as he wanted to back off and let her have control of her life by making the choice of what else was being done to her jalopy, one look at the beat-up, old, blue Honda was all he needed to decide that she wouldn't be driving anywhere in the death trap.

"As you can see, the tires are bald." Luke pointed at the left front tire as they approached the car. "There's a slow leak in the radiator. I put some Bar's Leaks in it for now, but it's gonna need a new radiator pretty soon. With the engine going the way it did, I'm not sure how much longer the transmission will last before it needs to be replaced or rebuilt, too. And that's not counting the cosmetic and comfort repairs it needs to the body and air conditioner, or the fact that it's missing a radio."

"Fuck," Bobby cursed under his breath.

"It's fine for now," Brie insisted, pulling her hand out of Bobby's, and reaching out toward Luke as if he was supposed to give her the keys. "It's not like I'm doing a lot of driving. So, we can fix all these other things a little at a time as they need it."

"No!" Bobby shouted. Brie jumped at his loud tone, so Bobby softened his voice to continue, reaching out to take both of her hands in his. "Brie-Baby, I can't let you drive this car. Not in the condition it's in right now. It's not safe."

"It was safe enough to get me from Georgia to here," Brie protested, giving him puppy-dog eyes to try to sway him to her opinion. "So, I'm sure it will be fine to go to and from the grocery store for a week or two. We can start with putting new tires on it next week when I get my next paycheck. Then the radiator and whatever else, every other week."

"Brie-Baby," Bobby groaned, closing his eyes because he was unable to look at her imploring expression without giving in to whatever she wanted. "I'm trying my best to let you make all your own decisions and be independent because I know that's what you need. But I can't bend on this, not when it comes to your safety. That car is an accident waiting to happen. Please, let me use it as a trade-in and get you something newer to drive."

"Why do I need something newer to drive when your car is almost as old as the two of us combined?" Brie tugged on his hand to get him to look back into her big, bright, blue eyes. "Your car is over three times as old as this one, ya know."

"Yeah, I know," Bobby chuckled, unable to hold back his amusement at her impertinence. "It's also a collector's item and in pristine condition, with a metal body, so it's safer in a crash than your fiberglass Accord."

"Wait, she's comparing her car to your Charger?" Luke laughed so hard he almost doubled over. Bobby nodded, trying not to laugh as hard as his friend. "Brie, darlin', you can't compare a car that's worth less than the cost of a new engine with a hundred-thousand-dollar Mopar machine."

"You've had me driving around in a hundred-thousand-dollar car?" Brie screeched, her eyes bugging out in shock.

"It's just a car," Bobby defended, shaking his head.

"No, it's not," Brie disagreed, shaking her head back at him. "That's like saying a painting by Picasso is just a piece of art. A car that expensive should be on display in a museum, so it can be appreciated by the car connoisseurs of the world."

"Naw, he just needs to take it to car shows once in a while," Luke interjected.

"Shut up, Lucas," Bobby growled at his friend, wishing his buddy hadn't escalated his disagreement with Brie by butting into their conversation.

"Now I absolutely have to take my car now, and do the other repairs later," Brie pouted, stomping her foot like a child demanding her way. "There's no way I can drive around in a collector's item I couldn't afford to replace because it costs more than four years of my salary."

Without any other ideas for how to quell her tantrum, Bobby dipped his head and covered her mouth with his, swallowing whatever she was continuing to try to say. When she quit trying to speak and returned his ardent kiss, he savored her taste for several long moments, making sure to leave her breathless when he finally lifted his lips from hers.

"How 'bout we go home and finish this discussion in private?" Bobby was ready to throw her over his shoulder and carry her to his truck if she protested.

"Oh, okay," Brie acquiesced, too dazed from his drugging kisses to continue to protest.

"If ya'll decide to use it as a trade-in on something else," Luke started as they walked back through the office toward the front of the garage. "I'll buy it from you for the cost of the engine."

"What?" Bobby and Brie simultaneously looked over at Luke in surprise.

"I need a junker to use in the auto body class I'm starting at the youth center," Luke shrugged. "Buying Brie's will save me from having to go look for one in San Antonio that's in bad enough shape to be educational for the kids, and still salvageable enough to be worth something to the lucky teenager who wins it in a drawing at the end of the class."

"Yeah, we'll let you know," Bobby nodded, knowing he'd still cover the cost of the engine Luke had put into the vehicle, and have Brie just donate it to the center to save all the red tape of titling it multiple times to sell it to Luke, then him donating it to the center, then the center giving it to one of the local teens. If he could convince his Aunt Susan's sister, Sarah Harper, who managed the local 4-H Youth Center, and was sort of his honorary aunt, to leave the car in Brie's name until they gifted it to one of the teenagers once it was repaired, then he wouldn't worry so much about Brie selling the car, and accidentally sending a signal to her father about where she was hiding.

"Wait, we didn't get my car," Brie argued as Bobby helped her into the passenger seat of his truck.

"Yeah, I know," Bobby nodded, shutting her door before she could hop out of the truck to go back for her car. He walked around and got in the driver's seat before continuing. "We're gonna discuss it at home, remember?"

"Why do we have to go home to discuss it?" Brie's insolence didn't stop her from buckling her seatbelt just after Bobby did, so she'd stay safe while he drove them home.

"Because I have a feeling the only way I'm gonna be able to convince you to let me take care of you is if I have this discussion with your lower lips." Bobby winked at his shocked sweetheart.

"But, we, uh, can't do that today," Brie stuttered, blushing brightly at his innuendo.

Leah Mae Wright

"Oh, Brie-Baby," Bobby grinned. "I can absolutely eat your pussy all day, every day."

"No, not now," Brie protested, looking mortified at the thought, which was confusing for Bobby, since he thought she'd loved how he licked her every day so far this year. "It's, um, shark week, so we can't now."

"Shark week?" Bobby chuckled at how weird she was being. *What the fuck is she talking about? Shark week isn't until like July or August.*

"Yeah, ya know," Brie drawled, starting to hum the theme to the movie *Jaws*. "Duh-dum. Duh-dum. Dun-dum, dun-dum, dun-dum, dun-dum, dun-dum, dun-dum, dun-dum."

"No, I don't know," Bobby chuckled lightly at her silly antics.

"You can't go swimming because there's blood in the water," Brie warned, raising an eyebrow at him before nodding down at her crotch. "Shark week started this morning."

Shark week? Blood in the water? Oh, fuck, she's referring to her period, Bobby realized. *Damn, she's adorable being too shy to just say that.*

"I'm not afraid of a little blood." Bobby knew he could just keep his mouth focused on her clit and wash his hands after fingering her. *Hell, that's not any more exposure to her blood than it'll be when I finally pop her cherry.*

"Gross, no," Brie gagged, unbuckling her seatbelt when he turned the truck off after pulling into the garage at home. "You're not touching me down there until the bleeding stops."

"Oh, Brie-Baby," Bobby crooned, getting out of the truck, and going around to help her down before continuing. "I guess it's a good thing we both already know that I can still get you off without even removing our clothes. Though I won't even do that if it risks making your cramps worse."

"Luckily, my cramps aren't too bad." Brie blushed shyly as they walked inside. "So, I'm willing to let you try to convert me to your way of thinking by doing those other things."

"Good." Bobby scooped her up into his arms and carried her toward the family room. "I'm thinking we need to just donate your car to the youth center."

"And if I had another vehicle to drive that wasn't so expensive, I'd agree with you," Brie nodded as Bobby plopped down on the couch with her on his lap.

"My car's really not that expensive," Bobby explained, adjusting her on top of him, so she was straddling him, his ever-present erection pressed into her center. He kept his hands on her hips, so he could grind their pelvises together. "I only paid like five grand for it. Luke was quoting you a price he'd seen recently for a show car like it online."

"But if you went to sell it, you'd be able to sell it for closer to a hundred-thousand than five-thousand," Brie argued while running her palms over his chest and shoulders, desire lighting up her eyes.

"But I'm never gonna sell it, so it doesn't matter," Bobby maintained, thrusting his hips up to press his hard-as-steel dick into the juncture of her thighs. "Even if I end up having to build a second garage to keep it in, so you can park whatever vehicle you end up with in the garage, I have no plans to ever get rid of the Charger. I hope to share my love of classic cars with a kid or two in the coming years, and plan to pass it down to the next generation to have something to remember me by when I die."

"Oh," Brie moaned, her breathing turning to more of a panting rhythm as his cock pressed against her clit.

Bobby wasn't sure if she was acknowledging his statement about keeping his car, or just responding to her increased state of arousal. But he couldn't think about cars anymore while enjoying her heat rubbing up and down his length. He slid one hand up her back to grip the back of her neck, pulling her mouth to his.

Their lips barely touched before she was opening for him, allowing his tongue to plunder her mouth. She timed the rocking motion of her hips in sync with his thrusts, so he moved his other hand from her hip up to cup her tit. With the way she responded to his kiss, her tongue dueling with his for dominance, he knew he didn't have to hold her head in place any longer. So, he pulled his right hand down to match his left, cupping her other breast.

He alternated between kneading her breasts and pinching her nipples between his thumbs and forefingers, hating the barrier of her shirt and bra between his hands and her bare skin. He didn't think the limit to touching her only over her clothes during her period should include her bountiful breasts. But he didn't know if they were more sensitive during that time of the month, and needed the barrier to keep his touch from being painful, so he didn't want to interrupt what they were doing to ask.

I'll ask her after I get her off a couple of times first. That way I can make sure it's all good for her, and maybe do a little more later if she's up for it. First and foremost, I don't wanna risk hurting her in any way.

They made out for what seemed like only minutes, but somehow turned into several hours. Bobby was surprised he was able to hold his own orgasm off while bringing her over the edge several times.

She eventually told him that while her breasts weren't more tender during that time of the month, she didn't think she could handle the temptation of taking all her clothes off if he removed her top and bra.

Bobby respected her wishes, telling her, "I'll wait until you signal me that you're ready for more by wearing an easy access skirt and sexy thong, then."

"Mmm, deal," Brie cooed, diving back into their amorous kissing session. Only pulling back briefly to add, "But what I wear to church tomorrow doesn't count as your signal for more."

"Of course," Bobby agreed between kisses. "Church dresses don't count as oral sex signals."

Chapter Ten

Sunday, January 13, 2019

The first two weeks of the new year seemed to be flying by for Brooklyn. In addition to settling into her routine for work on the ranch and finishing her fourth book on New Year's Day, she'd also decided to donate her car to the youth center, so Bobby wouldn't worry about her being unsafe driving it. He insisted she keep driving his Charger, at least, until everything was cleared up in Georgia, so they wouldn't set off any red flags to her father about where she was by buying her a car in her real name.

After talking to Kay and Tia the first weekend of the month to let them know she'd finished the book, she'd emailed the manuscript to Kay, so the older author could help her edit it before submitting it for publication. She wasn't sure her real story was going to have the happily ever after ending for her and Bobby that Mary Kate and Adam had in the book, but she was hopeful with every day she spent with Bobby that life could imitate art in her case.

She was convinced that she'd fallen completely, head over heels in love with him, and knew she'd be devastated if they weren't able to stay together after things were cleared up in Georgia. It was that lingering fear in the back of her mind, that she would have to move back to Macon without him, keeping her from saying those three little words to him.

Well, that and the fact they hadn't made love yet. Brooklyn knew that she wouldn't be able to hold back the L-word when they joined their bodies together the first time. She also wasn't sure how much longer she could hold out without begging him to make love to her.

Since New Year's, he'd continued to make sure she was satiated every night, spending hours giving her pleasure with his mouth and

"

fingers, but she was starting to really feel guilty for not reciprocating. She didn't think she could really count the few orgasms he'd had while dry-humping during her period because they happened at the same time as her own climaxes.

He kept telling her that as much as he wanted her to touch and taste him too, he couldn't let her do anything more than touching him over his clothes until she was ready to go all the way. Brooklyn wasn't quite sure she completely understood why he felt that way, but she was trying to be patient and let him progress their relationship as slow as he felt necessary.

It's so hard, though, when just him rubbing my shoulder while we're sitting together in church is enough to make my nipples hard and my panties wet, Brooklyn thought as they sat there talking with his sisters while everyone finished eating at the potluck dinner after the services. *Wondering if he's going to set me up on the kitchen island when we get home to eat me for dessert again is almost enough to make me come right here in my seat. Jeez, the things that man can do with his tongue.*

Brooklyn unconsciously fanned herself, trying to cool down some of the heat building up inside her from thinking about the way Bobby had licked and kissed her everywhere over the past couple of weeks.

"You alright, Brie-Baby?" Bobby looked at her with concern.

"Oh, uh, yeah," Brooklyn sputtered, dropping her hand when she realized she was fanning herself where everyone could see. "Still feel a little warm from the spice in that chili," she lied, trying to cover her racy thoughts while sitting in church with Bobby's whole family. *Lord, forgive me for lying in church,* she silently prayed.

"I guess chili that spicy is an acquired taste," Bobby's sister, Becky, smiled at Brooklyn. "Give yourself a few more months to get used to it and it won't seem so spicy anymore. That's how you'll know you're officially a Texan."

"Maybe," Brooklyn replied, smiling back at Becky. *But I doubt a few months with Bobby will be enough to keep him from getting me hot and bothered with just a brief thought about all the things I love having him do to my body.*

The small talk around the table switched to what everyone wanted to do that day, since it was one of the rare days it rained in January, which was apparently the driest month of the year for the area.

"I really need to spend the afternoon grading essays," Charlotte sighed, trying to bow out of participating in a family game day.

"You really shouldn't have to work on your birthday, Char," Bobby commented, smiling at his sister.

"Yeah, don't you have time during your day at school to grade papers?" Becky arched an eyebrow at her sister.

"Normally, I do," Charlotte huffed in frustration. "But the new English teacher started this week, and I've had to spend my planning period, when I'd normally have graded these papers, babysitting him."

"Why are you having to babysit him?" Becky looked quizzically at Charlotte.

"Because he can't seem to comprehend the fact that he can't change the syllabus in the middle of the school year," Charlotte complained. "With only two English teachers and three grades to teach, we have to split the seventh graders between our classrooms, but they should still be learning the same thing, no matter which teacher they're assigned to."

"Right, I remember you saying something about how your class schedule had to change at the beginning of the year because of having so many more seventh graders than sixth or eighth graders," Becky nodded her head at her sister.

"Yes, exactly, that's why we did the lesson plans for the whole year before classes even started," Charlotte elaborated, balling her napkin up in her fist. "But Ian doesn't want to follow the lesson plans we already have in place for the year. He wants to do his own thing, which is going to end up causing problems for the kids, who are in different classes but trying to study together when they get home. And he can't seem to comprehend the need for some students to study together, like he thinks learning language arts is a solitary endeavor."

"Ian?" Becky inquired, looking really excited at the mention of the new teacher's name. "As in the guy who came to Christmas a couple of weeks ago?"

"Yes," Charlotte admitted, looking around to see who was close enough to overhear her before she continued speaking. "As if it wasn't bad enough that Mom was trying to play matchmaker with us at Christmas, now Lisa Walker is pushing us together at work."

"You didn't seem to be the only one Ma was playing matchmaker with at Christmas," Bobby commented, grinning. "I couldn't tell from the other side of the room who all was being set up, but it looked like she and Aunt Susan were both trying to find spouses for all their kids."

"I don't think the guys had it near as bad as us girls," Becky nodded at Bobby in agreement. "Since there were only a couple of single women in attendance, they almost left it up to them which of the guys to pick from. But with the new teacher and so many single male wrestlers in town for the holidays, they had a match for each of us girls picked out."

"Was that the problem?" Brooklyn queried. When both Charlotte and Becky looked at her like they didn't understand her question, she elaborated a little more. "That she had you paired up with guys you weren't interested in? Couldn't you have, like traded places, so you could pick the guys you really wanted to talk to instead?"

"Have you met our mother?" Charlotte raised an eyebrow while giving Brooklyn an incredulous look.

The girls all giggled before Becky explained, "Even if we could've convinced Mom that we weren't interested in her top picks for each of us, it wouldn't have mattered. Other than Ian, all the guys at Christmas had been here for Anthony and Kay's wedding, so we already knew them, and knew we didn't have chemistry with them either."

"Well, we didn't at least," Charlotte corrected, motioning between herself and her sister. "Not sure about Jen and Julie. They seemed happy to spend more time with Liam and Dion."

I'll have to ask Hazel and Susan how all their matchmaking plans are going tomorrow, when I go spend the afternoon cooking with them, Brooklyn thought, wondering if the "Matchmaking Mommas of Heart's Destiny" could be the series title for the books that Kay wanted her to collaborate on in the future. *Or at least a good plot theme for the series of books.*

With the way Brooklyn had been thinking about more romantic plotlines since she'd started dating Bobby, combined with the reading suggestions Kay had given her, she was seriously considering taking Kay up on the offer to work together on a romance series. Teaming up with another author was a good way to get her feet wet in the new category, without having to write scenes about things she'd never done in real life.

Although, I might enjoy following Kay's suggestion to ask Bobby to help me with "research" for writing those racier scenes, once we finally do the deed. But should I really call it "research" while talking to him about it?

No, I shouldn't, because that's not why I'm ready to go all the way with him. I want us to be intimate because I love him. Using the things he's teaching me about to be able to write better in the future is just a bonus.

Oh, I should try writing an oral sex scene now that I have some experience with that. If Kay likes what I write, then maybe I should switch genres and write a romance series with her.

As everyone else settled on things to do that afternoon before they all met up that night for Charlotte's birthday party, Brooklyn put together the plan in her head to spend the afternoon writing. She'd jot down her notes on the series ideas she had, as well as write her first oral sex scene with a couple of unnamed characters for Kay to read while she was home that week.

And if it looks like I'll be needing more "research" for future sex scenes, then maybe I'll tell Bobby I'm ready to go all the way in the next few days.

~ ~ ~

Monday, January 14, 2019

Bobby was struggling as the weeks went by, trying to keep himself in check and not pushing Brie for more than she was ready for in their relationship. If it weren't for the multiple masturbation sessions he indulged in daily while in the shower, he'd be suffering from a serious case of blue balls. While he thoroughly enjoyed the time he spent each day pleasuring Brie with his mouth and fingers, it was getting harder and harder to hold himself back, when she was getting bolder in her exploration of his body with her wandering hands.

It hadn't been too bad on the nights when she was wearing her leggings and t-shirts when he got home from work. They'd fallen into a routine of him showering off the day before dinner, talking while they ate, and then cleaning the kitchen together before cuddling on the couch while watching television. Cuddling often led to more kissing, dry-humping, and Bobby reaching into Brie's clothes to get her off with his fingers. The dry-humping was enough to keep him satiated, even though he didn't always come that way.

But since he'd pointed out the easy access of the dresses and skirts in her wardrobe, and she'd started wearing skirts almost daily to provide him that easy access to be able to lift her skirt and eat her out on every flat surface in his house, Bobby was having a much harder time controlling his inner caveman. Having her sitting on the counter in the kitchen, or bent over the dining room table, with easy access to her wet cunt, made it very tempting for him to drop his pants to his knees and plunge into her like an animal in heat.

After that one time on New Year's Day, he'd avoided actually stripping her out of all of her clothes to maintain some semblance of control, but he didn't think he'd last much longer with the taste of her on his tongue and not having more barriers between them. With the way she'd started slipping her hands under his shirts to run her palms over his abs and pecs, Bobby knew it was only a matter of time before she ventured into his pants, and he wouldn't be able to stop himself from taking her all the way any longer.

Fuck! I have to quit thinking about how tight she is and how sweet she tastes, Bobby thought, willing his erection to go down while he was at work. *It's totally inappropriate for the police chief to sit at his desk with a boner.*

His desk phone rang, bringing him back to the moment and easing the pressure behind his zipper.

"Chief Burleson," Bobby answered the ringing phone, knowing his hard-on would wither as soon as whoever was on the line spoke, giving him a police matter to focus on instead of Brie.

"Good afternoon, Chief. Lieutenant Burleson calling with an update for you," Bobby's brother, Jake, announced over the line, causing Bobby to chuckle at his brother's formality.

"Hopefully, it's good news," Bobby wished as his laughter faded.

"Well, it's not great news, but it's better than no news." Jake sounded like he was smiling on the other end of the line. "My FBI contacts have reported back. They've started the deep dive into the embezzlement case, but they said it'll probably be a month or two before they have enough to make an arrest. I've made it clear I can help them get the proof sooner, if they can get me a warrant to review the company files. But we'll have to wait and see if they'll follow through with that or not."

"Okay," Bobby drawled out the word as he waited to see if his brother would have any more news about Brie's safety while waiting for the feds to arrest her father. When Jake didn't immediately go into more details, Bobby prodded, "Anything else?"

"They didn't seem as receptive to believing my info about Brooklyn not being kidnapped," Jake sighed, no longer sounding happy. "I was basically told the only way they'll drop the search for her is if she comes to them to go into protective custody while everything's being settled with her father. I refused to give them any information on her whereabouts or how I know she wasn't kidnapped…"

"You better not fucking tell them where she is," Bobby bellowed, cutting off his brother mid-sentence. "She's already in my protective custody. Nobody else is gonna be watching over her but me."

"I know, brother," Jake grumbled, sounding irritated. "That's why I didn't divulge anything other than the fact I'd had a long-time confidential informant tell me he'd seen her, and she'd told him she'd gone into hiding to keep from being forced into being a pawn for her father and Clayton Donaldson in their embezzlement scam."

Bobby blew out a frustrated breath before thanking his brother for his discretion.

"No need to thank me." The jovial quality returned to Jake's voice. "You'd do the same for me if the situation was reversed."

"Absolutely," Bobby agreed. "So, uh, when you talked to them, were you able to get any info on where they're looking for her?"

"Not much. But I did find out they don't have any real leads to go on, either. They can't even find footprints leading into or out of her father's estate. And all of her traceable electronics and credit cards were left in her room. The way she disappeared without a trace has the feds looking at whether Barns or Donaldson are responsible for her disappearance, since they were the last two people to see her the day before Thanksgiving."

As much as Bobby liked the idea of Bradley Barns and Clayton Donaldson being put under a microscope, he hoped the feds wouldn't get caught up in pursuing the missing persons case and not the embezzlement they were actually guilty of, causing the whole mess to drag out longer than necessary. "They're not focusing solely on that, though, right?" Bobby wanted to make sure the financial crimes were brought to light sooner rather than later. "They're looking into the embezzlement at Ashbury, too?"

"From what I understand, when the cadaver dogs didn't find anything at either of their estates, and nobody ever called with a ransom demand, the kidnapping case has gone cold," Jake explained. "They still have people looking for her, but they're not exactly looking super hard, or have an idea of where to look even if they were. But with the suspicion being on her father and Donaldson, I think the feds will work harder to put them away for the financial crimes, since they can't find evidence of foul play against them with her disappearance."

"Okay." Bobby blew out a breath he hadn't realized he'd been holding. "So, we're stuck in a waiting pattern, for the month or two it takes them to build the embezzlement case?"

"Yeah, pretty much," Jake admitted, huffing out a breath of his own. "Like I said, not great news, but not bad news either. At least we know it's going in the right direction. And since nobody seems to have a clue where your girl is, she can probably quit trying to disguise her identity."

"You think?" Bobby pictured his girl with her naturally blonde hair and blue eyes.

"Yeah," Jake crooned, the smile coming back to his voice. "Even if someone in town thinks they know who she is, they're not gonna turn her in. At least, not to anyone but you. So, she should be able to relax a little and feel free being herself."

"Yeah, you're probably right. Thanks, Bro." Bobby really wished he was a more patient person. The next couple of months were going to be tense with not really being able to do anything to help Brie, and having to wait for the feds to finish their investigation without his input.

The brothers talked for a few more minutes about life in general, how Bobby felt getting closer to Brie, how Jake hated dating in the Navy town where he lived, and both of them laughing at how their mother's matchmaking antics seemed to be focused on their sisters for the time being. When the brothers said their goodbyes, Bobby sat at his desk for a while thinking about everything Jake had mentioned.

Not only about what was happening with the case in Georgia, but also about the possibility of Brie not having to keep dying her hair and wearing her colored contacts whenever she went somewhere off the ranch.

Is it gonna be weird seeing her as Brooklyn when she quits dying her hair? I mean, she'll still be Brie, but she'll look like Brooklyn. Will that change how it feels to be with her? Will it change her personality at all? Fuck! I hope going back to her natural blonde hair won't trigger her to act like the scared, subservient woman she was when she first arrived here.

He pondered for quite some time, trying to figure out what he could do to make things easier for Brie to be able to continue growing into the confident, outgoing woman he was falling in love with, and not have any steps backward into the hell of her former life when she saw her old self in the mirror every morning. All he wanted was for her to be happy, and he knew she'd been happier in the last month when she started coming out of her shell with him than she'd ever been in her life back in Georgia.

I just have to keep making her happy, he decided as he started packing up for the afternoon. He wished he could go home to her right then, but he'd already committed to spending a couple hours teaching a new class at the youth center, and knew he could never skip out on that time and disappoint the kids who were waiting on him to spend some time teaching them about caring for horses. *Maybe I should invite her along to learn with the kids and help me supervise them? Let her get to know the part of me that's looking forward to being a dad, so maybe she can picture our future family, too.*

Fuck! Talk about not being patient! I need to quit trying to plan our whole lives together, and focus on making sure she's so fucking happy with who she is here that she never reverts back to the repressed woman she was in Georgia. I don't think I'll survive it if she decides she'd rather go back there than stay here with me.

Fuck! Yeah, I would. I'd just have to move to Georgia and win her back. I'll get used to her high-society world, if that's where she wants to live. Just as long as she wants to live with me.

~~~
~~~

Brooklyn was a little nervous getting ready to go bowling with Bobby and a group of their friends and his family. It was the first time she'd gone off the ranch without wearing her colored contacts, and she hadn't dyed her hair that Wednesday for the first time in almost two months. It wasn't completely back to her natural platinum blonde, but it was much lighter than it had been at any point since she'd started dying it back on Thanksgiving. Though most of the people who would be in their group at the bowling alley already knew her real identity, she was nervous about appearing in public as herself, or as close to herself as she could be until the dye finished fading out of her hair, for the first time since her reported disappearance.

Bobby had updated her the previous Monday that it didn't appear as if the authorities in Georgia had a clue where she was, so she was probably safe to not be in disguise, even around town. She'd still been leery of the ramifications of being recognized while out in public, but Bobby reassured her that even if people in town recognized her, they would only report her to him. She trusted his opinion that the townspeople of Heart's Destiny were trustworthy, and would keep her secret if they did figure it out, so she hadn't gone and bought more hair dye to color her hair again this week. But her first outing looking more like her old self still increased her anxiety.

It's fine. I'll be with Bobby and his family and my friends who already know who I am. They'll all protect my identity with the other people there this afternoon. I don't have to worry about his other friends who'll be there that I haven't really met yet. Bobby wouldn't have invited anyone who he didn't trust to know the truth. This is no big deal. Just increasing my circle of friends and strengthening my bond with Bobby over a new activity.

She pushed her worries out of her mind as she made her way from her bathroom to her bedroom, where she'd left her clothes when she went to take her shower. *If Bobby comes out of his room and sees me in only this towel, maybe I won't have to worry about anyone in town recognizing me because we'll stay home and make love instead of going bowling.*

Unfortunately, Bobby didn't come out of his room in the brief moment it took Brooklyn to walk from her bathroom to her bedroom, so that possibility was dashed for the night. She thought about how frustrated she was getting at him not pushing for them to go all the way yet. She'd figured out that if she wore a skirt and was downstairs before he left for work, she didn't have to touch herself in the shower to have a morning release. And he always made sure she came at least twice every night before they went to their separate beds, so she hadn't had to masturbate before bed since the beginning of the new year.

But even as often as he was pleasuring her, she still longed to be more intimate with him. Although she assumed the orgasms would be even better when they started having sex, that wasn't the reason she wanted to be with Bobby. Even her guilt, for not giving him as much pleasure as he gave her, wasn't the reason she was starting to feel ready to consummate their relationship. It was all the time they spent getting to know one another through deep conversations and learning who he truly was as a man. The more she got to know the kind-hearted man, who deeply loved his family and friends and lived to protect and serve his community, the more she fell in love with him.

But even though I'm madly in love with him and want to give myself to him heart, body, and soul, it probably won't be tonight, since he told me to wear jeans instead of an easy access skirt, Brooklyn thought as she pulled her clothes off the hangers to get dressed.

She moved to her dresser and took out a set of her virginal white cotton undergarments, thinking the full butt of the bikini panties would be more comfortable under jeans than the skimpy sexy thongs she'd started wearing since being given more than one pair by her friends on Christmas Eve.

Even if we spend some time making out on the sofa when we get home, he probably won't see these tonight. But maybe that's a good thing. As much as I love it when he uses his fingers and tongue to make me come, keeping my clothes on and dry-humping means he's more likely to come, too.

Brooklyn couldn't contain her smile as she finished dressing while remembering the times Bobby had come with her while rubbing their pelvic regions together on the sofa over the past three weeks. It didn't happen every time, but Brooklyn loved knowing that she'd been the reason he'd started to lose control on the few times it had happened. *If only his control would slip just a little more, so I could actually find out what his penis feels like inside me.*

Maybe once the girls see us together this afternoon, they'll be able to give me some more helpful advice on how to progress our relationship than what they've given me in the past. Not that I've gotten to do more than practice with produce with their previous advice since Bobby won't take off his pants when we're canoodling. Brooklyn giggled at her own internal use of Tia's word for fooling around.

She slipped her debit card in one of her back pockets and her cell phone in the other before heading out of her room to go meet Bobby downstairs. Brook didn't risk taking anything with her real identity on it with her, except when she thought she might have to drive and might need her driver's license, so she left her purse on her dresser as usual for when she went somewhere. That habit had actually come in handy a month before when she didn't have anything but her debit card to use as identification when Bobby took her to the bank to add her to his checking account. He still found out her real identity a couple weeks later, but at least the bank officers weren't clued in about who she was to be able to blow her cover.

"Damn, maybe this wasn't such a good idea," Bobby groaned, walking up behind her as she turned toward the kitchen at the bottom of the stairs. He gripped her hips and leaned down to whisper in her ear as he pulled her back into his front. "Watching you bend over to bowl in those sexy-as-fuck jeans is gonna make me too hard to be able to focus on the game."

"Then maybe I won't be the only one throwing gutter balls all night," Brooklyn joked as she leaned back into Bobby's strong embrace.

"Yeah, I'm more worried about throwing punches than throwing gutter balls." Bobby chuckled as they moved into step side by side to head out to the car.

"Why would you be throwing punches?" Brooklyn didn't understand his meaning.

"To make sure all the other guys know not to look at your hot ass." Bobby smirked as they buckled up for the drive into town.

"Don't be ridiculous!" Brook shook her head and giggled at her possessive boyfriend. "With the way you're always touching and kissing me, they'll all know to keep their hands and eyes to themselves. And hopefully, all the girls who normally ogle you will realize you're off limits now, too."

"Oh, Brie-Baby, you should know by now that the local girls don't ogle me." Bobby squeezed the hand he was holding on the console between them in his truck. "They might stare at my brothers, cousins, and friends, but they learned a long time ago that I'm not interested in any of them, so they don't even bother looking in my direction now."

"Uh-huh, sure they don't," Brooklyn snickered, remembering his confession about his previous hookups in town. "That's why Tammi gives me the stink eye every time I go in the H.E.B."

"Don't even get me started on all the reasons you never have to worry about Tammi Jo Willis!" Bobby grimaced as he shook his head.

"I'm not worried about her," Brooklyn smiled at Bobby and squeezed his hand. "I was just pointing out that she's a local and she ogles you."

"Yeah, well, I don't think of her as a local," Bobby smirked. "'Cause I've blocked her from my mind completely, so I don't have nightmares about having to deal with her."

They both chuckled before changing the subject. Bobby tried to go through the list of people that would probably be at Lover's Lanes that afternoon, telling her about several people she hadn't met yet that were friends of his sisters and cousins who were going to be there.

When they arrived, she finally met all the Walkers, whom her girlfriends had mentioned back when she first got to know them in the coffee shop six weeks earlier. She was also introduced to a few of the ladies she remembered seeing when she had her hair, nails, and makeup done for going out with her girlfriends five weeks earlier.

Though she'd met Kayla, Lexi, and Cassidy that day, she hadn't remembered their names. She remembered Amy, Randi's best friend who recently moved to Heart's Destiny, from meeting her at Christmas. The other two girls, Kara and Sierra, were people she recognized from seeing them around town and hearing them mentioned by Bobby and his family, but she hadn't been introduced to them before.

It was quite a large group with fourteen women and ten men, taking up half the lanes in the bowling alley. The guys asked where Kenzie and Heather's brothers were since they were feeling outnumbered. Brooklyn learned that Kenzie's brother, Nick, owned the Book Nook and might come hang out later when the store closed for the evening. And Heather's brother, Dusty, was on duty at the police station, so Bobby didn't have to be officially on call and could enjoy a night off.

With it being such a large group, they opted not to choose teams, playing every man or woman for themselves. Since there were half a dozen people bowling on each lane, they took the extra time waiting on their turn to bowl to chit chat and get acquainted with everyone around them. Brooklyn had a blast making new friends, feeling happy and at home all afternoon, especially when Bobby had his arm around her when they were sitting together.

They bowled a couple of games before Nick Martin showed up. They played another game including Kenzie's brother before deciding to go to Tully's for the rest of the evening. It felt kind of strange going into the bar with Bobby, making her feel torn between wanting to stay by his side or hanging out with her girlfriends, when all the guys wanted to go play pool and all the girls wanted to pick songs on the jukebox and dance.

"Enjoy your girl time," Bobby instructed her, apparently seeing the indecision written on her face. He hugged her to his side for a brief moment, bending down to kiss the top of her head before releasing her. "I'm gonna go beat these guys in a couple games of pool while ya'll gossip, and then I'll come back in here and spin you around the dance floor before we head home."

"Okay," Brooklyn agreed, smiling up at him. She grabbed his hand just as he was about to walk away toward the back room, where the pool tables were located. He stopped in his tracks and turned to look at her, giving her the opportunity to reach up and clasp the back of his neck to pull him down, so she could kiss him on the cheek before he left her side. "I'll save the songs I want to play on the jukebox for last, so we can dance to them."

"You two are so cute together," Becky cooed, smiling when Brooklyn joined the rest of the women and took a seat at the table with Becky and a few of her friends.

"I think that's the first time I can ever remember seeing Bobby smile," Sierra confided, grinning beside Becky. She poked her friend in the side before continuing. "He was always scowling at us when we had sleepovers as kids, and he's always so broody and stoic whenever I've seen him around town since we grew up."

"Bobby used to smile all the time when we were in high school," Cassidy told them.

"That was more of a smirk," Lexi chuckled, butting in before Cassidy could finish her thought.

"We called it his panty melting grin my senior year of high school," the waitress giggled, walking up to their table to collect their drink orders.

"Hey Melissa, have you met Brie?" Becky introduced Brooklyn to the waitress by her alias.

"Not officially, but I've seen you around," Melissa nodded at Brooklyn.

"Nice to meet you," Brooklyn smiled, unsure what else to say at the introduction.

"You're a little older than us, aren't you?" Lexi asked Melissa. When Melissa nodded to Lexi, she continued, "So when did Bobby's grin turn into a smirk?"

"Probably his sophomore year," Melissa declared with a grin of her own. "After spending his freshman year flashing those dimples to drop the panties of half the junior and senior girls, myself included."

"Gross, I really don't need to hear about my brother and his former player ways," Becky grimaced, sticking out her tongue and making a playful, gagging face.

"Yeah, judging by the way Brie's turning green, we should probably drop the conversation about Bobby's man-whore days," Heather chortled, joining them at the table and giving Brooklyn a side hug that she wasn't sure how to interpret.

Is the hug meant to show she's teasing, or to comfort me while I hear about his former sexual exploits?

"Ignore them, Brie," Kenzie advised, taking a seat across from Brooklyn and shaking her head at the other ladies around them. "I told you not to pay attention to anything anyone says about Bobby in the past. He's different with you because what ya'll have is special."

"Yeah," Ashley added, grinning at them as she pushed another table up to theirs and took a seat. "Just enjoy his bedroom skills without worrying about where he might have learned them."

Brooklyn felt her cheeks heat and knew she was blushing from thinking about the skills Bobby had already shown her. *And we haven't even made it to a bedroom, yet.*

Leah Mae Wright

"Don't tell me he's still holding out on you," Heather implored, turning Brooklyn to look her in the eyes.

Did I say that out loud?

"Wha-what?" Brooklyn stuttered, not sure what she was even asking her friend.

"By the way you're blushing and stuttering, I'm guessing you still haven't done the deed with Bobby yet." Heather circled a finger in Brooklyn's direction, giving her a strange look. "I seriously thought you were just holding back giving us details on the phone and would give us the scoop tonight, but with the way you're still acting all shy and virginal, I don't think you've taken any of our advice to get to the bow-chicka-wow-wow."

"Yeah, I'm gonna go help my sister and cousins pick out music on the jukebox," Becky cringed, standing up from her chair at the table with Brooklyn and the other girls. "I don't wanna lose my nachos from hearing anything sexual about my brother."

"Keep anyone related to Bobby at the jukebox," Sierra suggested, waving Becky off. "I'll signal you when we quit talking about the hunky Burleson boys, so you know it's safe to come sit back down with us."

"Okay, now that she's gone," Lexi remarked, motioning at Becky's retreating back. "Talk. We need to know all the dirty details about you and Bobby."

"How 'bout I get ya'll a round of drinks first?" Melissa saved Brooklyn from having to speak when she wasn't sure she'd be able to tell them about her relationship with Bobby without dying of embarrassment. "Brie looks like she might need some liquid courage before she'll be comfortable opening up."

"Good idea," Cassidy agreed, smiling at the waitress. "How about a couple pitchers of sangria?"

When the other ladies all nodded in agreement, Melissa left to put in their drink order. As soon as the waitress was out of earshot, Sierra started the inquisition. "So, you're dating Bobby. Tell us all about how that got started."

"Good idea, work her up to the dirty talk," Ashley praised Sierra's approach, leaning in conspiratorially toward the other women.

"Well, um," Brooklyn started, not really sure how to explain how she started dating Bobby. "We met the first night I got into town, but we didn't see each other again until a little over a week later when I started working as his cook and housekeeper."

She briefly explained how he wasn't happy with her moving into his house at first and how she'd avoided him for the rest of her first week on the job. Then she told them about how she couldn't avoid him when she was expected to participate in Burleson family activities on the weekends, and how that led to them having dinner together and talking every night.

Brooklyn wasn't sure how to explain his confession of love at first sight without exposing her alter ego to the women she'd just met that night, so she glossed over it as him telling her he wanted more just before Christmas and that they'd been dating ever since.

"So, wait, he just declared that you're his girlfriend," Sierra exclaimed, looking shocked. "He didn't ask you to be his girlfriend?"

Brooklyn shook her head, thinking that negative response was enough of a reply, so she didn't have to come up with an explanation.

"Of course, he just declared it," Lexi laughed. "All those Burleson boys are too alpha to risk being turned down by asking."

"Like anyone would turn them down," Ashley scoffed, fanning herself, as if she was being heated up from her own thoughts.

"Good point," Cassidy nodded, pointing to Ashley. The girls all giggled as they acknowledged that none of them would turn down the opportunity to date one of the Burleson men.

Melissa delivered their drinks, and everyone had a drink in hand before Heather continued the interrogation. "Okay, now that you have your liquid courage, how far have ya'll gone on your dates?"

Brooklyn took a large gulp of her drink, giving herself time to formulate her answer. When she finally sat her glass down and swallowed the fruity red wine, all eyes were on her.

"We've, um," Brooklyn started, knowing her cheeks were as red as the wine in the pitcher of sangria on the table. "We've mostly just kissed."

The expectant looks aimed at her from around the table told Brooklyn that she couldn't stop there. *Why does this have to be so embarrassing?* Brooklyn thought while trying to remember what acts constituted which bases when using the baseball analogy for describing sexual activity.

"We've both spent time on second base," Brooklyn finally admitted. "And he's gone to third a few times."

"He's gone to third, but you haven't?" Heather tilted her head with a quizzical expression on her face.

"I'm not really sure," Brooklyn admitted sheepishly. "Does dry-humping count as third? Or is it still second since all our clothes were still on?"

"Oh boy, here we go," Cassidy proclaimed, tossing up her hands.

"We have different opinions on what constitutes second base versus third," Lexi explained, motioning between herself and Cassidy. "She thinks anything above the waist is second and below the waist is third, regardless of whether clothing is removed. I think touching over the clothes is second and touching without clothes is third, regardless of whether it's above or below the waist."

"And Kayla thinks heavy petting of any body part with or without clothes is second base and oral is third base," Cassidy continued explaining for her friend.

"So, you'll just have to describe each act in detail, so we're all clear on what you mean, instead of using bases as a cop out," Heather smirked.

Brooklyn couldn't stop herself from laughing at the goofy grins on her friends' faces. "Okay, yeah, I guess it is kind of hard to figure out with three different descriptions of the bases," she admitted when her laughter died down. She took a deep breath and looked around the room to make sure none of the guys were close enough to hear her before metaphorically pulling up her big girl panties and telling her friends, "All our clothes stayed on when we dry-humped. I've run my hands up under his shirt to touch his torso, but he won't even let me touch him with my hands below the waist with his clothes on, much less under them. But he's removed my clothing to touch and kiss me everywhere."

Brooklyn covered her face with both hands, mortified that she'd actually admitted all that to her friends.

"You go girl," Heather cheered, pulling Brooklyn's hand away from her face to give her a high five. "Nothing to be embarrassed about."

Kenzie, Ashley, and Sierra agreed with Heather, giving Brooklyn their own words of encouragement, and sounding happy for her to be finding love with Bobby. Cassidy and Lexi looked at each other before turning to look at Brooklyn. She felt slightly uncomfortable under their inquisitive stares.

"So, ya'll kiss, like a lot?" Lexi tilted her head as she examined Brooklyn. "Like more than just the chaste kissing ya'll have done all day?"

Brooklyn nodded, not comfortable talking about how much time they spent just kissing every night.

"And he's gone down on you?" Lexi queried. "Like actually eaten your pussy?"

Brooklyn knew her blush deepened at the other woman's use of such crass wording, but she nodded again to confirm her new favorite way to come, not that she would tell any of them that.

"Your friends are right," Cassidy professed, her lips turning up in the slightest smile. "What you have with Bobby is definitely special."

"Really?" Brooklyn couldn't contain herself from asking.

"Yeah," several of the women agreed in unison, nodding at her like she was surrounded at the table by a half-dozen bobbleheads.

"It's no secret around town that Bobby Burleson doesn't kiss," Cassidy explained. "Hasn't since he started high school."

"And even the buckle bunnies know not to ask him for oral," Lexi confirmed. "So, if he's doing all that with you, then yeah, you're definitely special to him."

"I knew she was special to him when he didn't try to get in her panties the first night," Kenzie confessed, grinning from ear to ear. "But now we've got to help our girl get him to quit taking things so freaking slow, so she can get in his boxers."

"Easy," Lexi smirked. "When ya'll get home tonight, pants him and drop to your knees. He won't protest once you get his dick in your mouth."

"Oh, please," Charlotte snapped as she approached the table where half the women in their party were sitting. "Tell me you're not telling Brie things to do with my brother."

"Sorry, Char," Lexi shrugged. "He's not giving our girl the goods, so we're offering her suggestions."

"No, just no," Charlotte glowered, holding up a hand in the universal symbol for stop. "Don't listen to any of their vulgar suggestions, Brie. If he's not going as far as you want him to, just tell him. I know it's embarrassing to talk about sex with a new partner, but it's a lot less embarrassing than the freaky things these girls would have you do to move things along instead."

Just tell him? Yeah, easier said than done.

Before Brooklyn could ask the girls for pointers on how not to be embarrassed when asking for sex, the rest of the women joined them and started dragging them out on the dance floor to learn a new line dance. Brooklyn put her plans for later that night with Bobby out of her mind, focusing on having fun with her new friends while trying not to trip over her own two feet on the dance floor.

<div style="text-align:center">~~~</div>

Bobby had been right about him being too hard to focus on anything but her while watching Brie bend over to bowl. Thankfully, he wasn't the only one of the group who wasn't interested in bowling for very long that evening. After only a few games, the group as a whole decided to head over to Tully's to shoot some pool and take a spin or two around the dance floor. Bobby was looking forward to getting Brie back in his arms to dance, just as soon as he finished the current game of pool he was playing, and the girls finished gossiping to decide on what songs to play on the jukebox.

When he heard the first few notes of a classic country line-dancing song, Bobby knew it would be a while before the girls got through all their picks of toe-tappin' music to put on something slower that he could appreciate dancing to with Brie. Resigned to needing to waste at least another half hour while the girls went through all the songs that seemed to have complex choreography that went along with them, Bobby called his shot, sank the eight ball, and asked his next opponent to rack the balls for the next game.

He spent the evening shooting the shit with the guys and ignoring any ridicule that came from his single friends over his newly coupled-up status. While the younger guys, like Dalton, Hayden, and Hudson Walker, and Nick Martin might not be ready to settle down, Bobby knew Luke, Landon, Leo, and Aiden Walker were all more interested in at least looking for a long-term girlfriend, so he thought their comments were more out of jealousy than disdain.

His cousins, JJ and Justin, were a lot more reserved in their comments, not picking at him like the rest of the guys. He knew his mom and aunt had been hitting them hard with their most recent matchmaking shenanigans, so they were less inclined to tease him about falling victim to the plot Hazel had used to set him up with Brie. From what he'd observed the week of Anthony's wedding and again at Christmas, Bobby surmised his cousins weren't far from falling for their true loves, if they hadn't already.

Should I ask Justin how he's liking working with Amy every day? Bobby wondered. *Naw, that'd just give him a reason to jump on the bandwagon with the rest of the guys about me and Brie. Speaking of Brie, this sounds like a slow enough song to be good for dancing with her.*

Bobby passed his pool cue to Luke, saying, "Finish this game for me. I'm gonna go dance with my girl."

Whatever the guys were groaning as he walked away was ignored as Bobby made his way to the table where Brie had just plopped down into a chair.

"Sounds like they're playin' our song, Brie-Baby." Bobby held his hand out to her. "And I need to have you in my arms on the dance floor while it's playin'."

Brie smiled and took his hand, letting him pull her up and out onto the dance floor. Bobby heard one of his sisters' friends say something about his "alpha actions," but he didn't bother paying attention to whatever the ladies were saying. All Bobby cared about at that moment was holding Brie in his arms as they swayed together to **What's Mine Is Yours** by Kane Brown.

He pulled her in close as they slow danced, settling his hands on her low back. She wrapped her arms around his waist and rested her head on his chest, right over his erratically beating heart. His heart wasn't pounding from the exertion of dancing to the slow song. It was from realizing how his feelings for Brie matched the lyrics.

Unable to stop himself, Bobby bent his head and softly sang along right into Brie's ear. He knew it was probably cheesy, and the guys would undoubtedly tease him about it mercilessly later, but Bobby hoped Brie realized he meant every word he sang. He didn't think she was ready for him to say "I love you" just yet, and he wasn't sure he wanted to put himself out there by saying those three little words before they had everything settled in Georgia and he knew she would stay with him in Heart's Destiny for the long haul, so he held back the sentiment that was on the tip of his tongue, and let the song speak for him. For now, anyway.

They spent the next hour dancing, taking turns serenading each other when favorite songs were played on the jukebox, and wondering how much longer they were obligated to stay there when all they wanted was to go home, where they could be alone. The more they rubbed their bodies against each other on the dance floor, the more Bobby's resolve to keep things from going too far started to slip. Deciding that he couldn't hold back any longer and needing to have Brie touch him more than he'd previously allowed, Bobby made their excuses, so they could leave the bar much earlier than he'd ever left a night out before.

As they drove home, Bobby ran through his plan for the night with Brie. He knew he couldn't take her to his room, or he'd definitely go too far, but he hoped he could at least let her give him a hand job on the couch without pushing her past her comfort zone.

But only after I've made her come a few times with my fingers and mouth. Brie always comes first. Then if she wants to try getting in my pants to reciprocate, I'll let her.

Bobby visualized how he thought she'd be tentative as she touched him for the first time while Brie sang along to the radio. When the song changed to one she didn't know and she started asking questions about all the people she'd met that day, Bobby pushed his fantasy about her wanting to try sucking his cock to the back of his mind to answer her questions. *I know that's never gonna be an option, so I should probably quit fantasizing about it anyway.*

"Seriously, none of them are dating?" Brie questioned, after going through a list of his family and friends, who she thought seemed like they would be cute couples.

"Nope, basically knowing each other since birth kinda kills any romantic vibes," Bobby replied, shaking his head at how Brie had started imagining book storylines for everyone she met to find their happily ever after.

"Are you saying that if I'd have grown up here in Heart's Destiny, you wouldn't be interested in me?" Brie crossed her arms over her chest defensively.

Bobby opened his mouth to reply, but quickly closed it, unsure how to respond to the hypothetical scenario. *Would I still be drawn to her the way I am if I'd known her since childhood?*

When Bobby didn't reply, Brie continued inundating him with questions and comments. "Are you only interested in me because you see me as a damsel in distress that you can rescue? Or would you still be attracted to me if I didn't have the baggage of my father and his cronies, trying to find and control me? See, I don't think that's it. When we first met, I certainly didn't see you as my knight in shining armor. I thought I needed to hide from you because you'd send me back to Georgia to be forced into marrying Clayton. But even though I didn't think I could trust you at first, I was still attracted to you in a way I couldn't stop, no matter how hard I tried. I think the intense connection we felt, and that several of the women in your family have described to me about feeling with their spouses, would be the same regardless of the circumstances of how or when we met. I may not have recognized the feelings if we'd met when we were little kids instead of now, but I still think I'd have felt it. Don't you?"

"Well, yeah, I think you're right about us," Bobby agreed, hoping to avoid being in the doghouse with his girl. "But if any of my siblings or cousins or best friends had ever felt something for any of our other friends, I think they would've figured it out by now and acted on it. That's why I don't think any of the couples you're trying to pair up in your head tonight are gonna actually get together."

"Maybe you're right about your siblings and cousins," Brie admitted as Bobby pulled down the driveway and hit the button for the garage door opener. "But I still think I saw some sparks flying with the girls and several of the Walkers. I just wish Kenzie didn't look so disappointed by your cousins not showing any interest in her."

Bobby wasn't sure if he should tell Brie about his detective, Dusty Deere's, long-time crush on his little sister's best friend, Kenzie, or not. On the one hand, it might make her not feel so bad for her friend, but on the other hand it might lead her to pulling her own matchmaking schemes like his mother, aunts, and their friends.

Naw, I won't tell her, 'cause then I'd hafta explain why he hasn't acted on it. I'd rather get her focused back on us and what we're gonna do when we get inside.

"Yeah, well, while I hope she finds Mr. Right sometime soon, so she doesn't have to feel disappointed in my cousins for long, I'd rather focus on us than who amongst our friends and family should be hooking up." Bobby unbuckled his seatbelt and got out of the truck.

"Yeah, and what exactly do you think we should focus on?" Brie wrapped her arms around Bobby's shoulders as he gripped her hips to help her down from the tall vehicle.

"You and me." Bobby nuzzled her neck as he slowly lowered her to the ground by sliding her body along his. "Getting naked on the couch."

"Mmm, I like the sound of that," Brie purred as she rested her face on his shoulder, giving him better access to her neck. Bobby trailed kisses down the delicate column, reversing course when he reached her collarbone to work his way back up to her mouth, wanting at least one deep kiss before they walked from the garage to the house. "Especially if you get naked tonight, too."

Fuck yes! Bobby thought as he claimed her lips with his. Holding her close while his tongue plundered her mouth, Bobby couldn't stop his hips from grinding his ever-present erection into her soft belly. Brie was so responsive, returning the kiss with fervor and pushing his need for her into overdrive.

Too impatient to walk slowly into the house, Bobby bent and lifted Brie over his shoulder as soon as they paused their kissing to take a breath.

"Oh my, Bobby, what are you doing?" Brie squealed, her hands landing on his low back as her midsection hit his shoulder.

Bobby kept one arm wrapped around her legs, reaching out with his free hand to slap the button on the wall to close the garage door as he rushed under it, practically jogging to the house. "Taking you in the house to have my way with you," Bobby announced, both of them laughing as he opened the back door and rushed toward the family room.

He tossed her on the softest part of the couch as soon as he reached it, following her descent to cover her with his body and get his lips back on hers. After the briefest moment of feigned protest, Brie was slipping her hands under his shirt, skimming her palms over his abs and around his waist, and pulling him closer to her.

Bobby shifted his weight, moving to only use one arm to hold his weight off of her, so he could use his other hand to cup her breast as they continued kissing passionately.

"Please Bobby," Brie begged, turning her head to break their kiss, so she could speak. "We need to lose these clothes. I need more than just making out tonight."

"Fuck, Brie-Baby," Bobby moaned, as Brie started kissing his neck like he'd done hers in the garage. "How much more?"

"Everything, Bobby," Brie breathlessly replied, just before Bobby claimed her lips again.

Fuck! Is she really ready? Bobby speculated while they kissed. *Should I let her explore my body first, or take her upstairs and make love to her first?*

I'm pretty sure with the way I've been fingering her for the past couple of weeks that she'll be able to take me without pain. Maybe it'll be best if I make love to her first? That way she won't see my size while giving me a hand job and get scared I won't fit inside her.

Tensing up at the sight of my size would be a sure-fire way to make it painful for her. Yeah, we'll skip over hand jobs for now. The size of my cock won't be nearly as intimidating after she's felt me inside her. As bad as I want her right now, I don't think I could hold back to let her play with me when I need her this bad, anyway.

Bobby pulled back from their kiss and wrapped both arms around Brie while putting his feet back on the floor, so he could pick her up. "Wrap your legs around my waist," Bobby commanded as he lifted Brie up into his arms while standing up from the couch.

"Wha-what?" Brie stuttered, seeming dazed from their kisses. "What are you doing?"

"Carrying you upstairs, Brie-Baby," Bobby informed her as she wrapped her legs around his waist and clung to him with her arms tightly around his shoulders. "I want you in my bed the first time I make love to you."

"Oh," she breathily sighed, her mouth forming a perfect O as she looked at him with a mix of surprise and excitement in her eyes.

Bobby took the front stairs two at a time, practically running to his room without looking where he was going as their mouths collided once again. Thankfully, he knew the way around his house like the back of his hand, stopping at the foot of his bed without running into it or any other obstacles in his path. Brie dropped her feet to the ground as they broke their lip lock to start trying to remove their shirts.

"Wait," Brie blurted, looking sheepishly at him when he had the hem of her shirt up to the bottom of her ribs.

Bobby stilled instantly; afraid she wasn't really ready for sex like he'd thought she meant by her statement when they were downstairs. "What's wrong, Brie-Baby?" Bobby inquired tentatively.

"I'm not wearing my sexy underwear." Brie had the slightest blush creeping across her cheeks, showing her slight embarrassment.

"Oh, Brie-Baby," Bobby chuckled, wanting to reassure her that she had no reason to be ashamed about what she was wearing. "You are what I find sexy, not your underwear."

"But I'm not wearing the thongs I've been wearing under my skirts for you." Brie looked down shyly. "I didn't think they'd be comfortable under jeans, so I'm wearing plain white cotton panties, like I've worn since I was a little girl. I wanted to wear something pretty and grown up for you."

"While I've appreciated all those sexy thongs under your skirts," Bobby began, stepping back and stripping off his own shirt with one hand while unfastening his jeans with the other, thinking maybe him getting undressed first would put her more at ease. "I'm sure I'll appreciate your plain white panties just as much because you're the one wearing them. And I don't intend for you to be wearing them very much longer."

Bobby toed off his boots before dropping his jeans to his ankles. He stepped out of his pants, using his toes to push his socks off with them, leaving him in only his red boxer briefs as he stepped closer to Brie. "Now let's get you out of these clothes, so I can show you how sexy I think you are no matter what you're wearing." Bobby gripped the bottom of her shirt to push it up over her head.

"Oh, okay," Brie conceded, lifting her arms as he removed her shirt before dropping them back down and placing both palms on his chest. Her eyes were wide as they roamed over his body. His cock twitched in response to her perusal, lengthening to the point that he was at risk of pushing past the elastic waistband of his boxer briefs and exposing himself to her before he even had her half undressed.

Bobby relished the feel of her hands on him, but he couldn't slow down to really enjoy the sensations because he needed to get her naked, so he could get inside her. He reached around and unfastened her bra with one hand, pulling it down her arms as he went down on his knees. He bent his head and lavished her breasts with open-mouthed kisses while reaching down to remove her sneakers.

Brie gripped his head, running her fingers through his short hair and moaning in pleasure as she held his mouth to her right nipple. *Ah, I know what my girl likes,* Bobby inwardly reveled, sucking on her hardened tip as he unfastened her jeans and started to slide them down over her hips, taking her panties with them, so they wouldn't cause her even the briefest moment of embarrassment. He moved to her left nipple, repeating the suction he knew she enjoyed the most from all the nights he'd played with her tatas in the past couple of weeks.

She was a perfect handful, a solid B-cup that was still perky from youth, which made titty time into a potential distraction from finishing getting her naked for Bobby. When his hands hit the floor along with her jeans and panties, Bobby released them and slid his hands back up her legs. He continued lavishing her breasts with his oral attention as he slid a single finger through her soaking wet folds.

"Oh, Bobby," Brie moaned, rocking her hips against his hand, her body language begging for him to push the digit inside her.

"Mmm, not yet." Bobby pulled his hand back from her core, lifting his head as he stood back up to his full height. Cupping each of her ass cheeks in his large hands, Bobby lifted Brie up into his arms, so he could move them onto the bed. He walked across the king-sized bed on his knees, until he could lay her down in the middle of it, resting her head on his pillow with her flaxen hair spread out over the slate gray bedding. "I need to taste every inch of you first, Brie-Baby."

He planked above her, holding his weight off of her as he kissed her mouth first. He maintained a plank position as he slowly crawled down her body on his hands and toes, trailing open-mouthed kisses down her neck, across her collarbones, and down her sternum. He took his time lavishing affection on her breasts again before moving across her abdomen to the top of her mound.

Brie spread her legs, allowing him to lower his body down to the mattress with his face at the apex of her thighs. He wasn't sure where he found the patience to take his time, savoring the taste of her on his tongue to bring her to her first climax of the night, but when he slipped a finger in her slick channel, he was glad he had. Even though he'd been using his fingers to stretch the small opening in her hymen enough to be able to accommodate his cock size for the past couple of weeks, she was still extremely tight.

Bobby suckled her clit as he slowly worked a second and then third finger inside her creamy cunt. He scissored his digits first, opening her adequately, so he could get deep enough to feel for her G-spot.

"Oh, yes, Bobby," Brie chanted repeatedly, her hips rocking involuntarily as her second orgasm built inside her.

Her hands were fisted in the comforter covering his bed, her head was thrown back with her dark blonde hair spread across his pillow, and her eyes were closed while her mouth was open. Bobby loved the view of her as he looked up her body, wanting to watch her every response, especially when her body convulsed in her second orgasm.

"Bobby, Bobby, Bobby!" Brie screamed, her voice rising an octave each time she chanted his name.

The walls of her pussy clamped down on his invading fingers like a vise, at the same time his mouth was flooded with her juices gushing from her core as she came. Hard. It was the hottest thing Bobby had ever witnessed. He gentled his movements, pulling his fingers out of her while she floated in ecstasy.

He pushed his body up and off the bed, shoving his boxer briefs down while she recovered from her intense O. The need inside him was so strong, he didn't even think about grabbing a condom before he was crawling over her and lining the purple, mushroom-shaped tip of his cock up with her opening.

"Brie-Baby," Bobby moaned reverently, causing her to open her sky-blue eyes and look up at him. "Are you sure you're ready for everything?"

Brie smiled, dropping her chin to her chest in a single nod.

"I need to hear you say the words, Brie-Baby," Bobby practically growled. "I'm barely holding back right now, but I can still stop if you're not ready."

"I'm ready." Brie wrapped her arms around his shoulders and pulled him down into a kiss.

Her passionately pushing her tongue between his lips was his undoing. He took over the kiss, keeping it slow and sensual, just like his cock was entering her, one leisurely inch at a time. It was agonizing trying to maintain control, so he didn't hurt her, but he knew it would be worth all the erotic torture he was enduring to make her first time painless.

"Oh," Brie moaned into his mouth, stiffening beneath him as he pushed the blunt head of his cock through the small opening in her hymen.

He felt the tissue tear to accommodate his girth and held still for a moment to allow any possible discomfort to pass. He wouldn't push farther inside her until he felt her relax. He focused on continuing to kiss her, hoping that would be enough to maintain her arousal as the pain turned into pleasure, so they could go on.

He tensed as she turned her head to break their kiss, fearing she was going to ask him to stop, and unsure if he could find the willpower to force his body to pull out of hers. His worries were short lived when she moaned, "More. Please Bobby, I need more. I need all of you."

"Oh, Brie-Baby," Bobby murmured, shifting his hips to push further into her tight, wet sheath. He sustained a steady amount of pressure as he tunneled into her, not stopping until he was balls-deep. "Fuck," he growled, drawing out the word to several syllables. "You feel so good, so perfect."

"So full," Brie cooed breathlessly, her fingers digging into the muscles of his upper back in the most exquisite way.

"You're so tight!" Bobby was barely able to hold himself still inside her. "I'm not gonna last long, Brie-Baby, but I have to move."

"Yes, Bobby, yes," Brie crooned, her inner walls starting to squeeze his cock as he brushed across her G-spot when he started to pull out.

He couldn't stand the feeling of not being inside her enough to come more than halfway out of her before he was thrusting back in. He wanted to set a steady pace and smooth rhythm, but how good she felt was too overwhelming, causing him to lose all semblance of control. His thrusts were frantic and frenzied as he felt the tingle signaling his impending orgasm building in his spine. His balls started to tighten the closer he got to reaching his own climax.

Wanting her to go over with him, he shifted his weight to one elbow, freeing his right hand to fondle her breasts. He lowered his head, kissing her continuously as the waves of euphoria washed over them. Her cries of pleasure into his mouth were unintelligible as her body started to spasm in orgasmic bliss. The way her inner walls rippled around his cock easily milked him of his own release.

"Fuck! Brie-Baby!" Bobby shouted, their breath mingling as he'd barely separated their lips to verbally express his climax. It was the longest, hardest, most intense orgasm Bobby had ever experienced as he continued to spurt streams of cum into her womb for what seemed like forever in his euphoric state.

Bobby rolled them across the bed, pulling her with him, so he could collapse and recover without crushing her under his weight, and somehow he still maintained their connection.

How the fuck am I still stiff inside her after coming that hard?

Laying there on his back with Brie on top of him was the most comfortable he'd ever been in his bed. *Because we're meant for each other.*

"Wow!" Brie lifted her head to look him in the eyes once they'd caught their breath. "That was…"

"The best." Bobby finished her sentence when she trailed off.

"Yes," Brie agreed, smiling up at him before resting her head back on his chest and closing her eyes.

Bobby knew he needed to get up and clean them up, but he couldn't bring himself to disturb her when she started softly snoring. He laid there for a few long moments, reliving the best sex of his life while holding the woman he loved in his arms.

When realization dawned that he hadn't worn a condom, he was slightly surprised to realize that he wasn't freaking out about it. It was the only time in his life that he hadn't worn a condom when he'd had sex. He'd been diligent with protection his entire life, not wanting to risk becoming a parent with the wrong woman.

But Brie is different. She was the right woman, so he wouldn't be upset if they'd just made their first baby.

I'll be fucking thrilled when we have our first kid. I just hope she wants kids and won't be upset if it happens sooner rather than later.

Once he was sure she was well and truly asleep, Bobby shifted her off of him toward the center of the bed, hating the feeling of his cock slipping from her soft, wet sheath. As embarrassed as she'd been at the thought of him touching her while she was on her period earlier in the month, he knew she'd be mortified if she awoke to realize that her blood had mixed with his semen to coat both of their sexual organs and thighs. He quickly went to the bathroom and grabbed a washcloth, wetting it with warm water to clean her up, along with a hand towel to dry her off after.

Once he'd gently wiped off the evidence of her giving him her virginity, he cleaned himself up, as well as the spot on the top of the comforter. He rinsed the blood out of the towels before tossing them in the hamper and returning to the bed.

Carefully, he moved the comforter down on one side of the bed, so he could roll her over between the sheets. He pulled her back on top of him once he joined her in the bed, covering them both with the top sheet and comforter, so there was no risk of her getting cold in the middle of the night from sleeping nude.

"I love you," Bobby whispered as he drifted off to sleep, knowing she wouldn't hear the words, but unable to stop himself from saying them. He spent the night dreaming of their future together. He knew he'd spend the rest of his life loving on Brie every night and raising a houseful of kids, just like his parents.

Chapter Eleven

Sunday, January 20, 2019

Brooklyn slowly drifted up from slumber, thinking her pillow was exceptionally harder than normal. As her eyes fluttered open, she realized that her pillow also had a smattering of chest hair that tickled her nose. Memories of the night before filtered through her mind. Bobby carrying her up the stairs to his bedroom, stripping them both of their clothing, and making love to her for the first time. She couldn't have stopped the smile from spreading across her face if she'd wanted to, as she settled into his loving embrace, where he was still holding her to his chest with his strong arms wrapped around her.

He had one hand on her butt and the other on the back of her head with his fingers weaved through her hair. She usually wore her hair up in a ponytail or messy bun to keep it out of her way while she was working, but Bobby seemed to have a thing for running his fingers through it whenever she wore it down, so she'd been wearing it down anytime they went out and at night after work when they spent the evenings making out.

As Brooklyn laid there listening to the steady beat of Bobby's heart under her ear, she reflected on how drastically her life had changed in the last two months. She'd gone from being a mostly sheltered little girl in a grown woman's body to actually feeling like the adult she was, and it was all thanks to the man holding her in his arms.

While making love with Bobby was her favorite part of her recent growing process, losing her virginity wasn't what made her feel like he'd helped her mature into the woman she wanted to be. Instead of ignoring her, like her father had done most of her life, or withdrawing affection whenever others were around, like Mary and Joe had done to

"

keep her safe from the wrath of her father, Bobby was open with his attention and affection for her, regardless of who was around them.

She hadn't realized just how much she'd needed that open affection until she'd received it from Bobby. But it was his attention, how he actually listened to her, thoughtfully discussed things with her, and encouraged her to learn new things to be able to follow her dreams that really made her feel like she was capable, worthy, and able to do anything she put her mind to because he would be there to support her in anything she endeavored.

Mary and Joe had tried to do those things for her when her father wasn't around, but it was still hard for her to believe in herself when her father undermined their encouragement. Somehow, she didn't think Bobby would back down from her father, even if he was blustering out orders like he did to Mary and Joe, so that made his support of her hopes and dreams feel stronger, more stable than she'd experienced before.

Maybe it's because we share a different kind of love than what I feel with Mary and Joe, too. With Bobby, it's romantic love, but with Mary and Joe it's more familial. Kind of like what I feel with the rest of the Burlesons.

When she really thought back over the last little bit of time, she could really see the way the whole Burleson family had welcomed her into the fold. They'd not just given her a job to be able to pay for her car repairs, but they'd also invited her to family events and helped teach her the things she needed to know to further her career as an author, as well as explained the basics of business she'd need if she ever had to take over running Ashbury Enterprises.

If I do get stuck having to take over running Mom's family business, I wish I could hire them to do all the daily tasks that they haven't been able to teach me yet. If it weren't for the fact that I know Mom would want me to have the company as part of her family legacy, I think I'd rather just sell it to the Burlesons, or some other business like theirs, so it would be run properly in the future. Even with all Bobby's help, and that of his family, I don't think I'm knowledgeable enough to be able to effectively manage all the different divisions of such a big corporation.

Brooklyn was pushed out of her melancholy mood by Bobby stirring beneath her. She'd rather focus on the fun, flirty feelings he brought out in her than on a future she didn't want anyway.

"Good morning, beautiful," Bobby growled, his voice deep and gravelly from sleep. He squeezed her tight and kissed the top of her head.

"Good morning." Brooklyn returned his kiss by brushing her lips over the hard pectoral muscle under her face.

"How do ya feel this morning?" Bobby moved his hand to tilt her chin, so she had to look into his eyes. "Sore?"

Brooklyn did a quick assessment of her body before replying. "No, not sore. I feel really good actually."

"Good." Bobby gave her a big, dimple exposing smile before his look turned more serious. "There's, uh, something we need to talk about this morning."

"Oh?" Brooklyn wondered what would put such a serious look on Bobby's face first thing in the morning, and hoped it wasn't a poor performance review from the night before.

"Yeah," he sighed, rolling them to the side, so he could release her from his embrace and push up into a seated position. He ran a hand through his hair, like he was stalling and trying to figure out how to break whatever news he had to tell her.

Brooklyn grabbed the comforter that had been flipped over them sometime in the night and wrapped it around her, so she could sit up without feeling too exposed in her naked state.

"I, uh, kinda got carried away last night," Bobby started, causing Brooklyn's heart to plummet into her stomach from thinking he regretted their lovemaking. "I was just so desperate to make love to you that I forgot to put on a condom."

"Oh," she exhaled forcefully, unable to fully express what she was thinking. *We had sex with no condom. Is he freaked out because he has a disease that I'll now have to be tested for? Or is he freaked out about possibly getting me pregnant?*

I mean, I didn't think about needing a condom last night either, so if it's pregnancy he's worried about, I'm just as responsible for the consequences. But if he's got an STI, then that's one-hundred percent on him to take the blame, since we both know I'm clean because of never having done anything with anyone but him.

"I'm clean, and I know you're clean," Bobby blurted, his hand nervously making another pass through his hair. "Fuck, I'm screwing this up."

"It's okay, Bobby." Brooklyn reached out to place a comforting hand on his forearm. "I didn't think about protection last night either. I don't know how likely it is that we could've conceived last night, but I won't hold you responsible if we did."

"Like hell I won't be responsible!" Bobby shouted, raising his voice in a way Brooklyn hadn't heard from him since the first night she'd worked and lived in his home. When she involuntarily flinched back, Bobby gentled his tone to apologize. "I'm sorry, I didn't mean to yell."

He closed his eyes and took a deep breath, obviously trying to calm himself down before continuing their conversation. Brooklyn didn't know what to say, unsure what this potential issue meant for them as a couple. So, she sat there, clutching the comforter to her chest, and focusing on her own breathing to remain calm, while Bobby figured out what he wanted to say next.

"We haven't really talked about the future." Bobby opened his eyes, so his hazel orbs could connect with her baby blues. "I didn't wanna push you too fast because you're so young and have a lot going on back in Georgia. So, I just kinda left it as us being together for now. I thought we'd have at least a few months, or hell, maybe even a year or two, before we needed to discuss what we both want for the future as far as having kids goes."

"Oh-kay," Brooklyn drawled the word out as two very distinct syllables when he stopped talking and didn't appear to have figured out how to continue. Everything he'd just said led her to believe that he wasn't ready for kids yet, so she was still sticking to her thought of raising their child on her own if they'd conceived the night before. But she wasn't able to explain her thoughts before Bobby continued.

"I'm still not saying this right." Bobby shook his head before reaching out to pull Brooklyn onto his lap and into his arms. "I adore you, Brie-Baby. And I'll adore any little ones that come along. Whether that's now or ten years from now, I want us to be a family. I just don't wanna take the decision to have kids or not away from you, and I feel like that's kinda what I did by not wearing a condom last night. I'm sorry I was so thoughtless."

"Oh, Bobby," Brooklyn sighed, throwing her arms around the most thoughtful man she'd ever met. "You weren't thoughtless. We were both caught up in each other and not thinking about any potential consequences."

"Does this mean you forgive me?" Bobby nuzzled her neck with his scruff.

"There's nothing to forgive," Brooklyn declared, turning her face to kiss his temple. "You didn't do anything wrong."

"Maybe not, but I'm still gonna make sure I grab a condom every time, until you tell me you're ready to start trying for our first baby," Bobby murmured against the sensitive skin where her neck met her torso. "Or until we find out we're already expecting."

"You're really going to be okay if we have a baby now?" Brooklyn wasn't quite ready to reveal her own excitement at the possibility.

"Brie-Baby, I will be thrilled if we made a baby last night." Bobby lifted his head to look her in the eyes as he spoke. He touched their foreheads together before continuing. "I'll probably feel a little guilty for forcing my family plan on you, but I can't think of anything more wonderful than making babies with you."

"I kinda like the idea of making babies with you too," Brooklyn admitted, giving him a wry smile. "But I'm also a little nervous about what's going to happen with everything back in Georgia, and how that will impact us actually being able to stay together to raise those babies."

"Brie-Baby," Bobby sighed, shaking his head, and making hers shake with him since their foreheads were still connected. "Nothing's gonna happen to tear us apart. You're it for me, Brie-Baby. If that means I have to go to Georgia to kick ass and fix shit for us to be together, then so be it. Even if you have to take over running your family business, I'm gonna be by your side to help you with it."

"But what about all your commitments here?" Brooklyn's eyes filled with tears at the thought of having to be in Georgia while Bobby had to be in Texas. "Your job and family, and your family business are all here. You can't just move to Georgia to help me run a company I don't even want."

"I'm already planning on taking vacation time from work when you need to go back to Georgia to deal with the legal issues there." Bobby pecked her lips with the briefest kiss. "And if you don't really wanna run Ashbury, then I'll help you set up the staff to run it for you. Or we could talk to my family about a merger with Burleson Incorporated, so your Mom's legacy can be shared with our kids and all their cousins in the future. Hell, even if you decide you wanna run Ashbury, we can split our time between here and Georgia and telecommute to work at our respective family businesses. I'm not planning on being the police chief indefinitely, so if I need to I can retire early from there instead of in twelve more years like I'd planned."

"I wouldn't want you to give up your job for me," Brooklyn protested, blinking back the tears that were still threatening to escape. "I know how much you love it."

"Eh, it's not like I need to put in a full twenty years to have the retirement money to live on," Bobby shrugged. "I can still give back to the community without wearing a badge. Besides, as much as I love police work, I love you more. So, if I have to quit my job as police chief to be with you in Georgia, then that's what I'll do."

"Oh, Bobby, I love you, too," Brooklyn shouted, punctuating her first declaration of love by pressing her lips to his.

Bobby quickly took over the kiss, just the way she loved having him kiss her. Passionately. Making her feel like he needed to kiss her more than he needed to breathe. She returned his zeal, ardently tangling her tongue with his, and hoping he felt as claimed by the kiss as she did.

They didn't waste a moment thinking about morning breath or needing to finish their conversation. Their desire for each other was too all encompassing for them to even register that there was even a world around them outside their two bodies trying to meld into one. Frenzied hands moved, ripping the comforter out from between them, so they could get closer. They were fervently yearning to be skin to skin.

Once they'd removed the encumbrance of the comforter, Bobby fell back onto the mattress, bringing Brooklyn with him as he rolled them to the edge of the bed. In a move that Brooklyn couldn't figure out how he'd done it, Bobby picked her up and stood from the bed. She wrapped her legs around his waist and her arms around his shoulders, clinging to him like she had the night before when he'd carried her up the stairs.

Bobby held Brooklyn with one large hand under her bottom and the other covering her upper back. He turned and leaned her back, breaking their kiss to say, "Grab the condoms out of that top drawer, Brie-Baby."

She did as he instructed, even though she would've been perfectly happy to continue going without them now that she knew Bobby intended to make them work as a family in the future. Still clinging to his shoulder with her left hand, Brooklyn reached out with her right to open the drawer and grabbed the box, not wanting to waste time opening it to pull out a single packet.

As soon as she had the box in hand, Bobby pulled her back up in a tight embrace and walked them into his master bathroom, heading straight for the huge glass-enclosed shower. The gray tiled walls of the shower matched the solid surface countertops throughout the rest of the house, just like the tiles in the guest shower she'd been using, but on a much grander scale with the master shower being at least twice the size of the standard tub and shower combo in the guest bathroom.

"Put the box on the top ledge," Bobby ordered, pointing with his head to where Brooklyn sat the box of condoms. He then turned around and did something with his hand behind Brooklyn's back to turn on the multiple shower nozzles, checking the water temperature before walking them both into the rapidly steaming enclosure.

"Fuck, I've fantasized about you in this shower so many times." Bobby crushed his mouth to hers once more, not giving her a chance to confess her similar imaginings.

She wanted to ask him about those fantasies to see if they matched up with the ones she'd had about him in her own shower, but she couldn't make a sound other than an impassioned moan while they exuberantly kissed with the water beating down all around them.

Bobby lifted her higher in his arms, trailing his mouth down her throat. "So. Much. Better. Than. My. Fantasies." He punctuated each word with a nip to her skin as he moved his way down to her breasts.

"Mine, too." Brooklyn felt the tip of his erection at her entrance in the new position, instead of smashed between their bodies as it had been when they walked into the bathroom. The way he was barely grazing her clit with the head of his penis was driving her to the brink with need. "Oh, please, Bobby," she cried out, not sure if she was begging for him to push inside her or just make her come with more pressure on her clit.

"Fuck, Brie-Baby!" Bobby raised his head and twisted around to press her back into the glass wall where he could reach the box of condoms. Still holding her under her bottom with one hand, he relied on the wall to hold her up, so he could reach with his other hand to get a condom from the box and sheath himself. "I love hearing you beg for my cock, but you have to tell me exactly what you want."

"I want you, Bobby, please," Brooklyn begged as Bobby bent his head to continue lavishing her chest with open-mouthed kisses, little sucks, and tiny nibbles.

"What do you want me to do?" Bobby's hot breath blew across her pebbled nipples. "Do you want me to keep sucking your tits? Or shove my cock in your tight little pussy? What does my dirty girl need?"

"All of that, please," Brooklyn pleaded, her hands in his hair, trying to guide his mouth back to her nipples, and her hips wiggling, trying to get him lined up to push inside her.

"Then tell me Brie-Baby," Bobby growled, his scruff feeling tantalizing between her breasts. "I need to hear your pretty little mouth say all those dirty words."

Brooklyn felt a little shy about saying the things Bobby seemed to want to hear, but having enjoyed hearing him talk dirty, she understood why he wanted to hear the same from her. "I want you to suck my tits and shove your big, hard cock in my tight, wet pussy."

"Fuck, yes, Brie-Baby," Bobby shouted just as he impaled her on his rock-hard erection.

"Bobby!" Brooklyn screamed, surprised by the sudden fullness she felt at his invasion. She wasn't quite sure what she was feeling in that moment. It wasn't pain, at least not the same as the night before, when he'd broken the barrier keeping them from joining for the first time. But it wasn't quite pleasurable either.

It was a completely new feeling for her. An intense fullness that was walking the tightrope between pain and pleasure, between hell and heaven. It was too much and yet, somehow, not enough.

"Fuck, sorry," Bobby groaned, pressing their foreheads together, so they were looking into each other's eyes. "You're so wet. I wasn't expecting to slide home so fast. I didn't mean to hurt you."

Seeing the look of concern on Bobby's face, Brooklyn knew he would stop if she told him she was even slightly uncomfortable. Remembering back to the night before, how Bobby had transformed the fleeting moment of sharp, stabbing pain into what seemed like hours floating in nirvana beyond anything she'd ever known, Brooklyn knew which side of that thin line she wanted them to fall on. So, she gave him a reassuring smile, and spoke the words he needed to hear to take them out of the purgatory they were in, and lift them both to the heights of heavenly bliss once again.

"You didn't hurt me." Brooklyn cupped his cheeks in her hands. "I was just shocked by the sudden fullness."

"Thank fuck!" Bobby brushed his lips over hers briefly. "I never wanna do anything to hurt you, Brie-Baby."

Bobby adjusted his hold on her hips, so he could control her movements, bouncing her up and down on his length in the most delicious way. He rounded his back to be able to keep his head bent low enough to pepper her breasts with sucking kisses each time he bounced her up and almost off his cock.

Brooklyn wasn't sure what the spot was deep inside her he kept hitting that was making her feel like she was about to implode, but she loved the way it felt. She didn't realize how much she was pulling his hair with one hand or digging her nails into his upper back with the other. All she could focus on was how wonderful he made her feel in that moment.

Her orgasm ripping through her felt like a series of waves crashing over her body, flowing from her core to her heart. "Oh, Bobby, I love you," she repeatedly whisper-shouted, barely able to form the words as she was overcome in a state of orgasmic ecstasy. She floated there in a sea of pleasure, unaware of anything around her other than Bobby and their connection.

"Oh fuck, Brie-Baby," Bobby shouted, lifting his mouth from her breasts as he plunged inside her one last time, holding himself as deep as he could go. Brooklyn felt his cock pulsing inside her as his whole body shuddered in release, only briefly registering how different it felt with the condom as opposed to how it had felt the night before without.

Obviously spent from his intense orgasm, Bobby stumbled backwards, carrying Brooklyn with him as he plopped down on the bench at the back of the shower. The hard landing on his lap would've been a lot more uncomfortable if he'd still been hard inside her, but thankfully, it was more shocking than painful in his softening state.

They sat there for several long moments, catching their breath, and enjoying the feeling of nirvana they found in each other's arms. Brooklyn wasn't sure just how long they stayed there, basking in the afterglow while holding each other in a loving embrace, but she was pretty sure it was long enough that they were going to miss breakfast before church. *If we even make it to church this morning. I wouldn't mind going back to bed for round three. Maybe he'll teach me how to use my mouth on him next.*

~~~

After being reprimanded by his mother for missing breakfast and being late for church that morning, Bobby was glad the conversation over Sunday supper had turned to topics other than what he and Brie had been doing that morning. Though he'd thoroughly enjoyed seeing her blush at his admission of them oversleeping. *Fuck, that blush probably told everyone that we weren't really sleeping late this morning. Considering all our extra time was spent in the shower and not in bed, I probably shouldn't have used that fib to cover for us.*

"How are the negotiations going on that land in Alabama?" Bobby's sister, Charlotte, inquired of his cousin, JJ.

"We've actually hit a bit of a snag," JJ admitted, shaking his head. "Actually, Brook might be interested to know that Ashbury Enterprises has stepped in to engage us in a bidding war over it."

"Oh, um," Brie stammered, looking like she felt guilty for whatever her father was doing with her family company. "I'm sorry, I don't know what land you're talking about, but I hope my father doesn't screw up the deal for you." She looked stricken as the color drained from her face when she turned to Bobby. "You don't think he knows where I am, and is trying to get back at your family for protecting me from him by messing with this deal, do you?"

"No, Brie-Baby." Bobby took her hand in his to reassure her. "There's no indication that anyone outside our circle knows where you
~~~

are, so I don't think anything he's doing business wise is related to you being here."

"From what my contact in Alabama has told me, he's only dealing with VP level executives at the various companies who have put in bids." JJ seemed remorseful for bringing up the topic of her father and her family business, his apology for bringing it up written all over his face. "So, I'm sure your father isn't the one actively looking at the deal we're trying to do."

"What are you trying to do?" Brie looked a little less worried. When JJ didn't immediately reply, Brie continued her line of questioning. "What are you, or I guess, what is Burleson Incorporated going to do with this land that you want to buy in Alabama?"

"Oh, we want to cap off the dried-up oil wells and put in a wind farm." JJ's smile showed how proud he was of how he'd been turning Burleson Oil into Burleson Energy since taking over running that division of the company. Since JJ graduated college and started working there, he'd been the one responsible for converting all the land previously owned by the company that had dried-up wells on it into renewable-energy-producing properties. Now that all the Burleson owned properties were profitable, he was branching out to buy land from their former competitors to help clean up any environmental issues and rebuild the job markets in areas blighted by defunct wells.

"And is that what Ashbury will do with the land if they put in the winning bid?" Brie obviously wanted to know more about the company her grandfather started, and her mother intended to be left to her.

"I have no idea," JJ shrugged. "I haven't seen any of the paperwork they submitted or anything like that. I just recognized the name of the company when my contact listed out the names of the three other companies who had submitted a bid."

"So, it's not just Ashbury we're having to outbid?" Charlotte looked way more interested in the details of this one business deal than she ever had over the other deals they discussed in board meetings.

"No, there's also a developer I've never heard of before, and another oil company that is probably considering the same things we are for the land." JJ turned to face Charlotte as he answered her question. "I'm not as concerned about their bids because they're much smaller companies, so they're less likely to have the capital on hand to outbid us without requiring a financial backer. And we all know how uneasy finance guys feel about the costs of environmental clean-up and the effect of those costs on their return on investment."

As Bobby's sisters, cousins, and Uncle Jon discussed the potential business deal, Bobby watched Brie, specifically focusing on her reaction to the discussion regarding Ashbury Enterprises. She was chewing on her bottom lip like she was nervous. The way she squeezed Bobby's hand without seeming to realize she was doing it, made him feel like she was having an involuntary negative reaction to the potential business conflict between their families.

Wanting to reassure her that they were still fine, regardless of the outcome of the land deal in Alabama, Bobby leaned over and whispered in her ear. "It's okay, Brie-Baby. Nothing going on with Ashbury reflects on you. Nobody in our family will hold it against you if Ashbury wins the bid instead of Burleson."

"I know that," Brie confided, turning to look into his eyes and giving him a slight smile. "I just feel guilty for not being able to do anything to save my mother and grandfather's legacies. Like I should be actively working on getting my father out of Ashbury, and instead I'm taking the coward's way out by hiding here."

Bobby hated knowing that she felt guilty for anything, especially staying with him, instead of being in Georgia to actively fight her father and his cronies. But he also understood her frustration and desire to be the one on the front line, defending her family legacy.

Maybe Josh had the right idea when he suggested I marry her, so she can take over the business before the feds indict her father and oust him from the company. It's the only way I've been able to figure out to help her gain control of the situation without a possible long legal battle. Hell, even when her father is arrested, she might still have to fight him for control of the company and the rest of her assets.

"If you had the option to go take control of Ashbury right now," Bobby started, holding her face between his hands to maintain eye contact with her as he finished his question, "is that what you'd wanna do?"

"Um, I don't know." Brie looked pensive at the thought of being in charge of her family business. "Maybe? It depends on what I'd have to do, and if it would give me the power to fire my father and Clayton, and not put me at risk of them forcing me to do their bidding."

"You definitely wouldn't have to do any of the shit they had planned for you," Bobby chuckled. "I'd have to check the by-laws at Ashbury, but I think it would give you the power to fire them both, too."

"Okay, then yeah, I'm interested," Brie asserted, even though she still seemed a bit tentative as she nibbled her bottom lip. "But, uh, what would I have to do?"

"Marry me." Bobby smiled brightly at the thought of walking down the aisle with the beautiful blonde beside him.

"What?" Brie screeched, pulling back away from Bobby with her jaw falling open in shock.

Not caring that everyone else in the room had suddenly quieted at Brie's outburst and turned their attention to the two of them, Bobby repeated himself. "Marry me." When she just sat there looking dumbfounded, Bobby continued laying out the reasoning. "If we get married, you'll have fulfilled the requirements to inherit the bulk of your family estate. That means you'd have control of Ashbury Enterprises, and could clean up whatever mess your father and Donaldson have made there. If I remember everything right from your mother's will, you can kick your father out of your family home and sue him for all the money he's stolen from you over the years, too."

"No!" Brie shook her head. "No, no, no. I'm not stooping to his level by getting married *just* to gain control of the company."

The way she put special emphasis on the word "just" made Bobby realize he'd blundered by not giving her a more romantic proposal. *Shit! Open mouth, insert size-thirteen foot!*

"Obviously, after last night and this morning, we wouldn't be getting married *just* for control of the company," Bobby argued, trying to dig himself out of the very deep hole he'd inadvertently fallen into with his lack of finesse when he attempted a proposal. "But like I told you this morning, I want us to be a family. Why waste time dating when we already know we wanna be together? Especially when getting married now is the fastest way to fix everything in Georgia, so you don't have to feel guilty for not doing anything while we're waiting on the feds, and it saves you a long legal battle over who controls your inheritance, even if your father goes to jail for embezzlement."

"Oh, Bobby," he faintly heard his mother, Hazel, comment from her seat at the end of the table.

"Wow!" Brie threw up her arms in exasperation. "If you really think dating is a waste of time, then, yes, we should definitely skip it. But if we're not dating, then that means we're not doing the stay home dates to watch movies on the sofa either. Or anything else that *'dating couples'* usually do."

Bobby thought her use of air quotes when she said the words "dating couples" was a little unnecessary, but he didn't say a word about it, not wanting to aggravate her further. *Fuck, I've really screwed this up. But damn, she's hot when she's pissed.*

In an attempt to get his mind out of the gutter, so he didn't pop a boner in the middle of his parents' dining room, Bobby smiled at Brie, hoping to charm her into forgiving him for his word vomit and get them back on track as a couple.

"I didn't mean that the way it sounded." He intentionally made his dimples pop because he knew she liked them. He reached for her hand, needing to feel their connection as they talked things out. "I don't think any of our dates, or other things we do together, are a waste of time. I just meant that I don't need to do all that to know I wanna spend the rest of my life with you, so we should go ahead and plan our wedding, knowing we'll be doing all that dating stuff for the rest of our lives together."

"No." Brie refused his reasoning, pulling her hand back out of his grasp. "I think we need to take a step back. There's too much going on, and it's all confusing me. Maybe we should go back to being boss and employee until everything is settled with my father and Ashbury. While I'm figuring out how to be my true self and settling into my new role in life, maybe you can figure out how this all went wrong tonight and what needs to change before I'll ever consider dating you again."

Fuck! Fuck, fuck, fuck! Bobby cursed internally, knowing his Ma would be after him with a switch if he uttered the words out loud in her home. *How the fuck am I gonna fix this?*

"If ya'll will please excuse me." Brie stood from her seat and picked up her dishes from the table. "I need to go spend the rest of the evening working on my next book."

"Brie-Baby," Bobby called after her as she fled to the kitchen with her dirty dishes.

He stood and took the first step to follow her, not wanting their first disagreement as a couple to end without being resolved.

"Give her space, Son," Bobby's father, Bob, advised him, drawing Bobby's attention back to the room full of family around him.

"How am I supposed to figure out what all I did wrong to be able to fix it if I don't go talk to her?" Bobby was unsure if he was talking to his dad, the whole family, or God, because he was afraid getting back together with Brie would take divine intervention at the moment.

"Oh, I think we all know how you screwed up," Charlotte smirked from across the table.

"Yeah?" Bobby plopped back down into his chair and glared at Charlotte. "Then please enlighten me, so I can fix it."

"Do you love her?" Bobby's other sister, Becky, looked at him with sympathy.

"Of course," Bobby answered, knowing his feelings for Brie weren't the problem.

"Does she know that?" Bobby's cousin, Jen, rolled her eyes and shook her head. "Because no woman wants a proposal that doesn't include the big L-word."

"Yes, she knows," Bobby barked, turning his glare toward his cousin.

"Does she really?" His mother gave him a sad smile. "Have you specifically said the words *I love you* to her?"

"Yes, Ma, I've specifically said the words," Bobby grumbled, irritated by his family not seeming to believe he'd told Brie how he felt about her. Maybe not in his ill-timed proposal, but he'd told her just that morning.

Fuck, that's the only time I've precisely said those three words when she actually heard them, though. Is that the problem? I need to tell her more than once?

"Oh, I think he's getting it now," Charlotte declared, nodding her head at Bobby. "I can see the light bulb turning on in his head."

Bobby was tempted to throw his wadded-up napkin at his sister, but he refrained, knowing that if he did, he'd never figure out the rest of what he'd done wrong that evening.

"So, I should probably tell her I love her more than the one time I've explicitly said it so far." Bobby acknowledged the first point his family was making. "And I'm sure I should come up with something more romantic when I propose again. But what else do I need to do, so I can earn back the right to even get a chance to propose to her again?"

"You can start by showing her that you're really listening when she's telling you what she needs." Charlotte's expression was wistful, making Bobby wonder if that was something she needed from the new teacher their mother was trying to fix her up with, more than an observation of what Brie needed from him.

"I can do that." Bobby nodded, thinking back to everything Brie had laid out earlier to try and determine what she truly meant by her words. "Maybe. I might need ya'll's help to decipher what she said tonight."

Bobby was grateful for how close-knit his large family was, and especially for all their help as they schooled him on how to be a better boyfriend the rest of the night. Though he'd never felt like he had a romantic bone in his body before, they taught him that being romantic was all about understanding your partner and putting them first in your life.

He'd misunderstood that lesson when he was younger, thinking it was all about sex. But now he knew it was more than just making sure Brie came first when they were making love. He had to really pay attention to everything she said and did to determine not just her physical needs, but also her emotional needs. Then he had to make sure he was putting her needs above his own, taking care of her before he took what he needed for himself.

He thought he'd been doing a pretty good job of that for the last few weeks. Not only in how he'd been working her up to a more intimate relationship by taking care of her sexual needs first, but also in how he'd been supportive of her writing career, shown her the friendly affection that she'd missed out on in her old life, and comforted her when she was worried about the legal ramifications of being born Brooklyn Brielle Barns.

Unfortunately, he'd completely missed the mark when it came to her need to feel loved. He'd tried to show her how he felt about her by using foreplay and sex, instead of making her feel cherished like she deserved. Armed with a new understanding of how he needed to be a better man to be Brie's man, Bobby walked home that night to plan out how he would woo the woman of his dreams. It would include saying "I love you" multiple times a day and showing his love in lots of little ways that didn't include his cock.

I hope you're prepared to be pampered, Brie-Baby. Bobby mentally warned her as he laid alone in his bed, which still held a hint of her smell from the night before. *Because I'm gonna do everything I can think of to win your heart, like you've already won mine.*

~ ~ ~

Friday, January 25, 2019

As Brooklyn went about her normal daily task of cooking for the Burleson men, she reminisced about all the little things Bobby had done all week to try to win her back. He'd left her notes beside the coffee pot every morning before he left for work. All of them were variations on the same theme of his random thoughts about her from the previous day, and all of them were signed with those three little words she'd only heard him actually utter once before that week.

In addition to the notes, he'd brought her home little gifts each day, too. All accompanied by a different bouquet of flowers, so he could try to figure out her favorite flower, since she hadn't been able to decide in order to tell him during one of their earlier talks about their favorite things.

It had started on Monday with innocuous things like bath bombs and bubble bath for her to go upstairs and soak after dinner. The bouquet of daffodils was accompanied by a card declaring the meaning of the flower as "asking for forgiveness" from the recipient. Brooklyn had started to feel guilty for her childish behavior in breaking up with him when she read the meaning, but she couldn't quite make herself tell him that she was the one who should be asking for forgiveness.

Tuesday, he'd spent way too much on a pair of boots for her to wear horseback riding, telling her she should break them in by wearing them all week before the weekend ride he'd scheduled for them. Those had come with a bouquet of red and white carnations with a meaning card, reading "fascination and love" that would've pushed Brooklyn to backtrack on the breakup, if he hadn't argued with her when she said the boots were too expensive.

He actually seemed to have listened to her protests about the boots being too much, going back to an inexpensive gift on Wednesday—a manicure set and ten-dollar gift card to Beautiful Destiny, so she could pick out her own favorite color of nail polish to go with it. With that, he'd given her a hanging planter of forget-me-nots, their meaning obvious in their name.

Thursday, he'd given her a silly joke book. She thought it was a strange gift until she read the meaning card tucked into the bouquet of yellow tulips that read, "sunshine in your smile." He didn't have to elaborate that he hoped the jokes would make her smile, instead doing the same thing he'd done every other night when he got home and handed her the gift of the night. He kissed her on the cheek and said, "I love you, Brie-Baby," before going upstairs to shower and change out of his police uniform to come back down for dinner.

She wasn't sure how much longer she could hold out through their nightly dinner conversations without telling him how sorry she was for not really listening to him on Sunday to comprehend that he didn't just want to marry her so she could inherit her mother's family company. But after talking to Hazel, Susan, Rosa, and the new housekeeper, Cait, on Wednesday after cleaning Justin's house, and the four of them all encouraging her to at least make him grovel until her birthday the following week, Brooklyn was determined to wait out the days to see what other unusual gifts and flower messages Bobby came up with in his attempt to reconcile with her.

Only four more days after today until my birthday, Brooklyn thought as she packaged up the meals she needed to take to JJ and Justin's houses for the weekend. *Surely, I can keep from throwing myself at him until then.*

Based on all the little tokens of appreciation and romantic flower messages, Brooklyn already knew that Bobby had forgiven her for her immature behavior. But she still felt like she needed to explain to him how her inexperience in relationships, combined with her horrible history with her father, had led to her not comprehending everything he'd said on Sunday and blowing things way out of proportion in her adamant refusal to marry him.

Leah Mae Wright

If she'd have truly listened to him, instead of getting hung up on feeling like she would be descending to her father's despicable level by marrying in order to inherit the company, Brooklyn would've realized that Bobby wanted to marry her because he loved her and not just to end her legal woes. She felt terrible for getting caught in a cycle of selective hearing, where she misinterpreted his statement about wasting time dating, causing her to break up with him when that was the exact opposite of what she wanted to do deep in her heart.

If I can figure out a way to end this mess with my father soon, and get back together with Bobby on my birthday, maybe I can propose to him on Valentine's Day. That'll give us plenty of time to make up, even if everything isn't resolved in Georgia, and it'll probably shock the pants off him after the way I refused his proposal on Sunday.

Resolved with a plan, Brooklyn loaded up the mule with the food to go to the houses on the northern part of the ranch. She'd split her cleaning time at Kay's house between the previous Friday and Monday since the family were working both days, so Brooklyn didn't think Kay would need her to do much if anything at her house that day. She grabbed her laptop bag, in case the woman she thought of as a mentor was free to go over their latest book plans while she was there that afternoon, before heading out of the house that she now considered her home.

It didn't take Brooklyn long to drive up to the northern part of the ranch to drop off food at both JJ and Justin's houses. Once everything was unloaded, she drove the mule across the gravel road to the driveway leading back behind Kay's house. She laughed at herself as she pulled down the driveway, thinking it was funny how she always used the front door when she entered JJ or Justin's homes, but she went to the back door at Hazel's, Kay's, and Bobby's.

I guess it's because I was taken in the back doors at those three houses on my first day of work, so the lesson to go in the back stuck from day one. But nobody ever told me which door to use at the other two houses, so I've gone with what I'd been taught all my life as the proper door to enter. Maybe if Hazel and Susan's matchmaking plans ever work on Justin and JJ, I'll start using their back doors, too, to go into their homes to visit with their wives.

"Knock, knock," Brooklyn called out, wrapping her knuckles on the door as she opened it to step through.

"Hi, Brie," Tia and Maria chorused in unison as they almost ran her over coming out the door at the same time Brooklyn was walking in.

"Hi," Brooklyn replied as the girls rushed past her.

"Bye, Brie," Anthony chuckled, stepping to the side to let her pass before running to catch up with his daughters.

"Oh, um, bye," Brooklyn replied, making sure the door was shut behind them before making her way into the kitchen, where she found Kay sitting at the table.

"Get run over on your way in?" Kay looked up at Brooklyn with a bright smile.

"Almost," Brooklyn replied, returning Kay's smile. "They seemed excited about wherever they're going."

"Always," Kay chuckled, placing a hand on her belly. "Thank goodness Anthony's still young enough to have the energy to keep up with them when I'm sidelined by morning sickness."

"Oh." Brooklyn hated to hear that her friend wasn't feeling well. "Is there anything I can do to help you feel better?"

"I'm already doing all I can," Kay assured her, motioning to the fruit and crackers on a plate in front of her. "My grandmother swore to me when I was pregnant with Tia that pears and crackers were the best for settling the nausea of morning sickness. But since it doesn't seem to be working as well as I thought it did back then, I'm thinking she just might have been old and senile, and I was still too young to realize she was yanking my chain."

Brooklyn giggled uncomfortably along with Kay, not really thinking there was anything funny about Kay being sick or her elderly grandmother's remedy not working, but not knowing how else to respond to the strange situation. When their laughter died down, Brooklyn stammered, "So, um, do you need to lay down or anything to let the nausea pass? Or do you still want to brainstorm our books?"

"No, I don't need to lay down or anything like that," Kay smiled wistfully. "I think I'm past the puking portion of the day. I just don't have the energy to go horseback riding all afternoon."

Kay tilted her head as she looked at Brooklyn, making her feel like the other woman was examining her closely. Before Brook could determine if she felt uncomfortable under Kay's inquisitive assessment, Kay voiced her concern for Brooklyn. "But before we start brainstorming, I want to know what's going on with you and Bobby."

"I take it you've already heard about me being an idiot at Sunday supper." Brooklyn slumped down into a seat at the table.

"I heard Bobby botched his proposal." One corner of Kay's mouth turned up in the slightest smile.

"Yeah, I don't think I'd actually classify what Bobby said as a proposal." Brooklyn shook her head. "More like a suggestion for how to fix all the legal issues in Georgia, not actually asking me to marry him."

"More like being a bullheaded Burleson and telling you to marry him, instead of asking." Brooklyn couldn't tell if Kay's words had been a statement or a question, but she nodded her head in agreement. "Yeah, that's a family trait. It took Anthony several tries before he got the command out of his voice to ask me to marry him, too. You might have to tell him what he's doing wrong a few times before he gets it right, but I'm sure he'll get there. Probably not too long after you give him the green light that ya'll are back together."

"Yeah, that's what I meant about me being an idiot," Brooklyn confessed with a self-deprecating shake of her head. "I got so discombobulated by the thought of being as despicable as my father by marrying to gain control of the company that I couldn't comprehend anything else he was saying. I ended up misunderstanding what he meant and broke things off when I shouldn't have."

"Yeah, well, I think the general consensus is that Bobby needed the wake-up call of a breakup to realize that relationships require work." Kay's smile showed in her eyes as an ornery gleam. "A little birdie told me he's been stepping up his romance game to try to woo you."

"Yeah." Brooklyn blushed at the insinuation in Kay's expression. "I feel a little bad for accepting all the gifts and flowers and stuff, when I should be the one apologizing to him. Once I got home and really thought about everything he'd said, I realized that being caught up on that one thought kept me from acknowledging all the feelings we've expressed to each other recently. Or how those feelings are really the impetus to why he suggested marriage and not gaining control of the company."

"Have you told Bobby that?"

"No," Brooklyn admitted. "We've talked over dinner every night just like before, but it's always about how my writing is going and what he did at work that day. I tried to apologize the first night, but he put his finger over my lips to stop me, and said he didn't want to discuss the events of Sunday night."

Brooklyn wiped a tear she couldn't stop from escaping down her cheek before continuing. "I've wanted to apologize every night since, but between him not wanting to talk about it, and the advice I've gotten from Hazel and the other women this week, I feel like I can't."

"Oh, you can't go by the advice of the matchmaking mommas," Kay laughed. "They're enjoying watching Bobby suffer after years of him rejecting all the women they've tried to match him up with."

"It wasn't just Hazel, Susan, and Rosa," Brooklyn chuckled lightly at Kay using the nickname she'd come up with for the group while brainstorming about their future book series. "Cait was there, too, telling me to make him grovel until my birthday next week."

"Cait may only be in her mid-twenties and not a momma yet," Kay disagreed, shaking her head. "But she's in cahoots with the rest of them with their plans to match up her brother, Ian, with Charlotte. So, I think she'll side with them, at least until they figure out who to match her up with."

"Yeah, I was kind of surprised when they didn't have her move in with Justin or JJ when she started working here on the ranch," Brooklyn admitted, both women grinning at the antics of the older women.

"No, I think they already have plans for both of them." Kay had a knowing look on her face. "I found out when my best friend was down here for my wedding that she and JJ have known each other for a few years. Deanna doesn't want to admit to having feelings for him, but I think they'll get together eventually, especially if the mommas have anything to say about it."

"You really think they'll get together when she doesn't live here?" Brooklyn was happy to have the relationship talk transition off of her and Bobby.

"Oh yeah!" Kay's grin turned into an almost smirk. "I'm sure Hazel and Susan will figure out a way to get Deanna to change jobs and come to work at Burleson, just like they did with Randi's best friend, Amy, when she was here for the wedding. She just started working at Burleson in the same department as Justin."

"I suppose it's only really a family business if the Burlesons' spouses also work for the company," Brooklyn joked.

"Speaking of family businesses…" Kay trailed off, transitioning to a new topic. "What's going on with yours?"

"I don't know." Brooklyn shook her head, her jovial mood disintegrating. "I hate feeling like I'm sitting around doing nothing to fix things there. But the thought of getting married to inherit it makes me feel slimy. So, as much as I wish I could do something other than wait on the feds to arrest my father, I can't think of any other option."

"Yeah, I understand you wanting to marry for love and not the company." Kay nodded her head in agreement. "But surely we can think of some other way of clearing up everything else. What does Bobby think of you contacting the Macon Police Department to tell them that you haven't been kidnapped?"

"He doesn't know how risky that would be because of not knowing who in the department might be on my father's payroll," Brooklyn stated, shrugging. "He had Jake tell one of his FBI contacts that I left to escape my father's plans for me, but they're more interested in the embezzlement case and haven't contacted me to verify anything yet."

"Ya know what?" Kay pulled her phone out and typed up a quick text. "I think we need more minds working on brainstorming how to deal with your daddy issues."

"My daddy issues?" Brooklyn chortled, thinking that was a funny way to describe the legal problems she had with her father.

"Oh yeah," Kay chuckled, quickly replying to whatever messages she'd received in response to the one she'd just sent. "If we ever collaborate on a Daddy Dom book, we're going to use your backstory to explain the heroine's daddy issues."

"Don't hold your breath on that one," Brooklyn snorted, shaking her head at her friend. "I barely feel prepared to write a sweet romance. I doubt I'll ever feel ready to write about dominance and submission and kinky sex."

"Oh, that sounds like a lot more fun to brainstorm about than the reason you called us over here." Charlotte walked into the kitchen from the front hallway.

"Who all did you call over here?" Brooklyn questioned Kay.

"Just Charlotte, Becky, Jen, and Julie," Kay replied without looking up from her phone. "Becky said she'll be here in a few minutes. She has to deal with one last thing at the playhouse. Jen and Julie are going to meet in one of their offices and Skype me any minute to help us figure out how to expose your father's misdeeds faster than the feds are moving."

Before Brooklyn could reply, Kay's phone chimed with the video call from Jen and Julie. Kay quickly answered it and set her phone up on the table, aiming it between her and Brooklyn, so they could both see the screen. Charlotte sat down beside Brooklyn, squeezing in to be included in the conversation.

After a raucous round of hellos, Julie took over leading the impromptu meeting of Burlesons and Brooklyn. Apparently, her role as the vice president of business diversification and asset management at Burleson Incorporated put her in the best position to look into the structure of Ashbury Enterprises, in hopes of finding loopholes that Brooklyn could use to take control before she got married, or turned twenty-five, as outlined in her mother's will.

"There's a twelve-member board of directors that has to approve any change of ownership," Julie informed them.

"Seems fitting to have a twelve-member board, since that's what we have at Burleson," Charlotte smiled.

"Yeah, but where we have ten of those members under the age of thirty, Ashbury's board is mostly made up of men in their sixties and seventies," Julie sighed, frowning. "I'm guessing they were friends of Brook's grandfather, but I can't be certain that they aren't people appointed by Mr. Barns, since he took over the CEO position and one of the board seats as the trustee for Brook's inheritance."

"Do you think it really matters who brought them onto the board?" Brooklyn knew the women around her had much more knowledge of how big business worked than she did.

"Maybe," Jen shrugged, giving Brooklyn a sympathetic smile. "If they were friends of your grandfather, then they might be more upset by your father's treatment of you and misuse of your monthly stipend. That might give them cause to side with you when you sue to have your father removed as trustee, which is the first thing I think you should do."

"No, the first thing she needs to do is clear up the whole kidnapping mess," Becky asserted, having just joined them in Kay's kitchen. "It's too risky for her to go back to Georgia to sue her father, when she doesn't know who to trust with the local authorities not to take her straight to him."

"I agree with Becky," Charlotte nodded, sliding over on her seat for her sister to join her on it, so they could all be seen by Jen and Julie on the Skype call. "We need to make sure the whole world knows that her father was trying to force her to marry that old geezer, so they can't kidnap her themselves, and drug her or beat her into going along with their plans."

"What about a press release?" Kay's sudden question caused everyone to look at her for clarification. "I mean, we don't have to convince a judge and jury to convict him of emotionally abusing Brook to keep her safe from him. We can convict him in the court of public opinion with a press release from Brook about how she had to escape his tyranny."

"Oh, yes," Becky squealed, nodding her head. "They won't be able to convince anyone she actually wants to marry that old fart, if she tells the whole world she'd just been acting the part of the blushing bride to appease her captors until she could escape their evil plans."

"I don't think we have to be quite that dramatic with it, Cuz." Julie rolled her eyes, laughing at Becky's over exaggerated expressions.

"Why not?" Becky flipped her arms around and turned her palms up. "Being overly dramatic is how her father and fake fiancé have kept the kidnapping in the news for the last two months. If we want to overshadow their version of the story, then we have to be just as spectacular in television appearances."

"Sorry, I can't cry on command like Clayton," Brooklyn lightly chuckled at Becky's exuberance. "And I doubt you have enough time to teach me to act that well."

"Sorry, Sis, but I think it will play better on television if we keep it more sedate," Charlotte advised, giving her sister a one-armed hug. "Let them keep showing their crazy to the world, while Brook appears more intelligent and in control of her emotions."

"I agree with Charlotte," Jen nodded on the phone's screen. "If she has to get the board on her side to inherit early or pick a new trustee to her inheritance, then she needs to look professional at all times in the public eye."

"Okay, so, will ya'll help me draft a press release?" Brooklyn looked around the room and at the phone screen to make eye contact with each of the Burleson women.

"Yes," the three women in the room with her stated in unison at the same time the twins on the phone chimed in with, "Of course."

"And we can get you the contact information for all the major news outlets from our advertising department," Julie added with a smile.

"Or set you up a company email address and send it for you, if you don't want to send it from your personal one," Jen continued her sister's sentence.

"Yes, thank you." Brooklyn wasn't really sure which she'd just agreed to, but was glad to do it either way. "After the press release, what's the next step?"

"Waiting to make sure it's gone viral." Becky reached over her sister to grasp Brooklyn's hand reassuringly. "We're not gonna take any chances with your safety, so you can't go to Georgia to hire a lawyer and sue your father for control of your inheritance, until we know he won't be able to pull something shady to make it look like you're married to that dirty old man."

"And when you do go to Georgia, you won't be going alone," Kay declared, smiling at Brooklyn.

"In addition to Bobby coming along to keep you safe, you'll have at least a few of the other Burleson board members with you, in case we need to do a hostile takeover of Ashbury," Julie insisted.

Brooklyn opened her mouth as if to speak, but quickly closed it because she had no idea how to respond to Julie's declaration.

"What?" Julie shrugged when she noticed Brooklyn's shock. "Without knowing who on that board might be in league with your father, we can't be sure they'll oust him, even when the feds arrest him for embezzlement. It might not get all your money and other properties out of his control, but it's a valid option for safeguarding the legacy your mother and grandfather built for you."

"I don't want to do anything underhanded to get control of the company," Brooklyn implored, her voice barely above a whisper from how choked up she felt over the whole situation.

"Don't worry, Brook," Julie smiled at her. "Burlesons aren't down with dirty business dealings. I might have called it a hostile takeover, but since Ashbury isn't a publicly traded company…"

"And neither is Burleson," Jen interjected, cutting off her twin's statement.

"It would really be more of a merger," Julie continued. "We'll explain to the Ashbury board that while you and Bobby aren't married yet, you will be joining our family eventually, so we want to join our family businesses."

"Pointing out how that goes along with the marriage clause they've all already agreed to should make a merger easier to get past the board than an early inheritance," Jen finished her sister's thoughts.

How do twins do that? Brooklyn wondered. *It's almost like they share a brain, or telepathically tell each other what they're going to say before they actually say it out loud.*

"Okay," Brooklyn agreed, thinking a merger with Burleson Incorporated would be the best way to save her family legacy without having to actually run Ashbury Enterprises herself.

As they all got started with coming up with a first draft of the press release for Brooklyn to put out, she got to thinking about the Burlesons and the multiple sets of twins in the family. Not only were there two sets of twins in the current generation of Burlesons, but Bobby's father and uncle were also twins, giving the family a total of three sets of twins in the last two generations.

I wonder if that increases the likelihood of Bobby and I having twins? Brooklyn pondered, lightly placing a hand over her currently flat stomach. *If we conceived last weekend, could there possibly be two babies in my belly now? That would certainly make getting up to the, at least, four kids I want a lot faster.*

Chapter Twelve

Bobby felt pretty good as he walked into the station Monday morning. While he still hadn't gotten Brie back in his bed, he felt like he was well on his way with the wooing he'd been doing the past week. They had cordial, friendly conversations every night over dinner, and she hadn't turned him away whenever he'd kissed her on the cheek and told her he loved her when he got home each evening.

She'd also been responding favorably to each of his little gifts and flowers so far. Well, mostly. She'd complained about the cost of the boots he'd given her, and would probably have similar complaints about the earrings and necklace he'd already purchased for Monday and Tuesday's gifts. But otherwise, she'd seemed to like the little things he'd picked out for her.

On Friday, when he'd given her a kit for making friendship bracelets and yellow roses, she'd insisted he sit at the table with her and learn how to weave the strands of thread together to make bracelets for each other. While he'd completely sucked at bracelet making, he'd still enjoyed sitting there and telling her the story of the real Yellow Rose of Texas. She'd thought the only meaning of yellow roses was friendship, and the **Yellow Rose of Texas** was just a song.

Bobby had enjoyed seeing Brie blush when he told her about how Emily Morgan became the accidental heroine in Texas' war for independence by using her feminine wiles to keep General Santa Anna distracted in a tent while Sam Houston's Texas Army defeated the Mexican invaders along the shores of the San Jacinto River. He glossed over how the Mexican general had probably raped the poor young woman, telling the story the way he preferred to think of it— portraying Emily as a courageous heroine, instead of as a victim.

Regardless of whether or not Brie picked up on the dark undertones of history, he could tell the sexual aspect of the story made her think of their intimate moments, which was exactly what he wanted on her mind.

With Brie spending so much time with his sisters and female cousins on Saturday and Sunday, he'd had to wait until they'd gotten home each night to give her the daily gifts. She'd giggled at his screw up on Saturday. He'd gotten her violets for their meaning of faithfulness, but when he went to get the aromatherapy gift set he'd just remembered that they were purple flowers, so he picked out the lavender scented set. Regardless of how he'd mixed up his flowers and scents, hearing her laugh had been worth the hit to his pride for screwing up.

He thought he'd redeemed himself Sunday night, though. He'd given her red tulips to represent passion and his declaration of love, along with a box of sensual massage oils. He'd even spent some time on his computer making up a coupon book for him to give her massages, like she'd given him for donuts at Christmas. That had earned him another shy little blush from Brie. He hoped she never grew out of her innocent blushing tendency because he loved being the one to entice the pinkening of her cheeks.

He still had two more nights of gifts and flowers planned. The earrings he had for Monday night were platinum infinity symbols and he'd paired them with irises because the flowers symbolized faith, hope, wisdom, trust, and valor. Those all sounded like great symbols to serve as a foundation for their relationship, in Bobby's humble opinion. For her birthday on Tuesday, he had a dozen iconic red roses ordered from Flora's Flowers and a platinum Key-to-My-Heart necklace to show his love for her. He hoped she would forgive him and take him back on her birthday, otherwise, he would have to scramble to come up with more ideas of little ways to show his love later in the week.

"You look awfully chipper this morning," Detective Dusty Deere greeted him, as Bobby walked past his desk on the way to his office. "You must not have seen the news yet."

Those words stopped Bobby in his tracks. "What news?" *Fuck! I hope it isn't something that will make Brie's issues in Georgia worse.*

"Shit, man," Dusty cursed, standing from his seat, and grabbing a tablet off his desk. "Did your girl not tell you before releasing her statement to the press?"

Fucking Hell! I thought Brie and the girls were just talking about drafting a press release this weekend. I didn't know they were gonna release it this soon, Bobby thought as Dusty turned the tablet around for Bobby to read the headline on the **San Antonio Star's** website.

I Was Not Kidnapped!

Heiress Brooklyn Brielle Barns has released a statement refuting her father's claims that she was kidnapped on Thanksgiving Day last year. Her statement alleges that her father, Bradley S. Barns, III, has been abusing his position as trustee for the estate of his late wife, Madeline Ashbury-Barns, since her death almost 19 years ago.

Ms. Barns claims that her father has been transferring money that was supposed to go to her each month into an offshore account that she has no access to, and essentially held her prisoner in his home since her 18th birthday five years ago. She also alleges that she was being forced to marry Clayton Donaldson by her father. Unsure what to do to free herself, she pretended to be the happy bride-to-be in order to appease her captors, until Thanksgiving, when she was finally able to make her escape from the palatial estate where she grew up.

Though Ms. Barns did not disclose her location, or how she's survived two months on the run with no income, it is believed that she has aligned herself with her father's business rivals at Burleson Incorporated, as that is where her emailed statement originated. Burleson Incorporated is a multi-billion-dollar corporation that is solely owned by the Burleson family of Heart's Destiny, Texas.

Bradley Barns has claimed that Brooklyn's disappearance was orchestrated by a business rival to prevent her from marrying to gain control of Ashbury Enterprises. With so many eligible bachelors in the Burleson family, his claims raise the question of whether the Burlesons intend to take over Ashbury Enterprises by having Brooklyn marry one of their own.

"Fuck!" Bobby exclaimed, unable to finish reading the article, and barely able to stop himself from throwing the tablet across the room.

"Whoa, Chief." Dusty reached out and rescued his tablet from Bobby's grasp. "Calm down. You know most of that article was just the reporter speculating for click-bait."

"Hell, I couldn't even finish reading the article," Bobby fumed, running a hand through his hair in frustration. "I got to the point where they were implying it was all a setup for Burleson to take over Ashbury and couldn't see anything but a red haze."

"Oh, so you didn't see the part where they're trying to figure out which Burleson bachelor she's taking off the market?" Dusty smirked.

"No," Bobby growled, drawing the word out menacingly.

"Yeah, I don't think you should read that," Dusty laughed. "Considering you weren't in their top five picks, and they knew not to consider Anthony since he just got married."

"Seriously?" Bobby looked at his friend and second-in-command in confusion.

"Yeah, their top guesses were JJ and Justin, since they work for the company in prominent roles besides being on the board," Dusty chuckled. "Third was Josh, claiming he could've used his SEAL skills to sneak Brooklyn out of her father's compound. They mentioned Jake, but quickly ruled him out, saying if he was the one involved with Brooklyn, then he would've used his cyber skills to wipe all the kidnapping stories off the internet."

"Wait, so if they ruled out Anthony for being married, and Jake for not using his computer skills to remove all references to the kidnapping from the net, how was I not number four on the list?" Bobby wished he'd just finished reading the article, instead of getting it secondhand from Dusty.

"They rounded out the list with Jen and Julie," Dusty crowed, his smirk back in full force. "I guess with gay marriage being legal both here and in Georgia, they figured the ladies were all tired of the patriarchy and would be taking over both companies."

"Well, I guess the good news is that the writers over at the *Star* aren't discriminating against the LGBTQ+ community," Bobby sighed, shaking his head. "Even though they've definitely taken a step down in journalistic quality to more of a gossip site since they quit putting out a print edition."

"Yeah, but they seem to be the only report I've found that's linked Brooklyn to the Burlesons." Dusty swiped on his tablet again before turning it around for Bobby to read a more reputable national news source.

Heiress Not Kidnapped

Brooklyn Brielle Barns has released a statement regarding her disappearance on Thanksgiving last year. In that statement, she claims to have left her

father's estate in the early morning hours of November 22, 2018, because it was the only time she could get away when she wasn't being watched by security guards and other staff hired by her father. Ms. Barns specifically stated that she'd been forced to appear at various social events with both her father and Clayton Donaldson, to whom her father had arranged her marriage, but she'd only acted the part of the blushing bride to appease the men until she could escape. She has spent the last two months hiding, living in fear of being forced to go back to Georgia to marry a man more than twice her age. Her wish now is to be left in peace while the proper authorities deal with the legal issues plaguing her life.

Her statement also outlined numerous crimes her father, Bradley Stanton Barns, III, and former fiancé, Clayton Donaldson, have allegedly committed against both her and the company she's set to inherit, Ashbury Enterprises. As this is an ongoing police matter, we will not be printing that list of allegations at this time, but we will be following up with the authorities once arrests or indictments are made.

"Well, that was short and to the point." Bobby handed the tablet back to Dusty when he finished reading the article.

"Yeah, and that's what I've seen most everywhere else, too," Dusty stated, looking more serious. "I just had to rag on you some about the *Star* article, but I don't think even the national gossip sites have posted anything about it, yet."

"Yeah, the *Star* reporter probably only noticed the email address because of being in the same city as the main office for Burleson," Bobby admitted, hoping his detective was correct in his assessment, so Brie's father wouldn't be able to use those allegations against them when they went to court to get him removed as trustee of her inheritance.

After overhearing the discussions Brie was having with his female family members over the weekend, Bobby had already figured out that she would need to hire an attorney in Georgia to deal with her father still having control of her finances with regard to her inheritance. He just thought she was going to wait until after her father was arrested by the FBI to release the statement they were drafting, so she wouldn't need an attorney, yet.

Now that the statement was out there, though, Bobby knew it was time to find her the best lawyer in Georgia to deal with the ramifications of everything coming to light before the arrests were made. He wrapped up his brief conversation with Dusty, making sure his second-in-command was prepared to run the office when he'd have to be out to go to Georgia with Brie, before going into his office. While his computer was booting up, he pulled out his cell phone and called an old Navy buddy that he'd kept in contact with over the years.

Blake Avington had gone through both A and C Master-At-Arms schools with Bobby when they first enlisted in the Navy. While Bobby had left the Navy after only two years, Blake had stayed in and was planning to retire after twenty years of service. He'd grown up in Marietta, Georgia, and had somehow managed to get stationed at Naval Air Station Atlanta, which was actually located in Marietta, so he could be near his family.

Bobby often picked on his old friend about being a landlocked sailor. But truth be told, if he could've been stationed at the base in San Antonio, where they'd gone through Master-At-Arms A-school, Bobby would've gladly stayed on a landlocked base to stay close to his family, too.

Bobby was really glad for Blake's location at that moment, knowing that his friend would be able to help him with finding a lawyer in Georgia, even though he wasn't actually in Macon, where Brie was from.

"Hey, Bobby, what's up?" Blake greeted him when the call connected.

"Not much that I can actually give you details about over the phone," Bobby replied, wondering if he might be able to finagle a way to see his old friend while he was in Georgia in the next couple of months.

They spent a few minutes giving each other a rundown of the various life events that had happened in their families, with Blake being shocked that not only was Anthony married with a growing family, but Bobby was also dating someone he could see walking down the aisle with someday.

"Damn, man, never thought I'd see the day when you seemed ready to settle down." Blake's laughter was evident in his tone of voice, even over the phone line.

"Yeah, well, Brie's special." Bobby's smile stretched from ear to ear as he thought about her for the millionth time that morning. "She's actually why I'm calling you. She's originally from Macon and needs to find a lawyer there to deal with some inheritance issues. I know Marietta and Macon aren't really close enough for you to know who I should call off the top of your head, but I thought maybe with all your family there, someone might have had some dealings with people in Macon to give me some suggestions of who might be our best option to call."

"Macon, huh?" Blake suddenly had an inquisitive tone to his voice.

Shit, did Blake figure out who Brie is from me asking about lawyers in Macon?

"Yeah, Macon," Bobby confirmed, hoping his old friend would understand his deeper inflection meant that he should drop the interrogation, at least for the time being. "Maybe we can work something out to pop up to Atlanta to see you when we go to Georgia to deal with everything."

"Yeah, I can't wait to meet Brie." Blake's light chuckling told Bobby his friend understood the implied message. "I'll have to give my dad a call to see who he might recommend. He and my brothers have done some security jobs down there, so I'm sure he'll be able to recommend someone for you."

"Speaking of Avington Security," Bobby transitioned to the other reason for his call to Blake, remembering the company run by Blake's father and three older brothers, which might come in handy to help him keep Brie safe when they were in Georgia. "I could probably use their services while I'm there, too."

"Yeah? How 'bout I call Dad now and have him call you on a secure line, so you can discuss everything that you can't tell me now?"

"That'd be much appreciated. And I'll make sure to tell him it's okay to fill you in on the details, so you aren't shocked when you meet my girl."

"Deal," Blake laughed.

They said their goodbyes before Bobby left his office and hopped in his cruiser to head out to a secluded location to wait for the call from Byron Avington. He trusted everyone in his old friend's family to keep Brie and her secrets safe. But on the off chance that someone on Bradley Barns' payroll had seen the article that linked her to his family, Bobby wanted to make sure any conversations he had, where he specifically mentioned her real name, were not in the middle of town, where someone might overhear him.

I might be overly paranoid, but I'm not taking any chances with Brie's safety. I'm sure it won't take long for that one gossip rag's version of the story to spread, so I should probably look into adding more security at the ranch, too. At the very least, I'll increase the patrols around the ranch and make sure everyone in the department knows to arrest any trespassers, whether they're reporters or her father's goons.

~~~

Tuesday, January 29, 2019

Brooklyn felt jumpy all day after the fallout from her press release the day before. Thankfully, she'd already delivered extra meals to JJ and Justin's houses, so she didn't have to leave the relative safety of her home with Bobby all day. Bobby had just told her to stay on the ranch
~~~

to be safe, but after he'd had to arrest a reporter for trespassing on his way home from work Monday evening, Brooklyn felt better just staying in the house until he was there to go with her to his parents' house for her birthday dinner.

So much for being excited about having my first real birthday party, Brooklyn thought as she finished up her chores. *Hopefully, it won't be my last birthday party here with Bobby and his family, so it won't matter if the memories are marred by reporters trying to crash it tonight.*

After Bobby had finally arrived home the night before and given her the most beautiful bouquet of blue irises and a set of silver infinity symbol stud earrings, their dinner conversation had consisted mostly of the extra security measures he was putting in place. He had all kinds of plans to keep her safe, not just the extra patrols of his officers around the ranch to make sure no more reporters were able to trespass on the property. Instead of ringing the ranch foreman's phone when someone put in an incorrect gate code, or didn't have a gate code, the security box was now ringing to Bobby's phone first. He'd also been in contact with several people in Georgia to make sure everything was set up to protect her when they were in the state to deal with her legal issues.

She wasn't sure exactly when they would be leaving Texas to go to Georgia, but she knew he'd scheduled an appointment for her with an attorney in Macon for Monday, February fourth. Brooklyn figured that meant they'd probably go over the weekend to be there for the Monday morning meeting.

I wonder who he's going to have the gate call while he's in Georgia with me? Or is he going to stay here to protect his family from the fallout, since we haven't exactly gotten back together yet?

Brooklyn pushed the troubling thoughts out of her head when she noticed it was time for her to start getting ready to go to the party. As she took care of her own needs in the shower, she resolved to make up with Bobby that night, so she wouldn't have to worry about their relationship on top of everything else.

She finished dressing in record time and had just walked back downstairs when Bobby walked in the back door, still dressed in his uniform. She was surprised that his hands were empty, having gotten used to him giving her flowers and a gift every day as soon as he walked in the door.

Wow, Brooklyn, quit being so greedy and narcissistic. Eight days of flowers and gifts is more than enough to last a lifetime. Unfortunately, she couldn't really disagree with the inner voice that sounded so much like her father. It wasn't that she really felt greedy or narcissistic for being disappointed that Bobby hadn't brought her a little something. She knew she didn't really need any of the little gifts or flowers. She'd just enjoyed feeling loved, even when they weren't actually making love every night.

"Give me ten minutes, Brie-Baby." Bobby paused on his way to the stairs to bend and kiss her on the cheek. "Then I'll be ready to go celebrate your birthday."

"Oh, okay," Brooklyn smiled at his show of affection, which meant more to her than all the gifts and flowers in the world.

True to his word, Bobby walked back downstairs ten minutes later, freshly showered and dressed in slacks and a button-down to match her little black dress, which she'd bought the week before while on a shopping trip with her friends. "Fuck, that dress might be a little too sexy for you to wear around my family," Bobby groaned, his eyes exploring her from her head to her toes appreciatively.

Yeah, well, it's way more conservative than the black lace bra and panties I'm wearing under it, Brooklyn mused, smiling mischievously at the thought of showing them to him later, if everything went as planned that night.

Bobby apparently misinterpreted her shy smile and looking down at the floor instead of up at him as her thinking he disapproved of the dress. "You look beautiful, Brie-Baby," he declared, snaking one arm around her waist to pull her into his hard body as he tilted her chin up with the other hand. "The only thing inappropriate about that dress are the thoughts I'm having about stripping it off you. Since nobody else in the family will be having those thoughts, I'm sure none of them will think it's too sexy."

"Thank you," Brooklyn smiled, barely able to thank him for his beautiful comment before he pressed their lips together.

It was a chaste kiss when compared to what they'd done previously, at least up until the last week, but it was more than enough to make Brooklyn feel weak in the knees. She gripped Bobby's shoulders to keep from falling, pressing her whole body against his and prolonging the kiss.

She only briefly felt the hardness of his manhood pressed against her belly before he pulled away. He flashed his dimples at her when he smiled, making her core flood with need for more with him.

"Please tell me that response means we're no longer broken up," Bobby pleaded, desire showing through in the amber flecks of his hazel eyes.

"Were we ever really broken up?" Brooklyn questioned, wishing they could erase all traces of their disagreement and relive the last week with multiple days of repeats of their first night making love.

"No, we weren't," Bobby declared, his voice sounding deeper and gravelly. "You've always been mine and always will be mine. I just wish I could take you upstairs right now and show you just how much I love you."

"But we have to leave for the party," Brooklyn playfully protested, pulling out of his arms just slightly.

"Yes, but be prepared, Brie-Baby," Bobby warned, swooping his face down to kiss her once more. "Once we get home tonight, I fully intend to ravish you for your birthday."

"Oh, that sounds like fun," Brooklyn giggled as Bobby gripped her hand to walk them out to the car to go to his parents' house. "I don't think I've ever been ravished before."

They were both chuckling as they made their way to the party, and were greeted by a chorus of "happy birthdays" as soon as they walked in the front door of Hazel and Bob's home. There were balloons and streamers all around the dining room to the right of the foyer. All of Bobby's extended family were scattered around the room, with the exception of his three brothers and Anthony's family, who were working out of town that day. They were joined by the friends Brooklyn had made in town and a couple of people she'd only met in passing at other events hosted by the Burlesons in the last month.

Wow, I can't believe so many people are here to celebrate my birthday, Brooklyn thought, blinking back tears. She was feeling exceptionally emotional since she'd only ever had Mary and Joe celebrate her birthday with her before, at least that she could remember, since she couldn't remember any birthdays before her mother passed away.

In addition to the three tables that were set up as usual for when the whole family gathered to eat together, there was a fourth table set up against one wall to hold the cake and presents. Right beside the largest sheet cake Brooklyn had ever seen, was a vase of red roses that she was ninety-nine-point-nine percent certain were from Bobby.

As usual, Hazel had the whole evening planned and kept them on schedule with her typical zeal. They started off with a meal of barbequed brisket to show Brooklyn how it was normally eaten, instead of how she served it in her Brunswick stew. She was almost too full for cake after eating a plateful of the delicious beef and the heavy sides of baked beans and potato salad.

The conversations flowed around the room, making Brooklyn feel grateful for being included amongst the friends of this wonderful family. Even the ladies, who were clearly pushing their matchmaking shenanigans on their children by inviting their potential dates to the party, were making her feel loved, accepted, and worthy of celebrating her life.

Her birthday was a much more joyous occasion when celebrated with the Burlesons than it had ever been back in Macon, sneaking a cupcake in the kitchen with Mary and Joe. The only way it would've been better for her, would have been if Mary and Joe were also there with her at the boisterous birthday bash.

As the plates were cleared from their dinner, Bobby's Uncle Doug came over to speak with them. Brooklyn felt slightly uneasy at his approach. Not that she was afraid of the man per se, but more that she was afraid of what he was about to say being bad news for her and Bobby.

"Ya'll doin' okay?" Doug slapped a hand on Bobby's shoulder when he reached their seats.

"Doin' great, Uncle Doug," Bobby replied, reaching out to shake the older man's hand with his right arm while keeping his left around Brooklyn's shoulders.

Brooklyn didn't reply, just smiling at Doug and nodding in agreement with Bobby.

"Figured with as much work as you gave me today," Doug teased with half of his mouth lifting up in a grin. "That you'd be worn out from dealing with twice as many reporters as you've arrested and sent to my courtroom."

"Naw," Bobby chuckled. "I only personally arrested the first one. I've put Dusty in charge of scheduling the other officers to patrol out here and making sure their paperwork is in order when an arrest has to be made. Don't wanna risk my last name being on the paperwork having an effect on the outcome in the courts, or look like anything improper is happening if the reports end up on the news."

"Smart thinking," Doug agreed, his smile starting to spread across his face. "Come to think of it, maybe it's a good thing I've had to remand them to Medina County, since we don't have a big enough jail here in town. Maybe I should transfer all their cases to the county level judge, too, seeing as how being related to the Burlesons could be considered a conflict of interest for me, as well."

"Wait," Brooklyn interrupted, confused by there being a bunch of arrests she hadn't heard about. "Just how many reporters have tried to get on the ranch?"

"Only the one actually made it on the grounds," Bobby assured her, squeezing his hand on Brooklyn's shoulder to comfort her.

"The other six I saw today were charged with harassment and obstructing a roadway," Doug informed her, reaching out to pat Brooklyn's hand to reassure her. "Did you tell your guys to add the obstruction charge because of the larger fine than harassment or trespassing?"

"Nope," Bobby grinned. "I didn't even mention how the roads around town are too narrow to accommodate large news vans parking on the shoulders. But I'd be willing to bet that charge was recommended to the other guys by Dusty. He's always threatening to arrest his cousin for it when they pull the firetruck out to clean the bay and block off half of Thoroughbred. So, I'm sure he can see the problem with news trucks parked alongside Rogers, Walker, and Burleson when they can't get past our gates."

"Any chance the reporters will back off after being arrested?" Brooklyn was worried the few they'd seen so far were only the beginning of how many would swarm to the ranch soon.

"Well, the ones who are sitting in county lockup won't be back," Doug proclaimed, smiling at her. "But I can't imagine they'll all stop poking around until everything is settled."

"And they'll probably be even worse when you go back to Georgia," Bobby's Aunt Maggie, who was married to Doug, added, her expression wary.

"That's why I have security lined up for us when we're there," Bobby reassured them. He opened his mouth as if he was going to say something else, but he was interrupted by Hazel announcing it was time for cake and presents.

The next hour seemed to fly by for Brooklyn. She laughed when she saw the pink icing message on the cake. It read, "Happy Birthday, Brooklyn/Brie."

"I guess everyone in town knows who I am now, huh?" Brooklyn pointed at the message.

"Well, I'd ordered it with just Brie," Hazel confessed, smiling at Brooklyn. "But when the story broke yesterday, I called Kara and told her to change the name, since I figured everyone knew. I guess I confused her, so she put both names."

"Guess it's a good thing I've gotten used to answering to either," Brooklyn replied, still chuckling lightly at how strange it felt to be able to be herself again.

After some very off-key singing and her blowing out the twenty-three candles on the cake, she was instructed to take a seat and sneak bites of the delicious strawberry cream cake while opening her presents. Bobby hadn't been joking back at Christmas when he said his female family members seemed to gravitate toward giving clothing gifts. By the time she finished opening presents, she practically had a whole new wardrobe. Though she wasn't sure how often she'd wear the professional dress outfits, other than when she had to go back to Georgia to deal with her father and the various legal and business issues awaiting her there.

Her girlfriends had given her gift certificates to Destiny Dresses, opting not to embarrass her in front of Bobby's family by giving her lingerie again. Though she knew she'd probably use the gift certificates for lingerie later.

There were also various gift certificates for massages, manicures, and other local stores from the male members of the family that seemed embarrassed by not knowing what to get her for her birthday. Brooklyn was practically in tears from the overwhelming outpouring of love from everyone around her.

"What's wrong, Brie-Baby?" Bobby reached out to brush his thumb under her eye to prevent any of the tears from falling.

"Nothing's wrong," Brooklyn cried. "It's just, so much. You guys didn't have to buy me all these presents. Just having you all here to tell me happy birthday was more than I ever imagined. Especially when I'm causing so many problems with reporters and..." Her voice trailed off when she couldn't stop sobbing to finish her sentence.

"Oh, Brie-Baby." Bobby pulled her into his arms and kissed the top of her head. "You aren't causing any problems. And none of this is because we have to. It's because we want to. I love you, Brie-Baby."

"We all love you," one of the women shouted, but Brooklyn couldn't tell who with her face buried in Bobby's chest. "But we can't all show you how much we love you with hugs and kisses like Bobby does."

A chuckle went around the room as Brooklyn pulled out of Bobby's embrace and wiped her eyes. "I love you all too." Brook leaned into Bobby, so he knew her words were especially true for him. "Thank you for all of this. I can't express just how much it all means to me."

"You still have one more present to open." Bobby handed her a rectangular gift box with "Brie-Baby" written on it in his handwriting.

Brooklyn opened the present to reveal a beautiful silver necklace with a heart-shaped lock and key dangling from it. "Oh, Bobby, it's beautiful," Brooklyn gushed, her voice breathy in awe. She wrapped her arms around his neck and pulled him down to give him a peck of a kiss. "Thank you. Will you help me put it on?"

"Of course," Bobby agreed, lifting the delicate chain out of the box, and using the attached key to unlock the heart-shaped lock that was essentially acting as the clasp at the ends of the chain.

Brooklyn lifted her hair for Bobby to put the chain around her neck and smiled up at him as he locked the heart in place at the base of her throat.

"I didn't realize we were going to a collaring ceremony tonight," Bobby's cousin, JJ, chuckled.

Brooklyn blushed at the innuendo, having understood what JJ meant from having read about a collaring ceremony in the BDSM romance book that Kay had recommended for her earlier in the month.

Bobby opened his mouth to reply to his cousin, but to Brook's great relief, his words were cut off by his phone ringing. *Oh, I hope his call is enough of a distraction to keep anyone else from asking what JJ was referring to. While I wouldn't mind trying some of the things from that book with Bobby, I don't want to try to explain any of them to his mother.*

"Chief Burleson," Bobby barked as a greeting when he answered his phone. His eyes narrowed and his mouth turned down in a grimace, making Brooklyn almost wish the phone call hadn't interrupted the conversation because she hated seeing how upsetting the call was for him. "Yes. We're in the middle of a family gathering at the moment."

Bobby paused to listen to whoever was calling him, while the rest of the room quieted and focused on watching his angry expression turn to one of resignation. "No, I'm not gonna open the gate to allow you to interrupt her birthday party when you're outside your jurisdiction," Bobby hissed, closing his eyes, and running a hand through his hair in frustration as the other person spoke. "I can have her there tomorrow afternoon," he growled into the phone, his voice sounding dark and menacing. "But she will remain in my custody at all times. No, I haven't arrested her. She hasn't committed a crime."

Bobby blew out an obviously aggravated breath before raising his voice as he continued his conversation with whoever had called him. "You can consider her in protective custody with the Heart's Destiny Police Department. And I will maintain jurisdiction, even when we leave the city of Heart's Destiny, because my department is the only one involved that she feels she can trust. And quite frankly, with demands like you're trying to make right now, I agree with her assessment of not being able to trust the Macon Police, GBI, or FBI at this time."

Brooklyn reached out and clasped Bobby's free hand in hers, hoping to calm him down some with the comforting gesture. He squeezed her hand as he looked down at her and gave her a small smile.

"Actually, I am the police chief here," Bobby bragged into the phone, his lips turning up even more. "So, as the highest-ranking police official in the department protecting Ms. Barns, I am officially denying your request to remand her to your custody for extradition to

Georgia. As I said earlier, I'll gladly accompany her to a meeting with your department tomorrow. But after the gross ignorance of the law you've shown tonight, Detective Johnson, I will be speaking with your chief tomorrow morning to make sure they're not only present for any interviews Ms. Barns gives to your department, but also aware of my suspicions regarding you and the false charges you're trying to bring against her."

False charges against me? Brooklyn felt lightheaded at the thought of being arrested by the Macon Police Department on her father's orders. Seeing her obvious fear, Bobby lifted their joined hands to his mouth and kissed the back of Brooklyn's, while the other man was talking.

"That sounds like the first good decision you've made all evening," Bobby stated, smiling, and winking at Brooklyn. "I'll set an appointment time with your chief tomorrow and let them decide if you need to be present for the meeting." With that, Bobby hung up his phone without even saying goodbye to the caller.

"Everything okay, Son?" Bob Burleson arched a curious brow at his oldest son as soon as Bobby pocketed his phone.

"Yeah, Pop, everything's fine," Bobby assured his father, not taking his eyes off Brooklyn. "But I have to make a few phone calls and charter a plane for tomorrow."

"Do we need to come with?" Julie looked back and forth between Bobby and Brooklyn. "In case we need to present our backup plan to the Ashbury board?"

"Not yet," Bobby sighed. "Tomorrow we have to talk to the Macon PD to clear up the mess Detective Johnson has apparently made there. It'll be at least a day or two before we'll be able to set up a meeting with the Ashbury board, and probably not until next week, after we've met with the attorney about requesting a new trustee for Brie's inheritance."

"Wha-what were you saying about false charges against me?" Brooklyn slightly stuttered her words at first from the fear coursing through her at what she might be facing the next day.

"Nothing to worry about, Brie-Baby." Bobby hugged her to him and kissed the top of her head. "You can't be charged with kidnapping yourself, no matter how that idiot tried to spin it just now."

Several people chuckled, questioning how the man had made it to the rank of detective with that lack of common sense.

Bobby explained his plans for the next couple of weeks to his family, so they could all prepare for a trip to Georgia, if they were needed to assist in saving Brooklyn's maternal family legacy. Once they all knew their potential roles, the party broke up, so Bobby could go home and make all the phone calls he needed to make before the next day.

Brooklyn was slightly disappointed when he helped her carry everything from the party to her room, kissed her goodnight at her bedroom door, and walked away to go make his calls. While she hadn't actually gotten the chance to apologize to him for their misunderstanding the previous weekend, she'd thought the way they'd made up earlier in the evening meant they'd be sharing a room that night at least.

I guess I'll have to wait until after we clear things up in Georgia for that ravishing he was talking about.

~~~

Wednesday, January 30, 2019

Bobby kept second-guessing everything he'd done since the night before as he and Brie sat in the back of the blacked-out SUV being driven to the Macon Police Department Headquarters by the Avington brothers. Well, maybe not everything he'd done, since he was confident in the ability of Blake's two oldest brothers, Barrett and Blaine, to help him keep Brie safe while they were in Macon. He was also pretty certain the flash drive full of evidence he was about to turn over to the FBI and Macon PD would be enough to land Bradley Barns and Clayton Donaldson behind bars for the remainder of their miserable lives. What he was actually second-guessing was how he'd put distance between himself and Brie as soon as they'd gotten home from the party the night before.

I should've had her cuddled up beside me while I made all the arrangements for our trip and reviewed all the evidence with Jake one more time. Hell, she should've been the one to review everything Jake
~~~

found as her "private investigator" because I guarantee the feds are gonna wanna hear it from her and not me. And if we'd have done all that together, I could've had her sleeping in my arms last night, instead of spending my night tossing and turning with worry in my big empty bed as she slept down the hall. And maybe, if I'd have asked her what she wanted, I wouldn't have booked a two-bedroom suite for us while we're on this trip. Fuck!

Bobby was silently kicking himself because of how dejected Brie had looked when he walked away after kissing her goodnight the night before. *Maybe one of the rooms on the floor I have booked at the hotel will only have a single bed available that we can switch to? I don't have to tell her that I've booked the whole floor. We can make it look like the Avington brothers and my family all have to check-in separately and we'll just be lucky to all end up on the same floor. I won't be able to handle it if she gives me that same look of disappointment when she realizes we have separate bedrooms in the hotel.*

The more he thought about it, the less he understood his actions in backing away from the intimacy they'd previously shared in the last sixteen hours. He'd gone from planning to spend the night making love to her at the beginning of the evening to giving her a chaste kiss goodnight and going to separate bedrooms by the time they got home around ten o'clock.

Was it that dumbass detective calling from the gate? Bobby wondered. *Was that enough to make me realize that we can't keep hiding from reality in each other's arms? Or am I just pushing her away now because I'm afraid she won't come home with me after this trip is over?*

Fuck! I should be taking advantage of every moment we have alone together to make sure she's just as in love with me as I am her, so we don't have to ever end our relationship.

Just as Bobby was about to pull his phone from his pocket to see if he could send a message to the hotel to give them a room with a single bed instead of the suite he'd scheduled, Barrett parked the SUV. *Maybe I'll get a chance to do it later,* Bobby hoped as he got out of the vehicle. He took Brie's hand to help her down from the backseat he'd just vacated, but he didn't release her hand as they walked into the glass fronted building with Barrett and Blaine following closely behind them.

After a quick introduction at the receptionist's desk, they were directed to the fourth floor of the building where the chief's office was located. Bobby was surprised they weren't asked to relinquish their weapons, but he assumed it was a professional courtesy offered to him because he'd worn his police uniform to the meeting.

"You guys have many dealings with police departments where they don't ask you to relinquish your weapons when you enter the building?" Bobby inquired of the Avington brothers as they rode up in the elevator.

"Yeah, they pretty much all know we have our concealed carry permits," Blaine stated without even the slightest change in his stoic demeanor. "Every once in a while, we're asked to lock them in the security office at the federal building in Atlanta. But most places know we're only going to pull our weapons to defend our clients or other innocent bystanders if necessary."

So, it's just me that's paranoid and doesn't trust everyone with a permit to carry a gun in my station? Bobby shook off the thought as the elevator doors opened and they were directed to go down the hall to a conference room for their meeting.

"I didn't realize you'd have an entire entourage," the Macon Police Chief, Andre Rogers, criticized as he extended his hand in greeting.

Bobby shook the man's hand before acknowledging the comment. "Yes, well, as Ms. Barns is aware of her father having friends in law enforcement, who might do her harm at his direction, I felt it best to bring in outside security to ensure her safety." Bobby walked to the head of the table and pulled out a chair for Brie. He knew it was a dick move to seat her there with him on one side of her and the Avingtons on the other, but he wanted her to feel like she was in the power position for the meeting.

"That explains why you refused to turn her over to Detective Johnson last night," Chief Rogers grumbled as he took a seat at the other end of the table.

Before Bobby could clarify his issues with Detective Johnson, the two FBI agents he'd also invited to this meeting entered the room and took the seats between the Macon Police Chief and Bobby. Once Agents Adams and Barclay introduced themselves, Bobby turned back to Andre Rogers and explained, "No, I refused to allow Detective Johnson to arrest Ms. Barns last night because she has committed no crime."

"In your opinion," Andre carped, a smug expression on his face. "But I can assure you that the warrant Detective Johnson has for Ms. Barns' arrest is valid."

"What charge are you arresting her for?" Agent Adams turned toward the Macon Police Chief.

"Kidnapping," Chief Rogers bellowed, appearing to adamantly believe it was a valid charge.

"Um, excuse me," Brie interjected, raising her hand as if she was a child asking permission to speak in class. "I'm not a police officer, so I could have this all wrong, but I don't think I can be charged with kidnapping myself."

Bobby barely contained his chuckle at how her statement confused the other law enforcement officials at the table. He caught the briefest smiles on both Barrett and Blaine's faces as well, just before Agent Barclay broke the silence with a chuckle.

"She has a point," Agent Barclay noted, still grinning at Brie, even though he was no longer laughing. "I hope you aren't really thinking of charging her with kidnapping herself, Andre."

"Surely, that's not right," Andre huffed, shuffling through the papers he'd laid on the table in front of him when he sat down. As he read what Bobby assumed was the arrest warrant Detective Johnson had given him that morning, Chief Rogers' face turned an extreme shade of crimson. "This has to be a typographical error. There's no way Judge Stevens would sign off on an arrest warrant for someone kidnapping themselves."

Chief Rogers stood from his seat and went to the door, opening it to say, "Jillian, please get me Judge Stevens on the phone." He walked to the side table behind Brie where the conference room phone was located. He leaned against the table while he watched the phone, as if that would make it ring faster. "We'll get this cleared up and a new warrant issued once the judge changes the paperwork to reflect who she's actually charged with kidnapping."

"That's going to be kind of hard since I'm the only one who disappeared," Brie snorted, not able to contain her laughter at the ridiculousness of the situation. Bobby and the FBI agents joined her in a light chuckle, while the Avingtons smiled more than Bobby had seen from the serious bodyguards since they'd arrived in town, reminding him more of the jovial men he'd met ten years before when he'd gone with Blake on leave to visit his family.

Andre didn't get a chance to state his displeasure at being laughed at by the others in the room before the phone buzzed with an alert from Jillian that Judge Stevens was on line one. He pushed the button on the phone to connect him with the judge, putting the phone on speaker, so everyone in the room could converse with the judge.

"Judge Stevens," Andre began. "We seem to have a problem with a warrant you issued for Brooklyn Barns' arrest."

"Give me just a second to pull up the file," Judge Stevens beseeched through the phone. "Okay, I have it. What seems to be the problem?"

"It appears your clerk listed Ms. Barns as both the perpetrator and the victim of the crime," Andre accused. "I need a new warrant with the correct victim listed, so I can arrest Ms. Barns while she's here in my office this afternoon."

"That can't be right," Judge Stevens faltered, the sound of papers shuffling coming through loud and clear over the phone line. "Brooklyn Brielle Barns is the kidnapping victim. Does she have a sister or other relative who kidnapped her?"

"No, your honor, I do not have a sister," Brie stated, turning in her seat to speak closer to the phone on the table behind her. "My father is my only living relative, but I was running away from being trapped in his home and forced to marry his friend, not kidnapped."

"You were trapped in your father's home before you ran away on Thanksgiving?" Agent Adams queried Brie.

"Yes, sir," Brie replied, turning her head to look at the agent as she answered.

"For how long?" Agent Barclay jotted down a note on the small tablet he'd pulled from his coat pocket.

"Um, my whole life?" Brie shrugged, her words coming out as a question instead of a statement.

"Chief Rogers?" Judge Stevens called out from the phone.

"Yes, your honor," Andre answered.

"I'm going to cancel this warrant as it's asinine to charge Ms. Barns with kidnapping herself," Judge Stevens reprimanded. "It sounds like you have some issues with your department that need to be cleared up before you bring me new paperwork with valid charges against Mr. Barns for the unlawful imprisonment of his daughter for a new warrant."

"That probably won't be the only charge on that warrant," Bobby informed the judge, squeezing Brie's hand and smiling at her.

"With whom am I speaking, and what other charges are you expecting against Mr. Barns?" Judge Stevens inquired.

"Sorry, your honor, I'm Bobby Burleson, the police chief for Heart's Destiny, Texas," Bobby introduced himself, directing his words at the phone. "I actually have evidence I'm here to present to Chief Rogers and FBI Agents Adams and Barclay for several charges against Bradley Barns and Clayton Donaldson, ranging from embezzlement to conspiracy to defraud both Ms. Barns and Ashbury Enterprises."

"Were the federal agents the other two voices I heard asking Ms. Barns questions?" Judge Stevens clarified.

"Yes, your honor," the agents replied in unison.

"Very well," Judge Stevens sighed, the deep breath he was taking audible over the phone line. "Chief Rogers, I trust that you will turn this matter over to the FBI and let them get their warrants from a federal judge."

"Yes, your honor," Andre acquiesced, his dejection obvious from how he hung his head, even though his back was to the room, so Bobby couldn't see his facial expression.

"And make sure your detectives don't bring such asinine charges to me for another warrant," Judge Stevens reprimanded.

"Yes, your honor," Andre conceded before disconnecting the call. He turned to look at everyone seated around the table in his conference room before saying, "I'll leave you all to handle any further investigation into this matter, while I go speak with my internal affairs department to look into the ignorant actions of my detectives."

He almost made it out of the conference room before turning back and looking directly at Brie and saying, "My apologies, Ms. Barns, for any inconvenience you've suffered at the hands of my department. You are no longer a suspect for any crime in the eyes of the Macon Police Department."

"Apology accepted," Brie smiled sincerely at Andre Rogers before he turned and left the room.

Once the chief left, the federal agents were eager to see the evidence Bobby had on a flash drive in his pocket. They pulled out a laptop to review everything that Jake had compiled for Bobby and were surprised to see not only the banking records proving that Bradley Barns had been stealing from his daughter for the last eighteen-plus years, but also copies of the search warrants issued by a federal magistrate in Washington, D.C. to go along with the financial records and email correspondence Jake had acquired from Ashbury Enterprises' servers.

Bobby wasn't a hundred percent sure how Jake had presented the case to a judge for the warrants through his office in Naval Intelligence, but he couldn't argue with the results his brother had gotten way faster than the FBI agents he'd contacted ever would. With the electronic trail proving the embezzlement charges and collusion between Bradley Barns and Clayton Donaldson to force Brooklyn to marry and sign away her inheritance to them, the agents thought they'd be able to arrest both men within a few days.

Going through everything report by report took a lot longer with the two agents than it had with Jake, but Bobby was relieved it was over by the time they left the Macon Police Department late that evening. As he just had copies of everything, the agents still had to get in touch with Jake, who had all the official legal documents and original records as he'd been the one actively investigating. When the criminal trial finally happened, it would be Jake who had to appear to testify to the evidence as well.

Bobby felt a little guilty for not being the one to do all the investigating for Brie. *She's my woman, I should be the one to take care of everything for her*, he thought as he sat beside her in the back of the SUV on the way to their hotel for the night. *Though she won't be for long if I don't figure out how to bridge the distance between us soon.*

~~~
~~~

Brooklyn was a nervous wreck as she rode in the back of the vehicle driven by one of the armed security guards Bobby had hired to keep her safe while they were in Georgia, but she was determined not to let it show. Her anxiety about how everything was going to go when she met with the various law enforcement and company officials once they arrived in Georgia had been the impetus for her putting on the façade she'd previously only needed to get by at the events her father forced her to attend. But now she feared the mask she was wearing was causing more harm than good by erecting a wall she didn't want between her and Bobby.

She'd believed that Bobby had backed off on her birthday because he'd needed time to go over all the evidence with his brother and make all their arrangements for the trip. Since she'd donned her façade to keep even him from seeing her nerves the next morning, she had to wonder if it was why he'd maintained a professional distance from her most of the last thirty-six hours.

It wasn't that he'd completely cut off all physical contact with her. He'd continued his normal gentlemanly behavior of assisting her into and out of the vehicles they rode in, as well as placing his hand on her low back to guide her through whatever buildings they'd had to enter. He'd even reached over and squeezed her hand during their meeting with the Macon Police Chief and the FBI Agents the day before, but he hadn't really kissed her since her birthday.

When they'd gotten to the hotel after their meeting with law enforcement, he'd insisted they order room service for dinner while he updated his family on the events of the day. She hadn't minded the idea of eating alone in their suite, but she felt neglected when he'd spent more of his time talking on the phone than talking to her. She'd ended up finishing her dinner and going to her room for the night without even saying a word to him, much less giving him a goodnight kiss.

She'd felt bad for sulking like a child over being neglected. She'd beaten herself up over it all night, thinking she should've been accustomed to being neglected after twenty-two years and ten months of the same treatment from her father. She couldn't understand how the last two months of having Bobby's undivided attention over dinner could've spoiled her to the point that not having it for one night could hurt so much.

The really scary thing was that she was more worried about losing Bobby than she was about all the legal issues she was still dealing with and possibly losing her maternal family legacy. She'd rather give up Ashbury Enterprises and all the money she stood to inherit than to give up her relationship with Bobby. And she had no idea, whatsoever, how to reconnect with him when he was sitting stoically beside her, but it felt like he was miles away.

I should probably ask him why we have to go to Ashbury Enterprises this afternoon, Brooklyn thought as she watched the streets of Macon pass by the tinted window of the SUV. *I thought all those calls this morning with the attorney were to schedule a meeting with the board next week, after we actually get to sit down with him on Monday. Going up there now doesn't make sense when we don't have a meeting scheduled with the board of directors.*

Just as she was turning in her seat to clarify what was supposed to happen when they walked into Ashbury Enterprises' main office, the bodyguard parked in the lot beside the office building Brooklyn had only been in a handful of times. *I guess I'll just wing it?*

As usual, Bobby helped her out of the tall vehicle and guided her toward the front door with a hand on the small of her back. The two bodyguards positioned themselves with one on the opposite side of her from Bobby and the other behind them in a way that made Brooklyn feel surrounded by the three large men. They made her feel small in a way she normally didn't feel when she was wearing heels that brought her normal five-foot-three up to five-foot-eight. She just hoped her father and Clayton would also feel intimidated by the three men with her, each being at least half a foot taller than either of them, too.

They were greeted by the building's security officers and asked to sign in before being allowed to even approach the elevator. Brooklyn was glad they weren't asked why they were there or who they were there to see, as she was barely able to sign her name at that point without trembling from the anxiety coursing through her.

"Do you know which floor your father's office is on?" Bobby prodded as he walked her toward the elevator.

"No," Brooklyn admitted, noticing Ashbury Enterprises listed on three different floors on the board on the wall beside the elevators. "I know the large gathering space where they have parties is on the tenth floor, but I've never been to my father's office."

Bobby pulled his phone out and swiped the screen a few times, presumably finding out where they needed to go from someone else since she couldn't tell him. Soon, they were all boarding the elevator where Bobby pushed the button for the twelfth floor.

I really shouldn't be the one taking over Mom's company, when I don't even know enough about it to know where the CEO's office is located.

"Relax, Brie-Baby," Bobby commanded, reaching over to tilt her chin up, so she had to look at him. "You've got this. All you have to do is ask his secretary to schedule a board meeting for next week. Once she's working on that, we can leave for you to show me your hometown."

"I don't understand why the attorney couldn't get the board meeting scheduled," Brooklyn confided, feeling her façade slipping as she bit her bottom lip nervously.

Bobby brushed his thumb over her lips, stopping her from continuing to bite them, before saying, "Because the secretary is acting like a guard dog and won't recognize the fact that he's representing you in making the request. Once she physically sees you in her office to make the request, she won't be able to deny it."

Just when she thought he was going to bend down to kiss her, the elevator came to a stop and the doors whooshed open. Bobby dropped his hand from her face, straightened his suit coat, and turned to lead her out the door.

"How may I help you?" The svelte blonde woman at the reception desk purred in a sultry tone, giving the three men in suits around Brooklyn an obvious once over.

"I'm Brooklyn Barns," she stated, standing taller and projecting an air of confidence she didn't actually feel. "I need to speak with my father's secretary."

"Oh!" The receptionist looked shocked at the request coming from her, instead of one of the men with her. "Let me see if she's available."

The receptionist continued to give all three men flirty smiles as she picked up the receiver and pushed a button on her phone. "Yes, Janice, I have Brooklyn Barns asking to speak with you."

She focused in on Bobby as she listened to whatever Janice had to say on the other end of the line, making Brooklyn feel the need to step closer to him and put her arm around his waist to stake her claim. Bobby wasn't doing anything to reciprocate the receptionist's interest, but it still made Brooklyn feel better when he put his arm around her shoulders to pull her in closer to his side.

"Yes, um, she has three gentlemen with her," the receptionist told Janice, her disapproval apparent in her tone. "Should I have them wait here or send them back with her?"

"We will all be going back with her," Bobby declared, his voice low and menacing.

"They're insisting on coming back with her. Maybe it would be best if you came up here," the receptionist squeaked out before hanging up the phone. "If you'd like to have a seat, Janice will come up here to speak with you in a moment."

"Thank you." Brooklyn was unable to go against her ingrained manners, even with the rude woman behind the reception desk. She moved over to the chairs lining the wall in the outer office and took a seat, while all three of the men with her stood defiantly around her. Brooklyn couldn't stop the slight smile on her lips when she noticed the receptionist was no longer flirty and now looked a little shaky, like she was afraid of the men who towered over the seated women.

Seeing that reaction caused Brooklyn to really look at the two bodyguards Bobby had hired. They were both at least as tall as he was, or maybe a hair taller, but they were both also a lot bulkier than Bobby's somewhat lean frame. *Bobby seemed so muscular when he was naked, but he almost looks skinny standing next to Barrett and Blaine. I guess between their size and stern expressions, the receptionist has a valid reason to appear to be afraid of them. And she probably doesn't even realize they're all carrying guns under their suit coats. I imagine she'd be calling security or the cops to escort us from the building if she knew that.*

Brooklyn almost giggled at her last thought, imagining how poorly that would go if Chief Rogers was the one called to remove them from the premises. Her brief grin faded, however, when she realized that Janice was being escorted to the front desk by both Brooklyn's father and former, forced fiancé.

Leah Mae Wright

"What's the meaning of this, Brooklyn?" Bradley Barns bellowed when the threesome got to the outer office.

Brooklyn involuntarily looked down at the floor, unable to break through the years of training to never make eye contact with her paternal figure. Seeing her reaction, Bobby turned toward her before kneeling in front of her chair. He gently tilted her chin up so their eyes could meet. She could see that he was in a state of heightened emotion by how much darker the amber flecks in his hazel eyes appeared. She'd loved that reaction in him when it was brought on by their passion for one another, but she feared his eyes were showing his anger at that precise moment. And she wasn't sure it was the best time for that emotion to come out.

He didn't say a word, just looked deep into her eyes, as if he was searching her soul to determine his next move. Brooklyn had no idea how she understood what he was thinking to realize that he was silently contemplating how to get her out of the uncomfortable situation without it becoming a traumatic experience for her, but she knew he would shelter her from her father's wrath, regardless of whether they stayed to confront him or walked away without saying another word. Having Bobby there to support her in whatever she wanted to happen next made it so much easier for Brooklyn to metaphorically pull up her big girl panties and stand up to her father.

Brooklyn leaned forward, brushing her lips lightly over Bobby's without realizing the Avington brothers blocked them from view of the rest of the occupants of the room. She stood, stepping between the bodyguards to address her father. Bobby stood beside and slightly behind her, lightly pressing his large hand across her lower back to show her his support. She could see the shock on her father's face when she looked him in the eye for the first time.

"I'm not actually here to speak with you," Brooklyn stated calmly, not even deigning him with the privilege of her using the moniker of father in reference to him. "Janice, I believe you are the person responsible for calling the board members to schedule a meeting. As you have refused to do so for my attorney so far this morning, I've come to personally request that you schedule a meeting with the board."

"You can't schedule a board meeting," Clayton shouted. "You don't even work for this company!"

"I may not technically work here," Brooklyn shrugged, slightly smiling at knowing she had the upper hand. "But I will be inheriting the company, so as the future owner of Ashbury Enterprises, I have every right to request a meeting of the board of directors to discuss how I wish to see my *mother's* legacy run."

She hoped the extra emphasis she used in reference to her mother wouldn't be too much of a hint that she was in town to sue her father to remove him as trustee of the estate she was set to inherit from her mom.

"Does this mean you've come home to fulfill your matrimonial duties?" Bradley's lips lightly turned up as if he was happy to hear she was getting married and taking over the company.

"My future plans will only be discussed in front of the board of directors." Brooklyn smiled sweetly, thinking it was best to keep the conniving coots guessing.

Janice had been diligently typing on a tablet in her hands from the moment she'd entered the outer office. "The soonest the rest of the board is available is tomorrow at two." She finally looked up at the crowd of people in the room. "If that doesn't work, we can schedule something for eight a.m. either next Wednesday or Thursday."

Thinking she needed to meet with her attorney on Monday first, Brooklyn was just about to agree to the Wednesday meeting when Bobby spoke before she had the chance.

"Tomorrow at two will be fine," Bobby declared in that commanding tone that made her insides tingle, removing his hand from Brooklyn's back to tap something into his phone, which he'd pulled from his pocket with his other hand. "But we'll probably need to schedule the meetings for Wednesday and Thursday as well."

"Who are you?" Clayton looked up at Bobby with disgust. "And what makes you think it's acceptable for you to schedule meetings on Brooklyn's behalf?"

Brooklyn felt Bobby start to growl and decided it was best they left without escalating the incident to the violence Bobby clearly wanted to inflict upon Clayton. "If you have those meetings scheduled, Janice," Brooklyn interrupted before Bobby could speak. "We'll be on our way. Have a good evening. We'll see you tomorrow."

Ignoring the indignation on her father's face, Brooklyn grabbed Bobby's arm, practically dragging him toward the elevator. Since he was over a foot taller than her (when she wasn't wearing mega high heels to go with her professional dress) and double her body weight, she knew he only followed her to the elevator because he wanted to, and not because she'd actually forced him to move. But as soon as the elevator doors closed, she still gave herself credit for getting them out of there without any bloodshed.

She waited until they were out of the building and back in the privacy of the blacked-out SUV before turning to look directly at Bobby. "Why did you accept the meeting tomorrow? Don't we need to wait until next week, after we meet with the attorney and when the court mediator is available?"

"Ideally, yes." Bobby reached over and took her hand in his. "But I didn't wanna take a chance on the board meeting tomorrow without us there and giving your father a chance to turn them against you before you even get to speak to them."

"Okay," Brooklyn conceded, lacing her fingers with his. "But since our attorney and the mediator won't be able to be there, what are we going to talk to the board about? It'll end up being a really short meeting that we'll get kicked out of if we just inform them of the lawsuit."

"I know Burleson buying Ashbury for a merger was supposed to be our plan B," Bobby started, looking at Brooklyn imploringly. "But maybe we should hit them with that option first. If the board goes for it, then you won't have to go through a mediator with the board to get a new trustee named for your inheritance next week. I think going straight to a judge with that will be a lot easier to win than having to fight your father and the board that he works with on a regular basis."

Brooklyn nodded her head in agreement, knowing that Burleson buying Ashbury would save her mother's legacy without her having to work in a job she had no interest in, and was actually the option she liked best of everything they'd discussed. Bobby lifted their joined hands to his mouth, lightly kissing the back of her hand before releasing it to pull his phone out again.

Instead of exploring Macon like tourists, since she didn't really know her way around to show him anything important in the area, they went back to the hotel for Bobby to spend the afternoon and evening going back and forth on the phone with his family members about who should fly out the next morning to be at the meeting. Brooklyn ended up going to soak in the jacuzzi tub in the bathroom off her bedroom, after another room service meal that was interrupted by his need to be on the phone.

She pulled up a book on her tablet and got a dose of romance vicariously through the fictional characters, since she obviously wasn't going to get any from Bobby anytime soon. *Maybe if the sale goes through tomorrow, Bobby will actually remember we're a couple tomorrow night? Otherwise, we'll have to wait until after shark week next week to make love again*, Brooklyn thought, realizing her period was due to start over the weekend.

Chapter Thirteen

Brooklyn was surprised when she woke up on Friday morning and heard several voices out in the living room portion of the suite she was sharing with Bobby at the hotel. Even when Barrett and Blaine Avington had stopped into their room to escort them to the Ashbury offices the day before, they'd been as quiet as they were when they were working, so Brook didn't think it was their voices she was hearing. Just as her brain was clearing enough for her to try to make out what was being said, a feminine voice joined in with the males who had been speaking and really confused her.

She scrambled from the bed, and after quickly taking care of her morning bathroom needs, she put on the fluffy white robe provided by the hotel to cover up the fact that she didn't wear a bra under her tank top to sleep. She felt a slight twinge of jealousy as she heard the woman's laughter immediately following Bobby's distinctive deep voice. Brooklyn felt herself flush at the thought of being jealous of Bobby making another woman laugh, feeling ridiculous for such a petty emotion. Though she and Bobby weren't actively engaging in the physical side of their relationship, she knew he wouldn't cheat on her with another woman.

Besides, I don't even know who it is yet. Instead of getting jealous, thinking it's a hotel employee or someone he's flirting with, I should probably wonder if it's one of his sisters or cousins who might be coming to the meeting today. And I definitely shouldn't feel jealous if it's one of them laughing at Bobby joking around, like he's always done with his family.

After her internal pep talk, Brooklyn cinched the robe tighter around her middle and focused herself with a cleansing breath before opening her bedroom door to go see what was going on in the other room. *See, it's his cousin. Quit being silly, jumping to dumb conclusions, and being jealous over nothing.* Her inner voice sounded an awful lot like Bobby's mother, Hazel, and Brooklyn couldn't contain the smile that spread across her face at thinking how nice it was to have her soothing motherly voice replacing the harsh inner voice of her father that had filled her head for years.

"Good morning, everyone," Brooklyn smiled, walking over to the seating area where Bobby was sitting on the sofa with his cousin, Julie, while his father and uncle were seated in the chairs across from them.

"Morning, Brie-Baby." Bobby reached for her hand and pulled her down into his lap. He gave her a peck of a kiss before pulling back in deference to their audience. "Sorry if we woke you."

"It's okay, I needed to be woken up." Brooklyn wrapped one arm around Bobby's shoulders as she turned to look at the others in the room. "It feels like I slept forever. What time is it?"

"Just after ten," Julie answered, smiling a knowing smile.

"Really?" Brooklyn squeaked. "I must have been more tired than I thought. I never sleep this late."

"I'm sure it's all Bobby's fault," Julie smirked, smacking her cousin in the arm that wasn't supporting Brooklyn's back. "You need to let her get some rest at night, Cuz."

Brooklyn was too shocked to speak, a bright pink flush spreading over her cheeks at the insinuation. She didn't get a chance to refute the reason for why she was tired, but it wasn't because Bobby was defending her honor.

"Why don't you go find a guy to keep you up at night, instead of worrying about when Brie and I sleep?" Bobby grinned at his cousin.

"Enough, kids," Bobby's Uncle Jon reprimanded, his expression stern except for the slightest upturn of his lips. "We hear enough matchmaking drama from your mothers, we don't need to deal with ya'll bickering about your love lives, too."

"You know it's only gonna get worse since these two succumbed to Hazel's scheming so soon," Bob chuckled, pointing at Bobby and Brooklyn.

Brooklyn was surprised to see Bobby's father lightly laughing, but she was even more shocked to hear him speak as he was normally a quiet man. That one sentence might be the most she'd ever heard him say in the two months she'd known him.

"Yeah, well, Ma didn't exactly have to do any matchmaking with us," Bobby confessed, his arms coming around Brooklyn, so he could squeeze her close. "I was makin' plans to pursue Brie from the moment I laid eyes on her. Ma just made it easier for me to catch her."

"Well, you could have at least put up a little fight against Aunt Hazel's plans." Julie shook her head at her cousin. "She feels so successful with ya'll that she's convinced Mom to help her with setting the rest of us up, and they do not have it right with who they're pushing toward me."

Brooklyn remembered back to her birthday party when she'd seen Julie and her twin sister, Jen, being seated next to a couple of the Walkers and wondered why Julie wasn't attracted to the fairly good-looking men. Brooklyn didn't think they were as handsome as Bobby, but she could still see they would be attractive to women who hadn't already met their one and only like she had.

She thought back to the first night she'd met the majority of the most eligible bachelors of Heart's Destiny and realized she'd imagined Heather and Ashley paired off with Leo and Luke, instead of Jen and Julie like Hazel and Susan seemed to be pushing. *Since Julie doesn't seem to be interested in the Walkers, maybe I can enlist Hazel and Susan's help in fixing Heather and Ashley up with them? But they'll probably only go for that once they've found the right guys for their daughters and nieces. Hmm? I wonder who Julie might actually be interested in dating? She certainly seemed more interested in the wrestlers she was hanging out with at Christmas. Maybe I should point that out to the Matchmaking Mommas when we get back home.*

Realizing she was thinking of Heart's Destiny as home, Brooklyn smiled. She rested her head on Bobby's shoulder as he and his family discussed the plan for the day. She wanted to get lost in her head, daydreaming about their future together as a family. But since they were discussing the best way to sever her ties with her father, Brooklyn had to remain in the moment and take an active role in making their plans for the day.

At least I get to do this planning while being held safely in Bobby's arms. And hopefully, when this day is over, I'll get to spend the night in his arms again.

~~~

Several hours later, Brooklyn walked confidently with her entourage into the Ashbury Enterprises' office. She'd put her mask back in place to keep her from hiding behind Bobby and letting him fight her battles for her, even though, deep inside, she really wished she could turn everything with her father over to him to handle. As the seven of them crowded into the elevator, she realized she was turning at least part of it over to him and his family. When he pulled her back into his arms, she knew she was more than capable of handling her portion with his loving encouragement. She just hoped the affection and support he was showing her that morning would continue after the meeting. She didn't think she could handle a third night alone in her hotel bed when he was so close in the room next door.

"You've got this, Brie-Baby," Bobby whispered into her ear. "I know you do. But if you need me to take over for any reason, just reach over and squeeze my hand, and I'll make sure your message gets across loud and clear without you having to say another word."

"Thank you, Bobby." Brooklyn turned in his arms to return the much-needed hug.

"No need to thank me for doing my job as your man." Bobby brushed his lips on the top of her head.

"Your job?" Brooklyn questioned, not sure she liked him equating her to an obligation such as work.

"Yeah, when we became a couple, we were each given responsibilities to do for each other," Bobby replied, lifting his head, and pulling back from their embrace just enough to make eye contact. "My number one job in life is now to take care of you and protect you from anyone or anything that could do you harm. So, putting your douchebag dad and dickless Donaldson in their place is my right as your man, your protector."

Brooklyn couldn't help but smile at the serious expression on his face. "And what exactly are my responsibilities toward you?" She tried to school her features to appear as stern as Bobby's.

"We'll have to wait 'til we get back to the hotel to discuss those." Bobby wiggled his eyebrows suggestively just as the elevator slowed as it approached the floor where they would exit. Bobby bent to peck
~~~

their lips together quickly before straightening and releasing Brooklyn from his hold.

She smoothed out his suit coat from where she'd wrinkled it with her arms around his waist before turning to watch the elevator doors open. The Avington brothers were the first to exit the elevator, looking around as if they were expecting an ambush before motioning that it was clear for the others to exit.

"Do they do that everywhere you go?" Julie quietly murmured to Brooklyn as the ladies followed the older Burleson men off the elevator.

"No, until today it was Bobby leading the way and they covered us from behind," Brooklyn whispered her reply.

"I much prefer being the one watching your behind," Bobby quipped softly, making Brooklyn giggle, and easing her nerves in a way she hadn't realized she needed.

The receptionist from the day before eyed them all with suspicion before saying, "Ms. Barns is the only one authorized to attend the board meeting."

"Please direct me to where the meeting will be held," Brooklyn instructed, not acknowledging the receptionist's declaration, or giving anyone else the opportunity to refute it.

"Down the hall, last room on the right." The receptionist pointed to a hallway going left from the receptionist's desk.

"Thank you." Brooklyn gave the receptionist a polite nod before reaching for Bobby's hand to give her the confidence to lead them all to the meeting.

As soon as she started walking away with Bobby beside her and the rest of their group following her, the receptionist shouted, "The rest of you need to have a seat here until the meeting is over! If you don't stop and come back to the waiting room, I'll have to call security!"

Bobby stopped and turned slightly back, unbuttoning his jacket as he did, so he could flash the badge on his waist to the receptionist. "No need for security when law enforcement is already here." Bobby then turned back toward Brooklyn to continue walking hand in hand with her to the conference room.

Once they were halfway down the hallway and no longer within hearing distance of the reception desk, Bob chuckled, "You're a little out of your jurisdiction there, aren't you Son?"

"I didn't say I was local law enforcement." Bobby shrugged as they continued walking. "But I'll be glad to send a text to Chief Rogers and the FBI agents we met with a couple days ago, if you think we need to get someone here with jurisdiction to convince the board to allow us to attend the meeting. They've all already been notified about it and are on standby to be able to be here at a moment's notice."

"I don't think that's necessary just yet," Jon interjected, a slight chuckle behind his words.

There were already a couple of board members milling about when they walked into the conference room, but they weren't seated yet. Bobby did as he'd done at the police station two days before, leading Brooklyn to the seat at the head of the table and pulling it out for her. He took the seat to her right with his father beside him. Julie took the seat to Brooklyn's left, directly across the table from Bobby with her father beside her. Instead of taking a seat, Barrett and Blaine stood sentry behind Brooklyn, making her feel as well guarded as the President with the Secret Service at his side.

"Ms. Barns," the white-haired gentleman, who had been fixing himself a cup of coffee at a side table, greeted her, walking up to stand between her and Bobby, and extending his hand. "I'm Leland Remington."

"Nice to meet you Mr. Remington," Brooklyn smiled at the distinguished gentleman, shaking his hand.

"I've been on the board since your grandfather started Ashbury Enterprises," Leland informed her, holding her hand longer than was necessary. "William Ashbury was a dear friend and has been sorely missed, as has your mother. You are the spitting image of Maddie, and I hope you have as insightful a vision for the future of the company as she did in her time here."

"Thank you, Sir," Brooklyn sniffled, feeling extremely touched by his words and having to fight back the tears they elicited.

"We don't normally allow outsiders to attend our board meetings," Leland started to explain, his eyes wandering to the people around her as he finally released her hand. "But I assume you have a reason for bringing an entourage with you today. I'd ask for introductions, but maybe those should wait until the rest of the board arrives."

"Yes, Sir," Brooklyn agreed, nodding at the older gentleman as he stepped back. "I have very valid reasons for having everyone with me today."

"I look forward to hearing them," Leland smiled at her as he took the open seat beside Bob Burleson. As the rest of the board members joined them around the table, Leland introduced each one to Brooklyn, though she knew she'd never remember all their names. "And of course, you know your father," he finished as Bradley Barns took his seat at the other end of the table.

"Yes, thank you, Mr. Remington," Brooklyn smiled at her grandfather's friend for his gracious introductions. "As I said earlier, I have very valid reasons for each of the people with me today, that I respectfully ask you to allow to stay for the meeting. Behind me are Blaine and Barrett Avington of Avington Security." Brooklyn motioned behind her at the two gentlemen, who refused the two seats offered to them by one of the other board members. "They're here acting as my bodyguards, so no unsavory characters can get close enough to cause me harm."

"I suppose I should've hired them last year, instead of the incompetent security firm I hired that allowed you to be kidnapped," Bradley sniped from the other end of the table.

Knowing she wasn't supposed to speak to her father about any of the details surrounding her disappearance to keep from accidentally alerting him about his impending arrest, Brooklyn didn't recognize his outburst.

"Seated at the table, you'll find one third of the board of directors of Burleson Incorporated," she continued her introductions. "Beside Mr. Remington is Bob Burleson. Across the table from him is Jon Burleson. They are the co-CEOs of the corporation. Beside Bob is his son, Bobby, and beside Jon is his daughter, Julie. The Burlesons are here to present you with an offer to purchase Ashbury Enterprises."

"I didn't realize Ashbury Enterprises was up for sale." Leland Remington looked from Brooklyn and the Burlesons to the other end of the table where Bradley Barns sat stone-faced.

Brooklyn hated not being able to read her father's expression to have even half a clue what he was thinking. But since he wasn't saying a single word about whether he wanted to sell Ashbury or not,

Brooklyn felt the need to fill the silence and make it clear that it was her wish to make this merger.

"I don't believe anyone at Ashbury has been actively advertising the business for sale," Brooklyn stated, briefly noticing the slight flinch in her father's expression that made her wonder if he'd been looking to unload the company once he had her sign her inheritance over to him. "But when I was made aware that I will be inheriting the company when I marry, I had to weigh the options for what would be best for the business to thrive in the future. As I was not informed of my need to know how to run a company of this magnitude before I completed my college degree, I don't have the education that I feel is required to effectively lead Ashbury Enterprises in the future. Therefore, after getting to know the Burlesons and their business acumen, I asked them to come up with a proposal that would preserve the legacy my mother and grandfather built, without the need for me to act in a role in the company I'm not adequately prepared to fulfill. I realize I won't actually have the right to make the decision to sell until after I marry and inherit the company, along with the rest of the estate my mother left me in her will, but I also don't see any reason to delay the inevitable. That's why I'm here today asking you to listen to their proposal and offer your input as to how we can move forward in the best interest of both companies."

Bobby reached over and placed his hand on her knee under the table, drawing her attention to him. The twinkle in his eye as he smiled at her was all Brooklyn needed to see to know he was proud of her for standing her ground and presenting her plan to the board.

"Very well," Mr. Remington nodded, as did several other board members around the table. "We will gladly hear the Burlesons' offer."

Julie stood and pulled a laptop from her bag. After reintroducing herself as the vice president of business diversification and asset management for Burleson Incorporated, she asked for assistance in lowering the screen behind Brooklyn and hooking her laptop into the network to be able to project her presentation where the whole board could see it. The Avingtons ended up having to move to the side of the room, so they weren't blocking the view of the screen for the rest of the people in the meeting. But after some quick shuffling and turning in their seats, it didn't take long before Julie was going through a slideshow of the details of the deal.

Most of the details went over Brooklyn's head, but she understood the basics. Once purchased, Ashbury Enterprises would continue to run almost exactly as it currently was as its own entity, but as a subsidiary of Burleson Incorporated. The only real difference would be that instead of answering to the board of directors, the new CEO would be accountable to the division of Burleson that Julie was currently running.

Even with her back turned to him while she was focusing on the presentation, Brooklyn recognized her father's huff of indignation when Julie mentioned a "new CEO" at Ashbury Enterprises. *Hopefully, his one vote on the board won't be enough to stop the sale and save his position in the company as the trustee of Mom's estate.*

Instead of paying attention to the details Julie was going over, Brooklyn tried to listen closely to the rumblings of the other board members. She wanted to gauge how they were reacting to the terms to see if there was any chance of them agreeing with her to sell the company to the Burlesons. Unfortunately, most of the grunts and mumblings didn't give Brooklyn the impression that they liked the deal.

At least, until Julie started talking numbers. The gasps she heard from the board members when Julie specified, "Burleson Incorporated is offering to purchase Ashbury Enterprises for the total sum of one-hundred-million dollars," made Brooklyn think they were offering way more than the company was actually worth.

That seems like almost double the total that was listed on all the company accounts Jake found combined. Surely, they wouldn't risk going in the red at Burleson to pay more than Ashbury is worth just to get me out of this mess, Brooklyn pondered. *Would they?* She got so carried away worrying about how this deal could possibly bankrupt the Burlesons that she almost missed Julie's explanation of the breakdown of how the funds would be distributed.

"Fifty percent of the purchase price would go to the Ashbury estate, with the other fifty percent being divided equally among the other eleven board members to compensate you for any income you would lose by no longer serving on the board of directors for Ashbury Enterprises," Julie pointed out, clicking to show a slide that broke that down to approximately four-and-a-half-million dollars for each of the eleven men and women on the board, except her father.

Oh, I bet that hiss was because he realized he's only on the board as the trustee of the estate, so he's ineligible to receive a slice of that pie chart for himself, Brooklyn thought, grinning at the way the Burlesons worded the deal to screw her father out of any income from the sale of Ashbury. *He's really going to hate it when the feds confiscate all the money he's stolen from me and the company over the years.*

I wonder how long it'll take the FBI to release that money back to me, so I can start paying Bobby and his family back for helping me get out of this mess? Or if the Burlesons buy Ashbury, will the FBI send the money he embezzled from Ashbury to them, so I'll only have to pay back eighty percent of the money they're talking about spending today? I don't know how much is in the estate accounts that Jake didn't mention when he was looking at them, but I doubt even adding that to the eleven million I'm having to sue to get back from him, and whatever I can get from selling the house, will be enough to pay the Burlesons back what they're overspending on Ashbury.

Brooklyn was snapped out of her mental rabbit hole of worry by the lights coming back up after Julie's presentation ended. She turned back around to face the board members as Julie took her seat beside her. As soon as she was back within reach, Bobby's hand reappeared on her knee. Brooklyn reached down and covered his hand with hers, rubbing her thumb over his knuckles as their eyes locked on one another briefly. She didn't want to squeeze his hand and give him the impression that she needed him to take over the meeting, but she hoped the light brush of her digit over his skin was as comforting for him as his hand on her knee was for her.

Not wanting to risk their relationship tainting the board's opinion on the sale of the company, they each quickly turned their attention back to the board members, who were asking questions about the potential deal. Jon Burleson fielded most of them, with Julie and Bob backing him up when the questions veered toward how things would be handled when Ashbury was in competition with other divisions of Burleson.

Unfortunately, either Brooklyn and Bobby weren't as subtle in their longing looks at each other as she thought they were, or Bobby not answering any of the questions being asked by the other board members threw up red flags for her father to point out.

Leah Mae Wright

"I appreciate the presentation, Ms. Burleson," Bradley nodded his head at Julie. "And the thoughtful answers to all of our questions from both Jon and Bob Burleson. But I have to wonder why Bobby Burleson is even in this meeting. The only thing I've seen from him so far are lecherous looks at my daughter that make me wonder if he's somehow manipulating a naïve young woman into giving away our company for far less than it's worth."

Lecherous looks? Brooklyn silently fumed, not realizing she'd squeezed Bobby's hand in her outraged state. *The only lecherous looks I've ever received are from your slimy sidekick, Clayton. Thank goodness, he's not in this meeting. Though if he were, I'd at least be able to point out the difference to you.*

"While I would normally not consider anything said by Bradley Barns as worth my time in hearing, much less replying to," Bobby fumed, pulling his hand from Brooklyn's leg to stand up. Instead of buttoning his suit coat as most men did when they stood in a meeting such as this, Bobby removed the jacket, exposing the badge on his waistband and the shoulder holster where he wore his service weapon. "I believe this deal will only be able to go through if I'm fully transparent with the board, who will be making the decision whether or not to sell Ashbury Enterprises. I'm only partially here today in my role as a board member at Burleson. I'm also here in my role as the Heart's Destiny Police Chief, as the legal authority that Ms. Barns came to for police protection from her father."

"Why does she need police protection from her father?" Leland Remington looked up at Bobby with wide eyes.

"That's an ongoing criminal matter that I'm not at liberty to discuss at this time," Bobby replied, dipping his chin toward Leland to acknowledge his question without actually answering it. "All I can disclose about it is that the evidence has been given to law enforcement officials with the jurisdiction to handle things here in Georgia, while Ms. Barns remains in my protective custody."

Brooklyn wasn't sure how she felt about Bobby speaking about her as if she were any other complainant, and his protective custody was only in the course of doing his job. On the one hand, she understood that their relationship could be misconstrued by the board and potentially detrimental to the sale of Ashbury to Burleson. But on the other hand, she was still a woman in love, who wanted to shout it to the world, and desperately needed to feel like that level of love was returned by her soulmate not being able to hide his feelings for her either.

She didn't get a chance to make a decision about whether or not they should be outed as a couple, though, because Bobby made the declaration plain as day.

"But even if I wasn't on the board of directors at Burleson Incorporated, or a police officer sworn to protect and serve, I would still be by Brooklyn's side in this meeting." Bobby turned to look down at her with love shining through his hazel eyes. "Because I will do anything for the woman I love." Bobby reached down and laced her fingers with his before turning back to face the Ashbury Enterprises board of directors. "Including dipping into my trust fund to pay double what this company is worth to safeguard her maternal family legacy from destruction at the hands of her sperm donor."

Dipping into his trust fund? Double what the company is worth? Brooklyn was so blown away by the first part of Bobby's last sentence that she almost didn't comprehend the end of it. When she realized what he'd just said, she didn't have a chance to react because of the commotion his words had incited at the other end of the table.

Her father was ranting and raving, as were several of the Ashbury board members. Brooklyn couldn't understand everything that was said with so many people yelling over one another. The cacophony of raised voices was headache inducing, making Brooklyn grateful for Leland Remington slamming his hand down on the table and shouting, "Enough!"

The unexpected outburst from the eldest member of the board was so shocking, it quieted the rest of the people in the room. "Regardless of the relationship status of Ms. Barns and Mr. Burleson, this is a board room, not a reality TV show. As the chairman of the board, I'm going to ask our guests to please step out of the room, so we can discuss their offer and vote on whether or not we wish to accept it."

"That won't be necessary, Leland," Bradley Barns boasted, sneering at his daughter. "As the trustee of the Ashbury estate, I'm the only person who gets to decide if the assets of the estate are up for sale. As long as I'm in charge of managing the assets of the estate, neither Ashbury Enterprises, nor any other assets of the estate, are available for purchase by the Burlesons or any other entity."

Leah Mae Wright

"That's what I expected you to say," Bobby snickered, a knowing smile spreading on his face and showing off his dimples. "That's why I asked Janice to make sure you were all available for meetings next week as well. Those won't technically be board meetings. Those will be meetings between attorneys and the court appointed mediator in the case Brooklyn is bringing to have her father removed as the trustee of her inheritance. As the outcome of the mediation will affect Ashbury Enterprises, it will be in the best interest of the Ashbury board to be in attendance."

Brooklyn noticed the fury written all over her father's face, but he didn't get a chance to express it.

Bobby reached over and picked up his jacket that he'd laid over the back of his chair. "I look forward to seein' ya'll at eight a.m. Wednesday morning and I hope that, well, most of you have a good evening." With that, he helped Brooklyn stand from her seat and walked her out of the conference room, still clutching her hand in his.

I guess he wasn't kidding when he said he'd take over and get my message across without me having to say another word, Brooklyn thought as she and her entourage exited the building.

<div align="center">~~~</div>

Bobby hated seeing his family leave the hotel to go to the airport to head back to Texas after dinner that evening. He understood that they needed to deal with a few things in the offices at Burleson on Monday and Tuesday, and they would be back in Macon for the mediation scheduled for Wednesday, and possibly Thursday, of the following week, but he also wished they could be there for the meeting he and Brie had with the lawyer he'd hired for her on Monday, if only as moral support.

Though, if he was truly being honest with himself, he was glad they'd left when they did, so he could have the whole weekend alone with Brie to diminish the distance he'd inadvertently put between them the past few days. He thought he was doing a pretty good job of bringing them back together that morning by holding her on his lap as they discussed the plan for the day with his family. But since he couldn't really kiss her the way he wanted to with an audience, much

388

less bring them together more intimately, he'd only been able to show his affection by holding hands with her the rest of the day.

Yeah, that's gonna change just as soon as we can ditch the Avingtons at the door of our suite, Bobby thought while holding Brie's hand as they rode up to their floor in the hotel elevator.

"Sure you don't need us the rest of the night, Boss?" Barrett double-checked just before the elevator doors opened.

"Naw, it's been a long day," Bobby replied, shaking his head at being called "Boss" by his friend's oldest brother, who was a couple of years older than him. "I think we all need to rest for the evening."

"Any plans for the weekend we need to be around for?" Blaine inquired as they stepped off the elevator to walk down the hall to the two suites they'd occupied for the last three days on the otherwise empty floor.

"Yeah, making sure neither Barns nor Donaldson get near them." Barrett smacked his brother in the back of the head with his open palm. "You aren't sneaking off for a booty call while we're on assignment. Even if they don't decide to do any sight-seeing this weekend and stay holed up in bed the whole time, we're still gonna keep an eye on the door to their suite to make sure nobody disturbs them."

Bobby couldn't stop his chuckle at seeing the Avington brothers acting more like the goofballs he knew from all the times he'd hung out with them while visiting with Blake, than the serious security professionals they'd portrayed all week. He knew they were more than capable of being serious when the situation called for it, but he preferred interacting with the more laid-back versions of the guys he'd come to think of as close friends over the years.

"I'd kinda like to see Brie's favorite places in town," Bobby mused aloud, stopping at their door, and reaching into his pocket to get the keycard to open the door to the suite. "But we don't have any specific plans. How 'bout I text you if we decide to go somewhere and need both of you. And ya'll can trade off monitoring the surveillance cameras in the hallway otherwise."

"Sounds good," Blaine nodded as Bobby opened the door to his and Brie's suite.

Barrett insisted on doing a walk through to make sure the room was clear before heading next door to the room where he and Blaine were staying. "Have a good night," he grinned as he left.

As soon as they were alone, Bobby closed and locked the door to the suite and scooped Brie up into his arms. "I've been dying to get you alone all day," he confessed before pressing their lips together.

"Oh," Brie exclaimed in surprise at being lifted off the ground, opening her mouth to allow him to deepen the kiss.

Bobby took advantage of the opportunity to explore the recesses of her mouth with his tongue, regardless of whether she intentionally opened for him or not. The way she wound her arms around his neck and returned the kiss with as much passion as he felt, let him know that she didn't mind the invasion, even if she hadn't intended for them to kiss right then.

Fuck! She tastes like heaven, Bobby thought as he carried her over to the couch in the living room portion of their suite. He sat down still cradling her in his arms, knowing they really needed to talk before he lost control and took things farther than kissing. Reluctantly, he lifted his mouth from hers. He relished the dazed look in her beautiful blue eyes as she opened them to look up at him and smile.

"I need to apologize to you," Bobby acknowledged, reaching up to brush her long blonde hair behind her ear after repositioning her to be more comfortable sitting on his lap.

"Oh?" Brie squeaked, the word coming out sounding like a question as she looked up at him in confusion.

"Yeah, I've been an ass the past few days," Bobby hesitantly admitted.

"No," Brie disagreed, shaking her head at him. "You've been distant, but you've been focused on making sure everything is lined up to take care of things for me when I've had no idea how to do any of it for myself. If anyone should be apologizing, it's me for being so clueless and unable to do any of this legal stuff without your help."

"It's the distance I've been putting between us that I wanna apologize for," Bobby elaborated, resting his forehead on hers, so they had to maintain eye contact. He wanted her to see in his eyes how sincere he was as he spoke his next words. "I was afraid you'd come back here and realize you'd made a mistake in leaving home. And I think I was subconsciously preparing myself for you to send me back to Heart's Destiny with my tail tucked between my legs, while you lived the life you really want here in Georgia, instead of coming back to Texas with me."

"Oh, Bobby," Brie vociferated, her eyes turning glassy with unshed tears. "No, that's never going to happen." She slid her hands up to the front of his neck to cup his jaw on both sides, holding his head in place, so she could pepper his face with kisses. "My only mistake about leaving Georgia was waiting so long to do it. My home isn't here. It's back on the ranch with you."

"Thank fuck!" Bobby returned her fevered smooches to her forehead, cheeks, nose, chin, and finally landed his lips on hers. "I don't think I could stand to live in my house anymore without you there with me."

They didn't speak for several long moments as they made out like teenagers. Finally, Bobby pulled back from their impassioned lip lock to make sure they were clear on their path going forward. "I know you're not ready to think about getting married yet, but please tell me that when we get home you'll at least move into my bedroom. I want us to live together as partners in our relationship, not because room and board is part of the employment deal you worked out with my mother."

"Yes, Bobby," Brie giggled with delight as she smiled up at him. "And if things go the way I hope next week, I may even quit my housekeeping job with your family."

"Good, I much prefer calling you my girlfriend than my housekeeper." Bobby gave her a dimple-popping smile. "But you may have to give Ma some time to find a replacement before you completely quit. As much as I hate sharing your cooking and cleaning with my cousins, they're gonna need the help until they each find a woman of their own."

"Actually, I have a replacement in mind." Brie had an excited twinkle in her eyes.

"Yeah, who?" Bobby was curious as to who she planned to move onto the ranch to match up with Justin or JJ.

"If the feds arrest my father and I get control of my mother's estate, then Mary and Joe will be out of a job when I sell the house here in Macon." Brie slightly lifted one shoulder in a questioning motion. "I know Mary can do a way better job than I've been doing. And even if ya'll don't have a groundskeeper position on the ranch, surely Joe can find a job doing landscaping for someone in Heart's Destiny."

"That's an excellent idea, Brie-Baby," Bobby agreed, smiling reassuringly at her. *And I'm sure Dad will like the idea of hiring Joe to keep the yards around our houses mowed, instead of having to pull a ranch hand off of other tasks to do it.*

Satisfied that they were finished discussing everything they needed to talk about before moving to making love, Bobby growled out the question he really wanted to ask her. "Now that all that's figured out, what room are we sharing tonight?"

"What?" Brie giggled, as if she thought he wasn't asking her a serious question.

"I'm not spending another night sleeping without you in my arms," Bobby declared, readjusting his arms, so he had one supporting her back and one under her knees to pick her up as he stood from the couch. "So which bedroom am I carrying you to, so I can ravish your delectable little body all night, Brie-Baby?"

"Aren't they basically identical?" Bobby nodded in agreement. "Then I don't guess it really matters. Though maybe we can rotate between the two of them, so we don't end up sleeping in a wet spot like we did before."

"How very thoughtful of you," Bobby grinned, kissing the side of her head as he carried her into the room he'd been sleeping in the past two nights. It wasn't that he didn't want to go to the room she'd been using. He chose his room first because he'd been hopeful when he was packing for their trip and stashed his box of condoms in his bag, which was in his room. And he'd been serious when he'd told her that he would wait for her to tell him not to wear one when they made love. "Coming up with a plan to keep me from sleeping in the wet spot, since you'll be sleeping high and dry on top of me."

"I'm never dry when I'm on top of you." Brie surprised him with her innuendo, even though she blushed when she realized what she said.

"No, you're not," Bobby growled, his voice going deeper with arousal. "And I love how fucking wet you get for me."

"Only for you," Brie uttered breathily, as he kicked the bedroom door closed and stalked over to the bed.

"Damn right, only for me." Bobby almost didn't recognize his own voice with it so husky with desire, as he placed her down on the floor beside the bed. She momentarily wobbled on her killer heels. Bobby steadied her with a hand on each shoulder, only thinking it might be easier on her if she took them off for a split second. The vision of her fuck-me pumps resting on his shoulders as he plowed into her quickly replaced any other thoughts of how he wanted them to come together in that moment. "Just like I'm only hard for you."

He slid one hand up from her shoulder to tilt her chin up, so he could kiss her again. He felt like he was parched and the only way to quench his thirst was to suckle every inch of her, starting with her luscious lips. His other hand moved down to unbutton the navy-blue blazer she wore over a white silk blouse. Her arms came up to encircle his neck, her fingers weaving through his hair as their kiss deepened.

He took his time, appreciating the taste of his beautiful Brie-Baby, before pulling back to savor every inch of skin he exposed as he slowly undressed her. First the blazer, then the blouse, revealing a baby blue lace bra that did absolutely nothing to hide her hard nipples from his gaze.

When she reached to start undressing him as well, he clasped her wrists to stop her. "No, not yet, Brie-Baby," he growled, lightly brushing his lips across each wrist before gently moving them behind her back. "I wanna finish unwrapping the most precious gift I've ever been given first."

"Oh," Brie moaned, her mouth forming a perfect O as she breathed out the word.

"Then I wanna spend the next few hours cherishing you the way you deserve." Bobby trailed his fingers back up her arms. "If you touch me too soon, I won't be able to maintain control, and this will be over before it even gets started."

"But I want to touch you," Brie whimpered, her hands coming back up to his chest.

"And you will, Brie-Baby," Bobby promised, lightly pushing her hands back down. "But not until I've made you come a few times first. Now keep your hands to yourself, or I'll have to tie you to the bed, so I can have my way with you."

Brie's mouth opened as if she was going to say something, but she quickly closed it, obviously changing her mind about protesting. Her eyes were wide and lit with excitement in a way Bobby had only seen when she was aroused by what he was doing or saying. *Fuck! I think she likes the idea of me tying her up. Guess it's a good thing I brought all my suits and ties on this trip. Hopefully, using them to tie her to the headboard won't be evident when I wear them in our meetings next week.*

Bobby didn't immediately go for the tie around his neck to give her a hint of what he was thinking. Instead, he went back to undressing her, knowing that he could only fulfill that fantasy for them once she was naked. *Well, naked except for those fuck-me pumps.*

Brie did well at holding still and not touching him as he slipped the zipper down on her navy-blue pencil skirt and let it fall to the floor. But as she moved to step out of the circle of fabric on the floor, she slipped one foot out of her shoe.

"No, leave the shoes on," Bobby commanded, his voice gruffer than he intended. "I've been fantasizing about them propped on my shoulders while I'm fucking you all day."

"Yes, Sir," Brie grinned, slipping her shoe back on before stepping away from the pile of her clothes on the floor.

As sexy as he found her baby blue lace bra and matching thong, Bobby couldn't wait another moment to have her naked and on the bed. He loved watching her shudder under his touch as he slid his hands up her sides to reach around and unfasten her bra. It soon joined the rest of her clothing on the floor. Then he went to his knees in front of her and looped a finger through the lace over each of her hips to slide the thong down her legs, which were surprisingly long for someone so petite.

He lifted one foot to remove her panties before placing it back on the floor, and lifting the other to do the same on the other side. Instead of putting that foot back down once her thong was no longer around her leg, Bobby dropped the panties and started kissing his way from her ankle, over her calf, to the junction of her thighs. He rested the back of her knee over his shoulder as he took a moment to feast on the heart of her femininity.

Before he could get lost in her taste, Brie brought her hands to his head, reminding him of his plans for the night.

"Don't stop," Brie protested as Bobby backed away and gently lowered her foot back to the floor.

"Oh, I'm not stopping, Brie-Baby." Bobby stood and scooped her up into his arms. He walked on his knees on the bed to place her in the center. Once she was laid out before him, he sat back on his heels and started removing his tie.

"Oh, Bobby," Brie moaned, her arousal evident in her tone. "Do I, uh, need a safe word like in the last series of books Kay recommended I read?"

Caught off guard by the mention of his sister-in-law, Bobby momentarily froze. *What the hell is Kay having Brie read?*

"Uh, no, not tonight," Bobby finally muttered, going back to removing his tie. "But if there's something you really like in those books, we can read them together to come up with ideas for when we might use a safe word later."

Brie's face lit up with excitement as Bobby moved over her to wrap his tie around her wrist. *I guess she likes the idea of coming up with some kinky fantasies for us to reenact from those books.*

Once her left wrist was bound, Bobby weaved the tie through the slats on the headboard before tying the other end of the navy-blue silk around her right wrist. He double checked that the bindings around each of her wrists were loose enough he could get two fingers between the material and her delicate skin, not wanting to risk hurting or marking her with them being too tight.

Once he was satisfied with the way she was secured to the bed, Bobby backed to the edge and stood. He removed his suit jacket, shoes, and socks as he observed the beauty laid out on the bed for his pleasure. He took his time putting away his gun and badge and removing his belt, so there wasn't anything he was wearing that could possibly hurt her, if it scraped across her porcelain skin while he was teasing her with his fingers and tongue.

"It's too bad we didn't remember to bring that massage oil with us on this trip," Bobby postulated as he crawled back on the bed. He knelt at her side and trailed a single finger from her shoulder down to the valley between her breasts. "Now would've been the perfect time to use it."

"I brought lotion," Brie offered, her voice coming out as more of a pant from the way he was teasing her by touching everywhere on her chest except her diamond-hard nipples.

"Mmm, maybe next time," Bobby promised, unable to resist lowering his mouth to her mounds a moment longer. "I'd rather just taste your sweet skin this time."

And taste her, he did. He licked and sucked every inch of her delectable body, eliciting moans and whimpers of pleasure from Brie like he'd never heard before, each and every time he made her come. He didn't know how he was able to move around the bed as easily as he was with his cock so hard it was pushing the limits of what his slacks could handle without ripping apart at the seams. He was getting close to the end of his ability to maintain control, wanting to be inside her more than anything else he'd ever needed in his life, but somehow he managed to hold out long enough for her to break first.

"Please, Bobby," Brie begged, her hips rocking on the bed seemingly of their own volition.

"Please what, Brie-Baby?" Bobby taunted playfully, sitting back on his heels between her spread thighs.

"I need you," she pleaded, their eyes locking on each other. "I can't take any more without you inside me."

Bobby would've teased her with his fingers until she specifically begged for his cock, but the sincerity of her desire for him in her eyes was his undoing. He backed off the end of the bed and made quick work of removing his shirt, not even caring that the buttons went flying across the room as he ripped it from his body. He barely unbuttoned his pants before shoving them and his boxer briefs to the floor. Then he walked over to where his suitcase was sitting on the floor beside the dresser, his cock bobbing the whole way in its extremely hardened state. He wasted no time in bending down to retrieve the box of condoms.

He took the whole box back with him to the bed, knowing he'd need more than one before the night was over. He ripped open the first foil wrapper he pulled from the pack, not caring that he'd spilled several more out onto the bed. He was crawling on his knees back between her legs as he sheathed himself.

Running his hands from her ankles to her knees, he lifted her legs and positioned those sexy-as-fuck stilettos on his shoulders. He hooked his elbows under her knees and gripped her hips with his hands. He lifted her off the mattress to perfectly line them up before plunging into the tight, wet depth of her perfect, pink pussy.

"Oh, yes, Bobby," Brie shouted as he breached her opening with his long, thick dick.

"Fuck, Brie-Baby," Bobby growled, not understanding how she still felt so tight when it was so easy to slide balls-deep inside her. "You were made to perfectly fit my cock, and only my cock, inside you."

"Yes, Bobby, only you," Brie panted, rocking her hips to match the rhythm of his thrusts.

"And only you for me, Brie-Baby," Bobby groaned, pounding into her in a manner that was way rougher than he wanted to be, but he was unable to back off and maintain control. He was being driven by the most powerful, primal urges he'd ever experienced.

Fuck, you need to ease up and apologize for being too rough, his higher brain was telling him, but the animalistic caveman inside him was in control, preventing him from stopping the carnal mating. Only the fact that Brie was matching him thrust for thrust and chanting his name repeatedly as she came alleviated his guilt for losing control.

As her inner walls clamped down on his cock like a vise, Bobby released his load in the latex that separated them. Even as he was floating in the heavenly state of nirvana that was his orgasm, he wished he was releasing his seed directly into her womb. Unwilling to push her into having their babies before she was ready, he kept that thought to himself, shouting her name in ecstasy as he released her legs. He brought their lips together in a passionate kiss as the final waves of sexual gratification washed over them.

"I love you," Bobby declared, planking above her, so he wouldn't risk crushing her under his body weight. "So much, Brie-Baby."

"I love you, too, Bobby," Brie smiled up at him with her love showing through in her eyes.

Bobby got up and dealt with the condom before untying Brie from the headboard. He took a few moments to rub her wrists, kissing all the way around them to make sure there were no marks from their earlier experimentation. He grabbed a handful of the condoms that had spilled onto the bed before scooping her up into his arms, planning on taking her to the shower for round two.

"Oh," Brie squealed, wrapping her arms around his neck as soon as the shock of being lifted off the bed passed. "Are we going to the other room now?"

"Not yet, Brie-Baby." Bobby carried Brie toward the ensuite bathroom. "Figured we'd clean up, or maybe get dirty again in the shower first."

"Are we going to get any sleep tonight?" Brie giggled.

"Nope." Bobby set her down in the shower before turning it on. He dropped the handful of condoms on the shelf meant for shampoo and soap. "I hope you're ready for a long night. Because I don't think we'll be doing much sleeping." *Or maybe a long weekend where we never get dressed or leave the suite.*

"Can you, um," Brie stuttered, looking down at his dick that was already hard again and begging to be back inside her. "Maybe teach me how to…" Her voice trailed off, but Bobby could tell what she was asking by the way she was licking her lips.

"You don't have to do that, Brie-Baby." Bobby shook his head, tipping her chin up, so he could look into her eyes.

"Isn't taking care of you my *job* as your girlfriend?" Brie asked cheekily as she placed both of her palms on his chest and slowly started trailing them down toward his cock.

Thor jumped in excitement at the thought of Brie's hands on him, but Bobby still shook his head in protest. "No, Brie-Baby, your job as my girlfriend is to let me take care of you."

"That doesn't sound like a very fair partnership," Brie frowned as she outlined his abs with her fingers that were rapidly heading south. "After all the times you've used your hands and mouth on me, I think I deserve equal time getting to touch and taste you."

"Fuck! Brie-Baby," Bobby groaned as her hands followed the lines where his obliques met his abdominal muscles creating the V cut that pointed straight to his cock. He couldn't even think to be able to form words when she tentatively touched him for the first time.

At first, she simply stroked her fingertips over his length, like she was trying to figure out how his dick felt different than the skin elsewhere on his body. Bobby grasped his own hands together behind his head, trying to keep himself in check. Her feather-light touch was so titillating that he was fighting to keep from exploding, especially when she trailed a single fingertip around the head of his cock and found that spot just below the crown that was super sensitive.

"Do you like a gentle touch like this?" Brie watched his dick's reaction, instead of looking up into Bobby's eyes. "Or do you like a rougher touch?"

"You can grip harder around my cock, but stay gentle on my balls," Bobby instructed through clenched teeth. It took all he had to keep from coming like an untried teenager when Brie wrapped both of her hands around his shaft.

He was long and thick, well more than two handfuls for her. He'd known she wouldn't be able to get her fingers and thumb of one hand to meet when wrapped around him because his girth was right at the point of being too much for him to cover the whole circumference with one hand, even with his extra-large hands. That was why he'd never really had a blow job; because the one girl who'd offered when he was in high school couldn't open her mouth wide enough to even get the head in. As petite as Brie was, Bobby didn't think she'd be able to suck him off either. Not without risking lockjaw from the attempt.

"Fuck, Brie-Baby," Bobby moaned as she used the drop of precum that was leaking from his tip to lubricate the movement of her hands as she lined them up to wrap all the way around him and stroked down to his root and back again. "I, fuck! That feels too good. You're gonna hafta stop."

"But I'm just getting started," Brie playfully pouted.

"And if you keep going, I'm gonna come." Bobby dropped his hands to grip her wrists, stilling her movement over his erection. "And I don't wanna come until I'm balls-deep inside you."

"But I haven't even tasted you yet," Brie continued to protest while grinning up at him. "And I don't think you'll fit balls-deep in my mouth. I might be able to get a third of you in my mouth, but I figured I could just use my hands on the rest like I've seen online."

"No, Brie-Baby," Bobby panicked, shaking his head, and pulling her hands off his cock. "I'm too big for your mouth. Hell, if I don't get you worked up and ready first, I'm too big for your pussy."

"Oh, Bobby," Brie cooed, pressing her naked breasts into his lower chest as she hugged him. "I think we both know that you're a perfect fit there."

"Yeah," Bobby had to agree. "And I can't wait any longer for that perfect, tight fit."

"So, you're not even going to let me try to see how much of you I can swallow?" Brie cajoled as Bobby reached for one of the condoms.

Bobby was torn on how to respond to her plea. He hated telling her no whenever she asked him for anything, but he also didn't want to let her try, only to achieve the same disastrous results as the one girl in high school, whose name he couldn't even remember. As much as he loved fantasizing about Brie sucking his cock, he couldn't, in good conscience, risk her jaw popping like what's her name's had in high school. He might not remember her name, but he remembered her having to go see Doc Hayes to deal with her TMJ issues, so she could close her mouth after the attempt. He wanted to explain why he was leery of letting her try, but he also didn't want to bring up his sexual history while they were both naked and about to have sex.

Apparently, closing his eyes and groaning as he struggled with his memories was not the right way to deter Brie from her goal. In the blink of an eye, she'd dropped to her knees and had her hands around his dick again. His eyes flew open to watch what she was doing when he felt her soft lips on his tip.

"Holy…" Bobby groaned as her mouth moved on him, quickly encompassing the head of his cock. The feel of her tongue in that sensitive spot where the crown connected to the shaft was his undoing. "Fuck!"

Bobby crushed the condom package in his fist, balling up his hands, so he didn't grip her hair and push farther into her hot, wet mouth. Not that his restraint did anything to stop her from sucking him farther into her mouth until he felt his tip hit the back of her throat.

Fucking hell! She was right about being able to take about a third of me in her mouth, Bobby inwardly admitted, unable to tear his gaze away from the glorious sight of Brie's pretty, pink lips wrapped around his dick. He was in awe at the amazing woman, and loved that she was the only woman to successfully give him this special gift.

Tell her that later, jackass, Bobby could practically hear his dick screaming at him in Thor's Asgardian accent. *Just enjoy the beautiful blessing she's bestowing on us right now.*

He wished he could stand there for hours, holding back his orgasm to let her lick and suck to her heart's content. But the way she moved her hands in unison with her mouth, bobbing up and down while swirling her tongue around his cock, was too good, too perfect, for him to contain the tingles that started in his spine.

"Fuck, Brie-Baby," Bobby shouted. "You have to stop. I can't..." His voice trailed off as she drew him to the back of her mouth once more, not stopping as he requested. He practically screamed her name as she sucked hard, not giving him any option but to shoot his load down her throat.

Bobby was seeing stars from the intensity of his orgasm. His knees were weak, causing him to fall back into the wall of the shower, barely able to stay standing. Brie's lips came off of his cock with a pop that would've been a frightening reminder of his high school experience had it not been for the fact that he was still watching her intently. *Thank fuck! That was just her smacking her lips.*

"Are you okay?" Brie looked up at him with concern written all over her beautiful face. "Do you need to sit down?"

"Yeah, Brie-Baby, I'm fine," Bobby choked out, but he still took her advice to sit on the bench in the shower.

"You don't look fine." Brie stood to brush her hand over his face, like she was trying to check his temperature by feeling his forehead. "You look like you're about to pass out."

"That's cause you just sucked all my life force outta me," Bobby joked, pulling her hand down off his forehead to kiss her palm before grinning at her.

"I guess you really are fine if you're able to joke around now," Brie giggled.

Bobby pulled her into his arms, resting his head on the pillows of her breasts before trying to explain what just happened. "You have no idea the gamut of emotions you just ran me through, Brie-Baby. You took me from the depths of one of my worst fears to the heights of ecstasy in a matter of minutes."

"How?" Brie pulled back from their embrace just enough that they could look into each other's eyes. "What's there to fear about a blow job?"

"Hurting you," Bobby admitted, flashbacks of having to fix his clothes and drive the girl to the clinic when he wasn't legally old enough to drive, making him shudder. "Having to go find a doctor to pop your jaw back into place in a city where I don't know anyone I would trust to take care of you."

"Bobby, you would never hurt me," Brie tried to assure him, running her fingers through his hair soothingly. "I mean, I suppose I could've choked if I tried to take more of you than I did, but I knew you wouldn't push me past my comfort zone. So, I don't understand why you were worried about hurting me."

"Because I've hurt someone that way before," Bobby confessed, lowering his head back to her chest because he couldn't look her in the eye while telling her about his past. "It was the end of summer, right before my freshman year of high school. My dad dropped me off at the high school on his way in to work that morning, so I could meet up with the rest of the freshman class and a few teachers and older students there to supervise us while we went through orientation. We were done with the school tour and stuff around lunch time. Since I wasn't old enough to drive legally yet, I was about to call my mom to come get me when a senior girl, who was there to help with the orientation, offered me a ride home."

Bobby took a deep breath as the memories flooded over him, finally recalling the girl's first name. "Her name was Cindy. I don't think she even told me her last name. But being a fifteen-year-old horndog, I didn't care what her last name was, I was just thrilled to be propositioned by an older woman. Instead of going straight home, she took me to the trails where all the teenagers used to go to make out. We started out kissing and I thought we were gonna have sex in the back seat of her car, but she said she only did oral on the first date."

Bobby clung to Brie, savoring the feeling of her running her hands over his head and shoulders to comfort him as he continued. "Fuck, I hadn't ever done anything but kiss at that point, so I was fine with whatever she wanted to do. She could see I was a nervous virgin, so she offered to go first. I got my pants and boxers down to my knees and watched her eyes go wide when she saw my erection. She made a comment about my size that made me feel pretty proud of myself, but in hindsight, it probably wasn't a compliment."

He felt Brie's light chuckle more than heard it, and wished he could find some of her humor at how guys always like to think they have a big dick. But he knew having a big dick wasn't always a good thing, so he couldn't laugh with her to lighten the mood.

"She licked me a few times before actually trying to open her mouth wide enough to suck me," Bobby continued morosely, remembering the loud pop making him shudder again. "She couldn't open her mouth wide enough to take in more than the tip. And when she tried to open wider to go over the widest part of the crown, her jaw popped out of place and locked. I'll never forget that loud popping sound."

"Is that why you fell back when I smacked my lips together just now?" Brie's voice was barely loud enough to be heard over the spray of the shower that was rapidly cooling down.

"Yeah," Bobby admitted, nodding his head against her tits. "But thankfully, I was watching you, so I knew it was just you smacking your lips and not another oral-induced injury."

"I'm sorry," Brie apologized, lightly stroking her hand over his hair. "If I'd have known, I wouldn't have done that."

"Not your fault, Brie-Baby," Bobby slightly shook his head, feeling a little less lightheaded now that his blood flow was redirected to his brain instead of his cock.

"So, what happened after her jaw popped?" Brie's voice sounded tentative, as if she wasn't quite sure she wanted to hear the rest.

"She backed off obviously," Bobby sighed, shaking his head. "She couldn't close her mouth because her jaw was dislocated. I yanked my pants up, made sure her clothes were all in place, and hopped into the driver's seat to take her to the clinic in town. I couldn't go back with her while Doc Hayes treated her, since we weren't related. His nurse called my mom to come get me, since I wasn't hurt, as well as Cindy's parents, since she couldn't drive home after he had to sedate her to pop her jaw back into place. I'm not sure what all she ended up having to do to treat her TMJ issues, but she was in some weird headgear when we started school the next week."

"And did ya'll ever have a second date?"

"Uh, no," Bobby confided with a self-deprecating chuckle. "She avoided me like the plague all year and moved out of town right after she graduated. I was so traumatized, I refused to do anything oral, including kissing, until I met you."

"Really?" Brie pushed him back, so he had to look up into her eyes. "But wasn't that the same year you told me you lost your virginity?"

"Yeah, two months later," Bobby admitted, shrugging, and realizing that it was kind of strange how other activities were limited, but he was still down to fuck so soon after the incident. "Apparently, once her jaw was no longer wired shut, Cindy told all the girls in the senior class that my size caused her injury. And while none of them were brave enough to attempt giving me a blow job, my size was still a turn-on for a few of them."

"Your size is definitely a turn-on for me." Brie grinned.

"Yeah?" Bobby raised an eyebrow at his impish girlfriend. "You sure it's not too much for your mouth? Your jaw doesn't hurt after sucking more of me than I ever dreamed possible?"

"Nope." One side of Brie's mouth turned up in a smirk. "But I've been practicing for the last month with a cucumber to make sure I could do a good job, so I've built up my jaw strength to be able to handle you."

"A cucumber?" Bobby couldn't hold back his chuckle at imagining Brie practicing her blow job skills while preparing their nightly salads.

"Yeah, the girls said to practice on a banana," Brie admitted shyly. "But after our first time dry-humping, I knew a banana wouldn't be big enough, so I moved on to a cucumber."

They both chuckled before Brie's expression straightened up into something more serious. "So, um, if you avoided all oral activities since then," she stammered. "Does that mean I'm the only girl you've kissed, um, down there?"

"Oh, I've done a lot more than kissed you down there, Brie-Baby," Bobby smirked, standing to lift Brie into his arms as he got his second wind. "But yes, yours is the only pussy I've ever eaten. The only pussy I ever wanna eat. And I think it's time I got another taste of your sweet, creamy cunt."

Bobby reached over to turn off the now cold water before placing Brie's feet on the bench in the shower. He sat back down and positioned her to straddle his face, so he could devour her delicate flesh for a while. "Let's see how many times I can make you come on my tongue before the water warms back up, so we can clean up."

Chapter Fourteen

Brooklyn walked gingerly on her way out to the SUV to go to the meeting with the attorney Bobby had lined up for her. It was impossible to not feel like she was bowlegged after spending the whole weekend alone with Bobby in their hotel suite. It had been more than she could have ever dreamed of once they finally got past the distance that he'd been putting between them. *And totally worth walking like I spent the whole weekend riding the horses on the ranch, instead of in a hotel in the city. Though, I suppose I was riding Bobby a couple of times this weekend.* Brooklyn stifled a giggle at her mental ramblings, not wanting to explain her laughter to Bobby with the Avingtons in the car with them. *I guess I understand what that old country song means now. As much as I like riding the horses, I much prefer riding my cowboy.*

She'd completely lost count of how many times they'd each come since Friday night, but she knew it was at least in the double digits for both of them. After he'd tied her to the bed for the first time, they'd taken turns giving each other oral pleasure in the shower for round two.

Brooklyn wasn't sure she'd really done a good job of giving Bobby a hummer for the first time, but he swore it was better than all the times he'd fantasized about her sucking him off in the shower since they met, so she supposed she did better than she thought. *Although, after hearing about the only other time he even attempted to get a blow job before this weekend, the bar for giving him good head was set pretty low.*

They'd finished up in the shower with another carnal coupling against the wall after he'd taught her how to put the condom on him.

Even though I'd rather not use them, it was certainly fun to tease him by playing with his penis while putting it on.

Once the hot water had built back up, they'd finished their shower by actually cleaning each other up before Bobby had dried them off and carried her to the other bedroom, where he held her as they slept the rest of the night. After dirtying the second set of sheets when they awoke the next morning, they got dressed long enough for housekeeping to change the bedding in both rooms and do a cursory cleaning of the suite while they ate room service on the balcony. They were back to their normal easy conversation over meals, and Brooklyn prayed it stayed that way, even after they went back to the real world outside their hotel-sex bubble.

Not wanting to be interrupted for anything, other than when their bodies demanded sustenance, they put the Do-Not-Disturb sign on the outer doorknob for the rest of the weekend. In order to decrease the need for changing the sheets, Bobby introduced Brooklyn to the joys of sex everywhere but the bed. The sofa, the dressers, bent over the back of a living room chair, pressed up against the sliding glass door going out to the balcony—no surface was off limits for them to use in their primal mating dance.

When Brooklyn had joked about needing to write down some notes on the different positions and props to use as reference material for the sex scenes she'd be writing while collaborating with Kay on a romance series, Bobby had taken it as a challenge to come up with the most creative ways to copulate. He seemed to love the idea of being her muse and was eager to help her research the various angles they could come together to give them both the ultimate pleasure. His only stipulation was that she not name a character after him, unless he was the hero paired up with a heroine named after her.

I still can't believe after helping me proofread my last book that he hadn't realized Sheriff Adam Appleton was based on him, until I told him yesterday. I mean, a sheriff and a police chief aren't that much different, and Adam is his middle name, so that should've been blatantly obvious. I'm not sure I'm buying his story about thinking I'd already named the character before meeting him.

Speaking of things I'm not sure I can believe, how were we able to make love so many times this weekend without my period starting and causing us to stop our wild romps, like it stopped us from doing more than dry-humping last month? Did it not come because I'm pregnant? Or am I just late from all the stressful meetings we had last week and how anxious I am about all the ones coming up later this week?

Knowing she'd been late a couple of times when she had to pretend to be a happy bride-to-be the previous summer, Brooklyn couldn't rule out stress as a factor in why she hadn't gotten her period yet. But knowing that was a possible reason couldn't dampen her hope that she was expecting her first child with Bobby. *I'm only two days late. How late do I have to be before a pregnancy test is accurate?*

Brooklyn didn't get the chance to ponder her possible pregnancy for long because the vehicle came to a stop, signaling their arrival at her new attorney's office. Bobby's smile revealed that he'd realized she was lost in thought, but he wouldn't ask her what she was thinking with an audience. As usual, he helped her down from the tall truck and held her hand as they walked into the nondescript four-story brick building, with the Avingtons keeping her shielded from anyone who might try to come up behind them or from her other side to do her harm.

Brooklyn really didn't think the added security was necessary, especially after seeing both her father and Clayton and how neither could compete with Bobby on his own, even if they teamed up against him in a fight. But when she'd voiced her opinion on the subject, Bobby had silenced her with a kiss before explaining that having them there freed up his mind to focus on everything else besides their physical safety. She couldn't complain about anything that gave him the peace of mind to be so free and open with her as he'd been all weekend without worrying about whoever her father might have hired to harm them.

She shook off the unwanted fear of what her father might do that would require the services of the Avingtons as they made their way to the third-floor office of Miles Garrett, the attorney Bobby had hired the previous week for her.

After a quick introduction to his paralegal, Kate, they were escorted to Miles' office. Since it wasn't a very large room, Barrett cleared the room as safe for them to enter before he and Blaine took their posts outside the door, ensuring nobody would disturb their meeting.

Kate introduced Brooklyn and Bobby to Miles before moving over to a small desk to the side of Miles' much larger one. Bobby held one of the chairs across the desk from Miles for Brooklyn to take a seat before sitting down in the chair beside her. Once they were all seated, Miles wasted no time in going over what he'd spoken with Bobby about on the phone the week before, making sure he had all the pertinent information correctly listed on the petition he'd filed at the Bibb County Courthouse the previous week, in order to set up the mediation on Wednesday. When Brooklyn confirmed the details of her claim against her father, the attorney transitioned the conversation to talking strategy for how to win her case.

"After looking over the will," the attorney, Miles, started outlining his strategy. "And the laws both here in Georgia and in Texas, I honestly believe the quickest way to resolve your issues would be to declare that you are common-law married."

"What is that?" Brooklyn didn't understand how she could be married without having had a wedding.

"In some states, couples can declare that they're married by meeting certain stipulations without actually getting a marriage license and having a wedding," Miles replied, leaning back in his chair. "Texas is one of them. Since you've been living together, if you claim that you're doing so as husband and wife, and have someone who can testify that you've represented yourselves as a married couple, then the two of you could technically be considered married by common law in the state of Texas. And the state of Georgia, while not having their own laws regarding common-law marriage, recognizes couples who claim common-law from another state as married."

"Aren't there specific time limits we have to have lived together to be considered married by common law?" Bobby reached over and took her hand to comfort her when he noticed her trepidation at using that tactic. "And what proof do we have to show we're living together as a married couple, other than someone saying we've represented ourselves as such?"

"No, there are no time limits or specific time requirements in Texas," Miles replied, smiling at their joined hands. "And just showing that you're sharing household expenses should be enough, since a lot of married women don't change their last names nowadays."

"How 'bout the fact that I added her to my bank accounts back in the beginning of December?" Bobby nodded his head, making it seem like he agreed with the plan. "Well, I added her alias to my accounts anyway. She was using her pen name as an author to stay hidden from her father."

"That's an excellent form of proof." The attorney nodded along in agreement. "Even if we don't go with the common-law marriage angle, we'll need to present the evidence of her using the alias to show that she was in fear of her father finding her as part of our case to get him removed as trustee."

"But there won't be any need to get him removed as trustee, if our common-law marriage entitles her to inherit the estate," Bobby presumed aloud, his words coming out matter-of-factly, almost cold.

Brooklyn's head felt like it was spinning at the thought of being married to Bobby without actually having a wedding. As much as she could see herself spending the rest of her life with Bobby and wanted to be married to him and raising kids with him on the ranch, she didn't want to do it on a technicality and skip the ceremony.

Brooklyn might not have enjoyed getting dressed up for the society events her father had dragged her to in the past, but she'd always dreamed of getting dolled up and walking down the aisle to the man of her dreams to start their lives together. While some people probably thought it was silly and unnecessary, she wanted the pomp and circumstance, the flowers, the church, the poofy white dress, and the romantic proposal. *Even if I have to be the one proposing because Bobby's first attempt at asking me to marry him sucked.*

"Brooklyn also wouldn't have to get the board of directors' approval to merge Ashbury Enterprises in with Burleson Incorporated either," Mr. Garrett elaborated, bringing Brooklyn back out of her runaway thoughts. "With Texas being a community property state, your assets would be shared. I'm not sure exactly how the merger would be worked out completely, since I'm not licensed in Texas, but I don't think it would need to be a buyout the way you've already presented to the Ashbury board."

"It doesn't matter how it would be done," Brook interjected, her exasperation coming through loud and clear in her voice. Brooklyn turned to look directly at Bobby before explaining. "Just like I told you a couple of weeks ago that I wouldn't marry you to get control of the company, I'm not going to sink to my father's level by claiming we're common-law married to manipulate the system either."

"I know, Brie-Baby," Bobby sighed, bringing their joined hands to his lips. Even the barest brush of his lips against the back of her hand was enough to leave Brooklyn tingling with the need to be closer to Bobby, but she couldn't act on that need in the middle of a meeting with her attorney. "I just thought it would be the least stressful way to go, and I know you're stressed enough right now, so I wanna take any of that off your shoulders I can."

"I know, and I love you for wanting to ease my burdens that way." Brooklyn leaned over to kiss him on the cheek. "But I think we're still better off going through mediation to have my father removed as the trustee and pushing for the sale of Ashbury to Burleson."

"Okay, if that's what you want," Miles conceded, bringing both Bobby and Brooklyn's attention back to him. "That's what we'll do. But we can always pull the common-law-marriage card out of our back pocket if the mediation doesn't seem to be going in your favor any other way."

Brooklyn nodded, not wanting to argue with her own attorney, but also not wanting to play the common-law-marriage card, even if it was the last resort. Thankfully, he accepted her nod as her agreement with his plan and went on to discuss the other things they needed to present at the mediation. When he asked if she had any witnesses that would be willing to testify to her state of mind when she left her father's home back in November, Brooklyn told him all about Mary and Joe Turner and how they'd helped her.

After a brief discussion with Bobby about where they should meet, the attorney picked up the phone on his desk and dialed the number Brooklyn gave him for their cottage. She knew that if they weren't home, Mary would forward the phone to her cell phone, so her father wouldn't complain about not being able to reach them when he had a task for them to complete. Brooklyn just hoped as they spoke with Mary on speakerphone that her father hadn't tapped their lines in the hopes of finding Brooklyn by her calling them.

Even if he's tapped their lines, all he'll hear on this conversation is that I want to see them while I'm in town. I'll wait until we're meeting face-to-face to discuss their testimony against him.

~~~
~~~

Bobby was doing his best to reserve judgement until after meeting the older couple Brie often referred to as her foster parents. Though she'd only ever described her relationship with Joe and Mary Turner in positive terms, he couldn't help but wonder why they hadn't helped her escape her father's prison of a home as soon as she turned eighteen, instead of making her suffer in that neglectful environment for almost five more years. It was only the fact they'd been the only people to show her love for most of her life that made him decide not to berate them for their roles in keeping her hostage in her father's home the instant they arrived at the restaurant where they were meeting for dinner.

Unsure if he could really trust them to have Brie's best interest at heart, however, he'd, at least, insisted on them meeting at a chain restaurant on the other side of town from their hotel. That had been a compromise they'd decided on before making the call because Brie didn't feel safe going to their cottage on her father's estate, where she knew Mary would suggest they meet. Since Bobby didn't feel comfortable letting anyone from her old life know where they were staying while they were in town, he'd asked her lawyer for suggestions on where they could meet the older couple to have a private conversation without giving away their hotel information to anyone who might inadvertently give it to Bradley Barns or one of his associates.

Brie had first argued that neither Mary nor Joe would give her father any information about her whereabouts, but she'd quickly backed down when Bobby insisted he'd rather be safe than sorry, if the older couple didn't know their cell phones were bugged and gave away her location without realizing it. Bobby had felt bad for how she'd blanched when he presented the worst-case scenario, hating being the one to burst her bubble of innocence about the possibilities. But he wouldn't risk Brie's life on the off chance that sending his daughter off to be raped by a man more than twice her age wasn't the worst atrocity Bradley Barns was capable of committing.

Bobby knew that if he was willing to have his daughter suffer like that, then he was more than capable of killing her to claim her inheritance as her next of kin. That was why he'd hired Avington Security to help him keep her safe. But even the best bodyguards on the planet were only effective when their protectee didn't tell her would-be assassin where to find her.

He shook off the morbid thoughts about her father when Brie jumped up excitedly from her seat beside him, scooting all the way around the circular booth hidden away in the corner of the restaurant to get out without waiting for him to move out of her way, where he'd been seated between her and the other patrons. He also stood as an older couple approached, needing to be the one to get Brie out of harm's way if either of the Avingtons had to subdue a potential attacker. *Not that these two look capable of harming anyone,* Bobby thought, shaking his head at Brie's animated excitement at their arrival. *No wonder Brie trusts them. He looks like Santa Claus without the beard, and she looks like his cookie baking Missus.*

"Oh, Brook," Mary Turner exclaimed, returning Brie's excitement with a warm embrace. "I've missed you so much!"

"I've missed you, too!" Brie shouted, returning the sixty-something-year-old woman's hug.

So much for maintaining our privacy for this conversation, Bobby groused, noticing how their loud greeting drew the attention of everyone in the restaurant. The Avington brothers both stood from their seats at the next booth over to block the view of the other customers of the restaurant, prompting Bobby to try and get everyone seated, so they'd quit making a scene.

"Why don't we all take our seats before we make introductions?" Bobby motioned toward the booth as soon as Brie and Mary released each other.

"Sorry, I just got too excited to stay seated," Brie half-heartedly apologized, giving Joe a quick hug before stepping back toward Bobby and scooting into the booth. Once Mary had scooted into the booth on the other side, Bobby and Joe each sat between the women and the rest of the room.

"Thanks, guys." Bobby nodded to the Avingtons, who returned the nod and retook their seats at the next booth.

"Mary and Joe Turner," Brie started, reaching over to grab Bobby's hand. "I'd like you to meet Bobby Burleson, my boyfriend."

"It's nice to meet you, Bobby." Joe reached across the table to offer his hand to Bobby to shake.

"It's nice to meet you as well." Bobby shook the older man's hand.

"I feel like I already know you, but yet I don't." Mary smiled across the table. "Brook's emails were very cryptic in telling us how she was doing as if she were a character in one of her books, but I couldn't stop myself from hoping she'd met her one true love when she described the young man helping Mary Kate lead her best life."

Bobby had to smile at the mention of the Sheriff Adam character from Brie's last book. He'd recognized the similarities between himself and the character when he'd first proofread the book. But he still found it hard to believe that she'd given the character his middle name and had only included him in the book after moving into his house. That meant she'd written two-thirds of the book in the six weeks she'd lived with him before publishing it. *Hell, more like the first four weeks she was on the ranch, since the last two weeks before publication were all spent proofreading and editing.*

"I certainly hope so, too," Bobby agreed, bringing their joined hands to his lips, and kissing the back of Brie's hand before returning them to the table.

"So, is life about to imitate art?" Mary looked anxiously between Bobby and Brie. "Are you in town to make the arrests that will keep her safe?"

"Not exactly," Bobby shrugged, shaking his head. "Brie used her artistic license to give Sheriff Adam jurisdiction that I don't have in the real world."

"In the real world, I'm having to sue my father to have him removed as trustee of my inheritance and get him to pay back the money he's stolen from me for the past eighteen years," Brie explained, her sweet smile evaporating at the mention of her father. "That's why I needed to meet with you both tonight, instead of waiting for everything to be settled. I need you both to testify on my behalf at the mediation later this week."

"Testify about what?" Mary questioned as her husband nodded somberly and jumped into the conversation.

"Of course, we'll testify on your behalf, Brook."

"Wait, you expected this?" Mary sharply turned her head to look at Joe. "That's why you insisted we pack our bags as if we were going on vacation before coming to see Brook tonight."

"I didn't know if she'd need our help with anything else." Joe told his wife, motioning toward Brook with one hand while clasping

Mary's hand in his other. "But I knew it wouldn't be safe for us to go home after seeing her, unless Bradley Barns is being arrested while we're here."

Thank fuck! They really are on her side in all this. Bobby realized that this elderly couple wouldn't have had the resources to help Brie escape her father's fortress if she hadn't earned them with her book sales, so they'd done all they could to keep her relatively safe by staying on the estate long past when they were comfortable working there to care for her when she had nobody else.

"Unfortunately, I have no idea when he'll be arrested." Bobby shook his head in frustration at how long the feds were taking to build their case. "But I doubt it'll be tonight."

"You've talked to the local authorities to set it in motion, though, right?" Joe's gray eyes darkened as he looked at Bobby imploringly.

"Yes, but it'll actually be the FBI who makes the arrests," Bobby informed him, hoping his small smile was reassuring to the older man. "Probably the end of this week or the beginning of next week."

"Good." Joe showed his approval of the coming arrests with a single dip of his chin. "We should be able to evade his goons until then."

Bobby didn't get a chance to discuss where they'd be staying as the waitress came to take their order. They all quickly perused the menus to place their order. Once the waitress had walked away from their table, Brie changed the subject, going over what they would need to testify about in the mediation on Wednesday.

Talking about their observations of life on the estate of Bradley Barns led to the older couple telling Bobby and Brie all about how they'd met while working for William and Susan Ashbury, when their daughter, Madeline, was a young child in 1973. They reminisced about watching both Madeline and her daughter, Brooklyn, grow up on the estate. Bobby loved watching Brie light up at hearing stories about how similar she was to her mother as a child. He also appreciated how the Turners seemed to gloss over the negative aspects of the estate transitioning from the Ashbury's control to Barns' control, so Brie didn't have to relive the deaths of her mother and grandparents while they ate dinner. Talking about how Bradley Barns had mistreated his daughter was more than enough negativity for one night.

By the end of the meal, Bobby felt like he knew the Turners well enough to be one-hundred percent on board with Brie's plan to invite them to move to the ranch, even if they chose to retire instead of working once they got there. They'd more than shown him their trustworthiness, as well as their love for Brie.

"Do you already have a place to stay tonight where you'll be safe?" Bobby inquired as he slipped his card into the folder to pay for their meals.

"I planned on finding a hotel for the time being." Joe nodded, even though his words didn't indicate he had a specific hotel picked out yet.

From the way Brie's hand squeezed his, Bobby knew she wanted the older couple to come to the same hotel where he and Brie were staying and being protected by the Avingtons.

"I think Brie and I would both prefer it if you stayed in the same hotel we're at." Bobby gently squeezed her hand back, and hoped she understood his unspoken message that he would protect them because they were her chosen family. "I've booked the whole floor to make sure my family is comfortable when they come back into town tomorrow night, so I'm sure we have a room for you already."

"I wouldn't want to impose and put your family out of one of the rooms," Joe started to protest.

"It's no imposition," Bobby stated. When the waitress came to pick up the folder with the dinner ticket and his credit card inside, he turned to her and gave her the instructions to put the Avingtons' meals on his card. "Be sure to put the charges for the two gentlemen in the next booth on my card as well."

"Oh." The waitress looked shocked, her mouth dropping open as she looked over at the Avingtons.

"They're my security detail," Bobby clarified. "I just forgot to tell you to put our meals all on one tab when we ordered."

"Okay, yes, sir," the waitress sputtered, taking a few steps over to the Avingtons' table to pick up their check as well before walking away to run his card.

Turning back to the Turners, Bobby continued explaining his thoughts about having them stay close. "It'll be safer for everyone if you stay where the Avingtons can keep us all protected. Besides, there are eight suites on that floor. Brie and I are in one, the Avingtons are in the one next door, and if the three family members who are coming back to Macon tomorrow each pick their own suite, we'll still only be using five of them. There's plenty of room and it's already been paid for, so there's no reason for you to risk staying somewhere else without security."

"Don't bother arguing," Brie interjected, shaking her head, and smiling. "The bulls aren't the only ones on the Burleson Ranch who are bullheaded. Though Bobby's mother, Hazel, swears it's a Burleson trait, I think Bobby and his siblings got a double dose of bullheadedness by inheriting it from both of their parents."

"You're absolutely right about that, Brie-Baby," Bobby chuckled, bringing their joined hands to his lips once more.

"Oh, goodness," Mary cooed, flashing a beaming smile. "I can't wait to see what a triple dose looks like when ya'll have kids."

Me either, Bobby thought, but couldn't quite make himself say, so he didn't put any pressure on Brie to make it happen sooner rather than later. *Me, fucking, either.*

~~~

Wednesday, February 6, 2019

With having so many more people to protect than just Brooklyn and Bobby, the Avington brothers had called in two more teams of bodyguards to make sure they were all covered, as they would be at different locations while the mediation meetings were taking place. Bobby had introduced Brooklyn to Brady as the third Avington brother, though she hadn't actually met his friend, Blake Avington, yet. The other three men assigned to guard the Turners and Burlesons had been introduced with the single names of Knight, Lincoln, and Miller, but she wasn't sure if those were their first or last names. Regardless, she was glad to know that Mary, Joe, and the three Burlesons, who had come back to town for the mediation, were all being kept safe while they were waiting to be called in to testify during the hearing-like procedures being held in the Ashbury Enterprises' office.

Brooklyn really hoped Bobby was wrong in his belief that her father could hire someone to hurt her, or anyone who was trying to
~~~

help her, but she agreed with his opinion of it being better to be safe than sorry. She certainly felt more comfortable having to see her father again for the mediation meeting with Bobby and the two bodyguards beside her. She wasn't sure she'd have been strong enough to go through all this with only the attorney, Miles Garrett, on her side.

While she knew having the extra security there eased her worries about any outside threats hired by her father, she also knew the mental strength to face her father came solely from having Bobby there supporting her. She appreciated the fact that he reined in his alpha tendency to take over, letting her make the decisions about how they were going to proceed through each meeting. He made her feel strong enough to speak up for herself, not only by making sure she was seated in the power position in every meeting they attended, but also by holding her hand to lend her his strength if she needed it.

So far, she'd only had to squeeze his hand to let him take over for her the one time, though that had been accidental on her part, brought on by her outrage. *He definitely handled the situation better than I would have with how mad I was right then,* Brooklyn thought as they took their seats in the conference room. *Hopefully, the mediator won't be offended if I get that mad again and have to call on Bobby to speak for me once more in these meetings.*

"I'm Mikayla Newman, Bibb County mediator," the thirty-something looking woman introduced herself once everyone seemed to have entered the room and the door was closed. "I understand that we're holding this mediation here, so the Ashbury board can observe, since the outcome will have an impact on the company."

There were several nods and "yeses" from around the room, but nobody said anything in response to her statement.

"As the board members are only here as observers, I would appreciate it if you would all please move your chairs along that wall," Mikayla directed, pointing to the wall of windows separating the room from the hallway to Brooklyn's right, behind where Bobby was seated in the first seat on the long side of the table beside Brooklyn, who sat at what she considered the head of the table. "I will sit in the central position on this side of the table." She motioned to the chair in front of where she was standing in the middle of the left long side of the

Leah Mae Wright

table. "With the attorneys on this side of their clients in the end seats at the table and any witnesses they have on the other side of the table."

"Ms. Newman." Miles Garrett dipped his head in greeting to the mediator from his seat on Brooklyn's left where the mediator had indicated he was to sit. "We were given instructions for our witnesses to wait to be called before coming to the building."

"That's fine, Mr. Garrett," Mikayla Newman replied, taking her seat. "Actually, that's probably best due to the space constraints of doing the mediation here, instead of in a courtroom."

There was some confusion when only half of the board members moved their chairs to the proper location and the other half appeared to be moving into the chairs the mediator had designated for witnesses for her father. "I was told there were twelve board members." Mikayla arched an eyebrow, pointedly looking at the people trying to squeeze together at the other end of the table and the two Avington brothers who were standing behind Brooklyn. "Why are there only six who are seated out of the way?"

"My client, Mr. Barns, is one of those board members," the attorney seated by her father explained before pointing toward the five board members seated beside Clayton Donaldson at her father's end of the table. "And these board members are our witnesses."

"And you are?" Mikayla Newman glared at the attorney, narrowing her eyes at him.

"Callen O'Shay, your honor," the attorney replied, smiling at the mediator, who appeared to be a few years younger than him, as if his smile would win him favors from her.

"I'm not a judge," Mikayla censured, blowing out a breath of frustration. "You can address me as Ms. Newman, not your honor."

"My apologies, Ms. Newman," Callen replied. "I'm a corporate attorney, so I normally focus on drawing up contracts. I'm not familiar with the terminology of the courtroom or mediation such as this."

"I'm afraid that's probably not all you're unfamiliar with," Mikayla sighed, turning to direct her next comment to Brooklyn's father. "Mr. Barns, as much as I hate to waste everyone's time here this morning, I would be remiss in my duties if I didn't offer you a postponement of these proceedings, so you can find a litigation attorney to represent you."

"I don't believe that's necessary, Ms. Newman," Bradley Barns stated. "As this is a conflict over the stipulations of my late wife's will, I'm sure Mr. O'Shay's knowledge of contracts will be more relevant than his inexperience in court procedures."

"Very well," Mikayla conceded, giving Bradley a single nod in agreement to keep Mr. O'Shay as his attorney. "As mediation is more informal than a typical court appearance, we can do a few things out of order for how they would be handled in a courtroom. Instead of asking the attorneys to give their opening statements, I'd rather ask what pertinent information the board members have to give as your witnesses, so I can determine whether their testimony will be allowed, or if they'll need to move over into an observational role with the rest of the board."

"They're here as character witnesses, Ms. Newman," Mr. O'Shay offered, giving her a sly smile. "As Ms. Barns is asking the court to remove her father as the trustee of her inheritance, he's asked his colleagues to testify to his position in the community and ability to fulfill the duties of his current role."

Turning to look directly at the board members, Mikayla Newman queried, "Can any of you testify regarding the location of the funds Mr. Barns has been managing for his daughter? Or to his treatment of her while in their home and not in public?"

The board members in question looked toward Bradley Barns before turning their attention back to the mediator and shaking their heads in the negative. Brooklyn could feel Bobby shaking through their joined hands and knew he was trying to stop himself from laughing at the obvious irritation of her father. Truth be told, she was biting her tongue to keep from laughing herself, as Ms. Newman instructed the board members to all move to the wall with their counterparts.

"Who are you and what are you here to testify to today?" Mikayla looked directly at Clayton Donaldson, who was still seated beside her father.

"I'm Clayton Donaldson, Ms. Newman," Clayton's mouth spread in what could only be described as a smarmy smile. "I'm Ms. Barns' fiancé, here to testify that she's in breach of contract for not attending our wedding."

"That's not pertinent to these proceedings." Mikayla shook her head. "But I'll allow you to stay, for now." She then turned to look at Brooklyn, or rather the two hulking bodyguards standing behind her. "Who are you and why are you not seated?"

"Barrett and Brady Avington of Avington Security," Barrett introduced both himself and his brother over Brooklyn's head. "We're here to protect Ms. Barns from her father, and anyone he might hire to harm her, ma'am."

"Very well," Mikayla nodded, an appreciative expression briefly flickering over her face as she looked at the two hunky men. "You may stay where you are, but please sit down to observe." She then looked directly at Bobby, raising an eyebrow when she noticed their joined hands on the table.

"I'm Heart's Destiny, Texas, Police Chief, Bobby Burleson, ma'am," Bobby announced before the mediator could ask. "I'm here to testify to the evidence uncovered after Brooklyn came to me to protect her from her father."

"Excellent," Mikayla smiled, looking around the room as she continued. "Now that the introductions have all been made and everyone is where they're supposed to be, we can get started with mediating the case of Brooklyn Barns versus Bradley Barns, the third. Though none of you will be sworn in with your hand on the Bible when you give your testimony, I do ask that you each raise your right hand and declare your intention to tell the truth as if you were being sworn in during a typical court proceeding."

"Repeat after me," Mikayla directed as soon as everyone in the room had raised their right hands. "I, state your name, do solemnly swear to tell the truth, the whole truth, and nothing but the truth, so help me God."

All nineteen people present, not counting Mikayla Newman, repeated her words, inserting their own name where appropriate. Brooklyn wondered how they would deal with the Turners not being present for the mass swearing in when it came time for them to testify, but quickly shook off the thoughts as Miles Garrett began his opening statement, so she didn't miss anything that was said during the proceedings.

"We're here today asking the courts to remove Bradley Stanton Barns, the third, as the trustee of the Ashbury estate due to his gross misconduct in that role for the last eighteen-and-a-half years," Miles began speaking from his seat.

I guess with mediation being informal, he's not supposed to stand like the attorneys do on television to deliver his opening statement, Brooklyn thought, turning in her seat to focus on the man speaking.

"In addition to presenting evidence regarding the millions of dollars Mr. Barns has embezzled from his daughter's monthly stipend for over eighteen years, we will also be presenting witnesses to the neglect and emotional abuse he's inflicted on her since her mother's death on August eighth in the year two-thousand. It is due to his ongoing behavior that we request the court either release Ms. Barns entire inheritance to her at this time, or appoint a new trustee that will ensure Ms. Barns receives her full monthly stipend, until such time as she fulfills the stipulations of the will to receive her full inheritance."

"Thank you, Mr. Garrett." Ms. Newman nodded once to recognize that he was finished speaking before turning her attention to the other end of the table. "You may now give your opening statement, Mr. O'Shay."

"Thank you, Ms. Newman," Callen O'Shay smirked, standing as he started to speak. "Mr. Barns has been an upstanding member of the community since he first started working at Ashbury Enterprises in nineteen-eighty-eight. He worked his way up from his first position in the mailroom to upper-level management before marrying Madeline Ashbury in nineteen-ninety-four. He served proudly in his role of Vice President when Mrs. Ashbury-Barns took over the CEO position for her late father. And when he lost his wife eighteen-and-a-half years ago, he valiantly stepped into the CEO position to lead Ashbury Enterprises into the new millennium. His extensive business acumen, as well as the love he has for his family, make him the ideal person to act as the trustee for the Ashbury estate. Therefore, we ask that you dismiss this frivolous case and let him continue to do the stellar job he has done for almost two decades."

Brooklyn sat stoically as she listened to the drivel her father's attorney was spewing. Bobby sneezed into his elbow beside her, and she turned to him, worried he might be getting sick.

"Sorry, Ms. Newman," Bobby apologized, when he noticed Brooklyn wasn't the only one looking in his direction. "Allergies.

Leah Mae Wright

Ya'll have different, uh, pollens and, uh, other allergens here than we have in Texas."

"Yeah, he's allergic to bullshit," one of the Avington brothers whispered behind her, causing Brooklyn to have to fight not to giggle. Bobby smiled over her shoulder, obviously also hearing what the bodyguard said.

It was only after hearing the bodyguard, who she thought was Brady Avington, speak that she realized Bobby had covered his own uttering of the word "bullshit" with a fake sneeze. *Hopefully, Ms. Newman didn't hear any of their comments to have a reason to kick them out of the meeting.*

"I actually don't have the authority to dismiss the case, Mr. O'Shay," Mikayla Newman informed them, apparently not hearing the opinion of Brooklyn's boyfriend and bodyguards regarding the other attorney's opening statement. "My role here is to see if we can settle the case out of court by determining an outcome both parties can agree on. If that's not possible, then I will be scheduling a court date for a judge to look at all the evidence to make the decision on how it's settled."

"If you're just here to settle things without having to go to court, then we can end this whole process right now by having my daughter fulfill the stipulations of the will to be able to inherit the estate," Bradley Barns stated, leaning back in his chair like he'd just won the case without a fight.

"And what stipulations of the will would you have her fulfill?" Mikayla tilted her head inquisitively at Brooklyn's father.

"The will specifies that Brooklyn will inherit the bulk of the estate when she turns twenty-five or gets married, whichever comes first," Bradley Barns stated, his lips contorting into a sneer. "If she doesn't wish to wait two more years to claim her inheritance, then she and Clayton can go to the courthouse right now and get married."

Oh, hell, no! Brooklyn hid her inner southern spitfire behind her mask of civility that she'd had to wear for so many years in the presence of her father that it was now second nature.

"No, fuckin', way that's happening," Bobby growled, pointing at Brooklyn's father, then Clayton. "I'll never let you send Brie off to be raped by that dirty old man."

Shit! Shit! Shit! How do I fix this, so Bobby doesn't end up in jail for murder? Brooklyn mentally questioned herself. She looked around the room, hoping for an idea of what to do to stop the yelling match between her father, Clayton, and Bobby. When her gaze met that of her attorney, she remembered his idea from Monday about claiming common-law marriage to get her inheritance. *Not really the way I want to do it, but it's the only way I can think of to settle everything now.*

"Stop!" Brooklyn screamed. "You're fighting over a moot point! I can't marry creepy Clayton when the state of Texas already considers me common-law married to Bobby!"

"Order," Mikayla shouted, slamming her hands down on the conference room table like a judge's gavel. "Everyone take your seats and don't say another word unless I specifically ask you to speak."

Once Bradley, Clayton, Bobby, and both Avingtons sat back down, Mikayla Newman turned to look directly at Brooklyn. "Ms. Barns, did you just say that you're already married?"

"Sort of," Brooklyn shrugged, not quite sure how to answer, since she didn't really consider herself married, but she could still make the argument of being common-law married.

"Explain," Mikayla ordered, obviously irritated by Brooklyn's non-answer.

Before Brooklyn could refer to her attorney to clarify the reasoning for considering her and Bobby married by common law in Texas, the door burst open and six men in tactical gear stormed into the room.

"FBI," the first one in the room shouted. "Everyone stay in your seats."

Brooklyn recognized Agents Adams and Barclay from meeting with them the week before, so she relaxed back in her chair to enjoy watching her father being arrested. *Can I win this mediation by default while he's behind bars?*

"Bradley Stanton Barns, the third," Agent Adams barked, walking past the agent that had entered the room before him to go over to the other end of the room where her father was seated. "You're under arrest for embezzlement, unlawful imprisonment, and human trafficking. You have the right to remain silent…"

Brooklyn couldn't focus to hear everything else the FBI agent was saying after her jaw dropped from hearing the human trafficking charge. She was snapped back into the moment by the sound of the cuffs being slapped on her father's wrists, only to realize that as soon as Agent Adams had quit speaking, Agent Barclay had started rattling off the same charges against Clayton Donaldson.

"Sorry for the disruption, folks," one of the other agents apologized as the two men were being carted out in cuffs. "We'll get out of your hair and let you get back to your meeting just as soon as one of you can direct me to the chairman of the board."

"I'm the chairman of the board." Leland Remington held up his hand from his seat on the side of the room only a few feet away from the FBI agent.

"Then if you will please sign here," the agent instructed Mr. Remington, holding a clipboard out to Leland, and pointing to where he was supposed to sign his name. "This is stating that you received the copies of the paperwork to charge these two men with embezzling from Ashbury Enterprises."

"Embezzling from Ashbury?" Leland questioned, pulling a pen out of his inner jacket pocket, and signing his name.

"It's all in the paperwork, sir," the agent informed him, removing a manilla envelope from under the paper he had Leland sign and handing it to the chairman of the board before departing.

Once the agents had all evacuated the room, Ms. Newman turned to look at Mr. O'Shay. "Don't you need to follow them to see about getting your client released on bail?"

Callen O'Shay sat there opening and closing his mouth like a fish out of water for several long moments before saying, "I'm not a criminal attorney. I don't think there's anything I could do to help either of them. Not that I would want to if those charges are accurate."

"Not that you'd be allowed to as part of the legal department of Ashbury Enterprises," Leland Remington corrected as he flipped through the papers he'd removed from the manilla envelope. "But after the whole board has a chance to review these documents, we might need to call you back in here to review their employment contracts, so we go through all the proper steps to terminate them."

"Is Mr. Barns position with Ashbury Enterprises part of the stipulations of the will as trustee of the Ashbury estate?" Mikayla Newman inquired.

"I'm not sure," Leland Remington answered. "I know his position on the board of directors of Ashbury Enterprises is due to his being the trustee of the estate and the company being the majority of the holdings, but I'd have to look back at all the paperwork from almost twenty years ago to know about the CEO position."

"Then why don't we adjourn the mediation for today to allow your board the time to review how his arrest will impact the company," Mikayla decided, closing the case on the tablet she'd been using to take notes on the meeting. "And reconvene tomorrow morning to discuss a way to settle everything we can without Mr. Barns in attendance."

Both attorneys quickly agreed, but Brooklyn had a question to ask first before she was ready to leave the room. She raised her hand to ask permission to speak, feeling silly for the childish gesture, but also unsure of another way to get the mediator's attention without being rude.

"Yes, Ms. Barns," Mikayla acknowledged Brooklyn's raised hand with a nod in her direction.

"Can we actually settle the suit against my father without him present?" Brooklyn silently prayed that it was possible.

"Depending on how everything was drawn up in your mother's will, your father's employment contract, and the corporate bylaws, we might be able to appoint a new trustee," Mikayla answered. "But if you wish to use the marriage clause to claim your full inheritance, you'll have to set a court date to get the judge to sign off on it. That would be a simple appearance by you and your husband, and wouldn't require your father to attend either. It's just not something I can do in these proceedings. As for the money your father stole from you over the years that you're trying to reclaim, he will have to be present regardless of whether it's in mediation to come to terms on a settlement amount or in court to get a judgement against him."

"Okay, thank you." Brooklyn gave the other woman a slight smile. "Hopefully, we can appoint a new trustee tomorrow."

"We'll see." Mikayla returned the smallest upturn of her lips before walking toward the exit of the room. She turned back to Brooklyn and added, "Be sure your witnesses and trustee candidates are present for tomorrow's meeting," before leaving.

Leah Mae Wright

"I will," Brooklyn replied to the mediator's retreating back. *Hopefully, the room won't be too crowded with the five extra people and their four extra bodyguards.*

Bobby extended his hand to Brooklyn to assist her out of her seat, so they could leave the board to their task for the day. They walked hand in hand out of the office, but Brooklyn was in too much of a daze from the events of the morning to pay attention to her surroundings as they exited the building and got into the waiting SUV. She just kept running through potential scenarios of what might happen the next day in her mind, trusting Bobby to get her safely back to the hotel.

<div align="center">~~~</div>

Thursday, February 7, 2019

Bobby was surprised to find that the Ashbury board had insisted on moving their meeting down two floors to the larger room where they normally held company-wide events, needing to be able to accommodate the larger group that came with Brooklyn to the second day of mediation. But even though the new room held several tables with space for them to all spread out, there were still only six people seated at the head table for the meeting—Mikayla Newman as the mediator, Brie as the plaintiff, with Bobby and her attorney, Miles Garrett, flanking her, and Callen O'Shay representing the company, with Leland Remington at his side.

He wasn't sure how the mediation could legally proceed without anyone really there to represent Bradley Barns' interest in the outcome but, being unfamiliar with the differences in the legal systems between the various states, he wasn't going to argue the point that would actually be against Brie's best interest. He may have been at the head table, but it was only because he was there to support Brie, so he just sat back to observe. He still kept her hand clutched in his, making sure she had a way to signal him, just in case she felt overwhelmed and needed him to take over for her.

Yeah, keep telling yourself that, Bobby imagined his inner caveman saying in a voice similar to the one he dreamed up for the speech pattern of his dick. *I'm sure it has nothing to do with how much I*

426

constantly have to touch her, like how I hold her all night every night after making love to her.

Bobby shook off his inner ramblings to pay attention to the legal proceedings going on around him. When Mikayla Newman opened the meeting, she repeated the mass swearing in that she'd done the previous day to cover the people who hadn't been there the day before. Then she started the mediation by turning to direct her first question to the chairman of the board. "Mr. Remington, what did you uncover in the documents concerning the corporation with regard to Mr. Barns' role as trustee of the Ashbury estate?"

"That Madeline Ashbury was as brilliant as she was beautiful," Leland Remington proclaimed, the elderly man's face breaking out in a huge smile. "She set everything up to be determined at the discretion of the other eleven members of the board of directors, as to who was the trustee since that person would also be appointed to the board to take her place and assume the CEO position."

"So, Ms. Barns didn't have to file suit against her father to have him removed as trustee?" Ms. Newman smiled.

"No, ma'am," Leland Remington beamed. "She just had to inform the board of directors of the need to remove her father and appoint a new trustee. Once we realized that yesterday afternoon, the board unanimously voted to remove Bradley Barns from all three positions, trustee of the estate, his board position, and as CEO."

Damn, that seems too fuckin' easy, Bobby thought, rubbing his thumb over the back of Brie's hand reassuringly while he waited for the other shoe to drop, knowing there had to be a but in there somewhere.

"Did you also appoint a new trustee?" Mikayla Newman relaxed back in her seat like she thought her job might be over already.

"No, Ms. Newman," Leland Remington sighed, ever so slightly shaking his head. "We wanted to discuss the possibility of releasing the full estate to Ms. Barns, in light of the common-law marriage mentioned yesterday."

Brie raised her free hand as if asking for permission to speak while adamantly shaking her head no to Mr. Remington's suggestion.

"Yes, Ms. Barns?" Mikayla Newman gave Brie a questioning look.

"I don't care if the state of Texas thinks living together and having both our names on a bank account shows we're married," Brie argued, dropping her raised hand to cover Bobby's where he was holding the one closest to him. "I won't consider myself married until I walk down the aisle and say, 'I do', and I won't sink to my father's level to cheat the system on a technicality by claiming otherwise."

"If you weren't willing to use the common-law marriage to claim your estate," Mikayla prodded, her expression one of critical examination as she observed Brie's response, "why did you mention it yesterday?"

"Because Mr. Garrett mentioned it to Bobby and I on Monday," Brie shrugged, darting her eyes at the attorney, while pressing both of her hands as close as possible to Bobby's hand between them. "And when my father started pushing for me to marry creepy Clayton again, it was the only thing I could think of at the time as an excuse for why I couldn't do what he wanted."

Her hands trembled over his as she turned to look directly at him, a single tear slipping down her cheek. Bobby reached over with his free hand to wipe it away as she continued speaking.

"I knew Bobby promised not to let them near me, and he's done an excellent job of that in the week we've been in town. Besides hiring security to keep me safe, he's stayed between me and both of them whenever I've had to be in the same room with them since coming back to Georgia. But when they started yelling at each other yesterday, I saw a scary side of my father that I've never seen before. It terrified me to realize that my own father was not only capable of hurting me or anyone willing to help me, but he actively wanted to have his friend torture and rape me to gain control of the estate, and they were both willing to kill anyone who stood in their way of making that happen. I thought if I could throw them the curveball of having to contest my common-law marriage to try to regain control of the estate, then it would give the FBI time to arrest them before they had the chance to order a hit on my boyfriend."

Bobby chuckled, not willing to point out to Brie that claiming him as her husband only solidified her father's need to eliminate him to get to her. *My girl's been watching too many unrealistic crime dramas. Maybe I should show more interest in the home improvement and travel shows she likes to pick to watch instead.*

"I'm still afraid that they have access to the millions they've stolen and stashed in offshore accounts and can order that hit from behind bars," Brie finished, her beautiful blue eyes glassy with unshed tears.

"Oh, Brie-Baby," Bobby crooned, releasing her hands to cup her face with both of his huge mitts, so he could pull her closer and lean in to press their foreheads together. "You don't have to worry about that. The feds have frozen all their accounts, and have forensic accountants going through them with a fine-toothed comb to be able to return every stolen dime to its rightful owners once they're convicted. They won't even have much left of their legitimate salaries after court costs and fines, not to mention what the IRS will take for any unclaimed income they've had by earning interest on the stolen funds. They're not gonna be able to afford to order dinner, much less a hit."

"You're sure?" With their gazes locked, Bobby knew she could tell if he was misleading her.

"Positive, Brie-Baby," Bobby assured her, pecking her lips as additional proof. "But if you're still scared, I'll keep up all our increased security measures until you feel safe again."

"As touching as all this is," Callen O'Shay interrupted, drawing their attention back to the rest of the room from the bubble of just the two of them that Bobby seemed to experience whenever he and Brie were together. "It doesn't solve the issues we have with the lawsuit Ms. Barns brought us all here to resolve."

Bobby pulled back from his connection with Brie, sitting back in his seat and clasping her hand once more to listen to the rest of the people in the meeting.

"Actually…" Mikayla Newman's eyes shot daggers at Callen as she spoke. "Mr. Remington resolved the majority of the issues with the lawsuit by informing us of the board's decision to remove Bradley Barns as the trustee of the Ashbury estate."

The mediator turned to look at Miles Garrett, Brie's attorney, before adding, "Mr. Garrett, you will need to revise Ms. Barns complaint with the court to merely asking for monetary compensation from her father for the funds he's stolen from her and mental anguish damages for his mistreatment of her over the years. As Mr. Barns is no longer able to be present for this mediation, the monetary portion of the lawsuit will have to be resolved in court, where a judge can make a decision regardless of whether he's able to attend the proceedings in person or via teleconference from his place of incarceration."

"I already have my paralegal working on the paperwork for that change," Miles replied, his lips turning up in the slightest smile.

"Excellent." Mikayla smiled serenely. She looked back and forth between Brie and Leland Remington with a thoughtful expression on her face. "Technically, my work here is done, since the board of directors of Ashbury has the final say with regard to who becomes the new trustee. But if you need help in making a decision on the matter, I'm happy to stay and assist."

Brie looked to Bobby first, then toward Mr. Remington, before turning to Ms. Newman and nodding her head.

"Your assistance would be greatly appreciated, Ms. Newman," Mr. Remington added, also nodding in agreement.

"Do either of you have someone in mind to take over the position?" Mikayla looked back and forth between Brie and Leland.

"Being unaware of needing to replace our CEO and board member, as well as our CFO, until yesterday, we've not had the opportunity to vet any potential candidates at this time," Leland commented, his lips thinning into a flat line.

"I had thought," Brie disclosed, shifting in her seat like she was uncomfortable with what she was about to say, "maybe one of the Burlesons would be able to act as the trustee. But I would hate to ask them to step away from their own company to act as the CEO of Ashbury."

"Them wanting to buy Ashbury would be considered a conflict of interest, as well," Leland pointed out.

"I'd also thought about Mary or Joe," Brie continued, shrugging. "But I know neither of them would want to be the CEO any more than I do. None of us are qualified for that job."

"Mr. Remington, are there any stipulations about Ms. Barns having to take over the CEO position when she inherits the full estate?" Mikayla's expression appeared to be triumphant, as if she'd just discovered a loophole in the documents that might satisfy everyone.

"No," he replied, looking to the corporate attorney to clarify.

"When Ms. Barns inherits, she will hold the twelfth seat on the board of directors, but she can appoint a proxy to vote for her if she doesn't wish to participate in running the company in any way,"

Callen stated, pulling out a document and pointing out the specific clause to Mikayla. "And the board could hire someone else for the CEO position."

"Are there any provisions for Ms. Barns inheriting without having to meet the age or marriage clauses?" Mikayla flipped through the document Mr. O'Shay had just handed her.

"Actually, the wording of those clauses seemed kind of murky to me." Callen leaned closer to Mikayla to point out the correct page for her to read the specific clauses.

Damn, I wish I'd have asked Uncle Doug to read the will, Bobby thought. *He'd have been able to clarify where I was confused by the legalese of those stipulations, so I might have a clue how her mother meant it to be decided.*

"My apologies, Ms. Newman," Miles interjected, having pulled out the copy of the will Bobby had given him to review it for himself. "I only gave the will a cursory glance, noting the highlights, instead of actually reading the specific clauses. But now that I'm looking at this specific passage, I believe Brooklyn's mother intended the board to decide when her daughter was mature enough to inherit, and only listed the age of twenty-five and condition of marriage as possible signs of adequate maturity to handle the responsibility of her wealth."

"That was my understanding when I read the will as well," Mikayla agreed, directing her words to Miles before turning to look at Leland. "Mr. Remington, would it be possible for the board to decide that Ms. Barns has shown adequate maturity to inherit the Ashbury estate at this time?"

"I would certainly vote that way," Leland replied, turning in his seat to look at the two tables behind him, where the other board members were sitting. "I know we would normally convene in private to take a vote such as this, and we can still do that if we don't have a unanimous vote, but I'd prefer we do a show of hands first to see if we need to discuss the matter further, or if we can count our show of hands as a unanimous decision to allow Brooklyn Barns to take full ownership of the Ashbury estate as the sole beneficiary of her mother's will."

When several of the heads nodded in agreement, Leland led the board to vote by raising his hand. Slowly but surely, the other ten board members' hands were raised. "Excellent," Leland cheered before turning back to look at the mediator. "Now that the estate is settled, I'll instruct the human resources department to place an ad in the trades for a CEO, in addition to the CFO position they're already looking to fill."

"I trust that the two attorneys present will be able to handle any legalities with transferring the assets of the estate into Ms. Barns' name," Mikayla smiled.

"Absolutely," both Miles and Callen agreed in unison.

"Then my work here is done. I'll leave you all to handle any other issues you have as a unified board of directors." Mikayla stood and collected her things, turning to look at Brie once more. "Congratulations, Ms. Barns. I'll be watching the papers for that wedding announcement."

"Thank you," Brie giggled as Mikayla Newman left the room.

"Mr. Garrett," Callen O'Shay stood and turned toward the other attorney. "If you'd like, we can go to my office to take care of the paperwork to transfer everything over."

"Lead the way, young man," the older attorney directed, standing to follow the corporate attorney after placing his paperwork back in his briefcase.

"So, that's it? We're done here?" Brie looked around the room in confusion.

"Not so fast, young lady," Leland bellowed, giving Brie a grandfatherly smile. "We still need to meet as a board to discuss the Burlesons' offer to purchase Ashbury you presented last week."

"Oh, um," Brie stuttered, looking at Bobby before asking, "Is that offer still on the table?"

"Only if you want it to be, Brie-Baby," Bobby replied, lifting their joined hands to his lips.

"I, uh, don't want your family to risk your business to spend more than Ashbury is worth," Brie softly whispered. "But I like the idea of merging the companies, so our kids and their cousins can share them both."

"Then let's work out a deal to make that happen." Bobby kissed her long and hard before turning to his family to get them to go with the Ashbury board back upstairs to the conference room where they could all sit around the same table and hash out the terms.

Bobby didn't actually care about the terms of the deal. He wouldn't have cared if she didn't want his family to buy into Ashbury

Enterprises at all. If she hadn't wanted to be responsible for the company, but also didn't want it to go to anyone but their children in the future, he'd have told the board to hold off for a little over a week until he received his inheritance from his Pappaw Jerry to purchase it solely with the money in his trust fund, instead of with the corporate coffers. All that mattered to Bobby was that his Brie-Baby was pleased with what was happening at the company her grandfather started, and her mother had run before leaving it to her. He was willing to do anything to make her happy. Thankfully, by the time they left the Ashbury offices that afternoon, his Brie-Baby was thrilled, her smile lighting up the evening and outshining the stars.

Chapter Fifteen

Sitting back in her seat on the private jet Bobby had chartered to take everyone home to Texas, Brooklyn reflected on the whirlwind of the past few days. Even after spending Thursday and Friday dealing with attorneys and transitioning all her assets into her name, Brooklyn still wasn't sure she wasn't dreaming rather than living her real life.

They'd worked everything out with the board of directors of Ashbury Enterprises on Thursday afternoon to facilitate the sale of the company to Burleson Incorporated. Julie was going to be spending quite a bit of time going back and forth between Texas and Georgia to make sure the company transitioned smoothly into the new ownership. They weren't going to be hiring a new CEO or CFO, instead turning over the duties of those jobs to trusted employees already working at the Burleson headquarters. Julie's brother, JJ, would also be making a few trips to the Ashbury offices to ensure the two companies worked smoothly together on the deals they'd both been pursuing before the buyout.

On Friday, Brooklyn and Bobby met with the attorneys to discuss what all she'd inherited in the Ashbury estate. In addition to the business and the home she'd grown up in, she'd learned that, between the various investments and trust accounts, she'd inherited enough wealth that she didn't think even her grandchildren's grandchildren would be able to spend it all, even if everyone in the next four generations never worked a day in their lives. She wasn't quite halfway to billionaire status, but it was still more money than she knew what to do with.

She also couldn't believe that Bobby hadn't even been phased when he heard the numbers, but she supposed after what he'd told her about his trust fund being almost double the size of her inheritance, she shouldn't be so surprised by his reaction.

"If it's too much, Brie-Baby, just do what I'm planning to do with most of mine—give it to charity," he'd advised, as if giving millions of dollars away was a normal daily occurrence.

That had led to a discussion about which charities they wanted to give their money away to, which led to even more dialogue about possibly starting their own charitable foundations. She'd thought about selling her childhood home, knowing that the bad memories would make it impossible for her to ever feel comfortable staying there again. But when they started talking about the types of charitable organizations they could start with their combined wealth, Brooklyn decided to turn the vast grounds of the estate where she'd grown up, which had once been a plantation during the Civil War era, into a safe haven for women and children escaping from abuse.

Her attorney ended up with a lot more work to do in order to set up the Madeline Ashbury Foundation, named after Brooklyn's mother, and transfer the house and liquid assets she'd just inherited into the foundation's name. Bobby had enlisted the help of Avington Security to oversee everything that would need to be done to make sure it was a safe and secure place for the people they would start to help in the coming months, while Brooklyn contacted the former Ashbury Enterprises board members with a job offer to oversee the foundation's daily activities, since she wouldn't be in Georgia to do so herself.

While Brooklyn and Bobby had been dealing with all of that, Bob and Jon Burleson had talked to the Turners about Brooklyn's suggestion for them to move to Texas, as well. She'd known Mary and Joe would never accept a large retirement package from her, even though they'd more than earned it with all their years working for her parents and grandparents before them. That's why Brooklyn had talked to Bobby's family about providing for the older couple, under the guise of having them work on the ranch.

Of course, the Burlesons welcomed the Turners as if they'd been family for years, just as they'd done with her from the moment she met them. They had the Walkers working double time to finish the repairs on the south bunkhouse for the Turners to have a place to stay until they could get a caretaker's cottage built on the north-central part of the ranch beside the ranch manager's home. *I just wish they'd let me pay for some of Mary and Joe's salaries and housing now that I have the funds.*

On Saturday, they'd all gone to Brooklyn's childhood home. Showing Bobby where she'd grown up hadn't been nearly as enjoyable as how they'd spent the previous Saturday alone in their hotel room, but it had been good for her to feel a sense of closure after the hell she'd lived through the last six months she'd lived there. While she didn't consider the previous twenty-two years she'd lived there as an idyllic upbringing, living with her father's neglect had been a breeze compared to having to do his bidding and pretending to be happy about it.

She'd thought she'd left on Thanksgiving with everything she wanted from the home, but when they arrived, Mary had shown her to a section of the attic where there were things of her mother's that the housekeeper had saved for her when she was ordered to remove all traces of Madeline Ashbury from the estate. So, in addition to the Turners picking up the rest of their belongings to move to Texas, Brooklyn also left her childhood home with a few boxes of things to go through and possibly pass on to her own children one day.

Leland Remington and a couple of the other board members, who were going to run the foundation for her, had also shown up to go through the house. Brooklyn went through every room with them, holding Bobby's hand for the strength to make decisions about what to keep for the future residents to use, what to sell to increase the foundation's funding, and what to box up to send to wherever the FBI agents informed her that her father's things would be stored while he was in prison.

In addition to making plans for the security system upgrade at the house, the Avingtons had gone through and changed all the codes and locks, so none of the security and other personnel her father had given access to in the past would be able to get back into the property.

All in all, Saturday had been a productive day, even if it had left them all too exhausted to do anything other than fall into bed immediately after a late dinner. *At least I still got to sleep in Bobby's arms, even though we only had enough energy to cuddle. And he more than made up for our lack of amorous activities last night with the glorious way he woke me up this morning.*

Knowing that they wouldn't have any alone time on their flight back to Texas, and once they landed they'd barely have time to drop off their things before going to the GWA show in San Antonio to watch their friends wrestle and James proposing to Randi in the middle of the ring, Bobby had woken her up by eating her for breakfast in bed. Brooklyn had decided rather quickly that she loved having Bobby as an oral alarm clock. She couldn't contain her smile as she mentally relived the memories of their morning mating. She squeezed Bobby's hand and leaned her head over onto his shoulder, knowing that was as close as she could get to him until late that night.

He released her hand and flipped up the armrest in between them, so he could wrap his arm around her shoulders and pull her in closer. Resting her head on his chest was the last thing Brooklyn remembered of their flight, instantly drifting off to sleep as soon as she heard the steady beat of his heart beneath her ear.

Brooklyn awoke a few hours later, surprised that she'd not only slept through the whole flight, but also through Bobby carrying her and all her things into his bedroom. *Is excessive sleepiness a symptom of pregnancy?* She wondered, remembering that Kay had complained about being tired all the time since finding out she was expecting. *I should probably go buy a pregnancy test tomorrow, since I still haven't started my period.*

"Sorry to have to wake you, Brie-Baby," Bobby murmured softly as he stroked her hair. "But it's time to get ready if you still wanna go to the GWA show tonight."

"Yes, I still want to go," Brooklyn nodded, all thoughts of her possibly being pregnant moving to the back of her mind as she focused on the excitement of being there for her friend's big night.

Maybe I should come up with some kind of big, grand gesture to propose to Bobby? As much as I would rather wait to have him propose in a more traditional way, I don't want to wait if we're already having a baby together. Now that we're home, I'll have to ask the girls to help me brainstorm some ideas for a Valentine's Day surprise for him.

~~~

Monday, February 11, 2019

Bobby was exhausted after his first day back at work in almost two weeks. He'd been thrown off his normal routine with the late night the night before, celebrating James and Randi's engagement, so he'd skipped his early morning run. But needing to review everything that had happened in the department in his absence had meant a day of paperwork that was mentally draining. Not to mention the couple of hours after work that he spent at the youth center, covering both his normal class time and Kara's, since she'd covered for him the week before.

Thank fuck, she had them baking premade cookie dough tonight, so all I had to do was supervise to make sure they didn't burn the place down, Bobby thought as he pulled his cruiser onto the ranch. *They wouldn't have had anything edible after class if I'd have had to help them figure out a recipe instead of just observing them watching their oven timers.*

He was a little concerned when he noticed the lights were all off in the house as he parked. But knowing how tired Brie had been the day before, he assumed she'd laid down to rest after writing all day. He planned to check to see if she was hungry as soon as he got inside, thinking he'd order a pizza for dinner, if she hadn't cooked anything earlier.

He'd removed his boots and jacket in the mud room and was just about to turn up the back stairs to head to their bedroom when he noticed the flickering of candles in the dining room. His socks allowed for a quick pivot on the hardwood floor to see the enticing scene Brie had set up for him. The table was set for a romantic dinner for two, and Brie was sitting there, smiling up at him with love and excitement shining in her eyes. He also noticed that there was a wrapped box, which he assumed was an early birthday present since his birthday was only a few days away.

"Brie-Baby," Bobby drawled, walking into the dining room. "What's all this?"
~~~

"Dinner," Brie chirped, clutching her hands in her lap, as if she was trying to hide her nervousness about something.

"Looks like a little more than dinner." Bobby took his seat beside her and reached over to pull one of her hands up to his lips. "But I guess if you wanna surprise me for my birthday, dinner and presents a few days early is the way to do it."

He wagged his eyebrows at her suggestively as he released her hand and moved to start serving up his dinner.

"I do have a surprise for you," Brie giggled, moving to assist him in dishing up their plates of roast beef, potatoes and gravy, carrots, and homemade rolls. "But it's not really for your birthday."

"Oh? Then what's it for?" Bobby grinned at his girl before digging into the delicious meal she'd made.

"You'll have to open your present to find out," Brie teased, giving him a coy smile.

"Do I have to wait to finish eating first? Or can I open it now?"

"You can open it now if you want." Brie's smile widened, showing she was obviously as impatient to give him the gift as he was to see what she'd gotten him.

Not able to torture them both by waiting, Bobby sat his fork down after taking his next bite, so he could pick up the box and rip off the paper. Once he got the box open, he found a black t-shirt with white writing. He had to pull it out of the box and hold it up between them to be able to read what it said. "We've got one in custody," he read aloud, confused by the message. "Release date 2019."

He assumed based on the unlocked handcuffs beside the release date that the message had some sort of reference to him being a police officer. It wasn't until he looked closer at the badge between the two sections of wording that he realized it contained one pink and one blue baby footprint.

Baby footprints. We've got one in custody. Baby footprints. Release date 2019.

Holy Fuck! Is the release date actually our baby's due date? Is this Brie's way of telling me she's pregnant?

Bobby sat there staring at the shirt completely speechless. He was torn between feeling like an ass for not protecting her the first time he made love to her, basically taking away her choice as to when she wanted to have children, and the ultimate elation of finding out the woman he loved was carrying his child. Not sure if he should apologize to her or shout with glee loud enough his parents could hear him from their house five miles away, he floundered for words for several long moments.

"Bobby?" Brie barely breathed out his name, sounding as if she was worried about him, or maybe his lack of reaction.

The trepidation in her voice caused him to instantly drop the shirt into his lap, so he could see her face to figure out his next course of action.

"Did you figure out what it means?" Brie's smile was tentative.

"Yeah," Bobby breathed out the word, hoping he read her smile right as being happy about their impending parenthood, and returning her shy smile with a wide dimple-popping one of his own. "My Brie-Baby is having my baby."

Thank fuck, I got that right, Bobby thought as Brie's smile widened and she lightly giggled.

"You know what this means?" Bobby tossed the shirt on the table, so he could stand and pull Brie into his arms.

"Yeah, that I'm going to spend the next few months getting sick," Brie pouted, wrapping her arms around his neck and her legs around his waist as he lifted her. "And then a few more months getting fat."

Bobby shook his head as he started carrying her out of the dining room and up the stairs to their bedroom, where he planned to spend the rest of the evening worshiping her the way she deserved. "No, Brie-Baby. Even if you gain a hundred pounds with this pregnancy, you won't be fat." Bobby peppered her face with kisses between the words. "And I hope the morning sickness won't be too bad, but if it is, I'll be right there to hold your hair back and help you clean up after."

"If neither of those are what you were referring to, then what does this mean?" Brie pulled her head back, so they could look into each other's eyes.

"No more condoms," Bobby grinned as he crossed the room to their bed.

Brie started to giggle again at his answer, but he couldn't wait a moment longer to kiss the mother of his child, so he silenced her giggles with his lips on hers. Their tongues tangled as he savored the way their roast beef dinner mixed with her naturally sweet flavor.

They made out for what could've been hours or only minutes, until Bobby couldn't wait any longer to get her naked.

He pulled his head back just enough to speak with their breath still mingling. "You're gonna hafta quit hanging on me like a spider monkey climbing a tree, so we can get rid of these clothes, Brie-Baby."

"But I'm wearing a skirt, so you have easy access," Brie argued, grinning, even as she released her hold to allow him to set her down on the bed.

"Easy access is fine for a quick fuck to tide us over during the day," Bobby shook his head, stepping back to remove his duty belt and walking toward his closet to lock up his gun. "But I'm not gonna make love to my baby's momma with all our clothes still on."

"Did you just call me your baby momma?" Brie screeched, sounding indignant. "Like we're some trashy, reality TV couple?"

"No," Bobby laughed as he returned to the bedroom sans police gear. He deftly unbuttoned his shirt as he stalked toward the bed where Brie was sitting with her hands on her hips. "I said I wanna make love to my baby's momma, meaning I wanna show you how much I love you and our child. I certainly didn't mean it as a derogatory term like on reality TV."

"You'd better not," Brie muttered, her eyes widening with desire as he let his shirt fall from his shoulders to the floor. She didn't get a chance to finish her thought as Bobby bent to cup her face and kiss her once more.

Once her hands left her hips and her palms came to rest on his pecs, Bobby softly trailed his hands down her sides until he reached the hem of her blouse. He continued to kiss her as he pushed the lavender top up, delicately stroking his thumbs over her still-flat stomach. *Fuck! I can't believe our baby is growing in there.*

He rolled the silky material over the swell of her breasts as he trailed his tongue down the column of her throat. He pulled his head back long enough to pull the blouse over her head. Brie dropped her arms to allow her top to fall to the floor between them before running her hands over the ridges of his abs and the planes of his pecs.

Fuck, I love the feel of your hands on me, Brie-Baby, Bobby mused, his mouth too occupied with tasting her cleavage to speak the words. With a flick of his fingers behind her back, he unclasped her bra. He bit down on the material between her tits to pull it away from the glorious globes he wanted his mouth on next. Once again, Brie lowered her arms to fling the pale pink scrap of lace out of their way.

Instead of returning her hands to his torso to continue rubbing him down while he licked her diamond-hard nipples, she reached for his waistband, impatiently unfastening his pants.

"Fuck," he groaned against her sensitive skin when she grazed his hard-as-a-rock cock while trying to remove his pants. "Stand up, Brie-Baby," he commanded, even as he pulled her toward him and backed up a step, essentially standing her up, whether she wished to follow his demand or not. "I need to get you naked. Now!"

"Yes, Bobby," Brie moaned as he suckled her breasts while pushing her skirt and panties down the surprisingly long length of his petite Brie-Baby's legs.

He went down on his knees, so he could slip the garments over her bare feet, continuing to trail open-mouthed kisses down her thin torso as he bent lower. He paused momentarily to pay special attention to the expanse of skin just below her navel, peppering the area with pecks to show his love for their child as well as the beautiful woman in his arms.

"I just realized that you were barefoot and pregnant in my kitchen today," Bobby chuckled, his breath blowing across her belly as he spoke, causing goosebumps to rise on her porcelain skin.

"Yeah, I guess I was," Brie giggled, running her hands across his arms and up to weave her fingers through the short hair on the back of his head. Bobby loved how effortlessly they could laugh together, even in the middle of making love.

His hands, which had been roaming to caress every inch of her, halted in their movement to grip her hips and lift her back up on the bed. As soon as she was seated on the edge of the bed, he slid his palms down her thighs, spreading them wide when he reached her knees. He needed a taste of her tangy sweet sex, wanting her to come at least once on his tongue and fingers before he allowed himself the ultimate pleasure of sinking inside her.

"Oh, Bobby," Brie cried out with the first tease of the tip of his tongue on her clit. He circled the needy nub with the pointed tip of his tongue several times before sucking it between his lips. She fell back on the bed, unable to maintain a seated position as she came, but Brie continued to chant his name as he brought her over the edge the first time.

Knowing her little clit was super sensitive, and direct stimulation right then could be perceived as painful, instead of pleasurable, Bobby backed off, opting to lave her folds to lap up all the sweet cream she was releasing with each wave of her orgasm.

Though he'd only ever enjoyed oral activities with Brie, after that first time in the early morning hours of New Year's Day, Bobby quickly decided that drinking from the well of her desire was one of his favorite sexual activities. After the previous month spent exploring all their options for preparing Brie for his sizable invasion, he'd decided that eating her pussy was definitely his favorite form of foreplay. If ever there came a time when he lost her, he knew he'd die of thirst from not being able to pleasure her in this way.

Needing to make sure she was opened up and ready for his thick cock, Bobby filled her with his finger as soon as she'd started to come back down from her first erotic high of the night. They'd made love enough over the last week and a half that he didn't have to stretch her out as much as he had before her first time, but he still wanted to be certain she was ready and wouldn't feel even a moment of discomfort when he intimately joined their bodies.

His middle finger and ring finger soon joined his forefinger in the tight, wet sheath of Brie's pussy. "Always so, fucking, tight," Bobby groaned, watching her back arch as his hot breath wafted over her super sensitive clit as he spoke, pushing the smooth, slick folds of her sex closer to his face.

Unable to resist, Bobby licked around his fingers, drinking down her sweet honey before returning his attention to circling her clit with the tip of his tongue. Enjoying the sound of her panting his name interspersed with cries of "please" that he knew meant she was close, Bobby suckled the little bundle of nerves in the way that he knew always drove her over the edge to ecstasy.

"Bobby! Yes! Bobby!" Brie screamed in pleasure as her inner walls clamped down on his digits like a vise. He held his hand still, reveling in the rhythmic movement of her creamy cunt as the waves of her second orgasm physically manifested as the rolling spasms of her pelvic muscles.

Though his cock would probably disagree, especially when it was still trapped in the confines of his boxer briefs, Bobby enjoyed watching Brie come more than his own orgasm. The vision of her writhing on his bed, knowing that he'd been the one—the only one—to bring her to the height of euphoria was heady, making him feel like a superhero.

He gently pulled his hand back, caressing her softly as she came down from the heavenly plane where she'd drifted away in orgasm. He placed one last kiss on her lower lips before standing and dropping his pants and underwear. He toed off his socks as he stepped out of the bundle of material at his feet. Scooping Brie up into his arms, Bobby repositioned her half-limp, sated body in the center of the bed before crawling over her.

He kissed and caressed her delicate flesh as he worked his way up from the foot of the bed to plank over her with his elbows supporting his weight on either side of her head. He took a moment to appreciate Brie's sweet smile and fruity floral scent while he waited for her to open her eyes after recovering from la petite mort.

"I love you, Brie-Baby," Bobby declared, his voice deep from his desire for her, as soon as her brilliant blue eyes locked on his hazel ones.

"I love you, too, Bobby," Brie smiled, wrapping her arms around his neck to pull him down for a kiss.

Bobby let her take the lead for a moment, reining in his inner caveman, so he didn't plunder her mouth and body like a wild animal. Once he felt in control, he shifted his hips to line up the blunt head of his cock with her soaking wet slit. He took over the kiss, slowing down the erratic lashing of her tongue with long, deliberate licks around every crevice of her mouth.

He pushed inside her slowly, both with his tongue and his cock. He didn't want this time to be like their previous, primal, animalistic fucking. He wanted to sensually make love to the mother of his child, the woman he hoped would one day be his wife.

Brie moaned into his mouth when she finally seemed to understand what he was doing. She, too, gentled her hands on him. She didn't dig into his scalp with her nails or pull the short strands of his hair like she normally would. She caressed him with all the love and tenderness he hoped he was showing her with his slow strokes in and out of her tight heat.

There were no hard and fast thrusts of their hips. Those were replaced by gentle, rocking movements of their bodies to glide together in perfect harmony. They spent hours uniting in the most intimate way, only pulling back from their kisses to look into each other's eyes and whisper sweet nothings. But always maintaining their core connection with sensual strokes of his hard flesh into her soft center.

Bobby adjusted the angle as needed, pulling Brie's legs up around his waist, so he could bring her over the edge by sliding the head of his cock over her G-spot with every push in and pull out. He made sure she saw the stars multiple times before he finally allowed his own release to wash over him, flooding her womb with his cum as he whispered, "I love you, Brie-Baby," over and over. Brie reciprocated the sentiment as she joined him in orgasmic nirvana one more time. They floated there in heavenly bliss together for several long minutes before Bobby rolled off of her, hating the moment his dick slipped free of her sheath. He ran to the bathroom, grabbed a wet washcloth and dry hand towel, and cleaned them both up before pulling her close to cuddle.

Instead of drifting off to sleep as they usually would after making love, Brie insisted they go back downstairs and clean up from dinner. At first, he thought it was just her tendency to be a neatnik, but when she went for a second serving of dinner from the fridge, he realized her appetite was being affected by being pregnant. So, they sat back down for a second supper with her in one of his t-shirts and him in only a pair of boxer briefs while they made plans for converting the second bedroom into a nursery.

An hour or so later, once they were back upstairs in bed, she told him about buying the test that morning and going back to the t-shirt shop they'd visited together just before Christmas to find the perfect shirt for telling him about the baby. Bobby couldn't help but chuckle at how she'd gone all the way to San Antonio to buy the test and took it in the bathroom at the mall, so the Heart's Destiny rumor mill wouldn't notify him before she had the chance to tell him herself.

"That's what Kay should've done," Bobby chuckled, shaking his head while holding her in his arms. When Brie looked up at him with confusion in her eyes, Bobby explained about the whole pregnancy test uproar at Thanksgiving when everyone thought Kay's test belonged to Randi. That led to him telling her more about his brother's medical history than he ever imagined he'd need to disclose to his future wife, but he was okay with that to know that there were no secrets between them that could cause a similar issue in their future.

Now if I can just figure out how to know when she's ready to start talking about getting married, so I can plan a proper proposal, Bobby thought as they drifted off to sleep, already planning a trip to Jeweled Destiny the next day to buy her an engagement ring.

~~~

Thursday, February 14, 2019—Valentine's Day

Since Brooklyn was no longer responsible for cooking and cleaning for anyone else on the ranch besides herself and Bobby, she'd spent her free time, when she wasn't writing, talking to all her new friends to have them help her out with planning a Valentine's surprise proposal for Bobby. She'd originally thought of doing something similar to how she'd told him about the baby, with a candlelight dinner and going down on one knee to give him his wedding band, instead of an engagement ring. But her friends talked her out of it by saying it was too cliché.

When she was having a writing session with Kay, she asked Bobby's sister-in-law for any ideas she might have. Kay had naturally called in his sisters and cousins, who all insisted she had to make it a public declaration. And by a public declaration they meant with the whole family and half the town as witnesses, and not just by asking him while they were out to celebrate the holiday in a restaurant.

All her new girlfriends had been a godsend in helping her set up the surprise. They'd introduced her to Florence at Flora's Flowers, so Brooklyn could order the biggest bouquet of flowers they offered for Valentine's Day to be delivered to Bobby at the police station that morning. They'd also introduced her to Harmony at Jeweled Destiny. Harmony told her that the earrings and necklace Bobby had gotten her for her birthday were actually platinum and not silver like she'd
~~~

thought, so Brooklyn could pick out the matching platinum wedding bands that she liked best to give Bobby when she popped the question. She'd also eyed the engagement rings while she was in the store on Appaloosa that backed up to the flower shop on the corner of Appaloosa and Angus, but ultimately decided the wedding bands were much more important than the big, flashy diamonds.

Kay had also pulled Anthony into the plan by convincing him to learn to play ***Growing Old With You*** by Restless Road, so Brooklyn could sing it to Bobby in the middle of the station, as sort of a singing telegram before dropping to one knee. They had it planned that Anthony would be the last of their friends and family to invade the police station, blocking Bobby's view of Brooklyn, who would come in behind Bobby's youngest brother, singing to his brother's guitar accompaniment.

In order to keep everything a surprise with so many people coming to the police station, they opted to park in the lot on Thoroughbred Street that fed into the back sides of the Destiny Playhouse, the Bank of Heart's Destiny, and Walker Realty, and walk alongside Longhorn Lane to the Heart's Destiny Police Department entrance on Mustang Lane. They were just waiting for the text from Mabel, the almost sixty-year-old receptionist at the Heart's Destiny Police Department, letting them know that Bobby had stepped out of his office to grab a mid-morning cup of coffee from the break room, so they could catch him in the main room, where everyone else's desks were located, on his way back to his office.

"Relax, Brook," Becky grinned. "You don't need to be so nervous. We all know he's gonna say yes."

"You don't think this is too much?" Brooklyn looked around the group as a whole. "When we came up with this idea, I didn't realize just how many people were going to be crowded into the station with me. Now I'm worried it's going to be super embarrassing for him in front of everyone who works for him."

"Oh, don't worry about that." Hazel waved her hand like she was shooing away Brooklyn's concerns as if they were gnats. "Bobby is the least likely of my sons to be embarrassed for any reason."

"Go time," Anthony announced, pocketing his phone, and adjusting the strap of his guitar over his chest. Brooklyn hadn't wanted to carry anything but the ring box, since she didn't have pockets in the red dress she was wearing, so Anthony had reached out to Mabel to be the one she alerted.

As the crowd started walking, Brooklyn noticed a couple of people coming from the businesses around them to join the group. Though she hadn't personally met them yet, she was sure they all knew Bobby, especially the firefighters, who came out of the backside of the building the fire station and police station shared.

She couldn't hear what was being said as the people at the front of the group entered the police department offices, but she very clearly heard Bobby ask what was going on as she stepped through the outer door because everyone else suddenly got very quiet.

"Valentine's flower delivery," Florence broadcasted. "Where would you like them, Chief Burleson?"

"Brie-Baby," Bobby drawled. "Care to come out from hiding behind all our friends and family to clue me in on what you're doing?"

She didn't reply as Anthony started playing his guitar and the crowd parted for her to step around them. "*Boy*," Brooklyn began singing, changing the first word of the lyrics to account for the fact that she was a female singing a song meant to be sung by a man. She continued adjusting the song about spending their lives together by changing the word "baby" to "Bobby" in reference to the man she was walking toward as she sang.

He was obviously not upset or embarrassed with his dimples popping out as his smile grew the closer she got to him. She stopped walking a couple feet away, knowing if she got any closer he'd pull her into his arms, and she wouldn't be able to drop to her knee for the proposal.

"Happy Valentine's Day, Bobby," Brooklyn beamed after ending her serenade.

"Happy Valentine's Day, Brie-Baby," Bobby chuckled as he reached for her.

She surprised him by dropping to one knee instead of stepping into his arms. "I'm not just here to ask you to be my Valentine," Brooklyn smiled up at him. "I know we've already decided to spend the future together because we love each other. And I know I screwed up when I said no to your proposal a few weeks ago."

"That wasn't a proposal," Bobby denied adamantly. "That was brainstorming possibilities."

"Sounded like a proposal to me," Bobby's Uncle Jon mumbled from somewhere behind Brooklyn.

"Well, even if that wasn't a proposal," Brooklyn argued, shaking her head at the interruption. "This is." She held the ring box up in her right hand, opening it with her left, so Bobby could see the matching platinum bands nestled inside. "I want to spend the future we've already planned, living together, and raising a family together, to be lived as husband and wife. Robert Adam Burleson, will you marry me?"

"I don't know," Bobby drawled, slowly backing away from where Brook was laying her heart out on the floor. "You're gonna hafta give me a moment alone to think about it."

He turned and walked into his office, leaving Brooklyn there speechless. She unconsciously closed the ring box and floundered for how to respond to him walking away from her proposal.

"What on earth is your son thinking?" Hazel hissed, presumably, to her husband, Bob.

Before Bob or anyone else could answer, Bobby walked back out of his office with his hands in the pockets of his uniform pants. With his right hand, Bobby reached out and clasped Brook's left hand, pulling her up to stand in front of him. Instead of answering Brooklyn, Bobby called his youngest brother, Anthony, over to his side and whispered something in his ear.

Brooklyn wasn't sure what was going on as Anthony stepped back and started to play his guitar again. She thought she recognized the tune, but since she wasn't super knowledgeable when it came to song or artist names, she couldn't quite place it.

"I've been racking my brain for the past few days," Bobby began, looking down at Brooklyn as he squeezed her hand in his. "Trying to come up with ideas for a romantic proposal, so I'd know what to do when you seemed ready to talk about gettin' married. Thank you, Brie-Baby, for not only lettin' me know you're ready, but also for givin' me the perfect idea for a proper proposal. But I have a different song in mind for givin' you an answer."

Bobby nodded at Anthony and the music changed slightly, going back to the opening notes of the new song he was playing, so Bobby could start singing *Take My Name* by Parmalee, also changing the lyrics to "Brie-Baby" instead of just "Baby" whenever it was used in the song, somehow without getting off beat with the music by adding the extra syllable.

Brooklyn's eyes filled with happy tears, knowing this was his way of saying "yes," or maybe hijacking her proposal for one of his own.

When the song ended, Bobby dropped to one knee and pulled a black, velvet box out of his left pants pocket. "I'll marry you, if you'll marry me, Brie-Baby," he suggested as he opened the box to reveal a diamond solitaire on a platinum band that looked like a perfect match for the wedding bands she'd picked out.

"Yes," Brook squealed as she threw her arms around his neck and her body into his. Luckily, his larger size kept them from toppling to the floor as he caught her in his arms, and they kissed like nobody was watching.

"Congrats, Chief," one of the officers hollered from somewhere behind Brooklyn.

"But you might wanna go finish celebrating with your fiancée behind a closed and locked door somewhere, like in your office, before we have to arrest you for indecent exposure," another officer yelled, laughing.

"Naw, they've still got their clothes on," another officer shouted, chuckling. "It's just lewd and lascivious acts at this point."

"There's nothing lewd or lascivious about kissing my fiancée," Bobby declared, pulling back from their kiss enough to stand, picking Brooklyn up slightly off her feet in the process. He quickly set her back down, making sure she wasn't wobbly on her feet before releasing his hold around her torso to grab her left hand and push the engagement ring on her finger. "Now it'll be obvious to anyone who sees you that you're mine."

"Well, then you need to show everyone you're mine by wearing the wedding band I bought for you," Brook replied, opening the box she still held in her right hand.

"Isn't it bad luck to put a wedding band on before saying 'I do'?" Luke shook his head as he slapped a hand on Bobby's shoulder.

"Only if you wear it on your left ring finger," Mabel, the receptionist at the Heart's Destiny Police Department, added. "But he could wear it on his right hand or on a chain around his neck."

"I still have Pappaw's necklace you can wear it on," Anthony offered, nodding his head at Bobby. "I'll bring it to you tomorrow."

"That work for you, Brie-Baby?" Bobby locked eyes with Brooklyn.

"Sounds perfect," Brook replied, handing him the box that contained both their wedding bands. "You can keep my wedding band safe there, too."

After what seemed like forever to Brooklyn, with his family, all their friends, and what seemed like half the town offering their individual congratulations, Bobby finally told everyone to leave, or he'd have to start citing them for loitering.

"Bobby!" Brooklyn chastised, playfully slapping his shoulder. "You're not going to cite anyone for anything when they're here because I invited them to celebrate with us."

"But then how am I gonna get rid of everyone, so I can get you alone to really celebrate?" Bobby wagged his eyebrows at her suggestively.

"That'll have to wait 'til after work." Hazel shook her head at her son. "Right now, we need to take advantage of having Anthony here with his schedule, so we can pick a date for your wedding when the whole family can be here."

"Actually, Ma," Anthony interrupted his mother's attempt to get started on the wedding planning. "Kay and I are cutting it close on time for our plans for Valentine's Day, so we're gonna head out. You're still good for watching the girls the rest of the day, right?"

"Oh, yes," Hazel gasped, suddenly looking flustered. "Sorry, I didn't realize you were leaving this early." She looked around to spot her granddaughters before turning back to her youngest son and saying, "Go, I got the girls. Just bring your schedule to Bobby's birthday party tomorrow night, so we can schedule the wedding and all the events leading up to it."

"Will do," Anthony grinned at his mother. "Thanks, Ma." He turned to look at Bobby and Brooklyn once more before saying, "Congrats again. See ya'll tomorrow."

Anthony and Kay pretty much led the way for the rest of the people to leave the police station. As everyone else started leaving, Bobby called out across the station, "Yo, Deere, you're in charge, man. I'm takin' the rest of the day off." He pulled Brook along as he walked toward his office, she assumed because he needed to shut down his computer and gather his things before they could leave.

Leah Mae Wright

"I actually need to go catch up with your parents and get my purse out of their car." Brooklyn pulled back in the opposite direction of the way he was going.

"I'll call Ma later and have her drop it off at the house," Bobby announced, not being deterred from dragging her into his office.

As soon as they were in the room at the back of the police station, Bobby shut and locked the door, pressing Brooklyn up against it and covering her protest with his mouth on hers. Instead of the sweet kisses he'd given her in front of all their family and friends, this kiss was fierce and possessive. Bobby took her breath away and Brooklyn didn't know if she ever wanted it back, feeling like she could live on him and him alone.

Their hands were everywhere, incessantly touching each other out of sheer sexual need. Before she could fathom what was happening, Bobby picked her up and carried her over to his desk. He shoved a stack of papers off onto the floor before setting her down on the smooth, wooden surface.

"Fuck, Brie-Baby," Bobby growled as he pulled back and removed his duty belt, dropping it into one of the chairs in front of his desk. "We're gonna hafta be quick and quiet, but I need to fuck my fiancée."

"Here?" Brook croaked, leaning back on her elbows on his desk and feeling naughty for wanting to have sex in Bobby's office. "With everyone out there knowing what we're doing?"

"They just think they know what we're doin'," Bobby smirked as he unfastened his pants and let them drop to his knees. He shoved his boxers down with them before stepping back between Brooklyn's spread thighs. "They don't really think I'd do you on my desk, but what they don't know won't hurt them."

Bobby winked at her as he pushed her dress up to her waist, revealing the red lace thong she wore underneath. "Fuck, Brie-Baby," he groaned in that low, sexy tone that drove her wild as his fingers trailed over the lace panel at the junction of her legs. "You're so wet and ready for me that you've soaked through your panties."

Yeah, my nipples are hard enough to cut through my bra, too, but I'm not sure it's safe for me to show you right now, Brooklyn thought as she nodded. "Yes, Bobby, so wet for you."

"I can't even wait long enough to take this sexy scrap of lace off you," Bobby growled as he pushed the material to the side and lined up the head of his cock with her slit. "This is gonna be hard and fast, Brie-Baby. But I promise I'll be slow and gentle tonight when we get home from dinner."

"Good," Brooklyn agreed, her voice husky with desire. "You know I love it hard and fast, just as much as you do."

She barely got the words out before Bobby wrapped one arm around her back to hold her in place as he shoved completely inside her with one thrust. He covered her mouth with his when she would've cried out in pleasure at the invasion, swallowing her scream. Brooklyn loved this feeling, when their lovemaking was so intense all she could do was hold on for the ride. She threw her arms and legs around him, latching onto him as he lifted her off the desk, so he could bounce her on his length without the noise of the desk sliding across the floor with each thrust giving them away.

With his big hands holding her hips to control her movement, he synced up his own pelvic thrusts to bring them both to the heights of ecstasy within minutes. As she felt the waves of her orgasm wash over her, she also felt Bobby pulse deep inside her, releasing hot jets of his cum into the core of her being. Their normal cries of each other's name were swallowed by their kiss as they panted for breath through their noses. Brooklyn wasn't sure if it was a lack of oxygen, or just the extreme intensity of their mutual orgasm, that made her feel like she was flying, her whole body going limp as Bobby carried her around the desk to drop into his chair.

"Wow," she whispered reverently when their lips parted, so they could each catch their breath.

"Fuck, yeah," Bobby replied with a chuckle.

When she could finally feel her legs again, Bobby helped Brooklyn extract herself from his lap. He reached over and pulled some tissues out of the box on the table behind his desk and cleaned her up as best he could without running water. He put her panties back in place, straightened her dress, and tossed the first bundle of sopping wet tissues in the trash can beside his desk. He then cleaned himself up and stood to fix his own clothing.

Once they looked presentable, he picked up the files he'd knocked off his desk, making sure the papers were all where they were supposed to be, shut off his desktop computer, and grabbed his laptop case, so they could leave his office for the day. Nobody said a word as they walked through the outer office, even when he paused to pick up the large vase of flowers to carry them out to his cruiser to take them both home.

Brooklyn was surprised when he stopped at Flora's Flowers before heading to the ranch. But she couldn't contain her laughter when he walked back out carrying the exact same arrangement that she'd gotten him, having apparently ordered the same one for her earlier that week.

"What's that saying about great minds thinking alike?" Bobby chuckled as he put the second arrangement in the back seat beside the first one. Brooklyn couldn't reply through her giggles. "Seems we're so made for each other; we even have the same taste in flower arrangements."

"Yes, it does," Brooklyn agreed, smiling at her fiancé as they drove home together for their first of many Valentine's Day celebrations as a couple.

<center>~~~</center>

Friday, February 15, 2019

Bobby couldn't believe just how much his life had changed since his last birthday a year ago. Actually, it hadn't changed a whole lot in the first nine months of his twenty-ninth year. It was the not quite three months leading up to his thirtieth birthday that had changed his life dramatically. If someone had told him the year before, on his twenty-ninth birthday, that he'd be engaged and expecting his first child on his thirtieth, he never would've believed them.

Hell, even if someone had suggested I'd be the next in our family to fall after meeting Brie at Anthony's wedding reception, I probably wouldn't have believed we'd be engaged and expecting in less than three months.

As he looked around the huge dining room in his parents' home where they were hosting his birthday party, Bobby had to admit, even if only to himself, that he was more than glad that his former skeptical self would've been epically wrong in not believing he was headed toward happily ever after. He had a hell of a lot to celebrate this year. His big extended family. The best friends a guy could ever ask for.

454

But most of all, finding the love of his life with his Brie-Baby, who would be having his baby sometime in October.

When they'd gone to see Doc Hayes that morning to confirm the home test was accurate, he'd given them a due date of October twenty-sixth, exactly forty weeks from the date Bobby knew they'd conceived. He'd only not worn a condom the one time, Brie's first time, until she told him they were expecting, and he could ditch the rubbers, so Bobby had no doubt about when they made their baby. Now he just had to convince Brie that it wasn't too soon to tell his family about the bundle of joy they'd be welcoming to the family just before Halloween.

She wanted to wait until they were past the first trimester to tell everyone, because she'd read something about it being the most likely time for a miscarriage. Bobby had been trying to explain to her all afternoon that it wouldn't jinx them to tell anyone early. Truth be told, he thought that if worse came to worst, and they lost the baby in the first trimester, he'd need his family to know to help him through the grieving process, like they'd all tried to help Anthony when his high school girlfriend and unborn baby were killed in a traffic accident a little over seven years ago.

That was the argument that had convinced Brie not to make him change out of the t-shirt she'd given him to tell him about the baby that he was wearing under his black button-down to the party. She still didn't think they needed to reveal their pregnancy news the day after they got engaged, when they weren't quite four weeks along yet. But Bobby had a feeling that when his mother started in with planning the wedding and events leading up to it later that night, Brie would cave and tell her, if only so she didn't have to lie about why she didn't want champagne toasts at each and every party his mother would be planning.

That was why he'd put on the baby announcement shirt as an undershirt before the party. As soon as Brie caved and told one person, Bobby planned on stripping off his button-down to show off the baby shirt as his best idea for how to tell everyone else. But only if he could get Brie to agree with his idea. The way she was nervously clinging to his hand as they mingled with their friends and family after dinner made him think it wouldn't take much to convince her.

Leah Mae Wright

Hell, if she keeps resting her free hand on her belly like that, someone's gonna guess we're pregnant before we get the chance to announce it.

Finally, his mother was able to wrangle everyone back to their seats and called Bobby over to the table of gifts where his favorite apple-spice cake with salted-caramel frosting was waiting for him to blow out the candles once everyone finished singing **Happy Birthday**. He pulled Brie along with him to the table, not only because he wanted to keep her beside him, but also because he knew she'd either drop her free hand down off her belly or out them to the whole room.

Bobby didn't really think of his actions as scheming to get his way like his mother would do with her matchmaking, but he wasn't completely blind to the similarities between he and his mom when it came to manipulating situations to achieve the outcome they wanted. *Fuck, I guess the apple really doesn't fall far from the tree.*

As soon as the singing was over, Bobby blew out the two candles in the shape of the numbers three and zero and took his seat to start unwrapping gifts while Brie and his mom cut the cake and served it to everyone. After opening a bunch of fishing tackle that he didn't have a clue when he'd have time to use from all the guys, more socks, jeans, and button-downs from his female relatives, as if he hadn't just gotten a whole closet full at Christmas, and a half-dozen graphic tees of his favorite Marvel characters from Brie, Bobby was wishing he'd thought to do like Anthony and Kay had for their wedding—suggesting everyone donated to one of his favorite charities in his name in lieu of gifts. Although, he couldn't really complain about all the love being shown to him that night, especially how Brie had gotten him every single one of the t-shirts he'd pointed out he liked back when they were Christmas shopping.

Bobby gave each person a sincere thanks as he opened each gift, but he tried not to interrupt the chitchat going on around the room to do so. Once his cake had been consumed, and all the presents opened, the party started to break up. As soon as the crowd was down to only family, his mother did as he knew she would at some point in the evening, asking, "When do I need to reserve the church for the wedding?"

"We haven't really decided yet," Bobby answered, knowing Brie wanted to get married before the baby bump started showing, but not having picked a specific date yet.

"How long do you think it will take to plan everything?" Brie tentatively looked between Bobby and Hazel.

"We had Anthony and Kay's wedding planned in less than a month," Hazel beamed. "But we had to cram everything into the week they were off work for Thanksgiving. If you wanna do your wedding week the same way, then we'll have to wait until they're off for Memorial Day."

"Actually, we'll be home on maternity leave around the end of April," Kay interjected. "Plus, James and Randi are already planning their wedding for the week they'll be home for Memorial Day."

"Goodness, really?" Hazel brought a hand to her chest in surprise. "Mandi hasn't said a word about them planning the wedding already."

"I don't know if they've had a chance to tell her," Anthony clarified, leaning over where he had his arm around Kay's shoulders to kiss the top of her head. "They were just talking about options Monday night in catering and were leaning toward then as their first available vacation days."

"I don't wanna wait that long to get married." Bobby looked over at Brie in the seat beside him to verify that was still the case.

"Randi won't be upset if we get married before she and James, will she?" Brie glanced at Kay for clarification. "I don't want her to feel like we're jumping ahead of her in line, but I kind of want to be married by the first week of April."

The first week of April, when she'll still be in the first trimester of pregnancy and most likely not showing, Bobby thought, nodding his head in agreement.

"Of course not," Kay waved off Brie's concern for her sister's feelings.

"We'll actually be home the first weekend of April," Anthony announced, looking at his phone, probably at his work schedule. "Well, we have to fly out that Sunday, the seventh, but if you have the wedding on the sixth we'll be able to be here."

"April sixth sounds like a good wedding date to me," Bobby nodded at his brother before turning his attention back to his bride-to-be. "How does that sound to you, Brie-Baby?"

"That sounds perfect to me," Brie smiled shyly.

"Do you think Jake and Josh will be able to stay an extra week when they come home for the first quarter board meeting and their birthday?" Bobby specifically looked to his dad for confirmation that he'd be able to have all of his brothers stand up with him at the altar.

"Possibly," Bob replied, nodding at Bobby, and pulling out his phone like he was going to text Jake and Josh to verify.

"What other weekends will you be home between now and then?" Their mom directed her question to Anthony, since his schedule was the only one that required travel on weekends. "We need to plan the wedding shower and whatever ya'll wanna do for a bachelor and bachelorette party in the next month or so, because ya'll can't do that the day before the wedding when we'll have to do the rehearsal and dinner."

"We'll be home the last weekend in February and the third weekend in March," Anthony replied. "I guess we'll have to do the shower next weekend and the bachelor and bachelorette party in March, since those are the only weekends we're off before the wedding."

"You okay with those dates, Brie-Baby?" Bobby wanted to make sure his family wasn't overstepping her boundaries by planning the various parties according to their schedule, instead of when Brie wanted them.

"I'm fine with whatever works best, so your whole family can be here," Brie agreed, smiling, and reaching over to clasp his hand. "But will your other brothers be able to be here then, too?"

"Probably not," Bobby shrugged, noticing how her smile dimmed slightly. "But they can Skype in for anything they can't physically attend."

"I just verified with both of them that they're scheduled to be here March twenty-seventh through April tenth," Bobby's dad, Bob, announced, garnering everyone's attention. "Apparently, they planned their vacations to cover the board meeting, their birthday, and Justin's birthday, so they could be here for as much family time as possible."

"Perfect," Bobby grinned at his dad and then his cousin, Justin, whose birthday was April seventh.

"But with already planning that much time off, they won't be able to be here any sooner," Bob confirmed. "And Josh won't be able to Skype for the wedding shower next weekend because he's currently gearing up for a mission and doesn't expect to be back in the country by then."

"Yeah, I got the impression at our wedding shower that neither one of them will be too broken up over missing that party," Anthony chuckled, obviously trying to change the subject off the danger their brother was about to be in as a Navy SEAL.

"I don't know about that," Bobby's sister, Charlotte, smirked. "Jake did win the how-many-kisses-for-the-missus game at your wedding shower."

"Yeah, because he got bored and sat back there counting them," JJ joked, laughing.

"He didn't count them, Uncle JJ," Tia defended Jake, smirking. "I helped him figure out the formula to estimate how many were in there based on how many we could see. But when we got an answer with a decimal, I rounded down and he rounded up when we put in our estimates, so we could split the candy between us when we won."

"Next time, I'm teaming with Uncle Jake," Maria pouted, crossing her arms over her chest. "Uncle Josh isn't nearly as good at math as he is, and he came up with answers that were way off for us."

Bobby motioned for Maria to come over to his side of the table. "How 'bout next time," Bobby suggested, scooping Maria up into his lap when she arrived at his side. "You and your sister team up together, so your rotten uncles don't con you out of your candy."

"I knew I should've teamed with you, Uncle Bobby," Maria declared, resting her head on his shoulder, and hugging him around the neck. "You would've just helped me win all the candy and wouldn't have wanted to split it with me."

"Hey, Ma," Bobby called out, clearly falling for his con artist niece's scheme to get some candy out of him. "If we do that game again at our wedding shower, make sure each of the girls have their own bag of candy kisses, regardless of who wins the game."

"Absolutely," his mother replied, just as Bobby noticed Brie picking up her napkin to dab at her eyes.

"What's wrong, Brie-Baby?" Bobby was instantly concerned about what had upset his fiancée.

"Nah-nothing's wrong," Brie choked out, unable to stop crying.

"Then why are you crying?" Bobby shifted Maria on his lap, so he could pull Brie into his side to comfort her.

"Be-because, I," Brie stuttered between sobs. "I just…" Her voice trailed off, becoming so faint he couldn't understand what she was saying, until her last two words came out a little stronger. "…good daddy."

"What?" Bobby tilted her chin up, so she had to look up at him.

"You're going to be such a good daddy," Brie sobbed, her voice just a little louder and less shaky than before.

"Naw," Bobby disagreed, shaking his head, and giving her a self-deprecating smile. "You're gonna hafta be the good parent. I'm gonna spoil our kids rotten."

He released his hold on Maria to use both hands to wipe away Brie's tears before giving her a peck of a kiss.

"Are ya'll gonna give me cousins soon?" Maria asked as soon as Bobby released Brie's lips.

"Oh, um," Brie sputtered, her hand instinctively covering her still-flat belly, as she looked back and forth between Bobby and Maria. When their eyes met, Bobby knew she was struggling with how to answer the precocious child. All he could do was grin, knowing he couldn't say a word about the baby until she did. "Yes?" Her final answer came out sounding more like a question, prompting Maria to ask again to be sure.

"Yes?" Maria tilted her head inquisitively. "When? As soon as when Mommy is gonna give me a little brother? Or do I have to wait until you turn thirty, so you're old enough to canoodle to make them?"

"Not quite as soon as you'll get your new little brother," Brie answered, giggling, and shrugging before continuing in a whisper. "Is Halloween soon enough?"

"Yes!" Maria squealed, throwing her fists in the air like a cheerleader would make a V for victory. "I'm getting a little brother in the summer and a cousin for Halloween!"

"I probably should've realized I couldn't whisper that to an excited little girl and still keep it a secret, huh?" Brie giggled when all eyes turned to them at Maria's outburst.

"Yeah, probably," Bobby answered even though he knew she meant the question to be rhetorical.

"Is it true?" His mother jumped up to come over to their side of the table to question them, her voice as high and shrill as Maria's had been moments before. "Are ya'll gonna give me another grandbaby this year?"

Bobby had to laugh at the shock on Brie's face at how fast Hazel had rounded the table to wrap an arm around each of their necks to pull them in for a hug.

"Yeah, Ma," Bobby answered, chuckling. "But only if you don't strangle us to death first."

"Oh, sorry," Hazel apologized, releasing the choke hold she had around each of their necks. "I'm just so excited about another grandbaby on the way. Tell me everything!"

"You don't need all those details, Ma," Bobby adamantly shook his head in the negative while Brie roared with laughter.

Glad she thinks the mortification that's written all over my face at thinking about telling my mother about our first time making love is funny, Bobby thought, though he couldn't help but chuckle a little with her.

"I didn't mean the details about the conception," Hazel huffed, waving off Bobby's incorrect assumption about what she was asking. "I wanna know when you found out, how far along you are, all that stuff."

"I suspected the possibility since the first weekend of February when we were in Georgia," Brie informed them, smiling at his mother. "But wasn't sure if my symptoms were because of a baby, or because of how stressed out I was while we were there. Then on Monday when I went into San Antonio to pick out Bobby's birthday present, I took a test while I was at the mall to know if I should buy the t-shirt he's wearing to clue him in."

"What t-shirt?" Maria looked at Brie like she was confused about what Bobby was wearing.

"This one," Bobby clarified, unbuttoning his black button-down to show everyone the shirt underneath.

"We've got one in custody. Release date twenty-nineteen," Maria read the shirt for everyone who couldn't see it with him seated. "I don't get it. How does that say you're gonna have a baby?"

"It's a play on words about me being a cop," Bobby told his niece. "See the baby footprints? That's how I figured out that Brie was telling me that we're having a baby."

Leah Mae Wright

"How do you know it's only one? It could be twins," Maria pointed out, looking back and forth between him and Brie like she still wasn't quite convinced.

"Twins are only hereditary through their mother's side of the family," Tia stated matter-of-factly. "So, unless Aunt Brook has a family history of twins, she's probably only pregnant with one baby, just like Mom, even though there are so many sets of twins in the Burleson family."

"Wait, does that mean Char or I are more likely to have twins than our twin brothers?" Becky gaped at their niece.

"Yes," Tia answered. "Because your mother gave birth to twins, you could have inherited her genetic tendency to allow for multiple egg fertilization, or if they were identical twins, the tendency for a fertilized egg to split. But even though they are a twin, neither Uncle Jake nor Uncle Josh contribute the egg to the conception process, so they'll only have twins if their future wives have eggs that are prone to split or release more than one at a time."

"You know way too much about this stuff for a thirteen-year-old," Bobby grumbled, shaking his head at his older niece.

"Tell me about it," Anthony agreed from his seat two spots down from his oldest daughter, who was schooling them all on human reproduction.

"Don't worry, Daddy," Tia reached over her mother to pat Anthony's hand reassuringly. "It's because I know all this that I won't be a teen mom and make you a grandpa before you turn thirty."

Bobby laughed along with the rest of his family, until Anthony replied to his daughter with, "Yeah, well, just because you're smart enough to keep from having a baby before you're ready, doesn't mean Connor or Cody aren't gonna try to convince you otherwise."

Realizing his brother was already having to deal with horny teenage boys sniffing around his oldest daughter killed Bobby's humorous moment. He quickly turned to Brie as his laughter died down, saying, "Brie-Baby, we'd better only have boys. Anthony may have a company full of wrestlers to help him beat the boys away from his daughters, but as police chief, I'm always carrying a gun. That could lead to me having to arrest myself for killing any hooligans who try to date our daughter."

"Didn't you say you planned to retire in about twelve years?" Brie grinned mischievously. Bobby could only nod in response, unsure how else to respond until she explained her thought process of why that mattered. "Then we're good. Even if this baby is a girl, you won't be police chief when she's a teenager, so the boys won't have to worry about you having a gun on you at all times to be a danger to them if you catch them flirting with our daughter."

"Maybe not at all times," Bobby's dad chuckled. "But they're still easily accessible in the gun safe in the closet. And sittin' on the porch cleanin' 'em is a good deterrent to boys comin' to pick your daughter up for a date."

"That worked quite well when our girls were teenagers," his Uncle Jon added.

"I guess it's a good thing Daddy can't get a gun past airport security," Tia giggled. "Connor's already too scared of him to sit next to me when I'm trying to help him with his schoolwork. He'd end up failing from not being brave enough to even ask for my help studying if he saw Daddy with a gun."

"Dude, what did you do to scare the boy that bad?" Justin chuckled.

Anthony just smiled and shrugged, obviously not wanting to disclose his secrets with his daughters present. *If we end up having a girl, I'll have to ask him about that again later.*

Not wanting to discuss the fatherly protectiveness that prevented them from dating much in high school and was obviously passed down to the current generation from Bob and Jon Burleson and their ancestors before them, the women changed the subject. They effortlessly took over the conversation to ask about Brie's due date and what pregnancy symptoms she was already experiencing.

Luckily, she hadn't hit the morning sickness phase of pregnancy yet, only complaining of being a little more tired than normal. And on that note, Bobby decided it was time to take his bride-to-be home, so she could get some rest.

After I spend at least an hour lovin' on her, but she can lay there and rest everything but her orgasm muscles then.

A couple of hours later, as he was holding Brie in his arms for them to drift off to sleep, Bobby said a silent prayer of thanks for all the good fortunes in his life. *Thank you, Lord, for blessing me with such a wonderful life. For my big family and group of close friends. But I'm especially grateful for Brie's love and the babies we'll have together. I don't know that I'm truly good enough to deserve her, but I'm gonna do everything I can to earn her love every day for the rest of my life.*

Epilogue

As she laid in bed, cuddled in Bobby's arms, the morning of her wedding, Brooklyn couldn't believe how much her life had changed in such a short time. She didn't want to dwell on the events of her life that led to her fleeing the state of Georgia back on Thanksgiving, but she couldn't deny that her car breaking down in Heart's Destiny, Texas, two days later had been a blessing in disguise. She was happy with the improvement in her daily living conditions, even in those first tentative days in town, and her happiness seemed to multiply exponentially with each day she stayed there and got closer to the people she now considered family.

Making friends for the first time in her life had punched the first holes in the walls she'd felt trapped behind since childhood. Being accepted and treated like one of their own by the Burlesons had knocked a few more bricks from them. But it was falling in love with Bobby that brought her walls down completely. In addition to being happy, she was finally content in her life on the ranch with him.

Not that they'd spent all their time on the ranch for the last couple of months. After their trip to Georgia to settle her mother's estate, they'd had to make a couple more trips there to deal with the legalities of setting up the Madeline Ashbury Foundation, review all the changes to her former home, so it could be used as a shelter for the women and children, who had started moving in there in March, and appear in court for both her case against her father and his criminal trial. Both her father and Clayton Donaldson had been convicted of their crimes. They would be spending the next twenty years behind bars and weren't allowed to have any contact with her.

Thankfully, that was all behind her, so she could finally look forward to more quiet days on the ranch with Bobby and the rest of her new family. *Well, mostly quiet, relaxing days.* Now that everything was running smoothly in the first Maddie's House location in Georgia, Bobby wanted to use a portion of his trust fund to set up a second one locally. Or something similar anyway. Brooklyn knew she'd be busy in the coming weeks figuring out how to incorporate a group home for orphans into what was previously a shelter for abused women and children. *But all the red tape of dealing with the Department of Children and Family Services for the state of Texas will be worth it to help all those kids.*

She was brought out of her mental musings by Bobby stirring beside her. "Good morning, my beautiful bride," Bobby mumbled, his hazel eyes only half open.

"Good morning, my handsome hubby-to-be," Brooklyn replied, lifting her head to press her lips to his.

"Mmm," he moaned as he deepened the kiss, repositioned her on top of him, and rubbed the underside of his shaft through her wet folds. "Gonna be an even better morning once I'm inside you again, Brie-Baby. Your tight, wet pussy is my permanent home and I need to spend every minute until we say, 'I do', with my cock burrowed deep at home."

"I don't think that's going to be possible," Brooklyn giggled, wiggling against his erection to position his tip at her entrance. "We can probably make love one last time as single people, but we have to hurry before everyone arrives to start getting ready for the wedding."

"Oh, no, Brie-Baby," Bobby growled between kisses down her neck, while rocking his hips to rub against her, ramping up her arousal to make her wet enough he could slide in easily. "One time won't be enough for me this morning. I plan on keeping you in bed all day. Then a couple hours before the service, we'll have our last time as single people in the shower. That should still leave us an hour or so to get dressed and ready for the wedding."

"You must not have been paying attention last night at the rehearsal dinner when your mom was going over the schedule for today," Brooklyn giggled, her hips rocking in sync with Bobby's as he slowly started to press inside her. "We've got to be up and showered by eight, so you can go hang out with the guys all day while we ladies get glammed up here."

"Unacceptable," Bobby argued, pushing her up to a seated position as he filled her to the hilt. A devious smile spread across his face as he tweaked her nipples. "They can all get ready elsewhere 'cause I need to be alone with you here."

"Oh, Bobby," Brooklyn cried out at the seductive sensation of his hands on her breasts. He knew they were more sensitive at this stage of her pregnancy, so he kept even his light pinches gentler than he had when they first started making love. But the way he soothed even the slightest pressure with his tongue was enough to make the inner walls of her sex start to clamp down on him as her climax approached.

While Bobby played with her breasts, Brooklyn controlled their slow, sensual coupling, rolling her hips to move him inside her without allowing him to pull out more than an inch or two. They still had hard and fast fucking sessions since her new doctor had confirmed that it was still safe with the baby. But as her baby bump began to show, Bobby seemed to prefer her taking control and riding him, keeping things more gentle, so he didn't worry about hurting either her or the baby.

The new OB-GYN in town had also corrected their due date to two weeks earlier than Doc Hayes had originally told them, but Brook couldn't think about that right then. She was too focused on the feeling of Bobby inside her at the moment.

"Fuck, Brie-Baby," Bobby groaned, his hands sliding down from her breasts to stroke across her stomach. "I love watching you ride me like this. And I can't wait to see the view when your belly is all round with our baby."

With his big hands splayed across her abdomen, Bobby dropped his thumbs down to swipe over her clit, sending sparks of desire shooting through her whole body.

"That's it, Brie-Baby," Bobby encouraged. "Take what you need. Come on my cock."

"Oh, Bobby, yes, I love you," Brooklyn chanted, riding the waves of pleasure that washed over her at his words.

"I love you, Brie-Baby," Bobby crooned, taking over control to thrust up into her as her orgasm carried her away to a place where she could no longer think, much less move.

Leah Mae Wright

She collapsed forward, pressing her tender breasts into his hard pectorals while he swelled inside her and came with a loud cry of, "fuck, yes, Brie!"

They laid there, floating on a cloud of mutual delectation, as they recovered. Brooklyn felt Bobby hardening again inside her and thought they were about to start round two.

"Mmm," she moaned, beginning to rock her hips once more.

Their plans for a second release that morning were thwarted by two loud knocks on their bedroom door and Hazel's voice ringing out. "Rise and shine! It's time to get ready for the wedding!"

"Ma!" Bobby shouted, grabbing the comforter to cover them as he rolled to the side to block Brooklyn from the view of his mother, who'd just opened the door to walk into their bedroom uninvited.

"Oh, good, you're awake." Hazel stopped in her tracks just inside the bedroom door. "Bobby, grab your stuff. You can shower in your old room at the house. Brook, chop-chop, hop in the shower. I've got the girls setting up the manicure stations downstairs."

Thankfully, after giving them their instructions for the next few minutes, Hazel turned and left the room, giving them a little privacy to get up and dressed.

"Remind me to change the locks when we get home from our honeymoon," Bobby grumbled, pushing up out of bed to go throw on some clothes.

"You know we could just lock the doors, right," Brooklyn playfully chided, giggling as she got out of bed to go get her shower before her future mother-in-law returned. She wasn't sure why he didn't plan on changing the locks while they were still in town, since they weren't planning a getaway until the next weekend, because Bobby didn't want to leave town before his brothers did.

"No, we've gotta change the locks first," Bobby sighed, shaking his head as he pulled a t-shirt on over it. "Since it's probably been over a hundred years since this house was locked, I doubt any of us could even find the keys to be able to lock it up now."

Brooklyn wasn't sure she'd ever get used to living in a town with such a low crime rate that nobody ever felt the need to lock their doors, but she was looking forward to spending her life trying.

She pushed up on her tiptoes to give Bobby a peck on the lips on her way to the shower. "See you at the church, Mr. Burleson."

"I can't wait to meet you at the altar, almost Mrs. Burleson," Bobby replied, his arm banding around her waist to pull her in for one more kiss before he left, so they could both get ready for their wedding.

Brooklyn took her time showering and shaving, making sure everything was as smooth as possible for her wedding night. When she was done, she threw on some comfy clothes, knowing she wouldn't put on her wedding dress until she got to the church.

She'd picked out a dress that was somewhat non-traditional. Instead of being solid white like most wedding dresses, hers had navy-blue ribbon and embroidered flower accents on the top layer of tulle to match the navy-blue tuxedos Bobby and his groomsmen would be wearing. Spaghetti straps, elbow-length matching gloves, and a bikini-style bodice provided the sexy factor, while the empire waist and layers of satin and tulle hid her baby bump.

She'd picked the high-waisted style that poofed out in yards and yards of material just below the bust because she wasn't sure how big her belly would be on her wedding day and didn't want to risk having to have her dress altered at the last minute. The navy-blue bridesmaids' dresses were a similar empire-waist style, but with fewer layers of material since they were chiffon instead of satin and tulle. They had a ribbon accent just under the bust and wider shoulders with cap sleeves instead of spaghetti straps.

Brooklyn hadn't intended to make the bridesmaids wear something so similar to her wedding dress. But since Kay was farther along in her pregnancy and showing much more than Brook, she'd asked for a similar, forgiving waistline as well. When they all looked at the dresses, Kenzie, Heather, and Ashley all agreed that they liked the style, so it was an easy decision.

When she got downstairs after her shower, she found all her friends and the female half of Bobby's family already getting their nails done for the wedding. The day turned into a whirlwind of activity and girl talk as they all had manicures and pedicures before having their hair professionally styled and their makeup expertly applied.

Apparently, the women of Heart's Destiny had wedding day prep down to a science. They had all the women who had to go home to get changed for the wedding done first, leaving the wedding party to be the last to finish with their makeup since they would be changing at the church.

Leah Mae Wright

Brooklyn had to giggle as she was being ushered to Kay's Jeep to ride with her bridesmaids, remembering back to the rehearsal the night before. Bobby wanted his three brothers and his best friend, Luke, to be his groomsmen, so Brooklyn had picked the four women she felt closest to in town to be her bridesmaids. Since Anthony and Kay were married, it was obvious that they would be paired up during the wedding. But none of the other six members of the bridal party were coupled up, so Hazel had taken advantage of the situation to push for a little matchmaking.

Bobby's mother had agreed with Kenzie, when she said it felt weird to be paired up with her cousin, Luke, saying that they all needed to be coupled with someone they'd enjoy dancing with at the reception. Hazel had put Heather with Luke, Kenzie with Jake, and Ashley with Josh, insisting that the pairs sat together at the rehearsal dinner, as well as the reception.

Brooklyn wasn't sure what the guys thought about the matchmaking momma's interference, but her girlfriends were all tickled pink and enjoying their time being close to the guys. Their giddiness on the way to the church at spending the evening on the arms of the town's most eligible bachelors was more than obvious.

As soon as they arrived at the church, they were ushered into the bridal suite to change. A few minutes later, Lexi, Kayla, and Cassidy popped into the suite to make sure none of them needed a touch-up to their hair or makeup before taking their seats in the chapel.

The ladies had a toast of sparkling grape juice and made sure the rituals of old, new, borrowed, and blue were all covered while Bob, Hazel, Joe, and Mary were in the room with them just before it was time for the ceremony to start. Bob escorted both Hazel and Mary to their seats as the ladies started lining up to make their entrance, with Joe staying by Brooklyn's side to walk her down the aisle.

The only time she'd ever seen Joe Turner tear up was when she'd asked him to act in the fatherly role she'd always credited him with to walk her down the aisle at her wedding. "It would be my honor," was all he'd said before turning away to wipe his eyes, so the tears didn't actually fall.

Brooklyn was fighting back a few tears of her own as she took his arm to take her place in the vestibule behind her bridesmaids. She and Joe stayed hidden off to the side as the doors opened for first Heather, then Ashley, then Kenzie, and finally Kay to walk down the aisle to take their places at the front of the church.

When it was finally time for her to walk down the aisle to meet Bobby at the altar, Brooklyn didn't notice the former Ashbury Enterprises board members who had flown in for the wedding. She didn't see the Avington family, including Bobby's friend, Blake, who she'd finally met on their second trip to Georgia, after their familial relationship was discovered. (But that story was something she'd let the rest of the family disclose when Kay told their stories in their future books.) She also didn't notice any of the other people in attendance, whether they were Heart's Destiny residents or people she'd befriended while visiting back in Georgia the past two months. Brooklyn only had eyes for Bobby, her hero cop with the hazel eyes and dimpled smile.

She couldn't tell you who said what, or when each part of the ceremony was performed. She only knew that she and Bobby had both said, "I do," and exchanged rings before sealing their vows with a kiss too passionate for church and walking back up the aisle toward their happily ever after.

<div align="center">~~~</div>

Bobby knew he was supposed to be enjoying every moment of his wedding and reception, but after what seemed like the longest day of his life, he really wanted some time alone with Brie to enjoy her more. He still couldn't believe that his mother had interrupted his plans to spend the whole morning making love to his fiancée, keeping them apart for eight hours while all the women in his family and the bridal party took over his house for a beauty parlor.

They wouldn't even let him stick around to watch Brie's beauty routine, insisting he go hang out with his father and brothers, so he couldn't see Brie until she walked down the aisle to him for the wedding.

Fuck! She was a sight to behold as she walked down the aisle, Bobby thought, grateful for all the layers of lace she was wearing disguising not only her tiny baby bump, but also his extra-large erection while he held her in his arms for photos in the garden outside the plantation house on the grounds of the Hunters' Bed and Breakfast. They'd taken a few at the church with their family and the bridal party, but Brie wanted more in the garden with all the tulips, which he'd finally figured out were her favorite flower. So, before they actually went to the reception, the bridal party, the family, and half the guests had joined them in the garden for more pictures.

Once the guests and family that Brie wanted pictures with had finally gone in to get the reception ready for their official arrival, they'd taken a few more pictures with the bridal party. Since both Brie and Kay were pregnant, they opted not to do a fancy, dancing introduction when they each arrived. He thought it was probably more because Kay looked like she swallowed a basketball and her balance was too thrown off for her to dance in her heels than because of Brie's barely there bump, but regardless of why, Bobby was glad to be able to send the wedding party into the reception while he got some alone time with his wife.

Now, if I could just figure out how to get rid of the photographer for a few minutes, so we can sneak off to consummate our marriage, Bobby thought as he posed for yet another picture with his new bride. They took standing photos, seated pictures, shots of them hugging, and even a couple of kissing pics. Bobby liked those last ones best, even though he couldn't kiss Brie the way he wanted to with the photographer watching his every move.

"That's it for the poses I usually do," the photographer, Philippe, finally announced, smiling at the newlyweds. "Unless you have other ideas for here in the garden, I should probably go get set up inside to get the best shots of your entrance to the reception."

Bobby knew he liked Philippe and his husband, Nico, from the first day they moved to town over a year before, but he really liked the man when he gave him the perfect excuse to keep Brie in the garden alone for a few minutes.

"I don't have any other ideas for pictures out here," Bobby grinned at the man with the camera. "Do you, Brie-Baby?"

"No, I think we've got all we need from the garden," Brie smiled at Bobby before turning to look back at the photographer.

"How long do you think you'll need to get set up inside?" Bobby probed as Philippe was packing up his camera and tripod to be able to carry them into the ballroom where the reception was being held. "We can walk around the garden for a little while to give you plenty of time before we come in."

"Oh, um." Philippe seemed to take a moment to think about his answer, studying the couple for a minute before giving Bobby a knowing smile and saying, "Give me at least fifteen minutes. Nico is supposed to be figuring out the best place for me to set up, but you know Nico. He's probably been too busy gossiping with your sister to have the primo spot scoped out for me, so I may need more time to decide where to set up before I can actually get ready."

Philippe's husband, Nico, worked with Bobby's sister, Becky, at the Destiny Playhouse, directing the plays the theatre put on, since Becky had other responsibilities with the entertainment division of Burleson Incorporated. But Bobby knew that any chance she got, his sister was hanging out with Nico to be as hands on as she could with the productions she considered her babies. It was good to hear that they'd also, apparently, become friends, instead of Becky just being an annoying micromanager like Bobby had feared.

"No problem," Bobby smirked, checking his watch for the time, so he didn't keep Brie occupied too long and risk someone coming out to catch them in a compromising position. "How 'bout I give you twenty minutes, just to be sure you're ready for us?"

"Perfect," Philippe agreed, kissing his fingers before picking up his things. "Just make sure you don't enjoy your newlywed status too much and end up with grass stains on that gorgeous dress before you make your grand entrance."

"Grass stains?" Brie questioned, looking down at the bottom of her dress while Philippe practically skipped toward the building. "I thought I've been good about lifting the hem, so I didn't get the dress dirty. And we made sure the bench was clean before I sat down. It's not dirty already, is it?"

"No, Brie-Baby," Bobby laughed, grabbing her hand, and pulling her down the path leading away from the plantation house. "It's not dirty."

"Then what was Philippe talking about?" Brie walked briskly to keep up with Bobby's long strides as they went around behind a row of hedges where they couldn't be seen from the windows looking out into the garden.

"I think Philippe recognized my desire to fuck my wife while we're waiting to make our entrance to the reception." Bobby looked over his shoulder to briefly wag his eyebrows at Brie as he pulled her along the path, stopping when they got to a secluded spot with a bench they could use to keep from getting her dress dirty, and banding his arm around Brie's waist to pull her in for a passionate kiss. He kept it quick, knowing they didn't have much time and needing to be inside her in the next couple of minutes. "As affectionate as he and Nico are, I imagine they had a similar tryst at their wedding reception."

"Oh," Brie gasped, her mouth forming a perfect O as she realized what he was about to do.

"Now, Mrs. Burleson, you have to decide how you wanna be fucked for the first time by your husband," Bobby growled, kissing her once more. He trailed his mouth down her jaw and over her delicate neck to whisper her choices in her ear. "I can only think of two positions that won't get your dress dirty. We can bunch it up between us and fuck standing up with your legs around my waist. Or you can bend over with your palms on that bench, and I'll flip your skirt up on your back and fuck you from behind. Which way do you want it, wife?"

"We'll probably tear the tulle if it's bunched up between us," Brie speculated, her eyes lighting up with excitement at the thought of outdoor sex. "So, I guess I'd better bend over."

"You'd better hurry, Brie-Baby," Bobby advised, releasing his hold on her, and starting to move his clothing out of the way by unbuttoning his jacket and the lower buttons on his dress shirt. "If we take too long and get caught, I might just have to spank that sexy ass while you're bent over presenting it to me."

Brie's eyes went wide, and she opened her mouth as if to speak, but no sound came out. She slowly sauntered over to the bench and made a spectacle of bending over and shaking her ass at him, though.

"Is that your way of telling me you want me to spank you, Brie-Baby?" Bobby moved up behind her and bent down to flip her skirt up without risking bunching or tearing it.

"I'm certainly willing to try it," Brie purred. "But maybe not when someone could overhear and come out to catch us in flagrante delicto."

"Fuck," Bobby groaned at the sight of her thigh high stockings, garter belt, and tiny white G-string, almost missing her words. When he realized what she said, his head popped up from where he was staring at her gorgeous ass to see her head turned, so she could look over her shoulder at him with her lips turned up in a mischievous grin. "Brie-Baby, we will definitely be exploring your desire for discipline when we get to our hotel room tonight."

"Oh, yes, Sir," Brie playfully saluted, wiggling her ass at him again.

Bobby wasted no time in unfastening his slacks and shoving them and his boxers to his knees. With the garter belt and stockings in the way, Bobby couldn't figure out how to remove her panties without removing the garter belt first or just ripping them off.

"Brie-Baby, remind me to replace this G-string later," Bobby growled as he looped his fingers under the tiny scrap of elastic bisecting her ass cheeks and yanked to tear it out of his way.

"Why?" Brie squeaked, her question quickly turning to an "oh" of acknowledgement when she felt the material being ripped from her body.

Bobby shoved the wet scraps of her panties into his jacket pocket, making sure his jacket and shirt were opened up enough to be out of the way as he lined the blunt, purple head of his cock up with her smooth, slick slit. He teased her with the tip, rubbing it along her opening to make sure she was ready for him.

Even though the doctor had told him it was okay to be a little rough without hurting her or the baby, Bobby still pushed inside her slowly, unwilling to risk hurting the woman he loved or their unborn child in any way. He gripped her hips in his big hands, preventing her from pushing back on him and causing him to enter her too fast.

"I love you, wife," Bobby moaned when he finally bottomed out inside her tight pussy.

"I love you, husband," Brie stated breathily, trying to fight his hold to circle her hips when he didn't move fast enough.

"You're really trying to earn that spanking," Bobby groaned, pulling out slowly before plunging back in. "But the only spanking you're gonna get right now is my balls spanking your clit while I fuck you from behind."

Bobby sped up his strokes, increasing the intensity only as much as his balls could handle hitting the front of her mound. He knew if the impact wasn't enough to injure his delicate danglers, then he wouldn't hurt his Brie-Baby.

Leah Mae Wright

"Bobby, Bobby, Bobby," Brie started chanting his name the closer she got to her climax.

"Don't scream too loud, Brie-Baby," Bobby grunted as he continued pounding his cock into her creamy cunt. "We don't wanna get caught and miss our honeymoon because we're locked up for fucking in public."

He half expected her to glare at him over her shoulder for the playful reprimand, but instead she clamped her mouth shut and hummed out her moans of pleasure as she came on his cock. The exquisite feel of her inner walls squeezing his dick took him over the edge with her, milking him of more cum than he realized he was capable of producing. Bobby pressed his lips together, biting down on nothing to keep from screaming out his own release as he repetitively spurted inside her.

His orgasm was so intense that he was seeing stars, his knees were weak, and he was unable to even form words in his head, much less speak them to Brie. Knowing their twenty minutes had to be up at that point, Bobby gulped in a few breaths to try to clear his head and regain enough composure to clean them up, so they could go into the building where everyone was waiting for them to arrive at their wedding reception.

Once he could actually see more than spots, Bobby slipped out of Brie. He then pulled his handkerchief from his pocket and wiped the evidence of their romantic rendezvous from the apex of Brie's thighs as best he could. He used the only dry corner of the handkerchief left to wipe himself off, but he wasn't very successful. He folded the cum-covered linen with all their bodily fluids on the inside, though he knew they'd probably soak through. He put the used handkerchief in the inside pocket of his jacket, hoping that it wouldn't be noticed once they were in front of all their friends and family at the reception.

"You okay, Brie-Baby?" Bobby wondered aloud as he carefully flipped her skirt back down to cover her lower half.

"Mmm," Brie replied, still not moving from her bent over position. "Just still floating."

Bobby chuckled as he righted his clothing, reveling in the knowledge that he was the only man who would ever bring Brie to that floaty, happy place she drifted in after an orgasm. Once he was back to looking like the proper groom, Bobby gently pulled Brie back up to a standing position, holding her back against his chest to trail kisses down her neck.

"Time to come back to earth, Brie-Baby," he cooed as she turned her head, so they could lock lips once more. When they released the brief kiss, Bobby maneuvered her, so they could start walking back toward one of the back doors of the plantation house. "We'll go in from the other end of the building, so we can stop in the bathroom and clean up a little better before anyone sees us."

"Yeah, it's a good thing Mandi keeps tampons in a basket in the bathrooms for her guests. I'm going to need one to keep from dripping all over the ballroom since you ruined my panties," Brie giggled as they made their way to the entrance farthest from the ballroom.

"Fuck, you're gonna make me jealous of a tampon all night now, aren't you?" Bobby groaned as he opened the door for her.

"Nope." Brie popped the P as she gave him a little playful attitude. "You did that to yourself by making me all drippy and taking away the only barrier that might have kept your little spermies from hitting the floor."

Bobby could only laugh at his silly bride as they split up long enough to clean up in the restrooms right outside the library. He wouldn't have normally gone into the handicapped stall, but it was the only one with a sink in the stall where he could wet a couple of paper towels to clean himself up without anyone who happened to come into the restroom seeing him with his pants down. Once he was as cleaned up as he could get, he relieved himself before washing his hands and going back out to wait for Brie in the hallway.

He wasn't surprised that it took her longer to clean up than it had him, slightly worried that she'd dripped on her dress on their walk in from the garden. As he stood there waiting for Brie, he heard voices from somewhere down the hall. That did surprise him because he didn't think anyone would be at this end of the building, when the reception was being held at the other end.

He turned his head to look and see if he could see anyone, but he didn't want to walk too far away from the restroom where Brie might not realize he was waiting for her. *And I don't wanna give away my position to whoever I'm eavesdropping on either.*

As he stilled his movement and focused on listening closely, he recognized his mother and Aunt Susan speaking with Luke's mother,

Leah Mae Wright

Karen, and Luke's Aunt Lisa. *Great, they're expanding their circle of matchmaking mommas.*

"So, who all have you set up together tonight?" Karen Walker asked.

"All the bridesmaids and groomsmen," Bobby's mother, Hazel Burleson, replied.

"Well, except Anthony and Kay," Bobby's Aunt Susan interjected.

"And we're still pushing Charlotte and Ian together, both here and at school," Lisa Walker, the principal at Heart's Destiny Middle School, added.

Oh, yeah, I bet they've been pushing them together a lot more than just at the reception and school while Ian's family has been staying on the ranch the past couple of weeks. Guess that's okay, though, since I know Ian actually wants to get with Charlotte when the whole cartel manhunt is over. Maybe I should help him out and suggest tossing the garter and bouquet to Ian and Charlotte when Brie and I go to throw them later.

"I made sure a couple of your boys were sitting at their table, so maybe one of them will fall for Ian's sister, Cait, since none of our boys seem interested in her," Hazel mentioned.

Damn, Ma must have missed the way Josh and Cait have been sneaking glances at each other when they think nobody's looking.

"And we put Justin and Amy together again," Susan sighed, sounding a little irritated. "Though I'm beginning to wonder if maybe we should try to match them up with other people, since they already spend so much time together at work and don't seem to be interested in being more than friends."

Yeah, they spend so much time together because Justin is trying to hook up with Amy. You'd think after seeing him stayin' at her house most of last month to take care of her until the doctors cleared her of whatever caused her to pass out, they'd realize that Justin is using the friend role to work into more. Bobby shook his head at his mom and aunt's impatience with their matchmaking.

"And we seated Lexi, Cassidy, Kayla, and Sierra with the rest of your boys, hoping we'll find a match there, too," Hazel continued. "But maybe we should've introduced one of them to Amy, instead of seating her next to Justin again."

"We'll try that at the next wedding if they don't get together by then," Susan decided, sounding a little more positive at the prospect. "Even if it's not a great match, maybe it'll be enough to make Justin jealous, so he'll step up and stake his claim on the woman he obviously belongs with."

I should probably clue Ma and Aunt Susan in on how Justin's been implementing some plans of his own, so they'll start helping him, instead of possibly screwing things up for him.

"What are you doing?" Brie whispered from where she'd snuck up beside him.

"Listening to my mother and her friends scheming," Bobby softly whispered, taking her hand in his and bringing it to his lips, unable to stop himself from touching and kissing at least that little part of her. "I figured I'd do a little recon while I was waiting for you, so I can warn my cousins, brothers, and friends about the matchmaking mommas' plans for them." *And help out the guys who actually wanna be fixed up.*

"No, don't warn them," Brie grinned conspiratorially. "It'll be a lot more fun watching as each and every one of them fall."

"Don't tell me I knocked you up and turned you into a matchmaking momma, too," Bobby joked, shaking his head as he led her down the hall toward the voices and the rest of the reception.

"Is that what did it?" Brie sassed, looking up at him with mischief in her eyes. "I thought it was Kay convincing me to try my hand at writing romance novels that made me want to match up all our friends. Or maybe just loving you so much and wanting all our friends to feel as wonderfully loved as you make me feel."

"With as big a heart as you have, Brie-Baby," Bobby agreed, pulling her to a halt just as they reached the end of the hall that opened up into the main entryway of the plantation house, where his mother and her friends were chatting. "I'm betting it's the latter. And ya know what?"

"What?" Brie smiled up at him with love shining through every part of her expression.

"Now that I know what true love feels like with you," Bobby replied, dipping his head to press their foreheads together and locking their eyes on one another. "I agree that I want all our friends to fall in love just like we have. So, I'm not gonna say a word to the guys."

He pecked her lips before straightening up to walk into their reception.

"I knew you were really a big softy, who'll sit beside me on the sidelines while we watch them all fall in love," Brie smirked.

"Hush now," Bobby hissed, shaking his head. "I'll only watch with you if you don't tell anyone I'm a softy. And you'd better make sure we have some good snacks while we watch all the drama unfold."

"Deal," Brie laughed as they surprised the women in the foyer and shooed them into the reception, so the newlyweds could make their grand entrance.

As they walked into the ballroom, where all their family and friends were gathered to celebrate their union, Bobby smiled, knowing it was just the first of many celebrations they would have in the long life he planned to have with Brie.

Bobby stopped just inside the door when everyone cheered their arrival. He pulled Brie into his arms, and whispered, "I love you, Brie-Baby," just before dipping her back and kissing her like he intended to for the rest of forever.

Want more of Bobby and Brooklyn?

Visit https://leahmaewright.com/bb-bonus-scenes for details and the
link to download your free copy of ***Bobby's Bride Bonus Scenes***,
which contains a couple of cut segments from this book and three
bonus epilogues, including scenes at her former home in Georgia as
they're setting up the Madeline Ashbury Foundation, how they assist
the victims of the Rodriguez Cartel, and Bobby and Brooklyn's first
night at home after their baby is born.

Spoiler Warning: While technically ***Adoring Amy*** is the next book in
the series after ***Bobby's Bride***, the events in ***Bobby's Bride Bonus
Scenes*** take place in the middle of ***Adoring Amy, Charlotte's
Wedding***, and ***Joshin' Around***. Bonus Epilogue 1 includes
information that comes to light in ***Adoring Amy***. Bonus Epilogue 2
also contains major spoilers for ***Charlotte's Wedding***. And Bonus
Epilogue 3 covers part of a scene that happens in ***Joshin' Around*** from
a different perspective. So, if you haven't already read ***Adoring
Amy, Charlotte's Wedding***, or ***Joshin' Around***, I'd highly advise that
you read those books before reading ***Bobby's Bride Bonus Scenes***. It
also contains graphic sex scenes and profanity, which is intended for
adult audiences (18+) only.

Author's Note

My apologies to anyone who was thrown off by my timeline discrepancy of mentioning the songs **Growing Old With You** by Restless Road and **Take My Name** by Parmalee as the songs Brooklyn and Bobby sang to each other in the proposal scene on Valentine's Day 2019. I knew at the time I put them in the book that the songs weren't released until 2022 and 2021, respectively, so there was no way either could have really been used for a proposal in 2019. But since none of the characters in my books are real people, they aren't burdened with the limitations you or I would've had back in 2019. Since my books are all set in the make-believe world in my head, I'm using my artistic license to have the playlist of songs I've been listening to while writing available three years ago when this story was set.

I hope that's not an issue for any of my readers, but it was the only way I could think of to pay homage to the songs that are influencing me while writing without risking my timeline getting ahead of the calendar. It's going to be hard enough waiting for Tia to turn twenty-one in 2027 to write her story. I didn't want to tack on another three years to that wait by setting these stories in 2021 and 2022 just so I could mention a current favorite song.

By the way, if you're interested in what I've been listening to while writing the first few books in the Heart's Destiny series, here's the playlist.

Growing Old With You by Restless Road
What's Mine Is Yours by Kane Brown
Take My Name by Parmalee
Soul by Lee Brice
Best Thing Since Backroads by Jake Owen

Small Town Boy by Dustin Lynch
Steal My Love by Dan & Shay
In Case You Didn't Know by Brett Young
Good As You by Kane Brown
Glad You Exist by Dan & Shay
Sunrise Tells The Story by Midland
Waves by Luke Bryan
Pretty Heart by Parker McCollum
With a Woman You Love by Justin Moore
My Boy by Elvie Shane
Never Say Never by Cole Swindell with Lainey Wilson
Forever After All by Luke Combs
Heart On Fire by Eric Church
One Mississippi by Kane Brown
Country'd Look Good On You by Frank Ray
Up by Luke Bryan
Steady Heart by Kameron Marlowe
Body Like a Backroad by Sam Hunt
Just the Way by Parmalee and Blanco Brown
Slow Down Summer by Thomas Rhett
Play It Again by Luke Bryan
U Gurl by Walker Hayes
Better Together by Luke Combs
You Make It Easy by Jason Aldean
Made For You by Jake Owen
Ride by Chase Rice
Blessings by Florida Georgia Line
Little White Church by Little Big Town
That's My Kind of Night by Luke Bryan
When You Say Nothing at All by Keith Whitley
Gonna Wanna Tonight by Chase Rice
Strip It Down by Luke Bryan
She Likes It by Russell Dickerson featuring Jake Scott

Next in the Heart's Destiny Series

Adoring Amy

Justin Burleson lived a charmed, happy life on his family ranch in Heart's Destiny, Texas. He worked in his dream job in the family business as the head of the research and development department in the Burleson Energy division of Burleson Incorporated. While he technically had a vice president title, he had the freedom to spend his time in the lab more than in the executive offices with the rest of his family. He appreciated being able to spend his time working on finding alternative fuels to help Burleson Energy be a more environmentally friendly company than the oil conglomerate his ancestors had started without realizing how damaging to the land and surrounding ecosystems their endeavors would be a hundred years later.

Unfortunately, spending all his time with his family, either at work or on the ranch, meant he didn't have as much time for dating. So, settling down, as his mother and aunt seemed to want for all their children, wasn't his top priority. It wasn't that he was reluctant to romance, more that he wasn't interested in romancing the women his mother kept setting him up with at every event in town. He wasn't looking for just any woman to marry and carry on the family name. He was seeking his soulmate.

Amy Lawton wasn't sure she was really interested in dating anyone seriously after growing up watching her mother's string of relationship failures. Dealing with her own abandonment issues after losing her grandparents was only made harder by feeling abandoned by her father and several pseudo stepfathers over the years. Not wanting to feel the pain of heartbreak when a man inevitably left the relationship, Amy put up walls and wouldn't let herself fall in love, like her mother and sister seemed to do each week with someone new.

When Amy came to Heart's Destiny, Texas, for her best friend's sister's wedding, Justin thought he'd finally met his soulmate. Their common interest in chemical engineering was far more important to him than their racial or socioeconomic differences. Justin didn't just see a woman of color; he saw a woman of character, a woman he wanted to get to know better.

Amy felt an instant attraction to Justin when she met him, but she was reluctant to pursue a romance with the man who was so obviously different from her and anyone she'd ever dated. Even though they seemed to have a lot of common interests when they talked about their professional lives, she doubted a Black woman white man romance would ever develop between them. Though she'd seen such a pairing work for her grandparents, her mother's string of failed relationships with mostly white men had made it clear to her that a multicultural romance would never last, so she vowed to save herself the heartbreak by keeping him in the friend zone.

When the Burlesons offered her more than double her current salary to move to Texas and work in their research and development department, Amy couldn't turn down the opportunity for career advancement. Justin wanted to use their daily interaction at work to move them from friends to lovers, but Amy was fighting her instalove with her possessive boss.

Could Justin show Amy that he's the man of her dreams and she's the woman of his? Or would Amy be too afraid to take their chemistry outside the lab?

DISCLAIMER: This multicultural, best friends to lovers, office romance book contains profanity, graphic sex scenes, shocking DNA test results, and emotional moments of meeting long-lost family. It is intended for adult readers (18+) who are not easily offended.

Books by Leah Mae Wright

Heart's Destiny Series

A Brief History of the Founding Families of the Fictional Small Town of Heart's Destiny, Texas – Free eBook
Courting Kay – Anthony Burleson and Kay Lee
Courting Kay Bonus Scenes – Free eBook
Wrestling with Randi – James Hunter and Randi Lee
Wrestling with Randi Bonus Scenes – Free eBook
Bobby's Bride – Bobby Burleson and Brooklyn Barns
Adoring Amy – Justin Burleson and Amy Lawton
Charlotte's Wedding – Ian Campbell and Charlotte Burleson
Joshin' Around – Josh Burleson and Cait Campbell
Dion's Dream Girl – Dion Davis and Julie Burleson
Destined for Deanna – JJ Burleson and Deanna Wolfe (Coming Soon)
Lights, Camera, Ashlyn – Darius Davis, Ashlyn Lawton, and Cade Starling (MFNB Trio Romance, Coming Soon)

Galactic Wrestling Association Series

Glossary of Professional Wrestling Terms – Free eBook
Fighting for Fiona – Rick Robertson and Fiona Harrison
Dean's Darlin' – Dean Hunter and Allissa Walters
Mistakenly Married? – Liam Connery and Rylie Long, Brent Crockett
and Aiken Pearson, & Josh Parker and Teagan Shields
Winning Rylie – Liam Connery and Rylie Long
Claiming Cage – Cage Dalton and Jaxon Nolen (MM Romance,
Coming Soon)
Blade's Botched Bump – Brandon "Blade" Braddock and Caitlyn
Sullivan (Coming Soon)

About The Author

Leah Mae Wright lives in Florida with her husband and fur babies. Her head has been filled with romantic stories for as long as she can remember, beginning with fairy tales as a small child growing up in Oklahoma and carrying through to countless ideas of her own throughout the years, as she's moved around to live in several different states. Now that her children are grown and life has slowed down, she's letting them out of her head, so they can join the libraries of her fellow fans of romance. Leah's literary world is a wonderful place that has no Covid, no real politicians, and a few unreal towns. Her favorite part about her characters living in her literary world is knowing that they are guaranteed a happily ever after.

You can keep up to date with Leah's future book plans at: www.leahmaewright.com – Be sure to sign up for the Newsletter to receive emails about new releases, sales, and freebies.
www.facebook.com/LeahWrightAuthor
www.amazon.com/author/leah_wright
https://www.instagram.com/leahmaewrightauthor/
https://www.pinterest.com/LeahMaeWrightAuthor/

Provide your feedback to the author at:
Leah's Literary World Facebook Group –
https://www.facebook.com/groups/1808643116190844/
LeahWrightAuthor@gmail.com
Leah@LeahMaeWright.com

You can also review Leah's books on Amazon, Apple Books, Barnes and Noble, Bookbub, Fictiondb, Goodreads, Google Play Books, and Kobo.